"In *The Red Heart*, James Alexander Thom continues his tradition of historic novels that make the story of North America come alive. He puts flesh and blood on forgotten names, and he breathes life into the stale past. He is probably the most important author of American historic novels writing today because he helps to interpret the diatant past for the mind and interest of the modern reader."

—JACK WEATHERFORD
Author of *Indian Givers*

"No one can evoke the past like James Alexander Thom. It is as if he opens a door and takes us into another time. This historical tale is a colorful adventure, tempered with the beauty of the Native American way of life, and illuminated by Thom's wisdom of the wilderness and its people."

—SHARYN MCCRUMB

"Stunning . . . A truly wonderful work . . . If you ever read this author, you will want to read everything he's ever done."

—*Bell, Book & Candle*

The Red Heart "is rich in details of the Indian culture and filled with all those emotions that drive Thom's other historical novels. . . . When it comes to telling stories about colliding cultures, James Alexander Thom is a master."

—*Muncie Star Press* (IN)

By James Alexander Thom
Published by Ballantine Books:

PANTHER IN THE SKY
LONG KNIFE
FOLLOW THE RIVER
FROM SEA TO SHINING SEA
STAYING OUT OF HELL
THE CHILDREN OF FIRST MAN
THE RED HEART
SIGN-TALKER
WARRIOR WOMAN (with Dark Rain Thom)
SAINT PATRICK'S BATTALION

THE
RED HEART

James Alexander Thom

BALLANTINE BOOKS • NEW YORK

A Ballantine Book
Published by The Random House Publishing Group

Published in the United States by Ballantine Books, an imprint of The Random House Publishing Group, a division of Random House, Inc., New York, and simultaneously in Canada by Random House of Canada Limited, Toronto.

BALLANTINE and colophon are trademarks of Random House, Inc.

www.ballantinebooks.com

ISBN 978-0-345-36471-5

Manufactured in the United States of America

First Hardcover Edition: October 1997
First Mass Market Edition: November 1998

To Sun Spirit and

her daughter Hasuwi,

The Singer

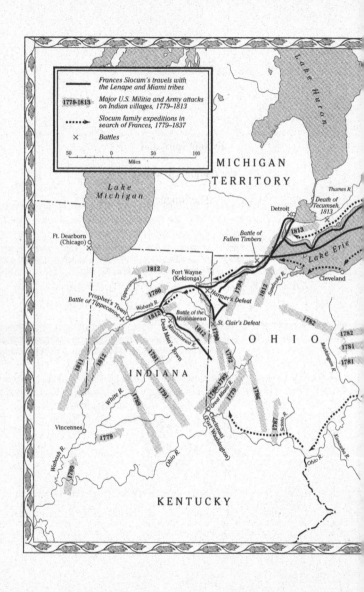

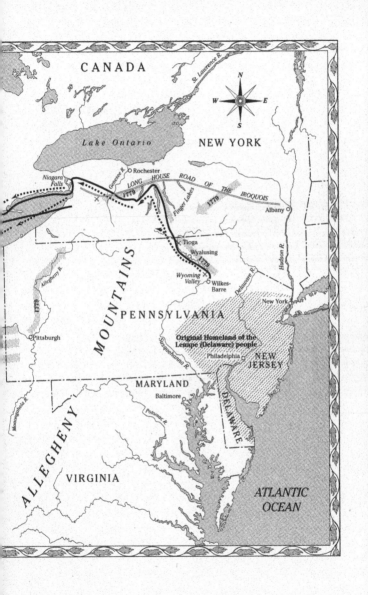

PROLOGUE

March 6, 1847
Valley of the Mississinewa, Indiana

E heh yeh!

The story is always going around. It is not before or after.

E heh! Fire is in the center, and the drum. Old Maconakwa, Little Bear Woman, dances with her People again. They do not hate her, after all! If they did, they don't now.

She is happy. She is not outside from them. To be outside from them would be unhappiness. For a while she feared she was outside.

She dances around the fire and the drum with the others. It is the thanksgiving dance for the maple sugar. Near the fire the ice melts in the ground. Her moccasins are wet and muddy, mud on the beads in flower designs, the leather dark with wet and mud, but her old feet feel only the dancing, not the cold, not the wet.

That handsome métis at the drum with the Miami men is Brouillette, husband of her first daughter, Cut Finger, who is at home too sick to dance but wanted her mother to be here dancing. Brouillette is such a good man. As good a husband to Cut Finger as Deaf Man was to her.

Maconakwa remembers Deaf Man as she dances. He was a breath away from death when she found him, but he lived and loved her forty more years. She was known as Wehletawash of the Lenapeh when she found him. Before that she was Frances, a little girl, a Quaker.

Now she is Maconakwa, dancing with her Miamis in a woods in the center of her square mile of land. There are white men all around her land, but here in the center is the woods to hide the fire-glow. Whites have a place they call Hell, and they can go there, for

1

all she cares. She is dancing with her People. Once her People could dance anywhere, but the white men all her life kept squeezing in. Now she can dance only in the middle of this square mile. This land is hers and the white men can't take it from her because their own law said so. So her People, the few who weren't sent away, they can always dance here. *E heh!*

E heh yo nah
Eh o weh
Heh yo nah
Eh yo weh heh
Heh yo nah!

Sung high, through their noses. The drum like a heartbeat, THAMP thamp, THAMP thamp.

If the white farmers outside the square mile hear it, they'll worry all night and try to get the sheriff to do something. *E heh.* Brouillette has spoken with the sheriff before of what the law is about her square mile of land. He showed the sheriff the Congress paper that said Maconakwa can always stay on this land. He told the sheriff the Congress law is above sheriff law and Maconakwa is not to be bothered. Brouillette talks strong.

See this old Maconakwa dancing toe-heel, toe-heel, toe-heel around the fire, mud underfoot, stars overhead, hot maple sugar-sweet breath condensing in puffs as she dances on and on. She is far older than the other dancers. They grow tired, but she is not tired and never will be as long as the fire burns and the drum's red heart beats. Her white relatives have papers that say she was born about seventy-four winters ago.

White men are always counting. Everything, but mostly money.

And time. Eh well!

See this old woman dancing. Strong square jaw. Eyes wide-set, glittering, blue-gray. A vermilion red dot on each cheekbone to show the Creator that this is one of His People. At the part in her hair is a line of vermilion. Her hair is white, but used to be bright red.

The song changes.

Eh o weh
Eh o weh o weh

Eh o weh
Eh o weh o weh
Eh o weh o weh o weh!

A tortoiseshell rattle in her hand, deer hoof rattles tied under the knees of the old men dancing: *tsh tschka tsh tschka tsh* with the heartbeat drum. They are a raggedy, hiding-in-the-woods People, and just a few. Most of the People were herded out at the points of soldier bayonets and put on canal boats and sent beyond the Missi Sipu. A few, like Maconakwa, learned white man tricks and got to stay in the homeland, keep some land, raise cows, churn butter, plow land, wear cotton clothes, count money, keeping the old Sacred Ways only in their hearts.

Like this.

The raggedy hiding-in-the-woods ones, the only trick they knew was to step off the path into a thicket or dodge into a hollow sycamore tree or vanish into the water of the Mississinewa when the bluecoat bayonet soldiers weren't looking. They loved their Miami People, but they couldn't leave the Miami land because they didn't believe they could be a Miami People anywhere else. These, Maconakwa thinks, are the real People. No government paper tricks, no special grants because of white blood in their veins, no sly money to the white men in charge. No, just wait till a soldier is looking the other way and vanish, and go hide on Maconakwa's mile, or Palonswah's, or Meshingomeshia's. Just don't go.

Eh o weh
Eh o weh o weh

See this old woman Maconakwa dancing, never growing tired. A woolen shawl. Calico blouse and skirt and a belt with a knife sheath on it. Red and blue woolen leggings, very fancy, and the beaded moccasins. Seven pairs of earrings shivering and glittering with her steps around the fire. On her breast under her clothing, two tiny medicine bags hanging by thongs, one stitched together almost seventy years ago and given to her by a Lenapeh woman, the other made for her half a century ago by her friend Minnow, a medicine bag with hairs on it, made from a soldier's scrotum. Maybe it is wrong to wear two medicine bags. The Old Ones knew, but they are dead and you can't ask them.

A medicine bag made from a scrotum. There are so many stories in the story of a life. The story of a life is round, like a circle, and always comes back around, and if you are of the People, there is always a fire in the center.

Eh o weh o weh
Eh o weh o weh o weh!

The story started when she was a little girl in Pennsylvania with Quaker parents, on a winter day in their log house, and at the start of the story she was daydreaming, looking into a hearth fire. There is always a fire in the center of a story, and you go around and around the fire.

PART ONE

Frances

November 1778–October 1779

PART ONE

Paris

CHAPTER ONE

November 1778
Valley of the Susquehanna, Pennsylvania

A gunshot and one angry shout sounded from outdoors, startling Frances from her daydream. The little girl glanced up from the glowing hearth embers to see whether her mother was alarmed. All of Ruth Slocum's children had learned to read the face of their mother, who feared little.

But Frances realized that her mother was not in the room. She must have carried the baby upstairs or out into the gray afternoon. Frances saw no one here but her lame brother Ebenezer and the took-in boy Wareham Kingsley; they both were standing stock-still by the staircase, mouths open, eyes boggling. Then Wareham Kingsley crouched and trembled. "It's Indians!" he moaned. His father had been captured by Indians in a battle, and the boy was afraid all the time.

"No," Ebenezer said, hobbling toward the door to look out. Several voices were yelling and screaming out there now. "Indians don't bother us. We're Friends."

Frances' heartbeat was racing, and Ebbie's statement was no comfort; she had hardly heard him, the screams from outside were so piercing. She clambered off the hewn-log bench beside the table and ran to be near her brother. The drafty puncheon floor was rough and cold under her bare feet. The boy Wareham, rather than going toward the door, was skulking wild-eyed into the staircase nook.

Frances, five years old, had been raised in serene faith that her family, being of the Society of Friends, were liked by all men, even Indians, and would never be hurt by them. But such faith was

7

shaken by the sounds of terror beyond the door, and she was desperate for her mother.

The log house had no windows; heavy plank doors front and back were its only lookouts onto the gray clearing, dead trees, river, distant forested hills. Ebenezer thumbed up the wooden latch, Frannie just behind him.

Outside the front door was a sight so ghastly it stopped the breath in her throat.

Wareham's older brother Nathan, in his soldier suit, was lying facedown on the door path beside the grinding wheel. He was all reddened with blood.

An Indian man was hunched over him slicing off the top of his head with a butcher knife.

Ruth Slocum had actually smiled at the three Delawares when they first trotted into the clearing, because Indians had always come as peaceful visitors. Now, mere moments later, she was running from them, carrying her infant son Jonathan clutched to her side. She dodged stumps and tried to get away, but also hoped to draw the warriors' attention away from her children. One of her first impulses was to flee around the cabin and up to the woodlot, where her husband and her father were cutting firewood, but they were unarmed, and she must not lead the warriors to them. So instead she raced down the long slope toward the river, where there were thickets and piles of brush to hide in.

After the three warriors had come straight out of the woods, she remembered, one had paused to raise his musket and shoot Nathan Kingsley. The youth had lurched and fallen beside the grindstone. The warrior had snatched up the very knife Nathan had been sharpening, straddled his body, and cut off his scalp. It had been as bloody as a hog-butchering, but stunning in its quickness. It must have been because Nathan was wearing army clothes, she thought. Those who live by the sword . . .

Ruth Slocum had run, even though she hoped that by killing the one in uniform they might have satisfied themselves, as all the Delawares knew her family were Quakers.

But she saw now, off to her left, two of the warriors pursuing her nine-year-old daughter Mary, who was shrieking and running toward the woods in the direction of the distant fort, dragging behind her little Joseph, the three-year-old. Ruth Slocum stumbled to a halt and cried after them, "Joey! Mary!" but they seemed not to hear her over their own screaming, and ran on into the autumn-yellow woods.

In the corner of her eye Ruth saw her one married daughter, Judith, running crouched toward another part of the riverside thickets carrying her baby brother Isaac; Ben, seven, ran ahead.

Now the Delaware men were laughing. Ruth Slocum, panting, mouth agape, glanced around and saw that they had stopped near the cabin and were pointing in amusement at Mary and Joseph, who were thrashing so recklessly into the woods that the boy's little breeches had torn loose and come down around his knees.

In this curious pause in the midst of terror, Ruth Slocum, heart still slamming, baby squalling under her arm, tried to make an instantaneous tally of her children.

Only two were in doubt; she had not seen Ebenezer or Frances. She seemed to remember that they had been in the cabin before the warriors came. Wareham Kingsley had been inside too. Surely they would have fled out the back door at once if they had seen Nathan Kingsley slain right out front. Perhaps all her children *were* safe, for this moment. The two warriors were returning to their comrade, who had tied Nathan's scalp to his sash and was reloading his musket. Hoping not to attract their attention, Ruth Slocum muffled the baby's shrieks against her bosom and side-stepped toward the thickets, trying to be invisible, craning to get a glimpse of her red-haired Frances and Ebenezer slipping away somewhere unharmed. Surely these Indians bore no malice to the Slocums. Surely they were only after soldiers—as soldiers should expect.

Frances was whimpering in the darkness under the stairs, feeling the waves of tremors in Wareham's body under her. She was still seeing in her mind the terrible scene of scalp-cutting. Then she became aware of her brother Ebenezer's voice, sounding breath-less and frightened.

". . . if thee wants anything, come take it . . . thee's always wel-come, but . . . please don't hurt anyone . . ."

And there were men's voices and laughter, but Frances could not understand the Indian men's words. She clutched her face with both hands to keep from crying aloud in terror.

The Indians really were in the house! She could feel the thump of their footsteps through the wood of the floor, as well as Ebenezer's scraping limp. He must be so brave, she thought, walking about with them and talking to them, after what they had done to Nathan. She did not know whether Wareham, huddled here in the dark under her now, had seen what they did to his brother.

". . . sugar in that crock there," Ebenezer's quavery voice was saying. "Does thee like sugar? There's salt too . . ." And still the thumping footsteps. Now the stairs creaked, mere inches above her. Wareham groaned aloud, and Frances was sure the Indians would hear him. "Up there's only clothes and bedding," Ebenezer's voice went on, "but thee's welcome to whatever fits 'ee . . ." The Indians were talking in their own tongue, deep-voiced, occasionally laughing, and Frances could hear heavy things being scooted and dropped on the floors. She could hear no voices from outside the house, and she wondered where her mother could be. The little girl began trembling even harder with a new onslaught of dread. She remembered something that had lately been in her bad dreams: some weeks ago one of her boy cousins from a distant farm had been carried away by Indians. Did they mean to do that to her?

Now the stairs were creaking again right above her.

"A heh!" one of the voices exclaimed.

And then a hard hand grabbed her ankle and she was pulled roughly, feet first, from her hiding place. She saw just above her a painted face with no hair or eyebrows and a metal ring in the nose. At that moment Wareham wailed in terror right next to her.

Her terror was so numbing that she wet herself and was flung out of her senses.

Ruth Slocum's whole attention at this moment was like a tense spiderweb covering the area of her children's jeopardy, and like the mother spider, she sensed by feeling the web where each child was.

She knew just where Judith and Ben and little Isaac were, a few yards upstream from her in a swampy thicket. She knew that Mary and Joseph would by now be almost at the edge of the clearing below the Wilkes-Barre fort, surely safe—unless there were more Indians than the three she had seen at the house.

It was the plight of the children in the house that now screeched harsh in her soul. She was almost certain that son Ebenezer and little Frances were still in the house, and she had seen the painted warriors go in the front door.

She was frozen between choices of action, wanting to run to the house and plead for her children and wanting to speed toward the fort and summon help. But the baby Jonathan cradled in her left arm was beginning to whimper and sob, either from the cold or in response to her own anguish, and he was the most helpless of them all. And the people in the fort would get warning enough when Mary and Joseph got there.

So Ruth Slocum remained fixed, hiding in the underbrush, and she prayed with all her concentration, silently, staring at the log house in the clearing as if to penetrate its walls.

O Light of God that liveth in every heart, she prayed, do guide those red men to be merciful. Do calm the hearts of my little ones until this bad moment passes. . . .

She heard a rustling in the fallen leaves, off to her left, and turned to see Judith, Ben, and Isaac approaching through the brush, crouched, pale with fear.

"Mama—" the girl began in a strained murmur.

"Judy, take the baby and hide theeself down. I simply *must* do something. . . ." She glanced toward the house again as she handed the baby to her daughter, and what she saw up there made her gasp.

Dim against the background of the dark-wooded mountains were several moving figures just emerging from the cabin door: the three Delaware warriors, each pulling after him a child. The red men were burdened with their weapons and by bundles of things from the house, and the children's resistance made them awkward. Ebenezer limped and hung back. Little Wareham Kingsley was so rigid with terror that the warrior almost had to carry him. Only Frances' voice could be heard. Dragged along by one arm, she was whining a singsong "Mama! Mama! Mama!"

Ruth Slocum discarded all caution. She strode out of the thicket into the clearing, brambles snagging her gray skirt, while Judith hugged the baby and groped, like the brambles, to keep her from going.

Ruth was unaware that she had set her jaw so hard that one of her molars cracked. She was hardly aware of cracking a shin on one of the stumps in the clearing, and falling onto her hands and knees and clambering back up to run toward the painted warriors. She was aware only that they were heading toward the brush with two of her children and poor Wareham Kingsley, and would be gone into the autumn evening before men could come from the fort.

"Turn those children free!" she cried. "Let them go! Please!"

They paused at the sound of her voice and glared back at her, frightful in their face paint but young enough to be her own sons. Her voice and her approach set Frances into a frenzy of crying and Ebenezer into an arm-wrenching struggle with the one who had him.

"Shame on thee!" Ruth shrilled, hobbling straight toward the warriors and scolding them as if they were mere bad boys. But then she saw lying before her the prone corpse of Nathan Kingsley, pale skull bone visible through his blood-matted scalp. She faltered, swallowed, clapping a hand to her throat. One of the Indians laughed, and another said something in a derisive tone. But none of them turned on her; they kept pulling the children along the path toward the woods, and she limped after them, trying to make herself heard over Frances' wails.

"Look thee! That boy Ebenezer, he's lame! It hurts him to walk! What good can 'e do thee?"

As if he understood her words, the warrior looked down and noticed Ebenezer's dragging gait. He stopped, said something, and released the boy's arm, pushing him away. The boy stood amazed for a moment, then, face shining with deliverance, went lurching back toward his mother. She caught him in her arms and ran her fingers through his hair.

But now the warriors spoke rapidly among themselves, glancing downstream toward the fort. The warrior who had released Ebenezer took from the others their bundles of booty and trotted ahead of them up the path toward the woods. They seized and lifted the two small children over their shoulders like meal sacks and hurried after him with swift, effortless strides. Ruth could see that there was no chance of catching up to them. Hands clapped to her cheeks, she screamed after them, "Frannie! Frannie! Oh my dear baby girl!"

This terrible moment, she felt with a dread certainty, would be her last sight of her red-haired daughter, the sunniest and loveliest of all her good children.

Frannie was vanishing into the darkening woods: slung over a warrior's brawny shoulder, curls blown wild, face wet with tears of anguish, her chubby arms outstretched toward her mother and home, her little bare feet kicking as if she were running in air, pink mouth drooling, voice now shrieking, "Mama! Oh Mama! Help me, Mama!"

Ruth stood groaning, supporting her trembling son Ebenezer, her face a rictus of agony. She saw the girl's flailing bare feet and thought of the new pair of little shoes that had been made for her to wear when the hard winter came, sturdy little leather shoes never yet worn, stored useless in a trunk in the house while their owner was abducted into a howling, stony wilderness soon to be white with deep snow and ice.

The horror of what was happening fully stunned Ruth Slocum, whose mind was accustomed only to peace and the Inner Light.

Suddenly her cracked tooth and barked shin hurt sharply. She stood staring over Ebenezer's shoulder at the grim woods where the Indians had disappeared. All her sense now was of the vulnerability of flesh to pain—of blood on cold ground, of a child's bare feet in winter.

Frances' terror was so numbing that she had to strain to draw breath. The last thing she remembered seeing was her mother standing on the path with Ebbie, dropping farther and farther back out of sight. Never before in her life had she seen such a terrible expression on her mother's face, and it had doubled her terror.

Now she couldn't see her. There was nothing back there but woods, branches, fallen leaves. She was aware of being carried, hanging head down, over someone's shoulder as her father sometimes carried her in play to make her squeal.

This man carrying her was as hard and strong as her father, but rougher, and was wearing leather clothes. Someone else was running nearby. Her dress was wet and cold against her bottom. Far back, as faint as a birdcall, her mother's voice was screaming her name.

That voice was so desperate that the little girl's heart twisted and she began screaming again into the dim woods toward her mother, toward her home.

The man stopped running. Frances felt herself thrown off his shoulder, and she fell onto her back in damp dead leaves behind a huge fallen tree. The fall jarred her. The Indian man, fierce and horrible without hair or eyebrows and with greenish stripes painted across his face, jumped on her astraddle to hold her down and clapped the palm of his hard hand over her face. His eyes were fierce. He pressed so hard her nose and mouth felt mashed. She could not draw a breath. The two other Indian men jumped down beside him, looking back, whispering sharply. She heard water running nearby. Wareham had been dropped on the ground too, and he cowered silent and white, as if asleep with eyes open, too terrified even to whimper. The Indian men were silhouetted against the gray light of the sky beyond leafless branches, and they were staring and listening back down the trail, their guns pointing back that way; a feather hung from under the muzzle of one, swaying in the slight breeze. The men looked fearsome with their shaved heads, feathered scalp locks, and nose rings, all looming blurry through the tears of her panic.

Desperate for breath, Frances tried to move, but the man tightened his legs on her and whispered something to the other two. He moved his hand so it was covering only her mouth, and she could inhale at last through her nose. It was runny and bubbly but she breathed, until she began to gag on mucus. She racked and gurgled and tried to cough under the crushing hand. Looking down at her, the Indian slightly lifted his hand from her face, but held it cupped above. Sucking a deep breath, her heart still pounding with terror and dismay, she emitted another forlorn wail. The hand clamped down as hard as before. She understood then, even in her panic, that they were trying to keep her still because someone was following them—perhaps her father and grandfather, or gentlemen from the fort. She realized that the Indian men themselves were afraid; these terrible, swift, strong Indian men were afraid because they had done something bad. Knowing that they were afraid somehow made her less afraid of them, though no less terrified of what was happening. She stopped trying to cry out, and listened. Over the sound of the running water she could hear distant men's voices, and dogs—hunting dogs, baying and yelping.

The Indian rose off of her with a quick move. A knife gleamed in his hand and he moved it down toward her legs. He cut her skirt and tore off a wide strip of it from the hem. The linsey-woolsey cloth was damp where she had wet herself, but the man wadded it and stuffed it into her mouth, and then with another strip around her neck and face, he tied the gag in. He grabbed her up and threw her onto his shoulder again, snatched up his gun and stepped down into a rocky bottom creek, wading upstream. The other two followed, one carrying Wareham and the other the sacks and bundles from the house.

Now as Frances looked down and tried to breathe through her runny nose, all she could see was the dark, fast creek water close below. She could not cry out, and did not even struggle, for fear the man might drop her into the cold stream.

She remembered then, as in a dream, her mother coming forth from hiding and scolding these bad Indians for bothering a lame boy, and she grew ashamed of herself for being such a sniffle-snot crybaby, not brave like her mother. This was very bad, what was happening, more frightful than anything before in her whole life. But, she thought, I don't ever want Mama to know I wasn't brave. Mama says if you're afraid, it's because you haven't faith in God.

I shall be brave. I shall be brave. I shall be brave. . . .

She was carried upstream until it was almost dark. The stream was narrow and fast and they were high on the mountainside when the Indians stepped out of the water and climbed through the woods. Now and then the man carrying the bundles would stop and let the other two pass, and would gaze back downhill with his gun ready. Then he would climb past them and lead again. Finally they stooped into a dark, low place and she was dropped rudely on hard, dry, rocky ground. The air was still in this dark place, and Frances looked about and realized that they were in a cave. She had been in a cave before. Her father had shown her a cave in the summertime. A cave far up a hillside, a cave, he had said, where Indians had camped for ages past.

In that cave her father had shown her smoked walls and fire pits, arrow points of stone, animal bones all broken and charred, fragments of pottery. He told her that Indians had lived in this valley probably since biblical times, or longer, and that perhaps Indian babies had been born in that very cave. He said that this valley had been their home for so long, they should be respected and treated well by the white people, who had only just arrived a short while ago.

He had said there was war going on elsewhere in the valley and that some people called Tories were paying Indians to help them fight, and that war was bad. He had told her the Slocum family was fair and kind to the Indians and thus would never be a part of the war, and that the Indians knew it and would never hurt them. She thought of that now, lying shivering in this cave beside Wareham Kingsley, a wad of cloth in her mouth to keep her quiet, three Indians with guns crouched in the front of the cave, dark against the violet twilight. That was the only time she knew of when her father had told her something that was not true. It had been while he was showing her a cave like this. It might even have been this very same cave. It too had been in the side of a high hill.

If it were the same cave, she thought, her father would know the way to it. Maybe he would climb up here yet this evening and talk to these Indians about the bad thing they had done, and they would give her and Wareham back to him and he could take them home.

That thought filled her with a warming hope. Exhausted by the worst day she had ever known, and now feeling like a leaf turning and turning in an eddy of water, she went to sleep dreaming that her father was carrying her home.

Ruth Slocum was waiting just inside the palisade gate when the armed searching party and tracking dogs returned to the Wilkes-Barre fort about midnight, and she knew they had failed. Her husband Jonathan, stocky, dressed in dark woolens, came to her slowly, shaking his head. Beside him was Ruth's father, Isaac Tripp, gray, tired, and grim. Now the poor man had lost two grandchildren: his namesake Isaac Tripp, from his son's family over the mountain, and Frances. The searchers filed in coughing and panting, hulking in the faint light of tin lanterns, some murmuring regrets to her as they passed.

Jonathan took his wife's arm, and her father took the other, and they walked her through trampled mud toward the armory. Though the two men had led the search for Frances, they carried no guns. They believed guns were for hunting game animals, not people, not even kidnappers.

"For all their weapons, our neighbors aren't a bold lot," he said. She knew from that remark that he would have gone farther than they were willing to. "Dogs lost the scent at a creek. Either went down it to the river or up it to cross the mountain, but whichever, they're headed north."

Ruth sighed, leaning against him. The report was not as bad as it might have been; they had not found Frannie's body. Or the Kingsley boy's. She had feared the Delawares might kill and discard the children when they heard dogs in pursuit. But north meant up the Susquehanna, where the Delaware villages were, where the Loyalists moved among the tribes and incited them to kill settlers. Such raids in the Wyoming Valley a few months ago had cost many lives and driven most of the settlers back down the Susquehanna, leaving only pockets like the Wilkes-Barre fort, and the farms of a few Quakers like the Slocums and Tripps, who had had faith that the tribes would never harm them.

Inside the crowded armory, dimly lit, smelling of tea and whiskey, the Slocum youngsters rose from a long bench and came solemnly to hear their father's report. Only Judith made any comment. "I feel in my heart the little ones are well."

"We need to pray that it's so," Jonathan said. And so in the hubbub they spent a while in silent prayer.

Then Ruth sighed and rose. "Let us go home," she said. "I am not at peace with idle hands, or among all these guns." She was thinking of the house standing dark and empty, of her spinning wheel and teasels and the kitchen hearth, all those familiars that would distract her from imagining her daughter's plight.

"Home?" her father exclaimed, jaw ajar. "On such a night?"

She swallowed and blinked. "They were but three young Delawares," she said. "Should three bucks at mischief drive a whole community to cower in a fort?"

"Mischief?" Jonathan said. "Killing and scalping a boy is mere mischief?"

"It was because he was in soldier clothes."

" 'Twas Giles' fault!" Judith blurted.

Ruth gave her a hard look to silence her. Giles, their oldest son, had taken up arms in the Wyoming troubles, which his father considered a sin against God's will as well as a betrayal of the family. It always seethed in Jonathan, though he strained not to mention it.

Ruth said only, "Our daughter's in jeopardy. There's no use placing blame on anybody. What happened this day is simply the way of an unenlightened humanity." But even as she spoke those calming, conciliatory Quaker words, she was trembling within, still envisioning her daughter's outreaching hands and kicking feet and thinking, O God, if she only had shoes!

"Come daylight," Jonathan's deep voice said beside her, "we'll go a-looking for the trail again. I truly doubt they'll hurt her. All the Delawares in this valley know we're Friends."

When Ruth looked at him, he was gazing into a corner of the ceiling with a wistful half smile on his lips, and she wondered how he could be smiling at a time like this. He caught her bewildered gaze and said, "Does thee remember the warrior who came and stayed with the Maddock children?" She stared at him, expression blank. "When they went away to Meeting," he reminded her, "and left their youngsters at home, with a kettle of stew? And that warrior from Wyalusing stopped in off the trail?"

"Ah, aye. Appalled that the parents had left them alone . . ."

"And so he stayed the week and took care over them till the parents returned. And then scolded them for negligence . . ."

"As they well deserved!"

"No man's without the spirit of God in him," Jonathan said, patting her wrist, "and I mean red men as well."

He was trying so hard to reassure her, she knew. She pressed her knuckles to her mouth, clenching her jaws so hard to suppress sobs that her cracked molar felt like a needle jab in her eye.

"Thee's right," he went on after a moment, "we ought to go home. Rest till day. Then I'll follow their trail again. Pray I can find them and remind 'em of the Lord's tenets of decency. They're afoot, and burdened. Mounted, I can probably overtake 'em. If I do, I'll turn their hearts, and bring the wee ones home."

Ah, Jonathan, she thought. What a faith thee has!

Frances was yanked from her nightmares by ungentle hands, and was at once aware that her mouth was full of something she could not swallow. In confusion and terror she tried to cry for her mother, but could make only groaning sounds.

She was being lifted in darkness. When she felt herself thrown belly down over a hard shoulder, it all came back to her: the Indians had her and were carrying her away from home in the night. She remembered being taken into a cave. She was cold and sore everywhere, and she knew that someone had her and would not let her go, someone who was mean and did not care anything about how she felt. There had never been a time like this in all her life, and she could see no hope for the end of it, no hope of being in the comfort of her family again. She heard a child murmur and sob, and remembered Wareham, who had been carried here with her. She heard a man's voice mutter harshly to the boy.

Then she felt cold rain on her back, and knew she was outdoors again. It was scarcely lighter here than in the cave, but she sensed the outdoors around her and felt the drizzle and heard drops falling on leaves. She could make out against the darkness the darker shapes of trees, and by twisting her neck she could look back and see the dim form of another Indian man, the one carrying Wareham. She could sense that they were coming along a high path and that the mountainside sloped away far down to the left. That much she could sense of the world around her, even in her fear and misery, and she knew she was still being carried in a direction away from her home. She remembered that there were sounds of men and dogs behind earlier, and the Indians had been hurrying as if afraid of them. But the night back there was all quiet now. She remembered thinking that her father was following them, and that he might catch these bad Indians and make them give her back. But somehow she did not feel that way anymore. She remembered only her last sight of her mother, standing hopeless and calling after her, farther and farther behind and unable to follow, until her voice had stopped calling through the woods. At the thought of that, the girl's eyes began streaming and she convulsed with sobs. With her mouth still gagged, she could only whimper and groan. Her mouth and jaws hurt from the gag and the tight strip that tied it in. She was about to wet herself again, and every step the man took jarred her and made that worse. Her nose ran and her feet ached with cold.

Without the physical discomforts, which kept bothering and annoying her in waves, she might have slipped entirely away into deathly despair. But finally she remembered telling herself yesterday to be brave. She would be brave and she would not cry out.

Now she realized that her hands were free, and there was no reason why she couldn't have been trying to get the awful gag out, no reason except that she had been too scared to think or to try anything the Indians might not like.

So she reached with her cold-benumbed hands and tried to claw the tight binding off. It cut even harder into the corners of her mouth. But the strip of linsey-woolsey was wet with rain and drool, and it stretched, and at last she worked it down past her lower teeth and then her chin, and then she was free to reach into her mouth and draw the spit-soaked rag out.

Never had she put into her mouth anything so delicious that it equaled the pleasure of pulling out that awful wad of cloth. She took deep breaths through her open mouth and lolled her tongue around, licking her teeth and palate, moistening them and ridding them of the woolen taste. She dropped the sodden rag on the ground.

The man behind her stopped and said something to the man carrying her, and he stopped and turned. The gag lay there on the trail, a pale thing that even she could see dimly against the wet-dark leaves. She wished she had not dropped it. Now they knew she was rid of it and probably would gag her again.

But the man carrying her just stood silent for a moment, then said something in his language to the other, turned and resumed his way. The one behind stooped and picked up the rag.

She did not say anything for a while, but, knowing she could talk, wanted to. Soon she built her nerve up to say, "Wareham?"

She felt the Indian tense, but he said nothing, and Wareham answered, "What?" Both of the Indians spoke to each other briefly, but kept moving along the path.

Speaking softly, she asked Wareham, "Is thee well?"

In a voice that sounded as if he were on the verge of crying, his answer came: "I'm so cold, and oh I need to pee."

How heartening it was to be speaking, just saying something. She had hardly ever had to go so long without chatting. "Oh, I too!" she exclaimed. "If these gentlemen understood a word of English, I'd tell them so, though I should blush to speak of such a matter to a stranger—"

"Heh-uh!" the man grunted, squeezing her so abruptly with his arm that she nearly squirted. She understood him to mean she must be quiet. Maybe these Indians were still afraid that her father would catch them.

And so she kept quiet, growing ever more miserable. The Indians walked on and on in the darkness, and after a while Frances became aware that the slope was going down the other way, and it was steeper, and the men were climbing down, and it seemed to be hard going on the wet path. The jolting got worse and the rain grew colder and colder, and Frances was becoming almost sick to her stomach from being carried so long this way. From time to time she remembered her mother's outstretched arms and anguished face and would sob awhile, being more miserable and afraid than she could remember ever having been, and afraid this would never end.

But her mother had always said, if thee be patient and behave well and have faith in the Lord God and keep His Light shining within thee, all will be well, by and by.

A sound like an owl's call very close by brought Frances awake, and she opened her eyes and saw nothing but water. Cold, dark gray water was running just below her. The Indian man who carried her was wading nearly waist deep. It was not yet daylight, but she could make out the form of the man carrying Wareham, just behind and to one side. In fear of being dropped into the cold river, Frances clutched at the straps and thongs that held the Indian's bag and powder horn and hung on to them.

Then she heard the owl call again, and realized that it was uttered by the man carrying her. An answering call came faint over the gurgle of the river current. Her Indian made the call again, and once more the distant answer returned.

They waded out of the river across a rocky, pebbly shore and passed through a thicket, ascending a low bluff. Now Frances began to sense the presence of more people. She could smell wood smoke and tobacco smoke. She heard and smelled horses. The man murmured cheerfully and was answered by other voices in the gloom.

When he stooped and slipped her off his shoulder with a long sigh, she was so dizzy in the head and numb in the legs that she fell down, among roots and icy mud. He walked away.

She was at last out of the grip of the fearsome man who had dragged her from her home and carried her on his shoulder a whole night long. She was on the cold ground and could not stand, but just sat slumped on the bare ground. She was too tired even to hold her bladder any longer, and she just relaxed and let go and was aware of the wet smell of her warm urine in the cold air and didn't know whether she was wetting her dress, nor did she care. It took her a long time to drain, and she sat in a stupor, aware of people walking around, and horse hooves, and some little yellowish fireglow here and there, though no flames were visible. She did not know where Wareham was. She felt cold sensations speckling her hands and bare legs, and gazed around and saw that the rain had turned to snow.

Snow, she thought. The first time it had snowed the previous winter, she and her brothers and sisters had had a celebration of it, running with outstretched arms and laughing faces upturned to the flakes. This was the first snow of this year, but it didn't lift her heart. It crushed it, made it hurt for her absence from her family. That first snow of last winter, she remembered in her memory's eye, had fallen on ground covered with bark and wood chips left from the recent building of the Slocums' hewn-log house. Falling on the unfamiliar ground of this riverbank, the snow was bleak and forbidding.

She heard the warrior's voice. He was coming back. She felt herself being lifted onto a horse, set astride its withers, and the Indian man got on behind her. He reached around her to hold the reins, then urged the horse forward to a place where other horses and riders were gathering. Frances saw sparks arcing and swirling in smoke and snow where some men were scattering and quenching campfires. The sparks looked warm and lovely. She was so chilled. She yearned for hearth fire.

With many men's voices speaking low, the horses and riders, and many men on foot, began moving uphill away from the river. The sky was growing pale with morning light, the steep ground lightening with snow, and Frances saw that the line of men and horses was long. She could hear the horses' hooves thudding softly, but the Indians trotting along on foot were silent as ghosts. She had no idea how they had come to this place or what direction they were going now, but was sure wherever they were going would be farther still from her family and home.

Her bare feet throbbed and tingled with cold. Her nose was running and she was so cold that she had begun to tremble. The only warmth in this whole vast, frigid night was from the horse's withers between her legs and the Indian man's chest at her back. The cold air crisped her nostrils and she sneezed, and sneezed again. She needed to cough after the sneezing, and then sniffled and shuddered.

Behind her the Indian was twisting, doing something. In a moment, then, she was enveloped in a blanket, which he was holding around her with his arms. It smelled of bear oil and horse and old wood smoke.

She had been so cold for so long that it was a while before she quit shuddering. Gradually the warmth of the Indian's body and hers within the blanket diffused through her, and her hands and legs tingled and buzzed with fatigue. The rhythmic motion of the walking horse lulled her. Her thoughts and fears dissolved and she could no longer keep her eyes open. The dim snowy forest vanished, and Frannie Slocum dreamed.

She was in the wagon coming from a place called Rhode Island, the place where she had been born. Oxen pulled the wagon, which had a canvas roof. The wagon creaked and swayed and jolted over the rough road, and the ride seemed to go on forever, taking her away from the home she had known, and the only solace was the nearness of her mother, who held her in her lap enveloped in a blanket, keeping her warm with her body.

Now and then she would come partly awake, and it was not her mother's body heat warming her, but an Indian's.

When she fully awoke, it was snowing heavily in the woods, the snow coming down aslant and sticking to the dark trunks and leafless limbs of the trees. The whole frightful thing that was happening came back to her, and her heart clenched with fear, and her chin began to quiver.

But she remembered then that she had sworn to herself she would be brave like her mother, so she did not whimper.

But her bottom was sore and the insides of her legs were chafed from the long time on the horse. The times her father and her brother Giles had taken her on horseback, they had gone only short distances, never far enough to satisfy her. She could remember leaning back against her brother or her father, feeling safe within their arms even though the ground was far below, knowing that because they cared for her, they would never let her get hurt.

But this was not someone who cared for her. This was a bad man who had stolen her from home and carried her roughly and put a nasty gag in her mouth.

Yet he was the warmth against which she leaned. His were the arms that had held a blanket around her and kept her from falling off the horse into the snow while she slept.

All this and she could not even see him, facing forward away from him like this. Perhaps it was better that she could not. Surely the sight of him would frighten her again. She remembered the glimpse of him as he dragged her out from under the stairs: the painted face, head hairless as an egg . . . She shuddered again. Her face was cold, and she raised the blanket's edge to cover it. The pee smell came up within the blanket, and she remembered she had wet this dress once or twice in her fright—either that or she had dreamed it. It was hard to remember what had really happened and what had been nightmare in the awful time since this fearsome man had come yesterday—it had been only yesterday, though it now seemed to have gone on forever.

Her chin crumpled and forlorn tears puddled in her eyes. How hard it was to be brave when hungry and far from home with no idea where she was going or what would become of her. . . .

Oh! Oh!

I did not pray once, she thought, jolted by shame. In all this time when I should have prayed, I have not! At night her family always prayed together in silence. Her mother had taught her to give prayers of thanks and prayers for strength and wisdom whenever her mind was quiet, and especially when her soul was unquiet. Now it was a terrible morning after the most awfully frightful night, and yet she had not spoken to God, not once in all this awful time, had not even thought of speaking to God!

Oh, she thought, I deserve to be as wretched as I am!

And so she tried now to pray, to pray inward to that part of the Light of God that her father and mother said was in every human heart.

Even in this bad Indian's heart. Neighbors who were not of the Friends' persuasion often scoffed at her father's belief that Indians too had the Light of God in their souls. Those neighbors sometimes had shouted at him that Indians didn't even have souls.

Dear Jesus Christ, she prayed silently as snowflakes touched her forehead, dear Jesus Christ who shineth in every heart, help me to be good and brave.

And shine in the heart of this man and tell him he should not be doing this bad thing because it brings grief to good people.

Or if my papa is following us, she prayed, remembering the Indians looking back the night before, if Papa is following, help him find his way.

As she understood prayer, it was not an easy or halfhearted matter. Talking to God and Jesus required great attention—or, as her mother called it, concentration. In trying to do that once, Frannie strained so hard that she besmirched her bed. That had been not much more than a year ago. Her mother had laughed softly and told her to strain above the waist, not below, when she prayed. So now Frannie prayed straining so hard around her heart that she shuddered, shaking so hard that she groaned aloud.

The Indian spoke, saying something right by her ear, and it sounded like a question. Startled by his voice, she turned, and there was his face. He had bent forward to speak to her. It was the first time she had seen his face since that first moment, even though he had been carrying or holding her ever since.

He looked different. He had wrapped some sort of a scarf or kerchief around his head to cover his baldness against the cold. His face was bony, brown-skinned with a sheen like grease, and in his nose hung a ring of silver. From cheekbone to cheekbone, over his nose, green stripes were painted. Paint on a face! She had never imagined paint on skin! But what was now more striking than anything else, was that this wild and powerful man was smiling.

This was so utterly unexpected that she blinked several times, staring at him. He repeated his question. She did not know what the words meant, but her mother had taught her to be polite when spoken to, so she replied:

"Good morning, sir."

"Eh, huh," he said, nodding once, and looked ahead, still smiling. His breath made steam in the air.

He smiles, she thought. Just like anybody. A man with paint on his face, who cut Nathan's scalp off, and who steals children—yet he smiles. She turned and faced forward, needing to think of this. She remembered her father always saying that Indians had souls too. If they smiled, it must be true.

By daylight she could see that several of the riders ahead were soldiers, not Indians. They did not look quite the way she thought soldiers should look, with red coats or big hats such as the king's soldiers were known to wear. Instead they were dressed in dull green and wore small green caps. But they were surely soldiers, for they were not Indians, and they were all abristle with muskets and swords and hatchets and sheathed knives. Most of the men on horses were these green-coat soldiers; almost all the Indians were afoot, trotting tirelessly through the deepening snow. Even in her wretchedness she wondered how anyone could run day and night without stopping. She saw one of the running Indians reach into a pouch at his side and take something out to put in his mouth. They could even eat without stopping, it seemed.

She wondered whether her own Indian had a pouch of food, and whether he would be so kind as to give her any of it. She had not eaten anything for a long time. Her mother had never in her life let her miss a mealtime, and this feeling of an empty belly was another thing to unsettle her spirit.

She remembered hearing her father say Indians never let anyone go hungry if they had anything to share.

But then, her father had also said the Indians would always be kind to her family. That had turned out not to be so.

She did not know how to ask the Indian for something to eat.

She sighed. Maybe she would just have to wait until he was hungry himself. Maybe when he ate, he would give her some.

A person who has a soul would feed you, she thought.

She was thinking about these things when she felt something touching her hair. She turned her head a little and saw that the Indian man had taken a thick strand of her hair between his fingers and was stroking it, pulling it gently and looking at it. Her heart tightened with fear. She had heard all her life about Indians cutting scalps off of people, and only yesterday she had seen one of them doing that to Nathan Kingsley. Now this man was examining her hair as if he might intend to take it. Her hair was a deep red color, thick and slightly wavy. Her mother called it her "crown of glory that fadeth not away," as it said in the Bible, and almost every day would find time to brush it with Frances sitting before her. All that had made Frances a little vain of her hair; she was aware that nobody else had hair quite the color of hers. Women in the settlement were always going on about it. There was one patch of it on top that was an even brighter red than the rest, and that was the part this Indian was now studying with such interest that she was afraid he must be coveting it. She sat almost breathless with dread.

But then the Indian man just made a little *mmm* sound in his throat and let go of her hair and smoothed it with his hand. After a while that particular fear faded and she was again thinking mainly about how hungry she was and having deep twinges of loneliness for her family.

The horses had climbed out of the river valley in the early daylight, and their path all morning had been along a high ridge where the snow blew hard, so hard sometimes that the river below was invisible. Now they began descending the other side of the mountain, going down a path so steep that the horses were almost skidding on their rumps. Frannie was always on the verge of slipping or falling forward over the horse's neck. But the Indian continued to hold her well.

She heard shouts coming through the snow from the head of the file, which was far down the mountainside, and she was peering down through the snowfall when she saw that Wareham was behind an Indian rider on another horse far ahead. She had not seen him for hours, not since the Indians were carrying them down the mountain on the other side of the valley the night before. He was too far away for her to try to say anything, but she was glad to see him.

Now from far ahead she thought she heard women's voices among the shouts. She had not heard a woman's voice since her own mother's, yesterday, crying her name. She wondered if she were only imagining women's voices. Why would there be women's voices out in an endless snowy woods? She wondered, with a wild new hope in her heart, whether the Indians and soldiers had turned around in the night and were taking her back to the settlement. All the women she knew of were there where she had lived.

Now the line of horses was rounding the bottom of the mountain slope and passing a stand of dead, barkless trees into a level clearing by a curving creek. Through swirling snow she saw a high wall made of upright poles, like the fort near her home. But it was not the same place. The buildings inside the wall were different.

Between the wall and the creek stood dome-shaped huts and long buildings, as gray as the tree trunks, though still so vague through the blowing snow and wood smoke that the scene was dreamlike. It was a village, and around it spread cleared fields, and there were lean-tos, brush piles, and a fence enclosing a herd of horses. The voices of women were louder and clearer now, and she saw women coming, running out through a gateway in the high fence and across the clearing to greet the soldiers and Indian men, clustering around the riders at the head of the column, crying out and laughing. The wind blew their long hair and made their capes and blankets flap and flutter.

They were all Indian women, and with them ran many children. Behind came Indian men walking, with blankets drawn close around them, some white or gray blankets, a few red, and those red blankets were the only bright color in the snowy, smoky scene that spread before her. Many dogs came running, barking, through the snow alongside the women and children.

Then, through the thrill and dread of all this that she was seeing and hearing, something else seized her whole attention.

It came on the smoke. It was the smell of food cooking, and nothing she remembered had ever smelled so good. She was so hungry that the aroma made her dizzy. She wondered if the Indian women would feed her. Her mother had fed Indian women.

She had seen Indian women only two or three times that she could remember. When they visited the settlement with their men and their children, they had always been shy, always soft-talking, never staring, hanging back at a distance. They had come to the house only after her mother went out and invited them to eat. But these women were not shy or quiet, they were bold. Their voices were loud and saucy, their ruddy brown faces wide open with white-tooth smiles. She had never seen white women act this merry. Several of them milled around the horse on which Wareham Kingsley was carried, and the man on that horse handed Wareham down into their upreaching arms. Other women came trotting farther back along the line, shouting to the Indian men, who laughed and shouted back at them. Frances had never seen men and women act so playful with each other, only children.

Some of the women had caught a glimpse of Frances and came running toward her. Their eyes were so sharp and dark it seemed she could actually feel them. The warrior let the blanket down and with one hand he lifted and spread her red hair into the wind, saying something to the women as he did so. Frances was intimidated by their response. They crowded close, chattering and squealing, reaching up to touch her. She shrank from them, pressing back against the man who had begun her day of terror but had grown familiar by his constant closeness.

The warrior said something in a laughing voice to one big, tall woman with a broad face and glittering black eyes. She worked her way in closer, face glowing with a smile, and the man hoisted Frances off the horse's withers and handed her down to that woman.

The woman's hands felt as strong and hard as the man's. She clutched Frances to her great bosom and turned with her, laughing, allowing the other women to examine her red hair. Then she started toward the village while a few of the other women trotted alongside, talking fast in their language, which sounded like singing. They thronged through the opening in the palisade, into the gray town, passing among round, bark-covered huts and outdoor bonfires, steaming kettles, pole frames with animal skins stretched in them, excited children and running dogs. The scent of cooking meat was everywhere, and Frances had to keep swallowing to keep from drooling.

She felt different from any way she had ever felt before. For the first time in her life she was in an Indian town—something she and her brothers and sisters had often imagined. For the first time in her life almost all the people around her were Indians, not white people. For the first time everyone was speaking words she could not understand. These people smelled different; their town smelled different. Like the Indian man who had carried her here, the women smelled of smoke and bear oil. Unlike the people at Fort Wilkes-Barre, these people did not have stinking breath or stinking clothes, and the streets did not smell like chamber pots.

Without the warrior's blanket around her, she was cold again, and every snowflake's touch chilled her. Her feet and legs were icy. Her forefinger, the one without a fingernail, ached terribly. Her heart was racing with fear and cold and vulnerability. The staring and touching of all the Indian women and children made her feel somehow ashamed, though she knew nothing she should be ashamed of.

Smoke from the roofs of the dome-shaped houses swirled in the wind. But the woman did not carry her into any warm house. She kept passing the huts and striding downslope toward the creek, bantering with others as she went, now and then pausing before a hut as if to show Frances off to someone who had appeared from within. It had become a small, moving, chattering crowd, with Frances, in the arms of the big Indian woman, at its center.

Then they were on the creek bank. The woman set Frances on her feet on a cold, gray, flat stone as big as a table and wet with melting snow. And there, with an abruptness that shocked her breath out of her, Frances was stripped naked; the woman pulled her long gray dress over her head and threw it to a skinny little girl, who held it up for a moment at arm's length between two fingers while holding her nose with her other hand. Women and children on the bank laughed. Frances remembered that she had wet the dress perhaps several times and understood what the gestures were about. Then the skinny girl knelt on the edge of the bank and plunged the garment into the cold running water of the creek.

Frances had never stood undressed before other people, never been naked outdoors, never been exposed to winter air without her woolen dress. Shivering, ashamed, wretched, hungry, scared, mocked, needing to pee, she shut her eyes and began crying. She sobbed in utter desolation.

Suddenly she was lifted and dunked into the creek. Gasping, she was turned about, lifted and lowered in the icy water. Her heart felt as if it would stop. For a moment even her head was pushed under. She choked and spewed water. Hard hands scrubbed her skin with what felt like sand and gravel. She lost control and let herself pee in the creek. She gasped and sobbed while rude fingers rubbed and rinsed between her legs and under her bottom.

Then she was lifted out and set upon the flat stone again, her quaking body stung by snowflakes that were colder than the creek water had been. She opened her eyes, still gasping and whimpering. She was raw pink gooseflesh and everything else in the world was gray. The big woman was kneeling barefoot beside her, wiping the water off her body with the edges of her hands. Someone handed the woman her moccasins and she pulled them onto her feet. Someone else gave her a red blanket. She swaddled Frances in it and picked her up and set off back up the creek bank toward the town, the whole chattering crowd again moving along with her. Warriors and green-coated soldiers were unsaddling and unloading horses, wiping guns and smoking pipes in the open area among the huts, and some of them paused to watch, laugh, and make remarks. Frances was barely aware of them, being in such a desperate and mortified state. She ached to the center of her bones and was murmuring, "Mama, Mama . . ."

She was carried through a low door into one of the huts. The interior was dense with smoke and strange smells. What first caught and held her attention was a fire. Inside a ring of stones in the middle of the room, it shimmered and flickered, red and yellow and lovely. She could feel its warmth on her chapped face. Her mother's own hearth fire had always been the most comforting thing in her world, and now as she looked into this living glow, it seemed to warm even the bleakness of her heart, even though she was being held here in an Indian house, far from her own family, surrounded by strange Indian people, their glittering dark eyes all staring at her. Rather than look at those eyes, she watched the fire and yearned for home, her heart swollen with exquisite pity for herself.

The big woman stood Frances near the fire and took the blanket off, rubbing her skin briskly with it as she did so. Frances felt her skin basking in fire warmth for the first time in what had seemed forever. Many of the people in the hut were women who had come up with them from the creek, but there were several already sitting by the fire wearing only leather aprons. Their breasts were exposed, but the women did not act ashamed, as her mother would have if people had come in and found her with her dress off. They were all looking at Frances, who now stood bare in the fireglow. The big woman had stripped off her own dress, which was wet from the creek, and was rapidly chafing Frances' skin with her palms, as if bathing her with the fire heat. The room was full of women's voices speaking Indian words, and it was a moment before Frances realized she was hearing something that she understood.

"Girl," an old woman on the far side of the fire was saying. "Girl. Zhaynkee's girl!"

The face beyond the fire was as brown and wrinkled as an apple left outdoors all winter, and was all but curtained by thick strands of long white hair. The old woman's breasts were flat as wallets and hung past her waist. She was pointing a bony hand toward the fire and saying, *"Tindeh* you like! Ahh, good! *Tindeh wehlee heeleh!* You like! Eh, Zhaynkee's girl?" She nodded her old head, smiling, encouraging Frances to answer, then she indicated the fire again with a wave of her hand. "Muhnuka'hazh gift to Lena-peh be that, *Tindeh. Wehlee heeleh!* Muhnuka'hazh, *waneeshee!"* She made an arc over the fire from right to left and made a noise like a crow's call. Then she smiled, nodded, and seemed to want Frances to answer.

Frances was too confused and aware of herself to comprehend much of this, which seemed to have been a story or something of that sort, but it was good to have heard a few words she knew. And, among the Friends, old people were loved and respected for their wisdom, and so she tried to produce a mannerly smile for her, and said, "Yes, fire is good. Willy-hilly. Thank thee." Then it was amazing to her how much braver and better she had made herself feel just by answering the old woman.

"Ah-huh!" several of the women said, nodding and smiling. *"Wehlee heeleh!"* And the big woman who had carried her said in her ear:

"Muhnuka'hazh is Crow of Rainbow." Then she nodded to the old woman and said, *"Waneeshee, Huma."* Then she exclaimed, *"Suhpahn,* for girl!" She pointed to something near the fire, and a woman handed her a clay pot. With a spoon-shaped scoop made of some kind of horn, the woman dipped up a steaming mass of yellow-brown paste from the pot and sang, *"Waneeshee,* Kahe-sana Xaskwim! *Waneeshee, Kukna!"*

She flipped off a dab of the stuff into the fire, then held the scoop to Frances' lips. It smelled so good that her mouth watered and she forgot the strangeness of eating without any clothes on. She sucked a mouthful off the edge of the scoop and swallowed it down, and then another and another. Its flavor was mostly corn, but she tasted maple sweetening and some sort of meat fat. She would have wolfed it all down at once, but the woman now and then set the scoop aside on the edge of the pot to slow her down.

Now, at last warm and fed and surrounded by kindly voiced women who seemed to care for her comfort, Frances began to grow drowsy and dreamy. Knowing that they spoke a little of her language, she tried to think of things she would want to ask them, particularly about whether she might be taken home, but she was too sleepy to think of how to speak to them. She watched wisps of steam rise from her gray dress that had been hung to dry on a thong stretched above the fire. She gazed at the hut's framework of bent saplings all lashed together and remembered the rafters under which she had slept at home. She watched the curling, swirling ascent of the cookfire smoke as it rose through the smoke hole in the roof toward the dull, gray, cold sky where snowflakes soared. Her hands and feet, so cold for so long, now felt hot and full of tickles and sparking sensations. Her sight blurred as she watched the fire. Sometimes a woman's voice or laugh would draw her attention for a moment and she would find herself gazing at brown-breasted women, some of them drawing smoke through little stone tobacco pipes, and although this was such a sight as she had never seen before in her lifetime, or expected to see, it was somehow familiar and as things should be and perhaps always had been, and she was no longer so afraid of what was happening to her, but instead was looking into the very spirit of fire, drawn by it deeper and deeper toward the beginnings, ever closer to some original fire with an original circle of firelit faces around it, feeling part of a vast family of all who had ever sat looking into a center of flames and embers.

She dreamed that she was thanking God for all the peace and solace within fire circles, but God was not necessarily called by His name, and her prayer of thanks was not necessarily in a language she had ever known. But she knew the whole meaning of the prayer and it glowed within her like the Inner Light.

In her own house with her own family, Ruth Slocum sat in silent prayer, concentrating on her lost daughter.

Her husband and her father and a few men from the fort had gone out on horseback the morning after the abduction, picked up the trail again and followed it up Wilkes-Barre Mountain to a cave near Laurel Run Gap, but then snow had come and erased it, and they returned disheartened.

Ruth could feel the presence of all her praying family now, even with her eyes closed. But where little Frannie would have been, she felt a terrible absence, an absence more intense than even her sunny presence had ever been.

But at least Giles, who had been gone in recent weeks, was home from soldiering for a few days. She could feel his presence there, and could also feel her husband's anger toward their soldier son. It was not good to feel the tension between people during prayers.

Her father Isaac now cleared his throat and quoted huskily, " 'Cast thy burden on the Lord, and He will sustain thee.' " She heard him sigh, get up from his creaky chair, and go to the hearth. That meant the prayers were over, and she opened her eyes to the sight of her husband Jonathan staring at their oldest son, Giles, with pain and anger ablaze in his eyes. That sent a chill through her, for she had seldom seen Jonathan show his offspring anything more than wistful reproach on the rare occasions when they disappointed him. She was afraid of what Jonathan might say, and when he spoke, she knew what was coming.

"Right yonder at the grindstone is where they shot and scalped poor Nathan Kingsley," Jonathan said to Giles, "and so I can only reckon they mistook him for thee, as he was in soldier clothes."

Ruth saw Giles, in his blue uniform, stiffen. "I doubt they gave me a thought, Father," her son replied in a voice tight with caution. "Nathan was a soldier himself, so they killed him."

Jonathan took a deep breath and blew it slowly out through thinned lips. "I believe they mistook him for thee," he repeated. "They have never come here hostile, until they saw thee in battle last summer. Thereupon they reckoned the Slocums to be partisan against 'em after all, and our friendship no longer trustworthy. And that put us in harm's way." He said this in the lowest but most precise voice, but from the response it provoked, he might have snarled or shouted it, because Giles leaped to his feet and stood facing his father with fists clenched at his sides.

"Well, I *am* partisan!" the youth cried out. "I am partisan against King George! But thee has no right to blame me for Nathan's death! I'll not bear the guilt of that! More shame to men who'll not even raise a hand to defy a tyrant king!" He was red in the face, breathing hard. He had never said anything to his father in such a tone, and Ruth was afraid her husband might explode from his Quaker calm and knock his son down.

Instead Jonathan said, without the slightest rise in his voice: "We Friends defy kings by not raising a hat to them. And I'll likewise defy generals, be their coats red or blue."

Giles was a grown man and a soldier, but Ruth could see that he was on the verge of tears. She saw that the younger children were agape at these cross words. Though she loved Giles especially as her firstborn, she would rather have had him stay away forever than bring this conflict of principles home. To Ruth, this soldier son was a strange and troubling presence, even though he was familiar in the memories of a lifetime. She herself had lain awake nights imagining Giles in the incomprehensible act of taking human life, of quenching the Inner Light of other persons.

Maybe he never had killed anyone, and she prayed that was the case. He had never admitted or denied that he had killed. Ruth believed she could surely intuit if he had, just by the sight of him, for surely he would have been transformed by it, from the Quaker boy he had been, to something entirely different. It was nearly a miracle that he was even alive. In the summer battle against the Tory Rangers, he had been one of the few to survive, having leaped into the Susquehanna and hidden under a log. She was glad that her son was alive, but she was not sure whether her husband was even glad of that, he was so disappointed in his son the soldier.

Giles had been moving his lips, groping for a reply, and now he said, "Father, thee shall never see as I see, no matter what I say to thee. But thee shall never make me feel guilt for what happened to Nathan Kingsley. Nathan himself would not, were he here in this room with us now. He knew he took his life in his own hands when he became a soldier." Giles raised his head back, proud of making a good point.

But his father was not impressed, and replied in that same quiet, exact tone: "Our lives are meant to be in God's hands, not our own. And whether thee'll assume fault for Nathan or no, the fault for our little girl's jeopardy rests squarely upon thee."

Those words like a knife in the belly made Giles flinch and bend.

And his mother felt the pain exactly the same.

CHAPTER TWO

Winter 1778
Valley of the Susquehanna, Pennsylvania

Ruth Slocum with an awl in her hand was repairing one of her husband's boots, which he had slashed open along the instep with a bad blow of a hewing adze. As she made stitch holes along the cut edges, she shook her head ruefully and thanked God again that he had not lopped his foot off at the ankle. The man was a prodigious worker, but frightfully lax about his own safety. He would always assure her that the Lord would protect him until his tasks were done. It was the same faith that had kept him from abandoning his lands in the face of the Tory and Indian raids, and of course a good Quaker wife could not argue against that kind of faith. But she could, and did, worry and pray in silence for his protection.

Just now Jonathan was up on the hill pasture pitching hay to the cattle in the snow, and she had some confidence that he would not hurt himself with a wooden hay fork—though her father Isaac and her son William should stay nimble to keep from being jabbed by it as Jonathan heaved and flung with his usual abandon. Will at sixteen going on seventeen was his father's main helper now that his older brother Giles had gone to the devil's work of soldiering.

Her own father still went into the fields, but he was failing, sleepless and morose over the fate of two abducted grandchildren, and always in pain from bladder stones. The poor old gent had to stand on his head or lie upon his side to urinate, which naturally he found humiliating and distressing as well as difficult. Nearly every day some member of this large family blundered upon him in such outlandish positions. But he simply could not pass water standing upright, and might well have been dead by now had he not heard of this recourse through the writings of Dr. Franklin.

Still, Isaac Tripp would never loaf at home when others were working, even though he could not do much. "No man's ever old enough to be useless" was his creed. Ruth Slocum loved and admired her father immensely but thought he had no more common sense about caring for himself than her husband had.

Or most men, she thought, pushing the steel awl through the boot leather. Having no second pair of boots, Jonathan was out there now in deep snow in woolen stockings and a pair of home-made moccasins, and probably his feet would be soaked and blue with cold when he came in. His clothes and hands were always needing to be mended or healed of cuts from axes, saws, and spokeshaves. Ruth had told him once, "I thank Heaven thee's a Quaker, for I believe if thee were a soldier, thee'd shoot thyself before breakfast every day, or sit on a bayonet."

How a body's got to worry about loved ones, she thought. And then that turned her mind to little Frances, about whom she had worried and prayed so ceaselessly for some six weeks that the child had become rather more like a sickness pain in the heart than a flesh-and-blood child who was somewhere out there in the wilderness at the mercy of capricious natives who might or might not have souls. Jonathan said everyone does, and the doctrine of the Friends said so, but Ruth Slocum's faith in that doctrine had wavered the day those men came out of the woods, killed Nathan Kingsley, and carried away her daughter. It did seem hard to believe that men with souls could do such things.

But then, Tories who were Christians had been doing such things. And her own son Giles was somewhere marching with a gun and bayonet and likely was doing things one would not believe a person with a soul could do. It was hard to take comfort from doctrines of faith while families were being torn apart. . . .

Ruth Slocum had to blot her eyes with her sleeve because her work with the awl was blurring through tears as she remembered her little girl's outstretched hands and kicking feet.

She had never for a moment believed that her daughter was dead. If the girl were dead, she would have felt a hole where Frannie's life had been in the weave of the family. No, not dead, but worse: suffering from cold and brutality and grief for the loss of home and family, perhaps little by little losing her faith in prayer, the Inner Light dimming day by day as she was dragged through the wintry forests.

Judith, sewing a child's garment across the table, said, "Mama, will thee be needing this needle? I'm nearly done with it."

It brought Ruth Slocum back into the room with her living, present children, those still safe around her. She dabbed her eyes again on her sleeve, coughed lightly, and replied, "No, dear. This'll need the harness needle, and sinew, not thread." She knew her daughter was looking at her and seeing her tears, and that made her angry at herself, because in times like these the offspring needed to see fortitude and good cheer. Judith's own husband, Hugh Foresman, was away as a soldier, and she, still scarcely more than a bride and dizzy in love, had difficulty enough keeping tears of fear and anxiety down without seeing them in her mother's eyes too. And, just as Giles bore in this family the onus of being a soldier, Judith bore that of being married to one, and that too kept her in a delicate disposition.

It was cold outdoors, and all the younger children were in this one room of the cabin or in the sleeping rooms above. Little Isaac and the baby, Jonathan, were asleep on and under blankets in the stair corner. Mary and Joseph were in blankets too, but were awake and murmuring child talk. Ruth looked at them and thought of how close they were, almost like a pair unto themselves within the larger family of brothers and sisters, even though Mary was eight years older than Joseph. Sometimes, rather, it seemed as if Mary were not so much Joseph's sister as a kind of submother to him. Ruth Slocum remembered the day when the warriors came, and remembered the sight of Mary rushing away toward the fort with little Joseph going so hard his pants slid down. If not for Mary, the Indians might well have carried Joseph away as well as Frannie. Close to the hearth, Ebenezer was sitting on a three-legged stool, working on a pair of scissors with a whetstone on his lap, a butcher knife and a mortise chisel lying on the floor between his feet. He was the family's sharpener and tinker; being half lame, he was not much good in the fields, and so had trained his hands to many kinds of work. Ruth watched him sharpening blades and it reminded her that it was what the Kingsley lad had been doing when the Delawares came and killed him and scalped him. Scalped him, yes, with the very selfsame blade he had been sharpening.

This was awful. Every thought came back around to that terrible day when they had taken Frannie away. There sat Ebenezer, whom the Indians had left because he was lame, and one was thankful for that. But if little Frannie's shoeless feet were frozen out there in that harsh wilderness, she would be lame too, and there was no way of knowing.

But Ruth Slocum still managed to sustain hope. She now hung on to the promise her husband had made her:

Come spring, Jonathan had vowed, he would set out north, to Wyalusing and the farther Indian towns if necessary, unarmed, and keep going from one town to another, confirming his friendship with the Delawares and his neutrality in the war, and ask them to find and return his daughter to her loving family. He would make it clear to them that only Giles, of all the Slocums, and Judith's husband Hugh, had taken up the gun, ever. He would convince them that his heart was still pure in peace and that he was not their enemy, and when they saw that, they would acknowledge their mistake and take his hand in friendship again, and they would go and get Frances wherever she was and return her—and perhaps her cousin Isaac and Wareham too. Jonathan knew the Delawares' tongue well enough that he could effect such a fair dealing. And in the event that they demanded more from him than just his friendship, he would be prepared to pay them a ransom. The Slocums and the Tripps were not poor people. Jonathan could certainly raise enough in money or goods to buy the children back, if that was what the Delawares wanted.

Of course there would be risk for Jonathan, going out among them like that after what had happened, and Ruth dreaded that risk. But she had faith in her husband and in the Lord God, and she could dream of him returning down the Susquehanna Valley next spring with little Frannie on the horse before him and his arms holding around her as he used to when he took her riding in the meadows.

Suddenly everyone awake in the room looked up and looked around at each other, eyes full of alarm.

"Those were guns," Judith said in little more than a whisper.

There had been two reports. And now before anyone could move, another boomed and rolled along the valley, its reverberations dulled by the log walls and softened by the deep snow outside.

Ruth Slocum left the awl sticking in the boot on the table and overturned the bench in her haste to get to the door. She hardly had a hand on the latch before Ebenezer was there at the door beside her. He sometimes called himself "the fastest limper in Pennsylvania." With all the other children in the room stirring in their places, Ruth Slocum pulled the door open a few inches, keeping a shoulder ready to ram it shut again if there was danger right outside.

The sunny snow was almost blinding. Squinting, blinking, she scanned the foreground and then searched up the slope toward the hill meadow where her father and husband and son had gone to work. The brightness made her sneeze, once, twice, three times, and she could not see anything up there.

Ebenezer exclaimed beside her: "Mama! It's Will a-coming, and he's limping faster than I can!"

And then, her heart leaping in alarm, she saw William lurching down over the distant crest of the snowy hill and heard him yelling, his voice so frantic his words were not intelligible.

She did not need to understand the words. Maybe she would not even have had to hear the gunshots, because there was a pain and coldness blowing through her so terribly that she knew somebody was lost to her. If only Will was running down the hill, it meant something had befallen her husband or her father.

It was as if a blizzard were blowing her, and she was swaying even though standing firm against the door, and through the white swirl of the blizzard and the watering of her eyes from the sneezing she could barely see the figure of her son William shambling and lurching down the hill toward the house with a ghastly slowness, kicking up snow and snow clods that sprayed around him. He came floundering, yelling down among the snowcapped tree stumps and the big dead gray trees that had been killed by girdling, his black coat flapping around him and his voice sounding hoarse and strained as crow calls.

Ebenezer shouldered the door open and clambered down the stoop to go out to William, and she heard Ebenezer say, "He's bleedin'!"

And then that was the last she remembered because the blizzard in her soul swept the last of the strength out of her and she was falling through whiteness.

Ebenezer helped the carpenter make the two coffins, one for his father and one for his grandfather. He said it was better to be doing something. He and the carpenter sawed and planed the boards for the coffins in the yard of the fort while Ruth Slocum and her other children sat in mourning inside. Near them in the room lay the corpses of their father and grandfather, under blankets on a table. The men who had brought the bodies down from the hill on a sledge had advised the family not to lift the blankets because both men had been shot and scalped, and Mr. Tripp had been speared and tomahawked as well.

The incident had been visible from the fort, and a man who had seen it happen kept describing it to everyone who came in to pay respects to the Slocums.

"The savages just shot from the edge o' the woods, then run out at 'em. That boy Will, he was behind the hay, and when Mr. Tripp and Mr. Slocum fell, he lit out down the hill, yellin' for help. Old Tripp, he was only wounded, and when a savage aimed his musket at Will, the old gent tried to grab it. That's when they cut 'im down with a spear and a hatchet. One shot down the hill at Will and only hit his heel. I saw the whole business but it was out of range for me to shoot. I like t' cried, bein' so helpless to do anything."

Finally Ruth, all red-eyed and trembling, said to the man, "Will thee please not tell it again? My children . . ."

"Ah!" He nodded, but looked insulted, and went outside, where he stood in the snow near the door and kept retelling it to everyone who came, and the widow and children could still hear it.

Then the banging of hammers on coffin nails began, and while that desolate sound was going on, Will came in on a stick crutch, his wounded foot wrapped in linen strips, through which blood was already seeping. The fork of the crutch he had padded with the folded leg of his boot, whose heel had been burst by the musket ball that hurt him. Will's face was drawn and pale from pain, his lips looked swollen, and his eyes glimmered, as from crying. The man who had been retelling what he witnessed came in with Will, holding his upper arm and helping him up onto the threshold, still earnestly apologizing for not having been able to help. The Slocum children and their mother all got up to gather around Will, but he warned them away with the brusqueness of his movements and stood there sagging on his crutch, looking down with wet eyes at the blanketed corpses.

"Lad," the man was saying, "if you'd not been behind the hay just then, you'd all three be lying there right now, three generations, not two! I saw it all, my boy, and how I wished I could have shot the damn savages!"

"Oh, yes. Shooting savages," William said in a musing tone. "Shooting savages. Yes, that's what's got us all this." He nodded toward the corpses. "This and Frannie." Ruth had come to stand close to Will, and she knew what he was saying.

The man looked puzzled. "What?"

"He means Giles in the army shooting savages is what brought this upon us," Ruth said in a flat voice, that statement she had kept herself from making while her husband was alive to believe it. She could say it to anyone now, and would even to Giles if Giles were here.

That night they were sitting vigil on a bench near the coffins in the cold room, a candle on each coffin. Ruth had been holding and nursing the baby, saying nothing, praying in silence for strength and wisdom to keep on sustaining her big family without Jonathan to sustain her. Or her father. She had no father now, and no husband. She had become a widow woman and fatherless all in one moment. Everything that had meant anything to her was all overturned, worse even than when they had carried Frannie away last month.

She felt Will looking at her and turned to look at his face looking at her in the candlelight. He was haggard from pain and fatigue and his red hair was lank. His breath clouded in the cold room.

She said, "Does thee want to take a blanket and lie down, son?"

"Thank thee, no, I'm well enough."

She took a long breath. " 'Tis thee and me now," she said. "Thee's the eldest son at home and we'll need thee as man o' the house. Thee'll have to take up what thy father had set himself to do."

"Giles is older than I."

She said after a moment, "Giles has rather forsaken us, as thy father thought. He's not the one to take up those burdens."

Will sighed and nodded. His brothers and sisters were not asleep, but were pairs of dull, sad, stupefied eyes all around. How little or how much of this they were comprehending, Ruth Slocum had no notion.

She felt benumbed. It was nearly midnight now. She thought, It proves again: thee cannot remember a day thee's failed to get through.

She said softly to William, "Thee worked close beside him; I suppose he'd told thee all he'd planned to do?"

Will nodded. "God willing, my foot will be well enough come spring to plow the north corner. . . ."

"Never thee mind that," she said. "We all can plow. What thy father'd promised to do come spring is go to the Indians and bring back Frannie."

February 1779
Wyalusing Town

Frances knew what the Indian women were doing because her family had done it the year before. She remembered it as one of the happiest times. Though it had been hard work for everyone in the family, and cold, wet feet for days, it had yielded something that tasted better than any other taste she knew, and her father and mother had told her it also meant that spring was coming.

She carried armloads of dry sticks from a pile of brush to the *tindeh* place, which was where the hot fire was kept burning under the steaming kettles. She was helping the other children of about her age. There were boys and girls going back and forth between the brush piles and the *tindeh* and they were cheerful and friendly to her, and mostly very pretty. She had some favorites already. At the brush pile there was an old man who was very strong, and he kept breaking the long branches into short sticks for the children to carry. He could break most of them under his knee with a loud crack. The ones that were too big to break that way, he would put between the trunks of a pair of twin trees and push until the limbs broke. He had a brown face, all wrinkles, and long white hair. His name was Kukhus, meaning Owl, and he was known as a *lehpawcheek*, which meant a wise one. He was about the same age as old Grandfather Tripp and he was a merry man, always saying things that made the women laugh. Frances remembered how her Grandfather Tripp had to be upside down to pee. This old man did not have to do that. She had seen him turn his back when no children were near, and then she saw where he had peed in the snow.

Just about everybody seemed to be working. Grown-ups carried pots and pails and skin bags of sap from the maple trees in the woods, and poured it into the kettles. The village was dense with smoke and steam. The people worked all day and all night. When someone got tired, she could go into a *wikwam*, as their little round houses were called, and sleep while someone else took her place at the kettles. There was much laughter and storytelling. In the *wikwams* the old *humas*—the grandmothers—kept pots of *suhpahn*, and hominy with berries and meat, steaming by the cookfires, and one could eat at any time. It was not necessary to wait for a particular mealtime, or a particular bedtime, as in her family, and Frances rather enjoyed the freedom to eat and sleep when she felt like it. And she liked the food here.

Frances thought of her mother every day, often every day, and always pictured her in her mind when she was praying, and sometimes she got an ache in her bosom from thinking about her and her father and brothers and sisters.

The Indian woman who had washed Frances in the cold creek took care of her as if they were mother and daughter, but so did all the other Indian women; she was just the main one. The woman was called Neepah.

Frances could now understand a little of the Indian people's language, just enough to obtain what she needed and be polite, and since Neepah knew a few words of English, Frances could ask her about the meanings of stories, and find out what some of the things were that she saw around the village. So much was new; so many things were done in ways she had never seen.

One thing it was hard for her to figure out was which children belonged to which women. There were several girls of different ages who were in Neepah's lodge so much that at first Frances thought they were all her daughters, but they did not sleep there. Women came and helped with chores, and Frances wondered if they were aunts. Then days would go by and those women would not come, but others would. They would sit around Neepah's fire and talk long, long, about matters Frances could not understand even if she knew some of the words. And now that the maple sugar was being made, all the women and children seemed to belong to each other, as if the whole village were one family. There were few men about, and none of them ever slept in Neepah's *wikwam*, though she fed any man who came hungry.

One girl perhaps one or two years older than Frances, the skinny one who had rinsed out her dress at the creek the first day, sometimes slept in the same blanket with Neepah. Her name was Numaitut, meaning the Minnow. She had a long scar on her thigh. She seldom spoke, but stared so hard one could almost feel it.

Frances now stacked her armload of sticks on the pile near the fire. Neepah said, *"Waneeshee, Palanshess."* That meant, Thank you, Frances. This language had nothing that sounded like the letter F or the letter R or those letters together, and when they tried to say Frances, it was "Palanshess." At home Frances had learned the alphabet and the sounds of the letters and had just begun to learn to read, and so she understood this about the difficulty with the letters. These people had some sounds she could not yet quite make either, though she was trying to learn and get used to them. One was the start of their word for corn, *xaskwim*, and it was easy to remember but hard to say because it was the sound you would make if a kernel of corn stuck on the back of your tongue and you tried to blow it out without offending anyone at the table. In fact the whole word sounded like someone hacking a kernel up but keeping it in the mouth to swallow again. That made it easy for her to remember.

Another sound they had was not even like any letter she knew, but was like the little popping sound you made deep in your throat when you said "uh-oh." It was in the middle of many of their words. She was trying to learn how to say the name of rabbit, which had it: *chema'mays.* Then there was the word for mouse—*axpo'kwess*—which had the popping sound right after the hacking sound and was very difficult to say. Sometimes when Frances was alone she would try to practice such words, and after a few times with the mouse word she would have to spit. She spent a great deal of her thinking time trying to learn their language because she was hungry to talk. She had talked all the time at home, so much that sometimes she was known as the Jibber-Jabber.

Here among these people there was so much to ask and so much to say, but it was all backed up in her, and would be until she learned their language.

"Palanshess," the woman said. Frances looked up. Neepah was holding out her stirring ladle so that some of the steaming amber syrup was running off into the snow, where it hardened at once. Frances smiled and thanked her. "*Waneeshee,* Neepah." She picked the little brown plug out of the snow, put one end in her mouth, and sucked the melting sweetness. Neepah nodded, and her tough, broad face was soft with affection.

That night when they were resting in the *wikwam,* the old *lehpaw-cheek* came in from the brush pile where he had been working and sat down on the other side of the fire, and the women fed him. He kept looking at Frances. He would smile at her, and when she smiled back at him, he would nod and chuckle and say something to the women.

When he had eaten, he set aside his bowl and withdrew a short, stone-bowled pipe from a raccoon-skin bag, and filled the pipe with a mixture of crumbs and flakes from a smaller bag all decorated with colorful quills. He leaned forward and held the end of a twig in the fire until it was burning, then lit the pipe with it, sucking on the stem and puffing. Then he turned the pipe around to point the stem in every direction, and resumed puffing, looking contented. The smoke had a thick, sweet, grassy fragrance. Finally he leaned toward Frances and said, *"Wehlee heeleh,* you."

"Waneeshee, lehpawcheek," she said, as it was mannerly to thank someone for a compliment. It seemed to please him. All his wrinkles gathered up in a smile.

He touched his chest with his forefinger. "Story from me," he said, then pointed to her. "Of *tindeh,* fire, ahhh, gift." He raised his eyebrows, and, thinking she understood, she nodded. *"Kulesta,"* he said, and she knew that meant "Listen."

"Long time before. Never cold, those time."

She nodded again, leaning forward, surprised and delighted not only to be hearing a story, but especially to be hearing enough English to understand.

"Muhnuka'hazh, bird name. Many color bird." He made an arc through the air before him, and somehow she thought she had heard and seen this before. He made the arc again and said, "Many color in sky, this so," and made the arc again, and she said:

"Rainbow?"

"E heh!" He pointed at her, grinning. "Yes. Muhnuka'hazh name Rainbow Crow." She knew that was what he said, though his pronunciation was odd. He went on: "Rainbow Crow sing so good." He tilted his head back, closed his eyes and whistled a lovely trill, with his fingers fluttering to show bird notes floating through the air, and she believed she understood that, although she had never thought crows sang beautifully, but really very badly. But then, she had never known a many-colored crow either, and this was his story, so she believed it and waited for more of it. She looked and saw that Neepah was watching her and watching the old man too, and was smiling fondly, like a mother. The girl Minnow snuggled at Neepah's side.

And the old man went on with his story, and it was hard to understand, and sometimes the story would stop until someone else in the hut thought of a way to say it, or sign it with hands, and even though the story stumbled along like that, Frances could nevertheless see the story bit by bit in her mind. It was of Rainbow Crow, who was beautiful to see and hear back in the ancient days before cold came, and of how Snow Spirit appeared in the world, and all the animals and people were freezing, and a messenger had to be chosen to go up to Kijilamuh ka'ong, the Creator Who Creates By Thinking What Will Be, and the messenger was to ask the Creator to think of the world as warm again so they would not all freeze to death. Rainbow Crow was chosen to go, and he flew upward for three days. He got the Creator's attention by singing beautifully, but when he begged the Creator to make it warm again, the Creator said he could not, because he had thought of cold and could not unthink it. But he did think of Fire, a thing that could warm the creatures even when it was cold. And so he poked a stick into the sun until it was burning, and gave it to Rainbow Crow to carry back to earth for the creatures, telling him to hurry before the stick burned all up.

Rainbow Crow dove down and flew as fast as he could go. The burning stick charred all his beautiful feathers until they were black, and since he was carrying the stick in his beak, he breathed the smoke and heat until his throat was hoarse. And so the Rainbow Crow was all black and had an unpleasant cawing voice forever after, but he was honored because he had brought *tindeh*, fire, for everyone to use. The old man finished the story by saying that the crow is still highly honored, and never killed by hunters or animals, and that if you look closely at the crow's black feathers, you can still see the many colors gleaming in the black. It had taken the old man a long time to finish the story because of the difficulty of the languages, and it was time to go back out into the night and take their turn carrying wood and stirring the maple syrup.

But Frances was happier than she had been for a long time, because she realized now what a wonderful gift fire is, to warm people and cook food and boil maple sugar, and because she now loved and respected Crow, whom she had never liked before.

A tall, limber pole swayed in the breeze outside the door of a *wikwam* near Neepah's home. The pole caught Frances' notice because of the two small decorated hoops hanging at the top. She stopped, stood in the snow, and squinted up.

Laced into the center of each little bright-painted hoop was a clump of long hair. The hair swung about when the breeze turned the hoops.

The hair in one hoop was rather the color of her own, but with gray in it. It reminded her of her papa's hair. The other lock of hair was like her grandpa's, all silvery white. The look of the hair reminded her of them, and made her think of her family, from whom she had been brought away, and the thought of them gave her a twinge of fright and sadness.

This Indian town was not a bad place to be in, and was always interesting, and the people took good care of her, but she hurt with a longing for her family. It was still not right that she was here.

She heard someone come close behind her, and turned to see the big woman Neepah, who took such good care of her, and the thin girl Minnow. Frances once had thought Minnow was a daughter of Neepah, but recently had learned that she wasn't. Neepah was just one of the women who had taken care of Minnow since soldiers carried her real mother away. That had happened while the soldiers were burning the town Minnow had lived in. It was a frightful thing to think of, and that was all Frances knew about it.

Neepah raised her chin toward the hoops, her way of pointing at things, and her face looked as if she had tasted something sour.

"From *wapsituk*," Neepah said in a hissing, mean voice. "*Mata* Zhaynkee. Bad English." Frances knew *wapsi* meant white; snow was *wapsi* to look at. English were *wapsi* people. But what did Neepah mean was from white people? Neepah was still looking distastefully up at the hair in the hoops, and with a strange, sickening feeling, Frances remembered what had happened to Nathan Kingsley in front of her house. The hair in the hoops must be the scalps of white people.

Bad English, Neepah had said.

Just then Minnow reached over and tugged a lock of Frances' hair, looked up at the hoops, bared her teeth and made her eyes fierce, then let go, smiled at her and nodded.

Shivering, from fright as much as cold, Frances thought of the words she had learned, enough to ask why such people were bad.

There then poured from Neepah a rapid stream of spitting, growling words, a few of them English words Frances barely recognized, others Indian words Frances partly followed, most flowing too fast to follow at all; but at length Frances understood that the bad white people had lied to the Lenapehwuk, Neepah's people, and cheated them, driven them from their homelands in the East, given them sicknesses, carried them off to make work slaves of them, burned their towns, destroyed their food, and killed them with guns and swords.

Neepah said something to Minnow, who pulled up her dress to expose the terrible scar on her thigh. Neepah managed to make Frances understand that when the *wapsi* soldiers took Minnow's mother away, they hit baby Minnow with a sword. At that time Neepah had had her own baby girl at one breast, and then had to take Minnow to the other. Neepah's face and gestures were at one moment violent and vicious, the next, tender and motherly.

Frances by now had forgotten the scalps on the pole, this was such a frightful story. Then she thought of what she had just heard, and asked:

"You have a *meeumuns*? What child is your daughter?"

The woman replied through thin, hard lips: "*Nagax'e. Ong ul.* Dead now. By more soldiers later. *Mata wapsituk!*" Again she jerked her chin toward the high-hanging scalps.

Frances looked up at them. It was hard to believe that people did such things to each other, even though she remembered Wareham's dead soldier brother with his bloody head. Cutting children and taking their mothers away, she could scarcely imagine. Those scalps up there that had reminded her of her papa's and grandpa's hair reminded her as well that not all white men were bad; her family could never have done such things. They were Friends. Friends never hurt anyone. She would have to tell that to Neepah, make her understand that her own people, though *wapsituk*, had never done such things.

It was some comfort to know that the hair that looked like her papa's and grandpa's could not actually be theirs, for they were Friends, not bad wapsi men, and so they would never be killed and scalped like that.

She saw Wareham Kingsley again that day. He was near a group of Indian boys who were sliding snow snakes. It was one of those wonderful games they were always playing, like throwing lances and shooting arrows at rolling hoops. The snow snakes were like walking staffs, curved at the heavy end, without bark, smooth and slicked with wax. The boys would trample out long icy grooves in the snow and then compete to make their sticks go slithering farthest along the channel.

Wareham was not throwing a stick. He was sulking, half watching. Frances had observed now and then that the Indian boys admitted Wareham into their rough games, but he usually dropped out, frowning and acting hurt. She thought he was silly not to play in those exciting games. She wished girls played snow snakes. She could feel in herself the grace and strength to make a snow snake go as far as any boy possibly could. At home among her brothers and sisters she had been a much praised hoop roller, able to fling a grapevine hoop so strongly and gracefully that it would roll far and steady, and the motion of flinging a snow snake seemed to be the same. If she ever got to be in a snow snake game, she would not be like Wareham, quitting and sulking. She would perhaps even win against boys. How that would surprise Wareham! she thought.

So she asked the old wise one, Owl, who was always breaking sticks for firewood, if he could find her a good snow-snake stick. He raised his eyebrows in surprise, but said nothing.

The next day he brought her a dogwood stick as pale as her skin, with a finger notch in the small end and a smooth, curved-up head with two brass tacks set in as eyes. It was a beautiful thing, and he had smoothed and waxed it till it was slick as bacon.

"Waneeshee, Muxumsah!" she exclaimed. She had remembered that she was supposed to call old men Grandfather. But he seemed stern and displeased. She went away, a little worried, to show the wonderful stick to Neepah.

The woman admired it, then said: "Did you remember what you are supposed to do?"

"Yes. I called him Grandfather and thanked him."

"But you gave him nothing? Palanshess, you must always give a person some *k'sha t'he* when you ask a favor! Here." She gave Frances a twist of tobacco for Owl.

"A ho!" he chuckled when she gave it to him. "Now may your snow snake go far!"

On a day not long after the sugaring was finished and there was still deep snow, Frances brought her new shiny stick to a boys' snow-snake game and had just boldly stepped up to throw when a boy's voice called her name and she looked up and saw a cousin.

He was behind a warrior on the back of a horse in a line of horses passing out of the village. Some of the horses carried green-coat soldiers. The horses were going out the gate of the palisade.

Frances stood holding her dogwood snow snake in a ready-to-throw position, and she was trying to remember that cousin's name when the horse he was on went through the gate and he was out of sight beyond the palisade. The boys in the game were yelling for her to fling her stick. She knew they did not like her being in their game, especially since some girls had come to watch her, and that the boys would like any excuse to put her out, so she couldn't just stand there. She leveled her stick and aimed its head along the icy groove, ran forward with her arm cocked and then stopped and gave the stick a hard underhand pitch very low, and the stick entered the groove flying level and straight. It was a perfect throw, the stick hissing and singing along the groove. The watching girls cheered, but the boys jeered, because her throw went farther than any of theirs had yet. She knew better than to toss her head and look smug, but couldn't help it. She tossed her red hair and smirked. That made some of the boys angry, and the girls laughed at them.

She kept doing so well that eventually the boys decided they were tired of the snow-snake game and took their sticks and left. It was only then that Frances thought again about seeing her relative, and she remembered who he was.

She had seen him only two or three times. He was called Cousin Isaac.

Isaac Tripp, she remembered. He was named after his grandpa, who was also her grandpa. He had lived on another farm Grandpa Tripp owned elsewhere in the valley. Now she remembered hearing, back in the summertime, that Indians had carried him away after the big battle in the summer. She could remember how upset Grandpa Tripp had been then, and she thought, I wish I could go home and tell Grandpa that I saw Cousin Isaac today and that he didn't look hurt, so Grandpa could stop worrying about him.

But if I could go there and do that, Grandpa could stop worrying about me, too.

For a while the girls played with Frances' snow snake. Later, as she plodded home with it, happy but tired, she wondered why she hadn't seen Cousin Isaac in the town before. During the sugar-making, everyone had been out and busy in the village, and she had seen several white people besides the soldiers. She had seen Wareham Kingsley many times. Maybe those other white people too had been caught by the Indians and brought here.

And then she thought, I wonder where those soldiers were going with him? I wonder if they were taking him home!

The winter sunlight slanting through the trees made long blue shadows on the snow. Between the *wikwams* the snow was trampled down hard where people had been walking, but it was very deep everywhere else. It was far up the sides of the *wikwams*. One morning Frances had offered to clean some of that deep snow down off the sides of the *wikwam*, but Neepah had stopped her, saying that snow kept the winter wind out, so the *wikwam* was easier to keep warm inside.

Frances and the women learned more of each other's words and ways every day, and Frances could understand most of the stories pretty well now. These people told so many. Most of the stories had animals in them that could talk to each other, and the things that happened in the stories showed how the animals had become the way they were. Like Crow. Most of the stories spoke of a time long before, when the animals, the four-leggeds, and the people, the two-leggeds, and the Winged birds and even the Fish, could all talk to each other and understand each other. Frances thought what a wonderful time that must have been.

In the beginning, when she had been brought here unable to understand or speak any of the Indians' language, she was lonely and afraid, but now that she could talk and understand, she was seldom lonely or scared. Sometimes now she would imagine being able to understand all the animals. At night she could hear owls and wolves, coyotes in the evenings, crows in the daytime, horses anytime in the village, and dogs, and sometimes she would think she almost understood what they were saying. She was never sure, though. But just in case, she did sometimes practice imitating their sounds and songs. Some of the boys could exactly make the sounds of almost any animal or bird, and some of those boys would teach her how, if she asked, though there were others who did not think that was something a girl should know. Like how to win snow snake.

A tall, gray-haired Indian man came walking toward her, wearing a fur hat with the animal's face still on it above his own face. It still had fangs. The man's face was sharp and narrow-eyed. He was carrying a gun and a pair of snowshoes. A few weeks ago she would have cringed in fright on seeing such a man approach. But she knew now that this man was just a hunter who was going out, and that he would put on the snowshoes when he was in the woods so he could walk on top of the snow because hunters had such long distances to go.

"Zhaynkee," he said to her, and his thin lips stretched in a smile with very white, even teeth, the kind of good teeth few white people his age would still have. She smiled at him, and he went on. She knew now that the word meant "English people." The old *huma* who lived in Neepah's *wikwam* had called her that for days before she learned what it meant. Many people in the village called her that, but they did not speak it as a hateful name. They might be at war with the white people, but no one seemed to dislike *her* for being a white person.

But maybe they liked her just because she was a child. They did seem to love children. Everyone was kind to everyone's children, and the children were hardly ever punished.

Here in the Indian village after these few weeks, Frances found herself to be much as she had always been at home: very much favored, and able to gain more attention and loving kindness than did even the younger and prettier children. Now almost six, she was very concerned with her place in people's affections, and tried to keep a close accounting of the ways in which she maintained it. At home her mother had always made much of her bright talk and her eagerness to learn everything. It seemed that the women in this village were pleased with her for those same reasons. She was learning their language quickly, and whenever she offered to tell one of their *lachimu*, or stories, back to them, they were delighted. Another thing they liked was her explanation of the beliefs of the Quaker Friends. She would remember as well as she could the things she had heard her parents say about that: the peacefulness, the fairness, the equality between people. They liked it that a Quaker woman could state her beliefs to her husband and make choices and decisions. "Lenapeh women too!" they would exclaim, pointing around to each other and laughing. And if a man happened to be there hearing, he too would laugh and nod his head. But then he would usually shake his head and flutter his hands in the air and make a sour face.

Another thing in Frances' favor here was simply her thick, long, wavy red hair. At home, in a family almost all red-haired, that had not been such a remarkable asset, though her mother had always made much of its thickness and luster and often sat brushing it for her in the evenings. Here among these dark-haired people it was her particular glory. She knew they were fascinated by it. Often they would reach out and play with its curls while talking to her.

She turned back the deerhide door flap of Neepah's *wikwam* and ducked into the warmth. It was so dark after the sun on the snow that she could barely see Neepah at first. The woman said in her own language, "I greet Palanshess home."

"*Waneeshee,* Neepah. Hello, Minnow."

Frances moved near the fire, sat close to Minnow on a mat, and slipped off her wet moccasins. She propped them on a fire-ring stone with the soles up, leaned forward in the fire heat, and rubbed her icy feet with her icy hands until her fingers and toes were hot and tingly. Then she told Neepah and Minnow, as well as she could in that language, about getting into the boys' snow-snake contest and doing so well at it that the boys quit and left.

At first Neepah laughed. Then she was quiet for a while, moistening a strand of sinew with saliva to soften it, then wrapping it tightly around a short handle to bind it to a flint blade. Then she said: "*Kulesta!*" Listen! It was the way a story always began. And so, happily, Frances sat playing with her toes and listened.

It was about Neepah Huma, Grandmother Moon. Neepah had been named for the moon, Frances knew by now, and so many of her stories were of Grandmother Moon, in some way. In this one, the time was very long ago when Grandmother Moon was young. If you looked up from the ground in those days you saw the Young Moon surrounded by stars all as big as she was, some even bigger in the sky. She was so wonderfully bright and shiny then, and the stars were so close around, that they all made night bright as day. All the stars were young men and they hung around Moon to court her. Young Moon thought she could be even brighter than stars. And so she shut her eyes and strained, making herself brighter and brighter.

Soon, Young Moon was so bright that the stars could not even be seen from here. Shamed, they went far away, silently. Young Moon had not even noticed their leaving, but she just kept her eyes shut and strained and shone even harder, until suddenly it was too much and, with a burst of smoke, she just burned out. When she looked around, she was alone. The stars were far away. And that is why Grandmother Moon now is the color of ashes, with dark smudges on her face, and is alone, and night is dark.

Neepah said, "Lenapeh women speak equally with Lenapeh men in Council. They are as strong as men. Some things we can do men cannot. We can create babies in our bodies. But we let them be best at things they like to do. Hunting. Fighting. As long as they think they are better at something, they like to stay near us. *Zhukeh lachimu kishalokeh!*" The story is finished!

Frances clapped. "*Waneeshee,* Neepah! *Wehlee heeleh!*"

It was not until she was nearly asleep that night, snuggled between Neepah's big warm body and Minnow's little skinny one, that Frances realized that the story had been meant to teach her not to outshine boys in the things they like to do.

After that snow-snake game, many of the girls came around to be friends with Frances. Snow was melting, though now and then new snow would still fall, and little by little the days were growing warmer. With the tree-sugaring finished, there was not much work children could help with, so Frances and Minnow and their many friends, girls their age, roamed the town like a little twittering flock of birds, flitting from place to place and amusing themselves with anything that came to mind.

To Frances it seemed that most of the people in the town were women and girls. There were few men and boys. In the mornings most of the men left at daybreak and were gone trapping and hunting. And many of the men, like those she had seen riding away from the town with her cousin Isaac, were often gone on journeys with the green-coat soldiers.

One of the girls one morning led them to a spot by the creek, downstream from the bathing place, so she could show off her grandfather, who was a canoe maker.

Even before they saw the smoke from the canoe-making camp, they were hearing the measured striking of the tools, like axe blows. The creekside glade reeked of ash and charred wood.

Frances had not expected to see people who were black, and nearly recoiled in fright at the sight of the men working in the smoky place. Their faces, clothes, and hands were as black as their hair, and when they looked up at the approaching girls, their eyes were red. Frances had heard of black-skinned people. Her mother and father had spoken of black people because the Friends were against the owning of slaves, who were black people or sometimes Indians.

These men working with tools were in the midst of fires. Huge fallen trees lay on the creek bank, with fires burning on top of them. The ground was covered with charred wood and ashes, and

the girls' moccasins were blackened at once when they walked
into the place. Everything was black, and when the girl's grandfather got off a log he was chopping to come toward her, Frances
realized that his skin was not really black, it was just covered with
soot and char. He was an Indian, with white hair grayed by ash,
and he smelled like soot.

The old man was kind to the girls and showed them how the
canoes were made. The top sides of the fallen logs were burned
until the burnt wood could be scraped and hewed out with stone
tools, something like the adze Frances' father had used in building
the family's log house, except his tool had been metal. Only two
of these Indians had metal tools, one an axe and the other a short-
handled adze. The men with the metal tools were cutting on an
unburned log, and their chips lay white and yellow on the blackened ground. The canoes were long and round-bottomed, hollowed downward by the chopping and scraping, and when the girl
asked her grandfather if the girls could get in one, he let them
climb into the unburned one. They all faced the end that was
toward the creek, ten girls with room left over, and for a little
while they pretended that they were canoe-riding in water, until
the grandfather told them they would have to get out and let the
men go on working on the vessel. Minnow asked Frances if she
had ever ridden a canoe in the water, and when she shook her
head, boasted that she herself had often ridden canoes, and not just
in creeks, but on the big river.

"I will sometime," Frances bravely announced. "I will ride in a
canoe on the biggest water there is."

They were hungry and started back toward the town, stopping
for a while by the *wikwam* of the *sakima*, the town head man. He
was sitting on a log in front of his *wikwam* with his eyes closed,
while a woman did something to his chin. "The woman is the
sakima's wife," Minnow explained as they went on. "She pulls
out those hairs that grow on a man's face so he will not have hair
growing there like the *wapsi* men." Frances, with a twinge in her
breast, remembered seeing her father shave his face hair off with
soap and a razor.

"My father did not let hair grow on his face," Frances said. She
did not want Minnow or the other girls to think she had come from
people with hairy faces. Sometimes Frances almost forgot that she
had come from another kind of people, but these Lenapeh seemed
so proud that they were not like white men that it would remind

her, and she hoped they really understood that her Quaker people
were not like those others. She felt that they would have to know
that in order to like her. They really did seem to like her, but when
they said things about the *wapsi* people, she was afraid they might
look at her *wapsi* skin and keep Lenapeh secrets from her. She
tried not to mention the *wapsi* people herself, but paid careful
attention to what was said of them. *Wapsi* just meant white. A
white person was *wapsini*. *Wapsituk* meant "those white people."
Lenapehwuk meant "we the People," or "us." But Lenapeh itself
meant "the Real People." Frances wanted to know how to say all
those things just right, so she always listened carefully to how her
friends said them. But for explanations she asked only Neepah.
Sometimes other older people would explain things, but she asked
only Neepah, who was the one she could confide anything to or
ask anything, like a mother. In Frances' heart, Neepah was the
center of this place.

When they came to Neepah's *wikwam*, she was outdoors pounding dried corn into meal. She stood over an upright section of log
that was hollowed like a bowl in the upper end. The corn was in
the bowl, and Neepah was lifting and dropping the pestle with
both hands. It was as long as she was tall, large at the upper end to
give it weight, slim as a child's arm the rest of its length. Neepah
could do this tirelessly, lifting and dropping it, giving it a little
turn, so the fire-hardened small end beat the corn into finer and
finer meal, fine and white as flour. Frances saw that this was the
pale kind of corn Neepah used for making dumplings. The bluish-
purple kind called *sesapsink* was used in other ways, usually as a
roasted meal that warriors or hunters carried dry in a pouch to eat
while traveling. Frances remembered having seen warriors eat it
without even stopping along the path when they had brought her
here. Sometimes the *sesapsink* corn was just scorched without
grinding and carried that way by hunters going far. Frances had
learned some of the secrets of *xaskwim* by watching and listening
to Neepah, but the woman had made it clear that there was much
more to know.

"The *wapsituk* learned from us how to grow corn," Neepah
would say, "but they know nothing about using it. They do not
even know it is sacred. To them, eating is just belly-filling. They
will eat any meat, even rabbit, horse, muskrat, woodchuck, which
we Lenapehwuk know are *kulakan*." She had explained that anything *kulakan* was forbidden by the Creator. And not just foods

were *kulakan*; so were many behaviors. Creator had forbidden many things, such as stealing and gossiping. No one must ever marry someone from the same animal-sign family. One from the Turtle Clan, for example, could not marry anyone else from that clan, but must instead take a mate from the Wolf Clan or Turkey Clan. It seemed there was so much to know to be Lenapeh; one had not to know anything to be *wapsini*. Among Lenapehwuk, for example, it was permissible to blow stinky air in the presence of some relatives, but *kulakan* to do so among others, and a child must learn such rules very young.

"In the pot by the fire is *m'sukatash*," Neepah told the girls. "It is still hot for you to eat."

While the two girls were eating succotash and warming themselves by the fire, Neepah came in with the flour she had made. She mixed it with a little water, in a big hewn-wood bowl that Frances had seen every day without really noticing. "It looks like a little canoe!" she exclaimed to Minnow. Minnow thought so too, and laughed.

Neepah chuckled. "Made just the same. Half a log hollowed out. This would be a good canoe for a baby." The girls laughed.

"We watched them making canoes today by the creek," Frances said.

"I knew that." Neepah was working the dough into little balls.

"How did you know that, Neepah?"

"Your feet and your bottoms are black. So, you saw the canoe makers. The hardest workers of all men. They work almost as hard as women." She looked in the succotash pot. "As I thought, you two have nearly eaten it all. We will make broth for these *suhpahnmush* to cook in." She told Minnow to put more wood on the cookfire and hang the iron kettle over it half full of water. She always told the girls how she was cooking so they would come to know. "This is dry deer meat," she said, dropping in several dark, thin leathery strips. "Now acorn meal. Now this is a little powder of dried squash, so the broth will not be thin like water. Now it will have to get hot and bubble a long while. Then we will drop the *suhpahnmush* in to cook. You will be hungry again by then. It will take that long. Almost night by then. Do you want to go and play? Or lie down awhile to rest? Or help me make string?"

So for a while they made string. Neepah took down from the roof a great wad of spruce root that had been hanging there. A mouse jumped out of it, landing almost in the fire, then scurried into the shadows under a bed. "Eh!" Neepah exclaimed, shaking the wad to dislodge any more mice if there were any. None fell. She sniffed the roots. "No. She was not living in here, that *axpo'kwess*. Where *axpo'kwess* lives smells like her urine. She was just in here stealing roots to make her nest." Neepah and the girls sat separating and untangling fine strands. Neepah soaked them in water and then twisted two strands together one way while Minnow twisted two strands the same way, and then, still pulling them tight, they twisted their double strands together in the other direction so they tightened up together. At the end of each strand, they wove in threads of a new length of root, still twisting and reverse twisting, so that the string grew longer and longer and there were no weak places. Neepah tied one end to a roof pole and pulled on it so hard that water squeezed out, but it would not break.

Frances watched until she felt she could help, and soon all three were making string quietly, humming, the broth seething fragrant in the kettle. She remembered how her father and mother had used lots of brown rope and white twine, but her father had always bought it. Her mother never made string, though she did spin flax and wool yarn for clothing. Frances worked the wet fibers with her fingers and remembered her mother's whirring wheels and spindles. She remembered too the wheels on the white people's wagons and carriages. She mused on this, which she had never really thought of: that white people used wheels for many things; even the grinding stone had been a wheel. But she had seen not one wheel here among the Indians, and yet they seemed not to need any kind of wheels, and could still do anything they needed to do without them.

Neepah had begun talking about something in a story voice. Frances' mind returned from wheels to the ancient days of which Neepah was telling:

"Lenapeh are the Grandfathers to many peoples, the many who speak a tongue like ours, the many who sing songs like ours. The Powhatan, the Nanticoke, the Mahikan, the Miami, the Ottawa, the Anishinabe, the Piankashaw, the Abenaki, the Micmac, the Shawnee, they all grew out of the first Lenapeh who came down from the ice mountains in the north and made homes all over Taxkwox Menoteh, this land on the Turtle's back. Many generations all lived in peace and sang the same songs. Now and then we had to have war with the Iroquois, and the Talekewi, who were large and pale and attacked us near Namesh Sipu, the Mother of Rivers, out that way." She jutted her chin toward the creek, westward. "But those other peoples grew out of the Lenapeh, and moved down other rivers, making towns, taking those other names, but still peaceful with us, and they knew us as the Grandfathers, and they still go many generations in peace. But since the *wapsituk* came, those happy ages have ceased. Now they have pushed us out from our homeland by the Eastern water, and divided all the peoples and set them against each other with lies. We are losing. Only once was there an honest and fair *wapsini*. We called him Mikwon, the Quill. His *wapsi* name was Penn."

"Ah!" Frances exclaimed. Neepah and Minnow looked at her, frowning. "Penn!" she exclaimed. "He was a . . . he was of the Friends, like my family!"

"Kweh-kuh," said Neepah.

"Yes. People call us Quakers. My family, like Penn . . . we are always fair and hurt no one."

"Hm. *Wehlee heeleh,*" Neepah murmured, tying off an end of the string and edging over to tend the cookfire. "But Penn Mikwon is dead now and there is not a *wapsini* who is our friend we can trust, not anywhere. Lenapehwuk were once the Grandfathers here, keeping peace on Taxkwox Menoteh, land on the Turtle's back. Now everyone pushes us and strikes us and tells us lies. The *wapsituk* are always so close we can smell them, but they will do nothing for us unless it helps them more than us. The *wapsituk* are many, but Lenapehwuk have not one to trust among them all."

"You can trust Friends," Frances insisted dutifully, always believing this of her people.

"You say it," Neepah replied, but there was in her face a look that showed her doubt, and that look troubled Frances, who wanted everyone to believe her, and Neepah most of all.

While the broth simmered in the afternoon, Frances and Minnow crawled everywhere in the *wikwam* looking for the nest of the mouse, and Neepah left for a while, telling them to keep a fire burning under the kettle.

They never found the mouse nest, or even saw the mouse, but while they were looking they talked about animals of all sorts, and Frances' thoughts eventually came to what she had heard about the turtle. She sat with both palms pressed to the floor, then asked

Minnow, "Do you really think there is a turtle holding up all this land? Mountains and everything?"

"All Lenapehwuk know that to be so. All other peoples too."

Frances squinted at her, doubtful. She had never heard such a thing until she came here. If her Quaker parents had known such a thing, they would have told her. They had said the world was a ball in the air, which floated and stayed steady without needing anything under it, always going around the sun. That in its own way was hard to believe—something able to stay up all by itself with nothing under it—but her father had pointed at the moon and said, "Do you see anything holding up the moon? God holds everything up where He put it."

Frances said now to Minnow, "Then what holds up the turtle?"

Minnow looked at her from the edges of her eyes. "What do you say, Palanshess?"

"I ask, what is under the turtle to hold him up?"

"Not *him*. It is Grandmother Turtle."

"Then I ask, what is under her to hold her up with the world on her back?"

Minnow looked uncomfortable, glancing around and tight-lipped. "Why do you ask this? Under everything is Turtle!"

"Then under Grandmother Turtle is another turtle to hold her up?"

Minnow shrugged. "Turtle is under everything. I told you. All people know that."

Frances was on a road of inquiry and enjoying it. This was like arguing with her older sisters at home until they flung up their hands, which she'd always taken to mean that she had won. "Then you say that under the turtle under the earth there is another turtle? And then what is under *that* turtle?"

Minnow took a long breath through her nose with her mouth shut tight and her eyes narrowed. Fists on hips, she exclaimed:

"See, Palanshess! It is Turtle *all the way down*!"

CHAPTER THREE

May 1779
Wyalusing, a Town of the Delawares

The first day of sunshine and real warmth after a long, rainy spring, Frances started to put on her ragged gray dress to go outdoors, but Neepah snatched it away from her and said, "Today this dirty thing will be washed in the creek."

Frances blinked. "I have no other garment!"

"That I know," Neepah said, folding the dress.

"But I want to go out there. This is a lovely day!"

"That too I know. Today we will all go to the fields and begin planting the *xaskwim*. But that is later, when the sun has warmed the ground. Go on now." She motioned toward the door.

"But I have no clothing on."

"On a day like this you need no clothing, little Pretty Face."

Frances was dumbstruck. Though she had grown used to sleeping naked, and was bathed at the creek by some of the women, she had never imagined just going out of the *wikwam* with nothing on. At the mere notion of it, she envisioned the expression of horror it would cause on her mother's face.

"Go!" Neepah exclaimed with a shooing motion. "You stand there making a mouth like *namesh*, the fish! Have you forgotten the language you learn so well, and do not understand 'go'?"

"But do you not see I have nothing on?"

A mocking little smile began to show on Neepah's lips. "Yes, I see that. How could I not see? Your *wapsi* skin gleams like Grandmother Moon. Go out and let Noox Keeshoox shine on you. Grandfather Sun will make your skin my color."

"I can't! This is bad!"

61

"How is this bad? Look out there and see. The little ones cannot wait for such a day, the bareness feels so nice!"

Frances hunched in the shadows beside the door, peering out. Everywhere in the village the voices of children were squealing and laughing. At that moment a small flock of girls, most of whom she knew and played games with, raced giggling and chattering down the lane between the *wikwams*, Minnow leading them. The sun dapple through the young leaves above flickered over their brown skin. Not one of them had on a stitch. A moment later four boys ambled past in another direction, carrying throwing sticks and a grapevine hoop. With their long hair hanging loose, they looked almost like the girls, except for their pee spouts. She had seen those on her little brothers.

Neepah said behind her, "Now you see. So go and feel good before the mosquitoes are born." And, moving swiftly, she took Frances' arm with one hand and put the other under her little white bottom and propelled her out. Frances spun around and tried to dart back into the darkness of the *wikwam*, but Neepah stood grinning with her arms barricading the door. The woman said, "You cannot come back in. Now while you are naked for bathing, go down to the creek and wash the winter off. You smell like a little *sheekak*."

Frances' mouth dropped open. She knew that meant skunk. Tossing her red hair and biting her lips tight, she turned her back on the insult and stamped away toward the creek, almost too indignant to feel shame for her nakedness.

Because she was so white, all the children playing at the creek looked her over with curiosity, but in a moment their attention passed and they went back to splashing and squealing. The coldness of the water made her shudder, but she went in and squatted with the water to her waist to hide herself, and also because Neepah had told her she smelled bad. And the water certainly was not as cold as it had been the times when the women bathed her in the winter. There had been days then when even though the creek had ice at its edges, it felt warmer than the winter air. Since being with these Indian people, she had endured cold of the kind that her mother had warned would bring on her death, but she'd not even gotten sick from it. Neepah had told her, "One is fire inside. My father told me this. When outside it is cold, Huma Shawanawunk, South Grandmother Spirit, blows on the fire inside you. She is even stronger than Muxumsah Lowunawunk, North Grandfather Spirit, who blows on your outside. That is all, and it passes." Frances had a hard time keeping track of all the spirit names, and sometimes thought these people lived with magic. And yet everything Neepah and the older women taught her seemed to prove true. Indeed she could endure cold.

Squatting in the water, Frances peed and shivered and watched the other children dive and tumble and splash each other. Ever since spring began bringing up the wildflowers and making the trees bud, the children had been in a high state of excitement—but not only the children. The grown-up men and women were intense and busy, seeming like children who are expecting something. Many worked in the center of the town on a great arbor called Xinkwikan, the Great House, strengthening it with new poles and sheets of bark. Neepah explained to Frances what the Great House was, and from what she had said, it was like a church. Her family, being of the Friends Society, did not have a church, but other people at Wilkes-Barre did. Frances had explained to Neepah that the Quakers prayed at home. Neepah had replied, "Lenapehwuk do the same. All the time. But in the Great House, in spring and fall, we make the Sacred Fire and give thanks to He Who Creates By Thinking. We prepare for doing that soon." And so the excited anticipation of that event hung in the air and animated everybody, and Frances could feel it.

Without someone holding her, Frances felt precarious in the water. She feared the deep places. Hardly any white people knew how to swim. Here in this creek were children even younger than she, as young as three years, even, who could paddle about without touching the bottom, or go down in one place and surface somewhere else. Minnow, who was well named, could go underwater from one creek bank to the opposite and back without coming up to breathe. But even though the little ones were like otters in the stream, they were always watched over by others a few years older, who helped them, or corrected them if they became too rough or reckless. They were like older brothers and sisters, even though from different families. Frances knew that if she got in trouble in the water, someone would help her. All the same, she stayed at the edge where it was shallow, taking no chances of falling into the current.

She knelt there and rinsed herself until she was chilly and felt

clean, and just when she was ready to get out into the warm sunshine despite her nakedness, she found Minnow standing on the
creek bank in her way, wearing nothing but a tiny bag the size of
a thumb, hanging by a thong around her neck. Sunlight filtering
through the high foliage shimmered and danced on her skin, making her look for a moment like a spirit of shadow and gold, and she
had appeared as unexpectedly as a spirit. Minnow said, "Neepah
tells you, wash your hair too."

And so Frances did, though she would get colder and the wet
hair would hang cold on her even after she got out in the warm
sun. When she was done, and wiped the water from her eyes,
Minnow was still there, and now the girl said, "Neepah says bring
you home when your hair is clean. So come now."

They were almost back to Neepah's *wikwam*, trotting along
between the houses and in and out among walking people and
horses and dogs, before Frances heard some boy laugh and shout
"Wapsini!" which reminded her that she was naked. For an
instant she remembered her mother and what she might think of
this, but then the sun and mild air and the feeling of cleanness
were so pleasant and all as they should be, and there was so much
happening now that spring had blossomed from the gray winter,
that she passed that shout out of her mind and hurried on to see
why Neepah had called her home.

Neepah had two covered clay pots sitting in the middle of the
wikwam, and a tool made of a stick and a big flat bone were on
them. She was sitting by the fire ring, where the fire was down to
ashes and embers, working on something very small when the
girls darted in through the doorway. Frances saw her quickly hide
the little thing under her hand and slip it behind a bundle, like a
child caught with something. Neepah got up in that graceful way
the women had, merely unfolding her legs and swaying forward
till she was standing erect, without using her hands against the
ground at all. She met Frances with a smile, ran a hand down over
her hair and acted like a dog sniffing around her, then said,
"Wehlee heeleh!" Not like the little skunk now. Now eat some of
that sweet hominy before we go and work in the field."

The girls ate. Frances loved the sweet flavors of maple sugar
and berries in the hominy, but much of her mind was on what
Neepah had so quickly tucked out of sight. She had come to trust
this woman like a mother, so it bothered Frances to have caught
Neepah hiding something from her. While she ate she slyly

watched Neepah pick the little secret thing up from behind the bundle and slip it inside the bundle. She pretended she was not doing anything, and Frances pretended she was not watching her. It was like being home among brothers and sisters, where they all had done sneaking, including Frances. They had seldom done anything bad, but even innocent things or good things had been done secretly, if only to know something the others did not. Frances hoped that Neepah would go outside so she could look in the bundle, but then she felt ashamed for having thought that. Anyway, if Neepah did go out and she peeked, Minnow probably would tell on her.

But it did not matter, because Neepah did not go out. When the girls were finished eating, Neepah stuck the scoop back in the hominy pot and picked up the tool and one of the covered pots and told the girls to carry the other pot by the rope net it was slung in. *"Kulesta,"* she said. Listen. "They sing as they go to plant! Come now. This is a day of joy and importance!"

And Frances could hear the distant voices of many women beginning to sing, a simple, repetitive, slow song that swelled and faded on the breeze. It was a strange and lovely sound. She had hardly ever heard singing before; the Friends did not favor it.

They walked through the village in the direction of the singing, catching up with other women and children going toward the gate in the palisade. The others were singing, and Neepah began singing the song with them. So did Minnow, but Frances did not know the song and did not try to sing it.

Eventually all the women and their naked little children were in a circle in an open field outside the palisade, a level bottomland where old tree stumps stood rotting. There was no underbrush in the field and no weeds. The ground was strewn with bleached dead cornstalks. The people in the circle faced inward, still singing, their bodies slightly swaying as they shifted their weight from one foot to the other. In the center of the circle was an aged *huma* standing with her white hair loose in the breeze. She held some kind of a bowl in her hands and smoke was coming from it. The old woman turned to face every direction, then bent to extend the smoke bowl toward the earth, then raised it toward the sky. The others stopped singing. Two motherly looking women stood beside the old one, looking very serious. They raised their hands toward the sky, palms up, and the old one began to pray. All the women in the circle, standing with their faces turned up toward the sun and holding their tools and pots and baskets, were totally quiet, and even the youngest children grew quiet. The scalp on the back of Frances' head tingled.

The *huma* began talking toward the sky. Her voice was feeble and Frances could not hear many of her words, but she did hear her speak to Kahesana Xaskwim, who she already knew was Mother Corn. The old woman often said *"Waneeshee"* and spoke of buds and leaves, of sun and thunder and rainwater, and she spoke about the prayer sounds one could hear when wind blows through the tops of trees. She said the People rejoiced when things began to grow. She spoke of the Three Sisters. Frances had heard the stories about Mother Corn, that she was the spirit that made plants give food the people could eat. But it seemed strange and wrong to her that prayers should be offered to someone besides God. She had heard that at home since she could remember: there is no one between thee and God; there are no priests and no sacramentals. Frances was not sure just what a sacramental was, but from what she had heard of them, they were the things that priests handled while praying, and she wondered if the smoking bowl might be a sacramental. Frances, who had never dreamed that she would ever be standing outdoors with no clothes on in a circle of Indian people, including grown women with their teats bare, was reaching back into her fading memories of what she had been taught all her life before, and she was a little frightened by all this. She wished her mother and father were here so she could ask them if this was right or wrong. Certainly they always knew what was right and wrong.

But even while she was thinking about these doubts, something was beginning to happen that made the doubts simply float and scatter away like the smoke from the old woman's bowl:

Those three women standing in the swirling smoke in the center of the circle slowly disappeared. When the breeze blew the smoke away, there were three plants where the women had stood. One, in the center, was a cornstalk tall and dark green with its shiny long leaves and crowning yellow tassel. The others were broad-leaf, twining plants; one's vines twined up the cornstalk, the other's crept over the ground. The plants were there where the women had been standing, and the singing could be heard again. But the women and children in the circle were not moving their mouths, and the singing seemed to be rising up from the ground. Frances could feel something rising up into her through the soles of her feet, and it was not any usual feeling like wetness or cold or heat, but the music itself, so that although she did not understand the words of the song, she understood that Kukna, Mother Earth, was singing that she was ready for seeds and would nourish them now. That was all the song said, though there were no real words to be understood. Instead of the words there was simply a tingling happiness that rose through her and went out through the top of her head into the sky, a feeling she had felt only a few times ever before, when she had been praying and knew that God heard her prayers.

In a moment the joy was gone and there was left only a memory of the singing, fading and echoing into the wind, and the three women were standing in the center where they had been before, the smoke swirling from the bowl, the three plants no longer visible. Frances looked around and all the women in the circle looked very happy, talking to each other and hugging each other and their children, and walking away from the circle into various parts of the field. Frances felt a warm hand on her back and looked up to see Neepah smiling down. "Palanshess saw them, the Three Sacred Sisters?"

"Sisters? I saw plants."

"*Wehlee heeleh!* Corn and beans and squash, they are the Sisters. Come now. We work." She hefted her bone tool.

Neepah's tool was a hoe. She chopped and worked the ground with the bone part, which she explained was the shoulder bone of a deer. The wooden handle to which it was fixed grew wet and slick with Neepah's sweat. She had braided her long hair behind her head so it would not hang all sweaty around her bent-down face. The sweat ran down her shoulders and dripped from the nipples of her hanging breasts, which quaked every time she chopped into the ground. The deerhide skirt tied around her waist grew dark and sodden with sweat. She was working harder than Frances had ever seen a woman work, although her own mother had always been busy working. This was the kind of work Frances had seen only men do, and all the Indian women were doing it, but they were singing as they worked.

Frances and Minnow helped Neepah, and it was hard work. The woman would dig a hole with the hoe, and chop the soil from the hole until it was fine and loose, without any clods. Boys brought baskets of creek fish up to the field, and it was the children's duty to keep bringing fish over, to drop one into each hole.

Frances at first did not like handling the slimy, scaly fish with their sharp fins and their smell, but after a while she got used to it. Neepah filled each hole with the loose dirt, covering the fish, and then mounded up the dirt to form a trough around the mound. She pressed three seeds of corn and two flat squash seeds into the soil mound and covered them. Every seed had been rubbed with bear oil, and so the bear oil and the sweat and the soil and the fish made a sticky and strong-smelling mud over everyone's hands. Frances and Minnow went down to the creek every few minutes to fill a pot with water, and that gave her a chance to wash the mess off her hands.

The hardest work was carrying the full water pot. She had never thought water could be so heavy. Neepah wet each mound of seeded soil with some of the water, then moved on to the next place where she had made a hole. She stopped singing now and then to explain things. The fish would rot in the ground to feed the little corn plant's roots, she said. "Kahesana Xaskwim likes fish," she said. "She told us that long ago and so we always feed her fish. The bear oil protects the little seed from mold until it has become a little plant. Then it can take care of itself and needs only water. If rain does not fall in the summer, we have to bring water from the creek. That is hard work in the summer. You will learn that to be so. You will feel so hot."

"I feel so hot now," Frances said.

"Not hot like summer hot."

"But very hot."

Neepah straightened up, leaned her hoe against her thigh and looked at Frances, turned her around and looked at her back and shoulders. "Ah, heh! I said Grandfather Sun would turn you red!" She rinsed her hands with water from the pot and then reached into the bear oil and with both hands smeared it over Frances' skin, especially where she was becoming sunburned. Neepah was dripping with sweat. Her body was big and thick and brown and strong. "Now is the hide of Palanshess so hot?"

"It feels good now. *Waneeshee*. But I smell like bear."

"Maxk'wah the bear is the brother of the two-legged. He helps us in many ways. I will tell you Maxk'wah stories one night. Now. Bring more water. Wash the pot out first so we can drink."

They worked on as the sun moved westward in the afternoon sky and grew hotter. Frances could hardly lug the water pot from the creek, she had become so tired, and the bear oil on her body and arms made the pot hard to hold. The women kept working and sweating and singing. Once, Neepah stopped singing and put down the hoe and shook her fingers down to spray sweat on the ground. She laughed and said, "I believe Mother Corn likes *pim* as much as she likes fish! Maybe our *pim* makes the corn grow."

"I do not know *pim.*"

"*Pim* is this," Neepah said, sluicing more sweat off her arms and flicking it on the ground. "Here is more *pim* to drink, Mother Corn."

The field was very wide, but most of it now was covered with the little planting hillocks the women had made. They were everywhere, about two steps apart. They were not in rows like the corn the Slocum men planted after making plow furrows.

Slocum, Frances thought, suddenly shivering with a strange feeling. She had not thought her family's name much, hardly ever since living in this village and learning the language of these people. Frances was still her name, by which she still thought of herself, and which Neepah still could not say right. But she had not heard or thought of *Slocum* for so long, she realized she might one day forget it if she did not use it somehow. It was a strange feeling, added to the other strange feelings she was getting from all this effort. She felt hot but shivery, and heavy but almost delicate enough for the breeze to blow over. And she still remembered seeing women turn to plants and then back to women, but it seemed as the afternoon wore on that perhaps she had only dreamed that.

But several times this afternoon she had felt that strange joy go up through her from the ground into the sky, like a prayer going up; it kept reminding her that she had seen what Neepah called the Three Sacred Sisters. *"Slocum,"* she whispered to herself, to get a hold on it again. *Slocum.* "Neepah?"

"I listen, Pretty Face. Ask."

"Where is the third Sister seed?"

"We'll plant beans later in these same little hills, not today. When the corn has a stalk strong enough for a bean vine to climb on and stay up from the ground."

"Does not the squash need to climb up?"

"No. It wanders on the ground. It grows wide leaves that cover the earth with shade so weeds will not grow in our field. The Three Sacred Sisters help each other, you see, just as you see all these Lenapeh women help each other now. And you, Pretty Face, you

have helped us well today. *Waneeshee.* You are not bad, for a
wapsini. Well, you *are* turning red, after all."

The pleasure rushed from the ground up through Frances again.
Neepah had called her a *wapsini*, but in a kind way, and made a
joke about her skin turning red from the sun. And she had called
her good. And she kept calling her Pretty Face.

Neepah chuckled. Frances laughed. There in the middle of a
busy field full of sweating brown women and pots and fish and
children, Frances laughed from pleasure. Even solemn Minnow
was laughing. This was a good time. But in the midst of their
laughter, Frances remembered Neepah hiding something from her.

Then they heard a rumbling. People turned and looked about. It
was the sound of hoofbeats, going fast. The women leaned on
their tools and watched a small band of riders come down off the
hillside out of the trees and race their horses in through the palisade. Some of the women turned and looked at each other. Then
for a while the women worked without singing. They would pause
and face the village, as if listening for something. But nothing
unusual was heard from the town, and the field was nearly all
planted, and so they worked until they were done.

The leading *huma* called out something from near the creek,
and all the women and children took their pots and tools and baskets down and set them on the ground on the side of the field along
the creek bank. Everyone was talking happily and laughing and
sighing with weariness. The children jumped in the creek, squealing with the shock of the cool water after the heat of the field.
Neepah motioned for Frances to go in the creek, and she went to
the edge and sat with her feet in the water, gasping and shivering.
Minnow dove past her like an arrow into the water.

Up the bank, all the women were stripping off their sweat-
soaked dresses. There were dozens of women standing there, old
saggy ones, strong, thick ones like Neepah, young ones with
nipples that pointed straight out. They all began singing then, a
different song from before, and set off walking, dragging their
dresses on the ground. Frances with her mouth hanging open
stood up to watch them go. She had never seen a sight like it. Their
brown and golden figures, shining with sweat in the afternoon
light that slanted from just above the treetops, filed around the
edge of the planted field. The children paid no attention, but kept
splashing and playing in the creek. Frances waded out to her knees
and then sat down quickly in the water until she was wet to the

neck, the cold water slaking the sunburn, and wiped her body and face with her hands until all the field dust and grit was off, though her skin was still a little slick with the bear oil. Meanwhile she kept watching the line of singing women passing along in the distance, dragging their garments and making dust.

"Slocum," she whispered to herself. "Slocum."

And finally when the singing grew louder, she saw that the women had followed the edge of the cornfield all the way around and were coming back to where they had started at the creek, and then the women whooped and laughed and charged into the cold water like children, except for a few old ones who eased in carefully, bathed themselves thoroughly, and rinsed and wrung out their clothes.

Then when they were dressed again in their wet clothes, with gooseflesh on their skin, and starting back toward the village with their children through the long shade of the trees, carrying pots and tools and baskets, the afternoon light growing deeper gold and the shadows more blue, Neepah said, "Those men came with something to tell that perhaps is not good. Men come home making happy noise if all is well." She sighed. "May I be mistaken. This is a joyful and important day, you will remember I said it would be. This was the day to plant and the Three Sisters blessed the day. There should be nothing bad brought to our village today. It must be to do with the *wapsituk*. When messengers come fast, it is usually that."

"Neepah, why did they all drag their garments and walk naked around the field?" She had been wanting to ask that.

"Why, to mark."

"Mark?"

"So all the little four-leggeds who would like to steal seeds will smell the *pim* of the two-leggeds, and will say, 'No, this field belongs to the Lenapeh, and we must stay out.' "

They walked on in the lovely waning daylight with the sun glowing in the pale green catkins and young leaves of the maples on the hill. Neepah finally seemed tired, breathing hard with the things she was carrying, and there was a grim and angry look about the way her mouth was set, and her eyes were glittering with anger or fear, and finally she spoke again.

"How good it would be if we could scent the ground of our country with sweat and the *wapsituk* would say, 'No, this land belongs to the Lenapeh; we must stay out.' But no. Even scenting it with blood does not teach them it is ours."

A few steps farther and she looked down. "You, Palanshess, I ask you, think that you are ours. May you not go back to such a bad people."

I keep telling you, Frances thought, my Slocum family are not a bad people! But something inside told her that this was not a good time to say that.

Neepah quickly built the embers in the fire ring into a small blaze to warm their food, but kept looking out the door of the *wikwam* and going out to talk to anyone who went by. They talked in quick, low voices. Frances knew that Neepah was hurrying and worried, which gave her a fearful feeling. It was the same as when she had watched her own mother to know whether everything was all right or not. But Neepah did notice that Frances was shivering, and told her to lie down in the bed and sleep until the food was warm. "I think you never were this tired," she said, "since the warriors first brought you here. Sleep a bit, Palanshess, or you might be sick. Minnow, go down and wash her cloth clothes at the creek right now and they will dry by the fire. She will need clothes. Tonight will be cool."

The sun had gone down beyond the forest, and through the smoke hole in the roof Frances could see that the wisps of cloud still had a tinge of red in them. She was looking at those clouds from the bed where she lay with a soft deerhide over her, and when she awoke there were stars outside the roof, and all around the fire women were sitting, talking with Neepah. Their words, through her weariness, were incomprehensible murmurs. Frances' body was so tired it hummed, and she closed her eyes again.

She dreamed of being in the cabin with her mother and her brothers and sisters, but her father and grandfather were not there and so she thought they must be up on the hill. The next time she opened her eyes and looked up, there was daylight sky outside the smoke hole and smoke was rising out into it and she needed to pee so urgently that she had been dreaming about peeing, and knew that if she had not awakened she would have done it in the bed. Her arms and buttocks and shoulders and thighs hurt where the sun had burned her skin, and her stomach was so empty it was talking, as her mother used to say. All of this came to her at once, with the awareness that she was alone in the *wikwam*. Frances remembered that she had gone to sleep waiting for supper to warm, and had not even awakened to eat it. As she slipped out of bed to run out and relieve herself, she saw that her gray dress was hanging near the fire on a thong. There were no voices outdoors, as there usually were after daylight.

Outside there was no one in sight, and so she just went around to the side of the *wikwam* and squatted on the ground instead of going down the path to the women's dirt trench as she knew she was supposed to do. The sun was not up above the trees in the east and it was still chilly, even though her sunburned skin was hot. She saw that she had little white blisters on her arms and thighs, and thus probably had them on her bottom too. The cool air gave her gooseflesh even on her hot skin, but it was above all the absence of people that made her shivery. This made an awful strangeness. She wanted to see Neepah, Minnow, anyone she knew. She had never been all alone before.

Hugging her arms around her body as she went around to the door, she heard voices at last. They were distant, muffled, many, and came from the center of the village, where the Council Lodge was.

She went into the *wikwam*. She felt her dress and it was dry, so she pulled it down from the thong and started to put it on over her head, but it scratched her sunburn, so she took it off and dropped it on the bed. She was perplexed and was becoming frightened, here all alone and feeling this way.

She remembered how the bear oil had soothed her sunburn the day before, and looked around for the little oil pot. She found it sitting behind a bundle, opened it and dipped her hands in. As she spread it over the hurting parts, she felt that she did indeed have blisters on her bottom as well. This time when she pulled the shabby, raveling little garment on, she could bear to have it against her skin. Squatting to replace the top on the oil pot, she was drawn toward the bundle. She remembered Neepah yesterday sneaking an unseen thing into it. She remembered that she had thought of looking in but had not had a chance because Neepah and Minnow were here. But now they were gone.

Half afraid, Frances went to the door and looked out, both ways. There was not a person in sight. She went back in and knelt by the bundle. Down inside her heart, her conscience started trying to shame her. But in her mind she thought that this was not an unfair thing to do, because Neepah was being sneaky about it and deserved to have it found out.

She slid her hand into the opening where she had seen Neepah put the thing, the voice of her conscience growing louder.

Then there came through her something that was not her conscience, something that was stronger. It passed through her as the good feeling from the earth had passed through her yesterday, but it was not a good feeling like that. It was a feeling as if her stomach might heave up. And she thought she heard a noise that was a part of that feeling—very faint, like a flapping of bird wings, and a shadow seemed to pass over. But when she looked up, her heart racing, the sky outside the smoke hole was still cloudless and bright.

She made her fingers crawl in the bundle, seeking deeper. She felt a strand, thin and threadlike, probably sewing sinew. Then she felt a lump, small and rounded and soft, like deerskin. The shadow passed over again and was gone, and there was the flapping, fluttery sound. But she kept probing.

Suddenly she went ice-cold all over, as if she had jumped in the creek. Something was scrambling over the back of her hand and up her arm. And as she yanked her hand out of the bundle, something stuck her finger. She had jerked her hand back so quickly that it flung something through the air. The little object hit the bark ceiling and fell to the ground in the light inside the doorway. Gasping and shuddering, she looked toward it and saw it move this way and that, and then it ran out of sight between the wall and the kindling wood stacked inside the door.

Axpo'kwess. A mouse.

Frances was shuddering and her heart was racing. A mouse was nothing to fear. But there had been those fluttering warnings and the strange feeling. And her conscience. And being sneaky while all alone with everyone unexplainably gone. She thought about the magic again. These people used magic smoke and changed from one thing to another, from women to plants. Was that mouse really Neepah, guarding her secrets? Or had Neepah put that mouse in the bundle to see whether she was sneaky? Was the hidden thing she had seen Neepah slip into the bundle yesterday a mouse? Frances felt almost sick from the dread of this strangeness and what it might mean. Her heartbeat was slowing now and she could again hear the faint voices in the distance, but still no laughter of children in the lanes between the *wikwams*.

She looked at the side of her finger where something had stuck her. A drop of blood stood on it. She thought at first that the mouse must have bitten her, but then she remembered, by the sensations that were still in her skin, that the sharpness had jabbed her finger after the mouse was already running up her arm.

Maybe Neepah had put a snake in there too, to catch her being sneaky. She drew back from the bundle, stood up, and sucked the blood off the stuck place.

No, she thought. Snakes eat mice. Neepah would not have put them in there together.

But of course there could be Indian magic that would make a snake not eat a mouse, she thought.

Frances had been among these people long enough that she had thought *axpo'kwess* instead of *mouse*, but there had not been much magic to scare her before, even though they told many magic stories.

But yesterday had been a strange day something like magic, with women becoming plants, and going around with nothing on and forgetting that she had nothing on. And then there had been the night, when she went to sleep without any supper, as she had never been able to do before, a sleep so deep and long it might have been a *spell*, such as she had heard of in old tales back home. Maybe Neepah had cast a spell on her.

And now this morning when nobody was around in the village. This seemed almost like part of the magic.

Neepah had said all those hard things about bad white people yesterday. I am a white person, Frances thought. Maybe she means to hurt me! Now Frances was afraid to keep looking for the hidden thing.

Her finger had stopped bleeding. She was calmed down from the scare the mouse had caused her. And though she felt vague dreads, there were two things that truly bothered her now. She was hungry and she was alone.

So she opened the pot by the fire and ate a scoop of sweet hominy, which was still a little warm. Then she went out of the *wikwam* and set out toward the sound of the voices and the Council Lodge.

When she came around the *wikwams* nearest the lodge, she found herself on the edge of the biggest gathering of people she had ever seen in one place. They stood or sat shoulder-to-shoulder, facing away from her into the clearing in front of the Council

Lodge, where someone was talking in a deep but excited voice. There were boys in the trees, and children were sitting on the ground looking between and around the legs of people standing in front of them. The people were all listening with great attention to the man who was inside the clearing talking. Sometimes the listeners would turn and murmur to each other. Other times the whole crowd would mutter and exclaim all at once at something the speaker had said. Frances could not see the man who was speaking, and she did not recognize his voice. She had heard the village *sakima* talk now and then to people of the town, but his voice was high and clear, not deep like this.

Since she could not see into the open place, Frances started around the edge of the crowd, looking for Neepah. She was sure she was here someplace, and though Frances had been upset and doubtful about her this morning, she needed her, and would not be content until she knew where she was. For one thing, Neepah was tall and strong and might hold her up in her arms or on her shoulders so she could see what important thing was happening on the Council Ground.

She went all the way around and did not see Neepah, and when someone in the crowd now and then would turn and see her, their faces were not friendly as usual. She wandered on, feeling a growing loneliness and fear, such a fear as she had not felt since her earliest days here in the Indian village.

At last she saw a place where she might be able to climb up and look over people's heads: a pole frame in which a large hide had been stretched for flensing. It was a little way back behind the crowd and so it was not being used for a perch by any children except one small naked boy who was at one end. He was a boy she had seen several times at the creek but had never known his name. He looked at her for a moment as she climbed up at the other end of the frame and then looked back toward the crowd. The frame was sturdy, being lashed to poles rooted in the ground. Now that she was standing on the lower cross pole, she could see over the heads of the grown-ups and see the man who was in the center talking.

He was a grand-looking Indian man whom she had never seen before. He was tall and lean, with no hair except a braid hanging from the crown of his head with a feather attached to it. He seemed to flash as he talked, because of little round mirrors attached to a fur yoke he wore over his shoulders; the mirrors reflected sunlight as he moved and talked, and he gestured as much as a storyteller. But what he was saying did not sound like *lachimu* stories; those stories were always told in a sort of singing way, and this was hard talk. His language was Lenapeh, but different from the way it usually sounded. Behind him were grim-looking men, strangers, and she saw the village *sakima* standing close by, listening. The Head Man usually was merry-looking, but now he looked worried.

There were some white faces there too. Some of the green-coat English soldiers were lined up behind the *sakima*, and one who wore a red coat and a black hat was standing beside the talker. White men were sitting on the ground in front of the speaker, looking up at him, but she was only high enough to see their hats. On a tree limb beyond the clearing, Wareham Kingsley roosted with some Lenapeh boys. He was very visible because of his pink skin. He looked as if he too had been too much in the sun yesterday. She thought for a moment of going around to where he was, but decided it would be too much trouble; she probably was seeing as well from here as she could from where he was.

The speaker whose voice she had been hearing all this time now stopped, and an excited murmur and a few shouts swept through the crowd. She had been too busy finding a place and looking around to pay much attention to his words, but from what she heard, she had the impression that he had been talking of things that happened far away somewhere in the direction he kept pointing. Now that he had stopped, there were other men moving around and saying things to each other, and shaking hands, and giving things to each other. She saw the English soldier with the red coat move to the center, where the speaker gave him a small belt of beads and stood aside for him. The soldier was tall too, and stocky. The crowd grew still and the soldier began speaking, and Frances, with some difficulty at first, began to comprehend some of the language she had not heard much for several moons. She recognized a few words, then gradually more, and then began to remember how sentences went together in that language. This Englishman had an accent that made him sound unlike the people at Wilkes-Barre, but she could understand and remember enough to follow his meanings.

The soldier was saying: "We are thankful that God has brought us to our Delaware brothers that we may speak the truth to each other." He paused.

A warrior standing beside the soldier then said in Lenapeh what the Englishman had just said, and then the Englishman held the bead belt out high in front of his face and said:

"You know that I can speak nought but the truth while I hold this belt." The warrior translated, and the crowd murmured its agreement, and the soldier continued, now with his hands at waist level and the belt lying across his upturned palms.

"All the things this messenger has just told you, brothers, are true. Those misfortunes in the West have occurred." The translator talked again and the soldier then resumed.

"Last summer, the Long Knife soldiers from Virginia did go all the way down the Ohio River, and there they did surprise the king's forts beside the Mississippi River. Those Long Knives took those forts because the English soldiers were away. . . .

"When our Governor General in Detroit learned of that, he led English soldiers and Indian allies down there to throw out the Long Knife soldiers. It was last winter when he got there, and he recaptured one of the forts. But then the Long Knives crossed the winter floods and surprised him there. They captured him and his soldiers. . . ."

And when the translator had finished, the English soldier said, "Now the enemy controls the rivers in the West."

To Frances this was a story of things very far away, probably having something to do with the war her father had talked about, the war her oldest brother Giles had gotten into, but so far away it was not very interesting. She had never understood war and did not like to hear about it. She perched on the pole, with the smell of the deerhide strong in her nostrils. Some fat flesh was still on the hide in the frame, and in the sun it was beginning to spoil, and flies were buzzing around it. She wanted to get down, but also wanted to stay on this high place, to search for Neepah. At last she saw her on the far side of the clearing, almost hidden by a low-hanging branch of a tree. Neepah was not looking her way, but at the English soldier, and seemed to be listening very intently. When Frances turned back to look at the soldier, he was saying, with pauses for the translator:

". . . your Delaware chiefs near the Ohio got smoke in their eyes, and they signed a treaty with the Long Knife government. Those chiefs were Killbuck, White Eyes, Gelelemund, and Captain Pipe."

The crowd responded with an uproar of fast, angry talk, and

Frances held on to the frame instead of getting down. A man's voice nearby shouted, "You lie to us!" Many other people in the crowd started shouting that, but the soldier held the bead belt up above his head with both hands until their anger simmered down, then he began speaking again.

"It is true that those chiefs made an alliance with the Americans. But they were deceived. Do not condemn them. They were made false promises by the Long Knives, and when the promises are not kept, the smoke will blow from their eyes and they will return their loyalty to their true father and friend, His Majesty King George. That will happen soon, but you can help it happen sooner by remaining true to your great *sakima* and friend, King George.

"Listen!"

"Kulesta! Heh!" the translator cried loudly, and the Englishman continued, talking more loudly because all of the people were muttering back and forth now. Frances could feel danger in the air all around. She bent her knees in readiness to hop to the ground and go around to where Neepah was, but paused to hear the soldier continue. He was almost shouting now, and his face was red, and he kept the bead belt high over his head in one hand.

"I bring you a warning, to save you! The Long Knives at this moment are preparing to march up this river—yes, this very river the Susquehanna. In spite of their promises to your Delaware chiefs in the Ohio, they are preparing to send one of their biggest generals up this Susquehanna and burn out your towns here, and destroy your crops, kill your children, and rape your women!"

As the translator began translating that warning, he was interrupted over and over again by shouting and screaming. The crowd was stirring, some people moving from place to place, people grabbing each other's arms, some women even breaking out of the circle to run toward the *wikwams*. All the chiefs and soldiers who had been sitting in the Council Ground were now on their feet, many shouting, trying to calm the people. Frances grew very alarmed by the shouting and by what she had understood of the warning, and jumped to the ground to run to the place where she had seen Neepah standing. Whatever this was, it seemed full of frightful dangers, and Neepah was the only protection and comfort she knew in this place.

* * *

In Neepah's shining black eyes Frances saw so many changes that she was almost afraid to speak to her. One moment she was plainly angry, the next she was brimming with loving kindness, then fearful, then impatient, and then tender again. As a child from a large family, Frances had learned to read as well from eyes as from words, and she had seen all these same messages in her own mother's eyes, but her mother's moods had usually held long enough for Frances to adapt her behavior to the ways her mother felt. Before this day, Neepah's moods had been steady and easy to read too, but now there was too much going on in her at once. Even Minnow sat abashed.

There was little doubt that the soldier's talk in the Council Ground was what had upset Neepah so much. Everybody had left the gathering in a high state of excitement. That was surely because of the talk of an army coming. Frances could understand the people's fear of that. It was alarming to her, even though, if she understood correctly, the army coming must be the same army her brother Giles was in, and would not hurt her. Perhaps her own father and mother had asked that army to come up the river to this town and get her and take her home. That thought was disturbing, but not awfully frightening.

But she did not want an army to come here and hurt Neepah or any of these Indian people. They had been good to her and fed her well and taught her much of their language, and told her many wondrous stories. The truth of it was, she had never had such a good time in her life, once she got over the fright and cold of being brought here. She had so many things she wanted to ask and tell Neepah, but was almost afraid to speak because of the storms she saw in the woman's eyes.

Finally, though, she did have to ask her about something she just could not understand. "Neepah?"

"I listen for your question, Palanshess," the woman said, though she seemed too busy with bundles and food pots to be really listening. She kept taking things out of one container and putting them in another, all in an agitated manner.

"Are you getting ready to run away?"

"The councils will decide. The Men's Council, then the women. Then all. If it is agreed to run, we will be ready."

"Should you not run now, if you believe an army is coming?"

"Armies are slower than Taxkwox," Neepah said. "There is time." Taxkwox, Frances knew, was the Turtle.

"You should run away," Frances said. "If they are slow they could not catch you and you would not be hurt. . . ."

The look in Neepah's eyes was ferocious, but just for a moment, then she looked very sweet and said, "You do not want your army to hurt my people, do you?"

"Oh, no! Neepah, if they are coming to get me, maybe I could just walk over to them and say 'Here I am, let's go home and leave Neepah's people alone,' and maybe they would. They could get Wareham Kingsley too. They would leave you and Minnow alone."

Neepah chuckled and shook her head, but when she looked up, there was nothing amused in her eyes. "Palanshess would go back then, do you say?"

As if she had been accused, Frances stammered, "I—I would want to make them leave thee alone. I would . . . Yes, I would like to go be with my family. . . ." In the rush of confused feelings, Frances was speaking both tongues, a jumble of words from both languages, unaware that she was doing so. "But I would not want to leave thee. . . . If thee could be friends with my mother and father, we could all be together now and then. . . ."

"Palanshess, sit there. We will eat. I have something you like. And I have a gift for you. And I have a story to tell. . . ."

"A gift?" Frances had been vaguely aware that her birthday had passed, in March, two or three months ago, but with no way of knowing when it was March. Her mother and father had always given her some small gift to mark her birthday, though they did not observe other holidays as other people did because to the Friends every day was to be a holy day. Only once a year, on their birthdays, did the Slocum children receive something called a gift. Frances said, "Do you know of my birthday?"

Neepah paused in her rummagings and looked at her with amused puzzlement. "Birth day?" She used the Lenapeh words for being born and for daylight. Then she tilted her head and said, "Every child is born. I knew you were born, yes. Even *wapsi* babies are born, I know. Though sometimes I have wondered are the *wapsituk* excreted from the waste hole like turds . . . But, Palanshess, you are *wehlee heeleh*. I know you were born."

"Then are you going to celebrate by giving me a gift?"

Neepah needed an explanation then of the notion of celebrating a birthday, and finally said: "I am grateful you were born. But when a baby is born, the baby is the gift. Grandmother Moon gives us the gift which is the baby. We give back thanks. You did not come to me in birth as a baby, but even so, I give thanks for you. You have been a gift to me."

"But you said you are going to give me a gift."

"Yes. Because it is something you will always need. That is why. Not because you were born. I do not understand why I would give a gift to you for being born. How funny you think, little *wapsini!*" Neepah seemed to be having a good time and feeling better than she had. She was smiling and chuckling, and only now and then did she look worried.

Neepah reached among stored things and got out a blackened clay pot about the size of her head. Minnow smiled and put wood on the fire. As it was burning down to embers, Neepah started a story.

"*Kulesta!* This is not one of our old stories, but a new one. Long ago, before the *wapsituk* ever came to Taxkwox Menoteh, our Turtle Island, we were warned they would come and we should be wary of them. By the time they came, we forgot the warning. We were happy to see them and feed them and learn about them. They came down off a wondrous large boat, such as we had never seen." As she talked, she spread the embers and put the pot on them and heaped more embers around the side, almost to the hole in top. While it was heating, she went on. "They brought down from the boat a strange thing to sit on. I forget its word. . . . All *wapsituk* sit on them in their house. My father learned to make them."

"A chair!"

"It is called a 'cheh,' yes. The *wapsi* head man sat on that 'cheh.' He laughed and was nice. He gave our men something to drink. They never had that before. It had bad medicine. It made some howl and some fall down. They could not think. But they still tried to be kind to the *wapsini.* He said he would soon go away in his big boat but would come back every year. He said he needed a place to leave the 'cheh' so he could sit on it each time he came back, and asked them to give him a piece of land big enough for his 'cheh.' They did not know about 'giving' land because it belongs to the Creator. But they said he was welcome to put on the shore there his 'cheh.'

"The *wapsi* head man said he would need a little space in front of his 'cheh' to stand on when he stood up. He asked for only as much land as he could cover with an elkskin, that would be enough, and he gave them another drink and they said yes. What the *wapsini* did then was not nice."

"What did he do?" Frances asked, because Neepah had paused in her story to get something from behind her.

"The *wapsi* head man got out a . . ." Neepah paused again, held up a hand, and made a repeated squeezing motion, saying, "You name the thing you cut with this way."

"Ah! Scissors! My mother has some. Scissors."

"So, then. With this thing the *wapsini* starts cutting around the edge of the elkskin, around and around, to make one long piece very fine like a thread. So when the elkskin is all gone there is all that elkskin thong. And he holds one end while his other men take the other end and go walk a long way where the Lenapeh live. They go west and then turn north and walk and then turn east and walk. When they are back at the shore the thong is around more than this village and the cornfield we planted in yesterday, and the *wapsi* head man then smiles nice and is saying, 'You gave me the land covered by this elk hide. Thank you. I will be back next year.' "

Frances and Minnow looked at each other. Neepah put a stick in the hole in the top of the pot and moved the pot out of the embers. Then she held her other hand over the hole, in a fist, and allowed a handful of corn kernels to pour down into the pot. Then she put a flat stone over the hole, leaned back, looked at the girls with a funny-looking smile, and said, "Our Lenapeh *sakima* could not think because of what he had drunk, but wanted to be nice, so he told the *wapsini*, 'It is what we agreed. You have this land and your "cheh" can sit here.' The Lenapeh were not happy. But they had promised. The story is finished. No, the story is not finished. That was only the beginning of a longer story, for each year the *wapsituk* came back, they gave more to drink and did more tricks like that. They have done such tricks all the time, and you see, we Lenapeh are now here in the valley in these mountains and we can no longer even go to that shore where the 'cheh' was."

The hot clay pot began making noises. Frances jerked back and looked at it. It was sputtering as if it had a woodpecker working in it. Neepah looked at Frances and chuckled. When the noise slowed and stopped, Neepah flipped the stone off the top of the pot. Steam rose from the hole and it smelled something like bread.

"Now," Neepah said, "eight generations since then, the *wapsituk* are still giving drink to our *sakimas* and doing such tricks.

Did you hear the messenger? They made some of our leading *sakimas* put agreeing marks on a treaty, but send an army up this valley to burn our homes." She shook her head and her eyes flashed. "So in Council tomorrow we will talk about it. Whether we run away or stay here and fight that army."

Frances thought of the messenger and of some of the things she had heard, and finally asked, "What does it mean, smoke in their eyes?"

"Smoke in the eyes is, you think a *wapsini* means his promises. Now. Here." Neepah covered her hands with a piece of strouding cloth, picked up the hot clay pot and turned it over, shaking it above a wooden bowl, and what had been a small handful of corn kernels now made a mound of curious-looking white things that nearly filled the big bowl and smelled very good. The woman then poured some maple syrup over them and stirred the mass with the stick. She picked up the bowl and extended it. "So, eat, my girls. Palanshess, I have not cooked you this before. It is a kind of *xas-kwim*. Eat it with fingers. Minnow is drooling. Look."

It was, indeed, corn. It was dry and crunchy to chew and sweet with the maple syrup. Frances believed it might well be the best thing she had ever tasted. She and Minnow sat and stuffed it in their mouths. Neepah ate a little but mostly talked. She said, "Since that 'cheh' trick, the *wapsituk* took our land and tried to give us their god. But we learned their god would not feed us. Our Creator feeds us. We went back to ours. A woman chief here had a *wapsi* name, Esther, but got mad at the *wapsituk* and changed back. We tried much to trust the *wapsituk*. No use. Ah! You ate it all!"

"It was so good! *Waneeshee,* Neepah!"

"Yes. So good. Now hear something else, eh? Listen. This is of great importance. I must tell you this because now the *wapsituk* will be coming here." She paused, eyes intense, and asked, "Did you ever know why our warriors brought you here?"

Frances remembered all that, which seemed so long ago. She shook her head. But then she thought, and said, "You were angry because the white men cheat?"

"Not for that reason. For a worse one. The *wapsi* soldiers killed a little girl." Neepah looked as if she were about to cry, something Frances had never seen in her face. Neepah said:

"*Kulesta.* On that day the soldiers attacked a hunting camp of my husband and other men of his clan, below here on this river.

The soldiers shot my husband outside the camp. His brothers tried to bring him back to camp; he was only wounded. But then the soldiers killed the brothers and my hurt husband, and they skinned them. Then they came into the camp. I was there with my baby daughter on one breast and Minnow on the other. I hid Minnow and tried to get away. The soldiers caught me. They chopped my baby's head. Some soldiers held me while others did things to me that I will not tell you. When they had all made themselves too limp to do it anymore, they stuck a tomahawk handle inside me and left me on the ground. They never found this girl." Minnow was making a soft moaning sound.

Neepah turned her head and spat on the ground. Frances could not imagine what the soldiers had done to Neepah, but she understood that they had killed her little girl, and that was terrible enough to fill her mind. She could not even speak, the thought of it was so bad.

"Listen, Palanshess. You were brought to me to be in the place of my daughter. That is why we take a white person. At your house, did they kill a soldier?" Frances nodded, remembering Nathan Kingsley, scalped, on the ground. She was only beginning to understand this. "Good," Neepah said. "That was for my husband. You are for me. White people have paid me back a girl. And you are a little girl I like. If I had not liked you so, I would have killed you to avenge my daughter. It would have been right for me to do that. But you are a gift." She reached over and took Frances' right hand in her left. Her eyes were so powerful that Frances could feel them looking at her heart. "You grow large in my bosom," Neepah said in a deep, low voice. "Whatever comes to my people now is in the hands of the Creator. But you are in my hands and I will not let you be lost as my first little girl was."

The intensity of Neepah's eyes and words was making the hair on Frances' head prickle, and shivers were cascading down her cheeks and back and even her legs. Her hand felt as if it would burst into flames in Neepah's hand.

The woman eased her grip. She leaned back, taking a deep breath and letting it come out in a long, shuddering exhalation. In a little while Neepah was smiling again, very feebly and with wet eyes, and she said, "I have a gift for my little girl."

She turned on her haunches, leaned back toward the bundle behind her, and slipped her hand inside. Frances remembered and opened her mouth to tell Neepah there might be a mouse in it, but the woman brought out her hand with something small in her palm. A thong hung from it. Neepah said, "I have not finished sewing it where the soldiers damaged it. Be careful of the needle. Look at this, Palanshess, this is my gift to you."

What she put in Frances' hand was a tiny deerskin bag, hardly bigger than the end of her own thumb, but decorated in quillwork with a picture of a turtle, nearly white but with a slight green tinge. It was attached to a loop of thong and had a tiny drawstring threaded through holes in its open end. In a place where a side seam lay open, a sharp little bone needle stuck through the leather. Frances knew it must have been the needle that had stuck her when she reached in the bundle. So the thing she had been searching for was to have been a gift for her. She flushed as she remembered her suspicions and her sneakiness. And something spoke to her, with no voice, but rather like an understanding that passed from the little bag into her palm, and told her that the needle had stuck her to protect the little bag from being seen by her too soon.

"This will be your medicine bag," Neepah said. "As you have seen, all my People wear these and they wear them always. I will tell you more about it later, because there is much to know. I will tell you this now: I made this for my first daughter. Now it is yours. What little things you carry in it will be of the greatest closeness to your heart. It already has some things in it that I have placed there. I did it yesterday. Take them out and see."

Frances, feeling as if she were bathed in some humming warmth, loosed the drawstring and turned the little bag upside down over her palm. When the three tiny things fell out, she understood why there had been a mouse in the bundle.

There was a corn kernel. There was a squash seed. And there was a bean.

May 1779
Wilkes-Barre

To Ruth Slocum, her son Giles was like a stranger in his own family. He sat arguing with her and his brother Will. The visit had started badly when she ordered him to leave his musket and bayonet outside. In exasperation he had fixed the bayonet on the muzzle and stuck it in the ground just outside the door. He was a militiaman and would not leave his weapon anywhere out of his sight. Where he sat at his mother's table he could see the butt of the musket sticking up.

"Will," Giles was saying, "thee's a helpless simpleton. They'll kill thee before thee's halfway to Wyalusing."

Ruth Slocum wondered if her son spoke in the Quaker way among the soldiers, and doubted it. Giles turned to face her and said, "Mother, has thee not lost enough already? Does thee mean to have Will go the way of Pa and Grandpa? How could thee even think of letting him go among the savages? Damnation!"

She swelled up, arms folded over her bosom, and her eyes flashed. "Giles, we do not swear in this house. Save that for thy soldier camp. And we do not call them savages. The soldiers call them that because they kill? Then thee's a savage too, if that's the case. And if thee hadn't taken up arms, thy father and grandf—"

Giles's fist slammed the tabletop. "Not that again!" he shouted. "I am not to blame for that and I'll not carry guilt about on my shoulders!" He glared at her and clenched his fists to keep from saying more angry words to her. "Don't let Will go, I pray thee."

"Not let him go? I *told* him to go! Your father meant to go and now he cannot because of what thee brought down upon him."

"I did not!"

Ruth Slocum leaned forward over Giles with her arms still crossed, and her narrowed eyes bore into his. "My son, in this house we do not swear or pound the furniture or shout at our mother. Now hear me. Of course I do not want to lose a son to recover a daughter, but William wants to go, and his foot is well at last, and I know of no other way to find our little girl. Tell me how a lad who'll risk himself for the sake of his own flesh and blood is more a simpleton than one who'll risk himself for a flag."

"A flag?"

"For a flag, as thee does."

"It is not for a flag, Mother! It is to throw off a king!"

"Giles Slocum, we Quakers have never let a king be upon us, and so we have none to throw off. We do have a daughter who needs to be restored to us, and soldiers cannot do that for us. A man with the Light of God inside him can go where an army cannot. William means to go up the valley and seek our Frannie."

"The army means to go up the valley," Giles said.

"What say thee?" William asked, sitting up straighter.

"Aye. General Sullivan's to go up this summer and thrash Tory

Butler and tame his sava—his Indians. I expect our boys will march with him."

"Oh, dear Lord," Ruth Slocum groaned, unfolding her arms and waggling her fingers at the ceiling before clapping both palms over her face. "If war comes up this valley now, it will scatter everything! Frannie will be done for certain if an army goes blundering up there!"

Giles sat pressing his right fist into his left palm, now looking at the tabletop. "Thee still believes she's alive, Mother, truly?"

"I feel it," she said, taking her hands from her face and lacing their fingers together at her waist. "Whether thee believes in such matters of the spirit or not, I believe a mother can tell. I pray. But I shall have to pray all the harder if an army goes through."

Giles kept putting his fist in his hand and taking it out. Softly now, not pounding. At last he looked at William, staring, studying him keenly. At seventeen, William was tough as hickory from hard work, and once last year at the fort he had inadvertently wrenched the shoulders of two nineteen-year-olds while separating them from a fistfight. But Giles knew that William was wide-eyed and naive, and too full of Quaker faith to realize what could happen to him even though he had seen his father and grandfather killed. Giles sighed, and said to William, "So there's nothing for it but thee's going, no matter how much sense I talk?"

"Yes, Giles, I mean to go."

"Well, then, so be it." He compressed his lips, narrowed his eyes staring at his upended musket in the door path, exhaled slowly through his nose, and nodded. "Then rather than enlist again, I'll go with thee. Perhaps we can get up there and seek around before the army's close enough to stir the hornet's nest."

Ruth Slocum gaped at her eldest son in disbelief. After all this troubling time as a soldier, he could still behave like a Quaker. But she saw the fallacy of it at once, and said:

"No, son, thee'll not. They *might* harm Will alone; if he were with thee, they'd kill thee both for certain!"

"He wants to go and I want to go, for Frannie's my sister as well. With all respect, thee can't forbid me."

"Son," she said, clasping her hands tighter to keep them from trembling, "if thee chooses not to enlist, I'll pray thanks for that, for I'm against your soldiering, but if thee lays down the gun and takes up a plowshare, then stay here and help us with the farming. I tell thee true, Will'll be safer without thee than with. Giles, listen to me. Five minutes' thinking without male pride and thee'll admit I'm right. Thank'ee for thy courage and care, but I beg thee, let Will go alone."

Giles turned to Will, who was smiling at him but hiding his smile behind a hand. "What say thee, Will? Want me along?"

"My deepest gratitude, Giles. But absolutely not. I'm scared enough all on my own, without a bullet bait alongside."

Giles's mouth went slack and he cocked his head back. "Oh, indeed, now! That's how thee feels about it?"

"It is, good brother. If thee goes, I don't."

Giles smiled. "Good, then. *I* go, so thee stays." He smirked between his mother and his younger brother, who were looking at each other. He laced his fingers behind his head with a smug look. Ruth Slocum looked at him and could almost understand why less pacific people could smite each other. He had them stymied. By threatening to go along, Giles could keep Will from going.

But after a moment of thinking on it, she saw another side of it, and a smile of equal smugness overspread her lined face.

"Well, thank the Lord," she said. "At least now I have one less soldier and two more farmers! Neither one goes!"

As for a way to find Frances, she would have to let the Lord give her inspiration, and she prayed it would be soon. For with every step an army took in that direction, any chance for her daughter's survival would fade.

Neepah had repaired the medicine bag the night before, and Frances had slept with it hanging around her neck, and had dreamed of the Three Sacred Sisters in the field. This morning Neepah and Minnow listened intently as Frances told of the dream. Neepah seemed pleased. It was very early and still not daylight outside as the woman built up the fire and warmed their morning meal, which was hominy with meat, nut meal, and dried berries. As they ate Neepah said, "You slept very still last night. It was a pleasure to hold you close, both of you, one little girl to keep each side of Neepah warm."

"*Waneeshee.* It is good to feel you hold me. In my family I had to sleep with many brothers and sisters and they woke me up all the time, getting up to pee, or letting stink-air in the bed and giggling about it, or talking all the time. I sleep all night long here."

"Minnow," Neepah said, pointing with her chin, "go out awhile. I have something to speak of with this one only." Minnow rose and went out, without pouting or protesting, as Frances might well have expected a girl to do upon being excluded from something. When she was gone, Neepah faced Frances and said, "Now, Pretty Face. Tell me an answer to this question: What does your name mean? What is a palanshess?"

"Frances? It has no meaning. It is a name, that's all."

"It is not something?" Neepah persisted.

"I do not understand. It is not a thing, it is only a name."

"I am Neepah. Means, like that crossing the sky at night, Neepah Huma. Grandmother Moon. I am Neepah because when I was born the full roundness of the moon was in the sky passing over. One should be named for a sign that is seen before you are ten days old. But when *you* were born your mother and father saw no palanshess because there is no palanshess thing, you tell me. How sad that is."

Frances looked at her, puzzled. "Sad! I was never sad because of that name." She never had been, but now she was beginning to wonder whether she was missing something. The Lenapeh children she knew all did have names of something one could see or imagine, many of them animals. Like Minnow. Now and then she had wished she had an animal name, though she had never figured out which animal she was like. Of all animals she knew, she liked horses best, but she did not think she was in any way like a horse.

Neepah said, "I have a name for you that means something, in our way. I have thought of it already. I have called you by it a few times. I crossed your path too late to see a sign to name you by, so I must name you by what I saw after you first came here."

"Is it an animal?" Frances was excited, wondering which animal, trying to remember any animal name Neepah had called her. Neepah held up a cautionary finger. "I would have called you Wehle Taxkwox. It was the name of my daughter, and you are in her place now."

Frances sank in her spirit. Wehle Taxkwox meant something like Pretty Turtle, or Good Turtle. She did not think of herself as a turtle, hard and cold and slow. The quill design on her medicine bag was a turtle, so she should have known. She was afraid her disappointment would show in her face and make Neepah sad, but she just didn't want to be a turtle in name, even a good or pretty turtle. However, Neepah had more to say:

"But I cannot give you a name another person had, for that was her own name and she has taken it with her to the Other Side

World where she still uses it. So I give you a name of what I saw of you at first, and what I see still more now: Wehletawash."

Heartbeats still quick, Frances blinked.

Wehletawash. It meant "Pleasing Face to See," or "Good Face." She remembered that Neepah had sometimes called her Pretty Face. This meant Pretty Face, but more; it also meant Good Face. Well! It was not an animal name, but it was certainly an agreeable name, and her mother and father used to say she was very pretty. And this name showed how Neepah saw her and felt about her. The more she repeated her Wehletawash name to herself, the warmer she felt, about it and about Neepah for giving it to her.

Neepah stood up, saying, "Wehletawash? Wehletawash?" Neepah would not be trying to pronounce "Frances" anymore. The girl looked up at Neepah, who said, "Now this day I will be in the Council Lodge. We have to decide what to do about the *wapsituk* coming. Such councils are long. May you have pleasure today. Wash yourself in the creek. Go to the field and help the other children scare away the birds and other seed stealers. Mind what the older children tell you. Don't play around the Council Lodge, because inside there we have to be able to hear each other speak on important things. But if you really need me, come and stand outside. The sides will be opened and I can see you. Remember, you are my Good Face. That is not just a pretty face, but a face with good in it. Come here."

Frances, Good Face, stood close. Neepah did something she had never done. She got on her knees and put her strong arms around her and held her tight. Good Face reached around Neepah's neck and squeezed. They stayed like that for a long time, breathing. Good Face felt warmth and strength pouring into her, it seemed, and thought she heard many voices, like the women's voices singing in the cornfield, but not just the same. Neepah was swaying on her knees as they embraced and breathed. Good Face could feel her medicine bag with its three sacred seeds, or perhaps Neepah's medicine bag, or maybe both bags, pressed between their bosoms, her little girl's bosom and Neepah's great cushioned bosom. There was a vibration where the medicine bags were, and heat, and though Good Face had her eyes shut she knew there was a glowing there also, which, it seemed, her heart was seeing. If these people did live by magic, this was some of it that she could see and feel herself.

At last Neepah patted her back and they came out of the

embrace, letting go reluctantly, and Neepah's round brown face was wet around the eyes but she was smiling, bright as a full moon. She wiped her eyes with the heels of her hands and stood up. "Now I go, Wehletawash. Live long and live well with your name. A good day with your new name will start you that way, so I wish you pleasure all this day."

"Waneeshee, Kahesana."

Neepah put her fist against her mouth and something quick like a pain came in her eyes and she hurried out.

It was not until Good Face was alone that she realized that she had called Neepah *Kahesana,* which meant Mother.

She went to the creekside after Neepah left. She went naked, by her own choice. She was Good Face; Neepah loved her. The medicine bag seemed to speak to the heart over which it lay. She could remember having been Frances Slocum, that name that did not mean something, and she could remember one by one all the family named Slocum who had been her family, but now that seemed to have been another life. She remembered that she loved her mother very much, and still had her mother in her heart. But now her mother was far away and had been for so long, and all the needs she had provided for were now provided by Neepah, so the needs did not make an empty place anymore.

Good Face squatted by the water with a stick of green willow stem and cleaned her teeth and mouth with the fretted end of the stick, one of those things she had never done as a Slocum but Neepah had taught her to do every day, like bathing. As she cleaned her teeth she saw that on her arms where the sun had burnt her, the little blisters were gone and her skin was white and dry and flaking off in patches. Because of the bear oil, the burn had not hurt since yesterday morning. She thought of the bear, which Neepah had said was the brother of the People, and was thankful for bear oil. She had a suspicion that if she ever met a bear face-to-face, she would still be scared, because bears were something the Slocums had always said were dangerous. But nevertheless she would be able to look in the bear's face and know they were related to each other, not from two different worlds separated by fear.

The sound of the running water was very soft, but it contained many voices, some clear as tinkling bells, others vague and whispering. It was like the sounds of voices in the Council Lodge, which she could hear even from the creek bank. That, like the water flow, was a sound of many voices. Neepah had said they would decide what to do about the army that would be coming. Good Face thought of how Neepah seemed more angry than afraid of the army, although afraid too.

She remembered when she had told Neepah that the army might leave her People alone if she went back with them. When she had said that, it seemed like something that might be done.

But she was Good Face now.

She went down into her favorite shallow place in the creek and waded in to bathe. The water was cold enough to give her goose-flesh, but she squatted down and got entirely wet, even her hair. She stayed still and felt the flow of the water nudging her and caressing her as it went past. She seemed to be able to feel the high places where the water came from and the low, faraway places where it went. Neepah once had told her that if she put a stick in this creek, it could float down to the river and farther and farther down, through many lands the *wapsituk* had taken from the Lenapeh, all the way to the Great Sunrise Water, which Frances had known by the name of Atlantic Ocean. She had never seen the ocean, but her mother and father had seen it when they lived in Rhode Island. Neepah had also told her that if they went over some mountains not far from here, they would come to creeks that flowed in another direction and down into seas that were not salt water like the sea but freshwater. Neepah had said that her own old father and mother lived up there by the fresh waters, near Sookpa helluk, Great Water Falling, a place where a whole huge river poured over a cliff, making so much noise and mist that you could hardly hear or see anything. Neepah said too that just like a stick in the water, people in canoes and boats could go from almost anyplace to almost any other place on Turtle Island. She knew that what Neepah called Turtle Island was what she had known as America.

Good Face thought of all that while feeling the water of the creek flow around her. She thought, if she could swim, she could start swimming right here and keep going downstream all the way. She knew that the warriors had brought her upstream from her home, and that meant she could float all the way back down there. To the place called Wilkes-Barre. Almost to the door of the house where her mother and father and brothers and sisters lived.

She heard someone calling the name "Frances." She turned

toward the bank and saw Wareham Kingsley standing there, white-skinned among the Indian children who were there washing and playing. Wareham had on his cloth breeches but no shirt. He had a frown on his face. That and his whiteness made him look out of place among the Lenapeh children. She thought of him as a *wapsini* and of how different he seemed from her. She waded out of the creek and sat on the creek bank beside him and told him the first thing that came to her mind about him, which was that she had seen him perched in a tree yesterday when the people were in the Council Ground.

Wareham looked at her hard, frowning even more, and said: "Talk English. I can't hardly understand that Indian talk at all."

Only then did she realize she had been speaking in the Lenapeh tongue. Trying to think English, she said: "Thee's been here as long as I. Why hasn't thee learned?"

He shrugged. "It's hard. I can't make no sense out of it."

She thought it was strange that he thought it was hard. But then she remembered that Neepah and several other of the women had praised her for learning things so quickly. And her mother and father at home had often praised her too, for learning such things as the alphabet so quickly. For the first time in a long while she thought of the alphabet, and about reading, which she had started to learn before she came here. She realized that she might not ever learn any more of that because the Lenapeh didn't do it at all.

"I saw thee in a tree yesterday while the soldier was talking," she said again, this time in English.

He nodded. "That was scary, wasn't it? I thought the Indians were goin' to hop up and kill that soldier. And he was just tryin' to warn 'em. You think if the army comes, we could escape and go home with 'em?"

The thought startled her. "Thee would go?"

"Well, sure, if I get a chance. I thought you and me, we'd try to escape together, since we came here together."

"Oh." She thought about that for a little while, looking at him. It was a troubling thought: that there would come a day when she would have to choose between two good things. She asked him, "Does thee have an Indian name?"

He drew his head back and looked at her with one eye squinting, which she knew was the how-can-girls-say-such-silly-things look that boys always used, and he retorted, "You know my name's Wareham! 'Course I don't have an Indian name!"

"Well, I have." She tried not to use a saucy tone of voice, though she would have liked to.

"Well, I wouldn't be surprised," he said. "Y' even run around naked like these damn Indians. Aren't you ashamed?"

"Isn't thee ashamed to cuss?" She hadn't been ashamed of nakedness since that first day of it, but now that he had asked her, she thought perhaps she should be. But she wanted to talk about her name. "My Indian name is Wehletawash," she said. "Good Face."

"Huh? What-a-wash?" He said it with such a mimicking tone that she knew he must be jealous.

"Don't the people thee live with even like thee?" she said. "They'd give thee a name if they did, I should think."

"I already have a name. Wareham."

"Wear-a-what?" she mimicked his mimicry.

He stood up quickly. He looked as if he might cry, and she felt sorry for him. It occurred to her that he must still be as lonely and scared as she had been in the beginning, because he couldn't even talk with them and he didn't have an Indian name. She had seen how poorly he played with the Lenapeh boys, and thought he must feel so bad because they couldn't understand him and he couldn't understand them.

"I'm sorry," she said.

He shrugged, and looked less miserable, and squatted down beside her again.

She saw that he was glancing at the place between her legs, so she covered it with her hand. She said, "I could teach thee to speak their language."

He shrugged again. "What for? I aim to get out of here as soon as that army shows up."

"I could give thee an Indian name."

"What do I want with an Indian name?"

"I'll give thee one anyway," she said. "I'll call thee 'Wapsi.' That's a good name for thee."

He looked at her suspiciously. "I've heard 'em say that word to me, a lot. Wopsey. How'd you know that?"

"Oh." She tilted her head and shrugged. "Thee's just a *wapsini*, plain as day. Go tell them thee's a *wapsini*, and I'm sure they'll agree."

She could tell he didn't like that. He had that smart-boy look on his face again, and he stood up. "G'yawn!" he said. "I couldn't hardly understand you when you were just a thee-thou Quaker. Now you're a naked-arse Quaker Indian and I can't understand you at all!" But then he surprised her by looking down at the water in the creek and saying, "I'm sorry I said that."

"I am too. We are friends, thee knows that." She too looked at the flowing water, and after a while she said, "Can thee swim, Wareham?"

"No. The bitsiest Indian tads can, but not me."

"Nor can I. But I shall learn. Does thee know, Wareham, if thee could swim, thee could get in this creek right here and go all the way home?"

"Really? That's the way back?"

"That's what Neepah said. My . . . the lady I live with."

"Then we're not lost after all!"

"No, I guess not."

He gave a soft whistle, looking downstream, and he seemed to be thinking far away, by the look in his eyes. "I think I'd like to learn how to swim too," he said.

"Well, then, let us do. I know a girl, Minnow, who swims well. I shall ask her to teach us."

"Yes. Ask her," he said eagerly, standing up. "You know what, Frannie? I really am glad you learnt their talk! The people I'm with, they talk some English, so I just ain't learnt theirs. Wish I had."

Good Face was plainly not Frances anymore, because she was having a hilarious time making loud noise. In that earlier life among the Quakers, she had always been told to be quiet and seemly—never to shout or screech, never to bang or stomp or rattle. Now she was making as much racket as she could, because she was supposed to. Out here in the field with Minnow and a dozen other children, she was supposed to shriek and howl at the top of her lungs and whack sticks against gourds. A few of the children had metal pans and tin pots their parents had gotten from white traders, and those children were the best noisemakers of all, the envy of the rest as they clashed and jangled their metal vessels together and bellowed *"Haooo! Haoooooo!"* and whistled like hawks or barked like dogs. But most of all, they laughed, as they climbed trees around the field of the Three Sisters or chased among its planting hills. Good Face hopped and whooped with them and her heart frolicked with the joy of freedom and noise-making.

It was the responsibility of the village children to infest the gardens and fields with commotion and scare out the birds and four-leggeds that would want to steal seeds. Maybe the scent of the women's sweaty clothes would have discouraged some four-leggeds, but it was essential to keep birds away from seeds and animals from the tender shoots. It was the children's task to guard the field in the daytime.

It was amazing how many birds there were and how interested they were in the newly planted field. "I wonder if birds can talk to each other," she said to Minnow.

"Yes. You can hear them." Minnow imitated crows perfectly.

"They must watch the planting and then fly away and tell all their friends."

"Yes, they do," Minnow said. *"Haoooo! Haooooo!"* She ran at a crow that was gliding in toward the field, and a flock of smaller birds veered away too, all turning at the same time as if the whole flock were one creature. Good Face had watched them do that again and again and wondered how they could keep from running into each other. Here in the cornfield, two running children could bump into each other, yet hundreds of birds, much faster and closer together, could turn at once and never collide. It was the first time she had ever marveled at birds, beyond wondering how they could fly. Being here to guard the seeds against birds was making her pay more attention to them than she ever had.

And it was the same with the seeds themselves. Her white Slocum family had grown corn, but she had never really thought about corn, or how it grew, or that something like a corn spirit had anything to do with it. It seemed that everything was different here among these Lenapeh People. Here, everything had a spirit, not just people. Both Neepah and Minnow had spoken of the spirits of the trees, telling her to listen to them talking when the wind blew in their leaves, and she had come to believe that indeed she could hear them talking, and even almost understand them. This truly was different from being *wapsini*. It felt so different sometimes that she could hardly remember how it had felt to be a Slocum. She could not forget that she had been, but could not remember it as anything real; it was as if that was something she had dreamed.

And this being a Lenapeh felt better than the old dream-memory. It felt wonderful when everything around had a spirit, when one could feel prayers rush up from the ground through one's feet and body and head and into the sky, when one could see women turn to plants and back to women, when one could get used to going naked, when one could have a noisy good time and not be called down to behave. It was good to learn something every day and hear new stories every evening; even the magic of the Lenapeh, if magic was what it was, was more interesting than scary. What these Lenapeh People said and thought and did was as good and kindly as what the Friends said and thought and did, but much more interesting and, she thought, more fun. If, when the soldiers came, they somehow got her and took her back, she foresaw that she would not be very happy to go.

Or at least it did not seem like it now.

It was certain that Neepah did not want her to go back with the *wapsituk*. Good Face thought about all the grown-ups talking about this in their councils, the men and the women talking and deciding things.

"Birds!" Minnow's voice interrupted her daydream, and off they went again, running through the sunny field, whooping and whacking with their sticks.

"Minnow," Good Face said when, at the height of midday, they stood puffing and sweating from all their darting about, "if Muh-nuka'hazh the crow was so good as to bring the People fire, how can he be so bad as to steal their seeds?"

Minnow's startling answer made her ponder: "Everyone is as bad as good, and as good as bad. Did you not know that?"

Other children came to the field a few at a time to scare crows, and Good Face and Minnow could leave to go to the swimming place. Minnow made Good Face lie facedown in the creek and let her feet go free from the bottom. Good Face, to her delight and amazement, did not sink. She was afloat, holding her breath. Then Minnow taught her to go forward by kicking her feet and stroking with her arms, and finally how to turn her head and breathe under her arm every fourth stroke. By the time Wareham appeared on the bank, calling for her by her Frannie name, Good Face had already swum the width of the creek several times, not as gracefully or as fast as Minnow yet, but truly swimming.

"You said you couldn't swim," he said, squatting on the rocks while she stood waist-deep with water draining from her hair. She remembered that she would have to speak English to him.

"Minnow taught me just now," she said.

"So quick as that? I don't believe you."

"Minnow!" she called across the creek in Lenapeh tongue, "come let us teach this *wapsi* boy to swim in water!" The slim brown little figure plunged headfirst off the far bank into the creek and did not reappear until she burst streaming out of the water right beside Good Face. The two naked girls stood looking at the pale, woebegone boy on the shore. Other children of all ages were sporting in the water upstream and down, their voices like cheerful birdcalls.

Minnow said to him in Lenapeh, her tone revealing her dislike of white people: "Take the leg clothes off and get in the water."

"She said don't swim in breeches," Good Face translated. "Take them off and come in."

Already pink with sunburn, Wareham blushed and shook his head. Good Face remembered her own recent embarrassment at being naked and understood, but remembered too how quickly nakedness had felt natural. Wareham's breeches were so filthy there was not a hint of their original color. Obviously he had never removed them since last winter. "Don't think I'm going to get buck naked with girls!" he stammered, and started to ease into the creek's edge.

Minnow fell backward into the water and began backstroking away, saying, "Tell that *wapsi* boy I will not stay near those dirty leg clothes! They will ruin the water!" and she laughed.

To Good Face this was getting to be funny, and she watched his face grow more perturbed when she told him, "Minnow won't teach thee in such filthy breeches. They'll make the water stink."

Wareham stood pouting and appeared to be thinking of just leaving. But Good Face knew how much he wanted to learn so he could perhaps swim home. At last, red-faced, he turned his back to the girls and started skinning the breeches down from his waist.

Minnow squealed with laughter. "They stick to him! Look! I thought his bottom would be white but it is brown! Ha, ha!"

"What's she saying?" Wareham blurted, looking back angrily.

"Never mind what. Come in the water and leave the clothes there. You must wash them later. But swim first."

As he waded in with his hands cupped over his pee spout, she could see that he was far more afraid of the water than she had been even in the beginning. And before he was within a body length of the girls, the smell of him was enough to make them turn their heads. "Wash awhile," she told him in English. "Then we'll teach'ee to float. Wash thy hair and face too." She remembered how she had had to be told that. She could see that he was glad to be in deep enough to hide his bottom parts, though scared wild-eyed by the current. He washed and sluiced his body up to the chest, but with his chin raised and lips and eyes shut tight. "Thee must go clear under," she urged him, "or thee'll not learn to swim."

"I had a dog could swim 'crost the whole Susquehanny with his head above water."

"We don't swim like dogs."

"I will!"

"Well, then, 'twon't be Minnow as teaches thee. Learn right or just forget about swimming home, Wareham Kingsley."

Minnow had disappeared underwater. Suddenly Wareham disappeared underwater too, his upflung hands flailing water as he went under. Then Minnow surfaced.

She came up laughing, shaking water out of her long hair. Then she dove under again and in a moment came up, pulling Wareham to the surface by his hair. He was thrashing, coughing and gasping air, eyes glazed with terror.

"Now his head is wet." Minnow giggled. Good Face had never seen this quiet girl act so delighted.

"Did you do that? Pull him under? What if he had drowned?"

"Eh! He is only a *wapsi* boy! So he drowns and never will be a soldier!"

"But you were going to teach him to swim, I thought!"

"To swim is to be wet. Now I have made him wet."

Wareham had finished coughing up water and angrily demanded, "What're you two sayin' about me in that damn Indian talk? She tried to drown me!"

Before Good Face could answer, Minnow disappeared underwater again, and was invisible for what seemed a long time. Suddenly Wareham uttered a wild yelp and cried, "Make her stop! Stop it, stop it!" and lunged toward the creek bank, wading furiously.

"What? What?" Good Face could now and then, by peering through the reflected daylight on the water's surface, glimpse Minnow's dusky body swimming near the bottom. When her head broke above the water, Minnow was at a respectable distance from Wareham and looking blandly innocent. Wareham was almost out of the creek, heading for his filthy breeches. "Wareham, if thee means to learn swimming, come back here."

"That damn little squaw-girl pinched my—pinched my—my . . ." His face was flushed from exertion, anger, or embarrassment, or all three.

Good Face looked at Minnow, whose eyes caught hers with mischievous comprehension, and Minnow giggled:

"Fishes bite, maybe, bite little worm!" She pinched her thumb and fingers together in a nipping motion, bared her white teeth and gnashed them, then laughed.

After that, much cajolery was needed to get Wareham back into the water for his swimming lesson.

It was late in the afternoon when Good Face and Minnow returned from the swimming place. Neepah came home from the Council Lodge while the girls were rebuilding the cookfire.

Neepah embraced the girls long and warmly and then began heating more dumpling broth. Several times Good Face saw her pause with the spoon in her hand and gaze for a long time at the wall. It was evident that she had much on her mind, but she did not fail to notice that the girls' hair was still wet, and she asked Good Face, "Did you learn swimming today?"

"I swam across. Then I got out. Then I got in again and swam back. Minnow taught me and I learned so fast!"

"*Wehlee heeleh!* Did you swim like a turtle with your head up?"

"No! Head in the water! Fast like a fish! Eh, Minnow? Tell her how I swam right, and fast?"

"Like a fish who is not as fast as a Minnow, but yes, fast."

"Aha. And the *wapsi* boy, did he learn to swim too?"

"Ah, no, Kahesana. He swam like a mussel. Always we had to lift him from the bottom."

During and after their meal, women from Neepah's clan kept coming in to sit by the fire and talk with her. Some of them were asking her to vote for running away from the army, and others wanted her to vote for staying and fighting. Some wanted to get away from the army but were afraid to leave before the spring thanksgiving ceremony for fear of offending Mother Corn, who would then not let *xaskwim* grow to harvest. Others thought they should retreat farther up the river to other old towns and replant the Three Sisters. Others argued that there was no place far enough that the army wouldn't reach it.

"Then it is not sure yet?" Good Face asked during a moment when only she and Neepah and Minnow were present.

"Good Face, we talk a long time on such matters. Even if we choose to stay and face the army, those who want to go away may do it and no one will call them cowards. Unlike the *wapsituk*, any one of us may do what he thinks best for the People, not just do what one big man says. But we try to think all as one, though it is not always possible."

Good Face nodded. She understood that. It was like what her father had always said was good about the Quakers. No man was above other men, and men were not above women. This seemed to be the way it was with the Lenapeh as well.

After they had eaten and a last few visitors had finished what was in the pot, Neepah knelt close to Good Face. "My own father and mother, elders, live near the English fort by Sookpa helluk, the Great Falling Water, that way near the big lakes. If you went to stay with them, they would be your *muxumsah* and your *huma* and would tell you all the stories and teach you the old ways of the Lenapeh."

"I think I would like that! Is your father a *lehpawcheek*?"

"*E heh.* He is a wise man and was long a great warrior. He makes those 'cheh' things to sit on and sells them at the trading store there. Would you like to live with them there?"

"I think yes! Which way is that from the army?"

"Away from it. Far up this river and then west."

Good Face understood what that meant, and it frightened her: still farther from where her Quaker family had lived. She was not sure whether she should run away from the army or wait here for it to come so her soldier brother could take her home and not bother the Lenapeh People anymore. She said, "If we went to the Great Falling Water, would we all be together, you and Minnow and I?"

"After the Council decides what to do, we will know that. If we flee, many of us will go that way, others to hide in the hills other places where they have relatives. If we do not run away, I will have to stay here because I am a speaker for my clan in the Women's Council and need to be where my People are, even if it is in war. If I stay, I would have a trusted man take you where my old parents are."

"I should rather stay where you are." Good Face was feeling a deep fear and sadness knotting in her breast.

Neepah gripped her hand. "If the army comes, you must not be here. If the *wapsituk* find white children here, it will be worse for everybody. If I have to send you away, it will not be for long that we are apart."

Good Face's heart was quickening with dread. "The *wapsi* boy who came here when I did, will he be sent away too?"

"For the same reason, yes."

If Wareham knew these things, she thought, wouldn't he wish he could swim home down the creeks and rivers!

But he would sink before he got there.

"Tomorrow I will be in Council again," Neepah said. "You two must go to the fields in the morning as soon as birds awake, and scare them away as you did today. You can protect *xaskwim* from the winged stealers while we decide whether we can protect it from the *wapsi* soldiers."

Good Face when she was a Slocum had never even thought of corn needing to be protected. But here were people who seemed to be more afraid for their corn's safety than for their own!

The old man giving the prayer for the first day of Spring Ceremony was the chief of the Wolf Clan, and Good Face stared at him trying to imagine anything wolfish about him. But no, he was just round and wrinkle-faced, a wise old *lehpawcheek* who looked too kindly to be wolfish. The hundreds of people of the village stood in a circle around him as he prayed in the center of the stomp ground with his face raised and eyes shut, holding in his upturned palms a string of *wampum* beads. Though the day was hot, Good Face was wearing her old woolen dress, and was very proud of it because Neepah had patched its tatters and had sewn on two little round designs of red, white, yellow, and black beads, one circle on each side of the breast so that her medicine bag hung right between them.

Neepah had also given her two purplish-white *wampum* beads to hold in her mouth during all the prayers of the Spring Ceremony. Between prayers she was to carry them in her medicine bag, but during prayers everyone was supposed to have the two little cylindrical beads in the mouth because *wampum* represented the Lenapehs' heart, and thus prayers given with the heart in the mouth had to be sincere. "But remember them and don't swallow them," Neepah had warned her, and so she kept them right on the end of her tongue and pressed against the roof of her mouth. Their hardness and edges reminded her of when some of her bottom milk teeth had come loose not long ago and she kept playing with them with her tongue.

"Elanzhuh'ndionq, waneeshe zhukeh," the prayer began in the old chief's deep voice: "My kindred, I am thankful now . . ." His voice was strong enough for everyone to hear but had a mumbly sound to it because of the *wampum* beads in his mouth. ". . . as we think on blessings we get when Kijilamuh ka'ong, the Great Spirit, remembers us. Now we have lived long to come all together for this time of living things coming up and growing. Now we rejoice when we see everything coming forth, and our Grandfather's trees are making buds. Now everywhere in the land comes green beauty, in our corn and the fruits we will gather. We rejoice in the heat of the sun, who has sympathy for us after the cold. And in our grandfathers the Thunders, who will give us water for the growing. Everything is done by the Creator, who makes it by thinking it.

"It is even said that all the *manitus* pray, and we hear them in their passage through the tops of our grandfathers the Trees; that is the wind we hear in the leaves. It should make one start thinking, and be a cause for happiness, O the good works of our Father, how they work for us all the year through. And this is the time to enjoy it and rejoice, my kindred."

"A ho," said the People.

As strange as a voice spoken with beads in the mouth was the beat of the water drum. It was as different from the *bump bump* of a dry drum as was speaking with beads from speaking without beads. Good Face tried to pronounce it to herself: an ordinary drum was *bump bump* but this was *boimp boimp*. It looked like an ordinary drum made of a hollow log, but inside, Neepah had told her, was some water and a piece of charcoal: air, fire, and water were inside it, she had said, all sacrednesses, and it was the moistness of the rawhide cover that made it sound different from a dry cover. "You must learn to hear," Neepah had said. *"Wapsituk* don't even know how to hear whether a sound is plain or sacred. *Kulesta!* Listen to our songs! Those are sacred sounds!"

Eh o weh
Eh o weh o weh
Eh o weh

Eh o weh o weh
Eh o weh o weh
O weh o weh o weh

They were sounds that made her feel both happy and longingly sad, all the men's and women's voices in harmony, even the children's. They all knew these simple songs. Good Face, who as a Quaker child had never sung with people, learned them and sang, and could feel sacredness in her heart from the singing.

Heh i yo na heh o weh
I yo na
Heh i yo na heh o weh
I yo na
Heh heh eh heh o heh o weh
I yo na . . . WEH!

In that first day of Spring Ceremony, as the water drum beat like a heart, as the men and women shuffled solemnly in their separate circles around the stomp ground with the drummers in the middle, with the voices all blending in the yearning, quavering songs, sometimes with sobs in their throats or lilts like birdcalls, Good Face realized that never in her whole life had there been anything she liked better than this singing. It was like praying, but without having to concentrate on thoughts or words.

They were having their ceremony of the springtime regardless of the army coming. The army was still down the river a long way, very slow, stopping at *wapsi* forts for long times, always watched by spies who brought messages about its size and its movements. After one long day when Good Face had sat in a tree watching Neepah speak before the whole Council in a loud voice with anger in her eyes, the decision had been made not to run from the army. Neepah had explained to her that evening:

"The green-coat soldiers of Butler have been promised to us. Cornplanter the Seneca and Old Smoke, and Brant the Mohawk, all those we can expect to help." She had explained who they all were and what they had done before to *wapsi* armies. "There will be time for Spring Ceremony before the army gets here. Perhaps they will not get here even before Corn Harvest Ceremony. But in time before they arrive, mothers and *wapsi* children and old ones will go up the river to stay safe ahead of the army. For one or two moons only, Good Face, you and I will be in different places. You will be with my father and mother near the Great Falling Water. If we defeat the Long Knife army, we will bring you back here before next winter and all will be as it has been before. If we do not defeat them, the rest of us will retreat to that place and we will be together again there. It is a good place too, a sacred place, the Great Falling Water."

Good Face had unthinkingly caressed Neepah's bare arms and asked hopefully: "Could not everybody go up to the Falling Water together and come back after the army is gone?"

"Daughter, the Three Sisters are growing in the ground here. We must stay here to harvest, if we can, so that we may live through the next winter. If we did not try to stop the army, they would destroy all the crops and starve us, and burn our houses so the winter would freeze us. That is how they do it."

"That is so bad! I didn't know armies did such things!"

"Good Face, may you not see what armies do."

That was what Neepah had told her that Council day. Now all that lay in the tomorrows. But for now, there was singing.

CHAPTER FOUR

August 1779
Wilkes-Barre

Ruth Slocum, now and then shaking her head with sadness and disbelief, watched the passing bluecoat army: trudging foot soldiers, horse soldiers, cannons mounted between tall spoked wheels, dust rising in sunlit billows.

Going off to kill people, and on such a scale! she thought.

The army had been encamped downstream for several days, near Fort Wilkes-Barre, waiting for supply boats to catch up, as the rumors had it; at last the army really seemed to be setting out upriver toward the Indian towns. How will we ever find a trace of poor Frannie after such a monstrous event as this? she wondered.

An army boat had put in at the riverbank, and an officer climbed ashore. He was crossing the broad bottomland and coming up the slope. "Hello there," he called up as he came, taking off his tricorn hat and waving it at them. Soldiers in the column paused and touched their hats as he passed among them. Ruth knew nothing of colonels and captains, but presumed this one was important. He was a strapping, Irish-looking sort of fellow. His face was livid with sunburn and he wiped his brow with a sleeve.

"He wants something of us," Judith said, working the churn.

"Lord in Heaven, what could they want that they don't already have a ton of, I wonder," said her mother. "I've counted a hundred boats so far, all heaping with stuff."

The officer stopped before the Slocums, who stood and sat in a cluster at the front of their cabin. All had their hands full of work, or full of their littlest siblings. Ebenezer was sharpening tools for the harvest, Judith churning butter, Will shaving a spoke to fix a broken wagon wheel, eleven-year-old Mary kneading a mass of dough that she had been squeezing and thumping on the board bench for more than an hour as she watched the army go by. All had been working, but also watching the passing army most of the day.

"Good afternoon, ma'am. I am Colonel Thomas Proctor," he said to Ruth Slocum, and she thought, hearing his accent, I was right. An Irishman.

"Good day, sir," she said. "I trust thee's come up to apologize for trampling our poor yard down to the bare dirt and cutting down everything that lives."

The officer raised his eyebrows and pursed his lips, and turned to look down the weedy, stumpy slope he had just climbed. "This is your yard, is it now! Well, ma'am, I've no apology to make, for I'm in charge o' the boats, and none o' my boys has set a foot on y'r lovely lawn. On behalf o' General Sullivan, though . . ." He bowed and swept the ground with his hat. ". . . so sorry about y'r poor verdure. I shouldn't think ye'd mind, since we've come all this way to save your scalps."

"Oh, do I humble thy soldier's pride? When I should be thanking thee for saving our poor scalps . . . Isaac, what?"

"What, laddie?" the officer said, bending to little Isaac, who had come up beside him to tug at his sleeve with one hand while holding up a palmful of yellow corn with the other.

"Thee's no kernel! *These* are kernels!"

The officer threw his head back and laughed. "Ah, right y'are, m' lad! I'm no colonel! Ha ha!"

Ruth Slocum half smiled. Military man or no, he was a cheery sort. "What can we do for thee, Mr. Proctor?" she inquired.

"*Colonel* Proctor, ma'am. I—"

"Excuse us our ways, Mr. Proctor. We don't believe in titles."

"Ah, you're Quakers, then, I take it? Very well, then, you agree with the laddie that I'm no 'kernel.' So be it, then. I'm just *Mister* Proctor, a poor wayfarer who's been overcome by curiosity as to why there's a family o' mostly boys and girls sitting out here in the open while what few menfolk haven't fled the country are all crouched down safe in that so-called fort down yonder. So I said to meself, '*Mister* Proctor, why not just walk up an' ask?' And so here I am, asking."

She nodded, still with that half smile, and indicated her busy brood with a sweep of the hand. "As thee sees, we've plenty to do keeping ourselves fed and functioning. No farming gets done in a fort."

"Begging your pardon, though, ma'am, aren't y' afraid o' the Indians?" He waved a hand vaguely upstream.

"Aye, we've learned to be afraid of the misguided ones, certainly. I don't think there are so many of those that you need ten thousand soldiers to persuade their better nature."

"Six thousand, ma'am, and, aye, we'll need them all, with Cornplanter, and Brant, and Red Jacket and all up there, and Tory Butler, the bloody murderer, in charge of 'em all. Don't ye think Tory Butler is . . . is . . . *misguided*? Is that what y' said?"

"Of course a Tory's misguided; he bows down to a king."

"Well, I'm glad to hear that. I'd wondered if ye were loyalists yourselves, havin' so little fear of 'em."

"No, Mr. Proctor. We're Friends." She looked down past the endless stream of soldiers and the endless succession of provision boats going upriver. Six thousand, she thought. All with guns. Dear Lord in Heaven, this beautiful river will be running blood. "Mr. Proctor," she said, "forgive me my lack of hospitality. Would thee like a drink of fresh, cold water? And I should like to ask thee something."

"I'll take it, thanks, ma'am. And what's the question?"

"Ben," she said to the eight-year-old, "kindly fetch a pail of cold water from the spring, hm? This has gone warm." She led the officer off a little from the youngsters, into a patch of shade given by a chestnut tree left standing when the house site had been cleared. He glanced back once at the riverbank where his long bateau nuzzled the bank where it was moored, eight rowers resting with their oars sticking straight up. Then she said to the colonel in a soft voice, so her children wouldn't overhear, "I have a boy there, the big one, who would like to go up the river with thee. Would that be possible?"

The colonel looked surprised, glancing at Will, then back to Mrs. Slocum. "Being Quakers, you don't mean as a soldier, eh?"

"Oh, no. Just to be escorted, not to carry arms."

"Well, I must say, ma'am, I'd have to be smarter than I am to see why I should take another appetite on board, if he doesn't intend to fight. Now, if there was any good *reason* for him to go up, perhaps I might put him on the oars, and free up a man to fight. What such a reason might he have?"

Her eyes had begun welling up with emotion. "To look for somebody. His sister."

"And why should his sister be up that way, may I ask?"

"Indians took her away, Mr. Proctor. Carried her off last fall."

"Oh, my! Misguided ones, I presume?"

"Yes, Mr. Proctor, misguided ones. She's still alive, I'm sure."

He cleared his throat. "How old is the girl?"

"Five. No, six now."

"Butler's Iroquois, no doubt?"

"No. They were Delawares."

"You know the difference, do you?"

"Of course. The Delawares were our friends. They thought most highly of my husband."

"Did they now! Where is your husband, by the way? At the fort?"

"No, he . . . he was killed. In January."

"Ah, ma'am, I am sorry. Thought most highly of him, did they? Excuse me, ma'am. I am truly sorry."

She swallowed and blinked and clenched her teeth until she could talk without quavering. "Listen," she said. "My husband was intending to go ask after her and try to bring her back. After he was . . . after his passing, Will there decided to go, but that didn't work out."

"They meant to go up by *themselves*?"

"Yes. But with thy army coming, the Indians would be in too much a passion. He'd not have been safe."

"Permit me to say, ma'am, that even in this army going up into that country, he won't be safe."

"We are aware of that, Mr. Proctor."

"I would consider taking him as an oarsman. I don't think he'd care for it much. . . ."

"He can do the work of two grown men, Mr. Proctor."

"I mean he'd not care for being with us as we do what we're to do. We're to lay waste to every Indian town from Wyalusing to Niagara. To leave nothing standing, not so much as a cornstalk. There will be deeds done that I doubt a Quaker boy would care to look upon. If he likes Indians, he won't like us. And the chances of finding a little girl in such a donnybrook, m' lady . . ." He shook his head, looking to the ground. "Well," he said then, putting his hat on and cocking a fist at his waist, "I'll have that drink o' water and get back to m' fleet. I'll take the lad if he can be set to leave in three minutes."

"Will," she called. "Has thee packed a kit?"

"It's packed, Ma."

"Then fetch it. Thee's going traveling with this gent!"

And as Colonel Proctor's boat pulled from the bank to rejoin the flotilla of supply boats inching up the river, she kept her eye on Will's red head, until the vessel was out of sight beyond the willows. Then she stood watching the rattling, jingling, scuffing, muttering files of bluecoats trudging up the hot, dusty road, thinking, I've seen thousands go by and they're still going by, and they're all going to kill and plunder where my little girl is! Dear Lord God, I've never understood why Thee puts the innocent in the way of the misguided!

But at least she had got Will headed up the river without Giles going, or interfering. Giles was away on a sojourn to New York, and by the time he returned, Will would be well away.

"Come inside now," she said to all her offspring, who were teary-eyed and worried after Will's departure. "We'll do better to pray for him and Frannie up there than to keep watching that prodigious and mortal folly march up the road."

They were in the house, seated all about in silent prayer, trying to shut out the steady din of the passing army, when Ruth Slocum heard hoofbeats coming close up outside the house, and horses blowing, then the rattle of a wooden wagon. The light from the open door was shadowed by the frame of a huge soldier when she opened her eyes.

"We are in prayer," she told the man. "Please go away."

"I'll be damned," the soldier said to somebody outside. "There's folks in here."

"What does thee want?" she said, getting up with that uneasy feeling that interrupted prayer always gave her. Her youngsters were all looking at the big man in the doorway. It was very hot in the house, though not as hot as out in the sun. Ruth Slocum's dress was soaked with sweat and stuck to her skin everywhere. If it had not been for this army overrunning the valley, she and her family would have been making trips down to the willow thickets now and then to immerse themselves in the river and refresh themselves.

"Foragers, ma'am," the soldier in the doorway said.

"What does that mean?" She was afraid she already knew.

The soldier chuckled. "Ma'am, it means we're here to relieve you o' whatever you have too much of."

"My good man, I'm sorry to say we hardly have enough of anything."

"Well, ma'am, you'll find that we can skim pretty thin." Then the soldier shouted to someone outside, "Abe! Scout that cattle path that goes up yonder! And look in that smokehouse." Ruth Slocum bit her lower lip and laced her fingers tightly together to brace herself for unpleasantness.

"We've no beef cattle now," she said. "And I must insist thee leave our milker alone. We've tots and tads to feed."

"Then I'll wager you've got cheese in the springhouse." He turned away from the threshold and went lumbering toward the spring. Ruth stepped to the door, her lips drawn fine, and looked out. There were soldiers chasing down squawking chickens and putting them in a big wicker crate on their wagon. Others were rummaging in the smokehouse. The big soldier came stooping out of the springhouse with a crock under each arm. He put them on the wagon and came back to the door. "Y'have any flour in there? Any meal?"

"Precious little. Not a smidgen compared with what thee has in those boats."

"Let me be judge o' that," he said, pushing past her into the room. "This is a big army to feed, and from here on up I reckon we'll find nothing but Indian food." His eyes adjusting to the dimness, the soldier whistled. "All these your youngsters, ma'am?"

"Yes, not counting three that's gone. Just about too many for the little victuals we've got."

"Lot of young ones," he said, sweeping along the mantel shelf for meal, coffee, and sweetener bags.

"Yes, lots," she replied. "That's why I'm asking thee, leave us a little something."

The soldier paused, and his searching eye fell on Judith. He winked at her. Judith lowered her eyes and flushed.

"She's married," Ruth Slocum said in a flat voice. "Leave her be."

"Well well. Where's her fellow?"

"He's away in the militia."

"Militia!" the man snorted.

All the children's eyes were on the soldier, not hostile, but curious, and he began to look uneasy. "Hm," he grunted, starting for the door. "Lots o' mouths to feed. But m' army's got lots more. Thank'ee for your generosity, ma'am. Before we go, I hope you don't mind if we harvest a bit o' your fresh roastin' corn there."

She stepped quickly in front of him and barred the door with a stiff arm. "I must beg thee, stay out of our corn. Leave us that, or I shall have to report thee to Mister . . . to Colonel Proctor." She was improvising, to stop this plunder.

"And who, pray, is Colonel Proctor?"

"A friend of ours. The man in charge of those army boats. Don't pretend thee doesn't know Colonel Proctor."

He brought his elbow down on her arm and shouldered past her and down off the stoop. "It's a mighty big army, ma'am. 'Fraid I don't know everybody's names yet. Abe! Take the wagon up to that cornfield and load up!"

"What is thy name, soldier?"

"Uh, damned if I know, ma'am. Like I said, it's a mighty big army, and I don't know everybody yet! Ha ha!"

Wyalusing Town

Neepah picked Good Face up in an embrace and held her for a long time, their hearts beating together, then lifted her up to the skinny old *lehpawcheek* storyteller, Owl. He set her on the saddle in front of him. Good Face looked down at Neepah and remembered the day ten moons ago when she had been handed down by a man in a saddle into Neepah's arms, that first day she had seen her, that very cold day. Now it was hot and everything was the opposite. Neepah stood looking up, chin quivering, and warned, "Don't go to sleep and let her fall off the saddle, Owl."

He laughed. "I have heard this one talk. She will keep me awake!"

Neepah reached up and held Good Face's knee and said, "Your *muxumsah* and *huma* are waiting at Great Falling Water. They will feed you and teach you as I have done. You tell her you need a good dress, not *wapsi* cloth. In that roll behind the saddle is the deerskin I tanned for it. I was going to make the dress for you in time for Green Corn Ceremony, but because the soldiers come she will have to make it."

"I will tell her." Good Face was trying not to cry because

Neepah had told her not to. Neepah had assured her over and over that she would be happy with the old people and safe from the army, and that they would see each other before long, after the army was chased back out. Good Face tried to be brave and believe all that, but it scared her to be leaving Neepah. Minnow waved at her with a sad face from a little distance. Minnow was to stay here with Neepah and other young, strong women and girls and help harvest corn until the army got too close. Good Face was almost, perhaps really was, jealous of her for getting to stay longer with Neepah. She sat on the saddle and tried not to look at Neepah's eyes too long or they both would start crying; she knew it.

Neepah said to the gray-hair, "I hate those soldiers for coming before Green Corn. At Green Corn the adopting medicine would have been spoken."

"Indeed so," said the old man. "But if you hurry and rub out the *wapsituk*, then at the fall ceremony the adopting can be said then."

"*E heh, lehpawcheek.* Yes yes. I will yank off the young soldiers' seed nuts and give them to you, then you can marry another young wife." They both laughed, sharp, cackling little laughs, and so did Minnow. Good Face did not quite understand what they were talking about, but she could tell they were laughing so they would not seem sad. She had noticed that these Lenapeh often laughed when she knew they were actually upset.

"The others wait for you to lead out, *lehpawcheek,*" Neepah said, looking toward the palisade gate. "You go now. May your path be smooth."

"*E heh.* May Nanapush the Creator's Helper stand by you until we next see you."

Good Face's eyes were blurry with tears but she had promised not to cry, and so as she rode toward the gate in front of the old man, she clamped her throat and bit her lip to keep from sobbing. This made a moan in her throat.

The old man was the leader of these who were leaving. As he rode toward the front, Good Face noticed that Wareham Kingsley was one of the people on foot. On a horse was a woman who looked like a *wapsini*, whom Good Face had seen in the village but never talked to. As Neepah had said, the *wapsi* people in the town were being sent away so the army wouldn't see them and get even madder at the Lenapeh.

Old Owl was an important old man, not just a storyteller. Neepah had said he was a Midewiwin *lehpawcheek*, who had much spirit help and was connected with elder Midewiwin in other tribes. Neepah had not tried to explain it further. Good Face understood only that it was a kind of good force that would help Owl have safe passage wherever he went.

She gazed over her shoulder at that field where she had first helped Neepah plant the Sacred Three Sisters, the corn and squash and finally the beans, and where she had run and made a racket with the children to keep away the seed stealers, and where she helped pull and hoe weeds. Leaving that field was almost as bad as leaving Neepah and the village. The corn was so tall now that even on horseback she could not see over the raggedy, golden tassels trembling in the heat. On their stalks were the ears of green corn, festooned with browning silks, and the bean vines twined up thick with long, young pods. And among all the corn hills wandered the squash vines low to the ground with their broad, shading leaves and bright blossoms. This was the season when the women and children had to guard the fields day and night, because the raccoons and other animals wanted to steal the sweet corn and beans.

Good Face looked longingly over the lush field, hearing the voices of people, and perhaps of spirits too, twining through the crops. Boys with bows rested on pole scaffolds above the corn, watching all around for the furry raiders of the crops. Some boys she had defeated at snow snake waved to her, and she waved at them. This was sad, to leave the crops behind. Good Face herself had become like a part of that field, of those Three Sacred Sisters, and often dreamed in her sleep of picking and eating the food she had helped grow there. In her sleep dreams she had even seen Kahesana Xaskwim, a green, beautiful woman with yellow cornsilk hair and kernels for nipples, beautiful and young, not the ancient, severe Mother Corn of the old story.

That afternoon, as they rode along the riverbank beside the Susquehanna Sipu, going ever farther away from the home of her first family, the *lehpawcheek* told her that story, talking quietly over her shoulder as she leaned back against him. "This," he said in a voice whispery and raspy as corn husks, "is the most important of all the Lenapeh stories for you to remember. It is the reason why we have the Green Corn time:

"Kulesta!" Listen! "This was long, long ago, long before the

coming of the *wapsituk*, when the Lenapeh lived close to the Sun-rise Water. . . .

"Some young people were trying to make each other laugh, so they began mocking sacred things. They said they did not believe in Mother Corn because they had never seen her.

"Of course she heard, and took back all corn. Everywhere all the kernels of corn flew like bug swarms away from the People, back to Mother Corn." Good Face imagined that, and it was a clear and thrilling and dreadful picture in her mind.

Owl went on: "Winter came with snow as deep as trees are high, and the Lenapeh were hungry. But their food corn had flown away, and even their seed corn for next spring.

"The People suffered much because of what the unbelievers had said, and they were starting to die. But then came an old man from the south—perhaps Nanapush, the Creator's helper, in one of his disguise shapes. He taught them to find oysters in the Great Water, so they had a little to eat."

He had to pause and explain to Good Face what an oyster was, and what it was like. They did not sound very good to her, especially when he declared, with chuckles, that they looked like what comes up when you hawk to spit.

"Even people who like oysters," he said, "soon get tired of oysters only. And so Nanapush, if that is who the old man really was, again took pity on them, and went through a hole in the ice in the middle of the water, to the world where Mother Corn lived. With him he took a Lenapeh boy who could sing beautifully and dance well, and he carried a big bag of oysters for them to eat on their journey. They caught some fish along the way. After a long time they came to Mother Corn's house.

"Kahesana Xaskwim was not happy to see human beings, because they had said they did not believe in her. She looked old and brown and mean, not green and beautiful." In her dreamy mind, lolling in the saddle, Good Face envisioned her that way, and it was sad.

Owl said, "Then Nanapush, if that's who the old man really was, gave Mother Corn fish to eat—"

"Ah!" Good Face exclaimed, remembering. "Kahesana Xaskwim likes fish!"

"*E heh*. And Nanapush, if that is who the old man really was, made her a shiny pair of ear bobs from oyster shells and gave them to her. Then he had the boy sing and dance for her while she feasted on fish, saying that the singing and dancing proved that the human beings really did believe in her. Then the boy begged her to give corn kernels back to the People so they wouldn't starve to death."

Old Owl didn't say anything else for so long that Good Face craned to look back at his crinkled old face and asked, "Did she?"

"What? Oh, *e heh!* Mother Corn wept with sympathy, and her tears were kernels of corn, which they collected in the bag. And as she wept corn seed she grew younger and more beautiful and greener. She was smiling then and she promised that if the Lena-peh would sing and dance and pray every spring, in just such ways, to prove they believed in her, she would never withhold the corn from them again.

"And so it has been ever since. We have to be thankful for what we receive, or we are not worthy of it and won't get it.

"And like everyone," Owl added, "Mother Corn looks old and brown and ugly when she won't give, but young and beautiful when she does give, for she knows that giving is a joy."

Good Face felt uplifted by that story for a while, but it made her think of things Neepah had been worried about, and she asked Owl after a time:

"But if soldiers come and keep the People from doing the singing and dancing for Green Corn, it wouldn't be the People's fault! It wouldn't be fair if Mother Corn made the People starve if the People *wanted* to do the ceremony and the soldiers kept them from it! Surely, Kahesana Xaskwim would know whose fault it was, and not make the People suffer!" She looked back at him again, imploring, but he shook his head.

"You cannot blame armies or make other excuses. Always remember, excuses are nothing. You must do all you can to be worthy, whatever it costs you, even if that is your life. Never forget to honor the gifts and their givers. Kahesana Xaskwim knows not of 'fairness,' she cares only to be thanked."

And so Good Face was left to ponder, as they rode up the river trails, whether Mother Corn was selfish.

She remembered coming up this river last year in falling snow, riding wrapped in a blanket on a saddle in front of a young warrior man whose tongue she had been unable to speak or understand. Now she was with an old man's arms around her to keep her from falling, just as her own Quaker father and brothers used to take her

riding, but she was going farther away from that family, still farther, and much had happened, and much had changed. Now she
was going farther from her birth mother and brothers and sisters,
but more than that she felt she was also going farther and farther
from the town where she had lived with Neepah and Minnow and
where she had been very happy.

Now and then she looked down at the river far below and
thought about how one could get in the river and float all the way
home. She knew how to swim. Probably Wareham was thinking
of this too. But he couldn't swim.

Poor Wareham. He didn't know how to swim or speak the language. He didn't get to ride on a horse and hear stories. He didn't
even have a name. Poor Wareham would probably want to jump
in the river and float home, if he weren't afraid of water. But he
couldn't.

She could. But she didn't really want to. It wasn't that she
didn't think about it. It was just that she was missing Neepah and
Minnow more than she was missing that earlier and more distant
family.

Although it was saddening to be riding farther day by day from
every comfort and affection she had known, Good Face was not
terrified or cold, as she had been on her other ride up the valley.
Now she was warm, sometimes almost unbearably so, and now
she could talk to the man who held her in his saddle, and be understood. Sometimes, however, after the first days of riding, Owl
seemed to pretend not to understand her.

She already knew that old men could be that way. Her own
wapsi grandfather had sometimes tired of child talk and acted as if
he couldn't understand. He once told her that he could not understand Blatherskite very well, and asked her to stop asking questions
in Blatherskite. She could still remember that word. Blatherskite.
"Grandpa," she remembered scolding him then, "thee understands
me perfectly well, for I'm talking English, not Blatherskite!"
Instead of arguing, he snored, pretending he had fallen asleep.

Now, old Owl sometimes would not reply to her questions, just
like her grandpa, and when she craned around in the saddle to look
at him, his eyes were shut and his head tilted. Well, she thought, I
do have a lot of questions perhaps.

Her grandpa, whom she had not thought of for so long, had
been a solemn but teasing old man, and she remembered him

vaguely and fondly now as she rode in a direction ever away from him.

And when she thought of her grandfather, of course she also thought of the rest of her family. She knew she had thought of them too little while she was in the Indian town. With Neepah nearby, always teaching and caring for her, and Minnow to play with, her mind and heart had simply been full of affection and wonder, almost like a spell of magic. But now in the monotony of the constant riding, with an old man who easily tired of talk, her memory and her heart often traveled back down the river, to an earlier life that had also been full of pleasure and affection. As she thought of her own family, she thought of herself again not just as Wehletawash, Good Face, but also as Frannie.

Slocum, she thought. Frances Slocum. Good Face Slocum. And she ran through her memory of the others in that family:

Mama. Papa. Grandpa. Giles. William, Ebenezer, Judith, Joseph, Ben, Mary, Isaac, and Baby Jonathan. She thought of them all and remembered their faces, as well as she could, and their voices. She thought of the way each of them had been with her, and remembered playing with the younger ones and being helped by the bigger ones. She remembered the warm jumble of children in the bed keeping each other warm on winter nights by snuggling, and remembered waking up chilled when both Joseph and Isaac had wet the mattress.

It was not that she had forgotten them. Even at Neepah's *wikwam,* when so much was happening and she was always living in magic and learning, their faces and names had swum up in her memory.

But now that she was being carried even farther from them, they all seemed to rush up in her mind and heart at once, and she missed them so badly that it was hard to swallow and she could not see without blinking. Whatever became of her, wherever she went, she must remember that she was daughter and sister of that family called Slocum.

They rode sometimes alongside the river, even crossing it at shallow places, to one side and then back, but often they were out of sight of the river altogether, going up steep mountainsides and along cliffs and ridges, through deep woods and swampy places where the air was thick with mosquitoes, past hunting camps and small villages without palisades. They rode past cornfields, and past fields that had been cornfields in earlier years, where dead stalks lay and the little planting mounds could still be seen. Good Face longed for Neepah whenever she saw women working in those fields, hoeing weeds while their children ran about and the babies in cradleboards hung on their mothers' backs or from tree limbs close by. The women would stop work and stand up straight to watch the line of horses and people go by. Sometimes one or two would come running out of the fields to greet somebody they recognized in the procession, or to ask what news they had of soldiers.

Often the people came toward the horse she was riding on because, it seemed to her, everybody in this valley knew the old man. Sometimes the people spoke to him in languages other than Lenapeh, but he understood them. If the travelers were near towns at evening, they were asked to eat and stay. Sometimes councils would gather so that Owl could talk to the villagers. Often, people from those towns would pack up and join him. He did seem to be very important.

As they went between villages through uninhabited places where there was nothing but cliffs and trees and rushing creeks, she wondered sometimes if they might be lost. Owl just laughed at that question, and told her that nobody but *wapsituk* ever got lost; the red people knew all the paths and where they went.

Sometimes the old man would get down to walk and lead the horse while she rode by herself in the saddle; sometimes he would ride and let her walk and run. Eventually he gave her the reins and let her control the horse herself. He told her she was a good rider. She was delighted, especially when she saw Wareham Kingsley watching her with sullen envy as he trudged along on foot. The *lehpawcheek* had just made her feel as good as she ever had.

They went on through steamy heat and chilly rain. Their clothes were soaked, then dried upon their bodies. They stopped to bathe wherever the path was near a good bathing place in a creek or the river. The river was low, running slow.

In all her life until now, she had never slept without shelter. Always there had been a roof of bark or shakes overhead and walls around. The first nights outdoors were intimidating, with distant wolf howls, rustlings in the darkness outside the fireglow, and the night wind, faraway thunder and lightning, or the sheer silent intensity of the stars, and she slept fitfully or stayed awake in fright or awe. When she would fall into exhausted sleep, she sometimes dreamed of bears, and in her dreams they were the dangerous bears her Slocum family had held in dread, not the friendly bears that Neepah said were brothers to the People.

Every day they passed people going both ways on the paths. Some of them were families going to other villages down the river, but most were warriors, long files of painted young men, bald except for their scalp locks, trotting silently with their muskets or bows or lances at their sides, usually with bedding rolls tied over one shoulder, their lean torsos and sinewy legs gleaming with sweat and oil. They all ran looking straight ahead, not pausing to speak. Some groups of warriors included a few of the green-coat soldiers.

She noticed that when the warriors passed, the *lehpawcheek* would hold up a greeting hand to them. They might glance up, but they did not respond. She thought they did not seem as friendly as the people she had known in Neepah's village, and said so to the old man.

He replied: "They have made themselves ready for war, and their hearts are on that other path. They will not look at the eyes of people who are not on that same path. When the fight is over and they go back to their villages, they will have another ceremony to purify themselves again and return to the good-heart path. I know about that. I was often on that path."

That was how he explained it to her. She did not really understand, but thought of it every time more of them went by with their strange cold eyes.

"Are they going down where the Long Knife army is?"

"*K'hehlah.* Indeed yes. They go to meet that army."

"I thought they were," she said with a nod. What would happen when all these warriors met the army was beyond her power to imagine, and she thought of it in terms of the one thing she knew: that Neepah, who had been like a mother to her, had stayed at her town and expected to be there when the army came.

One day they crossed a river a little way above a place where two rivers met, and after riding on for a while they came around a bend and saw ahead of them an Indian town of many *wikwams*. Up the side of a hill above the town were the gray shapes of many dead trees, a swath of them among the live green trees of the forested slope. She had seen that at other towns and knew that the dead trees were the ones whose bark had been peeled off to cover the *wikwams*. Owl told her the town was called Tioga.

Soon she could smell the smoke of fires and the familiar scents of corn cooking in many ways. She was hungry, very hungry.

Now over the hoof steps of the horse she began to hear a sound like a heartbeat. It was a drum, she realized soon, a drum beating in the town.

And as the column moved around the bend, she saw something she had never seen at any of the other villages. "What are those white things?" she asked Owl.

He said they were the cloth lodges of the British soldiers. They stood in a double row, straight and high-peaked and conspicuous, outside the palisade. "This village," he said, "is where English Soldier Butler camps."

"Are those soldier drums?"

"Ha!" he laughed. She turned and looked up at him, and his old face was wrinkled with a smile. "Not soldier drums. It is the drum of Green Corn. Rattles too, hear? This is good!"

That gladdened her heart. She remembered that if the People thanked Mother Corn in that ceremony, there would continue to be corn for the People. The people in the column seemed to be gladdened too. They were talking cheerfully, and despite their weariness they were moving more quickly toward the town.

The drum continued as they rode into town, and there were few people among the houses. Between the huts she had glimpses of a large pole arbor, and it was toward that arbor that the travelers were hurrying. It had no roof, just long rafter poles joining at a peak in the center.

Suddenly two hideous creatures leaped into the path with such terrible quickness that Good Face screamed and the horse shied. The old man's hard, skinny arms tightened so instantly to hold her and control the mount that her ribs hurt.

The creatures were covered with wild, shaggy, yellowish-brown hair. Their faces were round, scowling, little-eyed, bright red except for black foreheads and chins. They did not look like any living face she had ever seen on man or animal. These two ghastly beasts were bounding and cavorting toward her, and she wanted the old man to wheel the horse around and flee, but instead he was using his strength to make it stay still. People of the procession were squealing and scrambling to get out of the way of the monsters.

Voiceless after her first shriek of terror, she heard Owl command her in a quick, sharp voice:

"Kulesta!" Listen! "Give them this or they will smear you with *mweh mweh!*" She felt him press something small into her palm and she almost threw it because of the disgusting word he had just spoken, but his hand held hers, pressing the object in so she couldn't fling it. She did glance at it and thought it was dried dog excrement such as one finds lying in the dust in one's path. "It's *k'sha t'he*, tobacco," he hissed in her ear. "Give it to him or you will get dung in your face!"

One of the monsters was beside the horse and reaching toward her face, and she could see in that instant that what had looked like a monster face was actually a painted wooden false face, and that what had looked like shaggy hair was actually shredded cornstalk around the mask; the clothing was made of corn husks. She saw that the creature's paw was actually a human hand, almost touching her face now, but she could see and smell that its fingers were actually thick with excrement. Mouthing a silent shriek of fear and disgust, she at last heeded the old man's command and thrust the twist of tobacco at the masked person, who took it with his clean hand and put it in a pouch at his side, one of two pouches he wore. Owl then handed him another twist of tobacco and he leaped away, toward others of the people nearby. She saw these people cringe and give things to the masked ones, then jump away and laugh. Off to one side she saw Wareham standing stock-still and wide-eyed. He offered nothing, and in a moment was standing there howling with a smear of excrement across his cheek.

Old Owl was chuckling. As her wild heart subsided and they rode on toward the arbor house, he said, "Those are the Mweh mweh alewehsa, the dung daubers. You give them something at once to show that you mean to honor Kahesana Xaskwim this day. The smallest gift, even an acorn, tells them your heart is for Mother Corn. If not, you deserve *mweh mweh* in the face."

In the dust and throng they were approaching the great arbor, and it seemed to stand in a field of tall corn. But as they rode closer she saw that the cornstalks were actually the walls of the structure. Hundreds of cornstalks, still green, were tied upright around the frame, screening the inside from view. She saw smoke rising from inside and heard, besides the drumbeats, voices chanting. A few of Owl's followers had gone to the corn wall and were standing close to it, some of them touching the stalks.

"May I go and see?" she asked.

"You must watch from outside, because it has already started without us. You will see it is much like the Spring Ceremony you were in." He dismounted and reached up to lift her from the saddle. "Girl, you are a red-hair and they do not know you in this town. Be quiet and respectful and stay out of the Great House. If they ask how you came here, say Owl the Midewiwin carried you."

No one even looked at her as she went to the structure. She sat on the ground at a place where she could peek in between cornstalks. The old man had said she could look in, so she did not feel wrong about it.

She could see just a little at a time through the small opening. She could tell that the round structure was very spacious and that so many people were inside it must be nearly the whole village population. Most of them were seated on the ground and seemed to be very calm and content. It did indeed look like the other ceremony. By the center pole a smoky little fire burned, tended by an elderly man who now and then dropped crumbled tobacco leaf into it and fanned it with a hawk's wing. Near him, just beyond the gap in the wall where she was looking in, was the drummer, a thick-bodied man whose hair was half grayed and hanging free to cover his face as he sat bent far forward. He struck a hard blow, then a soft, then a hard, making the strange water-drum tone. Someone was shaking rattles.

Around the inside walls of the structure there stood women and girls wearing aprons and necklaces and holding bowls and spoons. A line of people was moving past very slowly, and every person would stop before each woman or girl, who would chant some words and feed from the bowl with a spoon. There was much murmuring and chanting, but the word she kept hearing over and over was *"Waneeshee."* It was all so kind and pleasant. It made her think of Neepah, the days in the cornfields, and the Three Sacred Sisters. She felt kindly and thought that somehow everything would be all right by and by. Everything in and around the Great House glowed in the golden sunlight of afternoon. She did not feel at all like a stranger in this village, even though she had just arrived.

"What are they doing?" a voice whispered in English right beside her. Startled, she turned and saw Wareham Kingsley there, squatting on his heels beside her. They had seldom been near enough to each other to talk during the long journey up from the other town. Now, remembering Owl's story about Mother Corn, she told him, as if Neepah herself were putting the words through her:

"They are all thanking Mother Corn, who feeds them. If they didn't thank her, she wouldn't feed them anymore."

"Hm." He squinted in between cornstalks. "Which one's Mother Corn?"

"Mother Corn is a spirit. Kahesana Xaskwim. She is the spirit who makes plants be food for people."

He pointed. "There's hundreds of people in there. Which one's the spirit?"

"Didn't thee learn anything? None of them's really Mother Corn, but all of them together, they sort of are."

Wareham hissed like a snake, turning a mocking face to her. "Girls nor Indians, either one makes any sense!"

"If thee doesn't like my answers, Wareham Kingsley, don't ask me things then."

"Well, who else can I ask? Ever'body else talks Indian."

"Thee could too, if thee were smarter!" she snapped. She was annoyed with him for breaking into the pleasure she had been feeling; it was like someone bursting into a prayer meeting. But at once she regretted her retort. And now she felt something very uncomfortable behind her and turned around.

Owl stood about ten feet behind her, staring at her with narrowed eyes. He put his palm over his mouth, frowning. She remembered what he had told her about being respectful, and realized that she and Wareham had been fussing perhaps a bit too loudly.

"I'm sorry," she whispered to Wareham. "I didn't mean thee's not smart. But thee could be more respectful and not so stubborn. Or thee could have learned to swim and floated down the river." It was hard to talk in English. If not for this Wareham, she thought, I might have forgotten it by now!

She was drooling with hunger when the feast began at sundown in the dance ground between the Great House and the harvested fields. Thousands of ears of corn had been baked in their husks in heated pits in the ground. There was also corn bread and hominy. Kindly women of the village served corn and kept serving it to the hundreds of people of the town and to the ones old Owl had led up the river. Also being fed were some British soldiers, and these were not all the kind she had always seen, in green coats. There were also soldiers in red coats, with long white leggings that came down far enough to cover the tops of their black shoes. They were big, red-faced men, and they stayed to themselves on one side of the bonfires. Their voices were loud enough to be heard all around, but they spoke in such odd accents that she could scarcely understand anything they said. Some of them stared at her, until Owl moved her away from them.

When the people had eaten all they could hold, they got up and did walking dances around the drum, a great, deep-voiced water drum struck by four men who sat around it, all their drum-sticks hitting in unison. The whole field seemed to throb with the drumbeats. Sometimes the drummers sang as they beat the drum-head, eerie tunes of only three or four notes descending, then repeated. Led by two figures in corn-husk clothes, men danced in one circle, with women in another circle inside, walking around and around the drum, each step first on tiptoe, then on the heel, in time with the drum, shaking rattles in time, laughing or with solemn faces, shuffling, swaying slightly. As night came on and the dancers were lit by firelight only, before Good Face's sleepy eyes the world became all color and silhouette in rhythmic motion. She was exhausted from travel and her belly was full, full of that wonderful hot corn made even sweeter by dipping in bowls of maple syrup. She had gnawed it right off the cob, holding it by the peeled-back, charred husks, and had not even kept count of how many cobs she cleaned off. Now, sitting in the grass, leaning back against the leg of old Owl, who sat on a log smoking his pipe, she was almost overwhelmed by sleepiness; she had even stopped swiping at the mosquitoes that whined around her ears.

But then the pulsing of the drum stopped at once. The singing and laughter trailed off, and somewhere toward the village there was a growing commotion of angry and alarmed voices that quickened her heart and awakened her even as the *lehpawcheek* took hold of her hand and stood up, lifting her to her feet. Hundreds of people were milling in the firelight, and she stumbled and bumped against hips and legs, clinging to old Owl's bony hand.

After much jostling and hurrying along in a throng of moaning, jabbering people, she found herself at the edge of a tense crowd arrayed in a circle around some chiefs and soldiers who stood opposite a bright bonfire in the Council Ground. Overhead the firelit foliage of great trees dipped and swayed, moved by the night breeze and the rising heat of the bonfire. The *lehpawcheek* picked her up, just as her father used to do, and set her on his right shoulder, where she could see, and held her braced there with his right hand at her waist.

"See that man coming forward," the old man said, pointing to a tall, muscular young man with a turban on his head and a ring in his nose. "He is Kyontwahgkeh, Chief Cornplanter. He will tell us what has come to disturb our feasting."

The young man began speaking, and his language was not Lenapeh. Owl said he knew the Seneca tongue and he would have to tell her later. She noticed as the young man talked that his ears were strange. Their rims had been cut to make loops, and one of the loops was broken, just loose flesh hanging. She had seen a few Lenapeh men with such cut ears and things hanging in the loops, but this was the first damaged one she had seen, and she was thinking how it must have hurt, when suddenly the people began trilling and wailing. It was a sound that made her scalp prickle and took her mind off the novelty of the ears. Owl himself burst out with shrill, sobbing yells, even as he held her on his shoulder. When the voices had died down a little, the chief called Cornplanter continued speaking. His voice was strong and clear even though he was speaking calmly, but his eyes were blazing with anger. Several times he stopped talking because the people's outcries became too loud.

It was a long time before the chiefs by the fire had finished their talking. Good Face was too heavy for the old man to keep holding on his shoulder, so he set her down and she stood in front of him, and he kept holding her hand as if afraid he might lose her. She could tell that he was distressed; his hand trembled. People were moving to and fro in the crowd, sometimes passing in front of her so that she could not see the chiefs or the Redcoat soldiers. Some of the old people who had come from Neepah's town were making their way to Owl and talking with him.

And old woman leading Wareham by the hand came, and while she was talking to the *lehpawcheek*, Wareham said, "What are they sayin', Frannie? What's all this ruckus?" He looked scared.

"I don't know yet."

"I thought you talked their language."

"That man's Cornplanter. He doesn't talk our language. I don't know what he's saying."

Finally the Council ended with some shouting, and everyone began leaving the Council Ground, all talking excitedly as they went away. Owl stood with the old people and children who had come with him from the Lenapeh town, now all in their own circle again, and they talked about what they had heard. Some of the old people seemed to have understood already, but many had not been able to comprehend what the Seneca chief had said.

The old man looked around at them and said: "It has happened, as we feared. The army was not stopped and keeps coming up the valley. They burn one town and all its crops. Then they march to the next town and do the same. They are too many for our warriors to stop. They have cannons that shoot through anything. They are a few days behind us."

Someone said, "Then we must hurry on!"

"Yes," an old woman said. "We must go on at daylight, toward Sookpa helluk, or the Long Knives will catch us and kill us!"

The old man held up a hand to calm them. "We should wait here for the people of our town to catch up with us, before we go on to the Great Falling Water. Cornplanter said many people are fleeing this way from the Long Knives."

"What're they saying, Frannie?" Wareham asked. He looked scared.

"Hush," she said. "I'll tell thee, but wait!"

Owl was telling the people, "It is hard to find brothers and sisters when everyone is running. Those left back there will be looking for us. We should not run away and be harder to find!"

"He is right-thinking," said an elderly man with only one eye. "We are not rabbits, to run away so fast."

An old woman mocked him. "You are just too old to run like a rabbit, or you would run. He, he he he!"

The old one-eyed man drew himself up tall, the bonfire's glow showing the bony face under his wrinkled skin. "Old woman with a bad mouth, you are wrong. If I can get a musket, I will go back down the river and meet the Long Knives. I have fought them often and I do not fear them, even though it was they who made me one-eyed."

Owl nodded. "Listen to me! Cornplanter promised that the *wapsi* army will not march beyond this town. Here is where they will be met by Cornplanter's Senecas, and by the soldiers of Butler, and the Iroquois of Captain Brant. Might not such warriors as those stop the army here?"

"They have not stopped it yet," said the same old mocking woman. "I think our men have forgotten how to fight."

Owl glowered at her. "We should use our mouths not to make ourselves afraid but to pray for more strength, Huma."

Good Face tugged at his sleeve. He paused and looked down.

"Will Neepah come here?" she asked.

"If she is well."

Someone asked, "Did our town there have Green Corn Ceremony?"

"No," he said. "The Long Knives came too soon."

"Ehhh!" someone sighed. "Our people will starve!"

CHAPTER FIVE

September 1779
Wilkes-Barre

Ruth Slocum was churning butter in the house when her daughter Mary called from outside.

"Mama! There's an army boat down there . . . and they're . . . oh, they're letting off Willie!"

She nearly knocked over the churn in her lunge for the door, calling, "Has 'e Frannie with him?" But a look down at the shore quashed that faint hope that she had been nurturing since the day William embarked with the army officer. The bateau, silhouetted against the river ablaze with afternoon sunlight, had barely touched the bank, letting Will spring ashore before it was pushed off into the current again and continued downriver, with three men rowing. Will picked up his kit from the ground where he had tossed it, glanced once at the departing boat without so much as a wave, and came limping up the slope. Running down to meet him, Ruth and her daughters stopped short when they got a look at his face.

His jaw was set and his mouth corners were drawn down. His eyes were circled with a bruise-tinged darkness and had a nearly mad intensity in them.

Ruth Slocum was almost afraid to touch her son, but she held out her hands toward him, squinting into his face, and said, "What, Willie? What?"

He dropped his kit and almost fell into her arms and, unlike the stoical and hardy lad he had become since his father's death, began shaking with sobs. The worst of all possibilities, the one awful dread she had not permitted herself to speak of to anyone,

130

struck her heart with such heavy certainty that she could barely gasp out the question. "Is she dead?"

For a moment he did not respond, as if he might not even have heard her. But then he stopped quaking, took a deep breath, looked at the sky, put his mother at arm's length, and answered simply, "I don't know. How could I know?"

Ebenezer had hitched down from the barn as fast as he could on his lame foot, and Judith and the younger children had come running from their chores, but all were struck meek and dumb by what they saw in his face.

Finally, Ruth Slocum said, "Come thee have some buttermilk, my son, and then we'd best meet for prayer."

She had known by the look of him that Will had things inside him that only prayer could bring out. After the family sat for a long time in silence with folded hands and eyes shut, flies droning in the room, cicadas shrilling outdoors, Will's voice began, soft and low, and quavering.

"Lord God, and my loved ones . . . I have watched men act as if Thy Light had never penetrated their breasts. Oh, may such abominations never be seen again on this earth, Lord Jesus. . . ." He was quiet awhile, then went on.

"Every soldier I talked to claimed himself a Christian. But they ran into that town—it was Wyalusing, the Delaware town— a-howling like very devils. They burnt houses down with children in 'em. Rode women down under hoof . . . stripped girls naked and took turns ravishin' them . . . laughing all the while or saying words too vile to repeat . . . slashed and burnt cornfields, beans . . . dumped out the wasted food. Didn't leave a stick standing in that town . . . skinned the folks they'd kilt . . ."

He fell still again, shoulders quaking. After a while Ruth Slocum's stomach stopped churning and her heartbeat settled down and she concentrated on her Inner Light to calm herself until she could speak.

"My children. Let us thank our Lord God for lighting the way of our own lives, for 'tis a world of wickedness we walk in. Pray your lost sister Frannie was somewhere far away from that. Pray that her captors not turn their grief to wrath upon her."

William cleared his throat. "Dear Jesus, forgive me for not averting my eyes from that carnage. I wanted to turn my back from it but my task was to look everywhere for Frannie."

Mary and Judith looked perfectly calm in their prayers, but tears were flowing down their faces. It was a long time before Will resumed.

"That officer named Proctor mocked me because I went sick to my stomach. When I told him I'd be no part of another such abomination, he was happy, as if he'd won something from me. And said he'd find me room on the dispatch boat. I reckon it proved his belief that Quakers are cowards. That satisfied him and he was glad I went up, just for that satisfaction."

"My son," Ruth Slocum said softly, "his satisfaction takes nothing from thee. He's badly misguided, but thee is not. The misguided need pity, and 'tis God alone who'll judge us all. Now this is becoming a conversation and it's time to say amen to our prayer."

Will looked up, his eyes shining now, though his expression was still stricken.

"When next I go seeking Frannie," he said, "it will be alone, or with other Friends. Not with soldiers."

Tioga Town

In her dream she was Frannie, but when she awoke she remembered that she was Good Face. But where was she? Over her head was the sloping bark roof of a lean-to shelter. Around her were many children among their blankets and deerskin sleeping robes, some still asleep, others sitting up and looking around. In a lane beyond some lodges, people were running, talking and crying out. Sunlight was just beginning to gild the treetops. Now she remembered this town, and Green Corn. She saw Wareham sprawled nearby, still asleep, his thick auburn hair full of leaf crumbs and dirt from the ground. The excitement of the people in the distance then reminded her that they were waiting for the people of Neepah's village to come up the river, and she scrambled out of her bedding in hopes that they were here and she would find Neepah. She had to pause between two lodges, impatiently squatting on the ground with her skirt spread around her while she made water, then ran out into the urgent throng of people headed down toward the river. Sunbeams slanted through the wood smoke that hung dense in the still morning air. Voices made a din. She saw old Owl nowhere.

At the edge of the village where the path sloped abruptly down toward the riverbank, she suddenly had a long view over the heads of the grown-ups and could see far down the hazy river valley. Mist was rising from the river, which was still in the shadow of the hills.

But the valley was not tranquil. Along the bottomland came a long, ragged procession of people and dogs and packhorses, straggling along the path between the cornfields, most carrying bundles and babies. They were being met and surrounded by the people who streamed out to greet them. Where the two streams of people met and intermingled, an eerie, piteous wail of voices arose. Her heartbeat quickened with the anticipation of finding Neepah and Minnow in that oncoming mass, though there were so many people that some were still coming around that far river bend from which she had first seen this village the day before.

And as she looked down the valley for a sight of the familiar sturdy figure of Neepah, scanning along the slow-moving line with her hand shading her eyes from the bright morning sun, she heard a deep, distant thump, like thunder from far down the river, and then again, then a few more times, and at each reverberation the voices of the people in the valley rose in pitch. Squinting toward the horizon to see what might have made such a noise, she saw what she thought at first might be thunderclouds, but were really not like thunderclouds. The way it hung low and dark, it looked like a pall of smoke.

She trotted down the slope into the bottomland, moving with the village people, and soon was engulfed in the milling crowd, darting among the crush of people dressed in skins, in cloth, in rags, or in virtually nothing. Almost all the crowd was women and children and elders, and she was surprised and frightened to see that many of them were bruised, burned, or bandaged, some even limping on bloody feet. Some people were so sooty, their clothes so visibly charred, they appeared to have fallen in fires.

As Good Face had imagined it, Neepah would have been leading her people up the river as if she were the chief or mother of them all. But now it was apparent that no one was leading, and there were so many people coming that Good Face was afraid she might not even be able to see Neepah or Minnow. Good Face was only waist-high to most of the people and could see only those immediately around her. She pushed between two groups of women who were embracing and lightening the loads of the new-comers, and almost ran into a dusty, naked little girl who was stumbling wearily forward, clutching a corn-husk doll to her bosom. Good Face had seen her before, but not in Neepah's town. This was a child she had seen in a cornfield in some little village beside the river, during the long journey up.

Wandering bewildered through the mob, confronted by scabbed-over wounds and seeping poultices and people with broken feet hitching along on forked-stick crutches, Good Face saw now and then some familiar face, but not Neepah, not Minnow, neither of her loved ones. She could not see them, but perhaps she could call them. And so she wandered erratically through the drift of wretched people like a twig in the eddies of a stream, nudging and turning about, a little redheaded girl in a colorless Quaker dress, calling, "Neepah! Neepah! Minnow! Neepah!"

In the din of desperate voices, hers could scarcely be heard.

The next day, Good Face shared Owl's horse with another girl, one with a hurt foot. The girl rode behind Owl. They were going farther up the river and then turning westward over high hills fol-lowing a well-worn trail. Now there were hundreds of people on the trail. They included most of the ones who had limped and stag-gered into the town the day before. They were from twenty or thirty villages that had been destroyed by the *wapsi* army, which was still following, still burning towns and crops. The leader of that army had been named "Town Destroyer." Cornplanter had promised he would stop Town Destroyer, but the people who had been driven farther and farther up the river would go on ahead to Sookpa helluk, the Great Falling Water. There, at a place called Fort Niagara, the British would feed and protect them until Town Destroyer was stopped and defeated and driven back down where he belonged. The old man had explained all this to Good Face. The *lehpawcheek* had explained also that the smoke in the morning sky had been from the burning towns, and that the thunder noises were Town Destroyer's cannon, which was fired morning and evening to tell the tribes that he was still coming.

It had been hard for him to make her understand anything, because all she could think of was that Neepah had never come. In all the hundreds who straggled in, Good Face had not found Neepah, had not found Minnow. She had called till she was hoarse.

Some families from Neepah's town had finally arrived, being the most tired and farthest behind because they had come so far, so many of them badly hurt, but none had been able to tell old Owl what had become of Neepah, even though he asked everybody who came from that town. Some had seen her in the morning before the soldier drums started. Some said they thought they remembered seeing her in the fields helping the women harvest some of the corn before the soldiers could destroy it. Some believed they remembered her running down a path with the warriors who were going toward the army, and one of those seemed to remember that she was carrying a lance as she ran down with them, and someone else said no, she was carrying a club. Finally Owl had said to Good Face, "They have come too far and are too tired and have seen too much since that day. When people are like that, you can ask them if they saw something and they will believe they saw it because by asking them you make them see it in their minds."

"Maybe she was killed," Good Face had said, almost weeping at the thought. She remembered soldier stories, remembered Minnow's scar.

"The people of the town were scattered," Owl said. "Some did different things. I have seen this. Some hide in the woods or the river and some go up in the hills. And then when the danger is past they come back to their town and find others who have come back. Then, when enough come back, they build the town again, or if few come back, they set out to find the ones who left. When a town destroyer comes through, it can take a long time for all the people to find each other. But these things have been happening to us ever since the *wapsituk* first came to the shore of the Sunrise Water and wanted a place to put their chair, and though it has been hard for us, we still remain the Lenni Lenapeh, the Grandfather People, the same as we have been since He Who Creates By Thinking first thought us into being."

The old man had patiently told her all that, even though he had had much to do and many to talk to. Then he reminded her:

"Neepah knows where you are going. Her father and her mother live close by to Fort Niagara, and I am taking you to them as she asked me to do. She knows the way there and she is a strong woman, and you will be her daughter, as that is her best dream. You have come a long way to be her daughter. Because of the deeds of this Town Destroyer, it is necessary that you must go an even longer way, but remember, you are to be her daughter. *Zhukeh kishalokeh*." Now I am finished telling.

And so she remembered his words as they came along this trail through higher country, which he told her was the land of the Seneca, who called themselves the Great Hill People because they had been born from a mountain here, and that was their creation, long ago. The trails here sometimes were so high and steep, traveling down into stony gray creek canyons and back up the opposite sides, that she could hardly bear to look down. Sometimes it seemed she was as high as the clouds, with nothing below but rocks and boulders and howling air and roaring, foam-white water.

It was a hard and slow way, through woods whose trees were so tall and dense that hardly a sunbeam could reach the ground, where boulders bigger than houses stood covered with bright green mosses or blue-gray lichens speckled with orange, where fallen trees thicker than a man's height lay black and rotting, or sometimes had been torn all to splinters by bears clawing for grubs. The old man pointed out to her such things, and showed her the kinds of flowers and plants that could be used for curing headaches and aching bones, the ones that would cure itching skin, the ones that had edible roots, nuts, and berries. "Neepah will want you to know all these," he would say, "because a Lenapeh woman knows how to feed and heal, and how to make everything anyone could need." There was plenty of time for him to teach her such things, because the old people and hurt ones needed to rest often, as did the horses with two or three riders.

Whenever they stopped and sat, other old men would come and sit by the *lehpawcheek*, and they would smoke their pipes and talk, while the women tended to sore feet and injuries and hungry children. There were no young warriors along with these people, except a few who had been too badly wounded to stay back with Cornplanter and Brant and Butler to fight Town Destroyer. On the first and second days here on the long trail, it had still been possible to hear the thunder of Town Destroyer's cannon in the morning and evening. Then on the third day, in the afternoon of a very hot and dry day, there had been a long rumbling from back in that direction, which then had grown faint and finally subsided under the rush of waters and the breeze in the trees, and during the time of that faraway thundering, the old men had smoked their pipes in a circle and prayed, and the women sat silently, praying too, with their jaws clenched and lips closed tight.

And then the tired and homeless hundreds got back on their feet or climbed onto the overloaded horses and moved westward again.

Owl told the two girls on his horse that this westering trace was the Longhouse Road. By what she saw along the way she understood the name. They passed through towns each day, and they were not like other Indian towns she had seen before. The bark-covered buildings were not *wikwams*, and were huge, some a hundred paces long, with several families living in each one. Pole palisades enclosed the towns. Owl told her that the Longhouse People were the tribes of the Iroquois. "They have always been mean to our People," he said. "But now we all have the same enemy."

To Good Face, the people in the longhouse towns seemed very different from the Lenapeh, the only Indians she had known; their language sounded strange, their ornaments were different, and they seemed unfriendly and scornful, though they did feed Owl's followers, let them rest within the palisades, and helped them take care of their sick and hurt ones. But even these cold-eyed Longhouse People knew Owl, and their head men came out to smoke and talk with him about the army coming on.

And in all these Longhouse towns along the way, drums were pounding.

Good Face had fallen into a dreaminess from the fatigue and motion of riding and was daydreaming of Neepah and Minnow, when they rode over the crest of a ridge. She heard a strong wind then, but when she looked up, the treetops were not moving at all.

She looked about, coming back from her reveries little by little to notice the heat and familiar discomforts of the saddle. She knew she was hearing wind, that she had not dreamed it, but the woods were still, the sun dapple on the trail was motionless, and midges were twirling in the narrow sunbeams. Behind, there were the sounds of the procession, which she had been hearing for so many days that she didn't even notice anymore unless she listened for them: the footfalls and hoof steps, dogs, drone of voices, horses snorting and blowing in the heat, and the old man's traveling song, barely louder than his breathing, which he hummed to himself sometimes for hours at a time, a song deep in his chest that she felt, as much as heard, when she slumped back against him in her sleepy spells.

He stopped humming and soon he said, *"Kulesta."*

"I hear," she said. "But what is it?"

Then a woman's voice back in the column sang out, *"Kulesta! Sookpa helluk!"* And after a pause, cheerful voices were calling those words back along the column, and people back there began laughing, and others began singing. Good Face remembered what the name meant, and turned her head to look back and up at the smile-creased face of old Owl.

He nodded. "Soon we will be at the end of this journey of sadness on the Longhouse Road. You hear the Great Falling Water. You will see it before this day is done."

They had been descending out of the high, steep hills for the past day of riding but were still going down long slopes through the woods, and she could see no sign of the falling water, nothing but trees, whose leaves were beginning to fade from green to yellow, sometimes edged with crimson. Now they rode on and on, the sound growing louder, becoming less a sound of wind and more a sound of thunder. The sound was so great that all the air in the woods seemed to rumble, and it covered all the sounds of the people and horses and dogs. They rode through the forest's edge into rolling land where dead trees and stumps stood and the ground was covered with grass and weeds instead of the little forest flowers and the ferns, and the afternoon sun was so bright and hot that she squinted and began sneezing. Then she was looking at more woods and patches of clearings, and, beyond the farthest treetops, something so unfamiliar that she almost felt dizzy for a moment: a blue, straight horizon more level than a tabletop. It was a confused instant before she realized that it must be water. She remembered her father's description of the ocean he had seen. She gaped at it, blinking, associating the flat bright vastness of it with the roaring sound. But the noise was coming from nearer by, from her left, and when she looked that way she saw something else totally unfamiliar.

It was like a white cloud floating and swirling above the treetops, shimmering with sunlight, dissolving into the blue sky above, a sky devoid of any other clouds.

The worn trail continued through clearings and clumps of woods, with the ruins of old villages here and there, sticks and bark rotting on the ground, a few arches of longhouse frames still standing weathered and gray, abandoned cornfields, the remains of pole fences.

The trail divided in two, and Owl rode to the left, through more woods. The very air seemed to pulsate, and the horse they were riding began fidgeting, throwing its head, trying to go toward the right. So the old man halted it, summoned someone with a wave of his hand, dismounted, and lifted the girls down while a tall boy took the horse's rein and led it aside.

She looked up at old Owl openmouthed. Under her bare feet she could feel the earth vibrating. It was the first time in her life the ground under her feet had not been solid and still. She reached for the old man's hand and he laughed, though she could not hear him. Then he walked her away from the horse. Other people had come near, and they all walked with him toward a line of trees beyond which the shimmering cloud of mist stood. As they walked through the woods she clung tight to his hand because she could tell there was something strange and enormous just ahead.

And then they were standing on the very edge of the earth, and below and before them was a world of rock and spray and cascading blue-green water. It was the most beautiful but most frightening spectacle her eyes had ever beheld, and her heart felt high and fast in her breast. She felt as if the whole world were about to wash away and take her with it. She watched fascinated as tremendous curtains of white water slowly fell, ever moving but never really changing shape, and burst into a churning, whipping whiteness on great boulders far, far below. The swift water in the chasm below roiled deep blue and milk-white, drifted over by mists. Even at the top of this cliff where she stood, she could feel the cooling mists moistening her hands and face. She had seen waterfalls on this journey through hills and woods, where creeks dashed musically down cliff sides, but here so much water was pouring so mightily that it dizzied her to try to look all the way across the chasm, and when old Owl let go of her hand, she gasped and sat down hard on the ground rather than try to stand unsupported in the presence of such din and motion.

Other old men had come to stand with the *lehpawcheek*, looking out over the thundering cascade. He extracted his smoking pipe from its fur bag and filled it with tobacco. He lit it as she had seen him do before, by holding a glass disk over it in the sunlight. He puffed smoke, drawing his hand along above the pipe stem as if to guide the smoke to himself, then turned the stem in a circle while saying something she could not hear but knew to be a prayer. Neepah had told her that this Great Falling Water was one of the People's sacred places, which she had presumed to mean like Jerusalem or Nazareth or something. She saw that many of the people had come close to the edge and seemed to be praying too, some with pipes, and many of the women praying as Neepah had, by holding their palms up and facing the sky with their eyes closed. Good Face felt that she ought to pray too, but was afraid to close her eyes so near this roaring, earthshaking tumult.

If Owl were still holding my hand, I mightn't be afraid to shut my eyes, she thought.

Just then she thought she heard Neepah's voice, faint in the roar of water, not speaking words, but nevertheless directing her to pray because she was in a sacred place. She did not look around for Neepah, because even though she had heard her voice, she knew that Neepah was not really here. Somehow she knew all this, and it was strange how she could. But she remembered that Neepah was never afraid, and she was ashamed of herself for being afraid to pray, of all things.

And so she did shut her eyes—though not till she had a firm grip with both hands on the grass on either side of where she sat—and she prayed a prayer that went swooping and soaring beyond any she had ever felt.

Good Face was relieved when they returned from the high place to the main trail and rode through more woods and fields, past more old towns and some *wikwams* with people still living in them. The roar of the water grew fainter as they went away from it, but it could still be heard for a long while, and sometimes when she looked back, she could still see the cloud of mist above the trees.

Then they were going down a steep slope toward a much lower level of ground, and she could look out through the trees on the slope and see the vast blue lake again, and when they came down off the slope they were on the river bluff, but not so high above the water now. Here on the low ground they began entering big, smoky villages of *wikwams* and skin tents and lean-tos. People came out of the camps and greeted those they knew among Owl's followers. Someone came and lifted the other girl off the back of the horse. People kept leaving the column, but Owl rode on.

And then at the end of the road, just beside the shore of the lake, Good Face saw a massive fort, far bigger than the one near her home at Wilkes-Barre, a fort with a huge, gray stone three-story building standing on it, so big it had seven or eight chimneys.

She thought the fort must be where Owl was leading the rest of the people, but he turned the horse away from the river and into a large cluster of *wikwams*, where he was immediately greeted by many who came running forth calling to him in the Lenapeh tongue. He greeted them cheerfully, and she thought these surely must be his own people. Again he dismounted and lifted her down, saying to the people crowding around, "This child is Good Face and I have brought her to be granddaughter of Tuck Horse and Flicker."

"Come, then, *lehpawcheek*," a young woman said. "Their lodge is this way. I have never seen hair so red and beautiful, Good Face, even though there are several soldiers in the fort whose hair is red."

"*Waneeshee,*" Good Face said to the young woman, being polite, as Neepah had told her always to be.

"*A ho!* She knows our tongue!" exclaimed the young woman.

"This is a girl who speaks much, and speaks well," old Owl said. They were walking through the village, and the smell of cooking was everywhere. The travelers had had nothing to eat all day but roasted cornmeal flavored with maple, and some berries, and the smell of meat cooking was making her mouth water. Several women of all ages had joined them, and some of them reached out and caressed her red hair as they walked along among the *wikwams* and cookfires.

"There is their lodge," the young woman said. "I will run and tell them you bring them a beautiful girl!"

The old man called after her, "Tell them I will give them this girl if they feed me!" He chuckled, but she felt sad. It seemed that she would be leaving someone else she had come to like.

The ground around this *wikwam* was strewn with wood chips and shavings. Slats and poles of fresh-cut wood leaned against the walls. Good Face remembered that Neepah's father was a chair-maker.

The young woman ducked in through the door of the bark-covered hut, and then came out followed by a man and a woman who did not look very old except for their gray hair. They had grave faces that were dark, round, and broad, and glowed in the golden light of the late-afternoon sun. The woman looked like Neepah, though with gray hair, so much so that Good Face wanted to run up and hug her waist. Instead she slowly walked closer, beside Owl, who was tired and walking with a limp. As they approached she saw that the woman did have an old face when seen closer. She had wrinkles and sagging eyelids and some spots that looked like freckles, even darker than the rest of her face. The old woman was looking straight at Good Face and was not smiling. The old man was smiling, but he was smiling at Owl.

The two old men put all four of their hands together and held them for a moment, nodding and smiling. Then they sat down on a log that lay near the cookfire, which was outdoors because of the hot weather, and the old man picked up a long smoking pipe that lay in the forks of two branches stuck in the ground. He filled the pipe while the old woman laid some dry sticks over the embers and fanned the fire with a turkey-feather fan. When the fire was flaming, the old man picked out a burning twig, held it over the pipe bowl, and sucked on the stem until he was making plenty of smoke. Then he turned the stem in a circle, pointed it at the ground and then toward the sky, and finally handed it to old Owl, who puffed more smoke, letting it rise out of his mouth into his nostrils.

The younger women sat and stood about, saying nothing, just seeming to wait, watching. The old woman picked up a small iron kettle and, with a pothook through its bail, hung it on a wooden frame to heat over the flames. She knelt and sat back, wincing, and then began morosely studying Good Face, who stood by herself being patient before the elders, as Neepah had taught her to do. Old people take their time and do certain things first, Neepah had told her. Good Face had noticed that was very true and that no matter how much one might want to start talking about things, it was no use to start until the elders were ready. Nevertheless, knowing almost surely that this woman was Neepah's mother, she kept looking at her, wishing she would smile but afraid that if she looked at her too boldly, the old woman would not like it. The young women had started talking to each other in low tones. Far away there was still the hushing, whispery sound of the waterfall, even though they had come down the river a long way from it. Other people, seeing the *lehpawcheek*, had come over to stand and sit around, but did not interrupt the pipe-smoking, and little children were gathering behind the adults' knees to stare at Good Face. She waited, feeling many eyes.

When the pipe burned out, the old man cleaned out the bowl with a twig and set the pipe back in its forks. He had not been looking at her, but now he did, with his knobby hands resting on his knees. He wore only a breechcloth and moccasins and a necklace of claws. His skin was loose and wrinkly and veiny, but underneath his muscles still looked thick and hard. There were not many places on his chest and arms that were not scarred. Across his cheeks and around his neck were tattoos of triangles and lines. His eyes were so small and deep and keen it seemed as if she could feel his gaze touching her like pointed fingers. She had heard Neepah talk of her father Tuck Horse, and she remembered the story that he had been a great warrior who fiercely hated the *wapsituk* and had been fighting them all his life. Remembering that she herself was *wapsini*, something that she had not thought about very much, she began to be afraid Tuck Horse might hate her because she was. He certainly did not appear very happy to see her.

Now old Owl, who seemed so skinny and tall in the presence of Tuck Horse, extended his hand toward her and said to the old couple:

"Your daughter told me to bring this child to you. She wants you to keep her here until the Long Knife army goes back and it is safe in the villages again. She asks you to be *muxumsah* and *huma* to this girl. I have traveled the Longhouse Road with this girl, and I can say with truth that she is a child who talks very much but listens well too."

"Has our daughter adopted this girl yet?" Tuck Horse asked.

"They did not have the ceremony. The army came too soon."

Tuck Horse said, "This cannot be my granddaughter, then."

It took Good Face a moment to grasp what Tuck Horse had said, and she thought she had misunderstood something in the language, for she still sometimes got one word confused with another.

But Owl, his head tilted, said, "Yes, she can be your granddaughter. Neepah will adopt her as daughter when they are together again, after the army goes away. She told me to tell you that is what she wants to do. This girl is to replace her daughter who was sent to the Spirit World by the Long Knives." Good Face was relieved to hear Owl explain it because she was alarmed by what Tuck Horse had said.

But now the old warrior squeezed his eyes shut and passed his hand back and forth across his face, saying, "Do not speak the name of that one!" And the man's wife was also squeezing her eyes shut and looking away. Then Tuck Horse looked hard at Owl, who sat with his mouth open.

"Listen, for you do not know this," Tuck Horse said, his voice deep in his chest. "You came slowly, all along the river. But the messengers came straight from Wyalusing like a swift bird many days ago. Our daughter whose name we cannot speak, she has gone past Keeper Grandmother and is . . ." He swept his hand up toward the descending sun and then down to the horizon. ". . . on the Path of Souls."

Good Face cried herself to sleep that night in the lodge of Neepah's old parents. When she slept at last, she dreamed of Neepah and the Three Sacred Sisters, who were corn, beans, and squash in the forms of young women. In the dream, Neepah and the Sacred Sisters all stood together on a mound of earth and swayed in a dance until their roots came free of the soil and they rose together into the sky. They were singing happily as they went up, but Frances stayed on the ground. She was Frances because the woman who had given her a Lenapeh name was dead.

When she awoke in the morning, she was still unable to keep from crying, and she was cold as well. After all the heat of the long summer, a cold wind had started blowing in the night, and then sometime while she was dreaming a rainfall had begun. She was sleeping barefoot and in just her dress and there was no fire inside the *wikwam* because the cookfire had been outside for the summer. She was curled up on a bed of boughs and grass that had been comfortable enough when it was warm and she was exhausted from crying about Neepah, but now she was shivering and wretched, and there was no warmth in her heart where Neepah had been for so long. She knew that she was now even farther away from her real family than she had been before. Even old Owl, whom she had grown to like very much, was not here now. Sometime during her awful grief of the evening before, the old man had left to go someplace where members of his clan were, somewhere closer to the fort.

She shivered and sniffled and tried to draw her legs up far enough that her skirt would cover her cold feet, but it was in vain because she had grown, and so much hem had torn and frayed. If she could have stayed with Neepah, Kahesana would have made her a deerskin dress. Or if she had been with her Quaker mother, she would have made her a new dress or repaired this one. But now Frances had no one to take care of her that way. This old man and woman did not seem to care for her at all, and they were still asleep in their old blankets on the other side of the dark, cold *wikwam*. She could hear the old man snoring softly. Frances wished she could have left these people and gone on with Owl. At least the old *lehpawcheek* had liked her.

She did not know really why Neepah was dead, but she remembered that she had had to stay at her own town because she was a leading woman of her clan there and she had said her people would need her there when the Long Knife army came, and so probably the army had killed her. Frances began to sob again.

The only person left from the beginning was Wareham, but he had never been any help. He was just a miserable, lost, whiny boy. And besides, she didn't even know where he was now.

She felt so sad now, with no Neepah, with the magic of her love and care gone, that she wished she had floated home down the river when she first learned how to swim. But now she was far from that river.

And what of Minnow? she thought. Did they kill her too?

It was so chilly, and the rain on the roof of the *wikwam* was so dismal a sound, a sound that made her think of winter.

She saw the old woman, Ulikwan, Flicker, stirring in her blanket. The woman got up a little at a time, first on an elbow, then groaning to sit up, then putting her feet on the floor, like somebody who was hurt. Seeing her efforts made Frances even more sad. This woman was so unsmiling and slow that it was hard to imagine that she was Neepah's mother. Ulikwan was a name that meant a kind of woodpecking bird, Neepah had told her, and had even pointed out a flicker to her. Frances thought of that as she watched the old woman get to her feet, draping her blanket over her head, and stoop through the door flap to go out into the rain. When Frances looked back toward the old people's bed, she saw the old man's eyes open looking at her, but he shut them at once and pretended to be asleep.

The old woman came back in with a kettle. She picked up some kindling from a dry pile inside the door and put it in the middle of the firepit in the center of the *wikwam*. She opened a little bag and got out some things, knelt in the gray light that came down through the smoke hole, and began striking sparks with a flint and

steel, into charcloth and tinder, just as Frances had seen her own
real mother and Neepah do on many mornings when their fires
had burned out overnight. When the tinder was smoking, the
woman held it in her palms and blew on it until it glowed on one
side and then flames burst out. She set it in the firepit and began
adding shavings and sticks until a steady fire was burning and
crackling. As the air in the *wikwam* filled with smoke, the old
woman moved a long pole that reached out through the smoke
hole. That adjusted the piece of bark over the hole so that a little
more light came in, and the smoke quickly drifted and curled up
and out. Then she hung the kettle from a pole above the fire. Now
and then she looked at Frances and saw her looking at her, but she
said nothing. That made Frances feel even more bleak and cold.

The old woman adjusted the fire under the pot and then with
pained movements got up and hung her rain-wet blanket near the
fire and went back to her bed, grunting and turning until she was
settled in under her husband's blanket with him, lying on her left
side facing Frances.

After a short while Tuck Horse muttered something to his wife
and she murmured back. Then she raised her head and said,
"Wehletawash." Good Face. Neepah's name for her.

"Ai, Huma?" Frances had not meant to call her Grandmother;
it had just come out, being the way these Lenapeh addressed the
old women.

"Surely you are cold," the old woman said, lifting the edge of
the blanket. "Come in here until the fire warms the lodge."

Frances nodded. She got up, hugging herself, and went around
the little cookfire. Their bed was between poles a foot off the floor,
and she sat down on the edge and sank back into the warmth and
smells of the old people's bed, the smoky, musky, leafy smells,
odors of tanned hides and tobacco, the night breath and sweat of
the old woman and man. The old woman enveloped her in the
blanket's warmth and with a warm arm drew her shivering,
clammy little body back close to her own body heat.

Better than the warmth itself was simply the terribly needed
closeness of someone. The old woman's arm was over her and
Frances could squirm backward until her cold back and bottom
were pressed to the old woman's bosom and belly the way she had
sheltered herself in the haven that Neepah had been during the last
winter. The old woman radiated not just heat but comfort. Tears
welled in Frances' eyes and made the little cookfire blur and

shimmer, but now they were not the tears of lonely misery, but the tears of gratitude. She put her cold hands between her thighs and felt her Inner Light growing and spreading and she prayed a word of thanks and sent it up with the smoke rising through the roof, and then her spirit floated down into someplace that, wherever it was, was home, even if only for this moment.

She awoke once because a strange, blaring sound penetrated her slumber, but its distant tones had died by the time she was awake. She was alone in the bed and knew she had been asleep for a long time and she should go make water, but she was too tired and comfortable to move yet and so she let herself fall into sleep again without thinking of anything, without even opening her eyes.

She woke up again and opened her eyes enough to see that the old woman was sewing by the fire and the old man was not in the *wikwam*. She still needed to pee, but not desperately yet, and all was calm in the *wikwam*, so she went back to sleep, aware only that the rain had stopped and people were talking outdoors.

Then suddenly she was awakened by the blanket being thrown off of her, and old Tuck Horse was standing over her saying, "Get up. Come." He took hold of her arms with his hard hands and lifted her so quickly onto her feet that her knees weren't ready yet and she almost fell down. He grabbed the hem of her dress and pulled it off over her head, and she was so startled to find herself standing naked that she almost wet herself. Tuck Horse threw her dress down on the bed and, seeing the little bag, he took it between his thumb and finger and looked at it and said, "Did my daughter give you this?" She nodded, shivering and pressing her knees together. He let go of the medicine bag and took her hand and wrist in his big hand. He pulled her toward the door, lifted the flap, and led her out.

Many women and children were standing around out in front of the *wikwam* as if they had been waiting for her, and they began talking fast and low when they saw her. Old Flicker stood there by the outdoor fire, holding a bundle in her left arm. The ground was cold and wet and squishy underfoot, with puddles of rainwater all about, and the sky was dull with low, ragged, fast-moving clouds. The strong breeze was making everything ripple, wave, and flutter—foliage, grasses, hair, feathers, clothing, even the water in the puddles. A man wearing a fur cap and a fur yoke covered with little round mirrors was kneeling by the fire. He scooped some embers from the fire with a shallow bowl, then crumbled some dry leaves over them to cause a thick white smoke. Then he carried it around her and Tuck Horse and Flicker. The old couple made motions of washing themselves with the fragrant smoke, which the wind dispersed at once. Then the man put down the smoking bowl and picked up a wooden bowl containing what appeared at a glance to be dirt, and turned to walk away, with everyone following. Tuck Horse led her by his strong grip. She knew some sort of medicine was being done and was a little afraid, but mostly she was in desperate discomfort from needing to pee; she was covered with gooseflesh and already starting to dribble as she walked.

They led her down a slope between two rows of *wikwams* and to the edge of a stony creek. There the old couple and several women stepped out of their moccasins and waded into the creek with her, while the man with the wooden bowl stood on the bank and began chanting softly.

The women immediately took her out of Tuck Horse's grip and dunked her entirely under the water, head and all. They let her up for a gasping breath of air but kept her body submerged and began scrubbing her skin painfully hard with handfuls of sand and gravel from the creek bed.

She remembered all this. It was what Neepah had done to her that first day. And, just as she had done then, she let loose and emptied her bladder in the creek.

It felt as if they would scour all her skin off every part of her body. It hurt so much that she almost cried. They dunked her head in the water again and twisted and pulled her hair to wring the water out. Neepah had not been nearly this rough or ruthless. It felt as if they were trying to scour her to death.

But soon they were done, and waded out of the water with her. She looked down and saw that every part of her was red from the scrubbing, and there were even places where little tendrils of blood were seeping from the abrasions.

Old Flicker opened the bundle she had been carrying, and with a wide swatch of clean cloth rubbed and patted her dry until her skin felt aflame. But then the old woman dipped into a pot of greenish grease and anointed her all over. It was bear oil with something in it, and at once it took away all the stinging and burning as if by magic.

Then the old woman stooped back to her bundle and lifted up a

folded piece of pale deerskin, which fell open and showed itself to
be a small, fringed dress, beautifully sewn. She helped her put it
on, and Good Face was astonished, then delighted, and exclaimed,
"Waneeshee, Huma!" For the first time, she saw a trace of a
smile, but Flicker shook her head.

Then, in her new dress, with people standing all around, she
was placed to stand between the old man and woman, with the
man in a fur cap standing before them. He was rolling tobacco
leaves between his palms to crumble them, saying:

"Listen, my People. I have been asked by Tuck Horse and his
wife, Flicker, to do this medicine." He walked around the three,
sprinkling tobacco crumbs over their shoulders, and returned to
stand in front of them, saying: "This girl, Wehletawash, has been
purified by water, by smoke and tobacco. The whiteness of the
wapsituk has been scrubbed off of her and her unclean garments
have been discarded. Now she wears a garment made for her by
this woman beside her, and she speaks the Lenapeh tongue and
wears a medicine bag given her by a person of this same family.
She is ready now."

He stooped and picked up his wooden bowl. A woman knelt by
the creek and dipped up water with a gourd spoon. The man said,
"Now each of you will put some of that water in with the earth I
hold here." Tuck Horse took the spoon and dribbled some water
into the bowl. Then he handed the spoon to Good Face, who did
the same, then gave the spoon to the old woman, who poured in
the rest of the water. The man swirled the bowl, then reached in
with his right hand and stirred and worked it inside the bowl. Then
he held it down for them to look in. It was now half full of a
smooth, dark mud. He said to Tuck Horse, "Could you separate
the water and the soil from each other?"

"No."

"Could you separate the water and the soil?" he asked the old
woman.

"No," replied Flicker.

"Good Face, could you separate the water and the soil from
each other?"

She looked at the mud, thinking that there must be some way
that the old ones just hadn't thought of. You could just let the mud
dry, she thought. But then the water would be gone. She looked up
at the man, who was staring hard at her, and she realized what the
answer was expected to be, and she answered, "No."

"Wehlee heeleh. Now listen and remember. As a medicine maker of my people I have shown with this mud how the souls of these three people are now mixed together so they can never come apart. Good Face is now their daughter, filling the place of one they had before." He made a mud spot on each one's forehead, and said, *"Zhukeh kishalokeh."* It is finished.

And then all the people around laughed and whooped and came close to hug Tuck Horse and Flicker and their daughter Good Face, who was bewildered but felt very good, and then Flicker bent down and put on Good Face's cold feet a soft, pretty pair of moccasins decorated with quills, the most beautiful moccasins she had ever seen, and told her, "Now you are beautiful, my daughter." And Good Face did feel beautiful, and they all went up to feast. Everyone was happy, and Good Face was fussed over very much, enjoying the attention and kindness she had missed since leaving Neepah's village. She felt encouraged to talk a lot, impressing the people with her ease in their language. As usual there was much attention to her beautiful red hair. The clouds cleared late in the afternoon and the sunset light from the horizon beyond the river flooded everything with a reddish-gold cross light. Just then she heard a strange, distant blaring sound, remembering that just such a sound had awakened her earlier that day.

"What was that, Huma?" she asked as the notes faded.

"That was the silver horn the soldiers at the fort blow in the morning and the evening, to tell them the sun is coming up or going down, so they can make their flag do likewise. You will hear that every day while we are at this place. But listen now, Good Face, and remember something."

"What, Huma?"

"Not to call me that. For, old as I am, I am not your grandmother but your mother."

Good Face flushed with embarrassment. "I will remember, Kahesana."

PART TWO

Good Face

1784–1794

CHAPTER SIX

July 1784
Wilkes-Barre

Ruth Slocum shaded her eyes with her left hand and reached up with her right to grasp Giles' hand and then Will's. High on their horses, they were silhouetted against the morning sun, faces in the shadows of their wide black hat brims.

"Godspeed, my boys," she said. "I'll pray every day thee finds her."

"Well, we've a trail of sorts," said Giles. She knew he was trying to sound more hopeful than he was. She had always had more faith than anyone in the family that Frannie was alive, and she was sure of it now. When prisoners were released after the end of the war, her nephew Isaac Tripp had returned to the valley swearing he had seen Frannie at a Delaware village.

And then, even more inspiring, Wareham Kingsley had been brought home, saying she was alive at Niagara as little as two years ago, living with an old Delaware man and woman and seeming to be well.

Her two eldest sons rode down to the river trail and turned upstream. They were leading a packhorse, and unarmed. They turned in their saddles and waved once before vanishing in the willows.

She had tried to dissuade Giles. As her husband used to say, Indians have long memories, particularly about promises and about grudges. Even with the war over and the new government trying to soothe the tribes, there might still be warriors who remembered that Giles had fought against them.

But he insisted on going, reminding her that it probably was his fault that Frannie had been carried off. He saw it that way, now

153

that the war was over. He had put aside the gun for good, and now without it was braver than ever.

Ruth Slocum stood in the yard sending her thoughts after them, her fingers covering her chin and mouth. Their hope for getting Frannie back if they did find her was the sum of one hundred guineas, which the Slocum family had raised by selling off a small piece of land. They hoped it would be enough to ransom her.

Ruth Slocum had no idea whether money would be of any importance to the Indians. If not, there were traders everywhere who coveted money and would know how to convert it to something the Indians wanted. A hundred guineas would buy a lot of whatever it might be that Indians wanted.

And if that was not enough, the boys could just come home and get more money. As the head of her family, she had plenty of land, thanks to her father and husband, rest their souls, and now that the war was over, land-hungry people were pouring into the valley.

She walked to the house and sat on the stoop, wiping her face with her apron. She was forty-eight years old, had borne ten children in nineteen years and suffered much grief, and she tired quickly these hot days. She left most of the field work now to Ebenezer, who was eighteen, and Benjamin, who was going on fourteen, though she could still get out and put in a good day in the harvest. She could in fact put in a better day of work than Ebenezer, who with his lame foot used up much of his strength compensating for his lack of balance. Mary was a strong and supple hand in the field now, being almost sixteen, but she usually stayed at the house taking care of the three littlest boys. All in all, Ruth Slocum's lot was much better than anyone would have expected for a widow of her age. There was never more work than family to do it, and then of course there was all the land, which just silently and invisibly grew in value year after year because it was so close to the fort and town.

Inside the house the little ones were talking; Ebenezer and Ben were up in the fields. Judith now lived with her husband Hugh, several miles away. Ruth Slocum still felt that all her children were under the web of her soul, no matter how far away they were. Even Frannie, about whose place she knew nothing, was still palpably out there somewhere. Ruth could feel the distance growing between herself and Giles and Will as they rode away, but they were still in that web of caring, and would be even if they went all the way to Niagara on their quest.

She didn't know what to think about the demeanor of the Indians these days, or what Giles and Will could expect. Officially there was peace. But all the Iroquois, and others who had been allied with the British, were abandoned by the Redcoats, who had promised always to protect them and their lands from the Long Knives. And since their victory, the Americans now claimed all the land east of the Mississippi—most all of which was still occupied by dozens of tribes who had not been consulted about the claims to their land. Though Ruth Slocum as a Quaker did not concern herself with such matters as states and nations, she knew from Giles that most of the tribes were seething and confused and growing defiant. Two great Delaware chiefs, Buckongahelas and Captain Pipe, had declared to their people that the Americans were evil and could not be trusted. Two years earlier a company of Pennsylvania militiamen had massacred a hundred unarmed Christianized Delawares in their mission town in the Muskingum Valley, and that act had convinced nearly all tribes, even the ones theretofore neutral, that the Long Knives had neither honor nor mercy.

The relentless progress of folly under flags and alliances gave Ruth little hope for peace and loving kindness among men. I reckon all one can do, she thought, is be faithful to one's Inner Light and harm no one, and pray not to be harmed by the folly as it goes roundabout. She sighed.

Lord God protect my sons, and help them find my little girl and bring her home safe and pure.

. . . though I walk through the valley of the shadow of death, I will fear no evil . . . Who shall ascend into the hill of the Lord? . . . He that hath clean hands, and a pure heart . . .

Niagara

"Daughter," said Tuck Horse as he sat on a log by firelight in front of the *wikwam*, "come and sit by me, and we will talk a little."

That surprised Good Face. Tuck Horse had never invited her to sit and talk. He usually talked only with men, or, in the privacy of their *wikwam*, to his wife Flicker. He had never been unkind or sour, but always watched her from a distance, as if this red-haired child who had come to him in his old age were something just to puzzle on. For nearly four years he had watched her grow taller and thinner, watched her lose teeth and grow new ones, watched her being a help and a comfort to Flicker, whose bones sometimes hurt so badly she could hardly move without wincing.

Now Good Face had just finished scouring the supper bowls with creek gravel, and she took them in the *wikwam* and came back out. He pointed to the ground near his knee, and she sat down on her heels facing the fire but with her profile to him. He had filled his pipe bowl, and with callused finger and thumb he expertly snatched up an ember and dropped it on top of the tobacco, puffing and tapping the coal down with his forefinger until his head was enveloped in a smoke cloud. She had often tried to handle an ember like that to see how he could do it, but it always burned her unbearably.

He puffed and did not say anything, and seemed to be studying the flames as if she were not there. Flicker sat on the other side of the fire, twisting strands of cedar-root bark and braiding them into rope. It was what she did when there was not good enough light to sew by. She would always say, "One cannot have too much rope." And that seemed true; there were always uses for it. Finally, Tuck Horse cleared his throat and said, still looking at the flames instead of the girl:

"What is fire?"

She was surprised. She had never thought about what it was. She did not want to give a bad answer. She thought then of the old story, and said, "It is flame from the Sun, that Rainbow Crow brought down for the People when they were cold."

"E heh!" he said, and she knew that had been a good answer. Then he said, "That is where it came from, but what is it?"

"I don't know, Father."

"Look at it." He pointed at it with his pipe stem. "Is it alive?"

She nodded. "It looks to be alive." She had never thought of that.

"It is alive. It moves. It eats. It leaves its waste, the ash. But you can move a hand through it, and therefore it must be a spirit instead of a body. But it is alive. Daughter, when your spirit leaves your body and you cross over to Awasakumeh, the Land Beyond, your body, which has been warm, becomes cold. Why do you think that should be?"

She guessed what he apparently wanted her to say. "Because the spirit leaves it?"

"Yes. That is so. The spirit in your body is fire. Like that. When it is in you and you are alive, you move. You eat. You leave waste. You are warm. And one more thing. Look."

He plucked some dry grass from the ground by his foot and leaned toward the fire, holding the tuft in the flame until it was burning, then he set it aside on the ground where it burned by itself. He said, "The fire can make more of itself. When you are alive, you can make more of yourself. Another proof that the spirit in your body is fire. My wife and I have made other life, just like this fire. Two sons. A daughter. All are gone across now. They did not burn as long as they were meant to, because *wapsi* soldiers extinguished them."

She had not known that her old parents had had sons, as well as their daughter Neepah. She looked down and held one hand in the other. "My *wapsi* family," she said, "did not believe in killing other people. We were called 'Friends.' "

He nodded. "I know of those people. I think that is right-thinking. But I do not understand what they do when it would be right to kill and they cannot."

She looked at him intently, surprised by what he had said. "Do you believe it is right sometimes?"

"Yes," he said. "When you are right and your enemy is wrong. I have had to do it often, when the *wapsituk* did evil things and I was there to stop them. Daughter, you had a brother in that Friends family. He became a soldier."

"Yes," she said. She had not imagined that this old man so far away from her family's home could know that.

"When he became a soldier, did he not believe that he was doing right?"

"I never asked him. But I do not think he would have done anything he did not believe was right."

Tuck Horse took hard pulls on his pipe stem to get another cloud of smoke up, then said, "That is a hard thing. When two enemies both believe they are right. I have not figured that out yet, how both can be right-thinking but not agree. Our people, the Lenapeh, we were told by the Creator that this land, Taxkwox Menoteh, the place on the Great Turtle's back, is for us to live on forever. Then comes a *wapsini* and he says his Creator means it for him. We believe there is only one Creator. A *wapsini* says he believes there is only one Creator. So I ask: Did the Creator lie? Or are there two Creators, one for us and one for them? If there are two, then everybody has been lying about the most important thing of all." He shook his head, frowning. "That is the only thing I do not like about fire. When you look at it, it makes you think, and thinking is troubling sometimes. Long ago in the beginning, we two-leggeds sat down to look at fire and we started thinking. From then on we have been thinking, and it makes it always harder to be good like the four-leggeds. The four-leggeds have fire spirit inside them, but they are too smart to sit looking at it and thinking." He shook his head again.

Good Face glanced over at Flicker, who was just braiding cord and listening and smiling. Then she began chuckling, her shoulders shaking, and finally she said: "Forty winters ago I first heard this. I thought, 'I want this man for my husband; he is a long-headed one!' Now after all this time, he still says the same about it. No answer yet! He he!"

The old warrior frowned at her, but then he began laughing too. They were both laughing and shaking their heads. Good Face felt a great rush of happiness. She loved them and she knew they loved each other, and she believed they had truly come to love her.

After a while she said, "My people too believed this about the fire inside. They called it the Inner Light. They believed it was a part of God inside each one."

"Yes," said Tuck Horse. "Like the piece of the sun that burns in each one like fire. How could it be any other way? Even if it is so that there are two gods—and may that not be so—they would surely agree on *that*."

Much of her time at Neepah's village Good Face had spent running and playing with other children, but it was not the same here with Tuck Horse and Flicker. Her old parents worked most of the time and they needed her help.

It was their age and the nearness of the fort and trading post that made life here different from life at Wyalusing. Tuck Horse caught fish, but was too old to be much of a hunter anymore, and there was little game to hunt anyway because the British had been here so long in such great numbers. So the old people made their living partly by supplying things the trading post wanted. Good Face went with them all over the countryside gathering reeds and rushes and roots and barks, vines and limber poles, berries, medicine herbs, cattails, plant fibers of all kinds, waterfowl eggs, and, always, much firewood.

Tuck Horse used much of the firewood to heat the steam pit

where he bent wood to make chairs, snowshoes, and handles. In the pit he would bury the clean, green poles in hot, wet sand. When he dug them out, they were so pliable that he could bend them into the curved shapes he needed and tie them to hold those shapes until they were dry, and would remain shaped just so. His only tools were a steel knife, hatchet, awl and auger, and a mallet of wood burl, but with these and plenty of cordage and fish glue he could make many useful things for the trading post. Flicker wove lovely baskets, tanned hides and pelts, sewed and decorated moccasins and pouches and sheaths covered with designs in quillwork and beads. Good Face grew strong from carrying loads along steep trails.

Tuck Horse was not proud that he made his living selling chairs to the British, though he was proud of how well he could make them. He and his people did not like the feeling of sitting on chairs, but the white people always needed them. Tuck Horse would shrug and make jokes about this strange work of "making wooden frames to hold their stinking buttocks up from the ground," and said that Mother Earth probably appreciated him for doing this. And if the whites needed these strange things, he needed the strange things they would trade him for chairs—beef, salt, sugar, bullet lead or gunpowder, or sometimes English coins. As for snowshoes, both Indian and *wapsi* hunters needed them in the winters, and he was proud of those, because his ancestors had made them too.

Good Face now and then asked to go to the trading place with her old parents. She was curious about it, and most of the Lenapeh people loved to go there and get things. But her parents' stern, silent looks discouraged her from asking often. They had serious reasons for not wanting her near the *wapsituk*, even the British ones who were their neighbors near Sookpa helluk. But they didn't like to talk about what those reasons were.

One sunny day on a steep path of the falling water gorge, Flicker pointed her digging stick at a clump of sumacs. "Here is much staghorn," she shouted in her ear over the roar of the falls, and set her basket down on the path.

It would have been stifling hot on the sunbaked face of the bluff if not for the cooling moisture that drizzled on them from the waterfall's soaring mist cloud. Through her feet on the slippery, narrow stone path, Good Face could feel the vibration of the

water's mighty pounding far below. She was not afraid of it anymore, not even on this precipitous place, but she could remember
well the first day she had seen the falls and was afraid even
standing on level ground above the gorge, because of the thrum-
ming of the earth.

Flicker now knelt at the base of one of the sumac shrubs.
Pinching tobacco powder from a pouch, she sprinkled some on
the roots and summoned Good Face to come down beside her.
"*Kulesta,* daughter, for you will need to learn the words of this
asking prayer."

"Pray loudly, then, Kahesana, so I can hear your words!"

"What?"

"Loudly, so I can hear the words. To learn the prayer!"

"E heh!" The old woman tugged her closer and spoke right into
her ear as if she were praying to Good Face instead of the spirit of
the sumac. "You, Plant Spirit! I come now for medicine! Two girls
in my clan sent me to give you this tobacco offering. They implore
your medicine to help them get well because they are pitiful! They
have got sick in their woman parts by copulating with English
fort soldiers. And I myself as their herb giver also pray from my
heart that you will take pity on those sick ones! I want their bodies
to get well forever of that which troubles them. For in you,
Staghorn Plant Spirit, rests the power to bless them with wellness.
Tobacco Plant Spirit prays with me that you will take pity on those
foolish girls. I am thankful to you and to Creator. *Zhukeh kishalokeh!"* I have finished asking!

She knelt there for a while after the prayer with her eyes closed,
and Good Face thought she could see a glow, like faint fire, passing
between Flicker's bowed head and the base of the sumac. Then the
old woman opened her eyes and straightened up, painfully, and
said, "I will pray another time for those girls to become smart and
never again do that with *wapsi* soldiers. And you either, daughter!
Now help me dig. These, together with the roots of the horse
hobble we dug yesterday, will make their disease go away in seven
days. If the plant spirits listen and say yes. That is why you have to
know the prayer words just as I have said them. Eh. While you dig,
I will gather the staghorn berries for the good sour tea."

Whatever it was that the two girls had done with the fort soldiers, Good Face vowed to herself she would never do. Not if it
made a girl sick.

And likewise, not if it displeased Flicker. The old woman was a wonderful mother, and she knew even more than Neepah had, if that could be.

Sometimes other girls or young women from Flicker's clan would come along to help gather plants, but usually it was just Good Face with her. In marshes, near the lakeshore, in the hills to the east, along the river bluff, certain things grew in some of those places and none of the others. Good Face loved the vast lake with its blue water extending as far as she could see, and she loved the excitement of swimming in it when the waves were breaking white on the shoreline so hard they could tumble her. She remembered her long-ago friend Minnow telling her about this great lake, and she still missed her after all this time, the girl who had taught her the joyful and useful art of swimming. Because her old parents required her help so much, she had few friends here, none like Minnow, smart and free, almost a sister. She still dreamed sometimes of being with Minnow in water, or near water, or scaring crows with much banging and shouting. She liked to believe that Minnow had escaped the Long Knife soldiers somehow even though Neepah had not. Flailing and falling in the surf of the lake while Flicker foraged sedately onshore, Good Face would daydream of playing with Minnow here.

If there was anything Good Face disliked about living here, it was that her old parents kept her too much to themselves. It was not only that they needed her to help them; they were afraid to let her run with other children near the fort or trading post. They made her stay at home when they went to sell pelts and chairs and other things at the trading post. "Too many *wapsi* people here," they would caution her, "*wapsituk* of the worst kinds, soldiers and traders and missionaries."

"I thought missionaries were good people," she said once.

"They too think they are good people," Tuck Horse replied. "Not good for us, though. They argue against the one true thing, our Creator. They also will steal your name and your spirit. Stay near home, daughter. Your red hair is like a flame in the dark."

She tried to understand why they worried so about her, but the dangers of the place were not apparent to her; as long as one didn't get in the river above the falls, what danger was there?

She would have liked to try to speak some English at the fort or trading post. Without the boy Wareham here, without Neepah, who had known a few English words, she was forgetting that language. Wareham had been gone a long time. After the war against the Long Knives ended, the Indians had been told to return any *wapsi* children they had, and Wareham's Lenapeh family, who had never actually adopted him by the mud-bowl ceremony, took him away somewhere eastward back along the Longhouse Road, then returned with Long Knife money they had been paid for returning him. To their unhappy surprise then, they had found that no one around the fort or trading post had any use for Long Knife money and it couldn't be used to buy much. So they had drilled holes in it and made a necklace and a bracelet to wear. Whenever an order came from the Long Knives to return *wapsi* children, Tuck Horse and Flicker would simply slip away to a hunting camp on the Canada side and stay for a season away from all white people. "We would rather have you than a necklace and a bracelet," they liked to tell her, laughing.

And so, although she was living near Englishmen, Good Face seldom heard a word of their language. She had a vague yearning to hear it, and sometimes ran English-language sentences through her mind for practice, but the lack of English didn't bother her much. The world she lived in now, all the people and places and plants and animals, all the prayers and songs, was Lenapeh, and English words were never quite right for the Lenapeh way of seeing and thinking anyway. There were no English words for the feelings one had in ceremonies, or for the kinds of relatives one had in the clans, or for the cleansing of both body and spirit that occurred when one washed every morning—it was not mere *washing*. There were no English words for the kind of tribute the Mweh mweh alewehsa demanded from the People before the Green Corn Ceremony, or for prayer smoke, or for *linkwehelan*, the search for one's sacred duty, or many other such things. In truth, there was not much use at all for English words, which were based on that other world's way of thinking and seeing.

Good Face dug sumac root and breathed the mist, and understood what it meant that the Great Falling Water was a sacred place. The power and size and thunder of the place made her heart swell up. The waterfall was always changing its appearance with the change of light and weather but was always constant and familiar. The frothing chasm was so vast it seemed to be a whole world itself. Sometimes in the roar of water she thought she could hear Creator speaking. Often when she and Flicker clambered along the paths here, or deeper down in the gorge by the river's edge looking almost straight up at the translucent, foaming curtains of water coming forever down, Good Face felt in her spirit something that was both fear and joy, a feeling like such intense prayer that she could hardly get her breath. It was one of those feelings for which there was no English word—nor any Lenapeh word either, that she knew of.

There were wonderful and terrible stories about Sookpa helluk that were easy to believe. Once, more than twenty winters ago during a war, Tuck Horse himself had seen horse and ox teams with British supply wagons tumbling and turning slowly through the air from the top of the cliffs to the bottom of the gorge, after Indians had stampeded them. He told her that in wars before the one she remembered, the one against the Long Knives, his People had fought against the British instead of for them. He had fought Redcoats often, he said, since he was young. Pointing from the bottom of the gorge to a high cliff one day, he told her where the wagons had come off the cliff and where they had burst apart at the bottom far below. He described it to her so long and happily that she could still see it in her mind as if she had been there herself when it happened.

Tuck Horse also had pointed out one day a place far down the cliff of the island that divided the falls. "There is a trail along that cliff that goes behind the falling water," he said. "I walked that trail when I was young. There was nothing back there but wet rock and thundering water. It seemed like the water was standing still and the rock was rising. I almost forgot everything and stepped over into the water to keep the rock from taking me to the sky." It had given her shivers just to hear him tell that.

"You must have been very brave," she had said with proper awe.

"I was young and brave and strong then," he said with a funny-looking smile. "Sometimes if I was in too much of a hurry to climb the cliff, I would just swim up the falls." He waited a moment for her to turn her unbelieving eyes upon him, and then laughed. That same day, he had pointed out great tree-trunk posts on the cliff of the island and told her that with big ropes on those, the British sometimes would lift big things, even boats, from the river below. "The *wapsituk* make much effort to do such things, daughter, though I fail to understand why they wish to work and think so hard to move things about, for whatever Creator put in one place, whether it is trees or game, he also put in all other places. But it seems the *wapsituk* are not satisfied unless they are having a hard time moving something back and forth, up and down, here to there. Heh heh."

And Tuck Horse had also told her stories about boats and canoes that got into strong current in the river and plunged over into the froth below. When she stood in the roar and the mist, the stories had a thrilling magic. She did not even think the same way here as she did in ordinary places.

She could remember one time when the waterfall had been silent. It had been in deepest winter, when it was cold enough for the trees to crack like gunshots and the snow to squeak underfoot. Her old parents had come up from the village, walking on the river ice, to see Sookpa helluk frozen still and silent. It had been a great wall of enormous icicles shimmering in the cold light of the winter sun, locked in absolute quiet, like a crystal mountain. Once she had seen that, she could always remember exactly how it was, even though it seemed impossible when she was standing here immersed in deafening noise and motion.

"Eh, daughter," Flicker said now as they put chunks of staghorn root into the basket to make medicine for the girls who had done something foolish. "Look." Flicker was pointing high with her digger stick.

There in the mist above the falls, far, far up, arched the rainbow colors, intense against a dark western sky. It was so beautiful Good Face nearly sobbed. This was a sacred place.

Sometimes Tuck Horse went away for days. Some of his absences had something to do with Owl, and other *lehpawcheeks* who were of that healing brotherhood called Midewiwin that Neepah had mentioned. During such an absence, old Flicker loaded herself up with a bundle of cured pelts and one of Tuck Horse's new chairs and got ready to set out with the awkward load, telling Good Face to stay home and keep the cookfire going until she returned.

Good Face saw an opportunity. "Kahesana," she exclaimed, "let me go with you and help you carry. Please! I know it hurts you to carry loads! I can help. And I can help you barter-trade, in their tongue!"

Flicker frowned and shook her head, but Good Face jumped to her side, grasped the chair, and looked up as pleadingly as she knew how, smiling to show all her eagerness.

At last Flicker said: "If you stay close by me. And no, do not talk English. Hide your red hair with that blue shawl. I do need you to carry, but I want no trading-store *wapsini* to get curious about you."

They set off up the lanes through the Lenapeh encampments, and as they approached the clearing around the fort, they passed the longhouses of Senecas and other Iroquois refugees. The air was smoky and dust drifted from the road, where wagons and carts, horses, oxen, and groups of Indians and white people walked and stood about. Through the gate in the palisade Good Face could see the stone building with its many chimneys and a high flag.

As they approached the store, Flicker pulled her aside whenever white people walked near. They wore every sort of garb, green soldier coats, red soldier coats, deerskins, frocks with braid and lace; the few white women she saw were either in dull and tattered dresses or shimmering, bright ones. She saw none dressed as she remembered Quakers. Most of the whites were so busy talking to each other that they didn't even notice her or Flicker, but a few, men and women, paused and tilted their heads to look at her, squinting, raising an eyebrow; a few even pointed at her. Though she was in deerskin and moccasins and her head was covered and she was brown-skinned from the sun, she suspected they could see she wasn't an Indian girl. Three riding soldiers passed very close by, looking, and one said, "Now how comes an old squawr to have such a red-haired colleen?"

The accent was odd, and she wasn't used to hearing English, but it seemed to her that the man had said something about a "red-haired queen" while looking at her. She quickly tucked away a lock that had slipped out from under her head shawl and fallen over her shoulder. The riders' voices were drowned out by other noises, and then the soldiers were gone.

She wished Flicker had not forbidden her to speak English in the trading store. Hearing the soldiers just now had stirred vague memories of words, faces, sensations, from that other life. And the sight and sound of rattling, trundling wagons brought back memories from a world in which, unlike her Lenapeh world, there were wheels.

For one dizzying moment the whole far memory of being a girl in a Quaker family, called Slocum, with brothers and sisters and parents and a grandfather all living in a log house near a river, suffused through her. It was strange that so much of that past life was still in her head but she thought of it so little.

She followed Flicker past strange-smelling, dirty, unsteady people, over a threshold into a big, smelly room; for the first time in many years she felt a wooden floor beneath her soles and saw a ceiling of straight beams instead of bent saplings, a room with corners instead of curved walls, a room with actual furniture: benches along the walls, a tablelike counter, and behind the counter, shelves, barrels, cabinets, a huge clerking desk. These all revealed themselves to her as her eyes became accustomed to the gloom after the outdoor brightness. She also began seeing a greater clutter of diverse things than she had ever seen in one place, even before her life with the Lenapeh had begun. Piled and hung everywhere behind the counter were colorful hanks of strung beads, clusters of powder horns hanging by their straps, leather bags, wooden canteens, harness, ropes, chains, blankets, bottles and jugs, hats, boots, belts with brass buckles, axes and tomahawks, shovels, knives, pots and kettles, tin cups, bolts of cloth, plumes, guns, white clay pipes with long stems, twists of tobacco, silver bands and gorgets, ribbons, whistles and tin horns, saws and scythes, and cloth bags of many sizes. Chairs that Tuck Horse had made were hung high on pegs.

Stacked everywhere too were animal hides both tanned and raw, bunches of dried herbs, baskets and beaded belts and bags such as she had seen the Lenapeh women sew, and several pairs of snowshoes she recognized as Tuck Horse's work.

And her nose was as busy as her eyes, identifying odors familiar from both her lives: tea and coffee and candle tallow and camphor and tarred oakum evoked her early childhood; tobacco, bear oil, sassafras, mint, sweetgrass, beaver gland, muskrat, brain-tanned hide, and wintergreen were more lately familiar.

But the strongest smell in the room by far was that of men who never washed or changed their clothes. Such men were sitting on the benches and working behind the counter, where Flicker was trying to barter with a tall, fat, stinking man who could not understand her. Good Face could understand some of his talk, though it was not the same English she had known as a child.

"Och, Benjy," he called over his shoulder to someone deeper in the room. "This auld hag's Delaware or Shawanoe or such-like. Doesna speak Iroquois. A'canna make nowt o' her blather!"

The other, who was measuring ribbon off a spool, replied, "John's never here when those buggers come in. Well, just hand-talk till she trades. What's she got there?"

"Mink and fisher skins. Fair good'ns. Well, old woman, what is it ye want for these, eh? What? What want? Oogum boogum! Gimme a hint, granny!"

Good Face, who had grown to be almost as tall as Flicker, leaned close to her and said in Lenapeh, "Kahesana, tell me what you want and I shall tell him in English."

Suddenly wary, Flicker answered, "No. Don't talk English here."

"Mother! Here's where it can be useful to us!"

Flicker hesitated, slightly shaking her head but apparently seeing the practical sense of that.

The man behind the counter was looking at Good Face now, and he said, "Hoot, lassie! Tha's nae Indian. Can 'ee understand me?"

"Oogum boogum!" she replied. He blinked and tucked in his chin, then scowled at her. She wanted to laugh. But she wanted more to speak English and help Flicker get what she had come for.

Flicker was looking peeved, and she said: "Was that English you spoke, when I asked you not to?"

"Oogum boogum? No, Kahesana. But he already sees I am *wapsini*. Let me speak for you in English."

Flicker narrowed her eyes in a cunning look, then said, "Speak, then, but do not tell him your *wapsi* name."

"And so then tell me what you want from this place, Kahesana."

"The metal needles that don't break, for sewing deerskin. And a bullet maker for the one my husband lost. And a piece of bullet metal."

Good Face bit her lip, frowned, thought hard for words. "Give needles, ah, lead . . . ah . . . bullet mold, to Mother, she ask for."

The man looked from one to the other of them and raised his eyebrows, then leaned forward and squinted. "I don't believe that's your mother, little lassie."

"My mother yes," Good Face replied, but she dropped her gaze for a moment as she said it, remembering her true mother.

"Aha!" he said. "She's not, is she? You're a captive, aren't ye, from the war? What's your name, lass?"

"Wehletawash. Good Face is my name."

Flicker said quickly in Lenapeh, "You are not talking about needles! This man is trying to find out who you are! Talk of the goods we need, or we must leave, daughter!"

So she asked again for needles and bullet mold and lead, and whenever the man asked her name, she would ignore the question, and after a long time they had three needles of different sizes, a bullet mold with squeeze handles, a bar of lead, and also a ladle for melting the lead. The man had told them they needed a ladle to melt the lead in because it was not good to use a cooking kettle for it. He had said he would trade all those items for Flicker's entire bundle of pelts, but Good Face had seen his eyes and sensed that he was being greedy, so she argued, and at last he accepted half the pelts for all the items. When that was done, the man leaned with his hands on the counter, smiled, and said, "Your 'father,' as ye call 'im, will need powder." He held up a small bag and said, "Gimme the rest of those pelts and I'll fill this with gunpowder."

Good Face said to Flicker, "This man wants the rest of the pelts very much, I think. He offers you that little bag of gunpowder for the rest of them. I think it might be too much because his eyes are greedy and untrue."

"You have done well, my daughter. Yes, they are all greedy. Tell him my husband has much gunpowder and that we are finished here."

"Plenty my father has now of gunpowder. No more need. So . . ." She had to think of the old word. "Good-bye."

"Wait, don't go, lass." He was tilting his head and smiling a smile that was obviously meant to look sweet, one of those false smiles she had seen all her brothers and sisters use to win things from their mother, and she herself surely had too. It was one of those kinds of smiles, but it was awful to look at because his teeth were rotten and dingy. He said, "Tell me your real name, lass, and I'll gi' ye a pretty." He held up his hand with a shiny little brooch between his thumb and finger.

"*E heh*. My real name I tell thee, so?" She held out her hand, while Flicker frowned warily, and the man held the brooch over it.

"The name first," he said with his false sweet smile.

"Good Face," she replied with an equally false sweet smile, and snatched at the brooch, but he palmed it even more quickly and shook his head.

"If ye really want this pretty," he said, shaking his head, "come back one day withoot granny there and tell me your name."

"Why thee wants so much my name?" Flicker had seized her arm and was pulling her toward the door.

"Why, p'haps I'll ask ye to marry me when ye grow up, lassie!

Ha ha! Ha ha! Fare thee well, then, little freckle face, if ye must go!" He clapped his hand over his heart and rolled his eyes toward the ceiling. Other people in the store were laughing as they hurried out.

"Wasn't that a funny man!" Good Face said.

"He thinks so," muttered Flicker. "He was always trying to make you say your *wapsi* name?"

"Yes. But I didn't say it."

"*Kulesta*, daughter. Those are greedy men. If you gave them your name, they would try to sell it, and that would be bad for us. Hurry along. I want us to be away from this fort."

"Sell my name? How? To whom?"

"Never you think of it anymore." She seemed cross, and was walking faster than she usually could because of her bone pains.

But when they were clear of the palisade she slowed down and was cheerful again. "Ah, ai!" she said, chuckling, hefting the bundle of pelts in which she had rolled their purchases. "*Waneeshee*, good daughter. You bartered well!"

The foliage was reddening. One day Tuck Horse and Flicker went to a Council, leaving Good Face to make corn-husk dolls with some of her friends, who were going to give dolls to their littler sisters. They would be red-hair dolls. Good Face cut off a hank of her hair and divided it to make the hair for three dolls. It was exacting work and time slipped by quickly, and Tuck Horse and Flicker returned while they were still working, looking quite serious. That evening as they ate corn cake and sipped rabbit-meat broth, Tuck Horse said:

"Daughter, our clan will leave this place, two days from today. We will spend tomorrow packing everything we can carry by horse or canoe, and what is left we will give to our neighbors who stay."

Good Face was startled. She loved this place and was still wrapped up in the project of the dolls. "Why? This is such a good place! Why should we leave a sacred place, Father?"

"Since the war between the Thirteen Fires and the British King ended, this place has been going bad and it will grow worse," Tuck Horse said. "The Town Destroyer and others who followed him have taken and ruined the lands of the Iroquois, the Six Nations, and those towns of our people who had dwelt among them. We all came here for protection and for provisions that the

British promised us. But now that we are no longer fighting for them, they are stingy. The British are throwing all their faithful allies into the hands of the Long Knives. The Iroquois are going to Canada. There have been so many people here for so long that there is no game left, and the soil has been planted until it needs to rest. This place is indeed a sacred place, but not a good place to live anymore."

She could not argue with what the Council knew. "Where will we go?"

He pointed westward. "That way. At the other end of the lake above the falls is a British place called Detroit. It is about twenty sleeps from here. There we can stay through the winter if the British there will help us a little. When the spring comes again we will go south from there to where most of our Lenapeh have been going, for a long time since the *wapsituk* came."

The thought of all that distance, still farther from all the places she had known, made her feel shaky. Somehow she had always felt that when the wars and flights were over, she would be returning down the same river. She had sometimes enjoyed imagining Tuck Horse and Flicker sitting at supper with her Slocum family, and being good friends, and her mother Mrs. Slocum admiring the beautiful quillwork designs in the dress and moccasins made for her by her mother Flicker.

But instead of going back toward her first family, they would be going the other way.

That night when Tuck Horse was away somewhere in the village smoking and talking with other old men, Flicker closed up a basket in which she had packed herbs and seeds for the journey, and said, "Sit here with me, daughter. I want to say something." They knelt near the cookfire. Flicker looked into the firelight, not at Good Face, as she began.

"All that my husband tells you is true. But he does not tell enough to make you understand, I think.

"Daughter, here by this fort we have been living with the Iroquois peoples because we were all being driven here by the Long Knife army. But the Iroquois people are not our friends, and they have done many hard things to us. They helped the British take away our lands in the east. Then they put us in the Susquehanna country and ruled over us by saying who our chief would be. They did this also to other peoples akin to us, the Twightwee, the Shawnee, the Nanticoke, who also had been cheated out of their lands in those parts. It is not in our hearts to live near these Six Nations Iroquois. Your father and I have many winters in our past and not too many from here forth, and we would like to spend the rest in a place far from all who have been enemies, whether red or white. Do you see?"

"I knew that not all the people here were the same. Owl did tell me once about the meanness of the Iroquois," Good Face said. It was always surprising to her to learn that so many people were always set against each other. First, English against rebels. Then white men against Indians. Now, Indians against other Indians.

"I want to say another thing for you to understand, daughter. You see that my husband and I are elders. Because we have so many years, we at first thought we should not take you as our daughter. But we soon became glad, and you have filled our days with goodness."

"You are good to me, Mother."

"My husband is still strong. But he has been hurt badly as a warrior. Some of those scars on him are from weapons that went all the way through. He cannot go far enough or move fast enough anymore to hunt, and our sons who would have lived near us and hunted for us, they were killed by the *wapsituk*. I am still strong. But age is in my bones and sometimes I can hardly move. The daughter who would have lived near us and helped me with work, she was killed by them too."

They both looked down sadly, thinking of Neepah. Then Flicker went on: "You would help me with my work, my new daughter. You do help me. But you are a girl not even ready to be a woman yet, and what I have taught you already about the things a woman must know and do is little compared with what I have yet to teach you. We might go to the Spirit World before you know enough to take care of us.

"And so you see, daughter, we want to go and be in a peaceful country with all our own people, all who can help each other. That was always the old way. The old ones and the young ones gave to each other. The parents gave everything to the children so they would grow up and be good. And then the young ones gave everything back to the old ones so they would be contented. That was always the old way. What you received, you gave back just as much. What is so bad about war is that it blows everything away before the giving-back can be done."

"Then I understand why. But I don't like leaving Sookpa helluk."

"*E heh*. Perhaps we will see it again. As a Midewiwin and trader, your father goes everywhere. And no matter what happens, the People always go back to see the sacred places."

The next morning Tuck Horse said they would travel to the place called Detroit by water, instead of land trails. He said the clan would go up above the waterfalls to get canoes ready. Up there on the upper lake, the one whose waters fell over Sookpa helluk, there was a fishing and boat-building town where canoes of both the dugout and bark kinds could be obtained.

Good Face dimly remembered sitting in a new canoe with Minnow and other children in the canoe makers' camp at Neepah's town long ago. She remembered boasting to Minnow that someday she would ride in a canoe on a great water.

Tuck Horse, Flicker, and Good Face gathered and packed everything they would be taking. They gave their *wikwam* and many of their belongings to people who would be staying at Niagara. A few things they had made they would sell at the trading store: snowshoes, one last chair, some of Flicker's quillwork and beadwork. They loaded their arms with these things and told Good Face to wait until they came back. She pleaded to go with them, to help them barter in English. To her surprise, they said no, she must stay here.

"I could help you carry, and talk in their language, as I did."

"No, daughter. We do not want you to be seen there. The traders are too interested in you, since that time."

She nodded obediently and watched them go, and thought about what Flicker had said about the traders. That they were greedy. That they would sell even her name, if they knew it. And that now they were too interested in her. She didn't understand that exactly, but she remembered the ugly-mouth man and felt that her parents were right.

Later in the day, when Flicker and Tuck Horse returned, they sat down on the logs by the outdoor fire pit. Tuck Horse put down his bundle. He was breathing hard. Flicker put some sticks on the embers. Tuck Horse got out his pipe and tobacco. Good Face was inside the door of the *wikwam*, rearranging the little bundle of belongings she would be taking. She could hear them talking low outside, and heard Tuck Horse say a word that made her scalp tingle: "Tsa-lo-cum," it sounded like.

She thought, *Slocum*? Was that *Slocum*? And she turned a keen ear. She heard Flicker say:

"They were trying to buy her name, I am sure. But the traders do not know what it is. They tried to get her to tell, but she did not. She is so good."

Tuck Horse said, "When I first saw them that other day, I was sure who they were. One of them I saw with the valley soldiers at Wyoming the day I was shot down."

"I am sure they were trying to buy her name," Flicker repeated. "I heard the word 'guineas,' and that is a word of money, is it not?"

"It is. My wife, it is good that we are leaving now. We should not wait even until tomorrow to start for the canoe camp."

"The fat trader looked at me when they were talking to him. I could see his memory working in his eyes. I was afraid they might follow us here if he spoke of her while we were there."

"I saw you keep looking behind. I too am uneasy. Let us get her and go. I wonder where she is."

"I am here, Father," she said, stepping to the doorway, and when they looked around at her, she saw they were startled.

"I will go and get the horse," the old man said. He picked up the rope halter and the pack saddle he had made the day before.

As Flicker carried bundles and cargo baskets out of the *wik-wam*, Good Face asked her what men they had been talking about, and Flicker replied: "A child should not listen from behind a wall."

"I did not mean to. Who were the men, Kahesana?"

"I do not know them. Your father saw them days ago and we both saw them today. I told you the traders are greedy and would sell names. There are *wapsituk* who come since the end of the war and will pay for names. Then perhaps they steal the people away and sell them to the Long Knife *wapsituk*. We want to be gone before they find you. You are our daughter in our hearts and we will not have you stolen from us."

It was an explanation that made sense to Good Face, and it frightened her so much that she too was eager to get away.

And yet she kept wishing she had been allowed to go to the trading post with them so she could have seen the men who were trying to buy her name. She had heard Tuck Horse say the name

"Slocum," she was sure, and now and then she thought of her father and brothers. "What did those men look like?" she asked.

"Wapsituk," Flicker said. "They all look alike to me. Some fat, some thin. They were *wapsituk*. That is how they looked."

They rode off the main trail for a last look at the waterfall. The sun was so low in the west that the roaring water was in bluish shadow, but the mist cloud above the farther cataract was so full of sunlight it looked like a sky-high flame against the blue. Tuck Horse smoked a prayer pipe there, as old Owl had so long ago, the first time Good Face saw the waterfall. Then they rode on up the river to the canoe camp on the shore of the upper lake. There they found the people of their clan who had already come up, and since it was dusk, Flicker made no shelter or cookfire. The other families gave them food, and then they slept in their blankets under the stars. It grew chilly, and Good Face woke up several times in the night shivering and thinking with dread of how soon winter would be here. She wondered if it would be warmer in the place called Detroit, where they were going, than here at Niagara in the winter. Then she thought for a while of her father, of the Slocum family, and tried to remember what he looked like. But she could not make his face appear. She could recall her mother's face fairly clearly, but it slipped away because she was cold and kept thinking of winter instead.

It made her sad that she could not remember them better.

In the morning, Tuck Horse led away the packhorse and went down to the lake with some other men of the clan. They came back later without the horse, and as they ate the morning meal they said they had traded the packhorse and one other horse for a canoe big enough to carry three families. It was a good, light canoe, they said, one made of birch bark by Ottawas from up north. It had been used the length of this lake and the Huron lake several times in recent years. It needed new pitch to seal some of the seams, and two ribs would have to be taken out and replaced because they had been broken by a hard landing on a rocky shore, but that could all be done today. Other families had already obtained canoes or dugouts and were fixing them up. The men had discussed whether to go along the north shore of the lake or the south shore, and decided that the north shore way was a little shorter and a little better protected from the west winds at this season, and so they would go along the north shore, which was the English Canada side.

Good Face listened to them talk about all that and thought she understood, although when she looked at the lake, she could see nothing but water to the horizon, coming in endlessly as waves sloshing and splashing on the shore. A little strip of land lay just off the shore farther south, where a small stream entered the lake, and the canoe-making camp was sheltered from the lake waves by that. There were many canoes on the bank, large and small, and men and women working on them, laying out sheets of bark on the ground, chunking on wood with tools, splitting off long slats of wood, soaking wood strips in water to curve them, the way Tuck Horse did when he made snowshoes and chairs. There were also men making dugout canoes by burning and scraping logs, as she had seen before. Many poles sticking out of the water showed where nets and weirs had been set to catch the whitefish and trout that were spawning in the shoals. Adding to the pall of smoke over the canoe camp were families smoke-curing fish. Good Face sat and smelled the odors that came to her on the cool wind blowing off the lake. Somewhere at the far other end of that lake was the place called Detroit, Tuck Horse had said. It was many days' travel and they would be in the canoes all day every day unless the wind was too strong, but they would travel close to shore and would go on land every evening to hunt and camp and sleep. He had assured her that they would never be out of sight of land, and that had made her less fearful of what lay ahead.

But she thought of the long distance in that direction, and now and then she thought of the men down at Niagara who were said to be trying to buy her name, and she wished, wished so hard that her heart ached, that she knew whether they were of her *Slocum* people.

If they had been, and had found her, what then?

She thought: I would have brought them to meet my old father and mother Tuck Horse and Flicker, and all would have seen that the others were good and kind people and they would have eaten together.

Beyond that she did not know what to think might have happened.

CHAPTER SEVEN

October 1784
Lake Erie

The six canoes were blessed with sprinkled tobacco and cedar smoke and prayers were given, and the forty-five men, women, and children arranged themselves carefully in the vessels. And then as the morning sun was rising over the treetops, they glided out of the mouth of the stream, heavy-laden and deep in the water. Good Face had just become used to the floating sensation in the smooth water of the stream when the canoe came out from behind the sheltering spit of land and was suddenly lifted and slammed by a breaking wave whose spray showered everyone and brought gasps and moans. She clutched and held a thwart in fright and exhilaration as the wave rolled under the vessel, lifting the stern for a giddy moment; then another wave slammed and sprayed over the bow and lifted it, and the wood of the canoe creaked with the weight of its contents and the twisting force of the waves. The paddlers, three men including Tuck Horse, laughed at the frightened voices of the women and children, which gave her hope that they were not in as much danger as it seemed. The paddler just in front of her, really not a man but a wide-shouldered boy of perhaps fourteen, looked left into the wind which was blowing his long hair, and his teeth were white in a grin of excitement. Soon the bow was steered straight into the wind, and the rolling grew less, and the waves sprayed out on both sides as the high prow cut through them.

Straight ahead now across a wide stretch of water was a low wooded land with clearings, and a palisaded fort so distant that it looked hardly bigger than a cabin. The wide stretch of water, Tuck

Horse announced, was the place where the lake overflowed into the Niagara Sipu—and he now frightened her by shouting, "If we had no strong paddlers and just drifted, that river would carry us to the Falling Water and we would go over!" Several children's voices responded, "Paddle hard, Muxumsah!" He laughed, laid his paddle across his lap, tilted his head on his shoulder, and made snoring noises until all the children were squealing with alarm. Then he put his paddle back into the water and the canoe continued plunging into waves. Even when the frightful space of the river was safely behind the canoes, Good Face felt a persistent terror at the thought of unknown depths of water below this frail canoe.

After the fear came the sick feeling. The constant rising and falling and rocking were having an unsettling effect on her insides. She had to keep swallowing, and the more she swallowed, the more nauseated she became. At last, with tears cold on her face, she yielded to an irresistible upsurge and spewed her morning's hominy over the side of the canoe into the frightful water mere inches below her face. Opening her blurry eyes for a moment, she saw the mess floating backward and saw a paddle blade rise from the clear water and sweep forward. Behind her, Tuck Horse said, "So soon, daughter. How bad for you."

After a long time of empty retching, her eyes weeping and nose running and body trembling, she was given a wad of dried vegetation passed forward from Flicker and told to chew it and keep swallowing her spit. She recognized it as wild tobacco that she and Flicker had gathered. The mere thought of its bitter flavor made her even sicker for a moment, but when Tuck Horse growled, "Chew it," she put it in and chewed and chewed the bitter mass and swallowed the nasty saliva. And then after a while the heaving urge diminished and was gone. Then, one by one, other adults and children in the swooping, bucking vessel leaned over the side and had to be dosed from Flicker's herbal supply.

For a while Good Face's only discomforts were from sitting cramped among bundles for so long and the cold lake wind chilling her in her spray-soaked dress. After a while a great hunger gnawed at her emptied belly, and then early in the afternoon the wind died down and the dazzling sun warmed the left side of her face, making her sleepy. But she couldn't doze because her bladder and bowels had begun urging for relief, and she was bewildered as to what she could do about them, and too embarrassed to ask in this canoe full of relative strangers. So she fidgeted, while the sun began to burn her face and reflect off the water so brilliantly that her eyes and head were soon aching.

She remembered that this voyage was to take many days, perhaps half a moon or more, and that almost all of the daytime would be spent in the canoes. Only half of the first day was done and she was so miserable she could hardly bear it. The canoe cut endlessly through the swashing water, and the paddles rose and fell and rose and fell, but the wooded shoreline changed so imperceptibly that she sometimes had the notion that the canoes were not moving at all. She wanted to give in and cry.

But other children in the canoe, and in the other canoes that sometimes were alongside or ahead, were not crying, even though some were half her age or less. Their little dark heads gazed about or slumped in sleep, but there was not a whimper or a cry from anywhere. And so she would not cry either.

Further into the afternoon she became aware that Tuck Horse's paddle was not dipping in the water beside her. She turned and saw that he was holding it across his thighs with both gnarled hands squeezed in fists and that he was facing into the sky with his mouth open and eyes tight shut, either praying or in pain, and she remembered what Flicker had said about his old scars and the wounds that had gone clear through, wounds so bad he could not be a hunter anymore. She realized suddenly how old and hurt he was, an elder with gray hair and loose skin, and yet he had been working with his paddle nearly the whole day long.

Then, as if he had felt her looking at him, he opened his eyes and caught her gaze, let out a long breath, smiled, and put his paddle blade into the water again, his strong yellow teeth bared in a grin or a grimace. And soon after that one of the paddlers in another canoe called and pointed ahead.

The shoreline, which had been parallel to their course, curved around in front of them, a low, brushy silhouette against the sun-blazed water. "I know this point," Tuck Horse said. "Out of the wind and a safe place for our first camp." His voice was tired and strained but he sounded happy. As the canoes approached the beach in the lee of the spit of land, eager voices could be heard across the water, and laughter. In a canoe off to the right one warrior was craning to scan the shore, his eyes shaded with one hand, his musket in the other.

"A good day of going, in the wind," Tuck Horse said. "Twenty such good days, I say we will see Detroit. Wife, we do well. How are your old bones?"

"Like old bones, husband. *E heh!* You might have to carry me ashore and dig me a hole to make waste in, and very quickly." Everybody laughed, all surely thinking likewise. Good Face certainly was.

But she was also thinking of what Tuck Horse had said:

Twenty more such days!

The next morning they left the camp at daybreak and paddled nearly a mile south to clear the end of the spit and then went westward again, following the shore as they had done all the day before. Gradually the head wind diminished and the waves became less choppy, to everyone's relief.

During the next few days a few distant ship sails were seen far over the water in the southwest, and Good Face did not know what the white shapes were until Tuck Horse explained they were the cloth wings of great English boats ten times as long as this canoe. She understood then. Her first father had told her of ships, which he had seen in the ocean ports of Rhode Island. She was pleased that she could remember that name. It was the place where she had been born, hundreds of miles back toward the sunrise. Thinking of those long distances, and of the long way they were coming now in the canoes, still westward, she wondered if there could ever have been any girl who had traveled so far in the world, or seen such far horizons of water. She remembered then, vaguely, a story in the Slocum family of an ancestor, who as a girl had crossed the ocean with her parents in a ship from Britain. That had been perhaps a greater distance than this.

But, Good Face thought, that girl was just in a ship. I have been carried by Indians and horses and a canoe.

As the days went on she saw many boats with sails, but the ones close enough to see in any detail were small vessels that could sail close to shore. Two or three of those, with both Indians and *wapsi* men on board, passed within shouting distance of the Lenapeh canoes, going the other way, skimming along with their sails bellied out with wind, their progress looking enviably easy.

One evening the canoes passed the mouth of a river where many boats and long canoes lay against the shore, and there were cabins and longhouses up on the low bank, with cooking fires smoking. Tuck Horse advised that they should not stop there for the night because it was one of the places where the Iroquois peoples were coming to live in Canada, since the Long Knives had driven them out of their own lands on the Longhouse Road. "Probably they would not trouble us," he said, "but as I have said, I no longer have to be near Iroquois, so let us go on to another place before we go ashore. I am sorry the Town Destroyer threw down the English King and took away the good country, but I am happy to make much distance between us and the Iroquois, and now perhaps we can try to forget all the bad things they did to us." Some of the other men in the canoe murmured agreement. Then Tuck Horse gazed ashore toward the flat lands they were passing and said, "But I will be lonely for mountains."

Good Face until now had never seen land that was flat. There had been mountains and valleys since she could remember, and mountains and cliffs and hills and waterfalls everywhere the Indians had brought her, until now. The land here was so level it reminded her of a floor, and some places along the shore the land was so low that there were only marshes and grasslands and swamps to be seen.

As if answering her unvoiced question, Tuck Horse said: "The ancient stories tell that this land was all covered with so much ice it smoothed out all the hills." That made her tremble.

Millions of birds were on the wing. The marshes were crowded with ducks and geese. Sometimes so many would rise on thundering wings it looked as if the whole shore were rising into the sky.

The voyage of the canoes settled down to a steady but unhurried pace. The days were divided between paddling westward and stopping to fish and hunt waterfowl. The paddlers had enormous appetites. And in this bountiful country, the young people could provide much of the meat, which delighted them, making them feel important and useful.

Good Face and other girls waded in the sandy, mucky shallows with a long fishnet, while others thrashed in the water and scared the whitefish into the net, where they got caught by their gills. Good Face could feel the struggles of the strong fish transmitted to her hands by the net, and at first was horrified, then thrilled. When they dragged the heavy-laden net ashore and she saw the size of the shimmering, lunging fish—some as long as the girls were tall—she realized that she was helping feed her Lenapeh People as surely as when she had helped in the cornfields.

The boys in the meantime would vanish among the reeds of the marshes with bows and arrows, nets and slings, then return lugging huge geese, mallards, and little coots. Some of the children brought in eels and turtles and eggs. The ease of food-getting was hard for Good Face to believe, and she loved the clean water, breezes forever whispering and stirring the reeds and brush, water waves and smoke moving, everything fresh and stirring, sunlight flashing off water, the vastness of open sky. And the novel flavors of the fish, fat ducks, eel flesh, all baked in fire-heated trenches, made her ravenous for every meal.

Good Face lost count of the days, but after more than a week of good weather, she saw ahead what appeared to be the end of the lake. Low land lay across the horizon. She turned to Tuck Horse, who was gazing ahead at the land as he paddled.

"This is the end of the lake so soon?"

"No, daughter. We are no more than halfway yet. That land ahead is only a long strip we must cross over. You will see."

They beached the canoes on sand and unloaded them. Women and children carried bundles and the men carried the canoes. They staggered through sand and blowing grass to the top of a low rise, and there on the other side was more of the boundless blue water as far westward as she could see. The waves rushed hissing onto the beach and drained back and rushed up again. White birds hung still facing into the wind overhead, then turned and drifted in easy arcs, mewing, floating on the wind without moving their extended wings. At great distances in the sky, chevrons of geese, thousands of them, beat their way southward over the vast lake, their strange honking voices faint and garbled beyond the whiffling of the lake wind.

Sweaty and sandy after the carryover, the people took time to bathe. The women crossed back over to the sheltered side with their girls and babies and stripped to wallow in the shallows, while the men and boys swam on the other side. Good Face splashed and dove in the crystal-clear water, which was not as cold as she had expected, while old Flicker stood in thigh-deep water nearby, stooping to slosh water over her sturdy brown body, lifting first one sagging breast to wash her belly under it, then the other. Young mothers squatted in the shallows and dipped their babies into the water and then lifted them into the sunlight, the women laughing, the babies squealing. The sun being so hot, most of the women and girls rinsed their clothes in the water, wrung them out, and put them on wet. Though covered with gooseflesh, Good Face had never felt so exhilarated. She wanted to run on sand, dive in water, and dry her face in sunlight all at the same time. The same mood seemed to be upon everyone, and feminine voices twittered along the shore like birdcalls.

Good Face was marveling at a white soaring bird when an angry shout went up and a woman was pointing up the rise. Good Face saw a boy spying from the brush. He was the young paddler from her canoe. The women scolded him by his name: "Like Wood! Shame, peeping boy!" They turned around and bent over to insult him with a mass display of their behinds. He scrambled to his feet and ran away over the crest. Flicker laughed and said, "We must tell the men what Like Wood did, and he will be in scorn for a while, as he ought to be."

As the people ate, the spying boy sat alone, head down. Then they reloaded the canoes and set off again toward the afternoon sun, their clothes already dried upon their bodies.

As she watched Like Wood's back, sweaty with the paddling work, she felt scornful toward him, as she believed she was supposed to, but she felt sorry for him too. He was a nice boy, and very pretty-looking. It was odd what he had done, that peeping.

Wilkes-Barre

Ruth Slocum shook her head at the sight of her son Ebenezer. The youth had just driven the ox-team wagon down from the bluff, loaded high with anthracite he had mined out from the hillside with a pick, and he looked as black and sooty as a charcoal burner.

Hands on hips, she told him: "Get thee down to the river and wash up!"

"There's no use in that," he said, "as I'll be just as black again after I unload at the smithy's." Ebenezer was one of the few youths enterprising enough to dig and sell the dirty fuel. There was no great enthusiasm for it outside of smithys' forges because it needed a bellows draft to keep burning, and there was still plenty of wood for charcoal making, though the hillsides were fast being denuded by settlers. The valley was becoming a landscape of stumps. "I'll just run in the house and have a bowl o' that stew and then be on my way down to—"

"Thee will not eat in my kitchen without washing first," she insisted, and pointed down toward the river, saying, "all over. Take soap down there and—" Her mouth fell open. "Our dear Lord! That's Will and Giles in a boat!"

But it was only Will and Giles. There was no Frances in the battered little rowboat with them.

They were a sorry pair of sojourners with a scary and disgusting tale to tell, including the theft of their horses on the way back.

They spoke of the bleak emptiness where the Indian towns had once flourished along the upper Susquehanna; they spoke of charred village sites and eroded cornfields where human skulls peeked out of the ground, of lawless woodsmen and bootleggers infesting what had been the Trail of the Longhouse all the way to Niagara, all masters at waylaying, fleecing, and demoralizing anyone who passed through, white or Indian. It was some of those, not Indians, who the boys believed had stolen the horses.

They told of the thousands of Indian refugees living around the Niagara fort, of the families of displaced Tories living there until places in Canada could be found for them. "What a monstrous thing war is," Will said, shaking his head and looking down at his hands on the table, "and its miseries go on long after the guns stop shooting." Even Giles, the former soldier, nodded in agreement.

They told over and over, in every detail they could remember, prodded again and again by their mother, what they had learned from the traders at Niagara: that there had been a freckled girl of about the right age, in the company of an old Indian woman who was probably a Delaware. But those traders, despite the offer of a hundred guineas, had claimed they couldn't help find the girl. Will said, "We got the impression the traders were afraid to say much."

"Some Delaware families decamped while we were there," Giles said. "They might have taken her away. The Indians played dumb."

"Did they say the red-haired girl had a bad forefinger?" Ruth Slocum asked her sons. "Did thee remember to ask 'em that?"

"We remembered to ask, but they hadn't noticed," Giles said. "They thought she'd only been in the store once, and the old squaw rather protected 'er, they said."

"And did she look well, or sickly? Did thee think to ask if she looked ill-used, or unhappy?"

"Of course we asked, Ma. We had just such concerns ourselves!"

"And they said?"

"That the girl was just like most any Delaware girl. Healthy, clean. Rather shy in the store. Though she did speak some English helpin' the old grandma barter."

Ruth Slocum clasped her hands in her lap and looked down with her eyes shut tight, trying to remember the hundreds of questions and doubts that had risen in her mind and out of her memory since the boys set out those many weeks ago. She remembered back beyond that time and remembered the terrible day six years ago. She remembered Frances being carried away. She asked:

"Did they say what she was wearing? Did they say whether she had shoes on her little feet?"

Ruth Slocum sat with her elbows on the table, stroking her eyelids and forehead with her fingertips. She finally had asked every question she could remember to ask, most of them more than once. Will and Giles were sitting with their elbows on the table too, trying to hold their tired selves up, sipping tea now and then. Ben was tending the fire at the hearth, but it was growing chilly in the room. Autumn was advanced and leaves were beginning to fall off the trees up in the woodlot. Ebenezer, still black with coal dust, got up from the bench with a sigh, saying, "Well, I don't want to miss anything interesting, so don't thee say anything interesting till I get back. I've still a wagonload of anthracite to drive to town. Want to go along, Will? Giles? There's folks would like to hear thee tell how it is from here to Niagara."

"Absolutely not," Ruth Slocum told Ebenezer. "One son covered with soot is enough."

"Aye, and we're too tired to go anywhere but bed. Thee has the glory of spreading news of our triumphant return," Giles said to Ebenezer. "By the way, what's thee doing with all the money thee makes selling that devil's dirt, brother?"

"I don't make that much. Some goes to our household here, of course. But I aim to save and build a mill up in Deep Hollow, where there's water power."

"Grist or saw?"

"Both, likely."

"Why, thee's a true factotum, Eben," Giles joked, tapping Will's elbow with a fist.

"Thee'll see for sure," Ebenezer replied, pausing at the door.

"I'll own a good part o' this town 'fore long. Advantage of being first in a place. One gets an early start. That's us Slocums. This one, anyway. I mean to have an iron forge one day too. I can fuel it right out of our own ground. Thee may call it devil's dirt, brother Giles, but mark my word, we'll all prosper on it."

"May we prosper," said Ruth Slocum in a strange tone.

The brothers, and even the younger children, turned to look at their mother, never having heard her speak such unexpected words in such an intense voice. She was staring at the far wall of the room so intently it seemed as if she were seeing through it and far beyond.

"Those traders," she said. "If they were afraid to help despite an offer of a hundred guineas . . . I know the greed of such people. We shall go a-looking for Frannie again. And if we can afford a ransom enough, by Heaven, I'm sure we'll get her back!"

"We . . ." Will leaned back wearily. "Thee means to keep looking, then."

"Why, how not?" she exclaimed. "We know she's alive and well!"

"Ma," Giles said, leaning forward and looking into her blazing eyes, "there were hundreds of children displaced and scattered about in the war. We can only *presume* the one those traders saw was Frannie. We're not *sure* of it!"

"Thee is not? Well, my son, *I* am."

Lake Erie

Good Face was dozing with the sunlight yellow on her eyelids when she heard, over the steady *slap slap* of waves, far thunder. The canoes were just coming out from behind another long spit of land that projected into the lake and she looked ahead to the west. There in the distance was the grim edge of a coming storm. Above and behind it were towering clouds reaching as if to devour the sun. The men called to each other from the various canoes, questioning whether there might be time to go on, up the windward side of the point, and reach the main shore before the weather struck. All quickly agreed that there would not. They turned the canoes about and paddled earnestly back the way they had come, into the sheltered waters behind the spit, and raced along looking for a place high enough to baffle the oncoming blow. Their haste was exciting and frightening. As the canoes were turned toward the beach where a low rise was covered with scrub, Good Face felt a blast of cold air so damp it made her shiver. She realized at that moment that there was an actual distinct smell that was the smell of a storm, and that she had become familiar with it while living outdoors among the Lenapeh, even though she had never heard or thought of a storm smell.

With bewildering quickness the canoes were emptied on the beach and carried a little way upslope into a copse of bushes, turned over with their bottoms facing the purpling western sky, and tied to the bushes. The thunder was cracking and booming, and though the sun was gone, constant scribbles of lightning, now here, now there, had replaced it for brilliance. As the women and girls dashed up with the bundles and baskets and blankets, the wind was shredding leaves from the whipping, shuddering bushes on the crest, marram grasses were bent almost to the ground, and the howling wind was full of spray and sand. The people all crowded under the overturned hulls, children squealing and men shouting, and suddenly the gray water offshore turned white, and the canoe hulls above began to drum with driven rain and pulsate and creak from the beating of the wind. Good Face cringed and squinted, heart racing, and prayed that the wind would not snatch the canoe and hurl it into the lake. The rope that Flicker had spent so much of her free time braiding was now holding firm this canoe, which was sheltering several families.

The deluge obliterated everything outside. Even the nearby beach was invisible in the seething, thundering gloom, which sometimes became a blinding whiteness. When such bolts of lightning flashed at the same instant the thunder cracked, she would then smell something which she could think of only as burnt water.

Though the canoe was a shield against the driving rain from the west, there was no true shelter from the whirling cold rain and spray. It came under and around and gradually soaked all the huddling people. Wetness spread through the sand under them and wicked up through their deerhide clothes. Tuck Horse and Flicker sat flanking Good Face, clutching a blanket around the three of them, and they did their best to keep warm with their body heat. They tucked the edge of the blanket under their feet to keep it from blowing free and exposing them to the chilling drafts. Eventually the blanket wool itself was so saturated that she could feel water dribbling down inside and trickling along her shins and into her moccasins. No one was speaking, or if they were, they could not be heard. Sometimes Good Face would imagine she could hear, through the drumming and howling and hissing, the cry of a baby. She thought of the few other times she had been caught out in such storms. Once, in the woods near Neepah's town, tree branches had crashed down where she and her friend Minnow were, but missed them. Once at the waterfalls, she and Flicker had been overtaken by storms while foraging, but Flicker had known the place so well that she led the way into a shallow cave under a solid rock overhang, and they stayed perfectly dry that time.

Further back in time, when she was a little girl living with her Slocum family, she had cowered and whimpered in her bedding under a cabin roof of pole rafters and shakes, but stayed dry, and once her family had huddled like this under the canvas canopy of their wagon, lightning revealing the curved wooden ribs under the canopy, thunder reverberating between the hills, in some journey she could still remember as if it had been a frightful dream. She could remember all those terrors so like this, when her life and soul had seemed as delicate and extinguishable as a candle flame, but she remembered too that in those times she had just hunkered down and prayed, and had always lived through it. She had seen many a storm in her young life, but had never known of anyone harmed by a storm, as her mother used to tell her to soothe her fears. But one of her older brothers, the one called Ben, if she remembered right, once told her that the spot of brighter red hair on top of her head was a lightning spot, and that she would be hit by lightning there someday if she didn't do what her brothers told her to. But then her sisters had told her that there was no truth in that. Still, sometimes when lightning was striking around close, she would think of that place on top of her head and it would tingle as if lightning were about to strike it. She felt that way now, which perhaps was not too bad because it helped keep her mind off her chilly, wet misery.

Eventually the thunder and lightning rumbled and flickered away, but the wind and rain continued until dark, and then kept on all night, and it was impossible to sleep or start a fire. It was the longest night she had ever known, and then when daylight slowly came, it kept raining. It seemed that she would never see anything again but the soaking sand being pounded and washed down by rain, and the water of the lake hissing and spattering with rain and rising and falling in gray waves, and a constant dribbling of rain-water off the edge of the canoe before her eyes, the dribbling water sometimes falling straight down but usually being blown in on the blanket.

Now and then she would hear a child's cry through the hush of rain, but the absence of complaining voices was almost eerie. Good Face felt as if she could fill the whole lakeshore with wailing for all the shivering misery she felt.

But the presence of the two stolid old people on either side of her kept her still. Wailing would only discomfort and disappoint them, and would not make her any less miserable anyway.

Then she realized, though she did not think it out in words, that those were surely the reasons why everyone else was bearing the misery in silence.

She snuggled closer to Flicker. The old woman, whose bones always hurt even in the best of conditions, did not stop staring out at the rain, or smile, or say anything. But she did reach over with her right hand and hold on to Good Face's forearm a moment, and squeezed it, and then clutched the edge of the blanket as she had been doing, and Good Face felt comforted, so deeply comforted that she in turn gave Flicker's forearm a squeeze, and they kept waiting, and tears ran from her eyes because she loved the old people so much.

The rain diminished and finally stopped the next day, but the wind kept blowing cold and too strong for setting out in the canoes yet. There were no trees on the spit of land for firewood, and the people could not cook or get warm and dry. At last Tuck Horse said there might be driftwood on the other side of the spit because that was the side where wind would blow it. He assembled women and boys, and with lengths of rope they set off up the slope to cross over to the windy side. At the same time, men with guns started northward along the beach to hunt for birds or meat. Many carried bows and arrows too because they had little faith in their gunpowder after so much rain and damp. Some boys went to the lake with nets and fishing spears, in faint hope of catching something when the water was so turbulent.

Soon a call came down on the wind and Good Face looked up to see the wood gatherers coming back with huge bundles of wood tied on their backs and braced against their foreheads by tumplines. They were staggering under their loads and grinning, some of them almost being blown over on their faces because of the wind on the back of their big bundles.

Fire starters crouched under blankets beneath the canoe shelters to strike flint sparks, but it seemed as if wind and damp and their own impatience were conspiring against them. No one could get tinder going, and the more Good Face watched their efforts, the more she shivered. Finally Tuck Horse yelled, "Haaa!" through clenched jaws, grabbed his musket and powder horn, knelt behind the canoe to load the gun with powder and patch but no ball, then charged the pan. He put a wad of tinder on the sand with a stick to hold it down and fired the musket into it. Flicker snatched up a remaining clump of the tinder with a smoldering piece of linen patch still in it and blew in it until she made flame, and cheerful yells went up. Within a few minutes every family had borrowed fire from Flicker and little blazes were burning in the lee of the canoes, smoke whipping away, and the people were as if reborn. Tuck Horse stood grinning, his gray hair streaming in the wind, and put a hand on his daughter's shoulder.

"See them come to life!" he said. "As I told you long ago, fire is life and it makes more of itself." She remembered his demonstration of that back in their camp at Niagara, and put her arm around his waist and hugged. She could hardly feel any real heat off the wild little flames yet, but she was already warmer inside, not even shivering for the first time in more than a day.

"Do you see something strange about this wood, daughter?" Flicker asked as they squatted between the canoe and the fire. Indeed, she had noticed that many pieces were not branches and twigs, but flat and squared like boards; some even had traces of weathered paint on them.

Tuck Horse said: "Those are pieces of *wapsi* boats. In the driftwood over there are many pieces of boats and ships. There is even an old wrecked ship in the shallow water. It looks like a dead giant animal with its ribs sticking out of the water." Her eyes went wide as she imagined it, and he explained. "Many ships are there at Detroit," he said, pointing west, "always going in and out. As you have seen, storms come up very fast on this lake and many ships get blown against the land or sink far out. I have traveled on this lake many times in the younger years of my life, and I can remember where many dead ships are. A big ship can bear mighty weather, but the Creator is mightier and he does not like to be mocked by *wapsi* fools who stay out too long on the great waters when the storms are plainly coming." He watched a piece of plank blacken in the windblown flames, with his mouth set in a hard line, and nodded once at the meaning of his own words.

"Yes," he said. "The *wapsituk* are such a people for forgetting that they are not gods but only two-legged animals. And then the big things they make die with them, when they offend the Creator by trying to push up against him." He gazed into the fire, filled his pipe and lit it with an ember, able to enjoy it for the first time in two days. He puffed, saluted the four winds, earth and heaven, then mused on:

"They have become a great bother to us for many generations. But the way they push up against the Creator, they surely cannot last many more generations, I believe. *K'hehlah!*" Yes indeed!

The water was calm now. Through the mist Good Face could see shorelands both left and right. She had been asleep, huddled between bundles for protection from the wind and spray, but now the wind was down and the waves were not very high, and that was why she had slept so well. The sky was still gray with smudgy dark clouds. Gazing around, she saw a few snowflakes spinning down and vanishing in the gray water. The voice of Tuck Horse, wheezy with the fatigue of paddling, said, "We are in the river of Detroit, daughter. It has been a long and hard way, but we have come and we are all well." She sat up.

The river narrowed and the canoes passed islands. On both riverbanks and on the islands there were clusters of *wikwams* amid cornfields already harvested, and here and there white men's square houses. She gazed at a windmill, its white sails turning. She saw wagons, and small herds of cattle and horses, piers and moored boats along the shores, light gray wood-smoke drifting. She was expecting to see a fort, but for a long time as the river curved to the right there were only islands, villages, and farms. The river was about as wide as the Niagara River had been at the fort, but there was no high land; no hills or cliffs were anywhere to be seen. Many small boats were on the water, some rowed by white men with oars and some moving along under sails of various shapes. And there were Indian canoes, some so small they carried only a small family, some even bigger than these in which the people had come so far on the lake.

She saw the ships' masts before she saw the town or fort. They were as tall as trees and strung together with ropes. For as long as she could remember, she had had in her mind an image of ships beside a town, from the description her father had told her, and that old picture in her mind was not very different from what she was seeing now, except that she always envisioned it with blue skies and plump white clouds overhead and sunny-sided mountains behind the town.

As the canoes moved closer she saw how big and solid the ships' hulls were, massive as walls, painted black and white. She could see men moving on the ships, and they looked as tiny as ants on a shoe. Two ships were anchored out in the river, but most of them were close along the shore, tied at wharves right along the riverbank. Two-story and three-story buildings with steep roofs were built on the riverbank slope, and a palisade of vertical logs ran from the water's edge far up onto the flatland to protect the town. Farther from the river rose the earthen ramparts of a palisaded fort overlooking the town. Carts drawn by horses and oxen moved slowly along the embankment above the river, going to and coming from gates in the log walls. Overlooking every gate was a blockhouse atop the palisade. On poles above the fort and the town there were flags blowing in the wind, the same kind of flag she had seen at the Niagara fort, blue with red and white lines radiating from the center. It was the British flag, Flicker had told her.

Flicker had been seeing that flag most of her life, either hanging above forts and trading posts or being carried by soldiers. That flag, Flicker told her, was the main reason why the People had not been able to stay in one place, as they had in the old times. Good Face looked at the flag and thought of what she heard Flicker say often about the British *wapsituk*: "They gave us a few pretty things and useful things and made many promises. But their promises were so false they have ruined everything, and if it would do any good, we would give them back all their needles and mirrors and guns and pots, and ask them to give back our lands and all our warriors who died for them." Tuck Horse would say sometimes: "If I had had the power to foresee, I would have killed the first British I ever saw and each one who then appeared."

Good Face gazed at the flags, which she thought were actually rather pretty, and thought of how these Lenapeh had learned to hate the British so much and yet still had to go from one British place to another in order to find what they needed.

* * *

Near the walls of the town, Tuck Horse found an ancient couple of relatives, named Joseph and Mary. Good Face was surprised to hear those names. They stirred her memory somehow. These old ones were living in a drafty house built square in the *wapsi* way, with oiled-paper windows to let in light, and a fireplace with a mud-and-stick chimney. They had a table and some wobbly, creaky chairs. They made much of Good Face and invited her to sit on one of the chairs. Though Tuck Horse was a chair maker, she had not sat on the ones he made to sell at Niagara, and this was the first chair she had sat on in six years. In the chairs at her Slocum home, her feet had dangled, too short to reach the floor, but now she had grown long-legged enough that she could touch the floor with her moccasin toes. These old people had a candle on the table. It flickered and guttered because the house was drafty, but it was good to see a candle burning again. Sometimes the Lenapeh burned sycamore balls soaked in bear or raccoon oil for light, but those were not as bright or long-lasting as a candle, and so most of the light in the *wikwams* was from the fire in the center of the floor. Good Face did like chairs and candles now that she remembered them, though she had not given them any thought while living without them.

It was while sitting on the chair and looking at the candle flame that Good Face remembered why the old people's names sounded familiar. She said, "Kahesana, may I speak? I remember that I had a brother named Joseph and a sister named Mary! I *thought* I had heard those names before!"

That amused the elders. The old man named Joseph said, "Joseph and Mary were the names also of the father and mother of Jesus. Do you remember that, child?"

She put her hand to her mouth, surprised again. "*K'hehlah!* Indeed yes, I remember now! Then you know of Jesus, Mux-umsah Joseph?"

"Very much of Jesus we know. Too much for our good we know. The missionaries called Moravians made many Lenapeh to be Jesus Indians, never to fight Long Knife Americans. No more be warriors, they said. Use guns only for hunting. Pray to Jesus all the time, they said, and if you learn anything of what the bad Indians are doing, tell the missionaries. So we would tell them and they would tell the Long Knives. We were moved here and there by those missionaries, then by chiefs who wanted to protect us.

You know *mekees*, the animals of shepherds? Yes? We were like the sheep of Jesus. Thus we were, two winters ago, when Long Knife soldiers came to our Jesus towns on the Muskingum Sipu, and pretended to be our friends. They tricked our chief, Abraham, to gather up our guns and give them to them. Then they put a hundred of our Jesus people in the church and the missionary's house. Mostly women and children and old men. Tied them up. Then, with a big hammer, smashed all their heads and cut off their scalps. Then those Christian soldiers burned down the church and house with the dead ones inside. . . ." He shook his head.

Good Face remembered hearing about that, at Niagara, but as this old Joseph told it, it was a story she could see in her mind, and much too horrible to think about. She looked with teary eyes to Tuck Horse and Flicker, whose old faces were cold and hard as stone now.

After a while Tuck Horse said: "Do you remember, old friend, when the missionaries came, I asked you not to go listen to their Jesus talk? Do you wish you had heeded my warning?"

"Do I wish that? Maybe yes, maybe no. Jesus did not do that to our poor people. Jesus was good, not hurting people."

"But he made you weak," Tuck Horse said.

"The missionaries made a strong warrior into a peaceful man named Abraham and he was easily fooled."

"Easily fooled is a kind of weakness," said Tuck Horse. "A serious weakness."

The old women had moved closer to the fire and were talking about their own weaknesses, aged bones, and were making willow-bark tea to drink for it. Old Joseph sat at the table with a dingy red blanket over his shoulders, telling Tuck Horse how the war and the end of the war had changed everything.

"We Lenapeh tried to be friendly with the Long Knives in the war, or to be neutral. They promised help and supplies but never gave them to us. Killbuck and White Eyes found out they had been fools to believe the Long Knives. Many Lenapeh have gone with Captain Pipe to the country south across the lake. Some of the Christian Lenapeh are there, but many were led east of here, to Canada."

"*E heh.* Like *mekees.*"

"Yes. Like sheep. As for the French, they angered the British by helping the Long Knives win the war. And so, many French have moved north up the river. Many other French have moved the other way, down to the end of the lake."

"That is a sad thing," Tuck Horse said. "Of all the *wapsituk*, the French are the least bad." He let pipe smoke stream up from his parted lips into his nostrils. His eyes were half shut.

"The end of war treaty told the British to leave the Detroit fort, but they show no sign that they mean to go."

"It is likewise at Niagara, from where we came," Tuck Horse said. "The British have two ways of keeping their promises, as you know: very slowly or not at all. But be satisfied they are still here. The British may be worse than the French, but the Long Knives are the worst of all. They want you so far away they cannot see you. Then if you go that far away they follow you and tell you that you should be dead. If they make the British leave Detroit, the Lenapeh will want to leave here too."

"You have heard that the Long Knives almost came here in the war," old Joseph said. "The general called Clark Long Knife, he sent birds to say he would come. It made the French happy and it scared the British so badly they built this new and stronger fort. But he got busy elsewhere and did not come."

"What I heard of this Clark was that he got busy burning the Shawnee towns south of here," Tuck Horse replied. "Another one of their great Town Destroyers. The Long Knives seem to have many Town Destroyers and corn killers. It seems to be a good way to make war. They might not win a war if they had to fight warriors, instead of women and children in the towns, and corn in the fields."

Good Face heard such a bitter and cruel edge on Tuck Horse's voice that she shuddered. But she remembered what had happened to all the old warrior's family.

"I don't know how long the British will keep this Detroit," Joseph said after a while. "We might be able to live near the British until we cross over to the Spirit Road—or to Jesus Heaven, if that's what is up there—for our seasons are few now. One does not enjoy living on and on when there is no village around, and no sacred times. Lately our people have been moved two more times by the missionary shepherds to places we never knew before. My wife Mary and I have talked of letting go of the earth before we have to endure this next winter. You see by this square shack we

live in that the *wapsituk* do not know how to make a warm
wikwam. All the heat of the fire goes up that 'chimney' thing, and
there is no way to pack grass in the walls to keep the wind out. . . .

"No, old friend," Joseph went on, with his whole face hanging slack, "we have not lived well as Jesus sheep. But it is not the
fault of Jesus. He did not tell his people to be the way they are.
What He told them, they are the other way, as far the other way as
they can be."

Joseph fingered kinnikinnick into the bowl of a smudged clay
tavern pipe, stood up stiffly from his chair and lit it over the candle
flame. The smoke was fragrant: there was red willow bark and
mullein and sumac leaf mixed with the tobacco, and some red
cedar too. In her years with Flicker, Good Face had learned to
know herb and medicine and smoking plants so well that she
could separate out the smells and see in her mind each of the
plants, just as she could tell by taste everything that was in a stew.
Flicker said such senses helped make a good healing woman, and
a good cook.

The thoughtful quiet, in which they smoked and thought of
their discontents, was suddenly shattered by what sounded like a
thunderbolt right on top of the shack. Good Face and her chair fell
over, and Flicker clapped her hands over her ears, screaming. Dust
filtered down through cobwebs. Tuck Horse stood up, bent forward with his hands on his knees, shaking his head. But the other
old man just smiled wistfully and blew another cloud of kinnikinnick smoke.

"It is only the evening gun of the British. They shoot it to say
the sun has gone down, in case nobody noticed. I am sorry my
house is right under the cannon. But if anyone else could bear to
live under that cannon, we would not have this place to live in."

Tuck Horse helped Good Face right her chair and get back on
it, and then asked the old man where he might find the people of
his clan that he had come so far to join.

The old man thought and sighed. "Few were ever here. You
know the river called Sanduskee, where we burned an English fort
for Pontiac, in that war? When one travels two days up that river,
one sees that the little river called Tymochtee comes in from the
right hand. Captain Pipe's Town is there on Tymochtee Sipu. On
the other branch of Sanduskee, Half King has his Wyandot town.
In a day's walk are six towns of Wyandot and Lenapeh, many

people. You know that is a rich and good country there and is as far from Long Knives as anyplace one can find."

Tuck Horse nodded, squinting at the ceiling with remembering. He said, "That has a good sound. Far from the Long Knives. Or British too."

"Perhaps there will be peace for you in your remaining seasons. If you get far enough from them. Two days' walk south of Captain Pipe, our other great *sakima*, Buckongahelas, has a town, and beyond him stand about ten towns of the Shawnee, on the Miami Sipu and the Mad. They are strong. They stand between our people and the Kentuck Long Knives. Near them is the trading post of Loramie, a man you remember, so your people can get what they need of white man's things without traveling far. Unless you intend to live a very long time more, you should live peacefully there among our people for the rest of your life before the Long Knives take that place too." He crinkled his eyes in a grim smile.

Tuck Horse grinned, but it was a grin without humor. "I will live in peace as long as I can. But I do not expect the Long Knives to stay out of that country and leave me alone. And my daughter Good Face as you see is very young, and she will surely have to keep moving much of her life to keep out of their way."

Now the old man and his wife turned to gaze at Good Face again, slightly smiling, and looking her over so long that she began to feel squirmy. Finally old Joseph said, "Tuck Horse, that looks to be a fine daughter you have got. You never were a man to avoid trouble, and I see that you are still the same. That red hair growing on her head can be seen like the flame of this candle. In a time when such things are happening between the *wapsituk* and the Real People, you may expect troubles to come around the way the dusty wings come around the candle."

"Ha ha! My old brother, you may be right. But this trouble, for once, I did not seek. She was handed into my life by no asking of my own. But I have come to see her as a gift from the Creator. She has been no trouble. But if trouble comes, I think her to be worth it. This one is marked to be a great woman among the People."

She had never heard him, or Flicker, say such a thing, and she wondered what he meant by "marked."

She wondered if it was the lighter hair on her head that her white brother had called a lightning spot.

CHAPTER EIGHT

Joseph and Mary, Ruth Slocum thought, as she listened to the vows making her daughter Mary the wife of Joseph Towne. *Joseph and Mary.* Aye!

That night the couple went upstairs to a bedroom in Ruth Slocum's grand new two-story house. Gradually the wedding guests who had stayed over went to their beds in other bedrooms and in the old log house nearby. Ruth and her thirteen-year-old son Isaac saw that every guest had a candle or lamp and a washbasin with a pitcher of fresh water. The tall clock was bonging eleven when the last guests were put away. Isaac tended to the guests' horses and then went to his own attic room. The younger boys, Joe and Jonathan, were already asleep, having exhausted themselves by the excitement of so much company and the mystery of matrimony, and perhaps they were dreaming of the thrilling idea that their new brother-in-law Joseph Towne would be taking their sister away to the wilds of the Ohio River country. Joseph meant to pioneer in that newly opened land.

Ruth Slocum was still too full of emotions, the whole bittersweet range of them, to think yet of retiring to sleep, so she sat alone in the kitchen where a single candle burned and sipped from a dainty teacup. In case anyone came in at this hour, she did not want to be seen with a glass of sherry, and so she took it from a cup. She used it seldom and sparingly, but at times like this it would help her go to sleep, or so she hoped.

It was Giles who had first brought any kind of liquid spirits into use in the Slocum family, having got used to it in his soldiering days. Will hardly touched it, afraid of making himself a fool if he

197

drank. Therefore it was Ebenezer who drank with Giles when any significant imbibing was done. Ebenezer rationalized that it cut the anthracite dust from his throat.

He also joked privately that because of his lame foot, no one in town would notice particularly if he staggered and reeled from it.

People in the town did notice, of course, because Ebenezer did most of his public imbibing down at Judge Fell's tavern, where he spent frequent evenings with the smithys, artisans, and millers who were his peers and friends. With proceeds from his coal-selling, he was already building his mill in Deep Hollow, hiring laborers to dig the sluiceway and making most of the machinery himself. As soon as the mill was done, he said, he would build a distillery, a logical next step in the use of grain and the making of money. He was bent on becoming one of the earliest millers and distillers in the valley. Because of these ventures, he was always too busy to consider going with Giles or William when they planned their excursions to the far country in search of Frannie. But he was always willing to contribute to the ransom money. And he had also helped finance the building of this fine new house for his mother, although much of it had been paid for by selling off sections of the land she had inherited from her father and her husband.

Now Ruth Slocum, a widow at the half-century mark in her life, sat with her sherry cup and mused, as she did at least once every day, on her lost daughter, whose unknown fate still brought tears to her eyes. She envisioned Frannie at Niagara, the last place where there had been any report of her.

Upstairs the telltale creaking of the nuptial bed was acceler-ating for the second time since she had been sitting here. It was disconcerting to be sitting here alone and aware of what was being done to her girl Mary, whom she knew in every detail of body and soul. She tried not to envision it. Joe Towne was obviously a lusty young man. She could only hope that Mary was being pleasured by it too, but she could still remember after thirty years the mixed pain and pleasure of being deflowered and then ridden through the night by her own husband. Jonathan had been twenty-two then, and though shy in manner, like a stallion for force and endurance.

"Oh my!" she murmured aloud, blushing at her thoughts and memories. Or maybe it was not blushing. Ruth had only recently quit having her monthlies, and was still overcome now and then with flushing and sweating that had nothing to do with embarrassment.

During these last few days before the wedding, Ruth had been in a strange and undefinable state of sympathy with Mary, something too deep and sanguine to be really understood or spoken of with the bride. It was as if she were feeling in her own veins, or heart, or head, or soul, every fear and every one of Mary's yearnings and sensations—as if they both were conduits of the same river of life, with the same flow passing through, daughter downstream from mother, but not separate; overlapping, rather. It was a part of the oneness that she had always sensed with all the children of her womb, so that she seemed to be able to feel their closeness or distance, but it was deeper and more intuitive with the daughters than the sons. She imagined that would be so because she had felt everything her daughters had felt inside, Judith, Mary, and Frannie, while the feeling of maleness surely was another thing.

And now thinking of this, or feeling it, she seemed to feel also the flow of Frannie's inner being, despite the distance and the long, sad absence. Frannie was now thirteen—no, fourteen, it would be—and surely in the tides of the moon by now, ripening, full of that mysterious moist power of fertility. . . .

Ruth Slocum shuddered and shook her head, blinking, unable yet to reconcile what she knew with what she remembered. For all these years since that frightful November day nine years ago, she had remembered her youngest daughter as the little five-year-old slung over a warrior's shoulder, reaching back, screaming in terror, red curls in disarray, bare feet flailing in the air, her little treasured chatterbox of a child, scarcely even of a gender yet; so abruptly had Frannie's age been frozen in her mother's imagination. And yet now she would be . . . perhaps shoulder height? With a young woman's lines, with breasts, probably flossy under her arms and on her netherlips. Not a five-year-old child, but a woman.

And then with a clenching of her heart, she thought of her daughter desirable and viable among a people whose mores surely were promiscuous, whose rituals surely would be lewd, whose males apparently did and took what they wanted swiftly and with no mercy. If Frannie had been helpless, cold, and miserable among the Indians as a child, what sort of degradation would she have to suffer now?

Ruth shuddered, thinking: I know what sordidness even Christianized men will do upon a helpless female when she has no mother to guide her, no menfolk to protect her. How would law-less warriors treat their chattel?

O God help my child!

Captain Pipe's Town

Good Face pulled strands of cord through the reed mats and tied them to the frame of bent poles. Flicker worked on the other side, doing the same thing. It was such a tiny hut they were building, no bigger than the little sweat lodges used for cleansing and healing. This little domed house would be big enough only for Good Face to sit in or lie down and sleep. The fire pit would be outside the door in front of the hut. Good Face was scared.

She would be staying here all alone four days and nights. She had never spent a night alone, entirely away from all other people, in all her life, not in her *wapsi* home so long ago, not in Neepah's town, not at Great Falling Water, not at Joseph and Mary's house at Detroit, not here at Captain Pipe's Town on the Tymochtee Sipu. Alone outside; that was the strangest and scariest part of this. Of course, the bleeding had frightened her at first, even though Flicker had assured her that it was what all girls did when they reached the age to be women. She had said it would stop in a few days, and from then on she would be a woman, not just a girl, and that it would happen once every moon for the rest of her life, except when she was pregnant, and would not stop until she was forty-five or fifty summers of age. This first time of the bleeding she would have to live alone in her own hut and do certain things and learn certain things. All the other moon-blood times for the rest of her life she would live in the women's moon lodge with other women who were bleeding at the same time, and would have their company. But this first blood time she would be alone, away from the town. Flicker had told her that this was a sacred time, the beginning of womanhood, and because she would be alone here, her Spirit Helper might come to her and give her her sacred name. Flicker was telling her the things she needed to know as they worked on the little *wiktut*, her own sacred moon-blood hut.

"Men have to have a *pimakun* lodge to sweat in and purify themselves, because they do not have this blood-flow to cleanse them out. That is why the sweat lodge is mostly for men. We have this bleeding time to take the poisons out of us. Tell back to me, daughter, what you have learned to be the ways of cleansing the body and thus also the spirit inside."

"One is *pim*, the sweating, Kahesana. That is for men."

"Yes, though there is a *pimakun* for women separately for certain purposes. Go on. Another?"

"Fasting, Kahesana."

"Yes. And the last?"

"Bathing in sacred smoke?"

"Yes, daughter. You remember well. Those are what we can do when we need to cleanse our own spirits. This, the bleeding, is a way Creator gave only to women so they can always be purified even if they do not know or remember those others. Women have to be pure because inside them is the place where babies wait before coming into the world."

Good Face, who had much confusion and doubt about blood coming from inside herself, asked everything she could think to ask about it. "Then is this blood that comes out of us so unclean that we have to be put away from everyone else?"

"It is medicine, daughter. It is very powerful medicine because it is part of all that is life and only women have it. It is thus a mystery to men and a taboo for them to be touched by it. Men do not know about the medicine of a woman's bleeding. They know it is a power and they fear any power they do not understand—just as you feared it until I told you about it. Men cannot understand how a woman can bleed for four days and not die. They bleed when they are wounded and they know they must stop their bleeding quickly or they will die, but we do not die, or even weaken, and they cannot understand this power we have that they have not."

"But how can I bleed four days and not die?"

"Daughter, the blood that comes out is only that which would have been a baby, if there was to have been a baby. This time there is not to have been a baby because you have not yet made one with a man. Please pull this string through on your side and then push it back through to me. I cannot reach around that far."

Good Face seized the strand and pulled it tight, and then with her needle stick she pushed the end back out through the mat.

"*Waneeshee.*"

"I still do not understand this all," Good Face said. "Tell me about the baby that would be but is not."

"*Kulesta!* Listen, then. Do you remember when your father told you that fire is life spirit? Do you remember when he held grass to the fire and showed that it could make more of itself?"

That was years ago, back at their camp near the waterfalls, but she could remember him showing her that and saying it. "Yes, I remember that."

"A boy is just a boy and a girl is just a girl and they cannot make life together. But when a boy becomes a man, he is like a steel striker, and when a girl becomes a woman, as you do now, she is like flint. Each one is ready to make fire, but one must touch the other for the fire to happen. Then they can make more of themselves. What you have in you now that you become a woman was ready to become the fire of a life, but it did not because no man struck it with the steel. That will happen when you have a husband who will be able to make the fire in there. But until then, what is in there in you, not being struck fire to, will let loose and come out. Every moon it will. Think of the blood as a life that would have been if Neepah Huma, Grandmother Moon, had said it is the time for it. Neepah Huma is the guide of this. She says when it will be or when it will not. If she says it will not yet be, then the life-fire-that-would-have-been is cleansed out so you will be pure each next time. You have to be pure inside when it happens because it will be a life, and as we have always said to you, a life is sacred."

Flicker had told her to keep a fire going day and night while she was here in the *wiktut* because she would be brewing oak-bark tea and drinking it all the time she was here. The tea was bitter and left her mouth nasty, but Flicker said it would make her feel better while she was in her moon because it would keep her passing water instead of swelling, and it was the swelling that made one feel bad, Flicker had said. And so Good Face was diligent about her fire and kept wandering out to gather dry wood for it.

The hut was built far from the creek. Flicker had told her that she was not to bathe during the bleeding time, even though she had gotten in the habit of bathing every day. "Your moon-blood is not to get in the streams," Flicker had said. "You are to return it to Kukna, Mother Earth, with a pinch of tobacco."

The other task she had to complete while she was here, besides keeping the fire going, was to make the corn necklace. She had an ear of dried *xaskwim* and a thread of sinew, an awl and a needle. She was to drill a hole through each kernel of the corn and string all the kernels on the thread. All the time she was drilling and stringing, she must be in a state of prayer, Flicker had told her. Then, when the necklace was full and complete, the power of the prayers would be able to go all the way around. It is the proper nature of prayers to go all the way around and meet themselves at the beginning, she had said. Prayers go to the Creator, and in being answered they return, and then prayers of thanks go back, and on and on, around and around.

Good Face was learning that hunger confused thinking. She couldn't decide whether to keep feeding the fire with sticks or go in the hut and try to sleep. There was comfort in the fire; it was indeed like a life, and gave her company, and kept wild animals away, and she needed it to brew the oak-bark tea.

But she was tired and she knew that if she slept, these days of solitude would pass more quickly. If she went in to sleep, though, she probably would lie awake worrying and thinking too much. In the quiet of the night the scratchings of a mouse could sound like the claws of a lynx or a bear. And she knew that sleep probably would not come because of her hunger. She had made the choice that she would fast while in the *wiktut*, so that a Spirit Helper might come to her, and give her a name, and tell her of her life to come. Now she wished she had not made that choice. After just one day without any food, she felt strange and vacant inside. With that emptiness too there were all those new and unsettling sensations of the moon time, and the sensations were so keen that she could hardly bear them. It was as bad as having mosquito bites and the itchings of the poison plants, as well as the hunger, and nothing she could do to relieve any of them. Her breasts ached and her nipples tingled. Between her hips there were feelings as relentless and annoying as the need to relieve herself, though she did not need to do that. These were feelings that made her squirm on her hips and yearn for something. She sighed, knowing that with all this and her fear of the night, it would be useless to go into the hut and try to sleep. So she leaned forward and put more sticks on the fire. The fire was beautiful. It was her friend. She finally went to sleep sitting up and looking at it until she was not seeing it anymore.

The second day she gathered wood and wished for food, sat listening to the distant sounds of voices from the village, sipped the bitter oak-bark tea, watched midges dance in the rays of sunlight that penetrated the treetops, and took journeys in her mind back through all the places and people she could remember. In those

journeys she visited her white mother, though she could not see
her face. Instead of seeing her, she felt as if she were in her body.
When her mind came back to the little *wiktut* under the trees, she
still could not see her mother's face. She could not remember it.
She had not remembered it for so long that she couldn't remember
when she had last been able to remember it. But it had been a long
time since she thought so much about her, and this was the first
time she had ever felt that she was in her mother.

She could still remember Neepah's face, though it had been
almost as many years since she had seen her.

That evening the mosquitoes came in great numbers, and since
she had no bear oil to protect her skin from them, she built up the
fire and fed green boughs and damp punk into it to make it as
smoky as she could, and stayed in the smoke even though it stung
her eyes and bothered her throat. After dark she had another time
of great doubt about whether she was thinking and behaving properly for this time. She thought perhaps the reason she was so
uncomfortable in so many ways was that she was thinking about
herself instead of being prayerful. That was something her mother
Slocum had taught her, and Neepah had told her that, and Flicker
too. All three who had been mothers to her had told her that: Don't
think too much of yourself.

And so she fixed the fire to send smoke up to the Creator, and
knelt in the firelight with both hands wrapped around her medicine bag, the tiny bag that contained the Three Sacred Sister seeds
Neepah had given her, and a pellet of dried mud from the first
Bread Dance Ceremony she had gone through, back in Neepah's
town long ago, a pebble from there, and one of her teeth that had
come out before the new ones grew in, several years ago. She was
not sure the tooth should be in the medicine bag, but it was a keep-
sake and something had told her to put it in as good luck, so she
had. With the bag in her hands she began praying with all her concentration, ignoring the feelings in her body and the smoke in her
breath and the whining of the mosquitoes, praying without words,
trying to see the things that should be so. It was said that Kijilamuh ka'ong could see the pictures in your mind of what you
prayed for, and when he saw them, he would make them be so by
thinking of them. And so that was how she prayed.

She had not known what she would pray for; she had not
thought about the future before. She had simply gone along day
by day hoping that things would be the way her old Lenapeh par-

ents wanted them to be. They wanted to live in peace, with enough to eat, with friends always nearby and enemies always far away, with Kijilamuh ka'ong's approval of their ways, with Good Face safe and happy and married to a kind man who would give her good children who would be their grandchildren. Those were all things that seemed good to Good Face too, so she tried to see them in her prayers. She tried to picture a handsome young husband, particularly the boy Like Wood in this town, but his face blurred in her mind and kept fading out. He was the boy who had paddled the canoe on the great lake. Once he had been shamed for spying on bathing women, but had grown up admired and esteemed.

Then she pictured something she had not expected to think of. She saw some white men and women, dressed in black and gray, who had come to her home to talk with her. They were asking her to go away with them. This was not something she was sure she wanted Kijilamuh ka'ong to see her thinking and so she stopped praying and opened her eyes.

She gasped; her heart slammed in her bosom.

A bear was on the other side of the fire. It was just sitting there on its haunches, looking at her. The closest she had ever seen one before was across the river. This one was less than five steps from her. It was bigger than a fat man, all black except for a brown muzzle and brown around its eyes.

For a moment Good Face was ready to leap up and scream and run, and would have except that she was frozen with fear and could not even utter a sound.

Then a strange calm passed over her. The bear's eyes were not angry or menacing. The bear reached up with a paw and rubbed its ear, then licked its paw and rubbed the ear again, and gave what sounded like a sigh. The *lachimu* stories said bears were kin to human beings. Maxk'wah was the bear. Good Face swallowed and spoke.

"Maxk'wah?"

At the sound, the bear cocked its head. It seemed to have known its name.

"Maxk'wah, are you my Spirit Helper?"

It did nothing and made no sound, but just by sitting there quietly it seemed to be saying yes.

"Maxk'wah, did you come to give me a name?"

The bear cocked its head again. It opened its mouth so that its red tongue and the white lower teeth showed. It looked as if it were smiling. Then it made a soft gurgling sound, not quite like a growl. It did not sound the least bit like words, and yet it seemed to have said, "Maxk'wah n'wah." If that was what it had said, it meant something like "small female bear."

And it did seem to be a female; though Good Face had no way of knowing, it gave the sense of being female.

A rustling sound came from the direction of the town, and the bear looked that way and suddenly rose on its hind legs. It gave a low growl, then turned to look once at Good Face, and as the sounds came closer, the bear dropped to all fours and vanished into the darkness. A moment later Good Face heard panting, snarling sounds, and then three yellow-gray dogs from the town ran through the firelight and into the darkness where the bear had gone, snarling and beginning to bark and bay. The sounds of pursuit faded into the woods.

Suddenly feeling very sad and dizzy, Good Face went into the *wiktut* and lay down on the bed of boughs. She was so terribly lonely that she wept for a while in the darkness. When she opened her eyes, it was daylight and a shaft of morning sun was shining through the door into her face. She could see just the speck of sun through the foliage, with long, shimmering rays blazing all around it. Birdcalls were twittering and chiming and chinking everywhere around the hut. She got up and went into the bushes to urinate. As Flicker had told her to do, she covered it with dirt and leaves and crumbled tobacco over it. There was still a little blood in it. Then she returned to the front of the hut. She thought the fire was out, and was upset with herself for not tending to it. But deep in the ashes there was still an ember, and she crumbled bark and twigs over it and blew on it until she had a small blaze going again, and she built it up and then gathered more wood. She kept thinking about the bear that she had dreamed of the night before. Or had she dreamed of it? She was not sure. It had seemed more like a dream than anything real.

The long hunger and loneliness were making her see things in a strange way. Tiny things were clear and large. She watched ants working on the ground and wondered what Creator had told them to do, and why. Then a bird with red stripes on its cheeks, like war paint, came scampering across the ground, licking up ants. It stopped and looked at her out of its left eye. The eye grew huge in the center of her attention and was studying her closely with understanding and concern. Then Good Face recognized the bird as the very kind that Flicker was named for, and knew, or believed she knew, that this was actually her old Lenapeh mother, come to watch her in her solitude. Realizing she was supposed to be in prayer all the time she was here, and that she had not been, Good Face lowered her eyes and tried to concentrate on praying.

She was in prayer for a long time, not just praying, but seeing things she had never seen before. She saw the sun go black, she saw towns burning, she saw blue-coated armies marching, and then she saw the strange white people in their black and gray clothes again coming to talk to her, and though they were speaking what she knew to be English, she could not understand it at all. When a mosquito bit her cheek and made her open her eyes, it was dark and the fire was almost out, but in its feeble flickering light she saw the bear sitting on the other side looking at her again.

This time she was not startled to see the bear. It was as if the bear had not been gone, but had only been unseen while her eyes were closed in prayer. She had the feeling that the bear was and would always be there. And again it gurgled the word meaning "small female bear."

"Maxk'wah n'wah," Good Face said. "Is that your name or are you giving me that name?" The bear, though it had appeared large the first time she saw it, truly seemed to have the air of a female about it, as she had sensed before.

The bear, without words, said yes, it was its name and it was giving it to her.

At that same moment there came the voice of an *ulikwan*, a flicker, and Good Face looked around to see the bird perched on top of the *wiktut*, saying, *"Weekah! Weekah!"*

Good Face was worried that the dogs might come again and chase away the bear as they had before, but none came. She remembered them baying off after the bear. She looked at the bear, wondering about that. And the bear, as if reading her thoughts, told her, without words as usual, I took care of the dogs. Now you. Do you not have something to take care of too?

Yes, she thought to the bear, thank you for reminding me. And she went back to work on her corn necklace. And though it was tedious and cramped her fingers, she bent close to the firelight and drilled the kernels, praying all the while, and while she was doing that the bear vanished. When Good Face looked up from her work, a very old woman was sitting where the bear had been.

Flicker had told her that this ancient one would come and teach her through her whole last night at the *wiktut*, and that what this old woman was going to teach her would help her to live her life well. But she had not told her who the old one would be. When Good Face saw the old woman sitting beyond the fire, she recognized her from far back in her memory, and was both surprised and puzzled.

It was the very old woman who had first talked to her in Neepah's *wikwam* when she had been taken there. She remembered that the old woman had talked to her about *tindeh*, Fire, and had taught her the Lenapeh words for "good" and "thank you." It was that very old woman, and what surprised her so much was that the old woman would be here. The last time Good Face had seen her was in that town beside the Susquehanna, during the war, just before the Town Destroyer came through. Good Face tried to remember her name, but was not sure she had ever even known it. It would have been hard to imagine the woman could look older than she had then, but she did look still older. She looked as old as Good Face imagined Keeper Grandmother must look as she stood guarding the door between life and death.

Now the old woman began, in a voice as dry and rustling as last year's leaves:

"When I saw you before, you were a girl. A *wapsi* girl, soft and frightened and unable to care for yourself. Now you are a woman. Much will be required of you. I have come to prepare you. My name is Maxk'wah n'wah. You will listen to me."

Good Face's jaw dropped open. Small Female Bear was the name the real bear had given to her—or so it had seemed. And of course maybe that had not been a real bear anyway, but a dream bear. Or had it been this elder?

I will know by and by, she told herself, and she said to the old woman, "Huma Maxk'wah n'wah, I am happy to see you and I will listen to you. *Waneeshee*. I thank you for coming to me."

"You will not like all of this," the old woman's voice rasped and rustled. "To be a woman is always hard, and to be a good woman is harder. A good woman will have cracks on her back like the Great Turtle, from carrying the world. It is the good women who carry the life of the True People around and around the hoop of ages. Men ride us from one generation to the next and they pretend they are more important. But they respect and fear our power.

They know that Kijilamuh ka'ong gave us the power to create them. Are you listening?"

"With my ears and my heart, Grandmother."

"Now that you are a woman, men will want to poke their little man-part into you. That will always be in their minds. When they look at you, your woman-power will make their back start to hunch and their man-part stiffen. Like everything, that is both good and bad. If they did not want to do that, we would all die out, and so that wanting is good. And the pleasure it can give is better than any other pleasure, even the pleasure of eating and laughing. That is what is good about the wanting.

"But it requires wisdom to keep the wrong men from sticking that thing in you, and to keep it from being done at the wrong time. Sometimes both you and the wrong man will want to connect your parts. Therefore you must know the difference between a right man and a wrong man and stop him if he is not right.

"Sometimes even the right man will want to do it at the wrong time. Therefore you must know the difference between a right time and a wrong time, and stop the man if it is not the right time. Are you still listening?"

"K'hehlah, Huma. Yes indeed."

"Therefore I will first tell you the difference between right men and wrong men. Then I will tell you about right times and wrong times:

"A right man is a man who is not your relative. You must not connect with any man of your clan. Promise that."

"I will not connect with any man of my clan."

The old woman nodded, looking hard at her from the wrinkled pockets where her eyes were sunk deep and dark, and said, "You came to us as a *wapsini* and so in your blood you are not really of any clan. All the same, it is against Creator's will for people in the same clan to connect, and therefore you will not.

"Other wrong men are these: *wapsi* men. Unclean men. Drunk men. Brutal men. Men who would not be willing to be your husband. Men who would betray the People. Men who are too lazy or selfish to provide—forever—for any children they make on you. Those are the wrong men. Say them back to me so I will know you know them."

Good Face repeated them all, in the same words.

"*Wehlee heeleh,*" said the old woman. Good. "Remember

those. Have you any questions about them before we go on to right and wrong times?"

"No, Huma."

That seemed to displease the old woman. She said, "You should have some questions, if you really want to know. Are you certain there are no questions about right or wrong men?"

"What questions, Huma?"

"You think. You will have to think when those times come. That is one of your responsibilities as a woman with a hole that a man wants to stick his thing in. You will have to think before you know whether some men are right or wrong. You had better learn now to start thinking about protecting that hole from wrong men. Because it is not just the hole, it is your spirit, which is sacred, and it is your children, who are sacred, and it is the People of your Lenapeh nation, who are sacred, and through that hole of yours is a way that all those sacred things can be harmed by wrong men poking into it. Think of your questions, because if you do not have any, you are not ready to protect the sacred things. Think. I am here for all night. I will not go away until I am satisfied that you are a true woman who knows what to protect and how to protect it."

Having to sit with the old woman's presence probing her like a needle made it very hard for Good Face to figure out what she was expected to ask, but when she thought back over the kinds of wrong men, she thought: I can ask a man if he is of my clan; I can *see* that a man is *wapsini*; I can tell a drunk man by how he acts. But the others . . .

"I have questions," she said. "Why are *wapsi* men wrong?"

"Because they do not care for the People. And because they are not clean. And because they usually have sickness in their man-parts, which then comes into the women they connect with. What other questions?"

"How would I know if a man was lazy or selfish or if he would betray the People?"

"Good," said the old woman. "Those are the questions you would have to answer before you knew whether a man was right or wrong to connect with. I am glad you finally thought of those questions."

Good Face waited for her to answer them, but the old woman just sat, nodding, until she had to ask, "Huma, how would I be able to know those things?"

"Young woman, there are many answers to that question. Some things you can ask a man and he will tell you. Some you may ask him and his answer will be a lie because he wants in your hole more than he wants to be truthful. Some things his relatives and friends can tell you. Some will be displayed as his reputation. And there are some that you might find out just in time, or too late. Too late is when he has already ridden on you and made children or broken his promises. In your years as a young woman and with the guidance of your mother and your aunts and the grandmothers, you will learn how to tell those things. Not all men will deceive. Some never will. Some will sometimes. The grandfathers try to teach the young Lenapeh men to be honorable and to respect women. After this ceremony, all the young men who might look on you will be asked to respect you. You will learn to protect yourself as well as one can. Sometimes your Spirit Helper will warn you. Sometimes a dream will warn you. Sometimes the Chipewuk, the spirits of dead ancestors, will come and warn you of what they know of a wrong man."

Good Face's scalp tingled. "Dead spirits?"

"Yes. They come back and guard us sometimes, or just to visit us because they are lonely for us. They are not like the dead spirits of the wapsituk, who are said to go up and sit on the clouds forever, being useless. Ours are always nearby when we are in need. That is why we always put a bite of food into the fire for them before we eat. That is why we turn the pipe stem all the way around before we smoke, to invite them from all sides and make them welcome. Always watch the crows and the deer. They have a kind of seeing that can see evil and deceit, and they will warn you. If you have had a Spirit Helper come to you here, think of your Spirit Helper when you have doubt."

She paused, and Good Face thought: Yes, I saw my Spirit Helper and I think it was you in the form of a small female bear. But she did not say that.

Now the old woman continued, "Even with all that help, there will be times when you will be deceived. When there is a right man, you will learn to trust him fully, and that is a relief to know. But when you cannot be fully sure, keep him out of your hole. Now we have spoken of the men who are right and wrong, and now we will speak of the times that are right and wrong."

"Waneeshee, Huma. Tell me about the times."

"One time that is always wrong is this, your moon time. You

will be away in the women's hut at that time, usually, but it could happen that you would not be. Your husband will be taught not to connect with you in your moon time. He believes that your moon-blood will bring him bad luck in hunting or in war if it touches him. Perhaps the game animals will smell your blood scent on him and know a man is near, and will flee before he can shoot them. If your husband is touched by your moon-blood before a battle, he will believe himself too weakened to fight, and he should not go.

"Another time that is wrong is when you have recently given birth, and have a baby at your breast. Your husband will have been taught that too. Therefore, for as long as you do not want to have a next baby, you may nurse the recent one and that will keep your husband from getting on you. It would not really hurt you to do it with your husband while you are still nursing, but keep him believing that, or he will have you carrying children all the time, more than you can well take care of. Men know little about the magic of life-giving, so you can use your husband's ignorance to keep the number of children from being too many for your health, or too many for the good of the People.

"Another time that is wrong for connecting are those times when Mother Corn is displeased with the People and does not give us good crops. Another is when Misinkhalikun, the Keeper of the Game, is displeased with our men and will not let them kill the game animals. When there is hunger, that is a bad time to make children. When the *wapsituk* armies are led toward us by Town Destroyers, that is another bad time to be making babies. You do not want to make children whose food will be burned in the fields by soldiers. You will not want to make baby girls who will grow up to be raped and spoiled by diseased soldiers. You would not want to make children who will grow up with no place left to live in. That is one reason why our People have had so few babies for several generations: because the *wapsituk* have been coming and doing that to us for all that time. You will know in your heart: when the hoofbeats and the bugles of the soldiers can be heard beyond the hill, that is no time to lie on your back making babies for them to spear on their long knives or to kick around like balls."

Good Face winced and shook her head; these were such incredible horrors as Neepah and Minnow used to speak of.

"I am sorry to have to tell you. They do such things." The old woman now took from her waist a misshapen, tattered old tobacco bag and drew a short clay pipe from it, and as she filled the bowl she pointed toward the fire and said, "You had better tend to your fire and keep making the tea. I have hardly begun to tell you the things you need to know to be a good woman for our People, and for your children." She lit her pipe with a burning twig from the fire and said, "Go on with the corn necklace. You must have it finished before I leave you."

And so Good Face, increasingly weary, her head beginning to ache from having to think and remember so much, her back sore from bending near the firelight to drill the little kernels, listened to the seemingly endless requirements of being a good woman. Her belly gnawed with hunger and she was dizzy. Sometimes the old woman would be the bear sitting over there beyond the fire, but then she would be the old woman again, still snapping out her advice, and as she had warned, it was not all good to hear. Once Good Face was startled to see an eagle feather waving just before her eyes. The old woman was pointing it at her and saying:

"Be clean! You stink now! You smell of sweat and dust and moon-blood. Your breath reeks from that tea. You smell like those *wapsi* women who follow the armies and never wash their behinds, from one moon to the next."

"I want to be clean! But Kahesana said I am not to—"

"I know, I know. And when you are cleansed after this you will feel like a Lenapeh person again, not filthy like a *wapsini*. Then you will bathe every day even in winter, and will never go to bed with dirt on your face or dust in your hair or an odor on your bottomside. If your husband wants to lie with his head in your lap, he will be able to breathe fresh air. When you speak in the presence of an eagle feather you must tell the truth. Now I put this feather to your lips and you will promise to be clean all the time."

"I promise that," she said, and she meant it.

Much deeper into the night, when even the distant owls had stopped talking to each other, the old woman was still wide-awake and giving advice, now about what to do if Good Face should have married what she thought was a right man but was not, or one who had been right until he got some of the white man's spirit water. The old woman reached around to her side and untied something made with a long leather braid. "This I give you as the one gift you can hold in your hand. The rest you will hold in your head and your heart. I will tell you what this is." She reached around the fire and extended it to Good Face, saying, "This is your head-cracker button. If a man does not treat you with respect, you may have to use it." It was a stone about the size of a duck egg, encased in leather at the end of the leather braid, which was of arm's length. "You know how to throw with a sling or a bola," the old woman said. "In that manner, whirl this until it hums in the air. You don't need to throw it. Just step close enough to him, and if he is too stupid to jump back, it will put his lights out."

Good Face blinked. She still remembered the teachings of her birth family, that one person does not inflict pain upon another. She thanked the old woman for it, but hoped she would never have to use it. Now the old woman said, "Practice with that. You have to know how to use it without putting your own lights out. Now I will tell you another way to change a man's mind when he wants to treat you badly.

"As I told you before, it will always be in men's minds to poke their thing in you. When they try that they are like an animal close to a trap. They are thinking of the bait and are not very smart then. Your hand is the trap and the little bag that hangs under his man-part is what you will catch. As you know, there is nothing stronger than the hand of a woman who works. You could tear off that bag and what it holds, if you twisted and pulled hard enough, but that is seldom necessary to change his mind, and you would not really want to do that unless you were truly through with him forever. It will surprise you how much respect a man will learn when your fingernails tell him he is in such a trap."

Good Face nodded and again thanked the old woman, but again she hoped sincerely that she would never be in a situation where she would have to use that trap.

When the night darkness was fading and the only sounds were the long shrillings of the morning insects but the birds had not yet begun to chirp, Good Face was sitting numb with exhaustion, feeling as if she were still swimming upstream in the ever-flowing river of Maxk'wah n'wah's words. By now the old woman was through advising on men and women and their body parts, and had been speaking of how a good woman must treat all the other people of her tribe and village.

She had already spoken of how a woman must be ready and willing to feed any person who came to her house hungry, and how she must be ready to assist any child as if it were her own, and how a woman was first a peacekeeper but must be ready to die like a warrior for her people if the time came for such an action, and how a woman must attend councils when the good of the tribe was at stake, so that she would know what would be best and speak in its favor. Now she said:

"There are many things that make the difference between a good woman and a bad woman, and I have spoken of many of them. Now I am going to speak of the worst thing a bad woman can do. For this, a person may be killed by her People."

That was startling enough to send a shock through Good Face even as worn down and benumbed as she was.

"Yes," said the old woman. "Even your own People are willing to kill you for this. It is something everyone is tempted to do sometimes, but you must never do it."

"Tell me, Huma, so that I may know never to do it, for I want to be a good woman. And to tell the truth, I do not want to be killed either."

"Truth is exactly what this is about, you see. The terrible wrongdoing I speak of is untrue gossip. It is the worst thing a woman can do among the People. It is worse to tell untrue gossip about a person than to murder a person. But it is done more often because there is such a temptation to do it. Some women find more pleasure in it than in anything their bodies enjoy. You look as if you do not believe this."

"I do not understand how it can be worse than killing someone. I always thought killing someone was the worst that can be done."

"Young one, if you kill a person's body, the pain is over quickly, and that person's spirit is free to leave and go to follow the Path of Souls through the stars to the Other Side World, which is a better place.

"But with untrue gossip you make a hurt that they feel as long as they live. You murder the honor they have among their People. Everyone who has heard the gossip will look at the one who was lied about and wonder whether the gossip was true. No one should have that done to him or to her. *Kulesta!* I will tell you a *lachimu suwakun*." A story of life.

"Long ago, or not so long ago, there was a woman who was jealous of another woman, and so she started a gossip about her. Later the gossip teller saw how wretched the other woman had become and so she was no longer jealous of her, but pitied her. So great and sincere was her pity that she went to her and said, 'I am sorry I lied about you. I beg you to forgive me.'

"The lied-about woman said, 'I would like to forgive you. But I can forgive you only if you can do this: Pluck the downy feathers from a goose's breast. Go about and lay one of those little feathers at the door of every *wikwam* everywhere.

" 'Wait a year then and go back and collect every one of those little feathers. Only if you can do that, only when you have gathered every one of those little feathers, can I forgive you. You cannot, because the lies you told about me are like those feathers, they have gone everywhere on the wind and you cannot bring them back.' Now the story is finished. Remember it."

A morning bird chirped. The breeze of dawn whispered. Across the fire from Good Face in the pale light, there was no old woman, nor was there a bear. There was only the smoke from the fire drifting off through the tree trunks.

Another bird spoke. Again it was an *ulikwan*, a flicker. It said, *"Weekah! Weekah!"*

And then she saw her mother, Flicker, standing before her in the smoke, holding a basket and a newly made deerskin dress. Her old face looked young compared with the face she had been seeing all night. And it was more kindly. Good Face realized that the old *huma* had not smiled all night because of the gravity of the lessons she had been teaching. It was good to see a smile, and it was so good to see Flicker that her eyes blurred with tears.

"We are through here, my daughter. You are a woman now, no longer a girl." Flicker was looking about on the ground. "The old auntie came to me this morning and said she was through teaching you. But I do not see her tracks. I see only your tracks, and dog tracks, and bear tracks."

"Yes, Kahesana. My Spirit Helper was here. It—"

"Se he!" Flicker hushed her, with an outstretched hand. "You saw your Spirit Helper and it is to be known only by you. I am full of joy that your Spirit Helper revealed itself to you. To some, no vision ever comes, and because you were born *wapsini*, I feared it might not bring forth for you. Add thanks for it to your prayers every day, for if you do not tell the Creator that you are grateful for a power, it will turn bad and you will have then even more trouble than an ordinary person who is without it. Always remember that everything is equally bad and good, so to balance you, but if you are not thankful for gifts, the bad will weigh more."

"Yes, Kahesana," she groaned, more tired than she had ever been. "It is as you have told me before, and I will remember."

"Now, come. We will go and bathe you and wash your old clothes. I have made for you a woman's dress. You will wear this and your corn necklace and the head-cracker button, when we stand you before the village and introduce you as a woman among them. I will paint the Creator's red dots on your cheekbones and vermilion in the part of your hair—though it will hardly show in the red of your hair!—and the women will give you gifts of the things a woman needs, and the men will be told they must respect you. Come, daughter. You are a woman and I am proud."

CHAPTER NINE

Summer 1789
Tioga Point, Pennsylvania

Ruth Slocum had never in her life been among such people, and it required all her courage and composure to keep her sons from seeing how intimidated she was. She suspected that Giles and William too were more frightened than they appeared, being apparently the only two unarmed men in the camp, and perhaps also the only sober ones.

Ruth and her sons had traveled the hard, dangerous road to this place on horseback, keeping their hopes high, because here, at the insistence of the United States government, Indians of many tribes were to assemble and bring with them the captives they had taken during the late war, so that their families might have an opportunity to identify them and reclaim them.

Ransom and compensation monies for the cooperating Indians had been promised, to give them an incentive to yield their prisoners up. But under the influence of rum and whiskey, many of these frontier whites were sniggering and blustering that if the savages did produce their relatives, they would be paid not in gold or silver but in lead and cold steel. This kind of ugly talk made the assemblage seem as menacing as a powder keg decorated with candles.

Giles muttered, with un-Quakerly rancor: "If these off-scourings of mankind start shooting and brawling, those Indians'll vanish so quick with their captives, we'll not get even a glimpse to see if Frannie's among 'em!"

"Then let us pray," said Ruth, "that a sight o' the poor things will bestir pity and gratitude in their bosoms and there'll be no violence."

218

"Yes, let's pray so," said Giles. "But just look at these murderous riffraff and tell me there's pity or decency in any of 'em."

"Remember," she admonished him, "it's our belief that the Light is in everyone."

William just then touched Giles' elbow and pointed toward a snag-toothed, one-eyed, slouching giant passing down the tent row, so festooned with pistols, daggers, and powder horns that he clanked and clicked with every step. Following him were four others of villainous aspect. Giles looked at them, then glowered, his jaw set hard, and nodded.

"What is it?" Ruth Slocum said, having noticed.

"Well," Giles said, "o' course it's been five years or there'bouts since we came up through these parts and got our horses stolen from us, but it takes about *twenty* years to forget a real devil's visage like that one, which was the last one we saw before our horses decamped." His big shoulders were hunching and his huge, work-hardened hands were clenching into fists and then unclenching. "Lord," he growled. "The curse of havin' a pacific creed! Thee will excuse me, Ma," he said, rising, "I do believe I'll follow those gents about and see what sort o' horses they've got."

"Don't 'ee dare!" she exclaimed, rising from the log she had been sitting on, then almost falling to the ground from the kinks and pains she had from days on a sidesaddle. Both her sons swiftly caught her and eased her back down to the log. "Goodness," she groaned. "Fifty-three years old and I'm hitched up like an old granny! Now, Giles, I'm begging thee don't go getting in trouble over horses thee's done without for five years. We're here to find Frances, not horses."

"I won't get in trouble," he said. "I'll just walk down to the corral and see if I recognize any beasts. Though I doubt anything'd live this long under churls like them."

With misgivings, Ruth watched her son go. Though he had forsworn violence on leaving the militia, she had little faith in his equanimity. He did have courage, and was strong and sinewy enough to feel the equal of anybody who might try to provoke him. Will watched him go too, but apparently had decided not to leave his mother here by herself. They sat gazing down through the sprawling, makeshift camp, which was made up of tents and brush huts and rickety lean-to shelters, aswarm with settlers, woodsmen, half-breeds, Indians, traders, and slatterns, as well as the officers of the prisoner exchange commission.

Will pointed across the valley at a ruin on the other side of the Susquehanna. "That was Fort Sullivan," he said. "Built the year General Sullivan rampaged up through here, when I came up with that colonel . . . Proctor, wasn't it? I'll tell thee, Ma, this place was like the gate to Hell. Armies and warriors passing through, prisoners bein' dragged away toward Canada . . . And this has been a war road for a long time, Ma. I reckon this Tioga here's about the best place to exchange prisoners, since most of 'em were carried through here back in those days. Everybody knows the way to Tioga. Shouldn't be many days before the Indians start coming in. They'll take their time, look things over first before they show any captives at all. No trust. Can't blame 'em, really . . ."

He trailed off, gazing up and down the valley he had traversed so many times in the years since his little sister's capture. Ruth Slocum knew he had little hope. He had tried to tell her that even if Frannie were still alive, she would be so Indian by now that she probably wouldn't want to return to the whites, and that whatever family had adopted her probably wouldn't bring her here anyway. He had told her all that, and she knew that it might well be true. But she felt in that deepest part of her soul that Frannie was still alive, and that if by chance she knew her mother was looking for her, she would want to return. Even though she had now been among the Indians more than twice as long as she had lived with her real family, the Slocums were still her real family, and who would *not* want, with all her heart and soul, to be with her true family?

"Eleven years!" she sighed. "Will, we'll have to remember to be a-looking for a young woman, not the little redhead waif we've been seein' in our heads ever since that day. Well, when they start bringing them in, the red hair'll narrow them down a good bit. Then that really bright red on top, I'd suppose that's still the same . . . and that poor mashed finger that lost its nail. And I just feel so sure I'll know her face the moment I see her. All us Slocums, we all have somewhat a same look to us, doesn't thee think, son?"

He turned and looked at her with wistful amusement. "Well, I can usually name off everyone at the dinner table. Especially Ebenezer. He's the black one."

"The bla . . . ? Oh, thee means his coal dust! Ha ha!"

"Ah, good, Ma! First smile I've seen on thee in days."

"Yes. Well. And does thee believe for a minute that Frannie

wouldn't recognize *us*? She'll have grown up and changed a lot, but *I've* not changed much, just grayer and wrinklier. And can hardly stand up 'cause I've perched on a horse too long. But she'll recognize me at once, surely she will."

"Ma, listen. It's not whether she'll recognize us, or we her. The doubt is whether she'll even be brought here. I'll be surprised if any Indian brings anyone in."

"Don't thee say that! We simply must have faith."

"I've hunted ten years, Ma. This is thy first time on this cold trail; thee hasn't seen how things are, so thee has faith."

"Yes, I do have. And enough for all of us, if thee has no more."

"Here comes Giles. No knives or bullets in 'im, that I can see. But no captive horses repatriated either." Will turned and looked at her, took a deep breath, shook his head, and said, "I don't expect any more luck repatriating a little sister either. But I look in the face o' thee, Ma, and I'll pray with'ee. And I'll keep on a-hunting, as long as thee's got the faith in it."

Thank God, Will was wrong, Ruth Slocum thought.

The Indians were coming to Tioga Point, and they were bringing their young white captives, who had been children when they were carried away.

Since they started coming, ten days ago, Ruth Slocum's heart had been like a kite in a whirlwind every day. Whenever she heard the shouts that heralded the arrival of another tribe or band, she hobbled out of the tent and down to the clearing with her heart soaring and her vision blurred by prayerful tears.

Then she would prowl, with scores of other trembling, haunt-eyed parents, along the row of sun-browned, half-naked captives who stood with their Indian families. Names would be said in timid and expectant tones, but there was hardly ever a response from the captives. The Indians seemed terribly anxious. Ruth went from day to day without seeing a red-haired girl, but some-times she would keep going back to some adolescent with sun-bleached auburn or brown hair as if believing that somehow little Frannie could have changed that much, and would peer into her eyes, saying, "Frannie? Frances?" until Will or Giles took her arm and led her away.

By the tenth day there had been very few reunions, and Ruth was beginning to understand how slim were the chances for anyone to find anyone in this vast country after so many years.

Each day most of the Indians would depart, and the white fathers and mothers reluctantly wandered back to camp, grim, teary-eyed, like herself, to wait for the next day. The heavy drinking went on in the camp every evening, and men filled the air with profanity and the sounds of brawling and retching, but during the days, at least, the gravity and expectancy of the search was so intense that it was almost like the quiet religious fervor of a prayer meeting. Every evening one of Ruth's sons would remain near her while the other went through the camp talking to traders and woods runners, even going into the Indian camps, to ask questions, to offer rewards for information. Giles would say, "Even if nobody's brought Frannie here, why, they have come from as far as Canada and Ohio, and we'd be fools not to test the wind while they're here." Ruth realized now how efficient and thorough they had become in this desperate business, and now and then the mere thought of their efforts made her throat knot up and tears leak.

There were here, among the ruffians and bootleggers, some decent families looking for their offspring, and Ruth had come to know some of the mothers, and to marvel and weep at their tragedies. And she had even had opportunities to talk with some Indian women, a Munsee, a Seneca, and a Nanticoke who spoke English well enough to tell their own tragedies, of husbands and brothers killed in battles, of children bayoneted and burned to death in villages by the Town Destroyer soldiers. The Seneca woman, about Ruth's age and very handsome except for burn scars over the whole left side of her face, had been living in this very town of Tioga the two consecutive years it was burned to the ground by Patriot generals, first one named Hartley, and then the one named Sullivan. Each time, she had lost a child. The Munsee woman's only son had been run through with a bayonet while trying to escape through a line of soldiers; immediately afterward her husband had gone down the river with a band of raiders and brought home a white boy to replace her son. "He is grow to be good son to us and we hope no one take him from us."

"Why then did thee bring him here?" Ruth asked.

"Fear your war chiefs. They threw English king and generals on their back and must be so mighty. We are afraid not to bring this boy back when they say."

And Ruth had prayed then that whoever had Frannie would one of these days respond just as that woman had. She thought it a shame that people had to do anything out of fear of mere men's power, but since that was the way the world functioned, let it bring her daughter back.

And now on this tenth desperate day, overcast and stifling, Ruth and Will Slocum were moving down the line looking over the captives. Giles had stayed at their tent to guard their meager belongings against the thievery that had grown more serious every day. The "half-human buzzards," as Giles called them, always descended on any frontier gathering, and blame could always be put on the Indians for the thefts and other felonies. Already, it was creating a tension and suspicion that threatened to dissolve this captive exchange. Thus Ruth Slocum knew that if Frannie did not show up soon, there would be no hope of finding her here at this assemblage, which had in its beginning seemed more promising than anything in a decade.

Just before her in line was a short, stout man in a clean linen shirt. Part of his right ear was missing, and at the crown of his head, in the midst of his thick brown hair, was a conspicuous, tender-looking scar where no hair grew. Will had noticed it and whispered to Ruth that there stood a man who had been scalped and lived to tell about it. It was fascinating but morbid, and Ruth tried not to let her eyes fall upon it or her mind think about it. As the short man moved along, he kept saying loudly, "Is there a Peggy Smith here? Peggy Smith? I'm your father Isaac Smith, if you're here! Peggy Smith?"

And then a female voice just ahead answered, "Me! Peggy Smith me!" The man stumbled forward eagerly. Then he stopped short.

The girl who had answered was about sixteen years old, wearing only a doeskin skirt and moccasins and a puzzled expression. She was ebony-black, one of several Negro captives who had been brought to Tioga in these ten days. The short man blushed as white men nearby began laughing. He shook his head. "Not my Peggy," he mumbled, and moved on, leaving people laughing, including the girl.

Then a tall, sinewy Indian man standing near the black girl peered at the man and called out to him:

"Eh, hey, you man Shuh-mith, you look to me!" When the little man turned to the voice, the warrior, grinning handsomely, bowed far forward and laid his finger on his black hair to point to a scalping scar just like Smith's. Then he straightened up, still grinning, and reached out his long right arm. Smith paused, and extended his, smiling now, and they shook hands, the tall Indian nodding and smiling and saying, "Brothers, brothers we, *e heh*?" He put his fist on top of his head and jerked it up, making a popping sound with his lips, and Smith, nodding and grinning, did the same. *"A huh! A huh!"* the warrior said, and then waved as Smith went on. Ruth quailed inside at the gruesome joke, and yet she herself could not keep from smiling at that momentary display of understanding between the two survivors.

She moved on, now and then saying, "Frannie? Frannie Slocum? Oh, please, is there a Frannie Slocum here?" She passed two more pretty adolescent girls, their faces sun-browned and freckled, but their hair was not red. One had a fingertip-size dot of vermilion on each cheekbone and more red in the part of her hair, which Ruth thought made her look like a hussy, and over her breasts she wore only strands of beads and claw necklaces. It was not Frances—her eyes were the wrong color—but Ruth thought: Wherever my girl is, they likely have her gaudied up all cheap and lewd like that and half bare, a shameless temptress who just doesn't remember the modesty she was taught. Oh, dear God, let me find my Frannie 'fore they make a slut of her!

And just then she heard a twangy male voice behind her say, "Heyyy, bub! I'll take that little darlin'! How much, eh?"

She knew without looking back that the man was speaking of the bare-bosomed one with scarlet on her cheeks, and she flushed with anger and stepped back, past Will, and snapped at the big, leering man: "Shame on thee, a father here to save his own child, and lusting over some other man's daughter!"

The man scowled at her, opened his mouth to say something, then saw big Will with a restraining hand on her shoulder and shut his mouth. "Sorry, ma'am," he said. "I—I—"

"This is no slave market," she scolded. "If some lout were slobbering over thy daughter like that, as one might be somewhere, how would thee like it?"

"He said he was sorry, Ma," Will said.

And the man grumbled: "I don't have a daughter. I'm here a-lookin' for my son. But you're right. This *is* somebody's daughter."

Feeling many eyes on her, Ruth turned and continued along the line, letting her blush fade. She knew she had lost her Quaker reserve because she had been imagining Frannie in the place of that pretty girl.

She was nearly at the end of the crowd now, looking close into one face after another, when Will's voice hissed excitedly, "Ma, up there's a redhead!"

Her heart leaped. She looked. There was a girl with thick red hair. "Frannie! Frannie Slocum, is it thee?"

When she was in front of the girl, she was so wild with hope that she was already trying to make the girl's freckled features conform to what she had been envisioning of her adolescent Frances. The girl was tall, round-faced, with full lips, with eyes that could have been Slocum eyes. She was modestly dressed in a deerskin tunic and moccasins and leggings, wearing the red cheekbone dots and around her neck only a tiny stitched leather bag. The girl was searching Ruth's face as anxiously as Ruth was searching hers, just beginning to smile self-consciously. "Oh, my dear," Ruth groaned, "is thee my Frannie? Doesn't thee know me yet, child?" She reached for her hand, but the girl became wary suddenly and cringed back toward the grandfatherly Indian who stood behind her.

"Ma, I don't think it's Frannie," Will said. "She doesn't know thee at all."

"Yet awhile, son. Frannie, does thee remember the name Slocum? Does thee remember wearin' plaincloth like ours? Does'ee know the names Giles and Will and Mary and Ebbie and—"

The girl said something in an Indian tongue, and Will said, "She says she knows thee not, Ma. I'm afraid this isn't—"

"Yet awhile! Ask her to show us her hands!"

Will spoke in her tongue. The girl, warming to his words and his good looks, meekly extended both hands. Ruth grasped them fervently and looked at them, hope collapsing in her breast.

There was no damaged fingertip. Every slender finger had a nail. Ruth sighed, looked across all the fingers again, then shook her head. Suddenly feeling a thousand years old, she lifted the stranger's hands and bent her face down to press her cheek against the fingers, then let them go, saying, "So sorry to've bothered thee, dear . . ." And she turned away from the crowd, blinded by tears, stumbling along down the slope with Will guiding her by an elbow.

"Thee's hopin' too hard, Ma," he said. "Thee can't wish somebody into being Frannie."

"Well," she said after a few more steps, "I'll see plainer tomorrow. And I'll not embarrass 'ee by scolding bystanders."

* * *

It was just as well that Ruth's hopes had diminished, because in the following days there was not one person presented who could have been taken for Frances. Ruth went to the assemblage every day, seeing things happen that wrenched her heart. Half a dozen parents found their sons or daughters, aunts and uncles found nieces and nephews, and a cousin found a cousin. In a couple of instances the reunions were tearful and joyous, making Ruth's heart ache with bittersweet sympathy and envy. But most often the captives who were identified by their relatives turned and clung to their Indian families and finally had to be taken away by force, or reconciled to the repatriation through long and tearful conferences with their Indian escorts.

And the last haunting notion Ruth Slocum had as her sons struck the camp and loaded the horses was that, dispirited and disappointed though she was, at least she had not had to bear the agony of seeing her daughter recoil from her and cling tearfully to the arms of an Indian mother. That would have been too much to bear.

Captain Pipe's Town

So this was what it was about, all the teaching of Small Female Bear and Flicker two years ago in her *wiktut*, and the giggly jokes of the women in the moon lodge since then, but now Good Face could not even think of the teaching or the joking because of the excitement down in her body and the wildness in the eyes of the young man who crouched over her and fondled every part of her, especially the untouchable parts. It was almost beyond belief that she and he were alone in a *wikwam* together all naked, neither wearing anything but a tiny medicine bag on a thong around the neck and she the vermilion spots on her cheekbones and he the tattoo marks across his forehead, and that he was going to put his thing inside her, just as the old woman had said men always want to do, and it was especially amazing that such a thrilling and frightening thing was permitted and approved of because each had decided the other was of the right kind. She was panting with impatience and the tingly place between her hips kept clenching and oozing. It was like the mouth of someone terribly hungry who smells rich food and drools for it. He seemed to know of her hunger down there, yet she was not embarrassed by his knowing.

His name was Tchaneegeu, Like Wood, and he was her husband beginning this night. Long ago shamed for spying on women, he had since become a warrior. He had fought Long Knives when they came up from Kentuckee to burn Shawnee villages. Around his left side, under his arm, he had a long scar from the sword of a riding soldier, but he had brought the soldier's scalp home, and no one mocked him anymore. Like Wood was not tall, really only about as tall as Good Face herself, but he was muscular and fine to look at, with skin the color of dark tobacco and straight white teeth in bow-shaped lips that gave him a heart-melting smile. He kept his eyebrows and all his hair except a scalp lock plucked out, and sometimes he reminded her of the warrior who had first taken her away from her *wapsi* family so many winters ago, as well as she could remember that man, which was only vaguely after all that time.

Like Wood was proud of being a warrior, and it had made a bold suitor out of him. From what Good Face had heard women confide in the moon hut, a man's bravery made him desirable as much as a handsome face and body did. Like Wood was both handsome and brave. But there was more too. Like Wood may have killed a man who cut him in war, but he also had something beautiful in his spirit that enabled him to make a flute and a love song to play through it for Good Face, and he had played it for her from a distance until her heart had absorbed every note, and all the little birdlike trills and sobs of the flute song, so much that whenever she heard it, she felt the yearning in her belly and hips. Even now as Like Wood opened her thighs to make room for himself, her memory of his flute song rose and curled and chirruped in her soul like the voice of a thrush.

He caressed her breasts and then her belly and then the inside of her thigh, making all her skin quiver, and said, "How much you please my eyes!" and his eyes were indeed blazing with delight. Once this past spring while bathing in a brook she had felt someone watching her, and wondered if he spied on her. He certainly could have done it many times, because he was one of those warriors and hunters who could slip up on anyone or anything, and had made himself a master of invisibility. The warriors often practiced that art because the Long Knife armies were always so massed and strong with weapons that only stealth and swiftness could kill them. She had often heard Tuck Horse speak of these things, for war was in the air again; already the Long Knives, from whom the People had fled so far in the east, were rumored to be encroaching from the south, into the O-hi-o lands they had been told to stay out of. They had attacked Shawnees, Wyandots, and Mingoes, and even their own friends the Piankashaws.

Now, even as Good Face's yearning grew unbearable, she knew that this was not a good time for them to be making a baby, because, as the old woman had warned her, one should not be doing so when the hoofbeats and the bugles of the enemy were coming close.

But the old woman had said also that this pleasure could be greater than even the pleasures of eating and laughing, and at this moment that seemed more true and more important than the warnings.

After the incredible pleasure, she was surprised to find that she could still talk and think. She got up to put more sticks on the fire, aware of his eyes on her, and then he asked her to stand beside the fire and let him look at her, which she did until his man-part was stiff again. He stood up from their bed and prodded her belly with it, and then turned her around and prodded her backside with it with his hands reaching around to hold her breasts and knead their nipples and stroke down over her abdomen. Soon she was on the bed on her hands and knees with him kneeling behind her doing it so forcefully that their skin was smacking like hand claps, and suns were bursting behind her eyes, and such an ecstasy exploded in her that she could not hold herself up, and when she became aware of anything again, she was lying with her face on the fur of the bearskin bedding, gasping for breath and realizing that she had been yelping aloud. Outside, people were laughing and making yipping sounds, probably imitating her own. Like Wood was lying sweaty beside her and breathing fast, and he laughed and shouted to the people outside, "Yes! Like Wood pleases his Red-Hair and she pleases him!"

Later he sat beside her on the bed playing the love song through the flute while she waited, nude, for him to be able again. She could have told the old woman now that this man was certainly a right man, not a wrong one, and she was wondering whether she would ever want to do anything again besides this. When she fell asleep before dawn from exhaustion, she saw her *wapsi* blood-mother in a dream, seeing the face as she had not been able to remember it consciously for years, and in her dream she was telling her mother that this husband was in every way a right man, in no way a wrong one.

And so they coupled, frequently and joyously, amazed at their ever-renewing need of each other, but even after a whole year of their marriage, Good Face's flint and Like Wood's steel had not made the fire of a new life. Every moon her blood came down, and she would go to the women's menstrual lodge, where the other women would joke with her about how hot she and Like Wood must be, judging by the sounds that came from their lodge so often. And she thought, yes, how hot, and one should not want anything more, but she did have another yearning, which was to have the fire of a life growing in her. She believed that in every way Like Wood was a right man to make a child with. And though there were war rumors, they were from far away; there had been peace and a feeling of safety here in the valley of the Tymochtee Sipu where her Lenapeh People had settled; because of this sense of peace, it seemed to be a right time to have a child, and she wanted a baby to grow out of their passion for each other, a baby to raise while there *was* peace.

She was in the menstrual lodge in the moon of the Green Corn Harvest with four other women when they heard a distant hubbub of excitement in the town. Then a messenger woman came hurrying up the sun-dappled path, her face full of distress.

War was coming again. The Long Knife *wapsituk* were making a new Town Destroyer army to come into this part of the country now.

The first thought Good Face had was that her Spirit Helper, the small female bear, had kept her from getting with child because this was coming.

And so she was thankful for the wisdom of the Spirit Helper. But she was not fully happy. She yearned to be a mother.

As an adult now, she sat in the councils, and there she learned why the *wapsituk* were building armies again. These were the rumors:

The armies would come northward from the O-hi-o Sipu to punish the Shawnee, the Miami, and the Lenapeh for having refused to go to a peace treaty the year before. The three tribes had said no, there will be no peace while the Long Knives keep

crossing the O-hi-o Sipu into our country. But the whites had
kept crossing the great river and cutting down trees to make forts
and towns and farms. They had killed much game on this side of
the river, and had even murdered Indian hunters here in their own
lands. And so instead of going to the peace treaty, the tribes continued to go down to the great valley of the river and attack the
wapsi intruders. That was why the army would be coming: to
punish the tribes for defending their own homelands. It was the
old usual reason: *wapsituk* wanted still more land, and having
whipped the English, the Long Knives thought they could move
into any land they wanted and punish any tribes that tried to keep
them out.

So it would be necessary to withdraw again from the path of
Town Destroyers. The Council decided to move the people north
toward some place too far away and too strong for the Long
Knives to attack. Such a place existed: the big Miami trading town
of Kekionga, which guarded the important portage between the
east-flowing Maumee Sipu and the west-flowing Wabash Sipu.
Good Face had been there with her family to trade, and she had
seen that Kekionga was not just one town, but a cluster of towns
around the Maumee headwaters. The chiefs there were powerful
and widely known: Peshewa, a half-breed trader whose French
name was Richardville; Le Gris, who hated the Long Knife *wapsituk* with a fury; and their war chief Michiconogkwa, the Little
Turtle, who had once destroyed a *wapsi* army that had dared
attack the place by sneaking up from the west.

Kekionga was always growing. Downstream along the Mau-
mee Sipu from the Miami chiefs' towns there were new villages of
Shawnee, who had been moving north to keep a distance from the
Long Knives.

And so the Lenapeh would do also. Surely, the Council said, no
wapsi army could come northward through the vast wetlands and
swamps to attack Kekionga, where the warriors of so many
nations now lived. The councils of the Tymochtee towns decided
to withdraw to that stronghold, if only long enough for the army to
wear itself out and go home. They would go after the Green Corn
harvest and the ceremony to guarantee Corn Mother's favor.

They set off in late summer, northwestward through the boggy
lands with everything they could carry, with rumors of the Town
Destroyers close behind.

                           *   *   *

Good Face had never seen such vast cornfields, so many dwellings. Many new *wikwams* covered the north bank of the Maumee Sipu, and the fresh bent-pole frameworks of many more, still not covered with bark. In every direction spread fields of corn, beans, and squash, with pole scaffolds for the crow scarers. These villages too had already harvested their green or sweet corn, but their flour corn, beans, squashes, pumpkins, and sunflowers were still ripening in the fields. Here was so much food no one should ever go hungry.

The Shawnee and Lenapeh refugees would be living a little farther downstream, and here Good Face and her parents began building a *wikwam*. They expected it to be only temporary, until the army was gone. But if for some reason they could not go back to their home village, they would be living here by Kekionga through the winter, and so they had to build well. They worked on the frame of their home as the leaves of the trees turned yellow and red, and most of the men went away to hunt for meat for the winter.

They did not even have covering over the frame before messengers came from the south, with the terrible warning that the army appeared to be approaching.

Old Tuck Horse said, mouth grim: "Joseph was wrong. Our old brother at Detroit. Do you remember what he said? That we were so old we might live out our years in peace before the Long Knives would ever come into this part of the country. But they are on our heels again. I am at a poor age for a man to be. I am not old enough to lie down and die in bed, but I am too old to go out and die fighting the *wapsituk*."

It was in this time of growing dread that Like Wood stopped giving Good Face the love pleasure. He explained that it was his need now to conserve his vigor for the war path.

She sank down inside. But she remembered the teaching: when the enemy's bugles and hoofbeats are coming close, it is a wrong time to lie back and make children. Instead, this was the time for young women to spread out through the fields and gather all the harvest they could, to harvest food for the winter, to gather food for as long as possible before the Town Destroyer arrived, and then get out of his way and carry the harvest farther northward toward safety. Children and old people would begin leaving at once, going northwestward toward the Eel River. The warriors would go and dance at the war post, and then Little Turtle, war chief of the Miami, would do what he could against the army with the warriors he had.

Unfortunately, he had few. Most of the men were hunting, and so far away that they could not be summoned in time. Despite the great size of Kekionga and the population of the nearby villages, fewer than two hundred warriors were here.

The size of the Long Knife army was fifteen times that many. It had three cannons. And it had come farther and faster than anyone could have expected. Never had the plight of the People looked worse.

Good Face pressed her forehead against her husband's chest and smelled the war paint on him, and said, "I shall pray that until this bad time is past, you will be invisible to the eyes of the enemy." Tears seemed to squeeze from her heart. She turned away and ran to get baskets and join the women in the fields.

Under the bright autumn sky the leaves and stalks in the fields were yellow-brown and dry. The distant treetops beyond the fields were glorious reds and golds, shimmering in sun heat.

Through these vast fields the women of all the tribes now moved swiftly, working together, yanking off corn ears and bean pods, filling baskets and bags and blankets. Their work made a constant rustling, hissing noise amid the dry plants, and they stirred up dust and grasshoppers as they dragged the swollen containers back out of the fields. They breathed the dust and spat mud. There was enough ripened food in these fields that the whole population of Kekionga, including all the refugees, would have had plenty for the coming winter had there been time to harvest and preserve all of it. But in this one frantic day of harvest there was time for the women to collect only a small part of it.

That night, Little Turtle's warriors built big bonfires on the river side of the town, then made an ambush line behind the fires. Soldiers coming to the river and seeing the fires would think that the people of the Kekionga villages were unaware of the army's approach. With so few warriors against such a large army, Little Turtle had to make tricks, and this was to be his first trick.

Good Face, with the women and children and old people, headed north away from the towns in the evening. They led packhorses, and every woman carried a load of food on her back, almost as much as a horse could carry. Even bone-sore old people like Tuck Horse and Flicker shouldered as much as they could bear.

That night they had to stop often to rest under autumn stars, and they looked back toward Kekionga, that place they had thought would be safe from any army. Good Face was thankful for the night silence, knowing that no shooting had started yet to endanger her beautiful husband.

Then the soft voices would come urging along the line, and they hoisted their heavy loads and moved on, in the darkness smelling the woods, smelling the horse droppings and sweat, smelling the precious corn and beans they carried.

They stopped again after the middle of the night, and it was then that the sputtering sound of gunshots and a drone of faraway voices rose in the night behind them. Good Face felt her heart race, and her mouth was dry with fear. But soon all fell silent.

They went on as daylight paled, then all that day, crossing into the Eel River valley. They stopped at dark that night. The sky in the south was full of red smoke. Town Destroyers and corn killers had again entered the country. Winter would come soon, and the shelter and crops of Kekionga were turning to ashes.

And somewhere down there, Good Face knew, either dead or hurt or in danger even at this moment, was Like Wood, the loving and handsome man who had won her with a flute song and brought her the greatest hope and pleasure she had ever known, or even imagined. She stood with her old parents, gazing at the red glow above the treetops, and it reflected in their eyes when they looked at each other.

"That army probably will keep coming on," Tuck Horse said. "They know there are more towns up here to burn. They won't stop coming until they are given a beating. But Little Turtle has too few warriors to give them a beating. I fear we will have to keep moving on." He sighed. "Why was I not born in the good days, before the *wapsini* first put his chair on the shore of Turtle Island?"

The next morning the families moved farther along the river. When they looked back, there was always smoke billowing up.

As they moved along the trail, they saw a small force of warriors going down toward the enemy. *"Wehlee heeleh!"* Tuck Horse exclaimed. "Hunters have heard the shooting and are going there! May many more do so!"

The next day, as the families were moving down the Eel River path, something happened not far behind them, something they could only hear through the woods and see nothing of, but something so terrible that instead of running in fear from the noise of it, they all stopped and turned to listen in fascination.

So many guns were shooting at once that their noise rolled like thunder for a while, and then as they diminished to single bangs and flurries of shots, a shrill pulsating wail of many voices rose, so many war trills they sounded like a shrieking wind, rising and descending and rising again. Good Face looked at the craggy visage of Tuck Horse, and even though he did not say anything, she could tell that he liked the sound of it; inside their wrinkled sockets his hooded eyes were glittering like an eagle's and his lips were drawn back in a frightening expression that could have been a snarl or a grin. The breeze was stirring his silvery hair. After listening long and standing tense, he at last opened his clenched jaws and emitted a sound like the hiss of a snake. She had never seen her old Lenapeh father look truly fierce before, and it was enough to make her shiver because she knew he was pleased with the killing going on back there.

It seemed a long time before all the banging and shrieking and yipping stopped. Then, not knowing what had come of it all, the old ones and the women and children lifted the bags and baskets of corn they had set down and resumed their way down the riverside path, talking fast and low to each other, looking back often to see if a messenger would come and explain something, or whether Long Knife riding soldiers might yet come storming down the path after them. Good Face staggered under her load, a blanket so full of corn ears that she had just been able to tie its corners together. It was heavy and awkward, always shifting its shape, the knots always digging into the flesh of her arms where she had thrust them through to sling the blanket on.

But even heavier than her load, and growing just as relentlessly heavier, was the thought of the shooting she had heard: How could anyone in it—such as her beloved husband Like Wood—not have been killed?

The evening turned cold as soon as the sun went down, but the refugees were afraid to build fires by which the Long Knife soldiers might find them. And so they huddled together in the darkness and shivered, because all of their blankets and hides were full of the corn and beans they had saved. Good Face wanted to untie her blanket, pour the corn out, and wrap herself for warmth until morning, when she could fill the blanket again. That made perfect sense to her. But she did not because if the soldiers came and they had to flee, the corn would be left on the ground. Someone later might then go hungry. Flicker had taught her that one does not do something selfish at the expense of the others. And so she shivered in the cold autumn night air and prayed for the safety of her warrior husband and all the other warriors who were back there prowling the edges of the army. She knew that Like Wood, if he still lived, was also out in the cold night without a blanket. In fact, when she last saw him, he was wearing nothing but breechcloth and leggings. And, like her and all these women, children, and elders with her, he would be very hungry. He had taken a pouch of cornmeal and maple sugar into battle with him, but that would be gone by now.

Here we are laden with food, and no way to cook, she thought.

Then a runner came. What he had to tell made the People laugh and shout. Three hundred of the Long Knife soldiers, coming this way, had been ambushed by Little Turtle and a hundred warriors. It was the battle they had heard. About seventy of the soldiers were killed and the rest fled toward the Maumee Sipu, where the main part of the army was still burning towns and crops.

Now it was deemed safe to build fires for a camp and prepare something to eat. The runner said the People should stay here, not go back toward Kekionga, because most of that large army was still there below and surely more riding soldiers would be sent out to fight. If they did, Little Turtle meant to surprise and kill more of them. This runner was a Miami, and did not know Like Wood or any Lenapeh warriors or if they were safe. A few warriors—six or seven—had been killed or badly wounded, but he did not know whether any of those had been Lenapehs.

And so again Good Face had to try to rest with that great doubt tormenting her.

The next day passed quietly. The sky in the southeast was gray with smoke, but so few guns were heard that they might well have been just hunters killing meat for the army. Some of the Eel River Miamis came up the stream bringing cooked food, and some blankets and hides, and helped the elders and children make lean-tos and brush shelters. Much of the day was spent shelling the salvaged corn, making it less bulky to carry, and the cobs were burned for fuel, while some of the girls were put to work under Flicker's supervision to braid cord from corn shucks. It was wonderful to have cord again. It was useful at once for making shelters and for tying up carrying packs and bundles for their great loads of food.

And so, by the time night fell again, this crowded camp of refugees from Kekionga beside the Eel River had begun to feel something like a community, although much of their quiet thought and yearning was still directed southwest toward their great town, where the sky continued to glow with fire smoke, and where they had sons and brothers and fathers for whom to pray.

The sun had just lit up the yellow treetops the next morning when a brief sputter of distant gunshots caused the wakeful to raise their heads and listen thoughtfully. And then when the sun was less than halfway up the sky, a closer, louder storm of shooting brought all the people to their feet. It was not as close as the other battle had been, but the gunfire rolled and rattled on and on, and as before, the war cries wailed on and on.

Eventually it dwindled to silence. And then for a long time the people simply waited, the dappled fall sunlight trembling in a breeze, the clear water of the little river flowing by, and they wondered, and they prayed.

The Long Knife army was gone at last.

It had been in the Maumee country almost a week. It had worked very hard to destroy everything, and had succeeded. It burned five towns of the Miami, Shawnee, and Lenapeh. It dug up the food caches, cut down all the vast cornfields and made mountainous piles of corn and beans and vegetables, hay and fence rails, and burned them to ash and char. It looted and burned the trading store. The whole valley smoked for days afterward, and whenever a breeze blew, black and gray ashes swirled up and then drifted down.

And yet the People were fiercely proud. They felt that Little Turtle and his warriors had defeated and driven off an army ten times their number. In two ambushes they had killed almost two hundred soldiers and wounded many more. They had so frightened the Long Knife general that instead of retaliating with his main force, he turned it south and fled to the O-hi-o. It was not likely another Long Knife army would dare come here again, and it was certain that if Little Turtle ever had all his thousand warriors on hand, instead of the two hundred he had had available, no *wapsi* army could ever set a torch to a single Kekionga building again. Kekionga was a good place, a great Miami town. It would be rebuilt. And crops would grow even better next year because of the burned ground and the ashes.

Thirty warriors had died in driving out the army. They were mourned and buried and honored. Many lay wounded, being healed and honored by the women.

In the eye of this whirlwind of emotion, Good Face quietly thanked the Creator over and over. Her husband had not been hurt.

Tuck Horse surprised his family. He came from a meeting of chiefs and elders, some of them Midewiwin probably, and announced that it was time to leave the ashes of Kekionga and go back to the Niagara country for the winter, or longer. He said the defeat of the Long Knife army here might mean the Lenapeh could now return to their homelands, and he wanted to learn for himself whether it was so. And he had it in his mind that it would be easier to feed his family back there, the Town Destroyers having burned all the food here. Though he was too old to hunt well, he could still make chairs to sell at the trading posts, as he had in the old days. With money from chairs, he could buy replacements for some of the things the soldiers had destroyed here.

Those were all his good reasons for making such a long journey. There was another reason he did not talk about to his family, but Good Face's husband knew it, and he told her. Little Turtle and the other leaders here needed to know what was happening in other places, and so they were sending spies out in every direction. These spies had to be people who would not arouse suspicion. An old craftsman and trader like Tuck Horse could go anywhere with his family and seem harmless. He knew Midewiwin everywhere, had wisdom and long memory, and knew many languages. He could observe and then reliably relate what he had seen, and could also carry messages. Like Wood said, "A great war chief must be like an eagle, seeing over all the land. Since he cannot go everywhere on wings and look down with his own eyes, he uses the eyes of his people and his friends who go everywhere. The eyes of your father can be trusted to see and know."

Like Wood was lying beside her with his cheek propped on the heel of his hand, in the faint glow from the dying night fire in their shelter, a hastily built lean-to, a temporary home so close to the charred ruins of Kekionga that the smell of ash was always strong. The Miamis had already begun rebuilding good *wikwams*, but the family of Tuck Horse would not need one this winter because they would be on the old trail to the east. Good Face could remember all those long travels from her girlhood, and although she was reluctant to go so far again, she was also eager to see the places of her memories: the waterfall, the hills, the long beaches.

She asked him: "Do you suppose the great Erie Water will seem as big to us now as when we crossed it as children? I have noticed that some places seem smaller when one goes back to them after a long while."

He smiled. "A water you cannot see across will still seem just as big, I am sure. You can tell me how it will have seemed when you come back, my wife."

For a moment she thought she had heard him wrong, then with a prickly flood of fearful sensation she rose on her elbow to search his eyes with hers. "Husband, you say you do not come with us?"

He stroked her bare shoulder. "Soldiers of the Long Knife army might yet come back to avenge our victory. The war chiefs ask that all of warrior age stay near. It is my duty as a warrior to be here if the Town Destroyers come again."

She bit inside her lips and blinked against tears, and through her head raced notions of how to avoid such a long and far separation from this beautiful man who was her passion. "I could . . . I could stay here with you, then, my husband. I could build us a good *wikwam* to keep us warm in the winter. I should not go east anyway, where the *wapsi* perhaps still look for me!" His face was swimming in the tears that she could not blink away. He rolled her onto her back and hovered over her, looking down on her with tender sadness in his eyes, a trace of a smile on his lips, but slowly shaking his head.

"Your old parents cannot travel so long and hard a road without your help. And because they will be spying on the *wapsituk*, there will surely be times when they will need your ear for that language."

She was shaking her head, trying not to show the weakness of her heart by sobbing aloud. "My husband, that is no reason. I hardly remember that language at all! I want to stay with my husband! My need for you . . ." She remembered the terrible unknowing when he was fighting the Long Knives within hearing distance of the gunfire; to be as far away as the other end of Erie while he might be fighting again to defend Kekionga, that would be more terrible an unknowing than she could bear!

But it would have to be, she realized finally. It was for the good of her old parents and for the good of the People. And so with a heart full of sadness and dread, she quit protesting. In the last glow of the campfire, he placed himself upon her and she opened herself to him with great pleasure and deep sadness.

Three days later she was in a log canoe with her old father and mother, yellow leaves spilling from the treetops in a cold autumn wind from behind them, the leaves falling to float on the clear green water, the canoe and the leaves sliding down the Maumee Sipu toward the Erie lake, her husband the warrior remaining behind while they started the long eastward journey that would separate her from her husband's warmth for a whole winter.

And then in a few more days they were on the deck of a small French sailboat with ten other passengers, Indian and white, speeding on the wind over the vast blue water toward the far end of the lake, the great white winglike sail booming and ruffling and the ropes and wood creaking, the deck slanting underfoot, wind moaning, waves bashing. What a thing a sailboat was, such a thing as she had long ago seen afar on the horizons of this lake! What a thing a sailboat was, and how exhilarating it was to ride in—until she began feeling dizzy in her head and unstable in her belly.

From that time on she was almost always hanging over the side, clutching the wooden rail and tarred ropes, vomiting even when there was nothing to vomit, strings of slobber from her mouth curving away in the wind, to be lost in the racing foam below. Sometimes she was sprayed not just by the lake water, but by the vomit of other passengers next to her at the gunwale. Everyone was sick except Flicker and the French sailors of the boat. This time Flicker had with her none of the medicine she had given to quell the sickness in the canoes so long ago. The old woman just sat with her blanket hugged around her as if holding her guts in place and refused to get sick. The Frenchmen laughed and joked in their strange language and worked their sail ropes, the smell off their filthy bodies making Good Face sick again every time she thought she was getting better.

With such misery, she sailed away from her husband, and if her heart was aching, she was now too sick to notice it.

CHAPTER TEN

Ruth Slocum, feeling the ember of hope begin to glow again for the first time since the prisoner exchange had dimmed it two years ago, sent her sixteen-year-old son Isaac riding to fetch Giles and Will. Then she began pacing, rubbing the arthritic knuckles of one hand with the palm of the other, constantly stopping at windows to look for their return. She saw her face reflected in the pane of a cupboard, and smiled at the anxiety in it.

After a dozen years, one'd think thee'd learnt a little patience, she thought. What's ten more minutes of them getting here, after all this eternity?

They came trotting, not galloping, she noticed, down through the stark bare hills where hardly anything had yet begun to show green. There were more houses along the river course now than trees. For a moment she remembered how her husband Jonathan had looked riding down from there—so much the way Giles looked now—but always when he had started down that slope, he emerged from woods. There were no woods anymore, and even the stumps were just decaying, misshapen lumps amid the over-grazed grasses of the slope. All the woods for miles around had been cut both for building and for charcoal-making. Even though Ebenezer could sell his anthracite coal to the forges as fast as he could mine it out, most of the smiths and forges were accustomed to using charcoal. The tarry-smelling smoke of charcoal pits was a constant miasma in the valley lately. It was not the beautiful place it had been a mere decade ago, but the important fact seemed to be that people were prospering here, and the Slocums, due to their early start, were prospering even more than most.

But, she always reminded herself, thinking of her father and husband and daughter, what we sacrificed for this prosperity!

She had tea ready when her sons clumped in with their muddy boots. As they stuffed sweet cakes into their mouths, she broached the news to them.

"Does thee remember," she said, "a certain officer by the name of Proctor who passed through here when General Sullivan's army went through? Will, I fancy thee does, especially."

"I do indeed," Will said. "The pompous war-eagle whose feathers got all ruffled when craven Quakers wouldn't call him 'Colonel.'"

"Well," she said, "it seems he's passed through again, some days ago, and didn't do us the courtesy of stopping by to say hello, but that's not the point, as I doubt he'd have remembered us. I've just learnt from Mr. Pickering the court clerk that the old soldier is on a mission into the Lake Erie country to mollify the Indians up there."

"Oh, really!" exclaimed Giles with a mocking half smile. "Now, how strange I didn't notice an army go through here."

"No army, son. Just a body of commissioners going to talk peaceably to them."

"Ah, that sounds better," Will said. "Whose commission, did they say?"

"The Secretary of War, Mr. Knox."

"Ah, yes, the old two-pronged strategy, or should I say two-tongued? Send a peace emissary around one flank and an army around the other. They're already recruiting a force to go try again what General Harmar failed to do last fall. Hah!"

"Don't thee make fun o' peacemakers, son. If he succeeds, the army mightn't have to go. Let's pray that. But I think you know I didn't ask thee here to talk idly about government schemes."

"Idly, indeed not," said Giles. "On the contrary, Ma, thee's surely got a scheme thyself, and it involves us. I'd reckon it goes like this: we race up the road after Mr. Proctor and ask could we attach ourselves under his protection, then go where he goes, to look for Frances. Something on that order, Ma?"

She couldn't keep from smiling. "Something quite on that order, yes, son. But I'd not 'send' thee on such an arduous errand again. I'd ask thee to accompany me till I catch up with 'em. Then thee c'd turn home, if thee'd a mind to . . . Thee's both journeyed so often on what's really just my forlorn hope. . . ."

Giles leaned forward over the table, tilted his head and wagged a forefinger at her. "Oh, no. That last expedition to Tioga aged thee ten years, and that was a mere jaunt compared with Erie. I'll go, but thee'll not. And pray thee, Ma, don't argue the matter."

"Giles is right," Will threw in. "He and I'll go. Thee's not hardy enough, and thee's needed here to watch the family's doings anyway."

"Further amendment to this grand scheme," Giles said. "Thee can stay here too, Will. Ma needs thee here for the planting, now that Eb and Ben are become millers and miners and whatnot up in the hollow. Besides, thee can't abide Proctor, nor him thee."

"I could go with'ee, Giles," sixteen-year-old Isaac said, squirming with eagerness. He could scarcely remember his sister Frannie, having been but a babe-in-arms when she was abducted, but Isaac and Joseph had both made her a legend and a mystery in their shared imaginations.

"Stop. Too many volunteers," said Giles, slamming his palm down on the tabletop. He was thirty-two now and as solid a man as his father had been, but his short military career in the Revolution and his travels in search of Frannie on the frontier had tempered him to a harder edge than Jonathan Slocum had ever had. When he raised his voice or banged a hand like this, he was usually heard out. "Faith in everybody's Inner Light is a lovely virtue, and I pray this family always has it. But there's not that much Inner Light burning strong out yonder right now, considering what's been done lately, by red man or white. While thee's explaining the Friends' creed, a bushloper will cut thy throat and a red man'll lift thy scalp. Until some magnificent saint of peacemaking goes over the land making all men's hearts right and bright, I'd as soon have as few members of my beloved family out there as possible. I'm only one, and I reckon I'm enough, and less at risk than the rest o' thee lambs'd be."

Ruth Slocum looked across the table at him, one eyebrow up, her lips compressed, appraising his words, remembering the trials and the hardships and the brutal people she had seen at Tioga. She nodded, finally, and said, "Very well, Giles. Mr. Proctor told Mr. Pickering he'd go the old trail to Tioga, then Painted Post, and the usual way past the Genesee, all o' which thee's been over. He left here five days ago."

"Then if I leave tomorrow, unless he's a fast mover, I ought to overtake him at the Horseheads or thereabouts. Work hard, little brothers. Thee'll miss me sorely at planting time."

Cattaraugus, New York

Good Face held Flicker's arm and steadied her on the mud-slickened path to the Long Knife soldiers' house, following Tuck Horse, who carried a bent-wood chair.

This was the last of the chairs Tuck Horse had made here during the winter. Now spring was breaking. The old man hoped to sell this chair to the *wapsi* soldier chief himself, and then his family could start the long journey back to Kekionga. Good Face was almost dizzy with impatience to go back to her husband. With this spring thaw, they could start on the long path of return. They would not go back by sailboat, but by horseback, and Good Face was thankful that she would not have to face the boat-sickness again.

They had been able to spend only a few days at the sacred Great Falling Water; then they came to this town to watch this peace-talking soldier chief. The town was Cattaraugus, halfway between Cornplanter's Seneca town and Niagara. The Long Knife soldier chief conducting this peace council was called Proctor, a hard name to pronounce. He was known to have been with the Town Destroyer Sullivan years before. He was mature and strong-looking. He was easy to like but hard to trust. It was believed that he was here to show a decoy of peace so the chiefs would be off guard, and so the chiefs had humored him by pretending to believe him. Tuck Horse in his days near Proctor's camp had sold three chairs to lesser officers. Now Proctor himself wanted one to use in the long councils. Good Face might be needed to translate in selling this chair, as the soldiers were using money. Her skin had paled during the long winter, and so Flicker had stained her face and neck and hands with dye from last year's walnut hulls. To hide her red hair, Good Face wore a bandanna over her head, as she had at the Niagara trading store when she was a girl.

The officers were not in council at this time of day, so a soldier led them to the cabin where the officers stayed. The soldier spoke outside the door, and the big man called Proctor came out, wearing his long blue coat with shiny boards and braids on the shoulders and shiny buttons on the cuffs and chest. He nodded to

Tuck Horse, peered at Good Face intently for a moment, then rubbed his palms together and turned his attention to the new chair. He put his huge hand on the back of it, pressing the chair down hard and twisting his hand to and fro. It was so tightly made it did not wiggle or squeak, and the officer stuck out his lower lip and nodded. Then he picked the chair up, as easily as if it were a twig, and examined the joints and the woven cane. Again he nodded, then put the chair on the ground and sat on it, moving his bulk this way and that, and the chair still did not squeak or wobble.

"Good work," he said. He held up his hand with fingers spread. "Five shillings," he said.

Tuck Horse looked at him long, unsmiling. Then he held up both hands with fingers spread.

"Ten!" Proctor exclaimed. "Ten shillings for a chair?" For some reason he turned toward Good Face when he said this.

She remembered "ten" as the *wapsi* word for all the fingers, and she remembered "five" for those of one hand. It was the way she and her little brothers had learned counting, and when she heard those words, most of the rest of them came back to her. At Kekionga she had often heard the number words, and now she could remember *one two three four five six seven eight nine ten.* She knew too that Proctor had said the chair was *good.* Proctor was looking at her eyes when she said, as well as she could remember to pronounce the words, "Five no. Ten yes."

The big man drew his chin down long but with a mocking smile barely showing on his lips.

"B'God! I was a carpenter before the army, and I know that's a fair-made chair, but no ten shillings' worth! Seven, then."

She had understood virtually nothing of what he said, but she knew *chair, no, ten,* and *seven.* She counted on her fingers and held up seven, then raised another, and said, "Eight." She had no idea what it was eight of, but she knew eight was closer to the ten her father wanted than to the five the officer had said at first.

Proctor, who was pretending not to like this haggling but had a sparkle in his eye that showed enjoyment, held up eight of his own fingers, looked doubtfully at them, shook his head. Then he half bent one finger and said, "Very well. Seven and sixpence. Lieutenant, get them seven shillin's and a half. And see if ye can find that Slocum fellow, who joined us at Painted Post, the Quaker who was looking for his sister."

A hot flush of fear went down from Good Face's scalp through her flanks.

Slocum!

"Why, sir," the lieutenant said, "I think he left just yesterday for Cornplanter's Town. Why, sir?"

"I have a notion," the colonel said, staring intently at Good Face. She understood hardly anything they had said, but she thought: He knows who I am. She said softly to Tuck Horse in Lenapeh, "Father, we must leave." She glanced at Flicker and saw a keen and suspicious look in her eyes; her old mother knew something odd was happening. The younger officer was walking toward a cabin.

"Leave?" Tuck Horse, looking a bit bewildered, reached for the chair. But the colonel's big hand came down on the chair back and gripped it.

"He wants the chair, Father. But we must go. I think they—"

"Then tell them to give me the money. We need it for horses to go back."

The colonel had raised a hand toward Good Face, then touched his lips and said, "You're that fellow's sister, aren't you?" She did not understand that, and was beginning to edge backward from his penetrating eyes when he said something she did understand: "Are you Frances Slocum?"

Her gaze fell to the ground. It was not in her nature to lie, but she was afraid to tell the truth. And she was backing away, glancing at Flicker, who, it seemed, now fully comprehended what was happening. Flicker came between her daughter and the colonel, taking her arm in a hard grip and turning her away from him, hissing in Lenapeh, "Tell him nothing! Husband, they will take her from us! We must leave now. Never mind this chair of sticks or the money! We must go!"

The colonel stood with his hand on the back of the chair, his other hand stroking down his chin as they edged away, backing and sidestepping, not quite running because they all feared he might send soldiers after them. The younger officer had emerged from the cabin, and the colonel told him something in short words, then the young one turned and hurried toward them. The colonel called out something, and the young officer called out something, and Good Face took her parents' arms to hurry them along. She heard the young man's trotting footsteps coming closer and turned to see him almost caught up, reaching for Tuck Horse.

When the officer's hand fell on Tuck Horse's shoulder, the old man stopped and whirled to face him, reaching at the same time for the knife that hung in a sheath under his left arm.

But the officer was smiling. "Here," he said.

He handed Tuck Horse a bag, shaking it as he did so to make coins jingle.

"Seven shillings six," the young man said. "B'God, I knew Indians are stupid, but not stupid enough to walk off and leave good money!"

And, not understanding him, Tuck Horse simply reached and took the bag, saying, *"Waneeshee."* He nodded once, and they walked away. When Good Face looked back, the colonel still stood with one hand on the chair back, still stroking his chin.

They did not wait to see whether soldiers would come for her. By the time the sun was halfway down the sky, they were on three horses, leading a packhorse they had just purchased, and on the trail that led through the woods south of the great Erie lake toward their distant home at Kekionga. Before next moon they would be home and Good Face would be in the embrace of her husband. She felt she had narrowly escaped from the soldiers.

Tuck Horse had learned more than he had hoped to learn: While the officer named Proctor was talking peace with the chiefs at Cattaraugus, the great Long Knife chief Washington was preparing another army to go this summer and punish Little Turtle for defeating the other army last year.

"I am sad to know of such treachery," he said, "but I am glad that I have heard of it. Little Turtle may already know of it from other spies. But the more his ears hear it, the more ready he will be to fight them when they come. We will be there. Ahhh! How I would like to be young enough to fight those treacherous people one more time!"

But Good Face was thinking: Let there be a while for me in my husband's arms before soldiers come again.

Kekionga

In her winter absence, her husband's passion for her had been waiting and growing, and for two days after her return, Good Face and Like Wood seldom left their bed.

Lying beside him naked, exhausted, and tingling between her

hips, their commingled sacred ooze cooling on the skin of her thigh, spirit glowing with love and gratitude, she dozed, dreamed, and awakened to new caresses. Once his flute song awakened her—or she dreamed that it had. They murmured and whispered, telling of what they had done and seen and endured while apart. Like Wood told her that the only real hardship he had had to endure was her absence, though he had gone on some long, cold winter hunts and a scouting journey as far down as the Long Knife fort on the O-hi-o. She said that the only hardship she had had to endure was *his* absence, though the sailboat journey going east had made her very ill. Returning by horseback in the cold spring-time had been so hard for her parents with their old aching bones that Good Face herself had to manage all the horses all the way back—finding water and graze for them, keeping them collected at overnight camps, calming and containing them when they smelled and heard things in the night, tending to their hooves along stony trails. She had earned her father's praise for her growing skill with horses, and she carried that praise in her heart.

She said now, "I came to know each horse as well as the people of my family." And she laughed. She liked the unfamiliar pleasure of making a story for her husband. "The packhorse, he was like my father, grumpy but able. The white-face mare was like my mother. She was wise and patient and could see far ahead."

"I too am your family," Like Wood said, smiling. "Was any horse like me?"

She tilted her head and looked at him for a moment, covered her smile with her fingertips, and said, "No, husband. We did not have a stallion that could make flute songs!"

A few days after their return from the east, Tuck Horse was asked to come and visit at trader chief Richardville's house and talk with chiefs of the allied tribes. He was to bring his family.

Peshewa Richardville, the kindly, smiling, but sly-looking chief, seemed as rich as the white men Good Face had heard of called *kings*. Here in his house the light of candles and lamps gleamed on silver pots and polished picture frames, the air was rich with the aromas of coffee and chocolate, and some of the women of the household wore shawls made of a cloth that was called silk and shimmered like moonlight on water.

Buckongahelas was here, the Lenapeh warrior chief with his long, strong, scarred profile and calm eyes. Here was Blue Jacket of the Shawnee, with a tawny face looking hard as stone until a narrow smile would barely show and his eyes would glitter. Between those two, the Miami war chief Little Turtle looked mild and harmless. He was not big. His forehead was shaved back to the top of his head, and his eyes were so large and guileless they looked like a child's. But his physique was compact and graceful, and plainly he was the light of intelligence to whom the chiefs all turned. It was he who did most of the asking and telling and nodding. He listened a long time to Tuck Horse, and it was good to see how keen the great chief's attention was. Good Face was proud of her father and knew that his thoughts and observations must be valuable.

But while seeming to watch her father and Little Turtle, she was covertly glancing at a strangely handsome young warrior who stood over Little Turtle's shoulder. Her eyes were drawn to him again and again.

He was tall, dressed in a close-fitting coat of nearly white elk-hide decorated with colored quillwork in designs of wildflowers, with a wide sash of silk around his waist, a small silver-trimmed pistol protruding from the sash, and a crescent-shaped silver gorget gleaming at his throat. Several times when she was sneaking looks at this man, his eyes caught hers and she would look down, feeling flushed. She hoped that her husband Like Wood did not see her and this warrior glancing at each other. It was inappropriate for a man and woman to be looking directly at each other. Their attentions would have been misunderstood.

She presumed that he was looking at her because of her pale skin and red hair.

Those were the very reasons why she was looking at him. His long hair was as red as hers, and his complexion as light.

That night she learned from her husband something about the red-haired man. Like Wood had seen them looking at each other but did not seem to be jealous.

The man was Little Turtle's son-in-law. His name was Apekonit, the name of a food root like a wild potato. He had been brought back from a raid beyond the O-hi-o when he was a boy of about eight, adopted by a Miami family, and, growing to be a considerable warrior, was favored by Little Turtle. He had married the war chief's daughter Wanagapeth, the Sweet Breeze. He could always be found beside Little Turtle, in battle or in Council. He had killed many *wapsituk* and was a good interpreter. Like Wood said all the Miami warriors seemed to hold him in high esteem and trust. Like Wood chuckled.

"The Wild Potato looked often at you. One does not see many red-hair people. I expect he will come near me one day soon and talk to me about my wife, to ask about this one whose hair is as red as his own."

She felt a twinge of the old caution. "He should not be told anything. They sell names, and might try to take me away."

He shook his head, smiling grimly. "Wild Potato would not. He hates them. On the O-hi-o he decoys *wapsi* boats into ambush, by his appearance. No. There is no stronger hatred for the whites than his hatred. He would not sell your name to them."

"Still, my husband, I ask you to tell him nothing," she said softly, mindful of Flicker's cautions. "If someone sold me away, we would no longer have our great pleasures together. We would never have a child together."

Good Face believed that in all the pleasures they had taken since her return, they surely had planted a child-seed in her, just as the women of the Maumee Sipu towns would soon plant the Three Sisters seeds in the sun-warmed ground, just as it was always supposed to be in the sacred cycle of the seasons. For they had loved hard and often in the fertile time of her body, and it was springtime. Flicker had dosed her with a tea made from the manroot plant, which might help her be fertile. Shrugging, the old woman had said, "Our people do not use it for this, but people across the Great Water want it so much that most of it on Turtle Island has been dug up and sold far away. It used to grow everywhere until the French started buying it from us. If it works for French, who are a sort of *wapsituk*, maybe it will work for a red-hair." She shrugged again. "There is a chance the *wapsituk* might be right about something."

But one day, before planting time, Good Face awoke knowing that her moon-blood was again upon her. Once more she would have to give up the anticipation of creating a baby human being in her belly. "I must leave for the moon hut today," she told Like Wood as he reached for her. He drew his hand back.

"*E heh.* Then Creator does not mean us to have a child yet. Creator sees another Long Knife army coming again this year, and does not want a child born to us when the Town Destroyers are in the land."

She rolled into a scrap of deerskin the few articles she would need in the menstrual hut, then peered in at him as she stooped to go out. "Such cheering things you say, my husband."

"I am a warrior. It is not sad to me that the soldiers come again. Last year I killed two. This year we will be ready when they come, and we will kill so many they will never dare to return!"

That was the way warriors talked, she knew. But what she remembered of last year was the rattle and thunder of distant gunfire, and the days of not knowing whether her beautiful husband was alive or dead. So maybe it was right that her blood was coming down. Still, it made her heart heavy with disappointment.

The women in the menstrual hut were talking about Wild Potato when Good Face came in. It was what Flicker called "tickle talk," just the giggly sort of chatter that women would never want their husbands to overhear. It was usually bawdy, but not mean like gossip. Good Face recognized most of the women, but in a town this large, with tribal groups always coming and going, she was not surprised to see a few strangers. The talk about Wild Potato, about how handsome he was, took a new turn when she seated herself by the fire in the midst of the women. One looked at her and said, "We were wondering if the hair of his man-part is red too." They all tittered and whooped.

She smiled, wishing to be pleasant, but her heart was heavy with the disappointment of not being pregnant, and with dread about the coming of another army, and this talk seemed so frivolous that it annoyed her a little.

One of the women, with a very saucy expression, turned to her and asked: "You are red-haired like him. Is your hair down there red too?"

Good Face could not keep from smiling at that, and almost laughed before she could answer. "It certainly is for the next few days."

They went into an uproar of laughter at that answer, and it made her feel better, to have made them laugh so heartily. There was always such comfort in being among women around a fire. From her first evening in Neepah's lodge so many years ago, when she arrived as a cold, frightened, hungry little girl, she had flourished in that comfort. With a twinge, she remembered that distant moment, remembered it with such clarity that she would not have been surprised to see Neepah's face among these laughing and chatting women. She gazed from one face to another around the lodge. There sat a stocky woman she did not know, one whose round face did remind her of Neepah's. Beside and slightly behind that one was a gaunt young woman, who would have been pretty except for her terrible thinness and the lines and traces of pain all over her bony visage. Her eyes seemed almost to burn with intensity, so that Good Face quickly glanced away. . . .

Then something like a wordless voice, like a birdcall, chimed in her heart, making it quicken, and she glanced instantly back to the burning eyes, which were fixed on her.

The skinny young woman got up and came around, and reached for Good Face's hands. Touching the nailless index finger, she uttered a little groan.

"E heh," she said. "I greet you, Good Face."

"You," Good Face said, "are Minnow?"

So quiet and intense were these few words that all the tickle talk fell silent in the women's lodge.

Good Face and Minnow looked at each other in silence for a time, memories rushing.

Minnow was so thin and sinewy and her embrace was so desperate that it was like wrestling a wild grapevine. The tears that welled in Good Face's eyes flowed from pity as much as from joy.

Together they remembered Neepah, who had mothered them and taught them. Sitting close, they murmured like sisters over childhood memories. Minnow laughed little, and when any tenderness revealed itself in her eyes or voice, she masked it quickly with some hard look or bitter remark. Eventually Good Face came around to saying:

"Never have I heard anyone speak of seeing the Long Knife soldiers harm her that day. Only that some saw her going toward the soldiers in the fighting. Always I have hoped she might not have been harmed. That is many summers ago, but sometimes still I pray she is alive and our paths will cross again."

Minnow made a short, sharp hiss, angry-sounding, but sad-eyed.

"You mock my hope?" Good Face queried.

"In This Side World our paths will not cross hers again. Only in the Other Side World."

"Then you *know* she is *ong ul?* You saw her dead?"

"*E heh.* Yes. Let us not speak more of it."

A dark weight squeezed Good Face's heart, though she had not really expected any other truth. "Please at least tell me what you—"

"*Tuk o! Tuk o kek o!* No! Nothing! There is nothing you want in your mind's pictures!"

The hard finality made her fall silent; it was true, she did not want to see it in her mind or put it in her memory if it was bad. All her memories of Neepah were pleasurable, even after these dozen summers since.

But Minnow herself could not keep from saying more, apparently. She breathed through clenched jaws: "Soldiers are slime serpents. They cut off pieces of her to wave and keep and laugh."

"Pieces . . ."

"Everything by which she was a woman. But also her scalp. Perhaps to brag they had killed a warrior. *E heh!* She was one!"

The intensity of Minnow's tone, and the words themselves, had troubled the women in the lodge and they had turned to look, frowning, not liking talk of killing in the moon lodge, a place of life. Good Face was trying to keep the bloody images out of her head; she did not want them; she was stirring inside as if she would be sick, and was beginning slowly to turn her head from side to side in a slow denial.

"Soldiers are slime serpents," Minnow repeated, loud enough now for everyone's ears. "I pray for a chance to skin off a soldier's nut bag someday. I will make a little pouch of it and give it to you, sister. In honor of *her.*"

Of her. Of Neepah, who had lost and suffered so much from soldiers. It was so long ago, but Good Face could still remember Neepah's story of a baby killed, Neepah's baby whom she herself had been brought to replace, and of something terrible the soldiers had done to Neepah even before, something so bad that she had not explained what it was.

Minnow, eyes narrowed, snarled: "I used to wonder why so many *wapsituk* always want to come and fight our people. But I believe I know. They want to come because of the things they hope to do to our women! They are slime serpents!"

Minnow was married, not to a Lenapeh but a Miami. This Miami was her second husband, she said. First she had been married a short time to a Lenapeh, but something terrible had happened, which Minnow seemed unwilling to speak of very much. She preferred to tell of the places she had been to in the years of flight: Canada, Detroit, several towns near the Erie lake, one on the Sanduskee Sipu. During those times, tribes were often mingled together in villages, as they were here at Kekionga, and the warriors allied. When her Lenapeh warrior husband had turned out to be bad, she put him out of their *wikwam*. Then she married the Miami warrior, and that was why she was here now. They had no children yet.

Minnow talked little, and that was about all Good Face learned about her in their four days in the moon lodge together.

But though she talked little, she seemed to bask in Good Face's presence, listening to what had happened to her in those lost years, listening, listening, sitting so close they touched. They were still like sisters even after the long absence. And Good Face, who in caring for her old parents and her husband had had little time for friendships with women her age, responded to this good listener by talking tirelessly. Had not her birth family had some name for her that meant a chatterer?

When their moon time was over, they worked together whenever they could, and there was much work to be done. Lodges were being rebuilt in the villages of Kekionga, and much tree bark was needed to cover them. Families crossed the rivers and went into the forests to cut and peel and stack bark. Early spring was the best time to peel trees because the bark was limber and sappy, easier to skin off in wide slabs without tearing. Good Face and Minnow worked together in one of the bark-harvesting camps on a riverbank, their arms and hands sticky with drying sap and blood-smeared from scratches and cuts. It seemed that working made Minnow talk more easily. She said, "My Lenapeh husband was handsome, like yours, but he became an empty loincloth. So I named him Empty Loincloth and made him leave forever."

Good Face almost laughed at the name, but Minnow was serious. This was apparently one of the bitter things in her. Good Face waited for Minnow to explain why she had called her husband that, then finally had to ask her.

"He began drinking *wapsi* spirit water and he became no husband, no good. He howled like a wolf. Cut his friends with a knife. Hurt his family. My ribs were broken when he kicked me. He stank too much to hunt, and could not shoot because of shaky hands. Worthless because of that burning bad drink. Empty Loincloth, too sick and disgraceful to raise a stiffness for me. After I put him out of the house, the Council warned him two times. Then the third time they put him out of the tribe, made him a no-person no one can see anymore. Of all things the *wapsituk* have done to us, maybe the bad drinking, *maxcheekwee menaxteeum,* might be the worst of all." She spat on the ground, and that revealed the heat of her anger most, because Neepah had taught them both as little girls that it is in bad spirit to spit on our Mother Earth without apologizing.

Some other things were being done in the improper spirit way. A few of the men possessed swords and bayonets taken from soldiers killed last fall, and because they were metal blades, they tried to use them to make the bark-cutting and peeling easier. Tuck Horse scolded some of the young warriors for slashing and gouging the trees with war weapons—particularly *wapsi* war weapons—which he said would bring bad spirit to *wikwams* covered with bark harvested that way. The young men soon enough learned that the weapons were not good tools anyway; swords made for cutting flesh were soon bent by wood, and bayonets pierced bark instead of prying it loose. Before long the bark was being taken in the traditional ways, peeled by tools made of wood and antler, after a tobacco offering was made to each tree. Then the long, wide, limber sheets of bark were loaded on rafts and pirogues and taken back to the towns, where they were laid over poles on the ground, crisscrossed with more layers of bark and poles, and weighted on top with stones to keep them from curling as they dried. It was a hard kind of work, sometimes in cold spring rain and on muddy ground. Everyone's hands were scratched and bruised and strained.

With his chair maker's skill with tools, Tuck Horse was more productive than any of the younger people, but he complained: "In the good days before the *wapsituk* started coming, this work only had to be done years apart. Now almost every spring we have to skin more trees and make new *wikwams* because the armies are always burning them. Surely Creator is not happy to see wasted so much bark from trees, and should stop the *wapsituk* from any more town-burning so the trees can rest. And we too."

Like Wood, overhearing his father-in-law, said proudly, "Buckongahelas and Little Turtle will keep the army from burning these towns again, if the Creator doesn't!"

Tuck Horse straightened slowly, painfully, and stared at Like Wood with a frown, staring until Like Wood felt it and turned. Old Tuck Horse growled at him, "Did I hear the husband of my own daughter say that? *Kulesta!* Whether the war chiefs can stop the army depends not on them. It depends on the wish of He Who Creates By Thinking. There are things that are so, in the Old Ways. Such as not using weapons to make houses. Such as always remembering that we are in the hands of the Creator. You are a good son. But do not forget the old true things. *E heh.* I have finished. Take that end and help me move these sheets of bark."

Good Face was relieved to see how graciously her husband took the scolding from her old father. For it seemed to her that whatever was happening to the People, the things that were so by the Old Ways would always be so and should not be forgotten. Living with her old parents had given her a solid faith in that. It was because of such faith that it had troubled her to see Minnow spit on the ground.

They had not planted together since they were little girls helping Neepah, but now Good Face and Minnow were working together as women in the moist, sun-warmed, scorched soil, hoeing the earth into little mounds, making holes to put in fish and water and the seeds, the fine dirt and bear oil making a dark slime between their fingers and thumbs, while children brought pots of water from the river, and the women's voices sang the planting song. This was the way it always had been, this was the way it was supposed to be. Kahesana Xaskwim, Mother Corn, had been asked in the prayer to make the seeds grow, these seeds that had been saved from the army the year before, and Kahesana Xaskwim had made her presence known, so every kernel planted in the ground was blessed and was full of hope. Good Face had braided her hair so it would not hang over her face. Sweat was running down her arms to drip on the ground, and she remembered Neepah saying that Kukna, Mother Earth, liked to drink *pim*, the sweat of women. In the side of her vision was Minnow, so spare and slender she looked like a boy with breasts, but wiry and strong and tireless, sunlight gleaming on her sweaty back and shoulders. Tools munched the earth and women's voices murmured in talk and song. The work was like a trance, or a long dream, and Good Face felt herself to be connected with all women who had lived before, as if they all were still alive and working and singing too, but elsewhere on the rolling circle of the world. It seemed that no one could die; everyone was always alive; Neepah, for example, must be somewhere else on the great turning circle, planting and sweating, just somewhere distant over the curve of the horizon, as well as all of the grandmothers and great-grandmothers a thousand generations gone. And always the corn would be sprouting and growing and being harvested. And all the men of all time would be hunting and fishing, protecting the women and children, growing old and wise and grumpy like Tuck Horse, full of knowledge and honor. . . .

The women had been planting for most of the afternoon when they began to hear a howling that sounded like an enraged panther. They straightened up from their hoeing and looked about. The noise was so uncommon and so piercing that it was hard to tell at once whether it came from upstream or down. Soon the women were sure it was coming from downstream. Then it was joined by wild squealings and yips like the night-sing of a coyote pack.

But coyotes never did that at this time of day. And there were some deep-throated screams beginning, as if men were being hurt. Children came running into the field to their mothers, alarmed.

Minnow was the first to act. She looked less scared than angry. There was a fire in her eyes that was frightening. She sent a runner upriver toward the town to get some men, but she did not wait for men to come. She spoke in a quick and hissing voice to the women nearby:

"Bring the tools and follow me!"

Good Face, though scared badly, followed Minnow with a few others, and they sped along the riverside path, running crouched and peering ahead through the lacy budding foliage. As they ran closer to the wailings, there were moments when the awful sounds simply trailed off to silence, then would erupt again. Though Good Face felt strong with the elk-shoulder mattock in her hand and was inspired to courage by Minnow's example, she was just as ready to turn about and run back as to go on. There were only four or five women coming; the rest had remained in the cornfield. Minnow ran ahead so fast it was hard to keep up with her, her stringy muscles moving under her sweaty skin, ribs and spine bones visible. It was astonishing that she showed no fear of whatever lay ahead.

Soon they were close enough that when the shriekings died down, they could hear scuffling and bumping sounds. Minnow sprinted on, glancing along both sides of the path. Good Face was beginning to stumble and gasp from the hard running.

Then they looked up the riverbank and there on a rise above the path were men who seemed to be crazed. To her horror, Good Face saw that her husband was one of them.

They were a hunting party that had left before daylight; Like Wood had risen and dressed and put fuel on the fire and then had rinsed the human smells off his body and smudged himself with cedar smoke. Smiling at her, he had ducked out the door with his gun and shooting pouch. It made no sense that they would be here, still so close by the town. But the horror of it was the way they were acting. She stood crouching with her hand over her open mouth, too stunned even to cry out.

They reeled about as if their legs were crooked and feet heavy. They crouched down and then thrust upward to howl and screech at the sky. They stumbled and sprawled on the ground, and crawled and cried. One was on his hands and knees, retching again and again with strings of drool swinging from his lips. Like Wood himself stood on limber knees with his toes turned inward, swaying, eyes nearly rolled back into his head, lips wet and slack, as if he were dying on his feet.

She cried out: "My husband!" But he gave no sign of having heard.

One of the men was clutching to his chest a keg, about the size of his head. Minnow pointed at it with a jabbing forefinger.

"I knew! *E heh!* I knew!" she shouted, her face a snarling fury. "The bad drinking!"

Even now the men were aware only of their own demons and did not seem to see or hear the women. Good Face was transfixed by the pathetic sight of her husband, and just realizing that he was drunk. Minnow, meanwhile, had run into the midst of the drunken men and with a wide, powerful swing of her open hand she slapped the warrior with the keg so hard that he staggered sideways and fell. When the keg hit the ground, spurting whiskey from its bunghole, she staved it in with one blow of her mattock. Only then did one or two of the men seem to see the women. They quit yelling and tried to focus their eyes on them, looking bewildered, as if these were only demons in another form. The man whom Minnow had knocked down was trying to get up, rising weakly onto one elbow; then he just shut his eyes and sank back to the ground, moaning.

These drinkers, except for Like Wood, were not husbands of those who had come running from the cornfield, so the women just stayed at the edge of the glade watching with disgust or amusement as the men staggered about. Their howls had diminished, and one man now dropped forward onto his knees and crossed his arms over his waist. He gushed vomit from mouth and nose and then toppled facedown in it.

Minnow, snarling in disdain, said, "Nothing can be done for them. Stay back where they cannot spew on you. *Eh!*" she shouted at the men. "Empty loincloths! Nothing in them but your body waste!" She turned and looked back up the path. "Here come men from the town to take care of these fouled ones. Come, we have planting to finish. Don't go to your husband." She seized Good Face by the arm and pulled her away from where she stood gaping and weeping.

And as she stumbled back up the riverside path toward the cornfield, the just-budding greenery of the woods shimmering through her teary vision, Minnow's voice hissed:

"May you never see your husband like that again. If I see the *wapsi* dogs who sell our men that poison water, I will break their head as I broke their keg. With that poison the *wapsituk* mean to kill all the People. Listen! When your husband can think and hear you again after this, tell him he can lie with you as his wife or he can lie in his own vomit, one or the other. Not both!"

"*E heh, numees.* Yes, sister. I should tell him that."

Minnow said, "My bad drinking husband told me that drink is great medicine, that it gave him visions. I told him no, visions are sacred. That is poison. I said, you insult the spirits by calling that poison craziness a vision. *E heh!* Somehow the *wapsituk* can drink that and not be crazed. Their god must protect them from poison."

Good Face, her soul saddened and in turmoil, tried to think of that as they approached the cornfield, where most of the women were still at work planting. She asked Minnow, "Do you think they have another god, not the same one?" It was one of Tuck Horse's old questions, which he used to ponder aloud by the campfire.

Minnow stopped in her tracks and looked at her, puzzled.

"Should you not know that better than I? I have never lived as a
wapsini, but only Lenapeh. You have lived both."

Good Face tried but could not remember ever feeling that she
had exchanged the God of her white family for Kijilamuh ka'ong,
the Creator of the Lenapeh, as she became one of the People.

"The name has changed," she said. "But so have all names, for
that was a different tongue. I now use smoke to carry my prayer
up, and did not do that before. But I do not remember changing
from another god."

"*E heh!* Maybe then the missionaries lie. They said we have to
turn our backs on Kijilamuh ka'ong and Nanapush and Misinkhalikun the Keeper of the Game, and turn our faces to 'God' and his
little boy 'Jesus' or we will perish. Some of our Lenapeh did that.
They have had ill fortune ever since. I do not know, sister. Some
of the shamans say the whites' god is stronger. Some say our Creator is displeased with us because we are trapping too many animals to trade fur for *wapsi* goods. And that we are being punished
for forgetting our true ways. And for the bad drinking. Neolin our
Prophet said the punishment would happen. I do not know. But if
the god is all the same, why does he take everything away from us
who honor him here in the land he gave us, and give it all to those
who would not stay over there where he put them?" She shook her
head. "Let us plant corn. This makes my head swirl around."

And so Good Face returned to the work in the corn hills and
tried to stop thinking of the terrible sight of her husband full of the
screaming demon. She thought of the choice she would have to
give him, between her or the poison water. To tell him that would
require courage. She did not want to make him choose, because he
might choose to leave her, and she did not want him gone.

She thought of the name Minnow had said, that name she had
not heard since the time in the house of old Joseph and Mary at
Detroit, that name *Jesus*. That was the son of God.

I had nearly forgot that name, she thought.

She had dreaded the moment when she would have to face her
husband with her displeasure, but she didn't face him alone. Her
parents too were angry and disgusted with what Like Wood had
done. And Like Wood, wincing with the pain in his head, and
shaky and nauseated, was disgusted with himself. He admitted
that after the whiskey seller had met them on the path and given
them each a drink of the liquor, he had become foolish and traded

the seller his good musket for the rest of the keg. Good Face could see that old Tuck Horse and Flicker were brittle with contempt. The old man said:

"Raise your head and talk to me. We are not speaking to our feet. Now, your wife is my daughter. You are supposed to feed and protect your wife. Without a gun, I wonder, how are you to hunt to feed her? Without a gun, I wonder, how are you to protect her against the Long Knife army, which as we know is ready to return to our country? I speak of my daughter, who is the delight of my aged years, and my wife's. When you became her husband, you promised to keep her in the sacred circle of your care and protection. Do you remember that promise?"

"I remember, Father. I have not forgotten. I was foolish one moment only."

"You were foolish one moment only, you say, but that moment is gone past and you still have no gun to hunt and protect with. There are many moments of foolishness in a life that live on and on, like a baby born from the lust of two who do not care for each other. Many of the treaties that have been moving our People out of the homelands for generations, those treaties were marked by chiefs who had one moment of foolishness and accepted rum. No man is all wise, but a man can avoid being a fool at any time he is offered the bad spirit drink. All he has to do is turn his back on it."

The young warrior had been lowering his head as he listened, and the old warrior snapped at him: "Did I not say we are not conversing with our feet?

"*Kulesta:* In battle you have proven bravery. But bravery must be guided by sense. A man howling at the sky and dirtying his breechcloth is not guided by sense. When the army comes this way again, will you drink from a keg and stand before them howling in their faces and pissing at their feet? That will not stop any army!

"*Kulesta:* I have lived two wars. I have seen them lost through moments of foolishness. If you are a fool in any way, your enemy will learn what your foolishness is, and he will work it against you. Keep looking up at my face!

"*Kulesta:* That Long Knife Nation knows that they can weaken us with the bad spirit drink because they know we are foolish for it. You saw them use your foolishness to take your gun and make you unable to think. Listen! Our enemy is not just their soldiers, it is also their whiskey sellers who come among us and disarm us and melt our brains.

"*Zhukeh kulesta!* Now listen: Before the soldiers return to this country, you must purify yourself from that poison. You must fast. You must sweat until the poison is all out of you. All your heart must be in this. You have this moment to choose: whether you will be the husband of my daughter and a protector of your People, or a fool who howls at the sky and vomits in the path of his enemy.

"*Kulesta:* You know that a wife can put her husband outdoors from her house if he breaks his promise to be a good husband. My daughter and I have spoken of you together, and she has told me that you will be one or another: her husband in her house, or a drinker of the white man's poison, away from her house.

"What you have done will be spoken of in Council. They will warn you. If you drink the poison water again, your wife will throw you out and the Council will warn you again. There will be no third forgiveness from your Council. You will be expelled like a turd from behind your People and you will be no one. That is worse than death. Look up! We are not talking to feet here!

"When you purify out your poison, remember first that your wife is ready to throw you out, and second that your People are ready to throw you out. This is not a little shame that can be snick-ered at and forgotten, like a boy spying on naked women. This is whether you choose to be worthy, or to be a reeking turd in a puddle of whiskey vomit. *Zhukeh kishalokeh!*" I am finished!

Like Wood's eyes turned to his wife. Good Face saw that he was afraid. He did believe that she might throw him out. Choosing to forgive him or not was thus a power she had. Never before had she known any power over anyone. It was not comfortable. Her friend Minnow had used this power, and it had made her proud but bitter.

"Go get clean," Good Face told her husband. And he went.

CHAPTER ELEVEN

Autumn 1791
By the Maumee Sipu

To Good Face, the endlessly beating war drum had grown as familiar as her own pulse. Over its beat rose and fell the shrill, quavering, nasal screams.

Above the roofs and treetops around the dance ground a few dim stars and a half-moon were dimmed by glowing smoke and soaring sparks. Around the roaring bonfire the war dance had gone on and on for most of the night, going on and on with that tireless slamming heartbeat of the drum, those chilling, trilling screams.

Everyone was here watching the warriors perform in their frenzy, putting themselves into a state of being that would allow them to kill or die, to be merciless or fearless. Good Face herself watched with a racing heart, staring so hard she scarcely blinked, a sweat of excitement trickling down her ribs and between her buttocks, watching the mad-eyed, grimacing warriors crouch, stalk, spring, whirl, jab, swing, enact all the swift and brutal motions of combat, their naked physiques painted and shiny with grease and sweat, exerting themselves until their veins stood forth and their muscles were ropy and knotted. She had been watching that dance for a long time, her unblinking eyes growing red from smoke and dust, her own body arching and feet shuffling, driven by the drum like all the other watchers. She watched the warriors spring to the center of their circle and strike the red-painted war post with their clubs and tomahawks, each time howling with murderous triumph.

And now she saw her own husband Like Wood stalk toward the post in a stealthy crouch, all his beautiful muscles gleaming in firelight. He leaped high with a tremolo scream and knocked a chip out of the very top of the war post with his sharp tomahawk.

That at last was too much for her, and she clapped her hands over her face. Feeling suddenly such an intense dread that it nauseated her, she staggered out from among the transfixed, yelping spectators and trotted, weak-kneed and stumbling, to her family's *wikwam*, where she gulped water from a gourd and stood wringing her shaky hands, gasping, turning to and fro as if lost, not yet knowing what was really wrong inside her. Finally, sobbing, she sat down on the bedding in a state of fear and shame and confusion, hands over her ears to shut out the drumming and howling of her People.

She knew the nature of their war dance. In her heart she was Lenapeh. She had come to understand, despite the tenets of her peaceable birth family, how a people must sometimes respond to force with force. She knew the Lenapeh were a peace-loving people—not just the women, but the men too—and that they had to be transported by this dance into that state of being where they could without hesitation send other people, the enemy people, out of this life and into the Other. She understood all that while watching the dancing build up; even her own soul had been involved—until that moment when she saw her own husband, whose body and soul she had known with the most intimate thoroughness, leap from a crouch with a pulsating shriek, just as he had those few weeks ago beside the river while the liquor demon's madness surged in him.

It was the sameness of the two kinds of madness that had all at once made her stomach turn over and a hopeless fear drain through her. It just did not seem that God, or Kijilamuh ka'ong, could mean for such madnesses to be—yet they were, and she and her loved ones were in their path.

The white men's army was not yet close enough to see or hear, but it could be felt. It came on the lips of messengers from tribes in the west and the southwest, where armies had appeared in the valley of the Wabash Sipu in the spring and then in the summer, burning villages and crops of the Kickapoo and of the Eel River and Wea tribes of the Miami Nation.

Now another army, three times as big as those, was coming through the Shawnee country from the south, coming to try to do again what it had tried to do to Kekionga the year before.

It was such a slow-moving army. Scouts came and told how the army had built two roads side by side, so its cannons and supply wagons could be pulled through the forests, and had built a fort on the Great Miami River, then left that fort to march on, to a place still closer, where it stopped again and began building another fort. The army loomed immense in the People's imaginations. The People, even the oldest ones, had spent their lives feeling the *wapsituk* coming on like a great dark storm, and always moving before it, looking back and seeing smoke in the sky where their homes had been. Of this year's army, the councils had vivid descriptions day by day. A young Shawnee chief of scouts called Tecumseh kept a relay of spies and messengers always reporting to Little Turtle and Buckongahelas and Blue Jacket; every day came a rider with the news of what the army had done the day before. The army from the beginning had been troubled by bad supply lines and bad discipline and weak, sick horses, but it was still coming on.

Good Face listened day by day as the Council discussed those reports of the oncoming army, and she could almost see it in her mind's eye; she imagined she could feel it creeping forward like a great beast from the south. It was a terrible weight on the soul and patience. It was not the natural way of the People to worry about any one thing for so long.

But the slowness of the army was actually a good thing. It was giving the war chiefs time to gather and organize many warriors for the defense of the country. This time the army would be met not by fewer than two hundred warriors, but perhaps as many as a thousand. Warriors from the Miami and Kickapoo villages had come, burning to avenge the destruction of their towns. And now besides the Miami and Shawnee and Lenapeh there were war chiefs and warriors from other nations—Roundhead and Crane, and White Loon of the Wyandot; Crippled Hand, Black Partridge, and Topenabee of the Potawatomi; Walking Turtle of the Winnebago, and Kathadah of the Ottawa. Little Turtle now had the support of all those famed chiefs, and the youthful energy and intelligence of his son-in-law Wild Potato, who had a talent for organizing and keeping track of many things at once. Almost like a white man's army, the warriors were named into groups of twenty, with four or five of each group chosen as hunters to bring meat.

Another advantage of the army's slowness was that it had still been at some distance when the crops ripened for harvest. Now the Three Sacred Sisters would not be standing in the fields for the soldiers to slash and burn. Whatever this *wapsituk* army might be able to do this year, it would not be able to starve the People.

The councils learned that the British in Canada had a new leader who seemed more bold about providing the tribes with guns and powder. It seemed as if the British were not as afraid of the Long Knives as they had been for a while. The longer the army took in coming, the more supplies could come down from the British.

But the best thing about the slow-moving army, heard over and over, was that its leader, an important old general whose name was St. Clair, did not know very well how to scout his path or defend the edges of his army. The army sprawled and straggled as it came along, and never had any pathfinders out in front. Such a weakness might give the tribes a chance to ambush the army before it even got to Kekionga. That could mean not only the women and children and elders would be in less danger, but that perhaps, for once, the towns themselves would not be burned.

Good Face learned as much of all this as she could, because she remembered from the last year the terror and confusion of not knowing what was happening. "Listen," Minnow told her one cold, dank day as they began skinning a buck deer, "even in men's matters a woman should not be ignorant. Remember Neepah: she always knew what was going on. And so she was like a warrior because she knew."

Good Face nodded, her heart twisting at the sound of that name, and she understood all at once what Minnow was saying. She thought hard, cutting skin around one of the buck deer's hocks while Minnow cut the other.

"Ever since I was a child carried away from home by a warrior," Good Face said, "I have been like a leaf blown before the storm of war. There is no sign of an end to it, as long as there are red men and white men on this same land. They make each other crazy, like drinking the spirit water, and their howling is like a storm. I see now that I must be stronger than just a leaf, so the storm cannot blow me away. To be strong, I must know what is happening."

"*K'hehlah!* Indeed that is true. Now you know the truth of it in your heart," Minnow replied, pinching an edge of the deer's leg skin up with hard fingers to get a grip on it. "It is for us to spring back like a bent stem, not blow away like a leaf. Women are what hold the People together. When men fight, we must be strong for them to come back to so they can devour more strength from us. No, not blown away like leaves!"

The buck deer was hanging head-down from the apex of a hickory-pole tripod, hind legs held apart by a stout stick, while Good Face and Minnow sliced with their knives along the hocks and forelegs and inward toward the slit-open belly. With the knife edges they separated the skin from the integument underneath until they could grip enough skin in their fists to start pulling down and peeling the hide off. Strong as the women were, it was hard work. Their breath clouded in the raw air. Minnow talked between clenched teeth, and Good Face knew at once that skinning the animal had started her talking of this:

"Somewhere in some soldier's house are tobacco pouches with nipples, and bracelets with hair. Made from my mother's breasts and genitals. I have seen this in dreams. The soldier shows those things to his sons when they are drinking whiskey together, and brags of how he raped her before cutting off those parts. My mother's," she hissed, black eyes glittering. "The same with Neepah's!"

"Sister," Good Face said with a shudder, "you should put such long-ago things out of memory and not keep speaking of them."

Minnow replied, "Pull. We have so much to do to feed our warriors. Now you see the beautiful shape of the thigh muscles in this good animal? When I was little, Neepah had strong legs like this. Neepah whom our hearts remember, eh? The soldiers who killed her at Wyalusing Town skinned her legs and her back, I have been told. And her scalp. And of course her breasts that once fed me, because you remember how big they were!" Suddenly throwing her knife down in the bloody mud, she yanked down on the hide with both hands, and with a hissing sound the deerhide peeled off all the way down to the buck's shoulders. Minnow made the move with such force that the tripod bucked and Good Face almost fell. "*Wapsi* soldier!" Minnow snarled. "This is you I am skinning! You are hanging up alive so you can feel it!"

The power of Minnow's hatred was frightening, and Good Face was speechless. She helped tug the skin the rest of the way down the neck. Then Minnow snatched up her sharp British-made tomahawk and with a quick blow severed the spine just behind the skull, and then with two more strokes cut the meat and arteries so that the head with its antlers fell to the ground and lay there still attached to the hide. Good Face knew that Minnow could do that because of the skill of a lifetime's butchering, but it seemed as if the hatred and anger had guided her hand.

Good Face thought of all the warriors who had left the villages just before the rains started and gone down to meet the army, and she knew that all of those thousand warriors hated the white men as much as Minnow did, and that they had all danced and struck the war post with at least that much fury, all of them, including her own husband. And so she wished, as she looked at the bloody mud and the cut meat and hide of the butchered animal before her, that there could be some way in which the warriors and the army would not have to meet each other.

But that was only a vague wish, and she did not pray for it because that would have been a prayer against the purposes of the People.

After five days of rain, Good Face one morning saw blue in the sky and frost sparkling on the ground. In the villages the women ground corn into meal, and made venison into jerky on pole racks over big beds of embers. They sliced squashes into rings and dried them in great quantities, and when they were not processing food for their warriors, they scraped and tanned hides and made moccasins. They stored huge quantities of dry corn and beans in underground pits and hid the covers of the pits so that if the army ever did get this far, the soldiers might not find the food.

Some people were beginning to believe that the army was not going to come any farther. According to reports from the Shawnee scouts, the army was still camped inside its latest fort and doing nothing. Many soldiers were sick, the spies said, and many were deserting in the nights and going back down the trail toward the O-hi-o. Tuck Horse came in one day smiling, lit his pipe at the meat-jerking fire, turned the stem to the four winds, and murmured some thankful prayer. Good Face and Flicker waited to hear what was pleasing him so.

Finally he said, with smoke seeping up from his smiling lips: "Some of the soldiers are hanging up."

The two women looked at each other, shrugged, and asked him to explain what he meant by that strange statement.

"They got caught running away and their general made them be hung up with neck ropes until they were dead."

Good Face put her hand to her throat. She faintly remembered that white men had a hanging punishment for bad men. She said to Tuck Horse, "You are amused by such a sad thing?"

"It is like this, daughter. The general worked well. He did not think they were very good soldiers, so he hung them up. Now, to my thinking, they are good soldiers. I should like to see all the soldiers good like those. Heh heh! Ah-heh!" He looked at her awhile, and when he saw that she was not smiling, he added, "I smile, daughter, because when an army is like that, it is less to be feared." He puffed on his pipe, then raised his nose and sniffed at the aroma of the drying meat. "The army horses are dying because the cold weather kills the grass. Dead horses cannot carry food from one fort to another. For once, I believe, our warriors have more food than the army. That is good. It is good what you are doing. May I have that piece of meat from that end of the bottom pole? It looks very good. *Waneeshee,* daughter.

"*Kulesta.* The chiefs have said that soon we will have to take jerky and corn down to the warriors. It will require strong women to help us old men with the packhorses. We will not go very close to the army. Will you go with us, daughter? You are good with horses."

Good Face felt a sudden prickling in her hair and a quickening of her heart. It was a frightening prospect, but it would take her closer to where her husband was. She looked at old Tuck Horse, who was now savoring the hot, smoky strip of venison.

"Father, I do not want to see killing. If I do not have to see killing, I will help."

"I think you will see no killing. That army is stopped. It is hiding in its fort. As long as it stays there, there will be no killing."

Riding with the pack train, Good Face thought about long-ago times when she had been on horseback. She could even remember when she had ridden with her white father as a little girl. That was like remembering a dream, because she could hardly believe she had ever been a child in a *wapsi* family.

On the second day, when the pack train left the banks of the Maumee Sipu and started south up the Auglaize, snow began falling and she daydreamed about being carried on another horse up another river, as a very scared little *wapsi* girl riding in front of a Lenapeh warrior whose arms held a blanket around her and kept her from falling off. She tried to remember the name of that river and finally it came back to her: Susquehanna.

I should not let myself forget so much, she thought. If ever I were caught by soldiers or found by my first family, it would be good to remember things. Like names.

Jesus was the name of God's son, she remembered. I should remember Jesus. She remembered the old Lenapehs, Joseph and Mary, at Detroit. They had still believed in that Jesus even though many of their own people had been killed by the white soldiers who believed in Jesus.

Christians. She remembered that word. She thought hard, watching the snow begin to fill the tufts of autumn-dead grass in the wet prairie the pack train was crossing. Then she thought of the word for her *wapsi* people:

Quakers.

"Quakers," she said. They were Christian too, but different.

The horse blew steam, as if answering.

The horse she was riding was a chestnut mare, one of the horses of the soldiers that had been killed near Kekionga last year. Only a few straps and pieces of its old army saddle remained, but the owner of the horse had fashioned a comfortable Indian saddle out of it, deerhide padded with an old blanket, and using the original stirrups. In her left hand Good Face held a rope that led a pack-horse and an army mule. Next behind her in line was Tuck Horse. Old grandfather-aged man though he was, he was still strong and skillful enough to lead five packhorses. She loved him very deeply whenever she turned and looked back at his white hair and his old lined face, brown and rough as jerky.

Tuck Horse was not his real Lenapeh name. He had given up that name long ago because of bad fortune with it, and she didn't even know what that name had been. Tuck Horse was the name he had used half his lifetime, but it was a sort of a joke name. Old Joseph in Detroit had told the story of how Tuck Horse got such a strange name. Once in a long-ago war he had been in some *wapsi* fort and needed a horse in a hurry, so he had just hopped on the nearest one. Long afterward the *wapsini* whose horse it had been saw him and pointed and yelled, "That man took my horse!" So the *wapsi* soldiers had called him Took Horse as a nickname for a long time, and he just kept it because he hadn't wanted to keep his old name. Old Joseph had a hard time telling that joke-story because, although he learned to be a Christian, he had not learned much English language. Joseph had said he never believed Jesus spoke English anyway.

So the name Tuck Horse was really only a nickname. Good Face smiled, remembering that.

She too had had a nickname. When she was little her family had called her . . .

She had been speaking Lenapeh so long that she wasn't used to making the English sounds, but in a murmur she tried to say it:

"Palahnee."

She had heard her white mother crying that name after her when she was being carried away on a warrior's shoulder. She could remember that. There had been a *wapsi* boy carried away with her, and when they were in Neepah's town, that boy had called her that nickname. She tried to remember the boy's name but could not. She wondered what had become of him. She wondered too whether her white mother was still alive. She would be old now, maybe dead.

She rode in the cold, thinking about that. About how little she remembered her real mother.

But anyway, if she had died, I think I would know in my leapeuhkun. She could not remember the English word for soul.

She sighed and drew her blanket higher around her neck. Riding long ways caused her to daydream and drift in memories.

This was low country the pack train was passing through. The trail was clearly marked, as the path worn by hooves and feet for hundreds of years filled with snow. She knew that people like Tuck Horse had traveled so much in their long lifetime that they knew all the trails between towns and rivers and would never be lost. Tuck Horse sometimes said that white men could not see what was before them, and that unless they had made a road with stumps and wheel ruts, they could lose a whole army. She glanced back at the old man again. He had pulled an edge of his blanket forward to cover the flintlock of his musket against the falling snow. Of the twenty riders in this pack train, five were old men and the rest were women. All of the old men and three of the women had guns. The rest of the women, like herself, had only knives and tomahawks and slings. It was not likely they would have to defend themselves, the pack train leader had said. The enemy was down in its fort, and all the warriors were around it. If any enemy were out in this countryside, it would be perhaps a few scouts, white hunters and Chickasaws hired by the general. There was always a possibility of danger when armies were on the move, but women and children were kept out of danger as much as possible.

Now Good Face heard excited voices from farther ahead in the pack train. The front of the column had left the little prairie and was in snowy woods, so she could not see what was happening yet. But as she rode in she found the pack train stopped. The riders were listening to someone who was speaking. Then a warrior, dressed in a blanket coat and wearing a fur *gustoweh* cap on his head, rode out of the crowd and trotted his horse swiftly northward, back along the path in the direction from which they had come. His face was serious and intense, and though he nodded to everyone he passed, he did not stop. He was no one Good Face had ever seen.

Then the leader of the pack train, a strong old man who was a friend of Tuck Horse, came riding back. He told the riders that the warrior had been one of the Shawnee scouts and was carrying the word northward to the towns: the army had come out of its fort and started north, but in less than a day the soldiers had stopped and set up a guarded camp where it seemed they intended to stay awhile. It was believed they were waiting for their supplies to catch up, because a column of packhorses was following the army.

"So the army is out," Tuck Horse exclaimed. "This late in fall they continue toward our towns? What a fool their general chief must be!"

The pack train chief gave a short, harsh laugh. "A fool, and he moves as slow as swamp water. Our warriors could starve while waiting for him to attack. So. Let us go on."

And so the column moved on. Good Face was a little afraid, knowing that the army was out of its fort and on the land. She thought of soldiers and what she had heard of them. She thought of them cutting off parts of women. She thought of Minnow's hatred of them, and wondered whether she was afraid of them now that they were riding closer. That evening when the little camp was set up and the horses were corraled, eating hay that some of them had been carrying, she hunkered in firelight under a brush lean-to with Minnow and asked her if it scared her to be getting so close to where the soldiers were.

Minnow replied: "I am not scared now. Maybe I would be if I saw soldiers. But if I saw soldiers I would run toward them, not away. I would skin one's balls, at least, before they could throw me down, and I would rejoice."

* * *

After all these days of riding, Good Face felt that she and her mare were one. The column moved slowly. The snow had stopped but each day was colder. Every day they were passed by messengers, and now and then an unloaded packhorse string would pass them, returning toward the villages. Occasionally the column was surprised by warriors from Little Turtle's force who were ranging the countryside hunting for fresh meat, and they would have more news about the army, which they told to Tuck Horse and the other old men, staying away from the women because they themselves were in the warpath spirit and any of these women might be in her moon time.

The reports of the army were so strange that sometimes they caused the old warriors to shake their heads and laugh. Sometimes the army would stop and sit for days in a swampy place as if to give the soldiers plenty of opportunity to suffer. Soldiers kept deserting. Two or three hundred loud-voiced women and crying children were always with the army, and as slowly as the army moved, those camp followers were even slower, often strung out far behind the soldiers. Sometimes the noise of the women and children and the arguing and complaints of the soldiers could be heard all night by Tecumseh's scouts, who were always all around the army. Sometimes the general could be seen, and he was obviously an old man with bad bones, so sick that he could not come out of his tent some days, and sometimes when the army was creeping along, he had to be carried on a litter slung between two horses. The general seemed always to pick the worst route, so his eight cannons and numerous wagons were often deep in mud. Tuck Horse relished these accounts of the army's miserable blundering, and he told Good Face and Minnow one night, "Ah, if I were young, I could be down there like a wolf going around that army, and all day and all night they would hear me howling and laughing at their suffering and their stupidity. I would shout to them, 'You, sick and hungry and cold *wapsi* army! This comes upon you for marching into a country that is not yours!' Daughter, may they all die here. I would like to be young so that I could be one of the wolves to kill them!"

It had rained again, and the world that had been brightly dusted with snow was gray and dun and black. The horses' hooves squelched in the sodden ground, churning up mud as the long pack train passed down the trail. But as the day grew colder, the rain turned to light snow again, snow that melted on the wet ground and failed to whiten the country. Even with a blanket over her head and shoulders, Good Face was chilled all through, often shuddering uncontrollably. At last, with dusk coming on, she became aware of many voices ahead, and Tuck Horse rode forward past her, leading his five beasts, and told her to stop.

She sat shivering on her saddle, becoming aware in the dim, snow-blurred evening light that hundreds of men were about. Their voices were a droning murmur. She could smell tobacco smoke and bear oil and horse dung. Though there were no bonfires, as one would expect in an evening war camp in such weather, she could make out the shapes of a few small shelters in the woods, with firelight gleaming faintly within. It was the kind of camp that could not be seen or heard from half a mile away, and so she presumed that it was Little Turtle's main camp and that the army camp must lie not far beyond it. This thought made her tremble as much with excitement and fear as with the cold. Her thoughts turned then to her husband, and Minnow's. They must be somewhere in or near this swarming, unlit camp.

Tuck Horse came back with the pack train leader, and they told the women in the column to dismount and wait beside the trail. Then the old men mounted and led their strings of animals forward into the camp, where a hubbub of low but cheerful talk droned and the horses nickered and blew. Minnow and the other women crowded together as if for warmth and waited.

"Listen to our men," Minnow said, and Good Face realized that Minnow's voice when happy was beautiful like music. "They welcome what we have brought. That makes my heart warm after this cold, hard ride."

"K'hehlah," another woman replied. Indeed yes. "May some of that find its way into my husband's belly, as it should if Creator watches over things proper."

Minnow said, "I wish I could find my husband and have him in *my* belly after all these days!" The women laughed in a bawdy way, and Good Face felt herself blush because she had just been having the same yearning.

She said: "Might we hope that we will be allowed to see our husbands after coming so far to feed them?"

"Do not even hope for it," a woman scoffed. "When the horses are unloaded, we will turn around and go back up the trail we came. This is not a place for us."

Good Face's heart clenched and sank, even though it was something she had known to expect. The men were on the warpath and thus in another world, even though right there amid the thickets.

After dark the women and old men took the unloaded packhorses a safe distance up the trail and made a small camp with a fire. They heated venison broth in a kettle and sipped it, with corn cakes to eat. Little was said, though everyone was brimming with strong thoughts, as Good Face could see by their eyes. Tuck Horse at length smoked his pipe and then began telling them what he had learned at the camp.

"Our warriors will probably strike the army before the sun comes up tomorrow." Everyone looked intently at him, and he went on. "The army sent some of its best soldiers back down the road for some reason, so it's now even weaker. Buckongahelas said the army camped this evening where the Wabash Sipu begins. He said the soldiers were so wet and tired they did not even build a defense. Just put up tents and built big bonfires to warm themselves. Buckongahelas said we will never catch an army so weak and stupid ever again. It is time to do it, now before they get up and move again. My friends, this night we will pray for our sons and brothers and husbands who are surely just now closing their trap around that miserable army."

His quiet words set Good Face's heart to racing, and her throat tightened. She thought of the long hatred between her People and the *wapsituk*, and of all the ugly and bloody deeds waiting to be avenged, and of the long treks the army and the warriors had made toward each other for so many weeks. She thought of her husband, whose body and heart she knew so well, and her dread and eagerness were so great and turbulent inside her that she could hardly breathe enough air.

A little later tobacco was offered to the fire, its smoke rising into the cold night air to carry their prayers up to the Creator above, and as if the smoke had caused it, the clouds disappeared and for the first night in a long time stars were seen. Tuck Horse sat by the fire and lit his long pipe, not his little personal clay pipe, and passed it for everyone to draw from. He turned the stem in all directions when it was handed back to him, touched the mouthpiece to Mother Earth, and then pointed it toward the stars. He closed his eyes and began speaking just audibly.

"Kijilamuh ka'ong, He Who Creates By Thinking, your children sit here offering you tobacco. We ask you to think of our sons and brothers and husbands all safe and not hurt. We ask you to think of them going home singing of victory over their enemy. We ask you to think of the soldiers all going away by other roads, by their wagon road back down to the Beautiful River, or by the Spirit Road back to their own creator, who sent them here by mistake. We ask you to think like that, and then to think of peace for us after they have gone, so that it will be so, as you think it. Now I am finished."

"*A ho,*" the others all murmured.

After the prayer, Tuck Horse got up from the fire and said, "Walk out with me, daughter." With her blanket drawn around her, Good Face followed him out under the stars, southward up a sloping meadow through wet dead grass growing crisp with freezing. At the top of the meadow they looked southward. In the southeast there were still some clouds, and there was a ruddy color to them. He pointed.

"Those are the army's bonfires," he said. "More times than I want to remember, such red in the sky was from our towns burning. This time I do not think that will happen. I believe this will be a time our People will always remember. I believe Kijilamuh ka'ong has agreed to see our prayers just as we sent them. I felt that it was so. Listen!"

In the distance a few guns were banging. Good Face's pulse began to race. "Is it starting, Father?"

He stood watching and listening. There were a few more shots. Then silence. One or two more. More silence. Above the reddish low line of clouds the brilliant stars blazed, thousands of stars. A faraway gunshot. Silence. Another shot. Then there was nothing but stillness. He said, "It is not started yet. Their sentries are frightened. As they should be." The old man stood looking that way and listening. He held an edge of his blanket as usual over the flintlock of his musket to keep it dry in the cold night air. Then he turned and led her back down the slope toward their little camp, where the fire twinkled, a warm yellow light in contrast to the cold-looking stars. At the edge of the woods he stopped. He put his old, gnarled hand against the side of her face and looked at her, his own face dark, only the whiteness of his hair visible in the starlight.

"Go and sleep," he said. "I will be on watch here. Do not worry about your husband. The Creator has put a protection over the People."

"You should sleep too, Father." She felt a great swelling of admiration and love in her bosom for this old man.

"Old people do not need much sleep," he said. "Go. Rest well. The horses like you and trust you, and you have done well for our People."

Good Face had slept the deep, undreaming sleep of one fatigued in body and soul, but she did not sleep late. When she sat up in her blanket, some stars were still shining, but the sky over the treetops in the east was paling. Others had already built up the campfire and were standing or sitting close by it, and she heard one of the elders say:

"Where is that old man Tuck Horse?"

Good Face remembered the night before and said, "He stayed up to guard."

"I know," said the elder, "but then he woke me to take the watch and I thought he came back to sleep."

Minnow said, "Give him time. He is probably squatting in the bushes as some old men do in the morning if they are not stopped up in the morning like some other old men."

"He must be stopped up himself if he has been squatting this long," said the old man.

Good Face stood up, a little alarmed, to look around in the half-light, and just then she heard coming from far in the southeast, a faint rattling and whistling, barely audible even in the windless quiet.

"*Kulesta!*" Minnow hissed. "The army plays its waking-up music. A shame our warriors did not kill them in their sleep."

"Maybe my father is with the horses," Good Face said. "I will go and see."

"He is not," said the pack train leader. "I have been to the horses already."

Good Face was bewildered and almost frightened. Her father should have been somewhere nearby, but he seemed not to be. The sky was growing light enough that she could make out individual trees and the bushes on the sloping meadow they had walked last night, and she could see the mass of the corralled horses and even the steam of their breathing. She thought then that perhaps he had gotten up early and walked up onto the hill to look off in the direction of the army again. Of course that was the kind of thing he might do, he whose long life had been so full of oncoming armies. She decided to go out onto the meadow and look for his tracks in the frost. She would go into the bushes first and make water and then start up the meadow.

She was taking her first step in that direction when she heard the first sputterings of distant gunfire. She stopped to listen and at once the gunfire ascended to a steady roar of crackling and echoes. The women and old men had leaped up from their places around the fire and were looking southward.

Now as the roar of weapons began to fluctuate, from ferocious thundering to sporadic sputters and then thundering again, Good Face began detecting another kind of sound. It was somehow a sound familiar to her childhood memory and it took her a moment to recall it: cowbells. But it sounded like hundreds of distant cowbells, and she could not imagine why there would be such a sound in a battle. But suddenly Minnow, then the other women, and even some of the old men, emitted the shrill, trilling war cry, and with her scalp prickling, Good Face realized that was what she had been hearing in the distance—the war cries of hundreds of attacking warriors, and her heart leaped with fear and thrill. Then the cannons started booming.

She could feel the great thumps through the soles of her feet as well as hear them. Somewhere she had heard cannonfire before, she knew, and then she remembered that it had been all those years ago when the old man called Owl was taking her up the river with the other people from Neepah's town, fleeing from the Town Destroyer. More than ten years that had been, and still there were Town Destroyer armies coming. She remembered that those long-ago cannons had boomed in the mornings, far down the river. These were much closer and louder. She knew they were not really close because of the distance of the red sky she had seen over the army camp the night before, but they were close enough that their bangs shook her nerves. She was already half frantic over the disappearance of her father, and now she was flinching at the thought of her husband who was, she knew, somewhere down there in the midst of all that shooting. The sun had started to rise and in its pale light the frosty grass up on the slope of the meadow shone like silver against the sky's deep blue. She remembered that she had started out to look for Tuck Horse's tracks up the slope, and she did see a faint line of bent grass cross-lit by the light of sunrise. Without a word she darted out of the woods and ran southward up the meadow, veering toward the trail. It came to her mind that her father must be up there where they had stood last night and that he was probably looking toward the battleground. Now she was sure she would find him there and she ran through the frosty grass up the slope.

Now she saw that the others were running with her, after her. Minnow passed ahead of her, running full tilt. The cannons boomed on and the rattle of gunfire and the ringing sound of the war cries she could still hear over the huffing and swish of her running.

At the top of the slope, heart pounding, she stood with the others and looked toward the south. There was really nothing to see except woodlands to the horizon, the remaining red and yellow leaves of autumn hanging like tatters on the trees, only the treetops yet gilded by the morning sun which had barely cleared the horizon; the low ground still lay in bluish shade. The sky was utterly cloudless, but above a distant vale, smoke was rising, and the people looked at that place and watched the smoke roiling up white and gray to a height above the trees where it leveled and spread like a mist. The faraway thundering and howling of the battle went on unabated, and the people on the frosty rise gazed in that direction with glittering eyes, not talking, but sometimes moving their lips as if praying. After a short time there were no more cannon shots, and Minnow shut her eyes, bared her teeth, and emitted another piercing ululation, then another and another, her palate vibrating.

But Tuck Horse was nowhere to be seen.

After a long time, with nothing changing except the angle of the rising sun, Good Face felt so immensely saddened that she had to do something besides listen and watch the drifting smoke, and so she began walking about, looking for her father's trail. The sun had dissolved the frost. Looking back toward the camp, she could see the traces of bent grass where this morning they all had come up the slope. She went back down that way. No one followed her or even looked after her. The smoke of the campfire hung along the treetops like a wispy little imitation of the distant battle smoke. The horses were still in the rope corral, nosing in the dead grass, a few watching her. She walked in a circle around the little camp, found a trail and followed it into a thicket and saw there where somebody had left body waste. She went back to resume her circle, and then saw another vague trail of bent grass. She stood and looked at it for a moment, her ears still filled with the drumming noise of the faraway battle. She could see where the trail led. It went southward toward the old sunken, long-trodden war road.

"Ah, no!" she said aloud, and bit her lip, looking down the path and blinking, hugging herself. Then in the bright cold sunlight she went back up the slope toward the people, who were still gazing toward the battle smoke, which was thicker now and billowing higher. It was mid-morning by now and the din had not diminished at all. Three of the women had sat down in a circle on the forward slope and were singing a lamenting song in unison, softly, mournfully. Minnow, still standing and staring southward, turned and watched her come up, then reached out and grabbed her arm. "What, sister?"

"My father," she replied in a voice almost choked with dread. "He wanted to be young and go on the warpath. I believe he has gone there."

Minnow stared at her for a moment, then pulled her close and held her and took a deep breath. And then she cried out:

"Ha! *Wehlee heeleh!* What a man is Tuck Horse!"

Good Face was astonished. She opened her mouth, about to cry. But then something struck her heart and she saw in her mind her father's craggy face and his yellow teeth bared, and though her eyes were blurred with tears, she laughed hard and sharp, over the rumble of the distant conflict. Tuck Horse now could be happy. Minnow threw back her head and trilled the war cry. And for the first time in her life, Good Face drew a deep breath and shut her eyes against the brilliant sky and, from her own glorying, swollen heart she too poured out the thrilling tremolo.

There came a lull in the shooting and shouting, and then it resumed after a little while. Now it seemed to be farther away as the listeners on the meadow interpreted it. At last the old man who was the pack train leader called everybody together. The three women who had been singing came, their eyes shining.

"I have never seen such a thing as this," the old man said. "No one comes running back from the battle. Always the armies pushed us back. But it is all going that way." He pointed to the southeast. "It must be that our People are chasing the army home. It must be that our People are winning. Listen:

"I was given charge of bringing food to our warriors while keeping you distant from harm. Now hear what I have been thinking. My friend Tuck Horse has gone down with his old gun, so it seems. After such a fight as that has been, our horses surely are needed. There will surely be dead and wounded to carry. Some of you women I know to be healers. Now I ask if any of you want to help me take these horses down, instead of back, if any healers will go that way instead of homeward. Listen:

"Any who do not want to go with me may walk on the path home, and will be fairly thought of. As for me, I would like to follow Tuck Horse that way and see whether I can do more good down there. That is all I have to say. Tell me what you will do, and we will go our ways."

Everyone chose to go toward the battlefield. By the time the horses were strung together and the riders mounted, the battle sounds had nearly faded out.

As the pack train moved down the trail, it was joined by other groups of people with and without horses, mostly Shawnee and Miami, surging eagerly but fearfully down the war road.

After passing through the encampment where the horses had been unloaded the night before, the accumulating crowd moved for a while through a deep woods and then down a gentle slope through fallen autumn leaves into open ground through which meandered a pretty little river. Here in the bottomland there still remained some snow on the ground. Beyond the shallow river the land ascended a few feet onto a level meadow, and upon that land there was a scattering of fires and dense gray smoke, and white shapes that revealed themselves gradually through the smoke to be not snow, but hundreds of tents, many of them burning. Riding down to ford the shallow stream, Good Face heard a hellish din of voices: screams, war trills, howls and laughter and wailing, a great buzz and ringing of excited human voices, male and female, and sometimes the piteous shrieks of hurt horses. Her own mare was becoming jumpy and stubborn, and Good Face was too preoccupied with controlling her and keeping her string of pack animals coming along to look over the confused jumble of unfamiliar sights yet, but the sounds were so demonic and eerie that she was almost afraid to look ahead. It was when her mare was about to wade out on the other bank that she saw swirls of red in the river water beneath her and recognized that it was blood. Her heart quailed.

She saw then that the snow on the low riverbank was a trampled, churned pink and brown slush of blood and mud. Her mare shied away from some lumpy thing in the mush, and when she looked directly at it she gasped.

It was a muddy snarl of limbs and clothing, part blue wool, part wet deerskin, a moccasin and a boot and a bare, bloody foot, a white face frozen with its mouth open and blue eyes staring up, a crimped, bloody hand, and the profile of a painted warrior's face: two enemies locked together in an embrace of death as intimate as her copulations with her husband. Then the mare scrambled up the slope onto the level ground and began whinnying, shying and wheeling, in a panic because there was nowhere to step but on corpses.

Minnow leaped off her horse, abandoned her pack animals, and darted past Good Face with a scream as shrill as a whistle. She leaped among the corpses, searching with crazed eyes, then knelt with a knife in her hand, slashing at uniform cloth, and in an instant jumped to her feet with a scream of triumph. "A fine medicine pouch this will be, see?" she screamed, holding overhead a severed scrotum. When Good Face's panicked mare danced past, Minnow was stooping to find another and was lost to sight beyond a pile of soldier corpses smoldering on a bonfire near the wheels of a cannon.

Other women who had come down the trail were darting through the carnage, stripping the soldier corpses that had already been scalped by the warriors. And the victorious warriors themselves were swarming over the field of dead soldiers, gathering their guns and swords and bayonets, pulling off their boots, coats, and capes. Good Face at last got her horses under control as they became used to the bloody mess around them, and for a moment she was able to scan the field, looking for her husband and father, before faintness and nausea blurred her sight and she doubled forward and vomited over the mare's mane. She was so dizzy she feared she would fall, but was loath to dismount because she did not want to walk on carcasses or on an earth stained with blood, vomit, excrement, urine, ashes, soot, and even teeth and hair. As far as she could see into the drifting smoke, there were dead soldiers and horses, sagging, bullet-riddled canvas tents, broken boxes and kegs, hats, spoked wheels, smashed trunks and jugs, shreds of wet paper, arrows, bloody cloth, stove-in drums, rags on flagstaffs, kettles, and creeping fires. Shaking her head, trying to swallow back another upsurge of nausea, it seemed she was watched by the staring dead eyes of a red-haired woman who lay sprawled on her back, drenched with blood from her gaping cut throat.

A red-haired woman, as she was herself. Good Face was transfixed by the dead, open eyes staring up at her. In years past she had tried so often to remember the face of her Slocum mother, and it was as if she were seeing it now. Her mother had looked like this.

And while she was looking at the dead woman, a wiry little Shawnee woman suddenly appeared and crouched over the body, grabbed a fistful of the red hair, sliced around its roots with a knife, put the knife between her teeth to hold it, and used both hands to yank the scalp off with a loud, wet popping sound. The little woman jumped to her feet, looked up grinning at Good Face, then gaped in astonishment. She cried something in Shawnee, pointed back and forth between the scalp and Good Face's own red curls, then shrugged and hurried away, leaping from corpse to corpse as if crossing a brook on stepping-stones, beginning to yip and yodel as she went. Good Face slumped forward over the mare's withers with her eyes shut tight and retched, again and again.

By the middle of the afternoon the looting of the battlefield had been organized by chiefs and chieftains. Good Face had given her mare and packhorses to a group of warriors led by Little Turtle's son-in-law, Wild Potato, and they were loading the packsaddles with army muskets, powder kegs, and tools. Good Face wandered off through the carnage looking for her husband and father. She had at last emptied her heart and hardened herself so she could wade in blood and trample over bodies without fainting or throwing up.

The dead on the ground were all white people. Wild Potato told her that the few dead warriors had already been carried off the field, and the wounded too. In the eyes of the red-haired warrior, she had seen great distress—even though, as a Miami leader, he was rejoicing in an unbelievable victory—and in that momentary, anguished glance she saw that they shared some terrible understanding, something she would need to think and pray on before she would know how to speak of it.

Wild Potato had not said much to her, because he was not fluent in the Lenapeh tongue and she had forgotten most English words. But by using a little of both languages he had been able to tell her that there were nearly a thousand soldiers dead, that the army of the Long Knives was no more, and that the attack at dawn had been so fierce and surprising that not more than twenty or thirty warriors lost their lives, and not many more than that were wounded. He did not know who they all were, but he knew her father and her husband, and did not believe either of them had been hurt. Wild Potato had said—or she thought he said—that no Lenapeh had been killed that he knew of, and then he thanked her for the horses, and his eyes seemed to glitter with tears; but maybe they had just been inflamed, she thought. Like the eyes of everybody on the battlefield, they were red and watery. Everyone living and dead who had been in the battle was sooty from the black gunpowder and the gun smoke; the whole world seemed still to reek of it.

Black gunpowder and red blood. Every warrior was totally besmeared and besprinkled with both—clothes, faces, hair, especially their hands and arms—as if they had been butchering game and wallowing in char all day. Red and black were the warrior colors; they stood for courage and death in the lore of the People, but it seemed to her this day that they stood for blood and gunpowder.

By now most of the corpses lay naked, their white skin bloodsmeared. Women and warriors had been stripping them for their woolen clothes, shoes, and boots, which would be so welcome this winter. Good Face saw a number of warriors, some of them wearing three-cornered soldier hats and long-tailed blue army coats, boisterously pulling down tents. As the tents fell and were rolled up, some of them were laughing, giggling like women and whooping like fools. Seeing that they were sharing a jug made of brown pottery, she veered away from them with remorse and loathing, remembering the time she had found her husband howling like a demon beside the river. Tents were collapsing all over the battlefield. They were a wealth of cloth, which could be used for clothing or to help keep the rain out of *wikwams*, cloth that was expensive at the British trading posts. And there were hundreds of tents here. Most of them were riddled with holes from the musket balls and arrows that had deluged this army, but holes could be patched. And the little tents could be used for what they were too: shelters hunters could take with them on their pack-horses when they rode out to the hunting grounds, shelters to sleep in during the rains and snows while the new villages were being built. Even in her stunned state of mind, Good Face was grateful for all this cloth and all these soldier things that could be used by her People, whose belongings had so often been burned by the Long Knife armies. So many guns, so much wool clothing, kettles, tools, gunpowder, and lead for the hunters. Little Turtle, Blue Jacket, and Buckongahelas—the war chiefs—had given their peoples more than a victory over the Town Destroyers; they had also given them things that would make their lives easier and more comfortable, without having to barter for years with the stingy British traders for them. In this way, war made a little sense; it seemed just.

Yet her heart ached for the People. It was still a madness that everyone seemed to have, the madness to kill and make pain, the madness of hatred that caused good people to act as if they were full of *maxcheekwee menaxteeum*, the drink demons.

CHAPTER TWELVE

Good Face separated out three little strands of her red hair above her left ear and began braiding. She looked in the mirror at the braid sometimes, but mostly at her eyes and face. It was such a novelty to see it, and she was quite taken with her appearance. It was a very pleasing face. It looked so much like her memory of her birth mother's face that she could now remember how her birth mother had looked. Or she thought she could.

Her husband, Like Wood, had brought the mirror home from the battlefield, one of the things he had looted from one of the big tents. It had been an officer's mirror, he said. It was set in a round frame of smooth, reddish wood with silver-headed tacks all the way around, with a short handle that had a hole drilled in the end, making it easy to hang from a limb or from the frame of the *wikwam*. He had worn it home hung by a thong around his neck. From the same tent he had brought for himself a fancy wig of curled white hair. He liked to joke that of the three scalps he brought back from the battle, this was the only one he had taken without a knife. He had just picked it up from where it lay on a box beside the mirror. In the frenzy of the victory, dancing around the blazing fires, his two blood-crusted real scalps had been displayed on the end of a long pole, but he put the wig of silver hair on his own plucked bald head. Had he only the wig as a trophy, he would have been considered a contemptible clown for dancing the scalp dance in a wig, but since he had killed and scalped two soldiers and had their brown-haired and yellow-haired scalps, he was not only a hero in the scalp dance, but a high-hearted and funny hero. After the three battles of his young life, Like Wood now had four

285

soldiers' scalps and a wig. To the pigtail of the wig he tied the eagle feather he had earned as a warrior. Tuck Horse disapproved of his son-in-law's clownishness in this manner, thinking it must offend the ancestor spirits to see the feather of a warrior's true honor attached to a white man's wig, which the old man considered to be like a mere fool's hat.

But Like Wood had scoffed, pointing out that some of the warriors wore their eagle feathers attached to the three-cornered soldier hats they had brought from the battlefield. "You are too serious, Father," he said, grinning, and Tuck Horse grunted at him and shook his head. Like Wood said, "You wear your eagle feather tied in white hair, Father. Why should I not, also? Ha ha!"

Tuck Horse himself had taken one scalp at the battle. He had walked down Girty's Town trail from the packhorse camp that morning before the battle, walked in the frost and snow to arrive at the stream just as the eight hundred warriors charged the army camp. He had shot one of the hunting-coat soldiers who were running away at the very start of the battle, even before the cannons began shooting, and sat down in the snow beside him to scalp him, unable to kneel because his knees hurt too much from the long walk. Then he had not been able to get back up because of cramps in his old legs. "By the time I could stand up again," he told them, "the battle had moved over across the little river into the main soldier camp, where I could not catch up, and my behind was almost frozen off from sitting in the snow. Once, the bluecoat soldiers made a hard charge with bayonets and drove our People back toward me across the river and they nearly ran over me before our warriors pushed them back in and killed them all. It was wonderful to see how our warriors danced in and out between the bayonets and clubbed the bluecoats down. Then the cannons almost broke my ears, but they only shot too high and tore up the treetops. But that was my last battle. It is no good to fight a battle sitting in the snow. I do thank Creator that my last battle was such a victory. It was better than when we killed the army of the British general called Ba-lad-ock nearly forty summers ago, when I was a young warrior. That was where I earned the first of my feathers. Now I have so many from fighting Long Knives that an eagle himself would want to borrow some from me to get well dressed. Hm!"

Good Face and Flicker had smiled at each other. He had been acting grumpy because he was so pleased with himself, and it pleased him to gibe at his son-in-law, of whom he was actually proud.

Tuck Horse was also proud of his red-haired daughter. She too had earned a feather, a hawk feather, for helping take the food down to the war camp and then the packhorses to the battlefield. It was for that feather that she now made the braid. The quill of the feather was decorated with green glass beads and had sinew strands by which it could be tied into the braid and worn with pride. Minnow and the other women of the pack train had been granted such feathers too. Now the three treasures Good Face owned were her hawk feather, her mirror, and the old medicine bag Neepah had put on her when she was a little girl. Minnow, whose Miami husband was burned on the chest by embers from a cannon shot, had been preoccupied with skin since the battle in two ways: healing her husband's burns with acorn oil, and tanning the soldier scrotums she had harvested from the battlefield. From them she was going to make medicine bags for herself and all the other pack train women. Good Face knew that was what Minnow was doing and that she was to be given one, but she felt strongly that she did not want it, though she could not tell Minnow that. She would not wear two medicine bags, and she would never discard the one Neepah had given her.

And she did not want a medicine bag with hairs on it, as those scrotums had.

Snow squeaked underfoot as Good Face and Flicker walked through intense cold toward the Council Lodge. Flicker moved slowly, leaning on a walking staff, bent with age and pain, squinting against sun-dazzled snow. "Not since Tuck Horse was young have I known a man who would be on his wife as often as Like Wood is upon you." Good Face blushed and smiled, but Flicker did not look amused, and went on: "Yet, every time the moon comes around, you go off to the women's hut. I wonder why you have no grandchild coming for me. I was a grandmother when I was much younger. I should like to be a grandmother again, as a woman should be when she is old."

"I too wonder why," Good Face replied. "In praying to Kijilamuh ka'ong, I try to make him see me with a baby in my arms."

The old woman nodded. "That is good. I shall pray more for him to see me with a grandchild. You are right. It is better to pray than just wonder."

"This probably would be a good time to have children," Good Face mused. "The Long Knives no longer have an army. After what happened in the battle, they would not dare to come and bother our People anymore. For two years Little Turtle has defeated their armies. Surely it is all over by now and we can raise children without fear."

Flicker stopped for a moment, leaned on her walking stick, and looked sideways at her daughter through squinted wrinkles. She opened her mouth to say something, but instead shook her head once, sniffed, and plodded on, face full of thought. Good Face wondered what her mother had almost said and why she hadn't said it.

Cedarwood smoke, a smell that Good Face loved, drifted up toward the high, cobwebbed ceiling of the Council Lodge, swirled under the smoke hole, and then rushed upward, carrying the prayers and words of the Women's Council toward Creator. The elders and clan mothers got up one by one and talked of the matters in their hearts, with the light from the smoke hole shining in their hair and making their jewelry gleam. These were beloved and respected women in the village. Though they worked alongside all the other women and cared for their children and helped them at childbirth, and were like aunts and sisters, here in Council they were strong voices for the wishes of all the women, and were invested with the power to debate even against the tribal chiefs themselves on behalf of the Lenapeh women.

Even so, they had to concern themselves with small and ordinary matters as well as grand ones. In this long Council these women listened to the women of their clans and spoke on every sort of matter. A Council always began with old matters and tried to resolve them before new matters were brought forth. This day there were tiresome discussions about the uses and the sharing of army tent cloth. Then there was much talk about the use of the portable forges captured from the army. After that there followed a long, tearful, angry dispute resulting in a second Council warning to a gossiping woman, who looked at the floor and clenched her jaw as she was told that if she gossiped again, she would be expelled from the tribe.

At last the Women's Council proceeded to the matter of the Lenapeh People's future now that the Long Knives had been so thoroughly defeated. They talked about moving back to the

Tymochtee Sipu country where they had been two summers earlier, where they did not have to mix with so many people of other tribes and enjoyed better hunting because the towns were smaller and not so close together. A clan mother reminded them that although alliances of tribes were good for defense, as had been so well proved, Creator had given Peoples their own languages and ceremonies so they could be distinct. Then Flicker asked to speak.

Good Face helped her stand up. She stood with her white hair glowing with sky light and her eyes, mouth, and cheeks sunk in dark shadow. Here among these councillors, age and frailty had power in themselves.

"Sisters and daughters," she began in her dry, whispery voice. "Many of you are too young to have dwelt in Lenapeh'hokink, our true old homeland between the Eastern Sea and the mountains, and so you may think *wapsituk* are few. When they come through the great woods, even their armies look small. A victory such as we had in the past moon makes them look even smaller. You think they were all cut down and that is the end of their armies.

"Do not soothe yourselves with such thoughts! Most of my long life I lived in Lenapeh'hokink, and I have seen their numbers. In one town will dwell more white people than there are of our People between Kekionga and the mouth of the Maumee Sipu, and they have more such towns than one can count. You have seen anthills, where so many ants swarm that the earth itself appears to be moving? It is like that in those towns. They are a people as white as the maggots of flies, and they breed that fast.

"Why do you think they keep taking our lands, as they have been doing for the last ten generations? I will tell you why: because they grow to be so many that they would have to stand on each other's shoulders if they could not spread out!

"*Kulesta!* Once there was a time when Taxkwox Menoteh, Turtle Island upon which we live, had upon it just enough red people of all nations that they could eat plenty and move about and be happy. There were many hundreds of hundreds, but Turtle Island is vast, and we were never crowded. If it became hard to get enough food, we stopped having babies. Surely there was not a better or happier land anywhere than Turtle Island. But then came the *wapsi* boats. On their boats were sickness rats, and the white people themselves were so dirty they had sicknesses our healers did not know. We died, they bred, and soon they were more in numbers than we.

"They put lies on paper and called our land theirs. Then they brought a race of black-skin people from across the sea, and made those black-skin people cut down the woods for them and plow the ground. They made those black ones breed like flies too, so they would have more people to work for them. They caught our people and tried to make them work, but we ran away and would not do it.

"But listen, my sisters and daughters: I am sure the white men are ten or a hundred times our number now. Even their black people are more numerous than we are now. If we had a hundred victories such as this one, they could just keep making guns for new armies and keep coming. They can grow a new army every season. We are foolish if we think that we have won over them! Next year, or two years from now, another bluecoat army will come back to make revenge for what we did.

"*Kulesta!* Our young men feel full of power now as they dance with their scalps. But our Buckongahelas, and old Captain Pipe, even Blue Jacket and Little Turtle, they know it is not over. They fear that we will never have enough warriors or guns or powder to stop those armies. In the councils now they are starting to ask: Where can we move next to keep a distance between us and the Long Knives? Farther down the Maumee Sipu? Westward down the Wabash Sipu? Northward into Canada? There are already red people there: Ottawa and Ojibwa in the north. Potawatomi and Kickapoo and Illinoi and Sac and Fox in the west. When we are pushed into their country, will they welcome us?

"Such pushing began many generations ago, even when we were more numerous than the *wapsituk*. Now they are as thick as maggots in old meat, and with their sicknesses and guns and their spirit water, they keep making us fewer.

"Sisters and daughters. Lenapeh'hokink, our homeland in the East, is now closed to us and full of white men. Soon this place will be likewise. I am sorry to darken your joy. I am an old woman who enjoys what she can. I am happy that my old husband got a soldier scalp in his last fight. But that was only *his* last fight with the *wapsituk*. Our children and our children's children will have to go on fighting those fights until we are all gone and there is no land left that is not covered with white men. That is all I have to say. Daughter, help me sit down again."

* * *

Walking slowly home in the cold, Good Face said as she helped the tired old woman along, "Kahesana, I have something to ask you, and it is this:

"I believe your words, which made the women in Council look at our tomorrows in a more somber way. But if the *wapsituk* will be coming into our country again, why do you want me to have a baby, as you said this morning? You have often taught that we should not bring babies when soldiers are coming."

The old woman compressed her lips, moved them as if talking to herself, then said, "It is true that I have seen enough in this world to give good advice in Council.

"But still, you are a daughter of mine by whom I have not yet had a grandchild. Good advice or not, the way of it is that old women want to be grandmothers. Why else would we bother to be mothers?"

Wilkes-Barre

Giles snapped the long whip and whistled, and the tired gray put just a little more life into his pace for the upgrade. The sleigh's runners hissed softly and the gray's hoofbeats were muffled by the deep snow. "Eh, well, Ma," Giles said, the words coming forth in a cloud, "almost home to a warm house. We've missed thee."

Ruth Slocum, swaddled in a heavy dark wool blanket on the seat beside him, turned to look at him past the edge of her bonnet, which essentially confined her vision about the same as the blinders on the gray's bridle. She was very fatigued from the long journey back from Philadelphia and not in as good a mood as homecoming should have inspired. She crinkled her nose and kept turning her blindered head to look over the town of Wilkes-Barre they were passing through in the twilight.

"I remember when snow was white," she said. "I can remember when air was invisible and breathing didn't stink and burn one's nose." From almost every chimney rose black smoke, and the snow was gray. In Philadelphia, where she had been for the big Meeting of Friends to discuss missionary work, most of the heating was still by firewood, and even though that city had been unbelievably crowded and noisy, teeming with people like an anthill, as she had thought, at least the smoke in the air had not been caustic like this. It was the anthracite. She hated to think it,

but her son Ebenezer had had much to do with bringing this on.
He was a big merchant in coal now. He had made at his foundry a
kind of deep grate on legs, in which the hard coal, if stoked dili-
gently, would burn hot and steady with an underdraft. He was
manufacturing the grates and had sold a few. It was becoming
easier to get coal than firewood in the valley, and Ebenezer expected to sell hundreds of the coal grates in the next few years. He
called it his "Grate Invention." But it required more attention than
most people cared to give a fireplace or stove, and so most of his
coal he still used for his foundry or sold to the blacksmiths and
manufactories in the town and in other towns downriver. Ebenezer was clever and was making a lot of money, but his works
were among those gradually turning this once beautiful valley into
something that now and then made Ruth Slocum think of Hell.

At the house, William and Isaac came out, embraced their mother,
and carried her trunk from the sleigh into the house, while Giles
unharnessed the gray and fed and watered him at the barn. By
the time he came back in, all were seated near the hearth, where
Ebenezer's grate glowed white and red, and a pot of tea was
steaming. Whale oil lamps were burning in their sconces. It was
warm and light in the room, but the mood was dark. On the
kitchen table was spread a broadside newspaper printed in Boston,
across the top of which were depicted thirty-nine coffins in two
rows. Over each coffin was printed the name of an army officer
who had been killed in the great defeat of General St. Clair's army
in the Ohio Territory. Ruth Slocum had seen the paper in Philadelphia, and was not happy to see that one of her sons had
obtained a copy and brought it into her house. It was bad enough
to reflect on the violent follies of man without having a paper
memorial to them lying on one's table, complete with coffins,
skull and crossbones, black borders, a picture of the slain General
Richard Butler, second in command, and a forty-one stanza elegy
in pompous and execrable verse glorifying the sacrifice of some
eight or nine hundred souls. Its headline was:

COLUMBIAN TRAGEDY
Containing a Particular and Official
ACCOUNT
Of the Brave and Unfortunate OFFICERS and SOLDIERS, who
were
Slain and Wounded in the EVER-MEMORABLE and

BLOODY INDIAN BATTLE,
Perhaps the most Shocking that has happened in AMERICA
since
its first Discovery

On the left hand of the page was a woodcut picture of an Indian warrior holding a tomahawk in his right hand and a bow in his left, in a formal and mincing pose. Ruth Slocum pointed a finger at it and said, "Has any of thee ever beheld an Indian who looked the least bit like that?"

William chuckled. "That's a Boston artist. I'd reckon the only Indians he ever saw were them who dumped British tea in the harbor. Meaning, that is, white men in disguise."

"I'm sorry," Ruth said. "Truly, there's nought amusing about it." She twisted one hand in the other so hard her knuckles whitened. "So many souls! Such a pity 'tis there's so much anger in the land. I suppose the truth is if it had not been those soldiers' souls dispatched, 'twould have been those of the Indians."

Giles nodded. "No doubt of that."

She sat gazing at her teacup and remembering the Meeting she had attended, and its purposes. She realized that at this dismal time, the Quakers probably were almost the only white people in America who would credit the Indians with having souls. The mission work of the Friends was to encourage peace and tolerance between the races, and help the Indians with food and tools and knowledge, not force them to believe in the white man's version of God. News of St. Clair's defeat had come during the missionary meetings, and Ruth Slocum could remember the feeling that had passed through the room, a great heaviness on the spirit, an unspoken understanding that what had happened at the headwaters of the Wabash would make every aspect of the mission work harder—but also more crucial.

The mission work had long been crucial for Ruth Slocum, once she'd started thinking about it. She had said once to her sons: "If there are missionaries out there in every tribe all the time, why, that'll be so much better than thee lads going to one tribe at a time to look for poor Frannie."

Giles had gone up the river in the previous spring and at Painted Post had caught up with Colonel Thomas Proctor. The colonel had not remembered anything about the Slocum family, citing twelve eventful years of war and public service as an excuse, but he allowed Giles to accompany his expedition.

Nothing had come of it. Colonel Proctor had seen a young woman whom he took to be Frances Slocum—she was with an old Delaware chair maker and his wife—but by the time Giles returned from a trip to nearby Cornplanter's Town, they were gone.

Thus Giles had once again slumped home to Wilkes-Barre with nothing better than an expanded knowledge of frontier geography and a greater pity for the displaced tribes of the Longhouse Road. Then the news had followed that Governor Arthur St. Clair of the Ohio Territory, one of President Washington's famous old Revolutionary War generals, was preparing to march an avenging army into the Indian country again, and any more searching this year had been rendered impossible.

And in view of General St. Clair's fate as described in the Boston broadside with its rows of black printed coffins, it seemed doubtful that any more quests through the Indian country could be made in the near future. Ruth Slocum sipped her tea, which had grown tepid, set the cup on the table, and gazed at the printed sheet. With a sigh, she said, "It seems to me that all God's work our Friends try to do is undone by army generals. Well, my boys, I'm a truly worn-out woman and I need to sleep for about a week. But first, let us pray for peace and mercy, and for our poor Frannie."

CHAPTER THIRTEEN

Spring 1793
Maumee Sipu

The field of corn was planted, and the Lenapeh women of the town walked around the perimeter dragging their sweaty dresses to scent the ground and discourage animals. In several parts of the field stood pole scaffolds where girls later would perch with lengths of trading-house cloth, pans and turtle-shell rattles, and bone whistles to scare off crows and other seed eaters. The naked women were singing.

Good Face, now twenty summers of age but still a childless wife, trudged tiredly with the other women, enjoying the mild sun and the caress of the spring breeze that were drying the sweat on her bare skin. She watched the women ahead of her, noticing how plump some of her friends had become during these peaceful seasons when no armies came to burn the crops and starve the People. Some of them ahead of her had filled out so that there were creases in the fat at their waists and their brown buttocks and thighs quaked with every step. Good Face herself was still slim in the waist and firm in the muscles, but her breasts had grown larger and so heavy that they tugged under their skin as she walked, and they bobbled in the lower part of her vision even when she was looking straight ahead, the sun-browned pair of them, and the women ahead of her were all made in that same unseparated symmetry of twos: legs and arms and buttocks, line of spine and cleft below, like so much of what grew in the world, paired—eyes, ears, nostrils, wings, the joined halves of a bean and paired lobes of fruits and nuts, of the lungs and organs of butchered game. A favorite design of the Creator, this of joined halves. She had been noticing it most of her life but had never thought about it in the front of her mind.

And into the divide of woman came the singleness of man, she thought, shuddering unexpectedly at the memory of her husband inside her. Lately he had done it less, only when he really needed relief, and sometimes when she wanted the pleasure, he would pretend to sleep too deeply to be aware of her yearning touches. A small cloud passed under the sun, and without the sunglow, she felt chilly in the still-cool breeze of early spring. Something was changing in him. Some nights he did not come home even though he was not away on hunting trips. Two days ago her beautiful mirror had disappeared out of the *wikwam*, and when she asked him if he had seen it, he looked down and then back up and said no and she knew he lied about it. She had started to challenge him, but he could have argued that since it was he who had given her the mirror, he could take it away again, whether she knew why or not. A thought had burrowed through her mind that, since he desired her so little anymore, perhaps he had given the mirror to another woman. She had heard her friends speak of such betrayals that husbands did sometimes. Of course, women did so too. She had never even considered it. She loved Like Wood only.

The sun had come out from behind the cloud. The women were walking cheerfully down to the river to bathe and wash their sweaty dresses. Good Face felt a strange, unpleasant caution. She felt as she waded into the water that someone was watching. She dove under the water, tense against its coldness, then surfaced, and as she squatted in the river with only her head and shoulders out, covered with gooseflesh, she scanned the fresh green foliage along the riverbank.

She saw the white man first, seeing a speck of pale color that was not the flowering of dogwood but the linen of a shirt. His eyes seemed to be upon her and so she pretended to be laving her forehead while looking at him between her fingers. He was not twenty paces away in a thicket on the shore. He was thick-bearded, and she recognized him as a man she had seen at Traders Town: a stalwart, burning-eyed man whom Minnow had warned her against as a woman grabber as well as a rum seller. Good Face stared through the thicket until she was certain there were no more than two men there, the other being better concealed in shadow but his form visible. She remembered what the women bathing on the lake beach had done a long time ago when they discovered the boy Like Wood spying on them, and, suddenly hot with indignation, she pointed and cried to the other women over their splashing and laughter:

"Look there! *Wapsi* men who want to see our hind ends!"

They followed her gesture and saw the two voyeurs, and charged like a swarm of hornets, surging out of the shallows, shrilling. This time it looked as if the women were going to attack the men, not just give them the backside insult; some of the women were grabbing up their grub hoes and mattocks and charging toward the thicket. Minnow was among those in the forefront, and Good Face had an awful notion that this white man's scrotum would soon be a medicine bag like the one Minnow had given her, which she kept hidden but never wore. Good Face herself was boiling up out of the river with the others with her wet deerskin dress in one hand. She was irate enough to go after the men with her hoe too, and was glancing around for it, but then looked up toward the thicket and what she saw made her halt, mouth falling open in astonishment, pulse pounding in her ears.

The two men having come to see naked women apparently were seeing more than they had meant to and now had broken from cover, sprinting across the sunny, new-planted cornfield, the white man in his linen baggy-sleeve shirt and brown pants running heavy-footed and stumbling through the fresh-worked seed hills, kicking up clods as he went.

The other was swift and light-footed as a deer, and it was her husband, Like Wood. Good Face was at once so heavy with shame that she just stopped on the riverbank and stood there with the cold, sodden deerskin dress pressed against her face, crying, the first time she had cried in years.

Ohhhhh, she thought in the direction of the shrieking women. Catch him, sisters. Kill him.

No, don't.

Yes, do.

No, don't.

Like Wood and the rum seller had escaped unhurt. Good Face felt wounded by shame, and avoided the other women, staying at home with Tuck Horse and Flicker, who were ill with fevers. She kept herself busy gathering and preparing dogwood bark into a strong tea to cool their fevers. She would not talk about what had happened, not even with Minnow, who came by now and then and tried to assure her that Like Wood had proven himself unworthy of a moment's despair. "He runs with a rum seller!" Minnow snarled.

After a few days, when her parents were over their fevers, Good Face went to her lodge and noticed that something was missing from among the belongings that hung from the *wikwam*'s supporting poles. With her index knuckle pressed to her lips she studied everything until she realized that what was gone was her husband's flute, with which he had first wooed her. The marten-skin case was absent from the place where it had always hung by a thong. Her sadness deepened and she tried to harden her heart against him, thinking that he would now be away in some other village, drinking rum and spying on women with his *wapsi* friend, and then, probably, using his flute to seduce whichever one he found most desirable. Her emotions were a jumble of jealousy, contempt, and remorse, all fed by her imagination. Sometimes she would even dream of his song, which he had made for her so long ago. Then one night she awoke in the dark and realized that she was actually hearing it. Through the smoke hole in the roof she saw that the treetops were illuminated by a past-full moon. Rising from the bed where she had been sleeping, she took up an old blanket and wrapped herself in it, drawn outdoors both by the puzzle of the flute song and a need to urinate.

The flute was so faint that the hiss of her water drowned it out. Standing, she wrapped the blanket about her again not because she was cold but because she was naked, as she always slept. In the moon dapple through the trees the *wikwams* of the sleeping town stood round, dark, and shabby like sleeping bears. Here and there came snores or soft voices, brief coughs. A crepitant, forced breaking of wind, as of someone farting as loudly as possible, followed by snickering and giggling in two voices and then two more harsh eruptions and more giggling. She did not smile even at that, but trod on silent bare feet toward the flute song. She did not think or know what she would do when or if she found the flute player. She could only go toward her song. This was very much like a dream.

Past the last *wikwams* a cornfield lay in the moonlight, a field of fresh dirt heaps not yet sprouted up enough to see, and there against the misty bluish silver of the clearing was silhouetted a sitting figure under a hazel bush. The flute went silent in midnote and the figure rose to stand before her. It was he. Slender, broad-shouldered, the gracefully muscled physique she knew so intimately and for which her body had been yearning so much. In this dreamlike encounter her anger and contempt barely muttered in her soul, as if from the wakefulness outside the dream. He came close, cautiously reached out, and put a hot hand on the side of her face. He wore only breechcloth and moccasins. The moonlight gleamed on his skull, and half the planes of his face were in shadow. She shut her eyes and pressed her face against the warm palm of his hand.

"*Waneeshee,* my wife," he murmured. "You heard your song. I am grateful that you came."

She opened her eyes and looked at him in the moonlight, which seemed to have doubled its brightness. In the air she smelled a sweetness something like flowers, vaguely familiar, but to some unpleasant part of her memory. In the next inhalation she smelled it again, and though sweet, it smelled unclean, perhaps like wet flowers rotting. She looked at him and said, "I had to follow my song." She did not want to say anything about the incident at the riverside, although the shame and sadness of it were beginning to stir in her dreamy soul. But this was a beauteous moment and she knew that she had not quit loving this man.

He took her hand and gently pulled until her hand moved back and opened and the blanket fell open. When he saw that she was naked, he gave that sigh of awe that she knew so well, and she thought happily: he does not spy on other women, he was looking at me. She let him look for a moment, and he breathed long and deep breaths, and then she groped for the blanket corners and wrapped herself in it again.

"My wife," he said, "follow me," and his voice was so tender a murmur that she followed him. They walked silent as spirits, not toward their own *wikwam* but around the edge of the town, along a collapsing length of what once had been a defensive palisade of sharpened posts when an earlier town had been here; she knew where she was even though she seemed to be walking in a dream. A secretion was slickening the insides of her thighs, and with an edge of the blanket in one hand she mopped it dry, surprised at her body's eagerness. He stopped in front of her.

"Wait here," he whispered, and she nodded. He moved away to an old *wikwam* near the end of the palisade, a *wikwam* that she knew to have been abandoned. It stood pale in the moonlight, and she saw that where its old sheets of bark had fallen and gaped, it was now covered with the canvas of one of the tents taken from the army. A faint, warm light shone through the fabric, shadowed by the structure's wooden ribs and bark slabs. So this is where he has been living all these days, she thought. In our own town, this close to me, staying away for shame. Pity and tenderness melded with desire as she stood waiting. She saw his shadow moving on the canvas as the firelight inside brightened. She remembered how he had loved to look at her standing nude in firelight. She heard his voice murmuring as he built up the fire and thought that he was humming a song to himself. At this unexpected thought of Like Wood being happy, a welling of tears made the moonlit and firelit images of the night, even the moon and stars, blur and swim.

His head and shoulders emerged from under the door flap and he gave the soft imitation of a bobwhite, which he had used to attract her attention when approaching home or seeing her outdoors; it meant please come to me.

She went and slipped through the door into the warm, well-lit interior, her heart swollen with bittersweet forgiveness and desire. She faced his silhouette as he stood intensely close before her. She had opened the blanket and let it fall away, and was holding a corner of it with one hand, when Like Wood moved aside and she saw her tack-studded mirror hanging from overhead, gleaming and glinting, and then she remembered that the sweet smell around him was the smell of rum and she saw the white man standing on the other side of the fire.

His shirt was off, his hairy torso was sweaty, his teeth were showing through his black beard in a grin, and his eyes, bulging and roving, were devouring her nakedness. As she started to swing the blanket around to hide herself, Like Wood grabbed her wrist in a hard grip and tried to turn her toward the big *wapsi*. She smelled the man's sweat and the thick aroma of spirit water in the place and saw a wooden chest and a jumble of small kegs and weapons and piles of hides. The man was breathing hard and making a sort of groaning, growling sound that she realized were words in the *wapsi* tongue, and though it had been years since she had heard much English, she understood him: "Oh, thank you, m'buck!" The man stooped, picked up a keg the size of a gourd, and handed it to Like Wood, who, with his flute in one hand, had to drop it or her wrist to take the keg. He tossed the flute onto a pile of furs near the door, reached and took the keg, nodding and grinning. He had done well to keep a grip on her wrist, because she was trying to twist loose and get out the door. He squeezed so hard she thought her wrist bones would break, and began talking to her rapidly in their tongue:

"*Kulesta!* Eh! He desires you even as I do! He is a good man, you will like him! Do this for me. Just one night! You will have a good time with a man of your own kind, a *wapsi* like you, and I will have a good time with this. Only one night, eh, my wife? What is wrong with that?"

She quit struggling for a moment so that he would ease his grip. She looked at him and he was blurred by the tears in her eyes. She tried to yank free, but his grip tightened instantly and he swung his other hand at her and the weight of the keg slammed her shoulder and glanced off to hit her on the temple. A sun flashed in her head.

She heard a man talking, and when she realized it was the rum seller's voice, she opened her eyes. Her head ached and the man was squatting beside her with two faces and two bodies. He had a rag wet with rum and was daubing at her head with it, and the smell rankled and the touch stung where she had been struck by the keg and there was a dull ache also in her shoulder. The white man had not covered her. She was lying naked on the fallen blanket. The man's two forms slowly became one and she could partially understand what he was saying to her. Like Wood was not in the *wikwam*, she verified by a quick glance around.

"There, now, miss. Sorry y' got bunged up 'ere. Your buck doesna handle himself well when he gets too thirsty, does he? Can y'understand English, miss? Ah, good! Now, pretty lass, I'll no' hurt ye. I'm a friendly, lonely en'p'eneur, and I have just damned utterly gone all atwitter in love wi' ye. Can y'sit up, m' dear?"

She nodded. It hurt almost as much to nod as to try to sit up, but she had all her will aimed toward the moonlit night outside that door flap a few feet away, and she could not get to it lying down. She knew pretty certainly that if she made a quick move, he, for all his love talk, would jump on her and keep her down, perhaps even knock her out again if she cried out. So she forced a smile and sat and tried to think of how to get out of this. It was hard to think of anything, and she was trying to remember how to say things in her old tongue and what to say if she could remember how. She could remember some words, but the Lenapeh did not put words together as the *wapsi* did, and it was the putting together of words that she had forgotten. She said, "Sir. This I want not.

Thee I want not. This was my husband did. Thank thee for be kind but go I do want?"

With a quick shrewd look in his eyes he swung around to sit on one hip, with his thick arm over her waist, and with a wet-lipped smile he said, "Now, me lassie, I did pay a muckle for the honor o' your company, and yeer handsome buck-o did make me a promise that y'd stay wi' me a night. Please be kind, and by God I'll be likewise. Maybe y'd like a sip o' heart-warmer. O' which I happen t' ave aplenty at hand." As he spoke his just-intelligible words, he kept sweeping her with his eyes, and with the palm of a sweaty hand he molded her breast and weighed it, and groaned. "Ha' ye ever had a taste o' sperrit water, me dear? Yeer buck-o likes it a lot."

She thought fast. The mirror turned slowly in the rising heat from the fire pit and glinted. She said, "No. Never have I. I would like, you say?" Some of that had come out in Lenapeh, but apparently he understood, for he gave a great grinning sigh and rose up to fetch some. But he grasped her wrist and pulled her up to stand with him, and kept a tight hold. As he pulled her toward the kegs, she held back and pointed at the mirror, which she presumed Like Wood had traded for spirit water. She pointed at her head wound and then the mirror. "I look? See my hurt?"

"Heh! Aye, the justifiable vanity of a lovely lass! Aye, well, it's no' so bad as it feels, so, sure then." He reached up, tugged the thong, caught the mirror as it slid free, and put it in her hand. Still holding her wrist while she looked in the mirror at the lacerated bruise beside her eye, he poured liquor over a cup while looking her up and down, up and down, now all dripping with sweat and lust, and half the liquor glugged out onto the tabletop around the cup. The more she smiled at him, the easier was his grip on her waist. "There, m' lassie," he panted, handing her the cup and freeing her wrist so she could hold both her drink and the mirror. But he was not so negligent as to let her near the door, and moved between her and the exit, both mighty arms at the ready to grab if she tried to dart out. She smiled over the edge of the mug and sniffed its repugnant aroma and kept smiling, and watched his eyes as they roamed over her.

"What was yeer name 'fore ye b'come a savage?" he asked. "D'ye remember? What would they'a named a pretty red-haired bairn, d'ye remember, or should I guess all night as I'm puttin' the auld skean dhu to ye. . . ."

When his gaze was on her lower parts, she pitched the rum into his eyes with one hand and with an arm toughened by woman's work swung the mirror at the side of his head. The splashed rum flared up in the fire pit. She stooped and darted to the doorway, snatching up the blanket as she went while the man roared and flailed about. Her last sight as she scrambled into the cool moonlight was the *wapsi* rum seller falling on his rump in the fire pit with his rum-soaked whiskers ablaze.

At home Good Face put all of Like Wood's belongings outside the door and left them there. Neighbors went by for two days, seeing them, knowing that he had by their tradition been divorced. On the second of those days it rained, and all his things made of rawhide, the quiver and rawhide chest and the painted rawhide envelope containing his war feathers, went soft and lost their shape and his gunpowder was ruined.

On the day when he slunk up to the door to begin carrying things away, neighbors were pretending not to watch. He gathered them up, eyes bloodshot from spirit water and forlorn for many other reasons. She was inside, peering out at this wretch she had loved so much, and he probably was relieved that he did not see her about. But when he had everything so loaded in his arms that he could hardly see over them, she slipped out of the *wikwam* that had been their home and stared straight into his eyes for a long time. Then, remembering the old puberty teachings, she set her teeth and reached down between his legs and got his scrotum in her work-hardened grip and squeezed and twisted and pulled until his knees began to buckle and he was about to drop everything. It had required a terrible provocation, but for the first time in her life she was angry enough to deliberately make someone hurt. Minnow would be proud of her.

"Now go!" she said loudly, releasing him. "Your name is Empty Loincloth!"

CHAPTER FOURTEEN

The old ones spoke true about vengeance, Good Face thought. It is never satisfied. As Flicker had warned the Women's Council, the *wapsituk* had raised another army to avenge the loss of the last one.

She walked on, legs burning with fatigue, back and shoulders and neck aching from the weight of the pack basket, her sweaty forehead chafed by the tumpline, her wrist sore from tugging the horses' lead rope. Her moccasins and leggings were soaked from the wet grass and weeds, and the wet leather was blistering her feet, the sodden leather of the moccasins stained red with blood.

It was as it had been so often before. The People were going along a river bluff with everything they could carry, and there was a bluecoat army somewhere behind them. Just as Flicker had warned them last year, the *wapsituk* had grown themselves a new army, a bigger and better army, and had returned to punish Little Turtle and his allies for killing all those soldiers.

She twisted painfully to look back at her old mother, who was on one of the horses she led. Flicker's eyes were shut with the pain of riding so long.

This army's general was not stupid, as the ones before had been. This general kept coming along all summer. He kept scouts out all around and his army tight together, and had built a fortified camp every night guarded by sentries who never shut their eyes. These soldiers were well-disciplined and seemed not to be afraid. This general never got into a place where he could be ambushed.

This general's name was Wayne. Everybody knew his name

because he was always sending ahead peace offers. Little Turtle had given Wayne the name He Who Never Sleeps, and finally Little Turtle had said the unsayable: that perhaps it would be better to smoke the peace calumet with this general instead of fighting him. To the other stunned chiefs, Little Turtle said he doubted it was possible to defeat three Long Knife armies one after another.

When the other war chiefs, still proud of their defeat of St. Clair, said they would not talk peace with Wayne, Little Turtle had astonished them by stepping down as their war leader. They had elected the Shawnee named Blue Jacket to replace him, and Little Turtle assumed command of his Miamis only. He would help the other chiefs but he would not lead them in a cause he believed was lost. So now it was Blue Jacket who was trying to stop He Who Never Sleeps.

It was steamy in the valley of the Maumee. There had been many rainy days during the People's retreat down from Kekionga, down past the towns at the mouth of the Auglaize, down past the Blown-Down Woods, down past the British fort. The path was churned to slick mud, and the work of walking made sweat flow from every pore. Good Face could hardly see the people and horses and travois dogs ahead of her on the path because of the sweat in her eyes. The still, hot, damp air seemed almost too thick to breathe. The People made wretched gasping and groaning sounds as they slogged along. And their spirits were low because Wayne had reached the Maumee lands before harvesttime. Just now the heat and exhaustion made it hard to think of anything else, but Good Face from time to time did think of the lost harvest, and that when winter did come, there would be nothing to eat and there would be no shelter.

Wild Potato had betrayed his father-in-law Little Turtle and joined General Wayne. He had gone back to be a *wapsini*. Good Face thought of that sometimes even in this misery. Tuck Horse said that betrayal had broken Little Turtle's heart and that was why he wanted to quit fighting. Maybe that was so, maybe not. She wondered how Wild Potato could have done that. She would remember his face and his red hair, and the way they would sometimes glance at each other, she a red-haired Lenapeh, he a red-haired Miami. She remembered the way his face looked on the battlefield two winters ago when the snowy ground was bloody and covered with dead soldiers, soldiers of their birth people. Sometime between then and now he had decided that his heart was white instead of red after all. Or at least she thought he must have decided that. One could never judge what was in another's soul, except by seeing what that one did.

As for me, she thought, I don't believe I will ever do what Wild Potato has done. It seems like the *wapsituk* are winning everything now and we are losing everything, but I still don't believe I would ever go back to that side. Maybe it is easier to live if you are winning. But these are my People.

She had been along this valley before. On foot sometimes, in canoes sometimes. She and her parents had come down this river to get on the French sailboat on the Erie lake. She knew this river's rapids and the Bull Head Rock in the river, and the British fort up on the north bluff, and the Blown-Down Woods, where a powerful whirling wind not long ago had blown down much of a forest on the north bluff of the Maumee Sipu, leaving a tangle of dead and splintered giant trees lying and leaning on each other. It was so hard to get through that these fleeing people had veered far northward around it, though the circuit added much distance to their retreat down the river.

Good Face slipped sideways on the muddy path and almost fell, but caught herself with her left hand and righted herself with a groan of effort and pain. She was top heavy with the pack basket, and its weight had jammed and sprained her hand and arm. The pain of it flickered behind her eyes like lightning, but no one even noticed. Eveybody was slipping, and many had fallen. She remembered telling Minnow, that year when the last army was coming, that she would not be helpless like a blown leaf again in front of these calamities—that she would try to know what was happening so she wouldn't be helpless.

E heh, but I feel as much like a blown leaf now as I ever did, even though I have tried to know what is happening, what is planned, what is hoped for.

She knew what was planned and what was hoped for. Blue Jacket planned to fight the army at the Blown-Down Woods, which was like a natural fortress in the general's way. Every army before had finally come too far, past a safe point, and finally been whipped. Wayne had come farther than the others and was ready to be whipped. Blue Jacket now had nearly as many warriors as Little Turtle had had the last time, and they were massing for an ambush behind and under the tangled big trees of the blow-down. Not even a smart, brave General Who Never Sleeps could push through a place like that filled with warriors; it would be like slapping a hornet nest. That, she knew, was Blue Jacket's plan and his hope, and she prayed that he was right. The British in their fort had promised Blue Jacket and Buckongahelas that they would help.

These refugees would go on down the river to Swan Creek, almost to the Erie Lake, and wait in safety there until Blue Jacket defeated the army at the blow-down and chased them back. Then the People could go back up the river and return to living at Kekionga, though they would have to rebuild homes again.

There were many parties of warriors passing the other way on this path, going up toward the fort and the Blown-Down Woods. They had ammunition and food supplied by the British. Whenever warriors passed, Good Face glanced to see if Like Wood might be among them. She had not thought about how she might meet his eyes if she saw him. For a while she had thought such things, but much happens in living, and such concerns fade away. He might be a warrior among these going to help Blue Jacket stop the general, but to her and her family, he was Empty Loincloth. Once, they had loved with passion, but her pleasure memories were pale compared with her memory of the drunken man who had tried to sell her to a rum trader.

She looked back. Flicker and Tuck Horse were still slumped on their horses with the bundles and bags all around them, swaying as if asleep, coming along still, coming along as always with a blue-coat army somewhere behind.

She could not see their expressions, whether they were awake or not; there was too much sweat in her eyes.

So she just faced forward and kept going along in the mud.

Two days later, in their makeshift camp at Swan Creek, they heard in the humid breeze from the southwest the muffled thunder of battle.

By the middle of the day those noises had stopped, and the people stood in mud amid their hasty shelters, Lenapeh and Shawnee, Miami and Ottawa, looking back up the river. Finally in the afternoon they saw smoke rising high in the southwest.

They had learned after years of such things that the smoke usually meant the army had won and was setting fire to everything. But they did not say it, and tried not to think it, because it might not be so, and they did not want He Who Creates By Thinking to think of it that way, for then it would be so, if it wasn't yet.

The smoke grew higher and thicker and darker late in the afternoon and came rolling down to drift over the refugees like a fog. But it was not cool and clean like fog. It was full of ash, and in it they could smell what was burning: wood and bark and hay, and green corn and animal hides—everything that could burn in towns and the crops around. Tuck Horse said, "What burners those soldiers are! The world is soaked by rain yet they can make it burn like tinder!"

Later the setting sun tried to come out from behind the clouds, but it came only as a dull red glow through the smoke. By then the news of the defeat had come down, and wounded warriors were coming, and those who were not hurt were smeared by their paint and sweat and others' blood and had no heart left at all.

The fallen timbers that seemed such a perfect place for defense had turned out instead to be a trap for the warriors, who were caught and pinned in the tangle by the boldly rushing bluecoat soldiers with their long guns and bayonets.

Then, worse, when the retreating warriors had run to the British fort for protection, the Redcoats had not fired their guns or cannons at the oncoming bluecoats, but had shut the gates and kept the warriors from coming in to take refuge, and had stayed in there like cowards, white faces peering over the walls.

"Did Blue Jacket forget," Tuck Horse sneered, "that British are *wapsituk* too, and that their words of promise are as brief and weightless as a breeze?"

In the smoky darkness that night in the refugee camp at Swan Creek, rumors and tales swirled around the bonfires; wounded men groaned under treatment, and the widows and children of dead warriors wailed. It was a sad, sprawling, shabby, muddy place, droning with confusion and despair, overcast by a dull red sky reflecting the upriver burnings. No leaders had come down from the battlefield to tell the People what was so, whether the army would keep coming down, what could be expected. Good Face went from fire to fire trying to learn anything she could, and finally made her way back to the cookfire where her old parents were resting. From a sooty kettle she served them a mush gray with soot. Just as she had gone from fire to fire to hear what she could, other people came to squat down beside Tuck Horse and see what he knew. Most of their talk was about betrayals. The people needed someone to blame for all this, and they felt that

Wild Potato and the British were the traitors responsible for it all. Tuck Horse as always had opinions, and he said:

"Here it is about Apekonit the Wild Potato: he has a hunger to be important. That is why he married the daughter of a chief who was always winning. Also it is why he joins now a general who is winning, now that the chief is losing. You will see, soon: what Wild Potato knows about Little Turtle and the Miami people will help the general put the chief under his boot, and it will make Wild Potato important among white men."

An old listener shook his head, gazing into the fire through the haze of his own pipe smoke: "What a people we are, always wanting to believe promises! Such a sad thing that we believe what we wish to see instead of what we do see! That has always been our weakness."

It was Flicker who responded then, from the other side of the fire: "So it is. But is that not how Kijilamuh ka'ong taught us to pray to him? By seeing what we wish? Are we then to blame our Creator for the times our hopes are betrayed?"

"*E heh!*" Tuck Horse grunted, with one emphatic nod.

Good Face was going to tell them that she could never have done what Wild Potato had done even though she too was born a red-haired *wapsini*, but she felt eyes looking hard at her, and turned to see Minnow standing just within the fireglow, looking at her with glittering eyes. Minnow summoned her with a motion of her head and withdrew into deeper shadow.

"*Kulesta,* sister," Minnow said when Good Face came to her and they stood in the humid night with mosquitoes whining around their faces. "Listen. I bring you away from the old ones to tell you this, because I want you to be strong and calm when you tell it in your family."

The tone of her voice made Good Face shiver with dread. "I listen, sister."

"One is gone who was a bad drinker and an empty loincloth. My husband saw him fall in the battle in the Blown-Down Woods."

"Like Wood?" She felt hollowed out. She had known this could happen for a long time. A year or two ago the same news would have been unbearable, would have made her scream and collapse; now it was just another part of all that was sad and dismal. It might have been better if he had been killed in the earlier battle, before he earned her disdain. She wanted to lean on Minnow because she felt dizzy, but took a deep breath and let her head clear and showed no weakness. "He was already dead to my heart," she said. "I feel no loss, but I honor him for dying on behalf of our People."

"Sister, you speak well. Hold me awhile."

The embrace, more than the news of the death, nearly wrung sobs out of her. She clenched her jaws to keep from quaking. Minnow was sinew, but her bosom gave heat. Minnow patted her back in the embrace and murmured to her: "The way of it is, we will all become bones in the earth. All these things that happen to us, copulating and planting, harvesting and killing, are what Creator gave us to do in our lives to keep us from thinking of being just bones in the earth."

Day by day, under the pall of smoke, the rumors came about what the army might do. Wayne had taunted the British in their fort and might attack it; he might even come marching on through here and destroy the British fort at Detroit, the People's last hope for refuge. In the minds of the People, Wayne was a powerful and terrible horned serpent spirit who would descend on them out of the smoky sky, though warriors who had seen him said he was just a fat man on a horse.

Flicker was weak and tired, but she got up and went about helping women heal the wounds of their warriors. Most were slash and stab wounds from soldiers' swords and bayonets, or gashes suffered in the wild retreat through splintered deadwood. Few warriors had gunshot wounds because the soldiers had charged with cold steel. But the warriors who had been shot had ragged wounds; the soldiers' guns had been loaded with both bullets and small shot.

Good Face helped her mother by gathering bark and roots, and cattail fluff for bandaging, and cutting bark for poultices and splints. She never saw Like Wood's body, because it had not been retrieved from the fallen timber battlefield, and she tried to give him no thought. But the daily sight of strong young bodies like his all cut and torn made her remember him more than she wanted to.

One day a Council was gathered in the refugee camp so that Simon Girty the partisan and Alexander McKee the trader could try to apologize for the shame of the British cowardice. Sitting in the crowded clearing, smelling cedar and tobacco smoke, which to her had become the very essences of prayer, feeling the presence of so many attentive people, she felt that the Lenapeh were still a living, sacred bond of people, still strong inside despite the recent defeat. She had not felt so comforted for many days.

Although they were apologizing for broken British promises, Girty and McKee made more British promises, and when the people realized that, they began looking around at each other with raised eyebrows, dropped chins, smirks and low chuckles. Nevertheless, the two men continued with their British promises: If the Indians would remain encamped here, they would be given provisions and blankets and ammunition, which could be brought easily by ships from Detroit. Some of the people, whose towns along the Maumee Sipu had been destroyed by Wayne, voted to stay here at Swan Creek for the winter, or as long as the British kept those promises, which they had reason to suspect would not be very long. Some of the people began, even before the Council was over, to exercise their love of gambling by placing bets on how many moons the British would keep sending the things they promised. Tuck Horse got up and made his feelings known to the Council.

"The British as always want to keep many of our Peoples between themselves and the Long Knives. Anyone who stays to protect Redcoats, after what they did at their fort, would be the worst fool. I will not stay here near the British. I will not go to Detroit near British. Wherever there are British, for the rest of my days I will go in the opposite way, even if I have to wade through Long Knives. That is all I have to say."

A few days after the battle, the Long Knife army of Wayne picked up its camp and moved. But instead of coming on down the valley, it began withdrawing up the Maumee Sipu.

Many warriors and chieftains, who had felt themselves whipped, felt a change of heart and a surge of courage. They saw the general's withdrawal as a retreat. Had he not failed to attack the British fort? Though he had burned everything in the valley, he was turning back. The fierce ones thus gathered and went up the river following the army like a pack of wolves following an elk herd, killing as many straggling soldiers as they could catch, while tormenting the army at night and keeping the soldiers from sleeping. Among those vengeful, eager warriors was Minnow's husband, a stealthy hunter, who vowed that he would get close enough to shoot arrows into *wapsi* behinds when the soldiers relieved themselves in the brush. The stories of such things came back to the refugee camps at Swan Creek and the People began to laugh again. The evil spirit of the Horned Serpent Wayne faded as the army went farther away upriver, and children could at last envision Wayne as a fat soldier on a horse.

But when the people began to wander a little way back up the river and saw nothing but ashes and stumps and charred rubble and smoking heaps of ruined crops the whole width of the valley, when they looked at the British Redcoats still in their fort with their mighty cannons they had been afraid to shoot at Wayne's army, they recalled that Maxa'xak, the Horned Serpent Grandfather Spirit, could assume other living forms—surely even that of a fat soldier on a horse.

Good Face one evening at sunset found Minnow sitting without expression beside the corpse of her Miami husband. Minnow's eyes looked harder than ever. Good Face yearned to go close and embrace her, but thought she could feel the force of Minnow's will pushing her away. So she sat down on the ground beside her, saying nothing, waiting to see what Minnow would want or need.

After a while Minnow said in a low, flat voice: "I could have kept him from going after them. But he wanted to shoot them in their hind ends as much as I wanted to cut off their bags."

"How could you have kept him from going?"

"I could have told him, but did not," Minnow replied, "that his seed is planted in my womb."

"That is the direction we go when we cross over to Other Side World," Tuck Horse said, pointing westward into the night with his pipe stem. "That way lies Muxumsah Wunchenewunk, West Grandfather, who takes our spirit to him when we are done with our bodies on This Side World. My wife and I are nearly done with our bodies, which are brittle and full of pain. But we can still walk and ride some, enough to go where we will never again have to see white British faces and red British coats. I say it is time for us to go that way, closer to West Grandfather."

Good Face was so moved by his solemnity that she sat a long while before asking him where in the west he wanted to go.

"Daughter, west of Kekionga there flows the Wabash Sipu. It is a peaceful, slow river, and almost its whole length there are no British or Long Knives. There are some French *wapsituks*, but they are married into the Miamis and other people who live on that river, and are easy to get along with. We might have peace there the rest of our years. I would like to go to the Wabash Sipu at once, so that we can find a place and make a house before winter."

Good Face turned to Flicker. "Kahesana, it is hardest for you to travel. What say you to such a long journey to a place you do not know?"

"Daughter, I can stay on a horse all day if someone puts me on its back. Or I can lie comfortably in a canoe. We still have our seeds and blankets, and hatchets, and your father's gun and tools. I am ready to take all those things and go to a peaceful place. And if my body cannot make it to the Wabash Sipu, my spirit can continue in that direction, which is the right way."

Good Face found Minnow at her husband's grave, which in the Miami way was marked by a tall red cedar pole with a ribbon and an eagle feather attached at the top to stir in the breeze. Good Face told Minnow where her family had decided to go. Minnow's mourning was more like an ember of anger smoldering than like grief. She was not one to sit still and weep. So she came away from the grave saying she would help them get ready to go.

Flicker could travel most comfortably in a canoe, and since the whole way from there to the Wabash Sipu could be traveled by water except a short portage near Kekionga, Minnow helped trade the family's old horses for a bark canoe of the Ottawa kind, light enough in weight for a man to carry on his shoulders. Tuck Horse made some repairs on it, and when those were done, Minnow said, "Red-Hair Sister, you are strong, but not strong enough to move a canoe and two old people up this swift river by yourself, or to carry it around the Buffalo Head rapids, or over the carrying trail by Kekionga. You will need help with this vessel."

Good Face knew that was true. Tuck Horse had been a strong paddler on the great Erie lake from Niagara to Detroit at the end of the long war, but that was so many years before, and his hands had become so bad that sometimes now the mere effort of putting a log on a fire made him wince.

"People will be going that way," she said. "Someone strong enough to help, I will find, and ask."

"You might ask your sister of the spirit, who stands here before you hinting."

"You, Minnow? You would go there?"

"The family of my husband lives over beyond Kekionga, somewhere beside that Wabash Sipu. Maybe they do not even know yet that the soldiers killed him. They are old. Probably they need me. I know their tongue well and could live with them. And I have a grandchild for them in me."

"Then come, please! I will not be so sad to go into an unknown country if my good sister of the spirit is with me!"

"*E heh.* We were already too many years without each other. If you tried to go away without me, I would follow you and slap your behind, one slap on every freckle."

For the first time in many days they looked at each other and smiled.

The weather was so hot and still when they started up the river that Good Face thought she would be unable to breathe. She knelt in the bow of the canoe and paddled on the right side; Minnow was in the stern, paddling and steering on the left side because she had been in canoes a great deal and knew how. Behind Good Face was Flicker, her painful old legs straight along the bottom of the vessel and her back resting on a bundle; and behind her, Tuck Horse, who was grumpy because they would not let him paddle.

This time of year the Maumee Sipu should have been sluggish and shallow, but because there had been so much rain, it ran high with a strong current. Because it was so hot and the paddling was so hard, Good Face and Minnow by mid-morning paused to pull their sweat-soaked dresses off. The sun beat and burned on Good Face's left side and arm and the side of her face, and she knew that with the sun and the sweat, she would be sunburned badly. As if reading her mind, Flicker spoke to her and handed forward a little pot of bear oil. Good Face spread it on her skin and handed the pot back. She found that it not only diminished the burning, but smoothed the friction of the paddle on her hand, which before had felt as if it might blister. The oil was passed back to Minnow, who also anointed herself, and they went on, straining at the paddles and gasping for breath. Oily sweat coursed constantly down their backs and ribs. By midday the heat was too great, and they put ashore on the left bank where a little creek ran in. Good Face and Minnow dove into the river to cool themselves while the old couple sat in the shade of cottonwoods and sycamores. For the rest of the day they paddled only a little while at a time, stopping for swimming and shade, until late afternoon when a light breeze came playing down the river and relieved the heat.

As they neared the British fort they saw burnt ground and trampled cornfields, and the ruins of villages and white men's houses. The countryside looked as if the sun had come down and rolled across the earth, flattening and scorching everything on both sides of the river. Tuck Horse gazed over the devastation and kept shaking his head and grinding his teeth.

It was almost dusk when they passed below the fort. The old man pointed up at its ramparts and palisades high on the bluff, silhouetted dark against the sunset's afterglow, sentries moving slowly against the ruddy background of sky, looking tiny as ants at this distance. "There stands a nest of cowards!" the old man shouted. At that moment a puff of smoke billowed from the fort, the evening cannon boomed, and the flag started down its pole. "Ai aie!" the old man cried, cupping his hands beside his mouth. "You dare shoot your cannon now, British *Zhaynkees*! The Long Knife is too far away to hear it!"

The next morning they paddled past the Blown-Down Woods and the countless buzzards that drifted above it. Good Face believed that Like Wood's body was still in there. Probably scalped. Perhaps skinned. On the air was a stink of decay.

She paddled with concentration, looking straight ahead at the water. She knew everyone in the canoe must be thinking of what had happened in there, to so many warriors, to the Indian nations.

But no one spoke of it. She swallowed again and again, eager to be away from that place forever.

At noon they began to hear the Maumee Sipu rapids ahead, a rushing, hissing sound, and saw bubbly foam drifting past the canoe. Now would come a hard part of their journey.

They sat in the canoe by the bank, with Good Face holding it steady by grasping a willow branch overhead, and studied the swift water coming down. It was Tuck Horse, with his long years on the rivers, who decided how they could pass the rapids. He explained thoughtfully, "In this season the water usually is so low one can get out and wade to pull the canoe up. Because of the rain, it is too deep and fast. We will have to take it out and carry it around by the path."

So they got out on the portage path, pulled the canoe ashore, unloaded everything, and made bundles. Two small bundles for the old couple, and one big, heavy one. There was the big bundle and there was the canoe. Good Face looked at it all and thought it would require two trips past the rapids, she and Minnow carrying the bundle, then coming back for the canoe.

But Minnow said: "Too much danger for two trips. You carry the big bundle on your back. I will carry the canoe. We will all go up together one time only. Less chance to get caught walking if there are soldiers around, or their scouts. We want to get past here quickly."

Good Face looked at her in disbelief. "You cannot carry that canoe by yourself!"

"*K'hehlah.* I can indeed. Maybe you think you cannot carry all the rest of that?"

Good Face looked at it and wondered whether she could, but said, "Yes, I can." All of it together would be heavier than the canoe, and she remembered that the rapids ran a long distance.

Minnow said, "Do you want me to carry the big bundle and you carry the canoe?"

Good Face looked at the long vessel and knew it would be too unwieldy, even if not too heavy for her, and said, "I can carry the bundle."

"Women argue," said Tuck Horse. "I will carry the canoe. You all get in."

They all laughed. When all the bundles were made and roped for arm loops and tumplines, Minnow lashed the paddles closely parallel to each other between the two middle thwarts, leaving just a little more than enough space to get her head between the paddles. Then the young women lifted the lighter bundles so that Tuck Horse and Flicker could put their arms through the loops.

"This is a baby's load," Tuck Horse grumbled.

"Men are babies," Minnow teased, and he grinned. "Complaining babies," she said. "Men complain if there is too much work, and even if there is too little."

Old Flicker laughed, standing under her load with drops of sweat running in rills down the lines of her face. Her wattled neck looked crooked as a buzzard's with the weight of the tumpline hauling back against her forehead, but she laughed.

Good Face looked at her big bundle and the canoe and simply could not see how either she or Minnow could get their loads up without helping each other, which neither could do because of her own load. Minnow said, "Squat in front of this and put your arms through." Good Face did so, but felt that if she tried to straighten up, all the weight would pull her backward. And even with her deerskin dress and the padding tied on the ropes, she knew it was going to hurt all the way. "Now stand," Minnow said, grunting and lifting, and when Good Face was up, the load was centered over her hips if she kept her forehead pressed forward against the tumpline. At once she was aching and sweating.

"Waneeshee," she gasped. "I am ready, but now I cannot help you."

"Do not all stand talking and watching," Minnow said. "You waste your strength waiting. Go on." Then she squatted with her left hip against the right gunwale of the canoe, reached across with her right hand to grip the thwart on the far side, and with one sure, swiveling motion that squeezed a groan out of her she rolled it bottom side up and stood swaying with the vessel resting on her shoulders, her head up inside it. Good Face was awed. She had seen muscular men hoist canoes that way, but Minnow was half the size of such men. And she was pregnant.

"I said move ahead," Minnow wheezed, swaying, shifting to get the weight balanced. "When I get going forward with this thing, I cannot stop to keep from running over slow turtles in my path!" She was laughing in gasps. Water from the bilges of the canoe was dribbling down onto the path.

"Ha! It's you who look like the turtle, under her shell!"

"I am too busy to laugh," Minnow said, her voice resonating from under the canoe. "Stop joking and move on or I will steer the prow of this thing right up the crack of your behind!" Good Face could hear how exhilarated Minnow was with having used her strength so well.

Good Face was also pleased and surprised with herself, that she could bear so much. But her neck, back, shoulders, and legs were being strained with every step she took. Her old parents were laboring hard up the path ahead of her and she could only imagine how their old bones must be hurting, their old hearts pounding. If they can keep going, she thought, I can.

In the middle of the rapids stood a high island of rock shaped like the hump and head of a buffalo. It seemed to take them an age to pass it, with the turbulent water rushing and gurgling below the footpath, so she kept a tense balance in order not to topple down the steep bluff and into the frothing water.

Soon her thigh and calf muscles were burning with fatigue, and she felt as if her neck bones were being ground like corn in a mortar. The shoulder loops felt as if they were gnawing through her flesh and bone, and her fingertips, curled inside the loops, were growing cramped and numb, her wrists in an agony of torsion. She needed to pull her fingers out, but they might as well have been in a beaver trap. She was streaming sweat.

Heaving for enough breath, she became aware of an opening out of the terrain along the path, and a leveling of the incline. She saw that they were coming out upon a gently sloping meadow, the path now grassy. She squinted through eye-stinging sweat to see the place.

On the trek downriver they had passed here a handsomely sited fishing village. It was now a charred and trampled waste, with a few scorched *wikwam* frames and debris strewn everywhere. Every pot or implement or scrap of hide or cloth had been smashed or torn into small fragments by the soldiers.

She desperately needed to drop the heavy load here and rest, but Minnow's voice grated, "Move! Move! You are about to get a canoe up your behind!"

She gasped in anger. It had been Minnow's idea to bring everything at once, and Good Face tried to retort. But her throat was too dry. With a grimace, she simply staggered on in pain and anger.

Suddenly, there in her way stood Tuck Horse and Flicker, sagging under their loads, heaving like a couple of blown horses. The sight of them swam and paled as she went dizzy, began to stagger . . .

She saw the canoe on the riverbank beside her, right side up, and Minnow was behind her lifting the great load off. Sharp pains stabbed through the ache of her shoulders and she drew her arms out, then turned to tongue-lash Minnow. But the wiry little woman was laughing, easing the pack to the ground and exclaiming in a panting voice:

"Oh, such a strong beast you are! That you could carry this without stopping!" Then she was lifting down the old people's packs and exclaiming to them, "What a daughter you have! You must be proud!"

Good Face stood blinking, muscles twitching, dizziness passing, trying to wring circulation and feeling back into her fingers, and astonished by Minnow's praise. Her anger vanished and she felt such a rush of admiration for this sinewy little woman that her heart swelled.

"Hurry, load the canoe," Minnow was already urging. "There must be army scouts near this portage! We must hurry on!"

Four days later Good Face smelled wet ashes, and as the canoe slid up the shaded green river toward a clearing on the right bank, she recognized a gigantic sycamore. This had been the Shawnee town of Blue Jacket. It was now a ruin, still smoking.

As they put the canoe ashore at sundown, near the mouth of the Auglaize, they heard the boom of a cannon from the south. Tuck Horse deduced that the Long Knives must now have a fort on the Auglaize. Being deep in what must now be army country, they hid the canoe and made a secluded camp in a thicket, off the Maumee trail.

That night when her parents and Minnow were in their blankets, Good Face went outside the little circle of campfire glow to wet the ground, and as she squatted with her dress up around her waist, still feeling the tight ache of the strenuous paddling in her arms and shoulder, hearing the hiss of her urine on the ground, she became aware of another sound, one that made her scalp feel cold. It was a sound like breathing, or perhaps more like snoring, with a groan or gurgle at the end of each breath. It could have been a bear, or a panther, though the sound had in it something hurt, pitiful, rather than menacing. With rapid heartbeat and slow moves, she smoothed down her skirt, and, moving stealthily sideways to keep from turning her back on whatever it was, edged back into the camp. There, she murmured into Minnow's ear and then squeezed Tuck Horse's arm till she knew he was awake, then told him. They all stayed low to the ground while the old man primed the firing pan of his musket and eased the frizzen back. They did not want to be seen outlined against the fireglow while pondering what to do, and Flicker suggested covering the fire with ashes to darken the camp. All this in whispers, murmurs. Instead, Minnow told them to put more wood on the fire and said she would slip out and around to see if she could see what was there. She took off her clothes so she could move silently and not give any handhold in case she had to fight someone in the dark, and took with her an old tarnished skinning knife of British steel. Good Face was both awed and chilled by Minnow's courage, but at the same time she knew that anyone who met that steely little woman in the shadows would also need courage, and luck as well.

As the firelight intensified, Tuck Horse slipped away to stand in its margins, blending into the shadows of a tree trunk, with his musket pointed toward the place where Good Face had heard the sounds. She prayed that he would not shoot Minnow by mistake as she prowled around out there. Good Face and Flicker stayed low to the ground near the fire, listening hard.

Then Minnow reappeared in the firelight, coming in behind Tuck Horse so stealthily that he did not even know she had returned. She pulled on her dress and said in a normal voice, "Make a torch and bring a blanket. That is a shot man lying out there and he is no *wapsini*."

Flicker always kept a few sycamore seed balls saturated with bear oil for use as candles. Good Face split the end of a green twig, clamped one of the balls in the end, and ignited it at the campfire. Carrying it as a torch, Minnow led the others into the bush, Tuck Horse just behind her with his musket ready.

The first sign they saw of the man was a glint of light on metal, then the sheen of sweat, and seeing where he lay, Good Face had a momentary twinge of embarrassment in having come so close to urinating on him in the dark.

He was not unconscious exactly, but seemed to be in a stupor. His eye was red and half closed but watching the light come toward him. If he had any weapon, he was hiding it behind him as he lay propped against a tree root. With the light close on him, he was hideous.

His head was swollen huge on the left side and smeared with yellow war paint and crusted blood, the one red eye a mere slit and the other swollen tight shut. His head was plucked bald except for a braided scalp lock at the crown decorated with a silver brooch holding the quill of a hawk feather. The metal that had glinted was either the brooch or the crescent-shaped gorget that hung by a thong from his neck.

Flicker limped forward and took the sycamore torch from Minnow. Then she knelt close to the wounded warrior, moved the light to and fro, and suddenly shook her head and groaned. Good Face peered over to see.

There under the large muscle of his chest was the hole from a musket ball, the flesh around it blackened and puckered. Unlike the other blood on his body, that coming from this wound was not dried but still issuing fresh and red. But worse than just the trickling of the blood was what she observed as the man breathed those gurgling breaths she had first heard:

With each inhalation, the blood bubbled. Flicker stated what she had at once presumed. "Air and blood. He is shot through his breathing chest. This is quite bad."

So, air was coming out through the bullet hole because he had been shot in the lung. At least that and maybe more. Good Face felt helpless. Surely this warrior would die.

But Flicker told them to carry him to the fire, and she rose painfully from her knees and limped, stooped, back into the light of the blaze before them.

When they carried him into the firelight, Flicker was already getting items out of the large bundle. She told them not to lay him down but to hold him standing. They wrestled with his limp form until one of the young women was under each of his arms; they were bearing all his weight. His head hung forward and his legs merely hung down, not supporting him in the least. He might as well have been a corpse. "Turn him so I can see all," she said, making a gesture, and they walked around him slowly until Flicker had been able to examine him all the way around by firelight.

"One hole only. Hmm. That ball is inside, then. Bad." She spread a wide scrap of clean deerhide on the ground. "Put him there, with the hole down," Flicker said.

"Lay him on his wound?" Minnow exclaimed.

"Yes."

They stretched him out prone. Flicker handed Minnow a bag. "Take this dogwood. Make a tea for his fever." She gave her another bag. "This is dried elm bark. Make a slick poultice. Hm. At daylight you must find a slick elm and get fresh bark." As Minnow turned away to cook the concoctions, Flicker told Good Face to slip her hands under the warrior's chest, one above the wound, the other below. Reluctant, she reached under the muscular, bloody, hot chest. Flicker then told Tuck Horse to clamp the man's nose and mouth shut, then she stooped beside the wounded man, put her palms on his back, raised her weight onto her arms, and pushed hard and slowly down on him.

From the wound came a sound like a person with runny bowels breaking wind. A long, wet, bubbly crepitation. Good Face almost recoiled in horror as blood and clots and mucus gushed out of the wound and flooded her hands.

"Now let him breathe in," Flicker said, and Tuck Horse released the man's mouth and nose. "Now shut him again." He did, and again Flicker pressed down, forcing more air and matter out of the bullet hole. She repeated this awful process until only clean blood was running out, then told them to roll the man onto his back.

"Ah! *Wehlee heeleh!*" she cried, pointing down at the dark mess on the deerskin. "There it is!" Among the gouts and slime lay the musket ball. "I feared I would have to probe for it. Or leave it in. Good, good! Daughter, offer Creator tobacco for making it come out as I prayed it to do! Oh, I am happy with that! Kijilamuh ka'ong means this man to live for something!"

Good Face shuddered, almost sick, the warrior's blood cooling on her hands and forearms. But her heart soared with gratitude.

For the rest of the night old Flicker worked over the wounded man. She put a hollowed fox bone on the bullet hole and sucked and spat, sucked and spat. She explored the wound above his ear that had made his head swell, and put an elm poultice on it, and then another elm poultice over the wound in his side. She had them brew dogwood tea all night and trickle it into the man's mouth. By daybreak they were all about to collapse from fatigue but the old woman was still working. They heard the morning cannon from the Auglaize, and Flicker looked up impatiently at Good Face and said, "Did I ask you to do something at daylight, daughter?"

"Ah! Yes, I go, Kahesana!" In her exhaustion she had forgotten about the fresh elm bark. She took the hatchet and went out looking. The woods were full of fog from the river. She paused to relieve herself, then began circling their little camp, looking for slippery elm. She came to the river's edge where their canoe had been pulled ashore and covered with brush to hide it. Nearby were several young elms, as big around as her thigh. She raised the hatchet and was ready to cut a line around the biggest elm at eye level when she heard men's voices.

She peered around with eagerness. If these were men of the tribes, they might be comrades of the wounded man, looking for him. They could take him to a village perhaps, where he could rest and heal more comfortably, maybe even with his family, and with a shaman to help him recover. Then she saw the men. They were in a long, black boat on the river, slipping through the mist, coming out of the mouth of the Auglaize. Oars were rising and falling, oarlocks creaking. She heard a man say words in English and she understood them.

"Swing left." The man standing in the stern had said it. It was English, the language of her childhood life. And she recognized the voice.

It was Apekonit, Wild Potato, the red-haired one! She peered through the foliage and across the river mist to be sure.

It was he, and he was within speaking distance, with a big boat full of rowers. There would be room in the boat for the wounded man, who was a Miami, she was sure, a Miami like Wild Potato; he could take the man to wherever he was going up the river and get good care for him. She raised her hand to her mouth and took a breath to yell for him. There was Wild Potato just across the river, hatless, red-haired, handsome, standing with one foot on a barrel and one elbow on his knee; she recognized him even though he was wearing not deerskins but a blue soldier coat. . . .

Then she remembered.

He had betrayed the Miami people and gone over to the Long Knife general.

She ducked behind the elm and watched as the long boat turned up the Maumee, and she thought hard. A strange feeling passed through her. She was so fatigued and hungry, she was seeing as if in a dream, with clarity.

Something had happened in Wild Potato to make him go back to the race of his birth. People of his own race would say that was where he belonged, that he had done right.

She thought of her own path, wondered where it was going. She had old parents who could not move without pain and would soon be taking the Spirit Road. She was traveling to a place she did not know, as all the Indians had been doing all this time because of the Town Destroyers always coming. She had had a husband, and was betrayed by him, and now had him no more, and if she found another husband, he would probably be killed by the white men's guns or ruined by their spirit water and she would perhaps be like Minnow, with a killed husband and a baby inside and going to another place she did not know, and so full of hatred for the *wap-situk* that she wanted to cut parts of them as trophies. They had started up this scorched-out valley with a heavy load of things that would have been worthless junk except that they were needed for staying alive, and now, just now, they had acquired still another burden, a stranger who had fought the white men and was dying from it and perhaps might yet die in their hands. Down that other river it would surely go on like this with the Long Knife armies always chasing and burning. She was twenty or twenty-one years old, she thought, and to judge by all that had happened in her memory, she and the Lenapeh People were on a long road to death.

How would it be going back to the world of white people? All that she could remember of her birth people was good, and surely they would welcome her back if she went there, being now in the bloom of womanhood and clean and healthy and strong. They, those whites, were the ones who would be on the bright path because they would have everything that had belonged to the Indians they were driving down this dark path.

Look at Wild Potato there, she thought. He must have understood all this, and he saw a moment when he could step off the doomed path and onto the bright path just by going back to his birth people, the winning people; now see him standing there so splendid and important that he can tell a boatful of soldiers which way to row that boat. If I were to call to him, he would know me, and would take us and the wounded man to a more comfortable place. And in the white men's midst I could do as he has done and step over onto the bright path, and stop being a leaf in the wind.

Wouldn't that be what I should do? Like him, after all, I was stolen away from my birthright people by these Lenapeh people. I didn't ask to get on this doomed road to death, they grabbed me and dragged me.

Her thoughts were getting jumbled now, and she realized she was thinking in her old language, English, that she had half forgot.

The boat was moving through the mist up the river and she was looking at Wild Potato's back now, but she could still call and be heard.

Or, she thought, even easier, I could run along the bank and catch up and get on that boat and nobody but those whites would know what happened to me. I wouldn't have to see Minnow or my old ones mad at me. People disappear all the time, now that the armies are always coming.

Anyway, if those soldiers in that boat saw that wounded man, they probably would just go ahead and finish killing him. If I just went and caught up with the boat, they'd never know the warrior or the others were back here and wouldn't bother them and they could just go on, wherever they mean to go. Flicker and Tuck Horse would grieve, oh, I know.

But I already have one mama and papa grieving, and they would be in joy. So it comes out.

She remembered the old repeated warnings about the white men buying names. They would buy my name, and that's how they could tell my birth parents where I am, she suddenly understood. It's what I should do.

Oh, surely it is! She remembered old dreams of people in gray.

Her heart was pounding with the anticipation of running after the boat, and she pressed her hand over her heart and its palm touched the medicine bag, the medicine bag Neepah had made for her and had filled with seeds of the Three Sacred Sisters, corn, beans, and squash. And in there too was a hardened ball of clay from the first Bread Dance. And certain small, beautiful stones, each with a story around it.

As she held the bag, she heard many voices. Maxkwah n'wah, the Small Female Bear. Telling her that would be her name too. And the flicker bird, at the moon hut, saying *"Weekah, weekah!"* her mother in that form. She heard the soft voice of Owl, the *leh-pawcheek*, who had taken her all across the Longhouse Road, safe on his saddle with his arms keeping her from falling, and telling her of the sacredness when she first saw the Great Falling Water at Niagara. She remembered dreams of a black sun. She remembered the sound of Like Wood's flute, her song, the song he had made for her before the spirit water had made him bad. She still had that song; it had not gone bad. And she remembered old Tuck Horse's voice as he talked to her on the hill before walking away that night to go and fight in his last battle. And she remembered the voice of Minnow, just a few days ago, bragging about her great strength . . .

Then she really was hearing Minnow's voice, calling her. She turned and saw Minnow coming toward the river, looking for her.

She called back in a hissing, warning voice. "Minnow! Be still!" Minnow heard her and turned and saw her, and Good Face put her forefinger to her lips and with the hatchet handle pointed up the river toward the boat of soldiers, and when Minnow saw them, she simply vanished from where she stood. When she appeared beside Good Face at the elm tree, they stood together watching the soldier boat go up, fading in the mist, up the Maumee Sipu toward old Kekionga Town. At last Minnow said, "Flicker needs the fresh bark and sent me to find you."

"I was about to chop bark when I saw the boat."

"It is good you saw it before you started chopping!"

"Yes." She was trembling, hoping that Minnow could not in any way see what she had been thinking, what she had almost done.

"If they had heard you chopping . . ." Minnow shuddered. "The spirits warn you, sister!"

Good Face, who for a moment had almost been Frances, let out a long sigh. "We had better cut the bark as quickly and quietly as we can. There might be more soldier boats."

They cut lines in the bark and peeled it off and it squealed and groaned as if a live creature were being skinned. It was, of course. But its purpose was to heal a man. Flicker would boil and pound it pulpy and glutinous and slip it into the wound, and day by day as she drew it out, the healing would follow it out to the skin and the man's lung would no longer leak and he would be well. What a good world Kijilamuh ka'ong had made, with everything one could need growing all around, and the knowledge of its use had been given to women.

They cut and peeled the bark, stopping often to look around and listen hard. Once Minnow said: "If the boat soldiers had seen you, you would have had to cut them instead of elm trees with this hatchet. That would have been good, but there were too many and they would have got you. Catching you here, they would have used you."

"Perhaps not. Seeing I am red-haired, maybe they would have just taken me away to sell my name."

"They might have done so. But after they had used you."

Good Face wondered after that whether it had been good or not that she had touched her medicine bag instead of running after Wild Potato's boat.

She was sure that touching the bag had made the memory voices and spirit voices come. They had kept her from going after the boat. Those spirit voices, the Chipewuk, stayed near to the People and did what they thought was right.

She had nearly gone another way, an easier way; she had been so tired and confused, she nearly had done that. But the Chipewuk called her back.

Something, maybe those same spirits, had sent Wild Potato the other way. Maybe they knew his heart was white, hers red.

CHAPTER FIFTEEN

Ruth Slocum knew that Giles was the one son she could depend on to arrange his life to accommodate another search for Frances. Once he had admitted that his soldiering might have contributed to her capture, and to the deaths of his father and grandfather, Giles had continued to hold that responsibility to heart.

Will was tied down for now; he had been elected sheriff of Luzerne County and therefore was not free to wander abroad. Benjamin and Ebenezer had the good intention of setting out to look for their sister when it became convenient, but they were in the saw- and gristmill business together five miles upriver at Deep Hollow, and business always called. Ebenezer was also recently married to the former Sarah Davis and keeping her always with child.

When Giles went, it would likely be Isaac or Joseph who would go with him, because of their undying fascination with the legend of Frances' capture. Now almost men, they both claimed to remember the awful day she was carried away, though everything they said about it was based on family stories rather than anything they could have remembered seeing at such young ages. Isaac could recount the story more vividly than anyone else in the family except their mother. The two of them longed to succeed someday where all the older brothers had failed, and fetch their long-lost sister home.

Now, on this particular snowy day, Isaac sat with his mother and Giles in her kitchen, discussing the prospects for another trip to the frontier.

Giles had a notebook he used primarily to record farm income

327

and expenses, an occasional noteworthy proverb, and facts he thought worthy of copying from the newspapers he read at Judge Fell's tavern every week. Now he had it open before him to the pages pertaining to General Anthony Wayne's victory over the tribes in the Ohio country. He ran his finger down the page and read his notes, while Isaac leaned over a smudged facsimile of an old British map of the region south of the Great Lakes, trying to make some connection between the rivers written in cursive script and those Giles was trying to pronounce from his notes. A difficulty was that the words on the map were strange, long strings of syllables representing the sounding out of Indian designations, most of which apparently had been renamed before or during General Wayne's campaign. Another difficulty was that there were now forts and settlements named in the newspapers that had not existed when the old map had been drawn, some thirty years before.

But the brothers had determined the location of the portage place between the Maumee River, which flowed into Lake Erie, and the Wabash, which flowed southwest toward the lower Ohio Valley. There, on the site of the great old Miami town of Keki-onga, General Wayne was building the final fort in his line of out-posts dominating the Ohio Territory. It had been named Fort Wayne in his honor.

"Colonel Ham . . . Hamtrack . . . no, I guess it's Hamtramck—either he's got the most confounding name in the country or I can't read my own hand—anyway, this Colonel Ham-whatever is in command of the fort, and listen to this:

" 'A former spy, William Wells, also known as Apekonit, who is a son-in-law of Little Turtle the Miami chief, was named by General Wayne to be the government agent and interpreter and the justice of the peace there at the fort.' Now there, family, would be a good person to know out there, because as the Indian agent, thee can be sure, he'll know every Indian in those parts. Now with Judy and Hugh living at Cincinnati, if they made some correspondence with that fellow Wells, or went up and met him, why, that neck o' the woods would be on the watch-out for Frannie, if she was ever through there—though I still feel she's up around Lake Erie some-place, maybe Detroit. . . ."

Giles tapped his thumbnail on his yellow incisors and traced through his notes with the forefinger of his other hand, then con-tinued, "The general has called the chiefs of all the defeated tribes to visit him at Fort Greene Ville next summer—that's not on that old map there, Isaac; they just built that one last year, and it must be 'bout midway betwixt Cincinnati and Fort Wayne—asked 'em to come and negotiate a permanent peace and new boundaries for the red men and white. Think o' that! Permanent peace, he says. Well, aye, permanent peace would be a blessing to all. To Friends, who believe in it and always did, and our missionaries, and of course we Slocums, who can't go a-looking for our girl when the Indians're all a-stir. But now listen to this, Ma, this is the best part I've saved till last:

"Those Indians who petition for peace, to show true good faith, says the general, they must bring in to him at Fort Greene Ville all prisoners and captives, even the ones that's been adopted. We ought to write to Judy and Hugh and see if they could go up there to Greene Ville and watch the prisoners return."

Ruth Slocum laced her fingers tight and squeezed her eyes shut, praying and remembering. She recalled vividly those scenes at Tioga more than five years past, all those hesitant, fearful, eager, reluctant people, the weeping Indians, the emotions cocked like gun triggers, the hardships of camp, the awful letdown. "I ought to go there myself," she said. "I'm not sure I could bear to have my heart millstoned down like that again, but I reckon if I bore it once, I could again." She shook her head and shuddered, then opened her eyes and her sons' faces were blurry. The memory of all that heart-misery at Tioga had made tears well up. But the thought that the chiefs might so earnestly sue for peace that they would comply and really bring in everyone! Any time the faintest gleam of a hope was glimpsed, her frantic heart would pump like a bellows blowing a draft through foundry coal to make it burn white-hot. Like that anthracite burning in the fire grate right there across from the kitchen table.

But Giles' big, hard hand came down gently on the back of hers. "No, Ma, not thee, not us this time, clear out there. We've already got relatives and missionaries in that part of the country. Besides, by the time we'd get there, they'd be done with all that. We couldn't even start out till spring. I hate to be too really frank with thee, Ma, but I doubt thee's strong enough—in body, I mean, not in will."

She knew he was probably right in that. She was nearly sixty years of age now and had borne and reared ten children, managed the estates of her dead father and husband, and done the rigors of traveling every year to the big Meeting of the Friends, coming down dreadfully ill after almost every one of those journeys. And now lately here in the Susquehanna Valley there was something mysterious always dragging down on her constitution. It had been written in a periodical back East that the burning of anthracite instead of wood produced fumes that were poisonous to lungs, eyes, and teeth, and that it even caused baldness. Ruth Slocum did not quite believe all that, but she did know that Ebenezer, and the blacksmith Owens, and she herself, were suffering from maladies they had not known back in the days when this had been a farming valley full of trees and fresh air and when they burned only wood for heat. Her breathing passages now where always raw and she had coughing spells and headaches.

Ebenezer and Benjamin coughed and raked their throats and blew their noses and their kerchiefs were black and their eyes were always red-rimmed, apparently because of all the coal rock they were forever chipping and shoveling. They had exhausted the accessible outcrops of the stuff and now tunneled into the hills for it, making filthy black caves where they labored in choking dust. They could have stopped at any time, but they enjoyed a sort of exhilaration in the money wealth they were gaining, and it made them heedless of consequences. She felt sometimes that if they gave up searching for their sister, it would be because they could not give up earning money long enough.

To her, that was an ugly notion, and not worthy of Quakers, rather more the way of the worldly.

Fort Wayne

It was a huge two-story fort the Long Knives were building here at old Kekionga Town, and in awe Good Face watched it grow higher and more massive.

She watched usually from the shade of a little shelter made under the overturned canoe, where the lung-shot man lay. He was going to live. As soon as they knew he would not die, they had put him in the canoe and come up cautiously from the Auglaize to this place. They expected they would have to slip across the portage place at night, past Long Knife sentries, before they could start down the Wabash or Eel rivers toward the villages in the west. They had presumed that the land around the new fort would be nothing but a deadly, hostile bluecoat camp, very hard to get around unseen, especially with a badly wounded warrior to smuggle through. Harmless-looking old Tuck Horse had gone ahead to look it over, and came back with the surprising news that there were Indians all over the place, living in hasty hovels and shelters right in the clearings within gunshot of the fort, the way dogs will hover near a cookfire waiting for scraps to be thrown to them.

"They are beaten," the old man had said. "They are waiting to be told what they may have and what they must do. They are waiting for Wayne to say those things. So we can go right by there. We can find food there. And perhaps a healer to help my tired wife heal this warrior. And people there can help us make the portage when we are ready to go on across. Maybe we will learn that there is something better to do than go down those other rivers." He was still a spy at heart and wanted to look around. Minnow was angry at him at first for saying those things. She had threatened to go on by herself rather than stop anywhere within smelling distance of the bluecoats. If she came near them, she said, she would want to kill them. Finally, though, Minnow had settled down, like boiling water lifted away from the fire. And now that she was here near the fort, she was always out among the People, getting things that Flicker needed to take care of the wounded warrior, asking about the family of her own husband who had been killed. But she kept a sharp knife in a sheath at the small of her back, which she intended to use if any bluecoat tried to touch her or Good Face or the old couple or the wounded Miami.

He was a Miami. Tuck Horse had learned something about him through hand-signing. The man could not yet speak, and whatever had hurt his head seemed to have deafened him. Flicker and Good Face took turns staying up and caring for him. His chest wound did not bubble anymore, even when the elm dressing was off. But he was still very weak and always in pain. He was thin as a skeleton, and although his head was not now so swollen, it was mostly the color of blueberries, the whole left side and much of the right side bruised.

The bluecoat soldiers could be seen and heard every day, at a little distance. They were working like slaves with their axes and saws, turning a forest of trees into a fort of log walls and buildings. They carried logs in wagons or dragged them with horses, and raised them higher and higher by pulling ropes attached to poles sticking up and out from the tops of the walls, and as the walls went higher, the lifting poles went higher. It was amazing how hard these Long Knives worked and what they could do. They were always shouting and banging and making dust, but they were making a place too strong to be attacked, and were making it right here in what once had been Little Turtle's strong town. They were also building big, solid houses of log and stone outside the fort. While most of them were working, there were always others around carrying their guns, among them bluecoats meeting near the walls of the fort with Indian men from the nearby camps.

Often, the one who had been Apekonit, the Wild Potato, was among the soldiers in those meetings. On the sunny days he would stand there talking to them with his black hat off and his red hair shining, the way Good Face had seen him standing in the boat of rowers at the mouth of the Auglaize. It was obvious that he was important here.

When he was near, Good Face was careful to stay in the shadows. She was not sure how bad or dangerous he was now that he had gone back to being a *wapsini*, but she was wary. She knew he would recognize her if he saw her, and although for a moment that day at the Auglaize she had been ready to reveal herself to him, the voices had warned her and she remembered their warning.

But even yet, despite those cautious voices from the Chipewuk, her eyes were drawn to the red-haired man, and her heart weighed again his return to his birth people. He had seemed a strong and confident warrior when he lived as a Miami, but appeared even more so now. There was no furtive, shame-faced look about him. It was plain that he had become some sort of a chief among the bluecoats, and that the bluecoats were now dominant in this land. Sometimes when Good Face was lurking in the shade of the canoe and the mats and skins that made additional shelter around it, she would imagine talking to Wild Potato in English words. She reached into her memory for English words, and with the ones she remembered, she tried to form the questions she might want to ask him. She practiced the questions in her head.

Is thee good in heart?

Is thee loved of Sweet Breeze wife anyway that thee came back bluecoat?

My birth people they love me if I go home of them?

My Lenapeh people have hearts bad at me if I go?

She had forgotten so much of that language. Of course, she thought, I could just ask him in Lenapeh and hand sign, as I did when I gave him the horses on the battlefield. He doesn't know our tongue very well, but I made him understand that time.

She would have to strain to make him understand her questions in English. But it would be in English, because she could not let her Lenapeh people understand her asking such questions.

She would be ashamed for them to know she even had such thoughts. Minnow, especially. She had heard Minnow often express her contempt for Wild Potato.

When Minnow spoke of him, one could tell she was again thinking of making medicine bags out of scrotums.

Tuck Horse slowly came in from one of his prowlings. He was always spying on the bluecoats as he went about, using his walking stick and walking more stooped than he really was, using his age as a disguise to seem harmless, understanding more tongues than anyone would presume he understood. Only English, it seemed, was unintelligible to him. By going about and listening, he had learned that the Great Serpent General Wayne had been calling the chiefs and chieftains of all the beaten tribes to go to his other fort in the south and talk to him about peace. Wayne was being cordial but firm, and was not offering them anything yet. He just kept hinting that if they wanted to keep their people safe, they should go there next summer and talk.

Tuck Horse sat and smoked for a while by the fire with a scowl on his face. Then he looked in at the emaciated, bruise-faced warrior. "Eh, young man," he said. "Can you hear me talking?" He asked it first in Lenapeh and then in Miami, but the man did not reply. "I wish he could hear me. I would like to talk with a Miami warrior like him about what his chiefs are doing."

"Tell it, Father. I would like to know too. And he might hear. Sometimes it seems to me he hears but cannot answer."

Tuck Horse aimed his pipe stem at the fort. "Little Turtle is here today. With him are his sons Black Loon and Crescent Moon. With him also is his nephew Richardville, called Wildcat. I saw them with Wild Potato."

Good Face flushed, having had Wild Potato so much in her mind just now.

Tuck Horse went on: "It unsettles me to see all those good men of that family hovering so close to the *wapsituk* fort. I hear they will build the Little Turtle a fine home near this fort. I do not like that."

"This was his old town," Good Face reminded him. "Why

should he not live where he used to live? This seems brave, that he has no fear of even these fort builders."

"My daughter, you will see that the reason he has no fear near them is that he will be sitting in the *wapsituk* lap. He will be near and he will know what they want because his son-in-law is their agent. They will all be wrapped in the Great Serpent's wishes because of the Wild Potato, who now wants to be called only by his *wapsi* name, Wells. Today I addressed him four times as Wild Potato just to see him grow as red as a true Miami." Tuck Horse spat viciously, then smiled grimly at the satisfaction of the memory. Then he said something that made her flush and start.

"Wild Potato asked me about you."

"What! Why? Has he seen me here?"

"No. He asked because he has *not* seen you. He remembers that I was the Lenapeh elder who had a young daughter with red hair like his. He thought I had lost you in all the troubles because he has not seen you."

"And you answered him how, Father?"

"I answered him only by asking him why he wanted to know."

Good Face thought that had been rude, but she would not scold her old father. Instead she said, "You truly hate Wild Potato for going back to his *wapsi* people."

"*K'hehlah!*" Yes indeed! "He has forsaken the Miami people who cared for him twenty summers, and you will see that he now means to profit by knowing them so well and by being married to the daughter of their *sakimeh*. He will hold the Serpent by one hand and the Turtle by the other and will smile between them and he will take a little of everything that passes between them. You will see, daughter. I observed his whole heart in his eyes, and I saw that his heart is not a red heart, but a pale one."

She had never told her father about seeing Wild Potato in the boat on the river, or what she had thought. "I hide from him," she said.

"That is good. Because one thing the Serpent General has been telling all the defeated chiefs is that if they want to have peace when they come and talk to him next summer, they must first show good faith by bringing him all their captives from the conflicts. I suspect that is why Wild Potato remembered to ask me about you. If someone paid for your name and took you back to the Susquehanna Sipu, Wild Potato surely would get some of that reward as it passed from one hand to another. Thus are things done by his kind."

This was all so close to the matters on her mind that Good Face was reluctant to look at her father for fear that he might read her thoughts. Working at the little fire, looking intently at it, she said, "Will we be here much longer? He will learn about me sometime. Even with a scarf or blanket over my hair I cannot be invisible."

Tuck Horse smoked thoughtfully. "We have been here longer than we intended, that is true." He sighed. "I wanted to get past these bluecoats, didn't I, and see them no more. But as you see, I am a bluecoat watcher. Hmm! But now there are no *sakimas* to tell what I learn. Heu! What use?" He squinted toward the fort, which loomed shadowy blue and enormous beyond the golden haze of sunlit dust stirred up by horse teams dragging logs. Everywhere echoed the chunking of the soldiers' axes in wood, and their hoarse yells. He sighed. "Now they have everything around here. I heard that they even found the cannons we took from the other general and hid. They found those and put them up in the fort they built there. I am an old man, and all I have seen all my life is the *wapsituk* getting everything. Even when we have a victory, they soon take that away from us too. I should have lain down and died with a smile after that last victory instead of living on to see this again." His pipe had gone out while he talked, and he snatched another little ember from the fire to relight it. "I do want us to go on soon. I have thought that now Little Turtle is here, we can take this hurt man to him. Little Turtle will know who he is and where his family might be found. Yes. That is what I should do. Tomorrow I will tell your *sakima* of you," he said toward the young man, "and then my family and I will go on to a place where there are no white men yet."

Then, to their astonishment, the injured man spoke.

"Ne she," he said, his voice gurgling and barely audible.

"What!" Tuck Horse exclaimed, leaning toward him. "He says no!" In a strong voice he asked the warrior in the Miami tongue: "Can you now hear my voice?"

"E heh." The voice was a whispery croak.

"Daughter, he is hearing us at last. Young brother, why did you say no when I said I would tell your chief of you?"

They talked together in Miami for a while. Good Face could understand a few words of it, though the man could still neither hear nor speak well enough to make any of it easy to follow. After a while Tuck Horse leaned back from the man and began:

"His name is Shapahcahnah, The Awl. Some sounds he begins

to hear now. For a long time after the gun spoke in his face he heard nothing because in his head was always endless thunder and noise like the whistle of a hawk, which still goes on. But now he hears a little. He thanks us for picking him up and healing him."

"It is Kijilamuh ka'ong he must thank," Good Face said. "And Kahesana. To what did he say no when first he spoke?"

"No, he does not want to go to Little Turtle. Not if Little Turtle befriends the whites. This is a man whose heart speaks with mine!" He leaned toward the scrawny reclining figure under the canoe, the young man whose face was still so purple with bruises that he was horrible to see. "I am glad you can hear me," he said to him in Lenapeh. "I have no warrior son ever to talk to. . . ." Then he remembered that he should be speaking in Miami. He did most of the talking because the warrior was too weak to speak much. Eventually the old man turned back to Good Face, seeming more satisfied than he had been for a long time.

"This man The Awl says he has no family that have not died. He is a war chieftain with no people left. Many died at the Blown-Down Woods battle and more at the Auglaize, where he was hurt. If we can wait until he is strong enough to travel, he wants to go with us westward where there are no more whites yet."

"Then may he strengthen quickly, Father," Good Face said. "I am troubled in my heart near this fort."

She truly did not like it. It kept her mind in two worlds, and both those worlds could not remain in the same heart. A person could not go two ways at once. Wells the Wild Potato was a doorway back into a world whose memories softened her and promised ease and comfort.

But while she had her family and Minnow, and even this hurt man to care for, she must turn her eyes from that other world. She must not look at Wells or speak to him even to ask anything. He was a betrayer; she was not.

She had to go down the rivers in that way toward West Grandfather Spirit. Down those rivers was an unknown. Perhaps it would be more of the same dangers, more of the same troubles, more defeats, more land forsaken and more freedom lost.

But for a while there was land out there in which people could be free to live according to the visions of Kijilamuh ka'ong, He Who Creates By Thinking.

PART THREE

Maconakwa

1800–1813

CHAPTER SIXTEEN

Autumn 1800
A Miami Town on the Wabash Sipu

Maconakwa, Little Bear Woman of the Miami people, arranged coals and hot stones in the fire pit to bake *lenapana*, the sacred hominy bread, for the funeral feast.

On a pallet of bedding nearby lay the body of her father Tuck Horse, he who had adopted her when she was a little girl called Good Face. He lay with his feet toward the west, ready to begin his journey to West Grandfather Spirit. Three lines of *olumun*, sacred red funeral paint, had been drawn on each temple from the corner of the eye to the ear, so the Creator would recognize him as Lenapeh when he came up the Spirit Path.

The scent of the slow-baking bread began to fill the house. The smoky heat rose among the bundles of dried mint leaves, sassafras roots, tobacco, and medicine herbs that hung among the roof poles, a mingling of the comforting odors for living on with healthy spirits.

It would be a Lenapeh ceremony to send Tuck Horse following close behind his wife Flicker on the Spirit Path, though their daughter, who was preparing his funeral feast, was now by marriage and by name a Miami, and was carrying a child who would live life as a Miami.

Maconakwa still felt she was Good Face when she glanced over at her father's corpse and thought of the life that had dwelt in it.

A man of many deep scars. She had known him only as an old man, but he had fought countless battles for his People before she met him at Niagara some twenty summers ago. She remembered him paddling in a canoe the whole length of Erie lake. She

339

remembered him walking away southward one cold, clear fall morning eight years ago with his old musket, disappearing from camp to go down to the headwaters of this very river and join the attack against the general called St. Clair. She remembered how he had always gone among the People before and after battles, learning whatever he would need to know to keep his family fed and safe. She remembered how his spirit had fought in frustration against the bodily pain and stiffening of age that had imprisoned him and made him less and less able to protect his People. She recalled that no matter where she and Flicker had gone with him in their hundreds of miles of flight from the Town Destroyers, he had already been there many times before and knew the way. She knew that the only reason so able a man had not been a chief was that his People were too scattered. He had always been on the path.

Now he was going farther. He was going to see Keeper Grand-mother, who would open the door for him and send him along the Spirit Path. And at the far end of the Spirit Path he would at last enjoy peace.

When she thought of that, she had to swallow hard to keep from groaning, and tears would flow over her eyes so she could hardly see to carve the *kinkinhikun*, his grave marker.

It was a plank split from cedar, as long as her leg. In one end she was carving a diamond-shaped hole, laboriously scoring its out-line and scraping out the fragrant wood with a flint knife. She was making it from her memory of Lenapeh grave markers. It would be painted with the same *olumun* paint as that on his face, and planted at the head of his grave with the diamond hole at the top.

A woman's marker was different from a man's. It was a cross with three diamond holes, one at the top and one through each arm. Tuck Horse had made Flicker's marker. It was so new its paint still shone bright in the burial ground. She had passed over in spring, and after Tuck Horse completed her *kinkinhikun*, he had begun to let his own life force evaporate out of his body like the steam from a cooling loaf of bread.

And so their daughter grieved for them both as she carved. She was no longer their Good Face, but Little Bear Woman. It was a Miami name, but it was the same as Maxk'wah n'wah, the name given her by the small female bear that had come to her in her vision, the first time she was in the *wiktut* with her moon-blood.

Now she had not been in the *wiktut* since the time of Flicker's funeral. She became pregnant shortly before Flicker passed over. Maconakwa had married The Awl in this Miami town two years after they arrived here by canoe. By then he had fully recovered from his lung wound and his head wound, though he could still not hear very well and said that the whistling noise inside his head, the sound like a hawk's cry, never stopped. It was so shrill and constant that he could hardly hear bird songs or children's cries, though deeper sounds, like thunder or men's and women's voices, he could just hear.

So after five years of marriage, The Awl and Little Bear Woman would soon have a son or a daughter, and The Awl was proud and intrigued. Sometimes when they lay ready for sleep he would draw the cover down and, propped on one elbow, use his other hand to caress and memorize the mound of her pregnancy, eyes thoughtful in the firelight and so absorbed that his narrow lips would be parted like a child's. It was wonderment to him that his family blood would live on. He had been the last of his own mother's children to survive the wars and illnesses, and he had come very close to Keeper Grandmother, but this red-haired woman and her old Lenapeh mother had brought him back from there to continue his family through this one yet to be born. She knew his love for her was strong, that it was built on gratitude.

Maconakwa missed his presence when, as now, he was away hunting. He was not a beautiful man, as her first husband Like Wood had been; he had never made her a song, never courted her with the flute. But he was as kind and as full of desire as Like Wood had been in the beginning, and she was confident that this husband was not one who would ever try to trade her body for a jug of the white man's spirit water. Though not tall and graceful as Like Wood had been, he was hard-muscled and quick and courageous, a keen hunter and trapper and thus a good provider. His dedication to his Miami People was as fierce and wise as old Tuck Horse's had been to his Lenapeh. This husband was a man upon whom one could depend—such a man as Tuck Horse had been. Maconakwa had learned to love the set of his narrow lips, often tilted with sly humor, and the steady boldness of his eyes. Flicker had said before the wedding, "Here is a man like your father. If you want this man, I sing no warnings in your ear."

And so Flicker had died content in knowing that her daughter's care was in the right kind of hands. Now Tuck Horse was following Flicker over to the Other Side. It would take four days for his spirit to leave the earth and start the journey on the Path of Stars. Little Bear Woman glanced from the carving of the grave marker to the profile of her father and she thought:

I know you would never have left me until you were satisfied that I will live well and be cared for as well as you cared for me. Now my good husband has assured you. But, Father, I am sorry you could not wait and see the grandchild who will be here so soon.

There were not many Lenapeh in this town, but the Miami people had been to Flicker's funeral so recently that they knew how to help observe a Lenapeh funeral. They came at sundown and sat holding a quiet vigil outside the *wikwam*, where Tuck Horse's body lay in torchlight. At midnight a shaman of the town arrived and stood beside the corpse. He held in both hands a bowl-shaped seashell in which herbs smoldered, giving off wisps of smoke to carry his prayers toward the Creator.

"Kiji Moneto! O Great Spirit! Please hear us!

"Now comes on the long road toward the Spirit Land this man. In his walk on Turtle Island there were always hard things in his way. He was driven from place to place by Town Destroyers. His flesh that he leaves here is covered with scars. He has told us that in the Land Beyond, the land his people call Awaskumeh, he will be happy to walk on paths that are only smooth and bright, and not stumble anymore over hard things. He is tired of pain and war and sorrow. He has always lived in a way to be worthy of a straight and smooth way to Awaskumeh.

"He has harmed no one but those who made themselves his enemies. He did nothing to make them his enemies; they came to him that way, and only those did he harm. He always kept all his promises and he never deceived. And so, let Keeper Grandmother open for him the door to the smooth and bright path.

"Kiji Moneto! Let him take no one else's spirit with him!

"Kiji Moneto! O please hear us and see him on the smooth and bright path, for if you so see him, so will he be. This is what we want you to do for our brother, who is worthy of it.

"Now, Kiji Moneto! This man's daughter will feed his friends who have come here. None of those here are sick. No women here are in their moon-blood. No one is here whom this man disliked. Thus there is no one here who should not be, for anyone who should not be here would trouble the start of his journey. The food for this feast was prepared by a virtuous woman, his daughter, and not touched by any woman in her moon-blood. And so all is right as he goes forth on his journey. When daylight comes, his friends will lay him in the ground so his body may return to Mother Earth and nourish all living things, just as they nourished him when he walked here. And so the Sacred Circle will go on. Though there are those who disturb the turning of that Sacred Circle, he was not one of them, and they were his enemies.

"Kiji Moneto! Please hear us! Our prayer comes to you on the smoke you see coming up from this place."

Maconakwa could not attend her father's burial the next day because she was pregnant, and it was believed that a spirit leaving the grave might take along the spirit of an unborn. So it was Minnow who made the small fire at the head of the grave every evening at sundown for three nights, so that the old man's spirit could take fire to keep him warm on his journey through the stars.

It was on that third night that her water broke and Maconakwa called out to her neighbors. Soon two old midwives hurried in and added wood to the fire, to warm and brighten the *wikwam*. They scolded her for not having summoned them earlier so they could have prepared the town's birthing hut for her. So her first baby would be born here in her own *wikwam*, which did not have a center pole to grasp with her hands while she squatted to deliver. It meant she would have to have a strong young woman to support her, or else hang on to one of the bent saplings of the *wikwam* frame, which in labor might be given so much stress it could break and damage the house—and which, in any case, was not convenient because the midwives could not move around her easily. She wanted Minnow to come and support her, but Minnow was tending the fire at the grave. It was considered bad to change fire tenders, and so she would have to stay out there at the grave and someone else would have to come and help. This gave the midwives even more to scold her about, and Maconakwa was afraid she had offended these Miami midwives. But then, while they were undressing her, she glanced under her arm and saw that one of the old women, even while scolding her, was smiling, and she realized then that this peevishness was just a part of the expected demeanor of midwives. Minnow had told her, so long ago that she had nearly forgotten, that these were the kindest and most generous of women and that they did what they did because of their love of new life, and often feigned grouchiness simply to make the birthing mother fear them enough to obey them.

They were brewing a tea of sumac leaves and berries, which would make the childbearing labor easier. It was ready by the time a strong and tall young Miami girl came in. She was a grand-daughter of one of the midwives.

Maconakwa had been told often by Flicker what to expect in this matter of delivering a child, about how it was supposed to come out, how it could hurt beyond all measure even if nothing was going wrong. But she had also told her of the things that sometimes do go wrong, and how it might feel if they did. Flicker had said, "You know your husband's body so well that you can see it in dark-ness by feeling it with your hands and your body, is that not so? And his man-part you know so well that you can see it with feeling even when it is hidden inside you, is that not right?" And Maconakwa had agreed, blushing, that even that remarkable fact was so. Flicker then continued: "You have known your own body many times longer than you have known your husband's, and so if you have been paying any attention to being alive, you should be able to see what goes on inside your body by how it feels. If you pay attention to your belly with its baby inside, you ought to be able to see how it is lying and how it looks and how well it is."

And so with Flicker's words in mind, Maconakwa had, for all the months of her pregnancy, seen the baby growing inside, so that when it began to move, she believed she knew each move the baby had made, whether a heel or an elbow had pressed sliding along the wall of the womb.

Now she was squatting on the floor of her own *wikwam*, which was round and domed as if it were a womb she herself lived in, and she was holding and being held by the smooth, strong, sweaty arms of the Miami girl, and her middle was by its own volition squeezing down hard, even when her own mind was too intently looking inward to remember to press and squeeze. And even though it hurt everywhere, she could feel a protruding pressure where there should not be one, and a twistedness inside, and she felt that the baby was not lying the way it should have been. She pressed down and her waist squeezed down and so much sweat was trickling down over her body that it was like squatting naked in the rain trying to excrete a blockage of waste. This was her first baby, but she knew it was not supposed to feel like this. Flicker with mere words had taught her how it should feel.

She gasped and groaned, and said to the midwife who was massaging the sides of her swollen abdomen, "Stop a moment. Your hands are confusing me! Stop touching and let me see!"

"*E heh*," the midwife grunted, apparently knowing just what she meant, and removed her hands. "Tell us, then, Maconakwa," the old one murmured, and looked at her, waiting.

Maconakwa concentrated inward, trying to see through the pain. It was like trying to see through smoke. A surge of contraction would scatter her concentration. Sometimes she would start to cry out from the pain, but she knew from hundreds of talks in the *wiktuts* that white women were scorned for their screaming, lying-down births, and she did not want anyone to think of her, "Listen to that red-hair *wapsini*. She must think *she* is the baby!" And she would just groan and hold back the outcry. And sometimes when she tried to see to her inside, she would remember instead the feeling of her husband inside her, and she would wish he were here instead of away hunting, where he had been for more than a moon, unaware even of the death of Tuck Horse. And he did not know that this had started, that she was trying to put his child forth into the Earth Walk. When he was gone hunting, she did not even know whether he was still alive. For even though the treaty the general called Wayne had made the tribes sign had stopped the wars and the invasions, *wapsi* men still wandered into the Indian lands and murdered hunters, or sold them spirit water so vile that the drinkers died of it. That general had died the year after the treaty, and perhaps that was why the white men were not behaving the way his treaty had promised they should.

But her mind was not supposed to be wandering to her husband. She was trying to see the baby inside her, and so she concentrated and felt with her inner feelings, until she was able to say, "It is turned some, that way. An elbow I think is up beside its head and tries to come first." She took her arms from the girl who was holding them and with her palms a little way apart in front of her sweat-wet belly she made a turning gesture several times to show the midwives how she thought the baby was lying wrong.

And so, with their incredibly strong, wiry arms, and the help of the young woman, they laid her back on the floor so she rested on her shoulder blades and the back of her head, and they lifted her legs and hips high, and the young woman stood between her thighs and held them and rocked her, swaying from side to side, while the old women prodded and kneaded the outside of her belly, trying to change the baby's position. The weight of her insides pressed on her lungs until she thought in panic that she would suffocate. These midwife women, Flicker had told her, would not put their hands inside to reposition a turned baby unless they absolutely had to, but some of them were very skilled at doing it this way, and so Maconakwa understood what it was they were doing and why, but it was hard not to feel desperate when one could not breathe.

Finally she heard one old woman say something, and she felt herself being lifted and set again on her feet, where she squatted while the young woman clutched her arms again, and this time when the next great shove rippled down through her middle and the heels of the old women's hands added to the squeezing and pushing, this time although the pain was almost unbearable it did not feel wrong. There was an unbelievably awful stretching and yielding that made her groan out all of her breath, and when she inhaled again she smelled excrement, and then followed a huge slumping and sliding sensation as if all her insides were extruding. Behind her eyelids were flashing suns, and in her loins maddening fire sparks, then more stretching and sliding. She was out of breath and so faint suddenly that only the young woman's grip kept her from collapsing. But when she opened her eyes, the young woman's face swimming in her vision was smiling, white teeth and sparkling eyes. And she heard one of the midwives say in Miami, *"Kwenanswa pelosaw! E heh!"*

She knew what that meant.

It was a girl baby.

Her eyes began to tear with joy, but a cautious joy, and she gasped, "Is she well?" When the woman answered yes, her soul soared.

One of the midwives held in the palm of her cupped hand a little heap of yellow-brown powder and crumbs, and she put it under Maconakwa's nose and told her to sniff it hard and quickly. Still squatting, naked, bathed in sweat and still not having seen her baby, she inhaled. Her nose and eyes immediately prickled and tickled and stung, and she knew this was sneeze-weed flowers all ground to powder; she was at once off into an explosive succession of sneezes, none of which relieved the need to sneeze again. She thought she would fairly die of sneezing, but when at last she was finished, nose draining and eyes watering, the afterbirth had been expelled.

At last she was washed of sweat and allowed to lie down in bed, and the infant's shrill cries diminished and stopped when she was laid on Maconakwa's bosom. She guided her nipple to its puckering little red mouth and, in a state almost dreamlike, gazed on its dark little head, the miniature hands, the little brown buttocks. She had created life! That truth was almost too much to encircle with her mind, but her soul engulfed it. The midwives had tied a little band around the infant's middle. She knew what that was for, having been taught everything by Flicker and Minnow, and by women talking in the *wiktut* over so many years. The band held a piece of puffball mushroom in place on the tied umbilicus, which would be left on till it withered and came off. The puffball would keep it from becoming inflamed or swollen.

The little lips were so strong on her nipple. Were it not for the delight they sent down her belly and up into her ears, the suckings would almost hurt.

She looked down at the little eyelids, as yet unopen, the line of fine black eyelashes. Clearly, this was an Indian baby. A few times her husband had wondered aloud whether his child would have red hair. He had not said anything against that, but she presumed from his tone that he would prefer a child that did not look in any way *wapsini*.

She wondered how many days it would be before he returned from hunting to see what she had given him, this infant. And just as she was thinking that, one of the old women said:

"Why doesn't The Awl come in? I told him, come when the child cries."

"You told him?" Maconakwa said, looking up in surprise at the wrinkled face. "He is here from hunting?"

"Go see if The Awl is outside and tell him he has a *kwenanswa pelosaw*," the midwife told the girl.

He came in at once and knelt by his wife and baby, his tunic dense with wood smoke, fingernails black from butchering and fire-tending and jerky-making, hair lank and greasy. In his angular face, cross-lit by the fire, glowed pride and tenderness. His hard, veined, brown hand reached toward the baby's round head, but he did not quite touch her, as if afraid he might hurt the little creature.

"They said it is a female child. Good!"

"Husband! I did not know you were here! No one told me! I am so happy!"

"How good it is that Creator brought me home just this day. A dream led me to return."

"They said you were outside while I was birthing. I did not cry out, not at all."

"Good. My wife I know to be strong." She could see in his eyes that his affectionate regard for her was as genuine as she always hoped. And when he examined the baby, she could tell that he was fully pleased as well. He said, "The midwife told me I could come in after the baby cried. I did not hear it."

"But they said you were just outside the door."

"Yes. But I did not hear. As I cannot hear birds and high noises because of the shrillness in my ears."

"And yet you hear me now, though we talk softly."

"*E heh.* But yesterday riding in wind, my own horse whinnied and I looked up, thinking I had heard an eagle."

She gazed at him tenderly for a moment, thinking, then said, "When the spring brings mayapple to fruit, I will put drops of its juice in your ears. Kahesana said that has given some people back their hearing."

He shrugged. "So we should try it," he said, but his face showed little hope for it. "So long as I can hear you talk to me, I am content." He bent forward and pressed his cheek to hers, and she was enveloped by the wood smoke smell on him. He murmured, "Forgive me that I was not here for burying your father. I only learned on returning to the town that he Crossed Over. He was a man full of honors."

She lowered her head and blinked. Then she said, "As soon as I became a person with no parent, I became a parent." Without a parent, she thought. Unless faraway white parents still live.

They sat in silence awhile. He was gazing at the baby, whom Maconakwa was gently caressing as she nursed. He stopped her hand suddenly and held it and looked at the damaged, nailless forefinger. Some deep and tender thought passed behind his eyes for a moment, so intense she felt her scalp prickle. "What?" she exclaimed.

He held the damaged finger to the baby's head. "Think of this name for our daughter," he said. "Keshkeneshkwa."

"Hurt Finger? Cut Finger?" It seemed such a strange name.

He nodded. "When I saw your hurt finger touch this baby so kindly, I was told, this is the name sign."

"Then," she said, "so it should be. Our daughter will be Cut Finger."

Pittston, Pennsylvania

In the front room of Will's new house at Pittston, Ruth Slocum slightly moved her grandson's cradle and looked down at the infant with foreboding. This was Joseph's first child, and she thought she saw an aura of death about him.

Every time she looked at him, she felt cold.

Jonathan was his name, after his grandfather. Sometimes Ruth Slocum, now sixty-four and full of arthritic pain, wondered whether she saw death around this child simply because he was named after her late husband, whose whole memory was overshadowed by his own violent death twenty years ago.

That would not be fair, she thought. Think that way and thee might well *place* a doom on the poor innocent!

She did not really believe in spells, or placing doom, or any such things; they went against her faith, which was a practical and no-nonsense kind of faith whose powers were strictly those of the Inner Light, always positive powers.

But still, this baby seemed to have no future she could see, no matter how positively she tried to see him. There was the aura, which was there whether she tried to perceive it or tried not to. And there was that dullness in the infant's eyes, eyes that were more like the sunken eyes of an old man than like a child's. This was the only baby she had ever seen that appeared to know already anything it might ever care to know about the world around it. This was a baby that seemed to have been born old, and Ruth expected that Joseph would be taught his first direct lesson about life's deep losses by this unfortunate child.

Hopeless or not, she never failed to pray for this baby. She prayed every day for all her other grandchildren, who were numerous. All her sons and daughters were as prolific in making children as she and Jonathan had been. Her children were all having just about one birth a year in each family. This baby Jonathan was little over three months old, but Ruth knew quite well—she wasn't deaf or blind yet—that Joseph was back upon Liz several times a week. She knew that because Joseph and Liz had been temporarily living in Ruth's house at Wilkes-Barre, using that same telltale upstairs bed with its distinctive squeak that neither carpentry nor tallow had been able to silence over the decades. Joe and Liz were about to move on up the Susquehanna to a plot of land up toward old Wyalusing, the old Indian town that had once been beyond the frontier but was now just a neighboring town where white people lived.

Wyalusing had been the place, it was believed, where Frannie had been taken right after her captivity. It was where her cousin Isaac had caught a glimpse of her one day—Goodness, Ruth thought, what, more than twenty years ago!—in one of those tantalizing incidents, so thrilling and hopeful then, so vaguely recalled now, of a search that had continued through a whole generation. She had grandchildren now who were about the age Frannie had been when she was taken away by those warriors. The roads were good enough now that the Slocums along the valley could reach each other's homes in day trips. She could remember the ordeal travel used to be, sometimes days of painful jouncing or horseback meanderings along steep Indian paths just to cross half of Luzerne County.

Her son Will had seven of her grandchildren here in his house overlooking the river bend, seven grandchildren in ages ranging from two up to thirteen. Will's wife Sarah was due again next spring. Will had been voted out of office as Luzerne County's sheriff last year, and often mused aloud about setting off for the Indian country again in search of Frances. But there was a silent resolve in Sarah to discourage it. Last time he had gone, with three brothers and a herd of cattle, Sarah was left with a babe in arms, two toddlers, and one on the way. The brothers had come back that fall unsuccessful as usual, half starved and so sick from exposure that Will had been less like a returned helpmeet than another baby to feed and clean up after. Sarah was stubborn and certain she was in the right, and it was pretty well accepted in the family by now that Will would not go traipsing in the wilderness looking for his sister again until Sarah was good and ready to let him go. Ruth admired and respected Sarah for that, though she did suffer through every year that passed without at least one of her sons going out on the far trails in that perennial quest.

Ruth gave the little chestnut cradle a lingering nudge; little Jonathan was sleeping now. She hobbled out onto the porch, where Will and Joseph were loafing away the beautiful fall morning. Loafing was a luxury neither often enjoyed, and so instead of sitting on the porch bench to talk, they kept strolling about, from one end of the porch to the other, chatting over their shoulders, gazing off up or down the valley, sometimes slouching with their shoulders against the porch posts. Back and forth they had been clumping in their boots all the time she was in the house. "Well, boys," she said, settling her full gray skirts on the bench, "if thee'd walked out that way as far as thee's tramped to and fro on this porch this morning, thee might be in Tioga by now." She didn't know why she had said "Tioga." Probably because she had just been thinking about the old quest.

Will, now thirty-eight, whose red hair was turning silver in the temples, had been pinching flaked tobacco into the bowl of a long, white-clay tavern pipe. He said, "Well, Ma, Sarah really doesn't mind if I walk to Detroit again, as long as I don't leave this porch." He chuckled. "Only sheriff in this country that ever served his whole term under house arrest! Heh heh!" He groped in the watch pocket of his black vest and pulled out his magnifying glass. Joseph smiled at Will's joke and shook his head.

Ruth watched her son go through his routine. He swung back the glass's hinged brass cover, glanced out at the location of the sun, turned a little sideways and held the lens above the pipe bowl, moving it minutely up and down until the sunlight was focused in the bowl and little tendrils of smoke rose out. After a while he carefully kept the lens in place while drawing his head back, closing his lips over the pipe stem and starting a hard sucking. The ritual took him perhaps two minutes of concentration, but at last he got a dense cloud of smoke drifting around his head.

"All that effort," Ruth Slocum sighed, "just to raise a stink!"

"Well, Ma," he said, "since I moved up here from Wilkes-Barre, fresh air's been about to kill me. No coal soot. This helps."

"I never thought I'd see the day my very own sons'd fall prey to that vice."

He hauled in a deep lungful, puckered his lips, and blew it out in a long stream. "Well, Ma, through this delicious smoke the world looks a little different. When I haze up the visible world out there, it helps me see better with my mind's eye. The mind's eye, see, is better than the real eye at figuring out how things are in the world."

"Is that so," she said, gazing up the river. "And how is the world through that haze thee's makin'? What I see with my real eye looks just about perfect, and I sh'd not want to change it." Up that way she could see perhaps three miles of the Susquehanna flowing in its graceful curve between mountains filmy with sunny mist, the woods mostly crimson and gold, the bottomlands buff and yellow with corn and barley and hay fields, mostly harvested already. A mile up, on the east bank, she could see where the little Lackawanna River flowed in. Will's house and the new little town of Pittston were situated on the outside of a lovely river bend where the Susquehanna proceeded more southwesterly, and when she looked downstream, she could see the defilade in Back Mountain, where her son Giles and son-in-law Hugh had escaped death in the massacre some twenty-two years ago; she could in fact see the sites of several forts from that war, now all silent and abandoned, thank God, she thought. And even before the Revolution there had been warfare and murder and mayhem all up and down this valley—those constant battles between the Pennamites and the Yankees encroaching from Connecticut and Rhode Island. Those little wars had been going on even when Jonathan Slocum brought her to this valley. One reason this river valley looked so perfect to her now was that at last it was peaceful. There hadn't been a battle here in years.

Offshore from the massacre site stood Monocanock Island, a mile long, and above and beyond it, hazy at seven miles away, stood the tiny structures where Forty Fort had been, above the next bend where the river turned southward again and ran down past Wilkes-Barre, her home. Wilkes-Barre wasn't visible from here at Will's house, but she could see the smudge of its coal smoke hanging in the gauzy air before Wilkes-Barre Mountain's lilac flank.

How beautiful it was, and it just kept adding to the fortunes of her family. What had started as mere frontier land purchases by her father Isaac Tripp had developed into assets by which the Slocums, it seemed, could not help prospering. Everything in the valley—land, ore, coal, wood, even falling water—kept turning into wealth. Her family, strung out now along these visible miles of the Susquehanna and its tributary the Lackawanna, grew steadily, inexorably, more wealthy with its landholdings and minerals and milling enterprises. Even those who had left for other parts—Giles to Saratoga, Judith and Mary with their husbands to Ohio—took with them stakes enough to ensure success in their new homes on the farther frontier.

She looked over the autumnal beauty of the valley and could scarcely believe what had happened here in the quarter of a century since she first saw it from the hard seat of a canvas-roofed wagon. She and Jonathan had had to stand up in the wagon to see over the top of the lush, windblown grasses. Many of the oaks had been five to seven feet in diameter in the trunk, and there were incredibly tall pines on the mountainsides. Indian tribes—Senecas, Mahicans, Shawnees, Delawares, Nanticokes, Iroquois nations— had been living in this valley continuously, it appeared, since the ancient days when they, or some long-lost older civilization, had built earthen mounds and fortifications. Missionaries of a sect called Moravians had come among them before the Revolution and taught them things that unrooted them, made them unstable and vulnerable to the influences the settlers then brought. . . .

Ruth Slocum knew, from her work with the Friends' missionary effort, a great deal about the usual effects of missionary work, and she knew they were mixed blessings at best. Mission work was intended well, but to the tribes, most missionaries were as bewildering as liquor and war. Often she read the reports of the conditions in which the defeated Indians lived—squalor, disease, helpless drunkenness and spiritual confusion—and her grief over the probable fate of her lost daughter would so torment her that even the great fortune of the rest of her brood was overbalanced by it.

Frances would be—referring to her perpetual mental calendar of her daughter's age—twenty-seven years old now. And when Ruth Slocum visualized her, she saw a drunken, greasy harridan in ragged animal hides, smeared with crimson paint, begging around forts or, worse, prostituting herself with soldiers, probably diseased, probably leaving a wake of abandoned or sickly children, doomed like little Jonathan in there—

"Ma. Ma!"

It was Joseph, leaning near her, silhouetted against the light of the broad sunlit valley. She had been lost in that dismal daydream again, and had not heard him addressing her. "Yes, Joe?"

"Did thee hear what Will was saying to thee? Is thee quite well, Ma?"

"What? Certainly I'm well." She realized that she had lapsed and was embarrassed. "I'm quite well."

"Well, thee was groanin'! We thought thee was coming down with a complaint."

She sighed. "Son, thee knows, as a family we've more blessings than any I know. To a pampered body, the littlest discomfort's an agony, bein' unaccustomed. Well, see, th'ordeal of our Frances I suppose will always sting like an open wound. Till she's found and brought back to this family where she can share our many blessings, I'll have pain, and thee'll see me show it."

Joseph put his hand on her wrist. "Ma, I've promised thee I'll find her. And I shall."

"And I'm not through either," Will said, standing over them, still puffing tobacco smoke. "Before long, Sarah will be so tired of having me around that she'll *order* me to go looking in the wilderness." The way he said it sounded more like a joke than a promise.

After their mother had gone back in the house, Will stood puffing and gazing over the valley. He was not looking Joseph in the eye when he said softly: "Joe, sometimes I wonder if we'd do better not to humor her."

Joseph frowned. "What's thee mean, Will? I don't get your drift at all."

"Ma's possessed by an idle hope, and we just help keep her possessed by it. By humoring her, I mean."

Joseph flushed, troubled, almost angry. "Humoring her how?"

Now Will turned and looked at him, his face hard, lined by the cross light. "Little brother, does thee really believe that girl Frannie's still alive?"

"By heaven I do! Thee doesn't?"

Will sighed, his face softening, and gazed downriver. "Joe, I always did, while I was hunting for her. I mean to say, I'd not have gone on those awful treks had I not had half a hope. But since that last one, to Detroit and back . . . the way those poor beaten savages live . . . Thee saw it. The sickness, the rum and whiskey. Above and beyond that, consider this:

"When General Wayne told all the chiefs to return their captives if they wanted peace, they were wanting peace desperately, and they brought in aplenty. Now, Joe, doesn't thee think that if Frances were alive, she'd have been brought in and exchanged then? Truly, realistically, thinking with the brain rather than the hopeful heart, Joe, doesn't thee believe she *must* be perished long since?"

Joseph opened and shut his mouth several times to answer, but the answer kept switching from yes to no and back to yes. Finally he answered. "Will, the wretches we saw were only the whipped ones, the beggars. There's a possibility, thee'll admit, that out beyond the army's influence, many still live free and sober and in their own beliefs. In that case, Frances might still be alive and healthy."

"Aye, she might. But in that case, how should we ever hope to find her?"

Joseph felt the logic of that hit him hard. But he had lived almost his whole life with his mother's hopeful dream of recovering her daughter, and he answered simply, "Nevertheless, unless a proof comes that she is dead, I shall presume she's alive. And by my conscience, then, I could never quit the search."

CHAPTER SEVENTEEN

Spring 1805
Near Fort Wayne

Maconakwa's husband was older than the other riders, but she knew that did not matter. In a footrace it might have mattered, because their legs and lungs might have done better than his, but this was a horse race with horses whose legs and lungs were fairly equal, while he had long been a master of horses.

Hundreds of watchers, including white men from the fort, lined both sides of the racecourse. Maconakwa held her daughter's hand and exclaimed to her, loudly over the drone of excited voices in the sifting drizzle:

"Now watch, Cut Finger. Can you see your father down there?"

The little girl nodded, pointing to the cluster of milling riders far down at the other end of the meadow. "There on the darkest horse!" She bounced up and down on her toes.

Maconakwa's stake in the race was not merely her husband's glory. She had helped him gentle and train several horses in the last four years, and this mare he was racing today had been her particular charge from the day it was foaled. She had raised the dark filly virtually alongside her daughter, Cut Finger. Working with her husband's small herd, she found that she had almost a kinship with them, could almost read their thoughts and make them read hers.

Raising, training, and trading horses had become the occupation of her husband, The Awl, more than hunting now. Fort Wayne was one of the main places where he could race and sell or trade his horses, because there were always great numbers of people. Here, where the Kekionga Miamis had prospered by controlling the portage, the Fort Wayne whites now prospered by controlling the Miamis, and the welfare of the tribe depended upon the whites. But with the white men at Fort Wayne had come their spirit water, which seemed to flow as plentifully as river water from the portage place, and it was ruining the People.

Little Turtle was tamed. He lived almost in the shadow of the big fort called Fort Wayne, near where his old town had been. The old chief lived well here, in a big house of the sort white men built, and he sat on furniture and ate with silver utensils. He enjoyed benefits stemming from his son-in-law's position here as the government's Indian agent to the Miami People. Wild Potato, now known again by his *wapsi* name of William Wells, had a big and rich farm near the fort, and he and his wife Sweet Breeze had given Little Turtle three grandchildren, who had Miami names they used when they were with their grandfather, and *wapsi* names the rest of the time; one of the boys even had as a middle name Wayne, in honor of the general to whom Wild Potato had betrayed his Miami People.

The Awl often wondered aloud how Little Turtle could have forgiven Wild Potato and come to trust him again. But he had. He had even gone east with Wells, wearing a blue suit and a black hat, to visit with the famous war chief called Washington, who had become *sakima* of the whole *wapsi* nation by that time. Washington had given Little Turtle a sword, since he promised not to fight anymore.

Then Wells had taken Little Turtle to see the next *wapsi* chief, called Adams, and on that journey Little Turtle had begged Adams to stop the flow of spirit water. It was the most desperate problem talked of in the tribal councils. In just one year the liquor had caused three thousand Miamis to die. They had never lost so many in a whole generation of war as in one year of peace, because in peace the liquor sellers could work.

Maconakwa secretly prayed every day that spirit water would not get into the blood of her present husband as it had the blood of her first husband. The Awl was a solid and cheerful man who did not seem as if he would ever weaken to it, but so had many others seemed before they succumbed, and then their lives had descended to dirt and cruelty and misery, the hurting of their families, and death. The present Long Knife chief, Jefferson, had not yet stopped the flow of spirit water into the Indian country, and sometimes in Council, Little Turtle hinted that perhaps the Long Knife chief actually wanted the red men to die off from it.

But of course as a signer of the treaty surrendering to the Long Knives, Little Turtle could not come out forthrightly and condemn them for anything. He did not like telling the tribal Council that the Miamis had to keep begging the Great White Father in Washington for everything that Wayne had promised them in his treaty ten years ago.

As the horses began lining up at the distant starting place, Maconakwa was delighted to see her old friend Minnow among the people lining the other side of the racecourse. Minnow waved to her, said something to some women with her, broke away from them and came trotting across the racecourse, wearing a nearly white dress of fringed elkhide and a mass of necklaces that jounced as she came running, laughing. That was not all that jounced, and Maconakwa hugged her, saying in Lenapeh, "So I see you are baby-carrying again, sister!" Minnow had married a hunter from Metosinah's Lenapeh village on the Mississinewa Sipu, about a day's journey east of The Awl's Miami town. The two women seldom saw each other except here at the fort and trading post, or when traveling to and from councils.

"And I see you are also, sister." Minnow laughed, putting her palm on Maconakwa's mounded abdomen. Then she frowned. "But you were pregnant last spring Bread Dance too, I remember. How is this?"

Maconakwa's heart clenched and she looked down and bit her lips. "That was a boy one, dead when he was born. I thought you would have known. I sent word to you by one of Metosinah's nieces last fall."

"No. I did not hear. Sister, I grieve for the loss you suffered." She put her cheek to Maconakwa's.

"*Waneeshee,* sister. May these we bear now be soundly born and live long, and grow to be like brothers or sisters, as we have been like sisters." It was good to be speaking the old tongue again. The Lenapeh and Miami tongues were not much alike. The Miami was softer in the mouth. Speaking the Lenapeh language had been more like uttering bird song, trilling and clicking, and Maconakwa missed it. Sometimes she thought Miami sounded as if the speaker was talking with a mouthful of stew.

Minnow pointed up the meadow. "I see your husband will run your dark mare. How does he treat you?"

"Always well. I would not change anything about him."

"*Wehlee heeleh.* I would pound his head bone into flour if I heard he was unkind. Remind him, you and your mother saved him to live."

"And you helped to save him too, my sister. But I never have to remind him. He thanks me often. And your husband? You are still well-treated?"

Momentarily Minnow's teeth bared in something that did not look good, but then she smiled. "Two times he drank the white man drink. The first time he was howling, like when we found your other husband on the riverbank. You remember how that was. The second time he struck me. Since that time, he has what you call *keshkeneshkwa* to remind him he will drink no third time."

Cut Finger, hearing her name, looked up, curious, but not more curious than Maconakwa, who said, "He has a hurt finger?"

"Like yours. I bit the end off and spat it in his face. I do not expect him to drink spirit water again."

At the thought, Maconakwa put her palm over her breast, blinked, and made a whistling sound. Just then an outcry swelled along the line of waiting spectators. With a rumble of many hooves, the racing horses were coming, and their riders' yipping cries were building. The encouraging howls of the spectators rose also, and Maconakwa began yelling her husband's name.

It was not a mere horse race, it was something more dangerous, requiring more skill. Each rider carried a lance in one hand and a quirt in the other. At this end of the meadow there hung from a tree limb a tough hoop of twined vines wrapped in leather, no broader than a hand. It was decorated with a long white goose feather, to help both the riders and the spectators see it in the melee. Twenty riders were coming at full gallop toward that hoop, which they could hardly see from the starting line, except for the goose feather under it. The winner of the race would be the rider who could thrust his lance tip through the little hoop and yank it from the limb, then get clear of the mob and race back to the starting line without losing the hoop off his lance. Upon a limb near the hoop crouched a trusted referee.

The broad rank of riders had started abreast, but as they all converged toward the hoop, they became a compacted mass, shouldering, elbowing, crushing inward, sometimes even slashed by others' quirts. The only plan in any rider's head was to be out in front when he reached the hoop, with his lance clear to penetrate the hoop. Getting there first was the best advantage, but it did not guarantee winning. Too many other things could happen.

The first of those other things began to happen now just as The Awl, on the swift dark mare, thundered past his wife and daughter, half a horse length ahead of the rest, his lance tip closing toward the center of the hoop. She did not see what happened. Perhaps another horse's hoof hit the hind leg or hoof of the dark mare and made her falter, or another horse's shoulder hit her rump, or somebody's lance hit The Awl's shoulder; Maconakwa, flinching against bits of grass and dirt kicked up by the cluster of hard-driving horses, saw only that her husband's lance missed the hoop by a hand's breath. Another lance hit the rim of the hoop and set it lurching, bouncing. At once the mass of yipping riders began reining in and around under the tree. Horses sat, reared, careened, fell, collided with others. Some lances hit the overhead limb and splintered. The hoop swayed and bobbled, now an almost impossible target. Now the riders still mounted were milling and brawling under the tree, madly jabbing and fending and thrusting at the wobbly hoop. Even over the yipping and howling and the whinnying horses, she could hear the clicking and clacking of the lances, and the referee observer sprang like a squirrel to a higher limb to get out of reach of the flailing lance tips.

Keeping a hold on the hand of her daughter, who seemed to want to run toward the melee, Maconakwa craned to see her husband and her horse. She saw the mare backing out of the brawl, saddle empty, and her heart seized with alarm.

Next she saw her husband run, stooped, out from between the dancing legs of horses. His tunic was bloody. He snatched up a fallen lance, or rather half of a broken one. Then he ran halfway around the screeching mayhem, grabbed the rein rope of the mare, and swung on. Kicking her flanks, he plunged back inside the churning mass. Minnow's voice was shrieking, hundreds of other voices were shrieking, and the knot of riders slammed and yelled and jabbed. An absurd thought flashed through Maconakwa's mind that her husband might be fortunate at such a moment as this to be deaf.

Instantly then rose a louder howl from the riders, and the mass of them began to break loose and stream outward in one direction like water flung from a pot. For an instant, near the head of that moving salient, she saw the white flash of the goose feather, the hoop bobbling on the end of an upraised lance, then another lance thwacking against that one, and there was another howl as the hoop disappeared and then it came flopping and jouncing out along the ground toward the spectators and the horsemen came veering after it. The watchers screamed and surged backward out of its way, snatching their children after them.

Almost at Maconakwa's feet she saw a lance slip through the hole in the hoop and raise it up. Dozens of hooves flung grass and clods among the spectators, and then the horses were thundering away down the field again, toward the starting line, leaving a wake of limping horses and dazed, dismounted riders and splintered lances all over the field. She heard a great, deep cheer at the far end of the racecourse as the contestants swarmed past the line. Someone had succeeded in taking the hoop down there, but it was impossible from here to see who had done it. The crowd of spectators, from both sides of the racecourse, was now sprinting down that way, cheering and laughing. Maconakwa, with her five-year-old daughter in tow and her belly heavy with child, was among the stragglers.

But even over the heads of the others, she could see the glorious and unexpected sight: her own husband, though nearly twice the age of any of the other riders, was the one in the center of all the cheering, sitting bloody but smiling on the dark mare, holding overhead half a lance, with the muddy, leather-covered hoop hanging from it and the broken, trampled goose feather swaying beneath.

Her deaf man and her dark mare had won the Little War of the Hoop!

Maconakwa was uncomfortable in the house of Little Turtle. The room had corners and straight walls and ceilings. She sat on a chair, which would have been constricting even without the great weight of a baby in her, and the edge of the chair pressed on the backs of her knees, making her feet tingle. And because of her swollen belly, she had to sit far enough back from the table's edge to give herself breathing room.

It was strange to be sitting on furniture. Maconakwa's mind and body had distant remembrance of chairs and benches, and of a table that held a plate of food just under one's chin, so when she held a silver fork to eat with, her hand remembered at once how to manipulate it. Her husband was awkward with it.

This was how dining was done sometimes in Little Turtle's big and solid square-cornered house near the fort, as he often had white people as guests. Now Maconakwa watched the *sakima* as closely as she could without seeming rude. He had magnificent eyes that glittered with delight or flashed with anger when he talked of the things that concerned his Miami People, but often those magnificent eyes squinted with pain, for he lately suffered from a rare kind of illness that made the joints of his hands and feet swell and redden. White people called it "gout," and it was an illness of excruciating pain with no known remedy.

Whenever her husband came up the river to the fort to Council with Little Turtle and the other Miami chiefs, she helped him understand some of the things that his ears could not pick out anymore. At first it had been only the high sounds, but now, he complained, it was like swimming underwater and trying to listen to men talking on shore. Whatever the gun blast injured in his head eleven summers ago, that had been just the beginning of the loss. Often he could understand nothing in Council except what she or other hand-signing interpreters could express to him. He had offered to retire as chief of his village and let his Council elect a chief who could hear. But in reply they said that his heart and brain were worth more than another man's ears, and voted to retain him as their village chief. They had said also that they did not wish to replace their *sakima*'s wife, who, though a red-hair born of *wap-situk*, was as good as a People could want their chief's wife to be. Thus Maconakwa and her husband were often in the company of Little Turtle, and in his councils, and were informed on matters he kept putting before the Long Knife government chief.

The latest main chief Little Turtle had met was a man who had never been a soldier. His name was Jefferson. It was presumed that since this Jefferson was never a war chief, he must therefore be a shaman of some sort, in order to be important enough to lead his whole nation. Little Turtle had described Jefferson as very tall, red-haired, and intelligent, but a soft speaker one could hardly hear. "Aha!" The Awl laughed. "Like me listening to anybody!"

Now at the table Little Turtle began speaking of things he had discussed with Jefferson. Little Turtle's voice was clear, loud and pleasant, such a strong voice that even The Awl could hear some of his words. Little Turtle was saying:

"He wants us to learn their ways of raising food and meat animals, so we will not have to range far to hunt. I told him it was always our way for men to hunt, but that we will learn to change, if we must to keep our people fed. We will have to learn that as our land grows smaller, as the whites move in closer."

Yes, Maconakwa thought, that is always their reason for everything they want us to do. They want us to get used to the shrinking of our country, because they mean to keep taking it. A *wapsi* chief named Harrison, who had been a young soldier of Wayne a decade ago, had made several treaties in the last two years, buying vast lands in the south and west. Little Turtle himself had signed those treaties, encouraged by Wild Potato Wells, and by signing them had made enemies in other tribes. It was a sad thing to think of, and hard to speak of in Little Turtle's presence.

"Jefferson," Little Turtle was saying now, "sends us some plows and hoes and wagons. Some good farmers, of a people called Quakers, will come and teach us to farm that way, and teach us many things."

Maconakwa was startled to hear that remembered name.

Little Turtle went on: "Brothers, I know my people well. I fear they will not want to help themselves in the new ways as much as the Quaker people want to help them. I fear our hunters will not want to put their hands to farm tools, or to making fences, or to raise pigs and cows. They will say, 'Our Creator did not instruct us that way; he told us to be hunters and go where the animals are.' But we will have to change, or we will starve.

"I know also, brothers, that those of our people who have learned the need for spirit water, they will be angry with me because I made Jefferson promise to keep it away from here. Some have already warned my son-in-law Captain Wells that it will go hard for him if they cannot get it to drink." Little Turtle rose, wincing with pain. "Brothers, listen well to me. What comes will be hard for us. We must pray that the Great Spirit will help our People see their true needs and change with them. You must help me persuade them it is good to cultivate the soil and bad to drink spirit water.

"I will send another letter to the Quakers and ask them to send their farmer-teachers quickly if they have not already. I ask you to prepare your people's hearts to welcome them. Without those Quakers, who are reputed never to cheat or make war, our people's troubles will grow ever worse."

Maconakwa sat on the unfamiliar chair seat remembering as well as she could what her Quaker family had been like. Truly, she could remember nothing bad. It seemed that they must really be different from all the other *wapsituk*. Her heart felt so big with thinking of Quakers that she felt she should speak for them. And so she signed to her husband, asking if it would be appropriate for her to speak; since this was not exactly a Council, she did not know the protocol for putting forth her own words.

He looked at her a little warily, but had faith in her judgment and sense, and he addressed Little Turtle, saying, "My wife Maconakwa asks if she might speak to us on a thought she has."

Little Turtle looked at her, and with a nod he raised his palm and motioned for her to stand, and told the people, "We know Maconakwa, wife of The Awl, she who is good to all the people and is a healer. Let us hear her."

When she stood, her right leg almost buckled under her. The hard edge of the chair had made her leg, as she remembered her white family used to say, go to sleep. She had to brace her palms on the edge of the table and keep wiggling her tingling foot and try not to seem awkward, even with the baby's weight pulling down.

"Our *sakima* the Little Turtle," she said, "tells us that those called Quakers are honest and right-thinking even though they are white-skinned. You might doubt—"

"Indeed we might!" several murmured, smirking.

"Hear me, my brothers and sisters," she went on. "I was born in a white-face family. You know that. You see me and know that. I have lived now for nearly thirty summers among the Lenapeh and the Miami, and these are my People.

"But I can remember that my birth family were those called Quakers . . ." She saw a widening of Little Turtle's eyes and heard several of the people in the room murmur with interest and surprise. "I remember," she went on, "that no lies were ever told in that family. No one ever hurt another. No one ever drank of spirit water. All worked hard and grew food and all did as they promised. If Quakers come here, you will be glad, I believe . . ." She hesitated then, wondering whether she had been too impulsive, or had given too strong a testimonial based on the vaguest of childhood memories, which are oftimes more wistful than true.

But then Little Turtle thanked her for saying what she had said, and told the people that what she had told was true, according to what he had seen of Quakers. She sat down, blushing, eyes modestly lowered, and it was not until she was seated and daring to look about again that she became aware that William Wells was staring at her. She was sorry she had spoken. She had long ago been warned that if he knew enough information about her, he might sell her name.

Little Turtle asked Wells to explain some things about the *wapsi* government and how it worked, and what might be expected to happen, and the deeds of the *wapsi* chief named Harrison, who lived at Vincennes, near the other end of the Wabash Sipu.

"All of your lives," Wells said, "you have seen the tribes being pushed westward. Perhaps you have thought that if the pushing continues, you can just keep moving farther west before it. You would not like going, but you believed you could keep going that way.

"But by his treaties, this man Harrison now has all the land from the Kankakee Sipu west to the great Missi Sipu, and so it is now useless for the tribes to think they can back away from the Long Knives by moving west. What is left of land that way is the place of Potawatomis, Kickapoos, Kaskaskias, Sauks, and Winnebagos. You cannot move in on top of them, and they can back off no farther because Harrison already has the land beyond them. The space for all the tribes grows smaller, and Jefferson has ordered Harrison to keep making treaties, which will make the land even smaller.

"That, brothers, is why you must obey the wishes of the great chief Jefferson, and learn the ways of the whites, so that you may live richly, as they do, on less land. If you raise your own meat animals instead of chasing game animals far and wide, you can live well on small pieces of land. That is why my father and I urge you to learn to live as the whites do."

After Wells sat down, and Maconakwa had sign-translated all his words to her husband, The Awl stood up. He faced Wells and Little Turtle, and he spoke, in his voice that had grown louder since he had grown deaf:

"Father, and brother, what you say raises in me much sadness and doubt, and I ask you to make something clear to me.

"If, as you say, the white man knows how to live richly on just a little piece of land, then why does he need so much that he keeps taking from us all of ours?"

Sweet Breeze, the wife of Wells, later came toward Maconakwa as the wives sat around a fire outside the house, some with blankets drawn about them, the spring nights still being cool. The men were inside the house with Little Turtle and Wells, all engaged in talks with Five Medals, a Potawatomi chief, about the matter of farming and livestock raising in the white man's way. The chiefs and chieftains in the house had been given cigars of rolled tobacco by Wells, and were smoking those, while outdoors most of the wives had drawn out their little tobacco pipes and were smoking their more familiar kinnikinnick mixtures.

Sweet Breeze in full maturity was still a beautiful woman, and her richly made white-fashion clothing, with ribbons and lace, reflected the wealth her husband was accumulating as the Indian agent at Fort Wayne. Though many of the wives here had known Sweet Breeze all their lives, and had been her playmates in childhood and her friends when her husband was Wild Potato, they now were reserved and distant in her presence, barely polite, either through distrust, envy, or fear. Maconakwa had no reason to dislike her, but because of her feelings about Wells, she was not very happy to see Sweet Breeze approaching with her eyes and smile set upon her.

Sweet Breeze for a while spoke of pregnancy and birth-giving. Maconakwa was interested, of course, but was worried by the looks they were receiving from the other women around the fire. At last Sweet Breeze brought forth what she apparently had come to speak of, saying:

"My husband helps my father write and read the letters that pass between him and the good people in the East called Quakers. They try to provide the tools and the teachers for which my father asks, because the government does not do well at filling its promises, but the Quakers do. And so my husband sends to them many letters that he often writes.

"My husband remembers you from far back in the days when you lived near us as Tuck Horse's daughter. He remembers seeing your red hair, like his. He never did know you were from Quakers. He never did know what your little-girl name was from your white family."

"That is so. I never did speak it, nor did my father or mother."

"This night," Sweet Breeze said, "he was surprised to hear that you came from Quakers. He asked me to inquire from you whether you remember your Quaker name from before."

Maconakwa hugged her arms across her belly, suddenly feeling a chill. "Does he say why he wishes to know?"

"He believes that when he writes to them, if he wrote your name to them, then your Quaker family might come to know where you are and you could be with them again."

Maconakwa remembered what her parents had said about selling names. It seemed as if that was what Wells wanted to do.

She said, "Why does he want me to be with those people instead of our Miami People?"

"When the chiefs went to ask peace from General Wayne, they were told to bring in all the white captives they had. Somehow that did not happen to you."

Maconakwa nodded. "Your husband went back to his *wapsi* people and was made important by them, but still he gets to remain with the Miami People who loved him and raised him as one of their own. That is all good, for him. But I, if I went back to my Quaker people, I would not get to remain with the Miami People."

Sweet Breeze's eyes widened, then she looked down, hiding some strong feeling that was showing in her eyes. She said, "Then I should tell him you do not remember the Quaker name you had?"

"Sister, that would be good for you to say."

Maconakwa was at Fort Wayne again three moons later, but this time she was not on furniture, but sitting comfortably on a fur robe on the ground, with her baby boy Waweah, Round One, suckling her. He had been named that because one of the first things he had looked at when his eyes opened was the full round moon in the sky. His name-sign made her remember Neepah, named for Grandmother Moon herself. Maconakwa was in the commons near the fort feeding Round One when she first saw the three Quaker farmer teachers who had come to Fort Wayne from the East. She was here this day because her husband had come to sell two mares.

Rain was drizzling down, and she had hooded her head and covered her baby with the edge of her woolen shawl. She looked long and carefully at the three men. In their broad-brimmed black hats and black coats and gray trousers, they looked as if they had stepped out of her earliest memories. They were indeed Quakers, and they looked just as she remembered her brothers, though older.

She tried to stay unnoticed, watching them talk to Little Turtle and some of the Miami elders, and her heart ached with a yearning even while it was shrinking with a fear.

She wanted to ask them if their name was "Slocum," and felt certain they would say yes. Surely these were her own brothers, whom she had not seen in almost thirty summers. Maybe they were the ones who had been at Niagara. She gazed at them from under her blanket hood so intently that she was sure they must feel it, and then one turned his head and looked straight at her, from less than ten paces away. At once she ducked her head down over the nursing baby boy and hoped to look like just any Indian woman, her heart racing with a fear that they would recognize her. She was not sure she wanted them to recognize her, at least not yet.

But they looked so good, so kind. They were straight and strong, as she thought she remembered her father and brothers had been, but didn't have the hard and arrogant look that *wapsi* soldiers and traders had. She thought these were men she could trust, whether they were truly her brothers or not.

She wanted to know whether they were her brothers, but she did not want Little Turtle or Wells or Sweet Breeze or anyone to point her out to them and say, "That red-hair woman there was one of your Quaker people."

And so she realized that while they were here, until she decided what to do about them, she would have a very narrow path to walk and would have to be almost invisible. A time would come when she would know what to do. It would be hard to wait till then.

If indeed these three Quaker men are my brothers, she thought, they have come to live among my Miami People now. If so, I could, like Wild Potato William Wells, be with my true birth people and yet not have to leave the people who have my red heart!

She held Round One snug to her bosom and wondered if he could sense the confusion of delight and dread stirring her heart.

You could grow up with Quaker uncles, Round One, she thought. Imagine our two peoples eating and laughing together in peace and trust!

Maconakwa had come to believe there was no more beautiful place than the site of her husband's village. Every morning when she bathed and prayed at sunrise on the bank of the Mississinewa Sipu, she marveled at the work of the Creator.

The village of which The Awl was chief was one of three Miami towns near the Mississinewa's mouth at the Wabash. It was more than two days' travel downstream from Fort Wayne, far from the white men and the trading crowds. It was known to travelers as Kakipsah's Town, the town of the Deaf Man. Sometimes traders and travelers presumed that his name was Deaf Man, and he let that be, and as time went on he let himself be called Deaf Man. It amused him. "I never knew why I was named The Awl," he would say. "I do know I am a deaf man."

"It does not please me to hear them call you Deaf Man," Maconakwa protested once.

"Eh! It does not displease me because I cannot hear it." Then he laughed.

Some Miamis had been living at the mouth of the Mississinewa Sipu since the first Town Destroyer attacked Kekionga—more than ten years—and they knew it was a good place, where no one would have to go hungry if left in peace, and here they did hope to be left in peace, at least for a while. Here was rich, dark, deep soil; here was a clear spring that flowed strong all the year. The river was narrow, flowing green between great trees whose high branches arched over and met above, then through marshlands and cornfields and garden clearings.

In The Awl's village lived about two hundred families. They were the people of his mother, who had been wife of the preceding chief. Taking in refugees and the orphans of refugees, and some half-French, or *métis*, men and women with their children, the village had grown from a few dozen lodges to its present size. Deaf Man's village had The Awl's large corral made of posts and rails, and the chief helped other families of the village to establish lines of good horses. A few families had come bringing white men's cattle, and the stupid, harsh-voiced tame birds called chickens, but most still lived in the old manner. They planted the Sacred Sisters in hillocks in the bottomlands, and they hunted, fished, and foraged. The river yielded huge fish that could be easily speared in the clear water by gigs or arrows, or trapped in nets and weirs, or even seized right out from under the riverbank tree roots by hand, with enough patience. There were plenty of deer and wild turkeys and a few black bears to hunt for meat and fat, countless flocks of waterfowl in the nearby marshes for meat and eggs, big turtles everywhere, with their delicious flesh and their useful shells. Boys and young men trapped the many kinds of small riverine animals for their meat to eat and pelts to trade.

Even if there had been no crops or game, the people could have foraged enough nuts, acorns, berries, and roots from the woods and marshes to keep themselves alive. Here the Creator had put plenty of everything a people could need. The only worry was that the *wapsituk* would eventually come and want this place.

Sometimes Maconakwa could almost forget white men for days at a time, here beside this bountiful river, but as they were always coming from the East, their shadow preceded them and troubled the morning prayer. And she thought of the Quaker teachers upriver.

Then one day early in summer a messenger came with blazing eyes and a tongue stuttering with the fearsome thrill of the story he brought.

It was the story of a miracle that had happened, and a prophecy of the end of white men's power. Maconakwa listened to the messenger with chills running down her back. Her husband summoned all the people to hear what had happened.

It had happened in a village of renegade Shawnees beside the Wapihani Sipu, the White River, two days' travel south. A terrible man who had long been an addict of spirit water, as well as a liar and a molester of women, a dirty and repulsive man called Loud Noise, had been struck dead in his lodge while lighting his pipe.

Then, as the family of Loud Noise was preparing to bury him, he came back from the Other Side World. He had seen Kohkumthena, Our Grandmother, as the Shawnees called the Creator of Life. She had changed him into a great prophet.

Our Grandmother had told him exactly what must be done to take power out of the hands of the *wapsituk* and return this whole land to the red people so that everything would be right as it had been before the whites ever came. Our Grandmother had renamed that man Tenskwatawa, He Who Opens the Door, and ordered him to lead all the tribes through the Open Door into a new time of purity and strength. By that Open Door the red people would become so strong and united that the *wapsituk* would have to slink back eastward and take their boats back to their original home beyond the Sunrise Water. The messenger trembled and his eyes glittered as he said:

"This man called He Who Opens the Door, who before had always muttered so drunkenly that hardly anyone could understand him, now shines with holy light, and will not take a sip of spirit water, and speaks with such clarity and power and strength that his voice is like a beam of sunlight coming down through dark clouds. He has come when our peoples have lost heart. Come and see him and hear him, and then you will believe."

"Who is that man? And where on the Wapihani Sipu is he to be found?" The Awl asked.

"He is of the Kispoko Sept of the Shawnee, son of a Shawnee war chief long dead. His family has been marked by signs; he was one of a triple birth." The people gasped at that. Even twins were rare; no one here had ever known of triplets. The messenger went on: "His older brother was born under a shooting star and was named for it: Tecumseh."

"We have heard of Tecumseh. Did he not lead the scouts when Little Turtle defeated the big army at the head of the Wabash Sipu?"

"That is the one. Now those brothers have left the Wapihani Sipu and they have bravely gone back into their homeland to build a holy town, back inside the boundary made by General Wayne."

Inside those boundaries! That was a boldness both inspiring and frightening. Maconakwa imagined the trouble that could cause with the whites, but it was stirring, to think of red men going back to their homelands. She saw flashes of fierce pride in her husband's eyes and the eyes of listeners in the Council.

"Where in that country?" The Awl asked.

"At the very ruins of Wayne's fort called Greene Ville, where that treaty was. Think of that!"

"*E heh!*" The Awl breathed. But after the messenger was gone, he wore a troubled frown. "This will sound very bad to Little Turtle. It pushes the other way against everything our *sakima* tries to do."

And, Maconakwa thought, against the Quaker teachers too.

In the heat of summer, Maconakwa sat in Council with the people of her husband's town. Most of the talk was of two things that surely would be affecting their lives.

The village Council Lodge had been built with a peaked roof and log walls like white men's buildings, with a smoke hole in the roof, where silvery daylight beamed down through high cobwebs and cedar smoke from the Council fire in the center of the room.

After the pipe was passed, The Awl said to his people: "We begin this Council with something on either hand.

"Our *sakima* wants his people to learn to live like whites, for there is less and less land to hunt in. We would have to learn money, and the care of tame animals. Men would make fences and plow the ground. Women would learn to make cloth. Little Turtle has put the Quakers' farming school half a day's walk below the forks of the Wabash Sipu, not close to any of our towns, so no chief will be jealous or take advantage of another. I will ask some families from this village to go and study the ways there, so we may learn whether it is a good thing. Some things we already know are good: no spirit water is allowed there. And unlike the missionaries, those Quakers do not mock our spirit beliefs or try to change anyone to their own. But," he added, "with white men matters, one must go and see for oneself whether they are as they are said to be.

"What we have on our other hand is that Shawnee man who goes straight to the Giver of Life and gets instructions about how the red peoples must live. People from all nations go to his holy town to hear those instructions. They will not be easy either. He says we must throw away everything the white men have brought, by having nothing to do with white men, by returning to the ways of our ancestors. Even to hunting with bow instead of gun, to making fire without a steel spark striker, to cooking without iron pots, to sewing without steel needles, to cutting without iron axes." The murmuring of the people made plain how hard it would be to give up those things that made daily life easier. Most of the hunters had grown up with guns in their hands and did not even have the skills to hunt with bows anymore.

"That Prophet," The Awl went on, "would forbid the marriage of red people and white people. I am only one of several in just this little town who are already thus married. We already have children of mixed blood. What are such of us to do? We must go and learn what the Prophet demands. If he said I must give up this wife, how could I follow him?"

Maconakwa's heart felt squeezed down by dread as she heard that.

"So you understand," he said to his people, "this on one hand draws us one way, to walk close with the white man. This on the other hand draws us the other way, to walk away from him. That which lies on either hand could bring us peace or could bring us death. We are going toward a forked road. Which way we choose to go will cause the good or the evil with which our children and grandchildren forever will have to live."

The silence and the grimness were as deep as anything Maconakwa had ever known in a Council.

"I, Shapahcahnah, The Awl, need the wisdom of my people. Pray for guidance. Listen to what your ancestors may whisper to you. Tell me what they put in your hearts.

"All our People will have to do this. And, like creeks flowing into a river, all our wisdom must flow to our *sakima*, so that he may lead us according to wishes of the ancestors."

E heh, Maconakwa thought. But then will Little Turtle heed the wisdom of the Old Ones or the wishes of the *wapsituk*?

CHAPTER EIGHTEEN

Maconakwa had never been among so many people, nor had she ever known a crowd so still, so awed.

She sat in the plaza of the Prophet's Town beside her husband and her daughter, with her baby son, Round One, suckling her breast. They were waiting for a miracle that had been promised.

They were waiting for the sun to go out.

There were hundreds of strangers here, from tribes and distant nations she had only heard of, some nations that had been enemies to each other for generations. Yet all now seemed to be one reverent, beating heart with one yearning, one fear: that the sun would go dark by the Prophet's command.

The Prophet had sent his warning far and wide: that if the rightful occupants of this land were to regain their former greatness and peace, there must be no doubters, and that when they saw him turn off the sun, there would be nobody who could doubt him, except perhaps witches. This day was probably the most important day in the whole long story of the red people.

Come to my holy town and see me do it, he had sent word by messengers, and thousands had come, some traveling many days. Doubtless even those who had stayed away, because they scoffed or because they couldn't travel so far, were watching the sun climb to the peak of heaven on this mild day.

Among the hundreds here in this great holy town waiting and watching, most were believers, already inspired by the thrilling words and flutelike voice of the Prophet, ready to renounce the white man's tricks and poisons and goods, ready to follow the spiritual path of the Ancestors as he prescribed it for them. Many

373

others were here who yearned but doubted, and had come hoping to see it proven because they so wanted to believe.

But still others were of a third kind: those who thought the Shawnee Prophet was a liar and a pretender, and had come to see him fail, as surely a man must who would try to command the sun. Maconakwa had heard some such mockers whispering and scoffing in the town. Among those scoffers were people who had known the Prophet when he was merely Lalawethika, the Loud Noise, a mean and disgusting one-eyed drunkard from the Kispoko Sept of the Shawnee. They snickered at the notion that such a deceiver could have become suddenly a sober and exalted spiritual guide for the peoples. That, they said, would be as much a miracle as the sun winking out.

Also among those who had come hoping to see the Prophet fail were his enemies, or spies sent by his enemies. There were many of those. Maconakwa and her husband, The Awl, known here as Deaf Man, had just recognized a square-faced, pockmarked tall man in a ruffled blue calico shirt and silk turban, picking his way carefully through the crowd of seated families with no expression on his face. He was a seldom-sober Fort Wayne Indian who made his living by doing whatever William Wells wanted done. The Awl pointed his chin at him and murmured to Maconakwa, "There slinks a dog who will carry back to Captain Wells whatever he thinks he wants to hear. If the sun goes dark he will say a cloud came under it." People nearby heard his remark because, with his deafness, even his murmurs were louder than he knew, and they looked to see whom he was looking at, though they were really not much interested in anything but the impending miracle.

Maconakwa knew that William Wells and Little Turtle were very worried about what was happening in this town, because the Prophet's ways went against almost everything they were trying to achieve. The Prophet had drawn so many followers that he had influence nearly as great as Little Turtle's, and he was trying to turn everybody away from Chief Jefferson's plan of making the Indians into farmers and livestock raisers like the whites. The past year had proven out her fear: Little Turtle would not listen to the Ancestors if they disagreed with the chief in Washington.

William Wells had approached The Awl and Maconakwa before they set out for this place, and had asked them to come back and tell him all that happened in the Prophet's Town. They had simply turned away from him without replying. They had come here to observe the Prophet's works for the good of their own People, not as a spy for a man they could not trust. And so Wells had sent this calicoed and turbaned Fort Wayne Indian to spy for him instead. They had also seen here a half-French spy named Brouillette.

Old Black Hoof, the principal Shawnee chief and another signer like Little Turtle of the Wayne treaty, had sent spies from his reservation town at Wapakoneta, having been troubled by the Prophet's antiwhite preachings there last winter. Here also were spies from the Lenapeh towns on the Wapihani Sipu, where the Prophet had gone witch-hunting three moons ago. There he had condemned four Christian Lenapehs to be burned for witchcraft. There were also Wyandot spies here, sent by Tarhee, the Crane, who had prevented the Prophet from burning four accused Wyandot witches.

This was a big and substantial town, for one built so hastily and recently. There were hundreds of bark-and-mat-covered *wik-wams*, and hundreds of tents and lean-to shelters made in the ways of the various tribes. There were shade arbors covered with boughs, and open-sided cooking huts where the women of the Prophet's tribe labored over big kettles trying to feed the thousands of pilgrims. They did their best, stewing together corn and beans, roots and tubers and berries scoured from the countryside, occasionally flavored with the meat of small animals snared or shot by the Shawnee boys. The large game had long since become scarce in this vicinity because of the nearness of the white people, and had been utterly hunted out now by the hosts at Prophet's Town. The creeks that flowed together below the town had been fished out, and waterfowl, turtles, frogs, and even snakes were hard to find.

Like most of the people here, Maconakwa and her husband had brought food to Prophet's Town when they came, and it was gone now. Like most, they ate only once a day, hoping that their own abstinence would help assure that everybody would get a little to eat every day. Many of the people were content to eat virtually nothing, having come here for spiritual sustenance instead, and numbers of them believed that fasting would lift their spirits closer to the Creator in this holy place during this holy time. Mostly it was only the children, too young to understand, who complained about being always hungry. Cut Finger, not quite six summers of age yet, tried to understand the spiritual explanation, and said she did, but she whimpered for food between explanations. It was better, Maconakwa had found, just to tell the girl that it was necessary to share the limited food because there were so many people. That she could understand and condone, because she was an unselfish child.

As for her baby boy, he was still on her breast, even now suckling vigorously as the family sat here in the midst of the great crowd. And although Maconakwa was hungry, and had been hungry for days, the baby apparently was still well-nourished by her milk. He did not cry and nothing was wrong with his digestion yet. His lively sucking sent tickles through her.

On one side of the vast plaza stood a long building with a pitched roof, where visitors slept if they did not or could not build their own shelters, or until they did. When The Awl and his family had slept in it, there were more than a hundred others dwelling there, all in harmony, all polite to each other even if they knew little of the others' languages. Facing onto another side of this central clearing was the round Great House, a roofless arbor where the Prophet prayed at his tribe's altar. Every day he preached, morning, noon, and evening, from a platform in front of the Great House. When he was on the platform, anyone in the plaza could see him. At this time, waiting for him to come forth and darken the sun, the whole great crowd was facing that platform, eager for him to appear upon it.

Maconakwa herself at this time could not have said that she believed the Prophet was truly a holy man. Since her Quaker childhood, she had vaguely held to the notion that everyone was holy because of the Inner Light; though among her Lenapeh and Miami families and friends she had never discussed that belief, it was an unsaid certainty at the core of her spirit. The Indian peoples among whom she had lived so long had never told her how to believe or worship, but she had come to accept their sense that the Light of the Creator was in every living thing, animals and plants as well as human beings. She could not remember what her childhood religion said about prophets, but it seemed that she had heard of such persons long ago—those who had talked to God and learned of things to come. All the Lenapehs and Miamis she had known lived always in a state of prayer. Even when killing their enemies, or tricking each other, they never left their state of reverence, but instead recognized that there was an equal weight of badness and goodness everywhere and in everything, like day and night, male and female, pleasure and pain, life and death, happiness and grief, and that as long as those opposites were known and balanced, the world would hold together and continue.

The preachings of this Shawnee Prophet had confused her beliefs. He stated that all the red man's old ways were entirely good and all the white man's ways were entirely evil, and that all would be good again only when all the white man's evil was expelled from the land—not balanced, but expelled. She did not know whether the Prophet had lost his ancestors' sense of the world, or had gained directly from Creator a new and true sense more correct than the old one. He even spoke of a terrible place where drunkards and other bad people went after death, to be tortured and burned forever. She had never heard of such a place in the red man's beliefs, but when she was a little girl, she had heard of something like that, terribly frightening, spoken of by white people. She seemed to remember that that awful place was *down*, while good people went *up*.

So she did not have an intuition yet of whether this Prophet was truly a holy man, even though his voice was like flute music and his words made severe pictures in her head when he warned of evil, bright pictures when he spoke of a world without white men. One of the things he taught was that red people and white people must not marry each other and have children because such children would have impure blood.

If that were true, really ordered by Creator, then her happy marriage and beloved children must be cursed.

From that fear, she almost had to hope that this was not a truly knowing holy man.

She held the baby closer to her bosom and reached to hold her daughter's hand. As she did so, she heard a swell of soft voices rise all around her. It was the crowd. They were saying,

"Ah-hai! He comes now!"

"It is time!"

"Now we will see it happen!"

"Or," somebody dared to say, "we will see it fail to happen."

The Shawnee Prophet was a homely man. But he looked magnificent. He had stepped out of his lodge at the edge of the plaza, wearing a long robe despite the heat, a black bandanna pulled down on one side to cover his empty eye socket, and a headdress made of a whole raven's skin with feathers, wings outstretched. From his nose hung a silver ring; big silver ear bobs dangled to his shoulders, and through his left earlobe were stuck three small ornamental arrows fletched with eagle feathers. He walked slowly through the edge of the crowd toward his preaching platform, holding in one upraised hand before him his short medicine stick, whose upper end was tufted with bright, downy breast feathers that trembled in the breeze and looked like flickering flame.

With him walked a man as unadorned as the Prophet was adorned. In breechcloth and moccasins only, with only an eagle feather tied into a braid on one side of his hair, it was his older brother Tecumseh, an erect, sharp-eyed warrior chieftain, who some said was the real builder and chief of Prophet's Town. This was a handsome, powerfully muscled man whose graceful excellence could not be overshadowed by the Prophet's pomp and finery, even though he did walk unobtrusively by the Prophet's off side.

By his form and grace, he appeared to be about thirty winters in age, but he was known to be close to The Awl in age, about forty. The pilgrims at Prophet's Town knew little about him because he never addressed them or preached. But people who had heard him in councils said that his voice and gestures and the sense of his words made listeners lean forward. In those councils everywhere, The Awl said, Tecumseh warned chiefs not to sign away any more land in treaties with the white man called Harrison. It was said that he knew the English tongue and could even read the marking language. But here in the Prophet's Town, where the purpose was to rebuild the peoples' spiritual force, it was the Prophet who stayed in the forefront.

As the Prophet stepped up onto his platform, the warrior Tecumseh stopped and remained standing beside it, letting all eyes follow his brother's grand and ominous progress. Tecumseh did keep shading his eyes and glancing toward the sun.

The droning voices of the multitude now dwindled down to expectant silence again. Hundreds were rising from the ground to stand and see the Prophet better, to be on their feet when and if he turned day and night around. Maconakwa's heart was pounding. She held her baby boy to her chest and squeezed her daughter's hand. She and her family stood looking at the Prophet.

And now that strange man, Open Door, the self-named Prophet who claimed to have looked in Creator's face, who professed that he could make Macotaweh Keelswah, the Black Sun, stood silent before the anxious multitude, pointing his medicine stick toward the sky. His mad-looking eye swept everywhere over the crowd, seeming to pin everyone's soul for an instant, before he began to declaim in his high, nasal voice that sounded like a flute, a voice that made the birds stop singing. His statement was brief, and was at once translated into the tongues of all the tribes whose pilgrims were there:

"That white man Harrison at Vincennes, the Land Stealer, he has been so bold as to challenge He Who Opens the Door! That Harrison told the red people, 'Make him prove his powers by a miracle all can see; ask him if he can command the sun!'

"Therefore, my children, so that you will never again heed the lying words of white men, I command the sun to be dark at midday!

"Now see it obey me!"

Maconakwa at that moment was taken by a terrible shivering thrill—not just because of the audacity of the words, but because she perceived that something was visibly happening to the daylight. Wails and moans arose from hundreds, who had begun to notice it too:

Shadows were dissolving, their edges growing indistinct; the colors of skin, clothes, leaves, dimmed toward grayness. The light changed as if the day had suddenly become cloudy, but there were no clouds.

What was happening was very slow, but there was no denying that the daylight was changing. Indeed she had heard the Prophet call for the sun to darken; indeed it was happening. She stood silent.

But almost all the rest of the crowd was being swept away with awe and rapture. Their voices moaned, keened, and howled like the winds of a storm as the day grew darker. A warm wind sucked dust upward from the plaza, and where sun dappled the shade under a hazel bush nearby, the shivering shadows were shaped all like little vague crescents. The Prophet still stood with his stick pointed at the sky. Dogs howled. The people's voices dwindled. Men and women dropped to their knees. Maconakwa's daughter hugged her thigh and Round One let the nipple out of his mouth and whimpered. Maconakwa broke out in gooseflesh as she wondered how dark it would get and whether it would ever get light again. Perhaps the Prophet could have angered Creator by commanding the sun, and it would go out and stay out and all

the world would die. There might be incredible danger in this
Prophet's boldness.

Now the world was full of a deep, eerie gloom, and when people
started looking up again, their voices crooned in amazement.
Maconakwa hushed her baby and raised her hand over her eyes to
peek at the sun through a gap between her fingers.

It was totally black and round now, with a silvery brilliance
around it. Bats were fluttering above the crowd. The Prophet's
voice piped in the half darkness:

"Do you believe me, my children? Are you eager to see the sun
again? Then I shall ask the Master of Life to remove his hand!" He
lowered his fire stick. Slowly, slowly, the light began to return to
the surfaces of all earthly things, trees, roofs, people. Birds began
to twitter as at dawn, the bats vanished. After a long while the sunshine was again warm and bright on heads and shoulders and
everything looked as it was supposed to look at noontime. People
rose, blinking their eyes, their faces shining as brightly from
within as from the restored sunlight. The Prophet stood on his
platform, uplifted face shining with tears or sweat, teeth bared.
His shoulders were heaving; he was either panting or sobbing.

Deep in her soul, Maconakwa felt that the Prophet had somehow known this Macotaweh Keelswah was going to happen this
day, rather than having caused it. But that did not matter.

Those who had seen it here, and those who saw it from villages
elsewhere, would believe that he caused it. And there would be
few if any doubters after this. Through fear or admiration, surely
every red person across the land would grant that he was the Open
Door through whom the happiness and greatness of the Ancestors
could be found again. This had been a day that might change their
lives.

Her daughter Cut Finger was babbling questions. Maconakwa
looked at her husband. He was staring at the Prophet, thin lips
drawn tight against his teeth in a grimace or a smile.

"E heh!" he exclaimed. "Our *sakima* will have to heed this!"

Maconakwa pulled the porcupine quills between the edges of her
upper and lower front teeth to flatten them, but her mind was wandering. Since her return to her husband's village from the Prophet's
Town, she had not been able to sleep or quiet her spirit, and often
gazed off, forgetting what she was doing. Now, trying to make
quillwork decorations on the top of her husband's moccasins, she

brought herself back to the task time and again only by pricking herself with a quill barb she had forgotten she was handling. Then for a while she would concentrate on the moistened quills, inserting the barb of one into the base of another to make a long enough quill strand to embroider with, but soon she would be gazing off again into the smoky, quivering, gold and green distance outside the arbor: the sun-dappled, breeze-stirred summer foliage among the *wikwams*, the cornfields and gardens in the clearing beyond. Nothing was ever quite still; leaves, grasses, water, clouds, smoke, children: everything was always astir with living, caressed by the wind spirits. All shivering and rippling, hushing and swaying, full of mystery, it kept her from attending to her work and from concentrating on the questions she was trying to answer in her heart.

Had that strange man actually made the Black Sun by commanding it?

Or had he merely used some foreknowledge of it to trick the people so they would not doubt him?

But then where would that foreknowledge have come from, unless Creator had given it to him?

And if Creator had seen fit to give foreknowledge to that particular man, might he not have seen fit just as well to help him make a miracle whether he had foreknowledge or not?

Her question was whether the Creator was truly coming to the red people, through that man who called himself the Open Door. If so, it would mean that Creator wanted the peoples to throw away the white man's ways and his goods.

And if that were so, the Quakers up at the river fork were doing something wrong by trying to make the red men work like white men.

But she believed that the people called Quakers would never do anything they deemed wrong.

She remembered a thought she had had in the past; it was something that her father Tuck Horse had spoken of sometimes:

That perhaps the red man had one god and the white man another god, and each told the respective people a different thing. Did that mean that one god would lie? Or did it mean there were two truths, each god telling its own?

No. How could that be? If there were two truths instead of just the one, how could anything in the world ever go right?

She had talked this all over, again and again, with the people around her, with her husband, with her friend Minnow. They all believed there could be only one truth, only one god.

But if there were only one god, why would he tell opposite truths to different peoples?

Was that god a trickster, like Coyote, set on making trouble?

She wondered how she could counsel and guide the women and children of Deaf Man's village if she could not answer this question within herself. What would she teach Round One, who slept by her feet?

She bent close over the moccasin on which she was trying to stitch the pattern in quills, most white, others dyed in berry juices and infusions of flowers, barks, and roots. Much work, knowledge, and patience was needed to make any little decoration.

Yet in the white men's trading stores, pretty things came in great quantities, already made scarves and ribbons of shiny surfaces and more colors than a rainbow, beads of deep and brilliant colors that could be used more easily than quills to decorate clothes and moccasins. Mirrors with carved frames and metal decorations. Where and who were all the white people who made all those pretty things, and how did they make them? The idea of people being able to make so many pretty things that they could sell them somewhere else was hard to comprehend. For a Miami woman to make decorations for her own family, she had to spend all the time she was not planting, harvesting, cooking, tanning hides, and house-building. A man was so busy hunting, meeting in Council, and teaching his grandchildren that he scarcely had time to carve any pretty thing for his family. There was something about the way whites did things that she just could not understand. Even when she thought back to the little-girl time when she lived among them, she had never seen white people making pretty things. As faintly as she could remember the house she lived in as a little girl, she was sure there had been nothing pretty made there. These Indian people who were now her people all had beautiful things, even though it took them days and days to make them out of the materials that Mother Earth provided. She could remember her Quaker birth mother endlessly working to make cloth, and then clothing from that cloth, but it had always been gray or black clothing, never with any color.

So many beautiful things could be made from feathers, the feathers of the many kinds of brilliant birds that Creator had made. All the red peoples made and wore things made with the delicate, shimmering, patterned feathers of birds: headdresses, fans, mantles, decorations to hang up in their *wikwams*. The white men at Fort Wayne sometimes killed thousands of the brilliantly feathered pigeons that flew over the forests, but never used their feathers for anything. Often they didn't even eat the birds, but just killed them and left them where they fell.

And what did the white men do with the furs, the beaver, mink, the marten, the ermine, that they bought from the red hunters? They never seemed to wear them themselves, in tippets or shawls or yokes, as the red people did. They sent shiploads of them away, but to where? Were there white people far away who dressed in furs, while the white people who lived here near the furs never used them? Were there two kinds of white people, plain ones and fancy ones? Were there some kind of white people far away who wore beads and furs and feathers and silver?

I wonder what the shamans of the white people wear? she thought. Perhaps they are the ones who dress in decorations. Perhaps they are beaded and feathered and colorful because they live closer to their god. Perhaps that is it. And traders and soldiers are more plain, because here, they are so far from their god.

I wish I knew the answers to these wonderings. I wish I could understand how white people are, so I could think whether their way is more right or wrong than ours. If I knew something of that, I could better guide our women and children, and help my husband be a wise *sakima*.

She thought of the Quaker teachers she had seen at Fort Wayne one day, those she presumed, on seeing them, to be her own brothers. In time they had proven not to be called Slocum, not a one of them. Their names, when she heard them, were all different. She made herself remember those names—Dennis, Ellicott, and Hopkins—in case it might someday help her to know them. After a while the leader of them, the one named Dennis, had gone away east to get more help, but he had not come back, and she had had to memorize another name, of one who came to take his place. McKinney. It was an easier name to remember because it sounded much like her own name, Maconakwa.

Those Quakers were growing a grain there besides corn. Little Turtle in Council kept praising the farm school. He told the Council he wanted to go see Chief Jefferson next year and ask for a grain mill for the Miamis. He also told the Council that some good was coming from Jefferson's promise to keep spirit water from being sold. It had not all been stopped, but there was less, and fewer Miamis had been killed and hurt by drunken Miamis. Little Turtle seemed full of hope for his efforts to make his people live like white people.

And he had warned the Miamis not to listen to the preachings of the Shawnee who called himself a prophet. "That man," he said, "would put you on a path leading back through stones and thorns, away from the help and friendship of our white brothers who care for us. He would soon have us raise the tomahawk against them, and then they would again raise it against us, and all we have tried to do would be in vain. That false prophet has fooled too many. Somehow he learned from white men that there would be a Black Sun, and then he made foolish people think he caused it. Already the white people around his town are suspicious about him and they want him to get out of that country, where he should not be anyway because it is in the lands we granted to our great brother General Wayne, when we signed the treaty making this peace we have so long enjoyed."

Those words of Little Turtle had made her husband's face crease with a smirk, and his eyes had twinkled, and later he said to her: "Having chosen the path he has, how very much our old *sakima* must fool himself to think 'our white brothers' care for us!"

She asked her husband then, "Do you not believe that the Quaker men care for us?"

"Perhaps they do," he replied. "But they are here for a nation that would like to see us be never more who we always were. They care only to have our land and keep us tame."

That was another thing Maconakwa wanted to know: the true purpose of the Quakers who had come here—what was in their hearts.

And so as she worked with the porcupine quills to make The Awl's moccasins beautiful because of her love and admiration for him, she was thinking of how much she would like to find a way to talk with the Quaker men. They could tell her so much that she ought to know. It would not be easy, for she had only the faintest memory of the whites' tongue.

But they have been here some time working among my People, she thought. They know some of the Miami tongue and can do some talk with hand sign. Surely we could understand each other.

The anticipation both delighted and frightened her. She wondered whether she would even dare try to meet them if the opportunity came. She would not want to make her husband suspicious or angry by talking with white men. Perhaps he might talk to them with me, she thought, but had little hope for that.

She murmured the name Slocum to herself. I could at least ask them if they knew Quakers named Slocum. I would not have to tell them that was once my name. It would not be like selling them my name and getting in trouble. The Quakers are not the kind of white men who would take you away if you did not want to go.

She thought long on this, as she worked the quills, as she cooked, as she nursed her baby boy, as she hoed in the corn that summer. A few families from her husband's village lived and worked at the farm school; perhaps she could think of a reason to visit them, and thus get near the Quakers without causing any suspicion. That, or something.

She prayed for a way to be shown her.

And then within four days she was at the Quaker farm school. She rode up the dirt road between rail fences toward the house the Quakers had built there, riding on one of the fine mares she and her husband had raised, carrying Round One in a sling before her. Though she had not weaned him yet, he was too big to be carried in a cradleboard on her back anymore. The Awl rode beside her on his dark racing horse, with their daughter Cut Finger in front of him.

It had been The Awl himself who said they should come here. She had not asked or even hinted. He had said:

"The Shawnee Prophet pulls the People one way; Little Turtle and his Quakers pull another. We have gone to see the Prophet, and now we should go and see the Quakers."

She had said simply and quietly, "That would be fair." She had not shown in her face that his idea answered her prayer.

As she rode through the teaching farm she assessed the white people's cornfields and gardens, and she thought they looked pitiful. The corn was planted in straight rows, and weeds flourished between the rows. The stalks were spindly and short, compared with what was growing near her village. The earth seemed dry and hard and parched. No squashes grew there to shade the roots of the cornstalks.

On the other side of the road was a bean patch, nothing but beans, growing up on tripods of poles instead of the cornstalks, and she marveled that so much work had been done to cut down poles and stand them up again just to do what cornstalks could do.

Both corn and beans seemed poor in their separate fields, as if lonely for each other's natural company. And she saw no squashes or gourds or pumpkins, those excellent things, anywhere. In other fields nearby, some kind of yellowish grass with seed heads grew among leafless dead trees that had been killed by cutting the bark all around—a desolate and saddening sight. That grass, she thought, must be the grain from which they make flour. The Miami word for it was *sahlomena*; she remembered Tuck Horse pointing it out to her near a *wapsi* town somewhere and calling it "weet."

There were no children in the fields to pull weeds or hoe or chase birds. The fields were utterly without people. It was as if these *wapsi* farmers had no love for the Three Sisters, but had just planted them and forsaken them. Mother Corn must be so sad to see these lonely crops! she thought. That must be why they look unwell. Why do they want us to learn their way? It seems such a sorry way!

Though there were several Miami families staying here, it appeared the Quaker men were doing most of the work. She saw them in their gray clothes, splitting rails, hoeing, repairing a wheel, while Miami men stood or sat in twos and threes and smoked and watched them. One of the men from The Awl's town smiled at his chief and pointed at one young Quaker man whose clothes were sodden with sweat as he swung a huge wooden maul to drive splitting wedges along a log. With each thud of the tool came a tearing, crackling sound as the grain of the oak separated a little farther. The Miami said, "I have been watching this skillful fence maker for a long time. Soon I may know how he does it." Then he chuckled, and pursed his lips around the mouthpiece of his smoking pipe. "Maybe if I watch him long enough, I might even understand why someone would *want* to make a fence! Heh heh!"

Then he said in earnest: "Sakima! You were at the town of the Shawnee Prophet when he darkened the sun. Is it true that he pointed at it and commanded it, and it obeyed? We saw it go dark here, and heard he did it just so. I would have liked to be there!"

When The Awl understood the question, he replied with a hint of a one-sided smile: "Not commanded it and it obeyed; I think he asked and it obliged. Heh. Probably you were better here than there. You learned to make a fence, but I didn't learn to make a Black Sun."

Then they both laughed so loud that the rail-splitter looked around and saw them. He smiled, set down the maul, wiped away sweat, and came forward to greet them. They could see sweat actually dribbling from his fingertips as he came. He had a round head with short, dark hair hanging in wet locks onto his forehead. When he learned that this was the chief of the Deaf Man's Town, he invited the family to sit on a log in the shade of an enormous poplar tree. Looking long out of the corner of his eye at Maco-nakwa's thick, wavy red hair, he went inside the house. Cut Finger found an orange and green poplar blossom that had fallen and was showing its beauties to her mother when the Quaker man came back out of the house, apparently rinsed off and wearing a dry gray shirt, though his breeches were still sodden with sweat. He was carrying a pitcher and cups, and called to the other two Quaker men as he came. Round One sat naked in the grass watching a leafhopper.

The white men were polite and conversed as well as possible across the language difference and their guest's deafness. Seeing that Maconakwa listened for him, and presuming that a red-haired woman would understand English, they tried at first to talk to her in plain English, but it was soon obvious that she could hardly understand them, and for an hour or so there was much difficulty getting anything across because their grasp of the Miami tongue was little more than the names for things. After a while the white men were glancing away toward the tasks they had been doing, as if impatient to start sweating over work again. Maconakwa realized that anything her husband wanted to know about their mission here he would have to learn just by seeing, and she knew that all the questions she had—about one god or two, one truth or two, where their hearts stood regarding the Indians—all those things would go pretty well unanswered. At one point she realized that the Quaker men were trying to ask about the Black Sun. While she was doubting that she could express anything about it, her husband said to her in quick Miami:

"We are to tell the white men nothing of the Prophet's aims or what happens there."

Soon it was obvious that this had been a futile visit for learning or sharing anything of importance. Everyone was awkward, and the few Miamis doing any work on the farm had stopped and were using this gathering in the shade as an excuse to sit down, smoke, and enjoy some good loafing and cool drinking water. Soon several of the men were smoking with The Awl and talking sign to him about the Shawnee Prophet, and he had half turned away from the Quakers to keep them from understanding any of it they might have been able to comprehend.

Maconakwa pounced on that moment, afraid that the visit was going to yield nothing whatsoever, and guiltily, recklessly, she blurted to the round-headed Quaker man:

"Know thee Quaker *Slo-cum*?" She enunciated the name with care.

He leaned forward and squinted at her, pursing his mouth in a quizzical smile. Then he shrugged and replied: "Slow come? Yes, ma'am . . . uh, it took us a long time to get here . . . and tools, well, I sometimes wonder if they'll ever get here. . . . It's such a long way from Maryland. . . ."

She did not understand any of what he was saying except that it seemed he had said, "Slocum yes." She searched her memory for English words, and, hoping they would understand that she was asking about the health of her Quaker family, she stammered,

"Slo-cum . . . g-good?"

"Well, ma'am, uh . . . coming slow is good enough, I suppose, as long as it gets here. We intend to be here as long as thee'll have us. . . . Say, ma'am, I've been looking at thee and thinking, by the look of thee, does 'ee happen to be Mr. Wells's sister, or something?" With his forefinger he pointed at her red hair and made a circle in the direction of her face. She understood "Wells" and "sister" and remembered that others had said they looked like brother and sister, but it vexed her. She was trying to find out something about her own good family, and this man mentioned a man she thought bad.

As she and her husband rode out with their children a little later, he said, "It was a pleasant day to ride. But I learned little."

She answered, "I learned that they know nothing of growing food! Such hard work to make straight lines, but their crops are in misery!"

"To like the strange ways of white people, one would have to go into their country, as Little Turtle does," he said, and shrugged.

She said after a while, "When I was there, I was just a little child and did not need to understand it. Now I am not there and I do need to understand it. Perhaps someday I would like to go there to see it and try to understand what I did not understand then. . . ."

He looked at her, frowning, and she added: "But I would not go unless my husband took me there and brought me home."

He smiled at her, then looked at her with that slow, wandering, up-and-down look in his eyes that told her he was thinking of getting upon her and inside her as soon as they could be alone together. Riding the horse always put her in the mood for that, so she started yearning to be at home instead of in white men's land.

Wilkes-Barre

"I am not long for this world," Ruth Slocum said aloud, though she was alone in the house. She put both palms on the table and leaned hard on them, putting her head down, shutting her eyes and gasping for breath. In her chest, as always lately, there was that tickly, bubbling impulse to cough, even though her whole abdomen ached from coughing all the time and sometimes she felt that if she coughed once more, all her guts would squeeze out through her other end.

She opened her eyes and saw swimming before her the letter case and ink stand on the table. She blinked to focus, then sat down on the hard chair, thinking that if this attack of misery passed, she would get back to the correspondence she tried to maintain.

It was all important correspondence, in her opinion, important enough to justify doing it however wretched she felt. Much of it was with her daughters Judith and Mary, both of whom were in Ohio with their husbands and who therefore, Mrs. Slocum faithfully presumed, always had some chance of running onto the trail of their long-lost sister. She had no clear notion how two housewives in that vast state would actually happen to find a woman in an Indian tribe, but they were almost certainly closer to where that tribe, whatever it was, might be. According to the newspapers and journals, there were still Indians in Ohio, including one troublesome Shawnee magic man who appeared to be stirring up the whole frontier with some kind of native evangelism. She had read in the journals about how he was drawing such crowds of pilgrims to his holy town that the settlers were in a state of fear.

All of her other correspondence was likewise important, being concerned with the Friends' committees on antislavery and the Indian missions.

She had taken up the abolition cause years ago, when the notion came to her that as a captive, Frances might have been used somehow as a slave or servant by the Indians. The notion of any sort of bound servitude always galled Ruth's Quaker soul, its bitterness exacerbated by her imaginings of her poor daughter's fate.

At this moment, with her sense of her own mortality whetting her inner vision, and the correspondence for humane causes lying before her on the table, Ruth Slocum had a stunning revelation: that most everything she had done in these last three decades of her long life had been influenced by her quest for Frannie.

Ruth was seventy years old now, wealthy, esteemed in her community and the Society of Friends, with many successful children and flourishing grandchildren—as much a satisfactory life as a woman could have dreamed of—but her driving force for three decades had been that one shortfall from complete happiness.

Every day of all those years, she had envisioned her little girl being abducted on an Indian's shoulder into the curtain of woods, her little bare feet kicking in the cold air, her piteous cry shrilling back.

Lord, it's true, she thought, feeling an eerie sense of shame, I am selfish in everything I do!

Selfish or no, I've done good things, she rationalized. But . . .

Even the lives of her sons had been altered by her obsession with that moment, she realized. Year after year, driven by her terrible anxiety, they had gone out into the frontier alone or in groups of two to four at awful risk and discomfort to themselves, to find the lost sister whom only she had consistently believed to be alive.

Sure, she thought, they might some of them have gone out yonder once or twice of their own hearts' volition. But 'twas for my sake they kept a-going.

Woman, she asked herself, has thee lived by the fortitude and serenity that the Inner Light is supposed to give thee?

I have lived a good life, she defended herself. Part of it being that I'll not have abandoned my child as long as there's a wisp of hope for her . . .

A commotion of clumping and clattering out front, and men's voices, jarred her out of her introspection.

Her sons Joseph and Isaac both tried to lunge in through the front door at once, their broad shoulders wedging them both into it for a panting moment before they got in and she met them at the central hall. Their sweaty horses, she saw, had been hastily hitched to a rail outside in the blazing sunshine. Both young men were wild-eyed and both tried to speak at once when they saw her standing there with her hand clapped on her throat. At last she sorted out from their bellowing the name of Frances. She groped behind her for a chair.

"Most surely her!" Joseph gasped.

"Redhead, remembers she was carried off in the war!" said Isaac. "Heard of our hunting for 'er! A chief's bringing her!"

"O thanks dear God," Ruth breathed as Joseph pulled the chair from the wall of the hallway and eased her back into it. "Thee saw her?" Ruth thought she would faint with joy.

"Not yet," Joe blurted. "Fellow bringin' lumber down to the Ship Zion Meetinghouse said he met 'em camped 'tween the road and river. He told the printer at the *Herald of the Times*, and he sure reckoned who they'd be looking for, and come and told me, and I fetched Isaac. We're on our way to their camp to bring 'em here!"

"We stopped here t' tell thee, Ma, so thee'll not perish of a heart-stop when we bring 'er home!"

CHAPTER NINETEEN

May 6, 1807
Wilkes-Barre

From where she lay propped up on pillows so she could breathe in bed, Ruth Slocum could see out the bedroom window onto the street that led north along the riverside, past neighbors' houses. She knew them well, all those neighbors, had seen them come and offer her money for this parcel of land and that, had seen them farm those parcels and raise their children on them, had eaten with them, had been helped by them and bothered by them, those being the ways of near neighbors; she had helped deliver their babies and the babies of their children; had seen them eventually divide their own parcels further and give them to their children or sell them to newcomers, who built still-closer houses on them, until by now what had been the farm of Jonathan and Ruth Slocum had become much of the town of Wilkes-Barre, and what had first been land-wealth was now money-wealth, which she and her children had aplenty—far more than they needed, and much of which they funneled into the Friends' missionary efforts and other causes they deemed worthy. She had seen much change.

The window was open to admit some spring breeze into the hot room, and noise and dust from the busy street drifted up all day: the clopping and whinnying and snorting of horses, the rattle and rumble of lumber carts and coal wagons, the clangor and clacking and banging of smithy shops and carpenters, the shouts of boatmen on the nearby river. And there was always the acrid smell of coal smoke, not just from the forges but from every kitchen. Since Judge Fell had modified an anthracite fire grate in his tavern to make the fuel still more efficient, virtually everybody was using it now instead of wood, which had to be hauled in from farther and farther away as the forests disappeared in the valley. Only by daydreaming through memory could Ruth see the Susquehanna Valley as it had been thirty years ago when Jonathan brought her here in a canvas-covered wagon from Rhode Island. All her children, the seven born in Rhode Island and the three born here, were adults now, most of them parents themselves, two of them—Giles and Judith—even grandparents. She could remember standing on a hilltop east of the valley with Jonathan, looking down into the breathtakingly beautiful, wide, curving, forested valley with the spectacular river winding through it, clear back before the Revolutionary War had swept through it.

All her ten children were still alive, she was sure of that. Whether they were in New York or here in Pennsylvania or out in Ohio, they were all alive and stayed in touch with her by letter.

Except Frannie, of course. Frances was still alive, Ruth knew, but her fate was still a somber cloud on the glowing sunset of her long life.

Somebody was sitting in a chair on the other side of the bed. She turned her head. It was Joseph. She had forgotten he was there. They had been talking, of little things. Then she had dozed, and awakened to gaze out the window, and he stayed, patient, studying his law book to pass the time.

"I'm sorry I'm not better company, Joe," she said.

"Company?" he said. "Why, I reckoned you were just prayin', like me." He put a finger in his place in the book. Praying indeed.

"Praying . . . remembering. Some of this, some of that." She raised a feeble hand and pointed out toward the street. "Right there. Right there where that fence comes out to the street. That was where the edge of the woods was. That's where I had my last sight of her. . . ." She shuddered and sighed, and the sigh made her chest wheeze and gurgle, and she began coughing. Her sight of the fence blurred, and she put a kerchief to her mouth and coughed till she was exhausted. Joseph waited till she was through, then reached over and put his callused hand on her wrist, leaning close to her pillow and looking out the way she was.

"I remember," he said. "Hair all tousled, feet a-kickin' . . ."

"Bare feet. And thee doesn't really remember it, son. Thee was but two then. Thee's just heard us tell it so often, thee's made a memory picture of it."

"I was going on to three, Ma. I do remember seeing it, clear as day."

She smiled at the rise of this silly old argument. "Dear Joe, thee was on the far side of the house, Mary a-leadin' thee by the hand toward the fort, and thee ran so hard thy breeches fell down. One would think thee'd remember that, losin' breeches and stumbling and falling down and all, instead of what thee imagined. Well, anyway, I accept now that that was my last sight of her, forever. For nigh onto thirty years I believed I'd see her again before I passed over. . . ." She felt as if she were talking in a rushing wind. "I . . . I s'pose I gave up that hope when that young woman came last year from the Senecas, wonderin' if we were her family. . . . That was the way my heart was meant to leap up in hope . . . and it did then . . . and I guess that's the only such a joy I was meant to have in this life. But when that poor woman came, and proved not to be Frannie, why, that . . . I do trust Frannie's alive, but that's when I gave up hope o' seeing her myself, in this life. . . ."

Joseph remembered that wonderful, awful day, the thrilling excitement of it, of riding with Isaac up to the little camp beside the river and seeing the old Seneca chieftain, a woman slightly behind him, timid, her face full of doubt. He remembered how he had stared at the red-haired, worn-looking young woman in deer-skins, and saying to Isaac, "Yes, that's just how she'd look at this age! That's Frannie!" But later, at home, the tears of joy in his mother's eyes had turned to tears of dejection when, remembering to examine the young woman's hands, all her fingers had proven normal, no crushed index finger. It had not been Frannie, just another sorry victim of war. The poor thing rested, then went on to look for her real family, a pursuit that Ruth Slocum had understood.

Thirty years of looking for Frannie, Joseph Slocum thought, putting his law book on the bed and his hand on his mother's wrist. His mind went back over the hundreds and hundreds of miles the Slocum brothers had traveled on the frontier, the rewards offered, the crafty-eyed traders, British, American, and French, all cunning in their peculiar ways, the suspicious, some-times compassionate, sometimes angry expressions in the eyes of red men, the clues that would inspire and then vanish . . .

And now of course with every passing year the trail would be more difficult. So many people who remembered those cam-paigns were dead by now, or vague with age. The tribes among which she might be living had been moved time and again, scat-tered like autumn leaves before the force of the white men's advance. If Frannie were still alive and among the Indians, they must have cherished her enough to keep her from being turned over in any of the prisoner exchanges, and likely would continue to keep her hidden. No word of her had ever come back by way of the Friends' missions anywhere, and would be even less likely to now, because of the resurgence of native religion sweeping the Indiana Territory; missionary work was faltering out there in the face of the feverish work of that fanatic they called the Shawnee Prophet. Finding Frannie seemed ever more hopeless.

Sometimes Joseph, in his own private soul, did think the family had humored their mother too much. It was like an obsession with her, not just ordinary hopefulness.

We do lose children, he thought, and we just have to accept that. His own first child, Jonathan, had died an infant, and he and Liz had had to accept it and go on. They vowed that if they ever had another son, they would call him Jonathan, to give that name another chance. But they hadn't tried to keep a lost soul.

Well, things go one way for a while, he thought, and then they go the other, and I reckon that by the time I can get myself and Will or Ben or somebody freed up to go searching again, the frontier will be simmered down and we can hunt safe and thorough. I can study a law book as well on the road as at home, I guess.

He thought about the upcoming yearly Meeting of the Friends. They were expecting Indian chiefs to come and report on progress and ask for more and different kinds of help. One called Little Turtle was expected to be there.

If I could get down to the Meeting, he thought, maybe I could ask some of those Indians personally if they know of Frannie. Maybe some of the mission teachers will be there and I could ask them. I'll go if I can. Ma used to always go, but she can't do it anymore.

He patted her hand. "Ma," he said, "I feel just like thee that she's alive yet, and with all the prayers and trying we've done on her behalf, the dear Good Lord will reward us when he's ready to. Never doubt, Ma. I'll find Frannie. Ma . . . Ma?"

He realized that there was no pulse or vibrancy in the old hand under his.

Ruth Slocum's face was gray and serene, still turned slightly toward the window, eyes lifeless but still on that place up the street where so long ago she had seen her little daughter vanish into the woods.

Deaf Man's Village, on the Mississinewa

From somewhere amid the midday shrilling of the insects, a voice was calling her, or so it seemed. Maconakwa was half asleep, naked, her husband's juices still oozing from where he had put them into her, and she was aware that he was asleep beside her. His presence was so comforting that she did not want to wake up. She could never at any other time sleep so richly and happily as she did when they had stolen time in the early afternoon like this to couple while the children were out playing in the village. There were not many opportunities for a village chief and his wife to disappear from all their duties to the People and to their children and simply take pleasure in each other and then doze off for a little while, some part of their bodies touching: a hand on a thigh, a cheek on a shoulder, or the front of one's knee in the back of the other's knee, while the raspy dry cries of the insects wound down out in the sunshine beyond the smoky-smelling shade of the *wikwam*, and the laughter and calls of the children mingled with bird songs. Perhaps the voice she thought she heard calling her had been simply the distant shout of a child, or of someone calling a child. Maconakwa's mind and soul hummed with sweet sleepiness, and shimmering, sparkling patterns of light billowed behind her eyelids. She was still tingling from pleasure but slipping into deep languor. When that voice sounded again, deep in her soul, she realized that it was a voice dimly remembered.

And it was not calling her Ningeah, Mother, as her little son would have, or Maconakwa, as women in this Miami town would have, or Wehletawash, as the Lenapehs would have. It was a voice mellifluous with love, but it was not the voice of Minnow, or of old Flicker, her Lenapeh mother, or of Neepah before that. It was a voice remembered from further back even, a voice in a dream memory.

Frannie! Frannie! That forgotten name, from so long ago.

She was being carried. Not by a horse, but somehow slung over someone's shoulder. Dead leaves covered the ground. Behind her, where she had been carried from, there was a woman with red hair and gray clothes calling after her.

Frannie! Frannie!

The woman in gray clothes was calling after her and reaching imploring arms toward her, wanting her to come back, calling for her. . . .

And so she went floating back toward her, to a still-earlier time, and as she drew closer, the agony in that white woman's face changed to happiness, tenderness. She was enveloped in the woman's arms and knew that it was her mother.

She awoke to cries: "Ningeah! Ningeah!" coming closer. It was Cut Finger's voice. Her husband was still breathing deep in sleep. One of the blessings of his deafness was that village or family noises never woke him. Maconakwa scrambled up from bed, drew on her skirt, and covered her husband's nakedness with a blanket just as her daughter ran in under the door flap calling for her. The girl, now seven summers of age, wore just a lap apron tied on by a thong around her waist, and her hair was long and black, thick and shiny. Maconakwa felt strange, knowing she had had some sort of a spirit dream, but was unable to remember it because she had been awakened so abruptly. And now looking at the panic in the girl's face, she cried, "What? What happens? Where is Round One?"

The girl's eyes were shimmering with tears and her mouth was drawn down in crying fright.

"Ningeah! Come! He is hurt!"

A thrill of alarm cascaded through Maconakwa from her scalp to her knees, and as she stooped to shake her husband awake she heard cries and shouts and wailing from somewhere in a distant part of the village. "Is it soldiers?" she cried to her daughter, remembering what had always caused such alarms in the earlier times. She was ready to sign to her husband that bluecoats were attacking; he was sitting up with unspoken questions dispersing the sleepiness from his face, at once alert to the urgency.

"*Ne she*, Ningeah! Drunk men fighting!"

"Aihee!" A bolt of fury almost blinded her. Since her other husband, she had hated what drunken men did; when they raged and fought, they often hurt others nearby.

When she ran out, she met other people running toward her with anguished faces. The Awl bounded out of the *wikwam* with just his hastily tied breechcloth on, barefooted, his musket and powder horn in one hand. The people were jabbering as they all ran back toward the edge of the village. By the time they got there she already knew the story of what had happened: a drunken man had thrown a hatchet at another drunken man and it had hit her son.

Round One lay in the lap of an elder woman whose tunic was drenched with blood. Maconakwa dropped to her knees beside the woman with a howl of grief and reached for her child.

It seemed a long while in which she knew nothing of what was happening or what people were saying or shouting; she was not even aware of what her husband said or did. She only held the child across her thighs and saw the gaping deep cut under his ear and jaw. There was no blood pumping out and she knew that he was already dead and there was no fixing and no medicine that could bring him back.

When she stood up with the little corpse in her arms, her heart as hard and dark and small as a musket ball, and looked around for the drunken man who had done this, she found that someone had already tied the man up to a pole where he sat with hands trussed behind him and his head lolling, eyes rolling, mouth drooling. He wore a deerhide tunic and there was vomit down the front of it. She knew him just a little. He was not twenty summers yet, a Miami from Fort Wayne who did not even belong in this village. He had one relative here, an aunt. His aunt was the woman who had been holding Round One as he bled. This aunt, strong and grim, walked with Maconakwa to the place where the tied-up drunken youth slumped in his ropes. The Awl was standing stock-still in front of the youth, so tense his muscles and veins all stood forth, trembling with a terrible rage and dismay, his eyes blazing. He was holding his musket tensely in his hand but looked as if he had not thought of using it either to shoot or beat the young man; it was as if he were more shaken by the senselessness of it than by anger at the drunkard. Even Maconakwa herself despaired at how useless it would be to kill the youth in vengeance, and the young man's old aunt, with tears in her eyes and jaw set, stroked Maconakwa's back and said:

"The demon is in him and he knows nothing. By the old law of our People, I give my relative into your hands, to replace the one you have lost."

It would be their choice whether to kill him, enslave him, or adopt him. When he returned to his senses he would have to stand before them and accept their decision when they announced it at Council.

But for this moment there was no sense of tomorrow or of vengeance or rightness; Maconakwa was in the bewildering present moment, heart feeling wrenched and shrunken, holding a little corpse whose blood trickled along her forearm while her husband's semen trickled down the inside of her thighs, while she stared at the limp form of a young man who might not even remember tomorrow what a tragedy he had inflicted while crazed by the spirit water. Two sons she had borne to her husband, and both had died babies. There was a moment of joy and pleasure when the seed of life was planted, but from then on being a mother was a story of pain and the constant risk of more pain.

At that moment the image of her dream came up like smoke in the darkness of her soul: a woman who looked like herself but in gray white-people clothes calling and reaching for her and then embracing her.

It could only have been her birth mother who had come to her in spirit. At such a moment. When her own son died.

Maconakwa sensed this, saw this in the roiling smoke of her soul, like a dim vision. But she did not think of it. She was at this moment beyond thinking.

CHAPTER TWENTY

It was true that the only badness in the young man had been the badness of the spirit water. Maconakwa watched him coming with her husband from the gunsmith's, and she thought, He is a fine boy. She would never have believed that she could feel affection for one who had killed her baby, but she had come to care for him like a son in the two years he had been theirs.

He had not remembered anything he did when he was mad with the whiskey. He had not remembered fighting with anybody or why he would have fought with anybody, and did not remember throwing the hatchet that killed the baby. When he awakened from the whiskey stupor and learned what he had done, he wept with anguish and knelt on the ground with his head down, waiting for The Awl to break his skull with a tomahawk, as he had known it should be. But The Awl, knowing it was the whiskey that had done it, and that it had been an accident even then, stood over him for a little while, and when the boy began singing his death song, The Awl had said, "We do not choose to kill you. No, you will replace our son. Get up and come home." It was understood that if they found they liked him well enough, they would tell the Council they wished to have a ceremony to adopt him as a true son.

They were beginning to think they would do so this year, and he was happy about it. His name was Kehkeon, or Clipped Hair, because his father had been a warrior of the Ottawa, whose fighting men wore their hair in a short standing crest. Maconakwa and her husband would give him a name of their choosing if they adopted him as their son, and that name probably would be Waweah, Round One, the name of the child he had killed. One

400

could change names. Maconakwa had been Wehletawash once. Her husband had just recently changed his name to Deaf Man, since that was how everybody knew him.

So this one probably would be named Round One, a name that would be both an honor and a burden upon him, as he would have to assume and fulfill the love they had had for the child. But Round One would be suitable for this one's name too because his face was broad and his head was large and round. She watched her husband and the young man mingle with the people near the fort and her heart was warm but bittersweet. Good things always came from bad, the Old Ones said, but they would not return to you unless you made yourself worthy. You had to keep being good no matter what bad things happened to you; that was how you remained worthy. Giving this youth a good place and letting him live well was the only way they could have kept the baby's death from being a sad end. This youth would live the good life that the baby had not been allowed. And now the baby was back with the Spirit Grandmother, from whence he had come, and babies were always happy to go back to her.

Another sad thing had been that Sweet Breeze, daughter of Little Turtle and wife of Wells, had passed to the Spirit World. Whatever one had thought of Wells, his wife had been good and true to her people, most believed, and they were sad for her because she had had to live so many years of her life shadowed by the doubts of her husband's heart.

Wells had long been spying on the Prophet for Little Turtle and for the white chief named Harrison. He had even warned the Prophet and Tecumseh to abandon their holy town near the old Greene Ville fort, telling them that was white men's land, telling them that the white men crowding into that country did not like having so many Indians there. That discontent had grown worse and more tense and dangerous until last year, when the two Shawnee brothers decided to heed such warnings and abandon their holy town.

But instead of making Little Turtle and Wells content, that move had made them even more angry and fearful. The Prophet had led his pilgrim families and Shawnee followers westward, right through Miami country, down the Mississinewa Sipu, right past Deaf Man's village, toward the Wabash Sipu, all in canoes and on rafts.

Little Turtle, afraid they would settle too close to Fort Wayne,

had ridden down to head them off at the mouth of the Mississinewa Sipu, despite his failing health, to try to scare the Prophet
away from the Wabash Valley. When Little Turtle and the Prophet confronted each other, something happened that no one
would have believed:

Little Turtle, he whose warriors had twice defeated the Long
Knife army and chased it out of the Ohio country, had been
laughed at, scolded, and told to go away—not by Tecumseh the
warrior, but by Open Door, the Prophet, who had been for most of
his life a drunkard and coward. And those standing behind the
Prophet had been not warriors, but just the elders, women, and
children who were hauling their baggage and tools and seeds into
the valley of the Wabash Sipu.

And most amazing, so amazing it had been talked of all the year
since, was that Little Turtle and his chiefs had turned around
before that scolding and ridden back to Fort Wayne!

But who, said others, dared defy a man who had commanded
the sun?

The Prophet and his followers then had gone on down the
Wabash and established his new holy town on old Potawatomi
lands near the mouth of the K'tippecanuh Sipu, nearly midway
between Fort Wayne and Vincennes. For a time there had been no
trouble.

But now, in the moon just past, old Sakima Little Turtle had
done something so much to the white men's advantage that it
might bring war upon all his Miami people again. With other
chiefs who were already tamed to the interests of the white men's
government, he had signed a treaty with Harrison giving the
whites a vast land east of the lower Wabash Sipu—land that had
not even been their land, but was occupied by several other tribes.
It was said that Harrison had given the signers very fine gifts and
some money to make them agreeable to signing.

Some of Little Turtle's own people believed that the old *sakima*
was so happy to give that land because he knew it would put the
white men's boundary uncomfortably close to the Prophet's new
holy town. Miamis did not like to think that Little Turtle could
have become so mean and spiteful in spirit that he would have
done it for that reason. Some quietly said that perhaps he was so
sick and sore in his old body that his mind was not well either.
Some blamed Wells. Others blamed money.

But it had made the world feel ready for war: that old sense that the whites were coming closer and that the warriors were acting all stirred up, like hornets who feel someone coming too near their nest. It was a sense she had grown up with, years ago, of everybody being ready to fight and talking about fighting. She could remember her Lenapeh father, old Tuck Horse, always being on edge, always proud and watchful and suspicious, bristling like a porcupine, ready even in old age to fight to protect his People. She could remember her mother, Flicker, always being ready for the worst to happen, always keeping everything packed in such a way that it could be carried off quickly if the Long Knives' army was seen.

Here anew was a feeling that she and all the people had always felt back in the days before the treaty at Greene Ville when the general called Wayne had finally whipped it out of them and made them tame. Since then, for some fifteen summers there had been peace. Everyone was used to it. Most of the children had grown up not knowing the dread of hearing soldier drums or booming cannons or seeing the clouds of smoke towering over the treetops where towns burned.

But even in the time of peace since that treaty, there always was pressure from the white men: the strange diseases that came and made whole villages of people sick to death, the whiskey sellers who were always around with their spirit water, which made false visions and mindless violence. The tribes needed to keep moving away from where the white men were numerous, in order to find game, but the people liked trading post goods and didn't want to move too far from those. Indian hunters were often found dead in the woods with white men's boot tracks all around. Accusations were made against Indians whenever a white man's horse or cow disappeared. Maconakwa was always hearing such incidents discussed in Council. And every year or so there came troubling news that some other part of the country had been sold to the white chief Harrison. Maconakwa could almost feel the Miami lands shrinking around her.

There had been marriages between white men and women of the tribes, and children born who had the blood of both races in their veins, children who had names like Charlie Williams as well as their real names. Of course, Maconakwa's own children were mixed-bloods, but because their mother instead of father was white, they would never have *wapsi* names. Cut Finger, now nine summers of age, had no white girl name. She did not look at all like a white girl, being pretty and brown, although when she stood in sunlight there was a ruddy light in her black hair.

Deaf Man and Clipped Hair sat down nearby, facing Maconakwa and Cut Finger, who were intently at work making buttons. Deaf Man smiled and held up an iron tool he had acquired from the gunsmith, then laid his old musket across his lap and concentrated his attention on it. Clipped Hair watched him, face set in similar concentration.

Maconakwa and her daughter were making buttons of deer antler, which they would trade at the trading store for a new iron kettle to take back to Deaf Man's village. Their old one had cracked and it leaked. They had brought deer antlers to an old Miami man who possessed a white men's saw. He had cut the antlers up into many little disks. Maconakwa and Cut Finger were now bent over these disks, Maconakwa twirling a bow drill to make two holes in the center of each disk for thread to go through, while Cut Finger smoothed and rounded the edges and polished the surfaces by rubbing them on a chunk of wet sandstone. They would give a fourth of the many buttons to the man with the saw as his payment for cutting the disks, and then they would trade most of the others for the kettle, keeping enough to trade in their own village or give as gifts. The trading store also had brass buttons and shell buttons made by white people far away, but those cost more than some people cared to pay, so the traders could use plenty of these antler buttons. Buttons were something that had come with the cloth clothes of the white people, and by now most of the Miami People had some cloth clothing, so they used buttons with buttonholes to fasten the clothing, instead of the customary ties and toggles. Therefore button-making was a useful skill. She and Cut Finger were good at it. Maconakwa had used to wonder how white people had enough time to make things to sell, and now here she was doing it herself. It was one of the things one learned by being around white people. The Prophet would not approve of this. Nevertheless, she said to Cut Finger:

"We need the kettle and will pay for it with these. But maybe the next time we can trade enough buttons for a little saw tool such as they sell in the store. Then if we had our own saw, we could make buttons at home whenever we had time. We would not have to pay that old man to cut button pieces for us."

The girl kept polishing a button in the wet grit on the stone, but after a while she looked at her mother and said, "If so, how would the old man get buttons?"

Maconakwa smiled. There were many answers to a question like that, but it pleased her that the girl's first thought had been for the old man. Cut Finger was always kindhearted.

Maconakwa twirled the drill and thought of getting a saw, the way her husband had gotten that gun tool today. She paused and glanced over at Deaf Man, watched him using his new iron tool on the musket, and said, "That looks like an awl. Maybe your father should change his name back." Cut Finger laughed.

Deaf Man didn't look up. Clipped Hair smiled but kept watching him. The tool was one that could be put into a slot and twisted until a screw came out and the gun's spark maker could be taken apart. The jaws that held the flint in place—what the gunsmith called the "cock"—had been loose. Deaf Man had now taken the spark maker apart, discovered that a bent piece of steel inside had come loose, and was fiddling with it, setting the piece in, turning it this way and that, pulling and pushing. He had watched gunsmiths before. "Aha!" he exclaimed softly. "That is how it does it! I have put the life back in this spark maker!" He put the mechanism back into the wooden stock, turned in two little screws, put down the tool, and sat cocking and releasing the flintlock. He was very proud of himself. *"E heh!"* He lit a pipe to celebrate his accomplishment, gazing proudly at his wife. "If the gunsmith had done that for me, I would owe him something of value. This is good! White men would not like it if all Indians could fix their own guns. This is a power."

He watched her for a while, looking contented. Then he took his pipe from his lips and surprised her with a question that had nothing to do with tools or guns. "I have noticed . . . has it not been a long time since you went away to, ah, the women's hut?"

With her eyes down on her work she blushed, smiled, and let him wait. When she looked up, still smiling, she saw in his face that he understood. He slapped his palms together. "Ha-ha!" he cried. "Deaf Man *is* good at making things!"

That evening the family ate turtle stew made from a snapping turtle that Clipped Hair had caught, and then sat talking about things they had heard among people around the fort. What they were speaking of was something Maconakwa had first heard of last year, something that happened far away but seemed to be very important. The white chief, Jefferson, who was known personally by Little Turtle, had sent two of his most favored young soldiers westward to cross Turtle Island all the way to the sea where the sun sets. One of them was a brother of the old Town Destroyer general named Clark. The two soldiers had made the journey there and back, taking more than two years and building two forts on the way, and brought back some chiefs of the distant lands to go and meet Jefferson. That was the story. They had completed their return two years ago, but the whites were still talking about it, as if going across land from one place to another were something very remarkable.

Deaf Man said, "It is told that those two men were soldiers of Wayne, when he made his treaty. I worry about what such men do."

Clipped Hair, who had heard the story too, said, "It is told that they went in peace all the way and back."

"E heh!" Deaf Man exclaimed. "If white soldiers can thus cross a whole country without fighting, why did they not come to Fort Wayne that way, instead of fighting everybody all the way here?"

Maconakwa said, "Perhaps they were Quakers, not soldiers, those two."

Deaf Man watched her lips and her hands as she said that, and chuckled. But then his face grew grim and his eyes hardened. "That story troubles me," he said. "I am suspicious of why they went there. I suspect that they made treaties with all the old chiefs of those nations out there so they could now say they own the rest of Turtle Island all the way to the setting sun. Where will our people go when Little Turtle and such men sell to Harrison this little land that is left since this last treaty? Where will we go if the great lands beyond the Missi Sipu were given to Chief Jefferson's soldiers by the tribes out there?"

"Husband," Maconakwa said, "we are not to go anywhere. Remember that Jefferson wants us to stay on small land and learn to be like white men."

"He wants us to. But what of those who do not want to? Those who want to live in the old way, as Creator meant us to on this place where he put us and taught us to use?"

"As the Shawnee Prophet says to do?"

"E heh. He and his brother Tecumseh will not be tamed like that. Or all those people they are teaching."

The youth Clipped Hair had been turning his face back and forth listening to them discuss this. He was a bright-minded young man and always listened and tried to learn. Often he heard things when he went with Deaf Man that Deaf Man could not hear at all. Now he spoke. "Some people talking by the fort today said that Tecumseh will kill any men who go out to mark the treaty lines on the ground. He said the lines are too close to Prophet's Town. That Indian people should tell the whites that Little Turtle and those others had no right to sell Harrison that land, and the treaty should be ignored."

Maconakwa signed all that to her husband. The hand language was hard when it had words like *treaty* and *rights* and white men's names in it. Deaf Man looked long and directly at the young man with a blaze in his eyes, and finally said:

"If Tecumseh kills any line makers, the white chiefs will send soldiers, and there will surely be war again. You have grown up in peace and have never fought. You do not know war. If it came, would you be with Wells and Little Turtle and stand still here like a white-man pig farmer, or would your heart be with those Shawnee brothers?"

"I know this much of war," said Clipped Hair through narrowed lips. "My father was killed beside Turkey Foot at the battle where the trees were fallen down. I was very small then, but I remember when he went and that he never came home. The soldier chief he fought there had the same name as this fort." He paused, and while he was thinking, Maconakwa and Deaf Man regarded him with appreciation, for he was a young man anyone would have been proud to have as a son; he learned much and thought well and spoke forthrightly. He had done his vision quest, and it revealed to him his Spirit Helper. He was a youth who prayed with fervor and sincerity in ceremony and never mocked, and he was a fast runner and a good horseman and an excellent hunter and trapper. Everything they could have hoped to make of Round One if he had lived to this age, this youth was. Now he looked up, his dark eyes thoughtful in his round face, looked at Deaf Man, and said, "If war comes, Father, which way will you go?"

Evidently Deaf Man had heard him or read his lips well enough to understand, because he said, "I am not your father; perhaps I shall be soon. But you know that every man does what his heart tells him to do after he has counseled in prayer, not what his father

or any other man tells him. I chose long ago to keep fighting the
Long Knives, even after we were defeated in that battle at Blown-
Down Trees. Now, my *sakima* Little Turtle has become peaceful
and friendly with the Long Knives, and I would not like to be
opposite him, because he is still a great man and still tries to protect his People, whether his way feels good to my heart or not. He
knows more about the whites than I do, and has talked to Chief
Jefferson, and maybe I just do not understand as well what is good
for us. Another thing:

"I was a good warrior once. But that was when I could hear
voices and footsteps and drums keenly. Hearing is as necessary in
battle as seeing, sometimes. My heart and body are still strong, eh.
But if I had to lead my warriors in a fight, being able to hear
nothing but the thunder and the hawk's whistling that always fill
my head, what would I do in an ambush? Or in a raid at night? My
own warriors would be at risk because of what a bursting gun did
to my head fifteen summers ago. If I had a brother or a son in my
war party, and he was hurt or killed because I cannot hear, I would
not want to have such a weight on my heart. You asked me and
that is my answer. But if ever I saw a bluecoat soldier coming to
hurt my family or my People, I would soon have his hair hanging
at my belt."

The *wikwam* at Deaf Man's village seemed half empty, even
though his whole family was here: Maconakwa, Cut Finger, and
Deaf Man himself. It was the absence of Clipped Hair, who was
really not yet even of this family, that seemed to leave such an
emptiness. He had been gone for more than a moon. Maconakwa
was big and full with a baby that seemed to be all knees and
elbows, but still felt an emptiness without the youth's rich voice
and eager ears and ready laughter.

On the advice of Deaf Man, Clipped Hair had ridden down the
Wabash Sipu to Prophet's Town to learn for himself whether the
Prophet and Tecumseh seemed to be leading the red peoples in a
better direction. Only his own heart could tell him, and he would
have to form his loyalty now, one way or another, because soon
the conflict would begin.

Warriors had entered the camps of Chief Harrison's line
drawers and broken their surveying instruments. Rumors ran the
whole length of the Wabash Sipu that Harrison was looking for
any excuse to bring an army up from Vincennes to Prophet's

Town and scatter all those Indians. Deaf Man often said, "Harrison cannot bear to see Indians who are not under his control." Harrison was always sending spies and messengers to accuse the Shawnee brothers of inciting the tribes to war, saying the bluecoats' old enemies the British Redcoats were helping Tecumseh. Little Turtle and Wells kept that rumor hot.

The truth was, as Deaf Man knew, that Tecumseh kept telling Indians everywhere not to attack any whites, nor even let themselves be provoked to fight. His purpose was well-known: simply to make all red men everywhere agree never to sign away any more land. When all the tribes were of one heart, all whites would be told to go back beyond the eastern mountains and stay there. The Shawnee names were in all mouths: Tecumseh, imploring red men to yield no more land, and Open Door the Prophet, who had made the sun go out as proof that he was the Creator's instrument to restore pride and happiness in the red people upon their rightful lands. The whole country was astir, full of hope and dread. Tecumseh could not let Harrison take one more clod of earth; Harrison could not let himself be stopped until he had all the land. It was as if all the conflicts of the white men and the red men of the last seven generations had come to focus in two men. Tecumseh was the blade of the red people, with all the weight of their destiny pressing him forward, and Harrison was the blade of his people, with their destiny behind him, and the two blades were now poised, pointed at each other and almost touching. It had been Clipped Hair himself who had described it in that word picture just before he rode off down toward Prophet's Town with five other Miami warriors who were as excited as he was and wanted to see for themselves which path to take. The choice would affect their entire lives, they knew.

The family missed Clipped Hair, and prayed for him every morning and night, this youth who had killed their child in drunken rage, but since replaced that son in their hearts.

Maconakwa and Cut Finger were making buttons while there was still daylight, and they bent in concentration over their work. Maconakwa prayed while she worked, prayed silently that something would happen, or change, in time to prevent war from starting. She did not want any more land to be sold out from under the peoples. But neither did she want to feel the day-by-day dread of war again. She did not want Clipped Hair to go and die as a warrior, and especially did not want her daughter Cut Finger, or her yet unborn baby, to grow up, as she had, in fear and in flight from Town Destroyer armies. She prayed for something to change the course of this dangerous confrontation, if anything could.

One thing not yet known was the heart of the new white men's chief in Washington. For some reason Maconakwa did not understand, the one called Jefferson had been replaced by another man. It was not that Jefferson had died. The Long Knife council somehow had a way of replacing its chiefs now and then. The new one's name, learned from Wells, was Madison. But no one knew what would be in his heart about the Indians. Maconakwa thought it would be well to pray that Madison liked Indian people.

The bit of the drill made its little plunge as it pierced through the other side of the antler, hit soft wood underneath, and stopped twirling. She pulled the bit out of the hole and set the button in the basket of those for Cut Finger to smooth and polish. She tipped her head back, eyes closed, and tried to shrug the ache out of her tired shoulders. When she opened her eyes, a low-slanting sunbeam flashed in them through the leaves of the big trees. It would soon be time for the sun to set. How quickly the days passed when one was making things. This was a most beautiful time of day, when the trunks and limbs of the huge oaks and maples were reddened by the sinking sun. The voices of the people in the village drifted to her ears from all around, and she could smell meat cooking and even distinguish the different odors of the woods being burned in the cookfires. She could smell the mossy freshness of the rocks from which the springwater ran, and the mud of the riverbank. This was such a good place where her husband had made his village, and she thought how bad it would be ever to be forced to leave it.

As if speaking directly into Creator's ear, she whispered, "May there be peace, not a war," and her whisper blended with the sound her daughter made rubbing a button on the stone. Her husband had lit a pipe bowl of kinnikinnick, with its rich good odors, and she could identify most of its ingredients, many of which she and Cut Finger had picked and foraged and dried for him—leaf tobacco, sumac leaf, willow bark—when the soft sounds of the evening were slammed through by a gunshot.

Then a shrill, yipping howl sounded, like a coyote's but in a human's voice. Deaf Man might not have been able to hear the distant voice, but he had heard the shot, or felt it pulsate in the air. He dropped his pipe, snatched up his musket and powder horn, and, following the direction of Maconakwa's pointing finger, sprinted down the riverbank edge of the village, calling for other men to come. Maconakwa and other women meanwhile gathered bundles and herded children toward safety in the other direction, thinking of soldiers, the baby's mass swinging heavily in her as she hurried on.

But it seemed strange that there had been only one gunshot, if soldiers were coming. And though the breeze was coming from that direction, there was not a hint of the noise or smell of an army: no rustle of men and horses moving through vegetation, no clink or rattle of arms, none of that stink of sweaty uniforms she knew so well from Fort Wayne.

And no more shooting. She stopped, holding her daughter's hand, looking back. She could hear voices back there, distant shouts, but their inflections were not like white men's.

She wondered then if it might be hostile warriors instead of soldiers. Old tribal grudges and hatreds had been stirred up by the tension between the Prophet's aims and those of the government Indians. And Little Turtle's last treaty signing had stirred the fury of Tecumseh's followers, as well as the tribes who lived on the land lost by the treaty. Some might blame any and all Miamis for what Little Turtle had done, and come raiding.

But still, there had been only the one gunshot, the one wild cry. She felt that this was no attack on the village, but something else. She turned Cut Finger into another woman's care and slipped back along the river path into the village. The evening sun was down beyond the dark trees, the village under the canopy of tree-tops lay in a green gloom, the twilight air rich with wood smoke from the abandoned cookfires. Two dogs trotted through the lanes between *wikwams*, looking for unguarded food. Slipping through the door of her own *wikwam*, she reached up and got Deaf Man's war club, a heavy, crude weapon he had made from the trunk and root bole of an ironwood sapling; only the handle was smooth, carved to fit his grip and comfortable in her own large hand. The loop by which it had hung was a leather thong looped large for his hand to go through. She ducked back out through the door and went toward the sound of men's voices. She heard her husband's loud deaf-man voice and knew he was all right, but there was an unusual strain of anger in his tone. Then she saw them coming up the river path.

Sundown had brought a wind that ruffled the surface of the

river and started the trees swaying; twigs and nuts rained down and leaves turned underside up. In the distance a muttering and grumbling of thunder began.

She saw that the men on the path were leading a horse, and then she saw that her husband was the man in front, and he was yanking a rope that was not the horse's halter but was instead around the neck of a stumbling, staggering man whose arms were held by two village men. She stopped in the path, her heart clenching and jaw dropping open. It was Clipped Hair, and in his face was the stupid whiskey craziness.

Deaf Man saw his wife and came toward her with wild eyes and hardened lips. "I was going for that," he said to her, reaching for his war club. He took it from her without looking at her eyes or waiting for her to say a word or ask a question. He handed his musket to one of the warriors and gave the club a slight toss to shift his grip on the handle.

Clipped Hair's eyes were rolling and senseless. On the wind, Maconakwa smelled whiskey and old vomit odors off of him, and she remembered the first day she had seen him, and a heat like fire rose in her face. She said nothing as her husband dropped the rope with his left hand and with his right cocked back the ironwood club. With a grunt and a whipping sound and a wet thud, the left side of Clipped Hair's skull was smashed in. He would not be their son Round One after all. Maconakwa's fists clenched against her swollen belly and her eyes were squeezed shut on hot tears, and so she did not see his body go sideways and lifeless like a dead tree falling over.

In the storm of lightning that came over that night, a giant sycamore tree in the village was shattered and split. In their *wikwam* Maconakwa's husband sat wordless with a face like stone, but she saw by the lightning flashes that tears were trailing down the deep lines that curved out around his hard mouth. So much rain poured down all that night that by morning the blood from Clipped Hair's execution had all been washed away off the river path.

Wilkes-Barre

Joseph Slocum raised his eyes after the eulogy for Will. He gazed at the brilliant red and gold foliage on the distant mountainsides above the curving Susquehanna and tried to find solace in their beauty, but the smell of the raw earth of his brother's open grave brought such an upwelling of tears that the far panorama blurred in his sight, and the late-October chill made him shiver—either the chill of the northerly breeze, or simply the chilling sense of mortality in his own generation of Slocums.

Three short years ago his mother had died right under his nose while he sat daydreaming. He had not been ready for that loss, but at least he had known she was old enough and sick enough that she *might* die, and so that had not been an utter surprise.

But here, down in the gaping ground below, just in the prime of his life at forty-eight years, lay William Slocum, justice of the peace for Pittston Township, formerly sheriff of Luzerne County.

Here lay William. After escaping from the Indians who had killed his father and grandfather, after traveling unarmed all over the frontier with his brothers looking for Frannie, after being sheriff for four years, after trekking right along through a hard and vigorous life limping because an Indian's musket ball had shattered his heel bone—good, strong, durable, brave Will Slocum had suddenly done this astonishing thing: died. Died and left Sarah with their brood of nine children. Nine, suddenly all fatherless.

Joseph took a deep breath of cold air and shuddered again.

"I needed thee myself, Will," he thought, looking down on the unvarnished wood coffin. "Needed thee to help me keep looking for Frannie." Some of Will's children around the grave had heard him murmuring and were looking at him with their sad eyes, making him realize he had spoken his thoughts aloud. He saw the children vaguely through a new wash of tears. Their dark wool clothes flapped in the wind and their noses were red.

It was true that there could hardly be a worse time for Joseph to go to the frontier, even if he could leave his four little girls and a new law practice. Probably would get scalped certain, he thought. He had read, and heard from Friends' Meeting, awful things about the territory lately: tame Indians siding off against the wild ones. Quaker missionaries and teachers being threatened. Government surveyors chased off by Indians. Spies all over. Witch hunts.

Just this summer, said the gazettes, the Shawnee Prophet's brother had visited Governor Harrison of the Indiana Territory, argued with him, called him a liar to his face, and threatened him with a raised tomahawk. Reports from Friends' missions out there said that even some of Little Turtle's Miamis had gone off to support the Shawnees' confederation, defying the very chief who had defeated two American armies.

To make it all worse, England and the United States were growling war at each other again. A War Hawk faction in Congress was clamoring for a Second War of Revolution against England, because the British were blockading American ships and inflaming Indian discontent in the Great Lakes. Joseph expected to be reading war news in every new gazette. There was even the safety of his sisters Mary and Judith and their families in Ohio to worry about now.

Beside Will's grave Joseph sighed and shook his head, and then the great lump came up in his throat and the tears again felt as if they were scalding his eyelids. It seemed as if all the awful sadness and folly and cruelty of man's brief whirl on earth had come to his brother's graveside to mock and torment him. He felt so useless. One tries to believe, he thought, in a higher and kinder sojourn in this life, but no matter how steady one's Inner Light burns, it might as well be burning under a hat, for all it changes the mass of men bent on their misdeeds.

Poor Frannie! Imagine what it must be like, he thought, to be living as an ignorant Indian woman in a hut, trying to feed and protect children, while armies are galloping all about, burning towns and crops.

He had Will to thank for those images of soldiers ravaging the Indian towns up the river—this very brother Will, lying deep in the ground now—what horrors he had seen: soldiers, professed Christians, killing, scalping, skinning, raping. . . . Well, Will was on his way to a better world, far above such atrocities.

Lord God, welcome my brother.

And protect all my sisters in the West.

Deaf Man's Village

Deaf Man stooped and came into the birth hut, which was warm inside and dense with the damp odors of childbirth. The old midwives moved back to make room for him beside his wife. He placed himself so that he would not block the daylight from the door. It was a day of misty drizzle, with little brightness, and he wanted a good look at his new child, who lay quietly on

Maconakwa's bare bosom. Sticking on the dark, damp wool of Deaf Man's blanket was a large, vivid yellow basswood leaf, which had fallen on him while he waited outside under the tree.

He looked back and forth between the baby and mother, back and forth, nodding and smiling, and occasionally would shake his head from side to side and chuckle. Finally he said, "Newewah! My wife, you do not even look tired!"

"This one gave me no work to do. She fell from me like that autumn leaf on you." He was trying to read her lips because she could not sign and hold the baby. But he saw her look at the leaf, and he looked down and noticed it, and picked it off and held the bright, heart-shaped leaf by its stem. It was beautiful with the light shining through.

"Ozahshingkwa, eh," he said. "Yellow leaf that fell easily. *E heh.*"

She was wondering whether it was the infusion of black-cherry bark that had made it so easy. The midwife had said it would. But surely not that alone would make it so easy, she thought.

"Ozahshingkwa," he repeated. "This is the sign. Yellow Leaf. A good name."

CHAPTER TWENTY-ONE

December 16, 1811
Deaf Man's Village on the Mississinewa

Maconakwa awoke in the middle of the night from a muddle of troubling dreams—towns burning, Indian men and women bleeding from bullet wounds, lights bursting in the night skies, horses and deer falling down, floodwaters rushing. She lay with her heart racing and tried to remember images she had seen in the dreams, to sort them out so she might understand what they meant. In the dreams, so many things had been happening in heaven and earth, so many different journeys, so many stories, perhaps not connected to each other, that it seemed she must have been dreaming for hours. She remembered a white man talking to her in one of the early parts of the dream, telling her she should go home to their people, and she thought that must mean the Quakers. She remembered seeing a basket woven in the shape of a man. She knew what that was; the Shawnee Prophet had had an effigy of himself made and blessed it with his own sacred powers so it could be carried to one village while he went to another, so his holy presence could reach more people than he could alone. In the dream that effigy had burst into flame; the picture of that in her memory was so vivid it crowded out other images she was trying to remember. The effigy had caught fire in other dreams she had had in the past moon. She thought she knew why: the real effigy probably had burned up last moon, when a Long Knife army burned the Prophet's Town.

Minnow's third husband had been killed in a battle with that army.

Maconakwa held her sleeping baby close and worried about the dangers. The war was starting up again indeed. Although the blame for it went both ways, depending on who was telling of it, the governor-chief called Harrison seemed to have been the one to start it because he had brought soldiers into lands he hadn't even made a treaty for—land where he didn't even have an excuse to be. He had invaded while the warrior chief Tecumseh was far away in the south, and while only a few hundred people were in the Prophet's Town following a great sickness, some white men's disease that had killed so many people in the town that doubts were raised about the Prophet's medicine powers. Many people who talked about the battle said that Harrison had proven himself a coward by striking only when he knew Tecumseh was gone. Others said that if he was a coward, how had he fought so bravely in that battle, always in sight on a big horse, when the bullets and arrows were flying so thick that they tore the bark off trees in the woods? Yes, warriors who had fought against Harrison in that battle were now scattered in villages all up and down the Wabash Sipu and its tributaries, staying low, telling their stories about how well the Long Knives had fought, waiting for their war chief Tecumseh to come back from the south and tell them what they should do now.

Many believed they saw the great war sign that he had promised would come when it was time to go to war against the Long Knives. A bright two-tailed flying star was in the sky night after night. Tecumseh was named for having been born under a flying star, and he had predicted that the war sign would be one that could be seen everywhere. Now everyone could see the strange flying star, and when he returned from the south, they would rejoin with him to help push all the whites out of the country.

People were now as sure of Tecumseh's power as they had been sure of the Prophet's power six summers ago when he made the sun go dark. The Prophet's own power was in doubt now—not only his medicine power—because he had promised that the Great Spirit would protect the holy town from destruction, and the warriors from white men's bullets. But few doubted Tecumseh's war sign, the two-tailed star.

Maconakwa held her baby, breathed the cold night air and the skin and breath smells of her sleeping family, and lay in the dark worrying about the return of war after such a long peace.

Now that there had been a real invasion by a white army, many warriors were hot for war. Even neutral Miamis, even people who had been taught by the Quaker men at the school farm, were ready to turn their backs on Little Turtle and Wells and join

Tecumseh when he came back. Her own husband had not yet made any such talk. When the survivors of the Prophet's Town battle talked with him, he usually just said he was too deaf to be of much use on either side. But how easily he had killed Clipped Hair! She shivered.

He was lying beside her now, breathing in that way that told her he was deep in sleep. That meant she would have to be the one to rise, leave the baby, fix the fire. It was a cold night and the fire had burned far down during her long dreams. She knew she ought to get up and fuel the fire before even the embers went cold. She could tell by the stars out beyond the smoke hole that it was not much past the middle of the night, far too early to expect those embers to last till morning. It was hard to believe she could have had such a long succession of dreams just between bedtime and midnight. In the *wikwam* it was almost pitch-black, and the night air on her face was so cold and dank that she shivered at the mere thought of getting out from the covers. The dreams had left her with a strange feeling of dread, as if something terrible were about to happen. She had a feeling that some strange power might have been let loose by the destruction of the holy town, where so many thousands of people had prayed so powerfully for years.

Perhaps, she had been thinking, that star moving through the skies was a sign not only for the warriors to go to war, but also, or instead, a last message from the Creator to all Indian people, women and children as well as warriors, telling them all to believe what the Prophet had been told.

She knew of many things the Creator had told Open Door that she and most people had not done. They had been told not to trade with the white men, and to stop using metal things made by the white men, and to stop getting spirit water, and even to destroy their personal medicine bags. But she still traded buttons and other things she and her daughter could make, for metal needles and awls and tools, which she used. And like most of the people she knew, she had been outraged by the order to destroy her medicine bag. Neepah had made it for her, and it contained not just the seeds of the Three Sacred Sisters, but other tiny things that had come to her in sacred ways from ceremonies and from living, such as a dried fragment from the umbilical cord of Cut Finger, and that of Round One, and now Yellow Leaf's cord was in it also.

She sighed. Now her mind was too wakeful and busy to go back and try to review the dreams; the images were vanishing one by one before her conscious thoughts, before the necessity of getting out into the cold room and building up the fire. And she could feel that she would need to pass water soon; she sighed and began to stir.

As long as she could remember, she had hated to get up in the cold.

She was just easing the baby down in the warmth beside Deaf Man when she heard an odd, whispery sound from outside the *wikwam*, and paused to listen.

Something, or perhaps many things, seemed to be passing swiftly along the ground outside. It was an unearthly sound, like small animals running and whimpering, yet at the same time seeming full of wordless messages, as if messenger spirits were rushing through the village, or a spirit wind when there was no other wind. She came out in gooseflesh all over.

The noise passed. But now in the distance she heard owls—not just one or two, as were usually heard, but as if all the different kinds of *meedagaws* in the woods in every direction were muttering to each other in their various voices. That was frightening, because to most of the peoples, the owl was a death messenger. Then there was silence. She listened for a moment, then slipped out of the bed, lifting an old woolen trading-store blanket off the top to wrap around her chilled nakedness, and groped in the dark for the heap of kindling wood that was in a recess by the foot of Cut Finger's bed. As she knelt by the slightly warm fire pit with a handful of dry twigs and bark fibers, she thought she heard wing beats everywhere outside, passing over, and twitterings.

Birds do not fly at night, she thought. Except *meedagaws*. And their wings are silent!

For many moons, since the springtime, there had been so many strange things in the earth and the waters and the heavens: countless thousands of squirrels rushing through the treetops southward toward the O-hi-o Sipu . . . endless rains and floods in the springtime, with no sun ever appearing. The two-tailed flying star. Perhaps all these were the signs long prophesied by Tecumseh and the Prophet.

Some people blamed the strange signs on the disturbance caused by a white men's boat as big as a council lodge that had passed down the O-hi-o Sipu, without sails or oars, rumbling loudly and giving off more smoke than a grass fire. The description of it had been told everywhere. Such a thing surely would have disturbed the balance and serenity of Mother Earth, and people everywhere worried and had dreams about it.

Maconakwa hoped to find comfort in rebuilding the fire in her lodge. Fire was a good, heartening spirit. On elbows and knees, shivering, she blew on an ember and crumbled tinder over it until smoke poured off and then a flame the size of a thumb leaped up, brightening the whole interior of the little lodge. Just the sight of it warmed her heart, even though her face and hands and feet were still icy. She laid on little sticks and then bigger ones as the yellow flames spread and climbed, crackling and fluttering and sparking. As the heat rose toward the smoke hole it carried the smoke up and out. She knelt, sitting on her heels, and turned her frigid hands this way and that over the flames to warm them. For the while she was absorbed in the marvel of fire, remembering how Tuck Horse had called fire a living thing that moves and grows and eats and helps people, and how it would, sometimes, like the bad in people, go out of control and destroy and harm other kinds of life. It was said that great evil boat had a fire in its belly that made it go. That could not be good!

Putting larger chunks of wood on until the blaze was lively and its bright heat began to push outward and fill the space of the room, Maconakwa glanced at her husband, daughter, and baby, whose faces were still closed in sleep. Standing up, at the very edge of the fire ring, she held the blanket open and let it fill with the wonderful dry heat. She quit shivering as the heated air enveloped her nakedness and flowed up toward the bent-pole ceiling where her dried herbs and strings of beans and bundles of sassafras root hung, so fragrant. The heated air was hottest and smokiest there under the ceiling, and she was having to squint to protect her eyes while her body warmed up. Far off in the night she heard wolves starting to wail and soon heard many wing beats again, and despite the bright comfort of the fire, she felt troubled once more; this was not the time of night when wolves sang or birds flew. Opening her eyes and looking up at the smoke pouring out through the smoke hole, she reached for a bundle of tobacco leaves hanging near her head. With one hand holding the blanket at her neck, she crumbled some of the brittle brown leaf into her palm and knelt to sift it into the fire, so its smoke would carry heavenward the prayer she was forming in her soul, a prayer for peace and safety and understanding.

The wing beats were coming again, but they were drowned out

by a rumbling that swelled quickly to thundering. The ground shuddered. She was rolled off balance. As she fell she saw the embers and flaming sticks of the fire leap and swirl, and the air was filled with sparks. She landed in the fire pit, gasping, but was immediately tumbled back out of it. Even as a scream tore out of her throat she thought that her *wikwam* had been hit by a shot from a Long Knife cannon. Everything was lurching, tumbling; the things hanging from the ceiling swayed violently, flew loose, fell, bounced, caught fire. The very earth of the floor was bucking like an untamed horse, and she, and her husband and daughter, all of them naked in the blizzard of sparks, mouths gaping and eyes wild with panic, tumbled about, unable to rise even onto their knees because of the trembling, tilting, side-slipping earth beneath them. Deaf Man and Cut Finger, hurled straight from deep slumber into this chaos, were crying out, but their words could not be heard over the rumbling, which went on and on. This could not be just a cannon shot, she thought. Turtle Island itself seemed to be shaking apart.

The old *wikwam*, dry, ground-rotted, and fragile after so many years as their home, was falling in bit by bit with every shudder of the earth; the mats and bark and thatch with which the dome-shaped house was walled and insulated were crumbling and coming loose from the arched-pole frame and falling inside all over the floor. Pieces ignited in the fire ring, and the flames spread. Sparks swirled up against the sooty ceiling.

Unable to stand or even crouch, Maconakwa grabbed for Yellow Leaf, gathered her in one arm, and tried to creep over the quaking floor and drag her out of the firestorm. Sparks and brands were raining on every part of her, burning and stinging like a flurry of wasp stings, and she smelled hair burning. She wasn't sure where the doorway was, and she knew not what terrors would meet them outside if they did get out.

But now the roof of the *wikwam* was catching fire and raining flaming debris down, and they would be cooked alive if they did not escape. Through a flaring blaze she saw Cut Finger crawling like a lizard, shrieking.

And at the same time that fire was spilling down, cold water was coming up, oozing and welling all muddy and bubbly from the earth under her hands and hips, stinking like fish and decay. As she crept forward still clutching her baby, finding at last what seemed to be the doorway, a hissing rush of cold water came spreading over the dark ground as if the river had overflowed its banks; it sloshed over her face and shoulders as though trying to wash her back inside.

Outdoors it was dark and cold, but not dark enough to obscure what appeared to be the collapse of the world. As she pulled her baby clear of the flaming lodge and saw her daughter and then her husband slithering through the swirling water, another wave of river water washed around her, quenching the pain of the many burns all over her body but momentarily blinding her again. Blinking and squinting and gasping, she glanced quickly around for someplace to go. Her heart quaked at the sight.

Water, full of debris and reflecting the fires and sparks of other burning *wikwams*, was rushing everywhere she could see, shallow but swift, now running one way, then washing back the other way.

She could see silhouettes of people crawling. Sycamore and cottonwood trees leaned slowly over, roots coming up; a big one was toppling toward a row of *wikwams* near the river's edge. People and dogs and animals, even wild animals—she glimpsed a deer and a raccoon—were floundering and sprawling, trying to get up, eyes panicky. Big birds were flying over. The air was full of smoke and steam as burning *wikwams* collapsed in the water. Some cabins built in the white man's way had already been shaken down, though they were not on fire.

Maconakwa lay stunned. She pulled and hugged her baby girl and Cut Finger close, looking for Deaf Man. He was just behind her, spraddled on hands and knees, silhouetted against the pyre of flame that their *wikwam* had become; he was looking back at it as if thinking of the things in there they would be needing when this ended, if it ended. She too thought of those things—the gun, the knives, tools, seeds, and garments necessary for even the barest sort of living. Foremost in her whole mind and soul was the knowledge that they had escaped being burned to death—but could yet freeze or starve or be killed by falling things, or drowned. Nearby villages too would be gone. . . .

And the great unworded question: What was this? Was this the consequence of the destruction of the holy town? Or of the evil fire boat? Was *this* Tecumseh's great signal that all men were to see?

In powerful storms, of which she had seen many, the skies were wild and turbulent with lightning and wind and racing clouds, only the earth underfoot still and solid. Now the earth was unstable and rumbling like clouds of a thunderstorm, while the sky stood still and clear overhead, the stars fixed, the two-tailed sign star still visible above the horizon. It was an upside-down storm. Who had ever seen an upside-down storm?

If this was a sign, a sign so terrible must foretell an enormous misfortune. She shuddered with fear, and then the tears came.

As is often so, it was the elders who brought calm and eased the fear. The old ones had felt the earth tremble before—though not so violently as this—and it had not ended the world. A white-haired grandmother called Acorn Top showed up in front of Deaf Man's burned *wikwam* as soon as the ground was steady enough to walk on, and she had a blanket to wrap around the naked Maconakwa and her baby Yellow Leaf, whom she as a midwife had helped birth.

"Remember," she said, "the land rests upon the back of the Great Turtle—and she is not a dead turtle, but one who needs to move, as anyone needs to move who lies still a long time."

When the earth was still and the waters had drained back into the river, Deaf Man and the old men prowled by firelight and torchlight in the cold mud and wreckage, gathering all the hurt people and bringing them to a bonfire where the old women salved their burns and soothed the terrified children. The elders kept bringing blankets and hides to bundle up the little ones against the winter night.

Maconakwa, with no clothes, found cord to belt the blanket around herself like a dress, and went to work making a bark splint for a boy's broken arm, trudging on numbed feet and kneeling in the icy mud, her spark burns hurting terribly with the blanket wool rubbing them. She worked with one hurt person after another, and the old ones' working with her inspired her, reminding her of her old Lenapeh mother Flicker, who had knelt on aching knees all night saving the life of The Awl. Cut Finger huddled near the bonfire with her baby sister Yellow Leaf and rocked her to sleep in her arms. Gradually the calm helpfulness of the old ones worked its way down through the tribe's other women, and down even to the children, who stopped whining and squalling and began bringing firewood, and water in pots for medicine tea, and taking charge of the smaller ones. Pain and fatigue and cold became things really not that important; the needs of the others made it all easier to endure.

By morning light they saw that most of the damage to houses had been from fires and falling trees. No house frames had actually been shaken apart, though the bark siding had fallen off several of the older *wikwams*. One cabin built the white man's way had been damaged by the collapse of its heavy stick-and-clay chimney.

Acorn Top and three old widows brought in moccasins and clothes and skins they had salvaged from the mud and cleaned up. Then Maconakwa directed the saving of the food cached in pits, so the water in the ground wouldn't ruin it. In the afternoon it was all being smoked and dried, when Maconakwa at last looked around and saw nothing else urgent she had to set a hand to. Suddenly such a weight of fatigue crushed her that she thought she must fall and die. But it was just then that she heard old Acorn Top's voice croak behind her, telling someone:

"This wife of our *sakima*! Eh! She deserves a feather!"

Maconakwa encouraged the town's adults to repair and rebuild shelters and *wikwams* at once, while the sun was out and the air was dry, before hard cold and snow returned. Everyone in the village was busy. There was no time to moan and whine.

Old Acorn Top kept working near Maconakwa, and when she sat to rest, the old woman would light a pipe of kinnikinnick and make her share it with her. And the old woman would give her suggestions on what could be done next. It was like having old Flicker back, a *kahesana* to amaze her with the endurance of the elders. Once again the old one heartened her by saying, "When bad things happen without warning, people need to be led to do what they know they should do, but don't think to do because they think Creator is angry. You are right-thinking, and you make them get busy."

Maconakwa smiled wearily, nodded, puffed the fragrant smoke, and gave the pipe back to Acorn Top. She remembered having thought, now and then, that she would be swept away helpless as a leaf on the wind unless she set her own will to stand steady and choose what to do and how to hold on. She remembered that she and Minnow had talked of such things. She reminded herself to pray for Minnow's safety in this, she who had lost still another husband. She would go to Metosinah's Town as soon as she could and see how the people were up there, Minnow in particular.

"Thank you for your kind words, Grandmother. I am honored by your esteem."

"*E heh*. I would like to fill your heart with strength. You will need it. The stars in the sky and the animals in the woods are troubled; you have seen that. And Mother Turtle herself is restless. I think she is not settled even yet. I feel it."

Maconakwa pressed the soles of her bare feet to the ground. The earth felt solid, as solid as ever. She remembered when she had stood on high ground long ago on a cliff above Great Falling Water, and was afraid to stand up because of the trembling ground. So long ago! But the earth felt solid and still now, as it should be; it was like the day after the Prophet had made the sun darken at midday. *We get used to the sun being bright at midday, the earth being still,* she thought. *They almost always are. May there be no more disturbances like those. May Mother Turtle sleep quiet the rest of my lifetime.*

But the old woman was right. Three more great shudders occurred in the next two moons, the last as violent as the first had been.

Warriors who believed that the quaking earth was Tecumseh's sign went to the Prophet's Town, which was being rebuilt from ashes. Tecumseh had stood among those ashes and sworn vengeance against Harrison, the general who had burned the holy town. A thousand warriors of many tribes were going to join him. Now, the time for war was here, as they had feared it would be. If Open Door had made the sun go dark to mock the general called Harrison, that general had made the earth shake by burning the holy town. Once again the white nations would be at war, as they had been all through Maconakwa's childhood, and once again the red nations would be in between them, dying on one side or the other. Tecumseh would be on the British side—not because he had faith in them, Deaf Man told her, but because they were against the Americans.

"As for me," he said, "I will stay here and be glad for whatever the bluecoats and the Redcoats do to each other, and for whatever Tecumseh can do to keep us from losing more land. I will pray that no Miami warriors shall die between the armies."

"Husband, I am pleased that you say you have no war to fight."

"At Spring Council most of the talk will be of war," he said. "As I have told you many times, I am an old deaf man, not fit to be a warrior anymore." He looked so morose saying it that she smiled and made eyes at him.

"Old?" she teased. "I know a part of you that never acts old."

"Ah hm! That is because there is a part of you that keeps that part of me from getting old!"

That night when the fire was low and their daughters were asleep, and they were quietly beginning to keep each other's parts young, she prayed that the Great Turtle would not shake the earth again—at least until they were through.

It was a good time of the moon for this. She was nearing forty summers of age now, and had two girls but no boy. She hoped to give Deaf Man a son, before she was too old. She had put the names of her dead sons out of her mind so that her heart could go on in happiness, but she went out sometimes to the mounded place where their little graves were and sat there.

It was true that war was imminent and this was not supposed to be a good time to create another baby. But one would be foolish not to have the joys of life and love just because of what angry men in governments far away were doing.

Barefoot on the grass, wearing only the ceremonial loincloth, Maconakwa gripped the hoop in her right hand, looked up at the top of the pole twenty feet high against the clean blue sky, and prayed, Kiji Moneto, see me throw this hoop over the pole so that it will truly happen, and we will have your permission to do our Bread Dance and honor you in the Great House.

The hoop was made of grapevine wrapped in hide, and it seemed to vibrate in her hand. In her mind she envisioned it flying up from her hand, rotating in the air, pausing at the tip of the erect pole, then coming down encircling the pole, and she sent that vision up to the Creator so that he would see it that way. The ceremony could not begin until someone succeeded in encircling the pole with the hoop. She could feel the hopes of the hundreds of people all pouring into her; they too were envisioning the hoop encircling the pole. Everyone wanted the ceremony, because a failure to observe the sacred Bread Dance would cause the People unimaginable troubles. And yet sometimes it seemed that Creator himself was not going to let them proceed. This was beginning to seem like one of those times. So far more than fifty men and women had thrown the hoop at the top of the slender pole, each being cheered and encouraged, but each time the hoop had fallen short or gone too high over, or hit the pole and bounced off. And each time another person had been chosen from the crowd ringing the field, and had gone cheerfully to try to throw the hoop onto the pole. It was like an athletic skill, but it was a wordless prayer for permission to start the important Bread Dance Ceremony. Seldom had Maconakwa had an opportunity to throw the hoop, and the two or three years she had, she missed badly or the hoop glanced off the pole.

It seemed a great responsibility. She felt an awful certainty that if she missed, everyone else would keep missing, and there would be no ceremony. Probably everybody else felt that urgency, but she had a heavy, powerful anxiety about it. And so she touched the edge of the hoop to her forehead with her eyes shut and prayed to the Creator to let her do it, and then she stepped forward and touched the base of the pole with the hoop, as she had seen a few others do. Then she stepped back three paces, moving the hoop in her right hand and staring up at the distant tip of the pole, hearing many people calling, "Do it well, Maconakwa!" and "Hai ai ai, Little Bear Woman!" She could hear Deaf Man's voice, and Cut Finger's, both very loud.

Half stooping, sweat beginning to trickle on her bare breasts, she extended the hoop back behind her right hip, stared at the tip of the pole, leaped off the ground, and flung the hoop skyward.

At the instant it left her hand, spinning upward like a rising wheel, she saw a redtail hawk crossing the sky high above the pole. Then with a pounding heart she saw the hoop do what she had envisioned: rotating, it slowed in its ascent, paused, tilted; the inside of the hoop made a small hard sound as it hit the top of the pole, and then the hoop fell wobbling and jouncing down the pole, and even before it hit the ground the crowd was howling and yipping and clapping. She clapped her palms to her cheeks and laughed with tears in her eyes, her heart swollen with thanks, and feeling not proud but joyously humble.

The hawk: she should have known when she saw the hawk, because whoever got the hoop around the pole was awarded a hawk feather for enabling the ceremony to proceed.

She went through the ceremony almost in a trance, calm at heart even though she knew the Council afterward would be mostly of war. The women at the blessing stations around the Great House honored her with warm smiles and kind voices, and hugged her tightly as she paused at each station, because she had thrown the hoop toss that made this beautiful ceremony possible. In their turn they put into her mouth a strawberry, representing thankfulness for the season's first fruit; corn bread, representing the women's crop-raising; meat, representing the men's hunting; sassafras tea sweetened with maple sugar, representing the blessings of the forest trees. When she stepped in the ashes and the mud, they murmured to her their meanings, of departed ancestors and Mother Earth, and told her to take a little of the mud from her toes and roll it into a tiny clay ball to be carried in her medicine bag. All these comforting rituals and words she knew by heart, from her years among the People. The vermilion dots were painted on her cheekbones, water sprinkled on her sun-hot shoulders, ashes dusted along her arms and brushed by a woman wielding a hawk's wing. The line of tribespeople moved slow and soft-voiced through these and all the other sacred stations, while the heartbeat drum thudded solemnly and cedar smoke from the ceremonial fire drifted in the sunbeams that leaned into the roofless Great House.

Then she reached the pipe bearer and received from him the beautiful, carved calumet pipe, and as she turned and blew prayer smoke to the six directions, she whispered the words of thanks for all of the world's continuing blessings that came in their seasons, finally and in particular thanking Mother Corn for the surviving seeds that would allow another year of planting to be done. In this ceremony the measureless gratitude of the People was like a richer air to walk through and breathe, and the ageless yearning for peace kept her from thinking of the war matters that would consume the Council after the ceremony and feast.

But last in the ceremony was the secret gesture by which one could vow to give one's life in defense of the People, a gesture one could choose to make or not make, and women could forgo without dishonor.

Her heart was swollen with love for the People, and she did the secret gesture, remembering Neepah, thinking of Minnow.

"Look at Sakima," Minnow whispered to Maconakwa as the Spring Council began. "His fine *wapsi* clothes cannot hide that he is sick."

Maconakwa could see even at this distance and over the crowd that Little Turtle was indeed gray-faced and pain-bitten, and she wondered if this might be his last Council. Yellow Leaf suckled while her mother studied the old warrior chief with both pity and resentment.

Under a huge shade arbor, several hundred people sat and

stood; others watched and listened in the shade of trees nearby. This Council Ground was in a narrow, beautiful lowland below Osage's Town, near the mouth of the Mississinewa Sipu. Upstream, the cliff called the Seven White Holy Pillars gleamed amid the green spring foliage of the river bluff; downstream the river flowed into the wide, hazy valley of the Wabash Sipu. To the north across the Mississinewa's mouth rose the roofs of the trading post of Godfroy. It was a wide, sunny, serene place, and the good spirit of yesterday's ceremony still glowed in Maconakwa's bosom, and she wanted to resist the bad feelings that the factions would certainly bring forth in the Council. The people had come from their villages, full of anger about Little Turtle signing treaties and Harrison's invasion of Prophet's Town, mystified by the flying star and the earthquake.

Minnow was among the many who believed those were signs to join Tecumseh and make war. "See how our old tame *sakima* keeps a traitor on each hand," she hissed. She meant William Wells and Five Medals, the Potawatomi chief. "This ground we sit on at this moment they may have sold to Harrison already. See the *wapsi* gift he treasures more than his own People," Minnow went on, voice full of contempt. Maconakwa knew she was talking about the sword that Little Turtle had been given by Washington, first Great Chief of the Long Knives, who was dead now. "He is actually proud to wear such a thing!" Minnow muttered. Sometimes it did seem, even to Maconakwa's tolerant mind, that he should be ashamed of it instead. But again she wished that Minnow would soften her tongue, because to many in this crowd, Little Turtle was still revered as *sakima*.

Maconakwa noticed that Wild Potato Wells had some gray in his red hair, as she did. It was said he had been replaced as the Indian agent at Fort Wayne for some reason reflecting upon his honesty, though he remained as a sort of judge, and still influenced Little Turtle as much as before. As always, the sight of this man troubled her. It had been so many years—eighteen or twenty, she could not remember exactly—since the day she had seen Wild Potato in a boat and almost called out to him to take her into the white people's world. To remember that moment still shamed her a little. And even though Wells had never known of it, it still troubled her to look at that strange man.

Here at Council were many Miamis whose blood was mixed with French, who had French names. The French, she knew, had

lived and traded along the Wabash Sipu long before the English or
Americans came. Near Little Turtle sat Peshewa, Wildcat Richardville, whose mother was a sister of Little Turtle. Wildcat had long
ago proven himself a brave warrior for the Miami, but had been
one of the chiefs who with Little Turtle had signed the Wayne
treaty and many others since. He was well-liked by the Long
Knives and had grown wealthy with special gifts and money from
signing treaties with them, as well as from his trading posts.

Near Richardville under the shade arbor sat another important
mixed-blood whose father had been French. This man was about
Maconakwa's age or a little younger, a man of huge frame, with a
broad, dark face and large eyes. He was important to this Council
because he had become the Nation's war chief, and war would be
this Council's strongest concern. He was known by two names,
Palonswah and Godfroy, and was a trader as well as a warrior.
After this Council he would be required to lead the warriors of the
Miami Nation to war with the Long Knives against the British, or
with the British against the Long Knives, or to keep them from
racing off to either side if the Council voted to take neither side in
the coming war between bluecoats and Redcoats.

She liked Palonswah; he was a good-humored and wise man
and a good friend of Deaf Man, whose advice he often sought.
Once when he visited Deaf Man, Maconakwa had asked him what
"Palonswah" meant, for she had never heard that word in the
Miami tongue. Laughing, he replied that it was the way they pronounced his French first name, which was François. And that had
brought back from her memory the way Neepah so long ago had
pronounced her *wapsi* name: Palanshess. She remembered her
white girl name, which she had forgotten. *Frances.*

She wondered sometimes how many generations would pass
before there would be no Indians left, just mixtures of tribal bloods
and white people's. She remembered the Prophet's warning against
marrying white people.

"That pretty man in a blue coat," Minnow said, nudging her, "is
another French-blood not to be trusted. He is a Harrison spy from
Vincennes."

Maconakwa recognized the man. He was less grave and more
elegant than the others, dressed with a ruffled shirt and a silk
turban of many shimmering colors. "Yes," she said. "Brouillette.
I know of him." She had seen him at Prophet's Town the day the
sun went dark, and at Fort Wayne in the years since. He was a

trader, but also a carrier of messages between Fort Wayne and the fort at Vincennes far down the Wabash Sipu. He was suspected of being an important spy for Harrison. But then, almost every half-blood was suspected of that, and for good reason.

"Watch your daughter," Minnow now whispered with a sly smirk. "She seems to have eyes for Brouillette's son."

Maconakwa had already noticed that. Cut Finger had been stealing long looks at the handsome boy, who was perhaps sixteen years of age, and the boy seemed to have noticed her interest. Maconakwa had been observing them with amusement and some anxiety for a while, and saw that whenever the boy caught Cut Finger looking at him, she ducked her head and visibly squirmed—but even then it would be but a few moments before she was looking at him again.

It was no wonder. The boy was beautifully handsome, even more than her own first husband, Like Wood, had been. Slender and elegant like Brouillette, he looked more Indian than French, with black, glittering eyes, and a lean, sculptured jaw overset by massive cheekbones; and his shoulder-length hair was so thick it made him appear even taller than he was. The youth had a proud, straight way of standing, but there was a lively merriment in his face that kept him from looking as severe as warrior-age boys usually tried to look.

The eye-play between the two made Maconakwa sigh with the realization that any time now Cut Finger would be having her first moon-blood, and, as pretty as she was, probably would be getting married before too many more years went by. She remembered for a moment her own first moon, and the vision she had had, in which the small female bear had come to her and given her the name she now bore.

Once begun, the Council covered every part of Miami life. The old arguments came up about spirit water, about selling one place or another to white men, about how the white men's goods and manners were disturbing and changing the sacred beliefs and even the ceremonies. As the afternoon sun moved over to stand above the bluffs, Maconakwa listened to everything, because the decisions and choices made in Council would affect the lives of her children, and even all the Miami children as yet unborn, and she was in the center of these people, one part of them, as an eyelash or a drop of blood is a part of someone. She watched her daughter and the Brouillette boy and mused upon their possible futures.

When Yellow Leaf stopped nursing, Maconakwa got up and carried her to a shady place where grandmothers were tending children, and Acorn Top took Yellow Leaf in her arms, smiling up. Maconakwa returned to her place beside Minnow while Little Turtle was trying to persuade the people to come to the fort's white doctor and get scratched with a medicine knife, to protect against the terrible *wapsi* disease called smallpox. He had let them do it to him, and claimed that he was now safe from the disease. Minnow snorted and said, "If a *wapsi* medicine man scratched me with his knife, I would at once cut his underpart off!"

Maconakwa shook her head. She turned to Cut Finger, saying, "Your baby sister is with the grandmothers over there. When you have had enough of gazing at that boy, go help—"

"Ningeah!" She tried to look indignant, but flushed and smiled. "I shall, Ningeah . . ."

Suddenly there was a stirring in the crowd, an excited drone of voices. The chiefs under the arbor had straightened up, some rising to stand even while Little Turtle was standing, and then they all looked off to the south. The attention of the crowd followed, and their many voices rose in excitement. She heard some exclaim, "Tecumseh!" and stood. Minnow gripped her arm; her eyes were blazing.

"Ehhh!" Minnow exclaimed. "This is a boldness that is needed here!"

The Shawnee walked swiftly toward the arbor, leading a small group of proud, lean warriors, while a few remained at the edge of the clearing, holding the horses on which they had arrived.

Maconakwa noted that Tecumseh's brother Open Door, the Prophet, was not among them. Then all her attention, like that of everyone else, turned upon the Shawnee war chief, this renegade who was held largely to blame for the fear of war throughout this country. She had not seen him since six summers ago at the Prophet's Town, when he had stood beside his brother who was making the sun darken. As then, he made her heart quicken.

He was not richly attired, as the Council chiefs were, but a grandness seemed to emanate from the natural power of his being, like the beauty of a panther. Though he was of middle years by now, perhaps five years older than she, he was tight-skinned, every muscle and cord of sinew clearly defined as he strode in. He wore no tunic, or even leggings, just breechcloth and moccasins, silver bands around his upper arms, a necklace of large bear claws, a silver dangler between his nostrils, and one eagle plume hanging from a braid in his shiny long hair. He carried a pipe tomahawk in his left hand, its long handle stem resting along his forearm, and except for that and a slim sheath knife hanging in the middle of his chest, he was unarmed—even though he must have known that in this Council sat several chiefs who believed he should be captured or assassinated. On his face there was neither fear nor severity. Though he strode in as straight and purposefully as an arrow, his face showed the pleasure of approaching men he respected, men who had been his comrades in war. Though he had an eagle's visage, when he went up among them and extended his hand toward Little Turtle, his glittering eyes and white-toothed smile made it clear why, as it was reputed, his companionship was enjoyed and cherished by everyone, even those who were at cross purposes with him. The chiefs under the arbor, though they must now be appalled and alarmed that he had come uninvited to their Council, stood and greeted him as if they could not help it.

Maconakwa felt uplifted by the sight of him though she knew his arrival meant trouble, and she laughed and exclaimed aloud with pleasure when Tecumseh took Deaf Man's hand and then clapped him on the shoulder. He said a few words, and then the pipe was lighted and passed again, which she understood to mean that Tecumseh himself would have words to add to the Council. There was no denying the fair-mindedness of Little Turtle, or the hospitality of Osage, whose town this was.

But it became apparent at once that however much they liked Tecumseh, they did not like what he was doing. One by one the chiefs got up and scolded Tecumseh for his continued defiance of American friendship offerings. They chided him for trying to lure Black Hoof and his peaceful Shawnees away from the Long Knives; they chided him for rejecting an offer of amnesty from Harrison; they blamed his harsh words to Harrison for provoking the governor's march into the middle Wabash Sipu country. They blamed him for everything that troubled them.

Tecumseh sat silently listening to all this censure, showing neither shame nor irritation, only shaking his head once or twice. When at last they had finished heaping upon him every bit of blame they could think of, and the translations had trailed off, Tecumseh arose and stood so that he could address the chiefs but also be seen and heard by the hundreds of onlookers. A young man stood up beside him, apparently to be his translator.

"Grandfathers, Fathers, brothers," he began. "The Master of Life, He Who Creates By Thinking, has heard my prayers for this day, and he has pictured me being allowed to speak my heart to you, and that is why it is now so. I have given you my pipe, so that whenever you look at it, you will be reminded that I came here this day to speak the truth to you.

"People of the Miami, of the Potawatomi, the Lenapeh! My people have long been your friends. Together we have fought the peoples of the Longhouse; together we have stood against the invasions of the Long Knives. Now, though you have signed treaties with the Long Knives and I have refused to do so because of my distrust of them, my heart still embraces the happiness and safety of your peoples. We differ only in seeing how the path to happiness goes.

"I have made long study of the treaties made by white men with our peoples. I can tell you every promise made in every one of those treaties. I have talked with the red men who signed those treaties, and I know what they were told by the white men who wrote them, and also I have read the treaties and have seen what is actually written on them. Those are not always the same, as the signers would have known if they could read the marking language on those treaty sheets.

"But even when the promises have been clearly understood, they have always been broken by the white men! I could stand here and count those broken promises until your ears would be numb and your hearts weeping for all you did not mean to give away, but did."

Minnow's knuckle nudged Maconakwa's knee, and Maconakwa saw her nodding vigorously.

Tecumseh went on: "Fathers and brothers! Not long ago nations from the East were pushed into Ohio by whites who broke treaties.

"Now we are in your land, this country the whites call 'Indiana,' which means the 'Land of the Indians.' But even the Land of the Indians grows smaller every season, because of more treaties, made by Land Stealer Harrison, and signed by many of you, the very ones here in this shade with me! Many of you signed treaties with that invader! I know each one of you who did!" He glared from one of them to the next, and they glowered and squirmed.

Then he continued, in a voice that Maconakwa seemed to feel as well as hear, as one feels storm weather coming.

"That great Land Stealer, Harrison, whom you call your friend even though he is the worst enemy your people ever had, that liar Harrison marched his army into our lands that he has not even stolen yet, and burned the holy town and endangered the women and children who had come there only to worship the Creator! Some of your warriors died when he marched in!

"You have stood here just now and blamed me for that attack on my own town! You say he came and attacked it because I have been urging war on him. But you know in your hearts that is not so! I have told my people to step back from war! I said, even if you must abandon a place that is threatened, abandon it for a while and step back out of the Long Knives' range. I said, wait until all red men can stand together, and then we can go see the white men's Great Father in Washington, and all speak to him together, telling him not to take any more of our lands, of which we have so little remaining.

"But," he said, and suddenly thrust a finger toward a Potawatomi chief, the Catfish, "though I had never told my people to war against the whites, my words were turned upside down by a pretended chief of the Potawatomi, who told Harrison I was provoking war! There he is, right before me! This man is a Bad Bird flying with lies in his mouth—as well as a deceiver who signs away land that was never his!"

It had already been seen often in years past that the Catfish was afraid of Tecumseh, and again this time he just hunched into his shoulders and looked down.

"Those men who put their hands to such treaties should have their hands cut off!" Tecumseh declared in a voice so strong and clear that all the hundreds could hear it, and they gasped, muttered, whooped.

"But now it is too late to try to keep peace with the Long Knives," Tecumseh exclaimed. "They now seek to start a war with the English in Canada, because they have long wanted the lands of Canada too. You know that; that is why you are here with your war chiefs standing ready to Council about it.

"You consider standing neutral in the war that comes, or, worse, helping the Long Knives. Some of you here, I know, believe you should instead stand with the Redcoats against the bluecoats. Come with me, then! Have no fear of your old tame chiefs! Come fight our enemy!"

That invitation stirred so much uproar in the crowd that Little Turtle rose, almost purple in the face, and exclaimed: "It is bad for you to come here to our Council where you were not invited to come, and ask our warriors to fight our friends! Are you through speaking?"

"After one plea, respected Father: I wish we people of Turtle Island, all the red people, were of one heart. I ask you to clear the smoke from your eyes and see that we all together have just one enemy, and he is the Long Knife. I have *tapelot*, great love, for the Miami people and the Potawatomi and the Lenapeh. Because of my love for them I wish you could see clearly as you used to before they blinded you with their favors. I warn you that when the war between the Redcoats and the bluecoats begins, Harrison will not care whether you are neutral or not. As the Long Knives have always done, they will run over all the people just because they are Indians.

"I have finished speaking. I hope your warriors will come with me as I leave!"

And when he left, a few warriors did rise and follow, leaving a silence behind. With racing heart Maconakwa looked at Deaf Man to see if he would get up and go too, hoping both ways. He did not get up. He was looking down. She wondered whether he had heard Tecumseh say "Come with me."

She looked at Minnow, whose eyes were ablaze with pride. She looked at Cut Finger, who had stopped gazing at the beautiful *métis* boy at least long enough to watch Tecumseh go. Maconakwa as a woman understood, as a girl could not, how Tecumseh was more beautiful than that boy. But he was a frightening man. Nothing around him could rest. Now, she knew, there would be no avoiding war.

And now the Council would have to decide war or peace with Tecumseh's thrilling challenge troubling them.

CHAPTER TWENTY-TWO

Maconakwa sat by the fire in Minnow's lodge and enjoyed the luxury of having her thick red hair combed by her friend, who was using a large, strong, trading-store horn comb.

The two women had not seen each other since Spring Council. Though their towns were not far apart, on the same river, Minnow had been living with Lenapeh people here in Metosinah's Town since her husband's death in the Prophet's Town battle, and easing back into her Lenapeh ways, had missed the rest of the year's Miami ceremonies. She groused that Metosinah was not fighting against the Long Knives, but *she* did not feel neutral.

Minnow was beginning to look old; so much weathering and grief had been visited upon her that her skin was traced all over by fine lines. But her little body was as hard and sinewy as ever under the thin brown skin, and her hands were so strong that now and then Maconakwa would wince and yip when Minnow dragged the comb relentlessly through a tangle.

Minnow chuckled and said softly, "Quiet. You will wake up our girls. One would think I am torturing you." Their daughters, who felt they were born to be friends, had whispered late in their blankets the night before. Now they, and little Yellow Leaf, were still asleep. It was very early on a bitterly cold morning. When Maconakwa had awakened to make water a little while ago, the first predawn light of a cloudless morning had shown her frost floating in the air. The river was beginning to freeze along the banks.

Most of the men of all the Mississinewa villages were out in the snowy countryside hunting. There was little food anywhere. The war between the English and the Long Knives had brought Long

Knife Town Destroyers again and again into the Wabash Valley, and as Tecumseh had warned in Spring Council, they had burned towns and crops without regard to whether the peoples were neutral or not.

As Minnow had said, hissing between her teeth: "Little Turtle's last gift to his people was to make them helpless, making them promise not to fight Long Knives."

Little Turtle was in his grave, lying under the ground with his Washington sword. He had died two moons after Spring Council, of the disease that had given him so much pain for so long. He was paid much tribute by people of many tribes, both his old friends and enemies, but some of the enemies had satisfied themselves by noting how appropriate it was that the disease, gout, was a white man disease which he probably got by his heart having turned white. They would make this joke and then look ashamed.

All through the late summer and fall the war had flamed and thundered through the valley of the Wabash Sipu, from Fort Wayne almost down to Vincennes. A fort named after Harrison, built on an old sacred place called High Ground, which the French called Terre Haute, had been surrounded and attacked by Kickapoo, Potawatomi, Shawnee, and Winnebago warriors, who had burned it severely but failed to take it from the soldiers inside. Fort Wayne had been unsuccessfully attacked and besieged by Winamac and Five Medals, who had turned against the Americans; Harrison marched up from Ohio and broke that siege, and in revenge sent armies out to burn all the Indian towns anywhere near Fort Wayne and destroy all the crops. In burning Five Medals' town on the Elk Hart River, the soldiers had robbed and defiled the burial place of an old medicine woman, and on their return march many had become very sick, one strong young soldier suddenly just falling dead.

"After that," Minnow had snickered in grim pleasure while speaking of it, "perhaps whatever other treachery those *wapsituk* do, they will leave our revered dead to rest undisturbed!"

"Perhaps," Maconakwa had replied, "but perhaps not. At the Place of the Flints up there"—she pointed toward the northeast—"the bluecoats plundered and burned the funeral hut of the old chief who had not been buried yet."

"May those soldiers die sick too," Minnow had hissed, "and may their spirits be afraid forever in the Other Side World, wherever their Other Side World is. It should be in the ditch where one empties the bowels!" Minnow's contempt for Long Knives was a thing to behold, but it was good to hear strong thoughts expressed in the old familiar Lenapeh tongue again, even when the thoughts were not pleasant.

But this morning Minnow had not talked about war. This was a rare time of quiet, warm friendship in a well-heated, snug *wik-wam*, surrounded by an outdoors too deep in snow and too frozen down for armies to travel in. The combing of Maconakwa's tresses was a luxury now that the tangles were out, and made cascades of pleasure flow down from her scalp through her shoulders, almost putting her in a trance. Now that she was receiving this rare treatment, the touch of a woman whom she loved like a sister, she could understand why at home her daughter liked it—almost begged for it—and understood too why her husband Deaf Man liked her to rub on his shoulders or thighs for long times when he was tired. It seemed that it was usually she who was combing or stroking them, rather than being combed by Cut Finger or stroked by Deaf Man—except of course when he wanted to warm her up to go inside her. She murmured that to Minnow now, and heard her chuckle.

"*E heh!* If you complain about *that*, I might just take this scalp of red hair! Heh heh! Be glad!" They laughed softly. They listened to the girls' sleep-breathing and the fluttering of the flames in the fire ring. Down by the river they could hear the slow rhythm of unshod hooves as some hunters went up the bank, perhaps three or four. The town was so still. There was no wind and probably almost everyone in the village was still in bed or indoors making breakfast out of whatever little they might have. This was a kind of moment that sometimes would make Maconakwa tingle with amazement, that somehow the Creator in the midst of hardship and fear would give creatures—two-legged or four-legged creatures—moments of such sweetness and comfort in their homes and burrows that they must be reminded of his presence and generosity. By these granted moments, she felt, the Master of Life keeps us from despairing. She had never known of a woman as fiery and tough as Minnow—nor one so selfless and kind. Now Minnow murmured close by her ear, still being quiet for their daughters' sake, "Do you know, sister, that here on this part of your head, the scalp lock place, you have a patch of hair that is lighter red than all the rest?"

Of course she knew. From the beginning she had been told of it by her birth mother, by her white sisters, by Neepah, by Flicker. "You have mentioned it to me before, sister."

"*E heh!* Perhaps I did. But I never told you that it is growing gray faster than the rest of your hair. I never mentioned that because I never look at you from up here behind. Yes, it is more gray than red here."

"Hm! I was just thinking what a nice moment this is, and you say in my ear that I grow old."

"Heh! It is not so bad. I have more white now than black. We women go through much. A man earns an eagle feather, and for the same surviving a woman earns a white hair. How great we are, you would presume by looking at our white-hair decorations!"

Maconakwa smiled. But then a bittersweet twinge went through her, evoked by the thought of silvering red hair. She said, "You have heard, Wild Potato was killed by the Potawatomi at Chicagou, in a fight by the great lake?" She remembered seeing at Spring Council that his hair had gone a little silvery. Tecumseh's allies had killed him.

"Ai. And that they cut his heart out and divided it to eat. They wanted some of his power. No matter. He had gone back around to white and it is better that he is dead."

There was so much to remember about Wells—how that other red-haired one had haunted her life with strange feelings of who she was and where she stood in the world. She knew all about him turning white, but in a way she was sorry he was dead. She said, flushing, "Would it be better if I were dead, as I am a white?"

Minnow slapped her hard above the ear. "Such talk! You are not *wapsini!*" And after a while she added, more kindly, "Only some of your hair is *wapsi.*" Then she leaned forward over the back of Maconakwa's shoulder and pressed her cheek against hers. "Come, sister. Let us see what we can make for our children to eat from a ring of dried squash I have saved. I pray our hunters have got at least a deer last—" She stopped and listened.

It took a moment to identify the rapid, thudding sounds that they had both noticed. It was the quick beating of hoofbeats coming fast: running horses out on the snowy, frozen ground.

Hunters coming in with so much meat they wanted to rouse the whole village? That was Maconakwa's hopeful first thought, and when she heard a yipping like coyotes, she thought that might be it. Men were like boys when they had something to show off. But then she heard a word of the yipping: *"Wapsituk!"*

At that, her heart jolted. The hoofbeats were closer, coming from upriver, and the next words she distinguished were "Soldiers coming! Up! Run!"

The two women looked at each other for an instant. Their gift of a good moment was over. They turned and grabbed their daughters, shook them rudely into wakefulness, and told them to get dressed. Maconakwa heard Minnow exclaim: "Soldiers coming in *winter*?" Dressing Yellow Leaf, Maconakwa babbled prayers.

But the next sound to come was a blaring, piercing song high in the cold air outdoors, a sound they had heard from the fort or from armies coming along the riverbanks so long ago. It was that signal thing the soldiers blew: a bugle.

Its echoes hung in the air while the naked girls scrambled for their dresses. Minnow grabbed her knife. And just as the two women and their daughters flung back the door flap and ducked out into the bright cold, a howling din of male voices—it sounded like hundreds of them—arose from the upriver side of the village, and the ground shuddered with hoofbeats. Women and children, many of them naked, came sprinting through the snow from that direction, screaming and yelping in panic. From behind them erupted a sputtering and cracking of gunshots. Splinters of wood and bark spun off the lodges and trees, and bullets whined and sang everywhere. Children tumbled in the snow and sprang up and stumbled on. Calling to Cut Finger, carrying Yellow Leaf, Maconakwa ran toward the river, clutching a blanket in her other arm. She saw blood drops in the snow. A naked old woman trying to crawl. Two or three saddled Indian horses without riders were trotting in confusion among the dwellings, shying and rearing in fear of the running people and the whining, whacking bullets.

She almost ran into a Miami man who was standing in the lane aiming his musket—at her, it seemed at first, but instead, over her—in the direction from which she had come. Just as she passed him, he fired, and her ears hurt and she smelled the powder smoke. Two more of the village men, one an elder, one hardly more than a boy, in nothing but breechcloths, stood aiming their guns back in that direction. Still running on the packed snow now on the slope toward the river, Maconakwa lost her footing and fell hard, wrenching her arm as Cut Finger tumbled over her. Picking up her screaming little girl and rising, she looked back and saw the horse soldiers coming at full tilt through their own gun smoke, and she had never in her life seen so many bluecoats at once; the whole

glaring white sunrise landscape was sundered by their mass silhouette, pearly sky above, snowy earth below, a moving wall of
horse soldiers between, so many they were engulfing the low,
domed *wikwams*, overrunning the brown bodies of the women
and little ones who ran too slow and too late to get out of their way.
She knew there were no more than ten or a dozen Indian men in
the town, and they were falling before the soldiers' guns.

The horsemen were close enough that she could see their
shouting faces and their shiny black plumed helmets. Minnow and
her daughter were nowhere in sight. Maconakwa's heart was
slamming in her breast and she was so full of terror that she was
hot even in the frosty air. She and Cut Finger ran through the shallows, breaking thin ice, and clambered through deep snow up the
other bank, grasping at the roots of cottonwoods and sycamores.
A woman with gray hair fell on the slope in their way, dropping
the crimson blanket she had been holding around her. Maconakwa
took hold of one of her arms and yelled to Cut Finger, "Help the
grandmother!" One on each side, they hauled her up into the
brush. She was heavy and groaning and they saw that she was
leaving blood in the snow. Maconakwa put her blanket around the
woman, noticing a bullet wound low in her back, then darted back
down the bank to grab up the woman's red blanket. She gripped a
sycamore root to keep from sliding back down to the water's edge.
The horse soldiers were still milling and bellowing and shooting
on the other bank. She felt a stinging jolt in her hand. A bullet had
barked the tree root right beside it. She clenched her teeth. They
were shooting too close to her children. She heaved herself up to
the top of the bank again, dragging the red blanket.

Now some of the soldiers had ridden down and were breaking
the shelf ice, starting to wade their horses across. A warrior's gun
banged just above her and a soldier fell backward over the rump
of his horse. He was in midstream, one foot still caught in a
stirrup, and the horse was lunging in the water, dragging him. But
then several other soldiers yelled and fired their guns. Bullets
sprayed snow all around her and she felt one whip through her
hair, and the warrior above, who had just raised his powder horn
to reload his musket, lurched backward and fell in the snow. Cut
Finger was still kneeling by the old woman and crying, her face
contorted in terror.

"Daughter! Get hold! Pull!" Maconakwa grabbed a fold of the
blanket in which the old woman was lying and Cut Finger grasped

the other side and they dragged it with the woman's weight along the snow, deeper into the thicket. She slid out of the blanket and was lying naked and bleeding in the snow, and so they turned back for her. But now the old woman seemed to be conscious and was trying to get up, so they whipped her own red blanket around her and helped her stand, and they limped away downstream through the snow away from the thunder of gunshots and the din of soldier voices. Looking back through the leafless branches, Maconakwa could see a few plumed helmets as some of the dragoons forded the river, but most of them were still up on the far bank. They were throwing the bodies of dead Indians into the water. Part of the army seemed to be going on down the river toward the other villages. One of those was the village of Silver Heels, who was not only neutral in the war, but a friend of Harrison's, and had tried to keep his warriors from joining Tecumseh.

As they limped and dragged on through the snowy bottomland with the wounded elder, seeing other fugitives from the village running or trudging along, generally northwestward and downstream along the bottomland, the army noise still roaring a few hundred paces away, the terrible piercing of the cold began to penetrate where only terror had been felt before, and Maconakwa realized that there was as much danger from freezing to death as from being killed by soldiers. Most of the people were barefoot, some dressed or muffled in blankets, but many were stark naked and bleeding. She wondered whether this old woman would live, and whether many others were back there lying hurt and freezing in the snow, and whether she would ever see Minnow again, and whether her husband and many of the other hunters had been near enough to hear all this uproar. Surely any men who were out hunting within half a day's distance must have been able to hear this and would be coming back this way to help their women and old ones and children. But of course, she thought with an almost bottomless dread, many of those hunters had headed out eastward in the past days, going upstream into the less populated country, which might mean they had already fallen into the path of this army. Her own husband had gone that way.

She groaned, and tried to hold Yellow Leaf close for warmth.

Downstream from Metosinah's Town were several bigger Miami towns, including Deaf Man's and Osage's, closer to the Wabash Sipu. Probably that was where the army was going: to burn the bigger towns. That could mean that if she ever got home to her own town, it would be no town, just ashes and embers. And even if her beloved husband Deaf Man were still alive, where would she ever find him if they had no village to go to?

This seemed like the end of everything. But one could not just stand in the cold and die. There were villages downriver whose people needed to be warned if they hadn't heard already. There was food to be foraged and shelter to be made for these who were naked in the cold. This old woman needed a bullet hole healed if that could be done, or a proper burial ceremony if not. Deaf Man needed to be found if he was still alive. And this girl Cut Finger had to be protected from the things Minnow said soldiers did to pretty girls. And Yellow Leaf had to be kept alive.

One could not just give up and be a leaf blown by the wind.

The old woman somehow kept on her feet, stumbling along, slow and heavy. Maconakwa and Cut Finger trudged on with her until the middle of morning, when at last some boys came up the river from one of the lower towns with a short string of horses and bundles of blankets. The fastest runners fleeing from Metosinah's Town had warned the other villages that a huge riding army was coming down one side of the river and cold, hurt people were coming down the other. Maconakwa helped the boys put the wounded woman up on a horse, and a boy led the horse back down. The boys asked if there were any others farther back who needed help, and Maconakwa said, "Surely so. But go with care. Some soldiers were crossing the river and may be back there following us." She saw that these brave boys had no guns, only their bows. Shivering violently with the cold, she asked about Deaf Man. He had not been seen since his hunting party left. She asked if there were any warriors down in those towns to meet the army and defend the towns. One boy said:

"Some hunters heard the war and they are coming in. But the towns on that side of the river, everyone has fled and crossed to this side. Chief Wildcat and Chief Silver Heels are calling hunters in, but there are few." He pointed downriver. "The hunting camp just around that bend, many of the women and children are there. They burn fires to get warm before they freeze. Go on, aunt. May your path be smooth."

"Thank you, young one. May your path be safe."

As they went on, more quickly now without the old woman, they followed the hoofprints. Here and there Maconakwa saw frozen blood drops in the snow, maybe from the old woman, maybe from others. There were many footprints, many of bare feet. She and Cut Finger had gotten moccasins on before fleeing from Minnow's lodge but their feet were utterly numb, and the thought of bare feet in this cold, crusted snow was so pitiful to think of that her heart ached for those whose toes showed in the prints.

But for us with moccasins, she thought, it is good the cold is deep. Our moccasins would be wet otherwise and we would have no toes tomorrow.

Thinking this, she tucked the blanket closer around Yellow Leaf.

She could not hear the army anymore. There were no gunshots, no bugles. But soon she saw rising from above the trees on the other side of the river great billows of dark smoke and even flakes of soot. Over there would be Silver Heels' Town, she guessed. A little farther on, as she and Cut Finger hobbled and clumped along on their deadened feet, both inside the same blanket, they saw more clouds of smoke rising and knew the soldiers had reached towns farther down and torched those too. She could hear distant shouting, soldier yells, but no gunfire. The reason, she presumed, was that the people had fled those towns before the soldiers reached them.

"Those people were not even their enemies," she said between chattering teeth. "Tecumseh warned them right. Friendly or not, if you are red, the soldiers will burn you out. Look," she said, pointing to the right. "We must stop now and do that." There were other refugees halted here and there in little groups, sitting and kneeling and rubbing each other's feet vigorously. And so she and her daughter found a fallen tree where they could sit. She pulled off Cut Finger's moccasins and began rubbing. Her hands were so numb she could hardly feel the feet. After a while her hands were painful and tingling as the blood moved through her fingers, and she could tell that the girl's poor feet were as hard and stiff as clubs. She rubbed until she was gasping with weariness. She and Minnow had not cooked or eaten this morning, and she felt hollow and shaky from hunger as much as from cold. "Do your feet feel anything yet?"

"They hurt," Cut Finger said in a quaking voice.

"Good. What hurts is not dead."

Then Cut Finger rubbed her mother's feet until they hurt. Maconakwa watched the girl's breath come out in frosty clouds.

While her feet were being rubbed she nursed Yellow Leaf under the blanket, which stopped her whimpering and shivering.

"Now," she said, "we must go on. That camp is not far. I see smoke that is not from towns burning." She thought: I have seen so many town burnings I can tell one kind of smoke from another.

In the refugee camp Maconakwa and Cut Finger dragged firewood and patched wounds and sheltered Yellow Leaf, and watched fearfully for the bluecoat soldiers to appear through the white bright haze. These people here were helpless. She prayed the hunters and warriors would arrive here first.

By afternoon the hundred hunters who had been close enough to hear the dawn gunfire had raced in from their hunting to gather with the chiefs of the destroyed villages. Deaf Man was not with them.

By sundown the ones who had not heard the shooting but had seen the smoke from the four burning villages had arrived, and warriors from the big Miami villages downstream had come up. Now the men with guns, Miami and Lenapeh together, numbered about three hundred. Deaf Man and his hunters trotted in at dusk. They had had to swing wide outside the valley to avoid the army, which had stopped after burning the fourth village and gone back upriver to Silver Heels' Town to make camp there in the ruins. The army was making a fort out of logs and limbs. Palonswah's scouts had seen all that and described it. The army had many guards posted outside the fortifications, and huge fires were burning inside the breastworks. It had grown still colder, and the soldiers, it could be hoped, were suffering very much. They probably were wishing they had not burned down the town, so they could have had snug *wikwams* to stay in, with hearth fires inside.

The scouts said the horse soldiers numbered eight or nine hundred. It was a huge army to have come here so far into the country in the snow. It was too big an army to attack with three hundred warriors and hunters, even men as vengefully furious as these, who had in one day changed from neutrals or friends of the Americans to bitter enemies. Three hundred warriors could not expect to defeat three hundred entrenched soldiers, and certainly not three times that many. It would be foolhardy to try to get revenge by attacking the eight or nine hundred soldiers now. It would be better to wait a few days until Tecumseh came down with his six or seven hundred warriors, who were somewhere in the Wabash Sipu valley. He could join with them and destroy this army that was so far from any fort. It would be easy, with Tecumseh, and messengers had already been sent to find and summon him. Tecumseh would be glad to find all these neutral Mississinewa warriors suddenly converted to his side.

That was the argument for waiting, and some of the chiefs used that argument.

But there was a more desperate argument for not waiting:

It could take several days to find and bring Tecumseh. In those days this army might turn and continue on down the river and destroy all the rest of the towns all the way to the Wabash Sipu and burn what little food was left—not much, after Harrison's raids at harvesttime.

But the strongest argument of all for not awaiting Tecumseh's help was that the army had rounded up about forty or fifty women and children in its morning attack and was holding them hostage in the center of its camp. If everyone waited till Tecumseh could come, the soldiers might kill them all or rape them or take them away with them back to their forts in the East.

There was no hope that three hundred warriors and hunters could defeat so many horse soldiers. They had already agreed on that.

But, some warriors and chiefs insisted, three hundred warriors might be able to break in through one side of the army camp, rescue the women and children, and get back out.

Maconakwa, shuddering and almost faint at the edge of this hurried war council, heard that. She was almost certain that Minnow and her daughter must be among those captives. Since the first minute of the raid, she had not seen them. They had not showed up at the hunting camp ·where the refugees had come. They might have been killed by the soldiers or frozen to death in the flight, but most likely they were among those captives.

She looked at her husband, Deaf Man. He was there close among the village chiefs and leaning far in, and there was cold fury in his eyes. She looked at him and again thanked the Creator that he was alive.

But she heard him vote yes, attack the army before daybreak and get our people out! And she knew that though he was alive tonight, he might not be tomorrow.

*   *   *

The glow from the soldiers' bonfires in the ruins of Silver Heels' Town could be seen from the war camp here.

It would require great courage to attack so many soldiers with so few warriors. It would require great fortitude to survive such a terribly frigid night without homes to sleep in. And so great heaps of firewood were brought into the war camp to make a huge bonfire for a war dance.

The drums beat and the howling warriors danced around the blaze for hours into the evening. They mimed stalking, springing upon the enemy with tomahawks raised high, lunging from a crouch with lances, pointing guns, bending bows, killing, killing, stooping to take scalps, and with each imitation felt the power come into them to do the real deeds to the whites in the morning. They yelped and sang the fearsome tremolo war cry, casting demonic shadows in the light of the roaring bonfire whose sparks swirled up in red smoke toward the stars. If the soldiers' firelight could be seen from here, this firelight could be seen by the soldiers, and surely the soldiers in their camp up the river would be able to hear these screams and war cries across that distance. It was certain that the soldiers would be more and more afraid the longer they saw this glow in the sky and heard this howling and, especially, the vibrant war cry that had not been heard for so long.

In the meantime, if the warriors had not had the great bonfire to dance near, they might have frozen to death, this night was so cold.

One of the dancers was the French-blood youth Brouillette, who had caught and held the eye of the girl Cut Finger last year at Spring Council. This boy Brouillette had never fought before. He would become a warrior at daylight because every able man and boy would be needed. Young Brouillette looked splendid as he danced, his deep eyes ablaze, his jutting cheekbones striped with war paint.

Maconakwa noticed her daughter watching the boy again, and this time not with sweet adoration, but with fear and pain. Much of the pain was in hands and feet that had nearly frozen that day, but much of it was heart pain. All the women and girls crouched or sitting in the big circle, watching the inner circle of ferocious warriors dance and scream themselves into readiness, knew that these dancers, who were their own sons or husbands or fathers or uncles or nephews, might be dead before the sun was up tomorrow.

It was the women who bore and nursed the babies who would

grow up to be fighters. The women had the most to lose when their boys and men went out to battle. That was why women in Council had a war vote. Sometimes the women would know that it was just the men's indignation or foolish pride or hunger for reputation that made them want to go to war and risk themselves, and at such times the women would vote against fighting.

But this time there was no question whether the warriors should go. The only question was whether it could be done, and how many lives it would cost.

Maconakwa saw Wildcat, the mixed-blood named Richardville, who usually looked like a French white man instead of a Miami. Now his face was painted for war and he looked like a Miami warrior in the glow of the war dance fire. In the war council this evening he had suggested that the warriors should only block the army from leaving the country, and keep them encircled until Tecumseh's force could come and help destroy them all. That sounded like a good plan, except for two bad possibilities: the soldiers might become desperately angry and start killing the hostages, and there might be another white army—another unde-tected army coming down from Fort Wayne, as one already had three months ago—which could get here before Tecumseh could. To prevent that, the chieftains and warriors had argued, the attack should be made now. And the people, being in a furious and vengeful state of mind, had agreed. So it would be before daylight, even in this bitter cold. No one had ever heard of battles being fought in such cold. It would be terrible.

But the horse soldiers had chosen this bitter cold time to come here, and so it would be in the deep cold. There are so many ways to suffer and die in war, Maconakwa thought. This is just another. And in deep cold, wounds do not bleed as much.

Yellow Leaf was swaddled and asleep in a brush lean-to. Maconakwa, chafing Cut Finger's frostbitten hands, felt a pres-ence and looked up. There stood the huge form of Palonswah the Miami war chief, with Deaf Man beside him. She had seen him earlier here and there, solemnly walking around the circle to talk to families whose men would be in the battle. He looked down at her and said in a deep, rich voice that she could hear even over the drumming and yelping:

"Little Bear Woman, wife of my friend. You sit here with red hair shining in the firelight and your face so different from ours. You are thinking hard. I wondered, and came to ask: Are you thinking, these warriors go tomorrow to kill people of my race? I hope it is forgiven that I ask you that."

She peered up at him, watching the sparks of the bonfire swirl up beyond him, and thought of the soldiers. She remembered how they had looked this morning, their yelling faces and their helmets, the beard stubble on their pale jaws, and thought about the strange question Palonswah had asked. And she answered in truth:

"I had no thought of that kind. Those soldiers are not my people. I have never known a people who could do what those men are doing. These Miami are my people.

"And, friend of my husband, it is forgiven that you ask, but please never ask that again."

After the middle of the night the three hundred warriors and hunters, men and boys, left the war camp and started up the river path toward the soldier camp at the ruins of Silver Heels' village. They dwindled from view into the frigid blue-gray night, their footsteps creaking in dry snow, the vapor of their breath freezing. They vanished beyond the leafless trees and bushes, into a silence still haunted by the pulse of drums and trilling of war cries. The high flames of their bonfire dropped lower and lower, to leave a huge, shimmering bed of embers still giving off smokeless heat under the piercing, clear stars.

Maconakwa and Cut Finger, like many of the other homeless families, wrapped themselves together with the baby to share body heat, trying to keep warm in the heat from the embers which reflected off the ceiling of the lean-to that sloped over them, open side toward the heat. They were spent. They prayed fervently, then held each other and let themselves fall asleep for a while.

Maconakwa dared not let herself sleep deeply because she knew that in this cold, feet could freeze, at the least, while at the worst one could slip off into the freezing sleep from which there was no awakening. Her husband had told her about the freezing sleep; once long ago on a midwinter hunt, he lost a friend to it and had nearly succumbed himself.

This night she was awakened now and then by what sounded like a gunshot but was only a tree splitting from the cold, or by the movements of those who were too distraught to sleep and kept throwing wood on the embers to keep a blaze going. Thus awakened, she made sure Cut Finger's feet were covered, and thought of Minnow and her daughter and prayed for them, and thought of her husband and prayed for him, and for War Chief Palonswah, who had asked her the strange question, and she prayed for him too. She would think, then, of where they would be by now, and try to envision the river path through their eyes. She knew the army had sentries out all night and people staying up to throw wood on their bonfires. She knew these soldiers would be suffering from the cold now, and perhaps sleepless fear, which they deserved for what they had done. Maybe they would be trying to rape the captives, but that was doubtful, the cold being this severe.

She would doze a little, then wake and try to send the love of her heart through the still night to the heart of her husband, to warm him and encourage him as he crept toward the American camp. She would doze again, awakened by a sore hip or by stinging cold on her temple, and would remember the pleasure of Minnow drawing a comb through her hair—less than one day ago that had been, though it now seemed ages ago.

Darkness had not yet begun to fade when the cold and hunger and hard ground convinced Maconakwa that any more rest was impossible. She got up stiffly, tucking the blanket around her daughters, and hobbled to the edge of the ashes where the great bonfire had been. Her feet and hands were so cold, so numb, that she wanted to wade into the hot ashes. Instead she set to work on the problem of how to feed these people. Women from Palonswah's Town had brought up dried provisions the evening before, and kettles. Women and children crept out of their bedding and came close, and soon all the little campfires were surrounded by women and children and elders who hunkered, gazing stupefied into the flames or watching steam rise from kettles. They talked little. They shuddered with their blankets and fur robes pulled up over their heads, and rubbed their hands again and again in the fires' heat. When they were not watching the kettles and the flames, they were squinting southward in the direction their warriors had gone, awaiting the sounds they dreaded and anticipated.

All the hunters coming in the day before had brought only a turkey and two raccoons and a rabbit. They made barely enough meat to enrich the thin stews of dried squash, acorn meal, corn flour, root starch, and elm bark the women from Palonswah's Town had brought.

Thin as it was, this fare gave off aromas that made the hungry, chilled people drool. Maconakwa found herself also tantalized by another scent, one she had come to know from when she had dined at Little Turtle's grand house at Fort Wayne. It was the white men's brew called coffee. It was rare, but almost everyone had sometimes drunk it, thickly sweetened. Women from Wildcat's Town were brewing it this morning. The refugees shuffled around the cookfires to get coffee and food. Most had lost their spoons and bowls in their burning towns, and had to wait to take turns with the tin cups some had brought, or eat from bark slabs. Maconakwa nursed Yellow Leaf as she and Cut Finger waited for the others to be fed. The dregs from the bottom of the kettle were delicious, but only a few sips were left, and the coffee was gone. She returned to snuggle with her daughters in their blanket and wait for day. No one knew what the day would bring, whether the army would remain in the valley or be driven out, whether the warriors would come back alive, so there was no use planning anything. With three hundred warriors gone to attack three times that many soldiers, whatever happened today could not be expected to end well.

Maconakwa was gazing through the tracery of bare treetops toward the paling eastern sky, praying, when she heard the first gunshot, then a quickening sputter of faraway gunfire. Her heartbeat raced and she prayed still more intently that none of those would hit her husband. She remembered that the first time she had ever seen him, he was nearly dead with a bullet in his lung. Cut Finger's eyes were open, full of fear, and Maconakwa tried to reassure her, saying, "It should not last long. They will just make a hole in one side of the soldier camp and bring out the captive ones."

But it did not end. The gunfire kept sputtering, diminishing, rising like far thunder. The morning was so intensely cold that she wondered how a man could even load a gun without his fingers freezing, and the snow was knee-deep. If a man fell he might not even be found in the snow. She imagined Deaf Man trying to run forward through the deep, crusted snow. She knew how easy it was to see game or horses or people against a background of snow, how impossible it was to conceal oneself in white snow with no foliage. Glancing around this camp as daylight came on, she could see the outline of every person, every tree, within three hundred paces, and knew that the soldiers could see the warriors just that clearly. And the shooting just kept going on and on. Soldiers always had better guns and more powder and ball than Indians, so most of that, she could be sure, was the noise of soldier guns. Her fear mounted, growing more and more terrible, and now whenever the gunfire began to slacken, she feared it was because all the warriors were dead. But then she would hear a wisp of war-cry sound. Once, she heard through the gun noise a strange, clear voicelike sound. It was a moment before she recognized it as a distant bugle.

It was a terrifying sound, even though so very faint. It was what she had heard loudly the morning before, when the horse soldiers came thundering through the town. She remembered that clearly, the sight of so many soldiers on horseback, a dark onrush across the morning snow. There are so many soldiers, she thought, even if our warriors do get inside and reach the captives, the army might just surround them and then they themselves might not get out. Or does the bugle mean the army charges this way?

I am imagining every bad thing that could happen, she thought. Better things could be happening. So much shooting for so long—perhaps Tecumseh arrived this morning up there and is helping them defeat the Long Knife horse soldiers!

I would rather be there with bullets whining around me so I could see and not have to imagine everything this way!

She remembered the lead balls yesterday morning whirring by and chipping bark. It did not seem that the fear and desperation she had felt then were worse than this helpless wondering.

And then she noticed that there was much less gunfire now. She could see by the brightness over the horizon that the sun would be up soon.

There was only silence now. A single gunshot; two more; one more; none. She heard the bugle again, an eerie, distant song. Two more gunshots. None. None. She rose, knees hurting, to stand and gaze upriver, as if by standing and looking toward the sunrise, she might see better what had happened so far up there beyond the trees and snowy slopes and creek banks. Or just to be standing when whatever was to come would come.

Everyone else was standing and looking in that direction.

She trembled in the cold, exhaled frost and prayed and won-dered, and the edge of the sun blazed through the winter-bare trees upriver, bringing pearly white light but no warmth.

* * *

Maconakwa was out in the deep snow gathering more deadwood for the fires when she heard the warriors coming back: crunching snow crust and low voices.

They brought back thirty warriors from the battle to be buried. One of every ten had been killed attacking the soldier camp, and many others might yet die of their wounds. And they had fetched back also the ones the soldiers had killed and thrown in the river the morning before. She put her hand over her mouth. These were dead with honor, all brought back to be buried and mourned properly.

The warriors had failed to get in and free the captives. The one blessing was that the soldiers had stayed there after the battle instead of pursuing them. "We killed many of them and wounded many more," Deaf Man said. "They are hurt badly and suffering the cold. I do not expect them to come this way again. I expect they will limp off east to their forts and lick their wounds." He was black with gunpowder and shaking hard, and his eyes were red. "They still have our people," he went on, voice quaking. "There were too many soldiers with good guns, and they had stacked wood all around their camp to shoot from. We just could not get in. When day came, they bugled and rushed out on many warhorses and swept us before them." He released a long, shuddering sigh and looked back along the line of horses with bodies over their backs. "We will have to burn the frozen ground to make graves." Then he gazed at the wide circle of ashes where the war dance fire had been, and she knew he was thinking that the ground was already thawed there. The war party had started there and would end there for these.

Maconakwa was thinking of Minnow, who, after all this, was still not here. Minnow and her daughter. And all those others still in the hands of the Long Knives.

Maconakwa worked in the cold to prepare food and medicine and to comfort the ones who had lost warriors. The thin, frost-bright air was woven with keening laments.

"They go away, the Long Knives," said a messenger who had ridden down in the afternoon to report what the scouts had seen. He described what the soldiers had done.

They had bandaged their wounded; they had medicine men with them who wore black clothes. They made litters to carry wounded soldiers on between horses. They buried the dead ones in the floor of a big ruined building, and then burned the rest of the building down to hide the graves. Then they formed into lines, many of the soldiers leading their horses instead of riding them, and opened a place in their breastwork to go out through, and started upriver along the Mississinewa Sipu toward the mid-morning sun. They had flankers riding along the outside and herded their captives along in the middle.

"*E heh,*" grumbled Palonswah. "By that direction they must be going to Greene Ville, not to Fort Wayne. Perhaps they know already that Tecumseh is on the Wabash Sipu and they are afraid to go that way and be caught by him."

"By their tracks through the deep snow from yesterday," the messenger said, "we believe Greene Ville is where they came from to attack us. They seem not to be Fort Wayne soldiers. And the one, Harrison, is not their leader. It is someone we do not know."

"Harrison is a general of bigger armies now," said Palonswah. "Now that Tecumseh and the British have captured Detroit, now that Mackinack and Chicagou have fallen to Tecumseh's allies, Harrison will be too busy preparing against Canada to ride with town burners like these. But know surely, Harrison sent these!"

"Then we will have no chance to shoot him?" a chieftain asked.

"Those who join Tecumseh might get such a chance. And I believe Harrison by his deeds has driven many of the neutrals and many of his own allies to join Tecumseh."

Palonswah mused, very grave: "One day sometime, Tecumseh will meet Harrison in battle. *E heh!* That is a destiny one can see. Even we who had smoke in our eyes and did not heed the quaking earth and the two-tailed star, even we can now see his destiny is to face Harrison."

On the second day after the battle, a scout who had been trailing the army walked in, hooded in his blanket, leading his horse. Slumped forward in its saddle, in her own tattered blanket, was old Acorn Top, so weary that she could barely hold herself upright. Maconakwa's helpers carried her into shelter, fed her meat broth and rubbed her hands and feet, and wrapped her in hides and blankets. They looked at her and wondered how she could be alive. Maconakwa gazed at her and remembered how she had helped her with the village people after the first earthquake. Acorn Top recognized Maconakwa and tried to answer her questions about what had happened.

"I was prisoner of the horse soldiers."

"How did you get away from them?"

Acorn Top croaked and wheezed, "I fell. They had their own . . . freezing feet and faces. Just went on."

"How did you keep from freezing to death in the night, Grandmother?"

"What is there to freeze? I am all bones."

"Grandmother, I want to ask you about a hostage called Minnow. . . ." But Acorn Top was slipping into sleep, and didn't answer.

The scout who had brought her back was warming himself at a fire, and Maconakwa went to thank him. With his blanket hood thrown back, she could see it was the young man Brouillette. She squatted by the fire and told him her name.

"*E heh.* I have seen you at Council," he said. "You are Deaf Man's wife, eh? You have a daughter, I think. And a baby."

So he had indeed noticed Cut Finger, even as she had noticed him. Maconakwa nodded. "We saw you there too. It was at Spring Council when Tecumseh spoke. You are Brouillette, eh?"

"I am Jean Baptiste Brouillette. My true name is T'kwakeaw."

T'kwakeaw. Autumn, that meant. She liked it that he called his Miami name, not his French one, his true name. His deep eyes, almost black, were not sparkling and merry as before. She thanked him for bringing Acorn Top back. "She might live. Tell me how you found her."

"She was lying in the snow, a little way off the wide track the horse soldiers trampled in the snow along the river. We passed by her unseeing in the evening, perhaps. We rode back past without seeing her again that night when we sought a campsite away from the soldiers. Then we found her this morning as we rode forward again to trail the army as it moved on. She looked so much like old sticks, we saw her only by bright morning."

"How can old ones bear so much!" Maconakwa exclaimed. "So, then the soldiers suffer much too?"

"Very bad. They were fools to come out in the winter. Probably when they started this way the weather was good. Who would expect a cold this deep to come down?"

"If soldiers stayed home, they would not be suffering."

"This," the youth said, "is their punishment for coming to attack people who were not their enemies."

"This, and the battle yesterday," she said. "You were in that?"

"My first one. *E heh.*"

"It was a terrible battle, eh?"

"*E heh.* The soldiers have good guns, many. Many spinning-bullet guns, not muskets. They sing as they go by, and you understand the song." Now his eyes were shining.

"So says my husband, who has heard many. Tell me, young Autumn, do you know the Lenapeh woman Numaitut, the Minnow, of Metosinah's Town? A widow, with a daughter younger than mine."

"*Ne she.* Is she among the hostages?"

"I believe them to be. The mother and the daughter."

"It is bad. The captives suffer even more than the soldiers."

"*E heh,*" she said. "And if suffering is punishment, as you say, Minnow's punishment is for what?" She sighed and shook her head and got up, thanking him again and wishing him a smooth path. From somewhere I feel Cut Finger watching me, she thought. She will want to know if he asked me anything about her. She'll be disappointed. Eh.

Then she sat back down near Acorn Top, to wait until the old woman could recover enough to talk, hoping she could tell her something about Minnow among the hostages.

But at sundown Acorn Top crossed to the Other Side World. Her breath quit. She was already almost a skeleton.

Maconakwa got up weary and sad to go and tell Autumn Brouillette. But he had already gone back up the river to rejoin the scouts and follow the army.

That night, Maconakwa lay between her husband and daughters in the lean-to, and he fell into exhausted sleep at once. She lay praying fervent thanks for his life. The warmth of her family's close bodies in the bedding soothed her and she was sinking under her own exhaustion, but her mind was flooding with thoughts, reminding her to pray for the spirits of those killed, the safety of the captives, Minnow in particular, and that somehow there would be enough food to keep the People alive through the winter.

Almost into sleep, she began thinking of her daughter Cut Finger and this young man Brouillette, called Autumn. She could see their lives coming toward a convergence that could not be stopped even if there were some reason to stop it. That youth had been like a warrior against the soldiers. But Autumn was not really

a warrior. Like the older Brouillette, he would probably be a
trader, a person between white and red people, perhaps a man who
wrote words and numbers on paper to keep track of goods and
money, as she had seen trading-post people do.

He may not be like that, though, she thought. His heart seems
red. If Cut Finger marries him, perhaps she would fare better in
her life because the white people with their money trade keep
coming, and they will surely change everything to their way.

And she is part white-blood by me and he is part white-blood
by his father, and so any children they had would be less Miami.
That boy is kind and has been brave, but I wonder if he ever went
out and sought his vision and found his Spirit Helper.

Or does he perhaps believe what the Black Robes teach, as so
many of the French-name ones do? Or does he believe a bit of our
way and a bit of theirs, making all his beliefs weaker? People
weaken when their beliefs weaken.

What will we become as my daughters become women?
Maybe, she thought, that will depend on what comes of this war.
And wars after this. I wonder if we can stay strong enough to be
who we have been.

The fire outside the shelter blurred with her sleepiness; now and
then a silhouette of a person passed before the firelight. In a camp
there was always somebody up, especially a camp where there
were dead to grieve for and wounded to heal. . . .

She heard intense voices. Something was happening. She
fought up from the heavy weariness and rose on an elbow. A few
people were moving quickly toward the riverbank. Then they
were coming back, voices excited. They were helping two stumbling, ragged, frosty apparitions out of the night. Maconakwa
inhaled a gasp and exhaled a groan. With pain sparking in knees
and ankles, she stood up, waking her husband and daughters as
she disturbed their covers. She called across the clearing:

"Minnow!"

Maconakwa limped through the stupefying cold toward the
woman and her daughter—or perhaps their ghost spirits, if those
were actually what she was seeing.

Fed on hot broth, fingers and toes rubbed with sumac-leaf tea,
bundled up warm in hides, at length Minnow could tell them:

"The soldiers grew too frozen to handle their guns. . . ." She
hesitated, sniffling, thinking long. "When they rode, their feet

froze worse. So slow . . . but their leaders wanted them to hurry. We told them, 'Hurry! Tecumseh follows!' Oh, that frightened them! Ha ha!"

"How did you get away, sister?" Maconakwa asked. She was working raccoon fat into Minnow's face to soothe the chapped skin and make blood flow to her skin. There was no bear fat anymore. There had not been bears for a long time.

"The army stopped often to rest. Make fires. Everyone sat . . . We lay down in the snow. Soldiers were at the fire, not watching well . . . We covered ourselves with snow, finally even our faces. In bright day we did this. We heard them shout to go and then they moved along. A horse stepped so close to my head, it pulled some of my hair out. . . . When we heard no more army, we got up . . . saw their backs far away. Warmed ourselves a little at the fires they left. Then we turned this way and walked. Sometimes we crossed the ice where the river bends, to make a straighter walk here. . . ." She wheezed and winced. "That is how we are back today instead of tomorrow."

Maconakwa stared into the sunken, glittering eyes a long time, thinking. Then she said, "Sister . . ." speaking softly, as if to herself more than Minnow. "You lift my heart. I had been worrying, whether our people are strong enough for what yet comes."

CHAPTER TWENTY-THREE

July 1813
Mississinewa Valley

There could not have been a more pleasant way to pass such a hot day. Maconakwa waded naked in the clear water among the white flowers and arrow-shaped leaves, holding and pulling the dugout canoe with one hand, groping the mucky marsh bottom with her toes. Usually she could break the tubers off with her toes, and when they floated to the surface, toss them into the canoe. Some she would have to bend down and twist off by hand, stooping and immersing herself as far as her shoulders, so even though the mid-summer sun beat down on her head and shoulders, she could remain cool, and when deerflies came to bite her wet skin, she could just slide down in the water.

The boat had become a floating forage basket. Its bottom was heaped with arrow-leaf tubers, pond-lily roots, cattail shoots, a catfish almost the size of her leg, and a heap of mussels. In the marshes and these shallow streams she could find enough food to sustain her family until the corn and gardens were ready for harvest. And then there would be the raspberries and currants and blackberries, and she had lived long enough in this valley to know where to find them all. But it was in the water that she preferred to forage, staying cool, avoiding the scratches and stings and the trickling sweats. Sometimes Cut Finger would come with her in the canoe to gather and fish, but this day the girl was back at the village, watching over Yellow Leaf and learning from one of Palonswah's sisters how to make dyes. And so this day, Maconakwa was in the kind of solitude that mothers in a tribe rarely have, and she was reveling in it. She did not have to talk, to guide, to answer questions, to watch all around for her children's safety. It was quiet without the talk, and she could think and see, making her mind as big as the sky or as small as an insect. She paused now and watched dragonflies and damselflies cruise through the air above the arrow leaf. Two damselflies flew by connected together, their dark bodies slim as grass stalks. They must be mating, she thought. Imagine doing that while flying in the air! It was one of the strangest thoughts she had ever had, and when she envisioned herself doing that with Deaf Man drifting through the air over the marsh, it was so funny and exhilarating that she nearly laughed aloud.

Deaf Man was still a husband of unflagging desire, even after all these years. She was glad of that. She reckoned her age at about forty summers now, and the weight of her breasts had pulled them down so that now they swung instead of jounced, and her belly after four childbirths was no longer smooth or flat. But she was still lean and strong and narrow at the waist, and could clench her inner parts in such a way as to make his eyes widen with delight when they were coupling.

But her hopes of giving Deaf Man a son diminished with each moon. Maybe he had had the seed for only two sons in him, and those she had borne him already, which Creator had chosen to take back. If no son comes, she thought, it is because the Master of Life, who is wiser than the wisest of us, does not think this is what we need at this time. Perhaps because of the wars. In the meantime, she and her husband could enjoy what they did, which often was so thrilling that she did feel as if they were soaring in air, like those two mating on the wing. Then someday all her moon-bloods would stop and she would no longer be fertile. That had happened already to Minnow, and her own time would come. We too are ripening crops, she thought.

These things passed through her mind while she stood in the water listening to the whine and rasp of summer insects and watched the linked damselflies vanish among the reeds and cattails. These were the ways one's mind could wander when one was in solitude. It was good to be away from children now and then. But only for a little while. Just a morning or afternoon away from them would make her eager to see them again, to know they were safe and well. Always in the back of the mind was the war danger.

It had been seven moons since the soldiers came down this valley and destroyed the towns in that time of terrible cold. The towns had been rebuilt. Most of the war had moved off beyond

Fort Wayne in the northeast and down the Maumee Sipu. It was said that the Long Knife soldier chief Harrison had built a huge fort at the rapids, and Tecumseh and the English Redcoats had surrounded and besieged it. Tecumseh's warriors had destroyed a whole army of reinforcements trying to reach the fort, but so far as was known, Harrison still held the fort. Maconakwa believed she knew just where that fort stood; she could remember portaging around those rapids almost twenty summers ago, with Flicker, Tuck Horse, and Minnow—little Minnow carrying that big canoe up the path all by herself. Not far from where the battle of the Blown-Down Woods had occurred. She could see it in memory.

Twenty summers, she thought, and it is still the same fighting: the Redcoats and the red men fighting against the bluecoats. What a terrible foolishness. So much pain and death!

If only the Americans would stay in place and leave everybody alone, she thought. But they never stop coming.

At least they had taken their war away from this valley, for a while. Many bands had gone to remote camps, to stay out of war's way.

Beyond the curtain of cattails she heard a burst of noise, as if someone had passed wind. She glanced up and saw a covey of little birds scattering into the air. The sound had only been their wings.

But what had flushed them out like that?

She felt a shiver of apprehension. Here she was alone, at a distance from her town. In the canoe was a knife she used in foraging, but no other weapon. Those birds had been frightened by something.

She started to ease the canoe back toward the creek and into the river, to start back for the village. She had gathered plenty and she was not comfortable here now.

Then she heard a noise she knew well: a horse blowing. It too sounded like a fart, but she knew it was a horse's mouth making that noise.

No one who knew this valley would choose to ride through this marshy ground, she thought. Perhaps a horse has strayed.

So she left the canoe afloat in the arrow leaf and waded toward and into the cattails, being careful not to splash water or rustle leaves. She almost cried out when a thick-bodied, dark-banded water snake came slithering past her knee. Frogs leaped, splashing into the water. She did not know whether she or the horse was alarming them.

Then, through the smell of mud and marsh vegetation, she detected an odor that made shivers run down from her scalp:

Soldier smells!

Crouching, she eased deeper into the cattails.

Something red caught her eye, high up, moving. It was not a redbird. She rose to look over the leaves.

She glimpsed for an instant the dyed-crimson, deer-hair roach headdress of a warrior, perhaps ten yards away, passing to her right, and then it was out of view. In the instant she saw the warrior's profile and bald head, she thought she noticed yellow paint in front of the ear.

Then the soldier smells were stronger and she heard sucking sounds. Rancid sweat. Hooves lifting out of the muck. Something glinted in the sunlight, something metal. More frogs leaped and more birds were darting over. Then she saw a tall, blue soldier hat, a face, another, then many more. The whole wetland beyond the cattail curtain seemed to be moving. Horses blew and she heard men's voices. She shrank down and edged backward, heart thudding.

It was an army. The warrior ahead must have been one of their scouts. It was known that some of Black Hoof's Shawnees and other treaty Indians were riding with the bluecoats because their own tribesman, Tecumseh, was their enemy.

Easing down into the water, she slipped through the arrow leaf toward the canoe. Soon the water was to her chin and she saw the low horizontal shape of the vessel just ahead. She grasped the line at its prow and pulled gently, guiding it toward the creek channel, into the shade of cottonwoods, toward the river.

Only when she was in the green water of the Mississinewa did she ease back alongside, reach with one arm across to the far gunwale, and pull herself into the craft. She knelt in the bottom of the vessel only long enough to tie her skirt around her waist, then grabbed up the paddle, dug it deep into the water, and propelled the craft downstream.

She paddled as hard and fast as she could without splashing. She was thankful that the village was downstream so she did not have to push the heavy craft against the current.

The river was narrow, overarched by limbs of the gigantic sycamores, cottonwoods, and willows. It was like gliding down a green tunnel in some places, broken now and then by dappled sunlight, brushy, sunny glades, and overgrown sites of former villages. She kept the paddle silent, not letting it swash or even dribble, and scanned the riverbank for scouts or soldiers or any sign of their presence. If they had skirted the marsh and gotten onto the river path ahead of her, she would not be able to paddle down to the town without being seen. She was certain she was ahead of the soldiers, but not so sure about their scouts.

A heron wading along the left bank suddenly raised its wings and took off, flying downriver. She had no way of knowing whether it had been startled by her approach or by someone on the river path. She peered all along the shoreline, trying to see through foliage; she listened for hoof steps and horse noises and voices with all her concentration. She paddled hard, silent.

I think I am ahead of them, she thought. I can keep ahead of walking horses, I believe. But not ahead of running horses.

May they be behind me. May they be walking.

She would not have to be very far ahead of them to give a warning in time. The people were very practiced at evacuating ahead of Town Destroyers.

If they were ahead of her, though, she knew she would have to abandon the canoe and run down the riverbank with her warning. She would hate to abandon the canoe with all this food in it. The soldiers would, as usual, slash and burn all the crops, and these gatherings would be needed.

Is there no end to soldiers coming? she wondered, with such a knot of frustration and indignation in her throat that she began weeping even as she paddled. The languid, shady, sun-dappled beauty of the rivercourse swam through her tears.

She was ahead of the soldiers. The People cleared out quickly but without panic. Deaf Man sent scouts up the river, and messengers down the river to warn the other towns.

The scouts came back reporting that there were too many soldiers to even try to ambush them or resist. So the people of the village went up a creek to hide. That night they watched the fires glow.

She had lost count of the times she had seen her homes burned.

When the army was gone, the people returned to the ashes and began rebuilding their huts and cabins. There was nothing to do but rebuild them so they would have shelter in the coming cold months and hope the Long Knives would not come through again this year.

All the unripe corn, beans, and squash, the Three Sacred Sisters, had been cut down, trampled, and burned.

In following days, messengers began coming. The town burners had been everywhere. They had burned all the Miami towns on this river, and on the Eel, and along the great Wabash Sipu. K'tippecanuh, the site of the Prophet's holy town years ago, had been burned again, its third time.

The chiefs presumed that the reason for all this was to crush the Wabash Indians so Harrison would not have to worry about them on his flank while he went north against Tecumseh and the British. Deaf Man said, "I look around me and I see that my People are beaten. This time we did not even fight the soldiers. We moved back and let them do what they came for. Now I fear that will be the way of it from now on. The Miami are warriors no more. Jefferson and Little Turtle wanted us to become farmers and traders and herders like the whites. I see that is all that is left for us—unless Tecumseh and the Redcoats can defeat Harrison in the north."

The message came late in the Hunter's Moon, while red leaves fell.

Tecumseh is dead.

He had been killed by Harrison's army in Canada, while trying to protect the tails of the Redcoats as they ran away from the bluecoats. The British had betrayed their red allies once more.

It was all over. The last free war chief was dead.

"Such trouble that man Tecumseh caused us by his life," Deaf Man said, drawing on his personal smoking pipe and gazing into the cookfire of their newly built lodge.

Most of what Maconakwa had to cook she had gathered from the woods and marshes. Boiling in the pot were roots and acorn meal and fish. She said nothing. She could tell by the look in her husband's eyes that he had things to say.

He went on: "When you found me dying by the Maumee Sipu, you remember, I was still a warrior in my heart. I count almost twenty winters since that day. You are a good wife, Little Bear Woman. You kept me alive then and you have made me content in my heart all the time since then.

"I have been more a husband than a warrior. I have done few of the deeds of a warrior in those long years. But in my heart I was a warrior. You saw that when the soldiers came in the cold, I went and fought them."

She nodded. She stirred in the pot with a wooden spoon. She looked at her sleeping daughters.

He said to her: "Hold on to my hand as I tell you this."

Surprised, she put the spoon in the pot and reached for his hand. He had narrowed his lips and was gazing at the far side of the lodge. His chin was quivering and his eyes were glinting. He took a deep breath through his nostrils and clenched his jaws and blinked. He said:

"As long as Tecumseh lived, I was a warrior in my heart and we had not yet been defeated. Now I am just an old deaf man. As a husband and a father only, I will keep doing my best, in whatever world the white men choose to leave us. Little Bear Woman, I am glad the white men never took you away."

She squeezed his hand in acknowledgment of such rare sentiment. Now with his pipe stem sweeping, he indicated the four winds and the arc of sky overhead. "Wherever the rivers went, we could go. Where the deer were, we could hunt them. From a hilltop we could look all around, and hear the Master of Life say, 'My Children, go wherever you please, and live long and live well, and be free.'

"But now the white man says, 'There is a line on the earth. Do not step across it because this land is mine.' And the lines grow closer and tighter. We are penned in. Soon the lines will cross our graves, and one white man will own our head bones and another will own the bones of our feet.

"Newewah, my wife, listen: Only the wind in the sky remains free. Soon a time will come when our spirits may mount the wind, and go through treetops, over water waves, into clouds.

"Then, Newewah, we will be free of those earth lines as Creator made us to be. I doubt if even Long Knife can draw lines to divide the wind." He looked down at their joined hands, stroking his thumb over the end of the finger that had no nail. "All I hear in my head is like the wind. When we ride it, Newewah, we must keep our hands gripping like this. So we will not become lost from each other in that wind."

"*E heh,* Nenawpamah," she replied. "Yes, my husband. That we must."

He had put aside his little clay pipe, and now he drew his long prayer pipe out from its leather cover, fitted the stem into the bowl, and filled it, saying: "Newewah, now let us smoke together."

"Yes, husband. We will send some smoke into the wind."

PART FOUR

Old Maconakwa

1837–1847

CHAPTER TWENTY-FOUR

"Here it is, Judge Slocum," said the postmaster, handing across the counter a thickly stuffed packet. "It's from Reverend Bowman, down at Lancaster."

"Ah!" exclaimed Joseph. "Sam Bowman. Remember him? Grew up just down the street there. Big temperance fellow in the Episcopal Church now. No doubt sending me more readings on the evil of drink. Well, now, what else has thee for me?"

"Mostly just journals, it looks like. Here."

"Thank thee, and good day."

"Beautiful day. Wish I could leave this office and go fishing, day like this!"

"Well, I don't know," Joseph said, pausing with his hand on the door. "I think the canal has just about ruined the fishing along this stretch of the river. I can remember how it used to be. And I do miss shad roe. The price of progress, I suppose."

"True enough, Judge. But even poor fishing beats the best day in the post office."

Chuckling, Joseph Slocum turned right and walked on Market Street toward the square. The market, Old Ship Zion Meetinghouse, and the courthouse loomed among the great shade trees. The city had been laid out with streets parallel to the riverbank, but the square had been set in like a diamond, at a forty-five-degree angle to all the other streets, which created a striking, angled commons in the heart of town. As he walked past the old Bowman house and angled down the west side of the square, his own grand three-story home, the first brick house finished in the town, came into view beyond the Meetinghouse. Three decades he had dwelt in that house with his wife Sarah, and they had raised five daughters and two sons. Only the youngest daughter, Harriet, now going on eighteen, still lived at home. His oldest daughter, Hannah, the wife of a state legislator, lived across the square. All the other children were married into good families, and Joseph Slocum himself, just past his sixtieth birthday now, loved this old town center, having seen every bit of its development. The courthouse just across the street from his house stood where the old pine-log stockade of Fort Wilkes-Barre had been when his sister Frances was kidnapped by warriors. Though now in the practice of law, Joseph still had the muscular solidity built on him in his early years as a blacksmith and farmer, and felt healthy and strong as a horse even though he was older than all the buildings he saw every day—except his mother's house, which he could see off to the east from his front door, in winter when the foliage was off.

As he crossed the corner of the square toward his house, he remembered sitting at her bedside when she died so quietly—died still believing her daughter Frances was alive somewhere out in the wilds.

Just about ten years ago Joseph had made his last journey out west to seek her. Missionaries near Sandusky had notified him that a white woman, taken during the War for Independence, was living as the wife of an old chief not far from their mission at Sandusky, so Joseph and Isaac had journeyed out to that part of northern Ohio. He could still remember the old chief, Between-the-Logs, a Christianized Wyandot. And he could remember the chief's big old wife, a fine, dignified woman who very well might have been Frances, but was unable to remember her original name. Joseph had believed that she was Frances—until he remembered to examine her hands and found all her fingers to be normal. That journey had taken up much of a season, and finally disheartened him entirely. Brother Isaac had sold his successful hotel in Tunkhannock and moved his family out to that rich land near Sandusky. He lived there still, building another fortune but still using his spare time to track out any clue that might lead to Frances.

Just almost sixty years, Joseph thought. If ever there were a people who don't know when to quit, it must be us Slocums. Even our children, who never knew Frannie, have fancies of going out to find her.

He shook his head. I guess in a way, that's turned out to be one of our rarest treasures in this family, he thought. We have every earthly possession or honor anyone could ask for, but we've got our own unsolved mystery legend as well.

Well, Frannie, wherever thee is, thank thee for teaching us the true Godly lesson of everlasting hope.

A buggy rattled by as he stepped onto the stoop at his front door and its occupant called a greeting to him, which he acknowledged with a wave before recognizing him. Oh, yes. One of the Catlins. Putnam Catlin's son George had gained national fame by traveling in the Far West, for seven or eight years now, painting portraits of the chiefs of the Plains tribes, and writing dispatches to the eastern papers about the life and customs of tribes as yet unaffected by contact with the white race. Joseph had read some of those accounts with deep fascination—not just because he remembered young Catlin, but also because the man was perhaps the only fellow from Wilkes-Barre who had traveled even farther among Indians than he himself had. Much farther, in fact. Joseph Slocum and his family had taken heart from George Catlin's writings, because he spoke often of the kindness and hospitality the Indians everywhere showed him. Years among them alone, without a military escort, and he had not only never been harmed, he had never even been allowed to go hungry. His accounts confirmed what had been written by Lewis and Clark a generation earlier, and it was a profound comfort to the Slocums to believe that their long-lost Frances lived, or had lived, among a race of people who were hospitable, generous, and, when left alone, relatively cheerful and peaceable.

When he pushed open the heavy front door, his ears and nose told him that all the life in the house was presently in the kitchen: bread baking, and the sound of women's voices. Harriet appeared, pretty despite her plain garb, and executed her little, smiling half curtsy with which she always greeted family members. "Hello, Papa."

"Hello, Harriet. Thee's baking, eh?" Although some branches of the Slocum family had drifted away from the Quaker forms, Joseph and his family had not, and were reserved, not given to hugs and touching. Enough affection could be conveyed by a cheerful countenance and a warm and lilting voice, day by day; when a real need for support or condolence arose, a tight embrace and a caressing hand was then much more eloquent, from having not been commonplace.

"Bread *and* pies," she said.

"Ah, I'll come out." The big house was gloomy, and the kitchen had south window light as well as aromas. He hung his black hat on the hall tree and followed her into the kitchen. There was his wife Sarah, crimping pie crust, and idling near the table was his ever-hungry son Jonathan, twenty-two years old, visiting at home. He had been born after the War of 1812 and given the name of the deceased first son.

Joseph, taking a chair, said, "I've something here from Samuel Bowman, remember him?" He laid the journals on part of the table that was clear of flour and dough and opened the packet. It held a page of the *Lancaster Intelligencer*, and a handwritten note from Reverend Bowman, saying that a printed letter, surely of great interest, had appeared in a special edition of the paper devoted mainly to temperance documents and thus had come to his attention. Although some Slocum brothers operated distilleries, Joseph did not, and so he heard occasionally from the reverend. Samuel Bowman said he could not explain why the printed letter, dated two years ago, had only just appeared.

Joseph set aside the letter, opened the newspaper page, and scanned it until his eye fell on the right place. He read for just a moment, straightened in his chair, and said, "Oh my! Harriet, would thee please get a cup of tea for me?" Responding to the tenor of his voice, Sarah, Harriet, and Jonathan looked up at him from what they were doing.

The letter had been addressed originally to the postmaster of Lancaster.

LOGANSPORT, INDIANA, Jan. 20, 1835

Dear Sir:

In the hope that some good may result from it, I have taken this means of giving to your fellow citizens—say the descendants of the early settlers of the Susquehanna—the following information; and if there be any now living whose name is Slocum, to them, I hope, the following may be communicated through the public prints of your place:

There is now living near this place, an aged white woman, who a few days ago told me, while I lodged in the camp one night, that she was taken away from her father's house, on or near the Susquehanna River, when she was very young—say from five to eight years old, as she thinks—by the Delaware Indians, who were then hostile toward the whites . . .

Dear Lord, Joseph thought, swallowing hard, let us not raise false hopes again. I'm too old. . . .

But the next paragraph already had him:

She says her father's name was Slocum; that he was a Quaker, rather small in stature, and wore a large brimmed hat; was of sandy hair and light complexion and much freckled; that he lived about half a mile from a town where there was a fort; that they lived in a wooden house of two stories high, and had a spring near the house.

He could remember all that from his own childhood, except the details of his father's description.

"What is it, Joseph? Something about your sister?"

"Yes," he said. "But let me read it through myself here first. There's something about it rings of a hoax."

She says three Delawares came to the house in the daytime, when all were absent but herself, and perhaps two other children; her father and brothers were absent working in the field. The Indians carried her off, and she was adopted into a family of Delawares, who raised her and treated her as their own child . . .

Joseph's suspicions were roiling. It's too pat, he thought—as if written by someone who's heard the story from our family, or read it. How could she have told all this detail after sixty years? How could she speak English well enough to speak of "freckled complexions" and "a large brimmed hat"? He had been disappointed too often on this matter to feel as excited as he should feel.

What might someone who knows this story hope to gain by hoaxing us? he wondered. It's known that we're well off.

But why would someone up to a thing like that send this letter to a town a hundred miles down the river instead of to Wilkes-Barre itself? He put his finger on the line about the Delawares who had adopted her.

They died about forty years ago, somewhere in Ohio. She was then married to a Miami, by whom she had four children;

two of them are now living—they are both daughters—and she
lives with them. Her husband is dead; she is old and feeble, and
thinks she will not live long.

   These considerations induced her to give the present history
of herself, which she would never do before, fearing that her
kindred would come and force her away. She has lived long and
happy as an Indian, and, but for her color, would not be suspected of being anything else than such. She is very respectable
and wealthy, sober and honest. Her name is without reproach.

The warmth in his soul from that paragraph told him he was
putting more faith in this remarkable communication than he
would have liked to do. But . . . a "wealthy" Indian?

   "Jonathan," he said, "would thee kindly go to my escritoire and
fetch those treaty maps, and while I finish this, see if thee can
locate a place in Indiana called Logansport." He had over the
years spent a good sum on maps of the ever-changing western ter-
ritories and states—wherever Frances conceivably might be—and
thought he remembered a Logansport, near the forks of the River
Wabash. Not far from old Fort Wayne, if his memory served.

   She says her father had a large family, say eight children in
all—six older than herself, one younger, as well as she can
recollect; and she doubts not there are yet living many of their
descendants, but seems to think that all her brothers and sisters
must be dead, as she is very old herself, not far from eighty.

"Oh, my," he groaned. "No, not that old."
"What, Joseph?"
"Oh, this is so . . ."

   She thinks she was taken prisoner before the last two wars,
which must mean the Revolutionary war, as Wayne's war and
the late war have been since that one. She has entirely lost
her mother tongue, and speaks only in Indian, which I also
understand . . .

Joseph nodded. That answers one doubt, he thought.

   Her own Christian name she has forgotten, but says her
father's name was Slocum and he was a Quaker. She also recol-

lects that it was upon the Susquehanna River that they lived, but don't recollect the name of the town near which they lived. I have thought that from this letter you might cause something to be inserted in the newspapers of your country that might possibly catch the eye of some of the descendants of the Slocum family, who have knowledge of a girl having been carried off by the Indians—This they might know from family tradition. If so, and they will come here, I will carry them where they may see the object of my letter alive and happy, though old and far advanced in life.

I can form no idea whereabout upon the Susquehanna River this family could have lived at that early period, namely, about the time of the Revolutionary war, but perhaps you can ascertain more about it. If so, I hope you will interest yourself, and, if possible, let her brothers and sisters, if any be alive—if not, their children—know where they may once more see a relative whose fate has been wrapped in mystery for seventy years, and for whom her bereaved and afflicted parents doubtless shed many a bitter tear. They have long since found their graves, though their lost child they never found. I have been much affected with the disclosure, and hope the surviving friends may obtain, through your goodness, the information I desire for them. If I can be of any service to them, they may command me. In the meantime, I hope you will excuse me for the freedom I have taken with you, a total stranger, and believe me to be, sir, with much respect,

Your obedient servant,
GEO. W. EWING

When at last Joseph had read through the letter twice and gone back through particular passages several times, he laid the paper upon the table, where it was snatched up by Jonathan, who started reading it aloud to the others while Joseph searched the Indiana map for Logansport. Yes, there it was, where the Eel River flowed into the Wabash. Breads and pies were forgotten; there were teary eyes, and head-shakings and sighs, and some little arguments over facts and dates. Joseph could see that his wife Sarah was balancing herself between joy and apprehension for another of his long absences. "I assure thee, I'll not be going that far until I'm somewhat more convinced than I am yet," he said.

"If thee does go, Father, may I go with thee?" asked Harriet.

"We'll discuss that as we work this out, the whole matter. Jonathan, before we get swept away by foolish yearning, let's ascertain—well, one thing, let's find out, if we can, why that letter was two years and a half getting into the *Intelligencer*. And we ought to write to that George Ewing, and get some more confirmation. If nothing else, let him know that the Slocums have finally heard from him! He's probably given up or forgot by now!"

"Oh, yes, indeed!" Jonathan exclaimed. "I tell thee, Father, whoever he is, he certainly seems a kindly and intelligent fellow! He says he lodged a night in her camp. Suppose he's an Indian agent, or a trapper, or trader, or something?"

"So well-spoken, I doubt he's a trapper . . ."

"Imagine," Harriet exclaimed, "having an aunt who lives in an Indian camp!"

"Thee's silly, Harriet," said Sarah. "What I like is, 'sober and respectable and without reproach.' "

"Well," snorted Joseph, "what else would thee expect of a Slocum?"

"Son," Sarah said, "on that map, see how far that place is from Sandusky. Or from Centerville, where Mary lives."

Jonathan rustled paper, scanned the sheet quickly, put his thumb on it one way and another, and said, "About two hundred miles—no more than that from either place."

"Well," she said, "it would make sense for somebody that close to Indiana to go and investigate her, doesn't thee think?"

"Oh, I'm sure Isaac will want to go there from Sandusky as soon as he knows of this," Joseph said. "But I could get there about as soon as mail would reach him. It's not the same hard trek it used to be from here, with the canal boats and steamboats and all." He paused and sighed deeply. He looked down at his hands, which were clasping each other firmly but still trembling. This had been such a giddy flurry of talking that he had hardly been able to take stock of his feelings.

"Son," he said to Jonathan, "I'll see if Sam Bowman can learn why that letter was delayed two years. I do believe we should attempt to write to that kind gentleman Mr. Ewing and find out whether that feeble old woman has survived through all that delay. Before we go running off into the wilderness, we ought to know that. Now I . . . I think we need to let the nieces and nephews know a little about this. . . . If thee doesn't mind, I think I could go meditate awhile . . . pray that she's still alive. Oh, it's a pity, isn't it, that

Giles and Judith, and Ebenezer and Benjamin, aren't with us anymore, to hear this happy news?" They had all dropped away over
the years, Benjamin most recently, passing just three years ago. Of
the ten children of Jonathan and Ruth Slocum, only four were
left—or, if the old woman in Indiana was Frances—and if she had
survived since that Mr. Ewing wrote his letter—then there were
five. He paused, leaning with one hand on the kitchen doorjamb.
"And if only Mama knew! . . . Ah, well, I guess she does, doesn't
she, if all our religion's true?"

"Joseph," Sarah said, "is thee well?"

"Yes, I . . . I just need to be alone a little while . . . and let my
heart catch up with my mind, or my mind with my heart,
whichever it may be."

He looked back at the three of them, his wife, son, and
daughter, each one's face tinged with the emotions this moment
had wrought. But not a one of them had ever seen Frances; they
had known her only as a family legend.

And even I, he thought, even I don't really remember her . . .
just through the story, same as they. . . . But she is my sister. And I
promised Ma.

                                    WILKES-BARRE, PA. Aug. 8, 1837

GEO. W. EWING, ESQ.,
Dear Sir:

At the suggestion of my father and other relations, I have
taken the liberty to write to you, although an entire stranger.

We have received, but a few days since, a letter written by
you to a gentleman in Lancaster, of this State, upon a subject of
deep and intense interest to our family. How the matter should
have lain so long wrapped in obscurity we cannot conceive. An
aunt of mine—sister of my father—was taken away when five
years old, by the Indians, and since then we have only had
vague and indistinct rumors upon the subject. Your letter we
deem to have entirely revealed the whole matter, and set everything at rest. The description is so perfect, and the incidents
(with the exception of her age) so correct, that we feel confident.

Steps will be taken immediately to investigate the matter,
and we will endeavor to do all in our power to restore a lost
relative who has been sixty years in Indian bondage.

                              Your friend and obedient servant,
                                        JON. J. SLOCUM

Joseph's lifetime of disappointments in this matter cautioned him to keep his excitement controlled, but his wife and daughters were in a tizzy. They were already rearranging the judge's residence to accommodate an elderly woman. Presuming that Frances would be unaccustomed to stairs, and probably rheumatic at her age, they intended to make over a first-floor parlor into a sleeping room, close to the warmth of the kitchen and with a direct exit to the privy. "She will be accustomed to a fire, of course," Hannah said, "though she shall have to get used to hard coal instead of sticks and twigs, I suppose." Harriet anticipated evenings spent with the old Indian aunt, as she was already calling her, learning each other's language and hearing tales of the Indian wars and secrets of Indian magic.

"And won't she be delighted to come into a Friends household where a woman's word weighs as much as a man's!" Harriet exclaimed. "She's probably been aught but a beast of burden and a slave to menfolk out there."

"Hmph! Like most *white* women we know in this world," Hannah remarked. Her husband was not a Quaker, and her life was a quiet struggle to keep her personal rights from being plowed under by her husband the assemblyman, who had simply not been raised to know better. Quaker dominance of the state government had faded after the Revolutionary War, which didn't help Hannah in her determination to make herself heard. She wanted to go with her father if he went to Indiana to see the old woman, and knew after eleven years of marriage that if she were to get leave from her husband to go, she would have to begin persuading him now.

"Dear ones," Joseph interjected with a smile, having overheard, "have I never told thee that in most of the Indian tribes I've met, the women have fully as much authority as the men, even in such matters as war and governing?"

"They have?" Hannah cried. "Now that is a wondrous good thing! Maybe I ought to go out there and stay! They must be more civilized than Pennsylvanians!"

While the family awaited a reply from the kind stranger George Ewing, the mystery of the long-delayed letter was solved by correspondence to Lancaster.

The postmaster at Lancaster to whom the letter had been addressed was in actuality postmistress, one Mrs. Mary Dickson, who at that time had been also owner of the newspaper called the

Intelligencer. Evidently finding the letter unworthy of publication, she had laid it aside, or perhaps lost it, among inconsequential papers at the newspaper office. Two years later the newspaper had been bought from Mrs. Dickson by an enterprising young editor named John Forney, who, discovering the letter, had deemed it important and published it, in that temperance edition that had caught the attention of Reverend Bowman.

Hannah Bennett's campaign for approval to go west, meanwhile, was failing, partly because there was as yet no indication that the "old Indian aunt" was still alive. And as the summer was growing long, the prospect of having to return in fall weather finally caused the family to agree that only Joseph would go—and perhaps Isaac and Mary from Ohio—and depending upon what was found, the younger woman might go in the next good season, perhaps with her sister to help bring the old woman home then. Joseph's daughters thus resigned themselves to staying in Wilkes-Barre and making preparations. In the meantime, the Wilkes-Barre newspaper had got wind of the story and printed an account of it, evoking many yarns and recollections from longtime citizens who had nearly forgotten the tragic story in those sixty years since, but suddenly were gifted with total and vivid recall. Some remembered that the boy kidnapped with her, Wareham Kingsley, had been among captives repatriated after the war and had moved to Rhode Island. Such details added much poignancy to the story, and it was one of the main topics in the valley that summer.

And it was in the midst of all that excitement that there arrived at the post office Mr. Ewing's reply to Jonathan's letter. A messenger came running to Joseph's house with it.

LOGANSPORT, IND., Aug. 26, 1837
JON. J. SLOCUM, ESQ., WILKES-BARRE,

Dear Sir:

I have the pleasure of acknowledging the receipt of your letter of the 8th instant, and in answer can add, that the female I spoke of in January, 1835, is still alive; nor can I for a moment doubt but that she is the identical relative that has been so long lost to your family.

I feel much gratified to think that I have been thus instrumental in disclosing to yourself and friends such facts in relation to her as will enable you to visit her and satisfy yourselves more fully. She recovered from the temporary illness by which she was afflicted about the time I spent the night there in January, 1835, and which was, no doubt, the cause that induced her to speak so freely of her early captivity.

Although she is now, by long habit, an Indian, she will doubtless be happy to see any of you. Should you come out for that purpose, and should it so happen that I should be absent at the time, show this letter to James T. Miller, of Peru, a small town not far from this place. He knows her well. He speaks the Miami tongue and will accompany you if I should not be at home. Inquire for the old white woman, mother-in-law to Brouillette, living on the Mississinewa River, about ten miles above its mouth. There you will find the long lost sister of your father, and, as I before stated, you will not have to blush on her account. She is highly respectable, and her name as an Indian is without reproach. Her daughter, too, and her son-in-law, Brouillette, who is part French, are both very respectable and interesting people. As Indians they live well, and will be pleased to see you. I may be absent, as I propose starting for New York in a few days, and shall not be back until some time in October. But this need not stop you; for, although I should be gratified to see you, yet it will be sufficient to learn that I have furthered your wishes in this truly interesting matter.

There are perhaps men who could have heard her story unmoved; but for me, I could not; and when I reflected that there was, perhaps, still lingering on this side of the grave some brother or sister of that ill-fated woman, to whom such information would be deeply interesting, I resolved upon the course which I adopted. In this it seems, at last, I have not been disappointed, although I had long since supposed it had failed. Like you, I regret that it should have been delayed so long.

As to the age of this female, I think she herself is mistaken, and that she is not so old as she imagines herself to be. Indeed, I entertain no doubt but that she is the same person that your family have mourned after for more than half a century past.

Your obedient humble servant,

GEO. W. EWING

CHAPTER TWENTY-FIVE

Maconakwa sat in a chair in her log cabin holding one hand in the other in her lap and looked at the gray-haired white man before her, and she was troubled and suspicious. His face was full of so much emotion that he seemed almost on the verge of tears. To her this made no sense, a visiting stranger acting like this.

The interpreter, Miller, who sometimes came with the fur trader Ewing, had brought this stranger here. This white stranger was saying something in English and Miller was translating it into Miami, and what she was hearing she did not believe. Miller said in Miami:

"This man says to tell you his name is Isaac and he is your brother. He came from over by the Sandusky to see you."

She held her hands firmly to keep them from trembling and kept her jaws clenched and stared at the stranger, determined to show nothing of her feelings, which at this moment were mostly fear. She said to Miller, "I have no brother by Sandusky."

I wish Brouillette were here, she thought. I wish Palonswah were here. His advice is always good. I do not trust this. It is another white man trick. They are trying to get the last of my land. That's what they always want and they will tell you any lie to get it. She could remember that some twenty summers ago an American general named Cass had made a land-taking treaty with old Peshewa Richardville, which promised that the Miami People could keep lands on both banks of the Wabash Sipu from the mouth of the Salamonie to the mouth of the Eel River, south of the Potawatomi lands; for that the white government built the Miami People a mill southwest of the town of Wabash. That treaty had

481

promised the Miamis they could stay there forever. Forever had
lasted eight more summers, until Cass and another general named
Tipton made another treaty that took all the Miami lands in
Indiana north and west of the Wabash Sipu.

After that followed fourteen more treaties that had eaten away
the Potawatomi lands farther north and west. Everything Tecumseh had predicted had come true. Now the Miamis had nothing
left but a square tract south of the Wabash Sipu, and now here was
a white man she had never seen before, who seemed to be lying
and was very eager, and so this was probably the beginning of
another trick to take more land. He had used the name Slocum,
and that was a very clever trick. She had told that name only to
Ewing, whom she had been foolish enough to trust. She now
wished she had never been sick enough to tell him that name, but
she had, and now they were using it as a confusing trick and she
could really understand now why all her People, both Lenapeh
and Miami, had advised her never to let her *wapsi* name slip out to
any white people.

"He is trying to tell you, Grandmother," said young Miller,
"that he is your brother, named Isaac Slocum. He wonders why
you do not seem pleased to see him, now that he finds you after so
long. He wishes you would answer." The white man was nodding
eagerly as Miller translated.

Do I remember somebody named that? she thought. She had
heard the white man name Isaac now and then, around the trading
posts. But if she had had a brother named Isaac, he was too far
back in the mists of old memory for her to remember the name or
the person.

That is cunning, she thought, pretending to be someone from so
long ago that one could not know his face.

It was a hot and damp day, and the September daylight was
bright where it fell through the trees. Here in her log house it was
gloomy and close, the only light coming from the door in the
middle of the riverside wall and the two windows with their shut-
ters open. She would have liked to go outside where a breeze
moved, but she did not choose to suggest that because if she did
go out, this white man might just take over her house. She said to
Miller, "I do not want to talk to this white man without my son-in-
law Autumn Brouillette here, or Palonswah Godfroy."

Miller did not translate that, although the white stranger looked
to him expectantly. This stranger seemed to have much patience

but no ability to see that he was not welcome. Maconakwa did not like to be inhospitable, and she always welcomed and fed travelers who came by, Indian or white, for her home was on a well-used trail that led from Ohio to the Wabash trading posts. White man Conner's trading store was a few miles up the river, and on the Wabash Sipu near its mouth was the largest trading post of them all, the one owned by Palonswah. Down near the Seven Pillars bluff were the Stinking Springs, whose waters were medicine. So Maconakwa and Deaf Man had built this solid log house here, with a peaked shake roof of the white men's style, a big enough house to feed travelers and let them sleep if they had no other place, and had never charged their visitors, as the white men did in their inns—they sell even their hospitality! she thought.

Even after the death of her beloved husband some six summers ago, Maconakwa had continued to welcome his old acquaintances, Indian or white, as well as strangers. She had even given food and drink to old soldiers who, she knew, had long ago been among those who burned the towns and killed horses and captured the women and children of the villages, back in those wars. Those wars had been long ago finished, and white men who came in peace were entitled to food and drink and rest, if they needed them. Only a few truly bitter and angry people, like Minnow, had remained hard-eyed and inhospitable to whites. Minnow had once cut a trader's cheek with a knife. And then her daughter had gone off with a white man, one of the canal builders, and since then old Minnow had grown so hateful that she would not go within speaking distance of *wapsituk*.

There were simply so many white people around now that it was hard to live many days at a time without encountering them. There were far more of them along the Wabash Sipu now than there were Indians; probably there had never been as many Miamis along here as there were whites now. The little reservation was like an island of Miami families in a sea of white people. One could hardly live anymore without some of what they called "dollars."

No, this was not the way she usually treated white people, and Maconakwa could see that young Miller was puzzled to see her so cold and hard. But this man had just put her on her guard at once. He was not just a passing-through white man, but someone who had come here earnestly wanting something of her and apparently willing to make the most outrageous lies to get it. She was sure all her brothers and sisters were dead, back in the East, and this man did not in any way resemble any Slocum person she remembered. Her memories were very cloudy, but she believed that if she were to see a Slocum now, something familiar would touch up pictures in her memory.

The only man she had ever seen in her Slocum family as old as this man had been a grandfather. She could not remember clearly the appearance of that grandfather, but it was not like this tall gray-hair standing nervous before her almost shining with his eagerness. This man just did not touch her memory at all.

Impatient, Maconakwa thought of offering coffee and corn bread with maple syrup, as she would have to any visitor, in hopes that after such refreshment he would be ready to go away. She unclasped her hands and slapped them softly twice on her knees, leaned forward to get up—then saw that the man was staring at her hands with wide eyes.

He reached for her hands, saying something. She recoiled against the back of the chair, turning and clasping her hands at the bosom of her calico blouse, over her medicine bag, afraid he was going to grab her arms and put her out of her house. She could not get this fear out of her mind, and she was not going to let him do it. But she heard Miller saying:

"Old Grandmother, he asks respectfully just to look at your hands! Please be kind to your brother!"

"Ah, you believe what he says, hah?"

"He will not hurt you. That I believe."

She inhaled long through her nostrils, keeping her jaws clenched, and with a scowl extended her hands. Gently, with one of his big, thick working-man hands, he took her left one and looked at it by the light from the open door. His touch was so easy and harmless, she realized with embarrassment that she had been acting like a frightened, unreasonable old woman.

"How came thee by that hurt finger?" the man asked in English, and Miller translated.

She looked at the nailless index fingertip that hurt in cold weather. She could remember. "Long ago my brother with a hammer struck it. He did not mean to hurt me. A child mistake."

Miller translated, and she watched with amazement the sweetness of expression that diffused over the stranger's face. His eyes looked up at her face, eyes shining, and on his lips was a smile as tender as a mother's over her baby.

"Ah, yes! I know," he said. "I think 'twas Ebenezer did that!"

Miller translated, and something turned in Maconakwa's bosom. *Ebenezer.* That was a strange name, but it made a memory. For an instant she could almost see the narrow face of a boy, the one who had done this with the hammer, and the awful look that had come over that face when she screeched with the pain.

Not this one. This one said his name was Isaac.

The man was saying something rapidly and fervently, and seemed very happy. Miller said, "He tells you that he knows you are his sister because of the hammer on the finger!" The stranger turned and talked rapidly to Miller, who said then: "He hopes you will be remembering. He is sorry he does not please you by being here. He will go back to the inn in town and wait there until another brother and a sister come. Then they all three would like to come and visit with you together. He says they should be here in days. He could not wait for them but wanted to see you today. Now he is satisfied you are his sister, and wishes permission to see you again when they come with him."

"Tell him," she said, trying not to show the wistful confusion that she was beginning to feel, "tell him when he comes next, I will have my daughters here, and Brouillette. And Palonswah maybe. I like to know what Palonswah thinks of such people coming and saying these things. Miller, I do not trust white people. You may tell him that if you wish, so he will understand why my eyes are covered like the snake's. But I will see him when he comes back with them. Maybe I will feel better when his sister is here with him. Now, please take him to town. I need to think by myself."

When they had gone down the trail and their horses were out of sight, Maconakwa walked out of the log house with a walking stick and went up onto the rise where the burial ground lay safe above the floodplain. Here on the grassy knoll, which her son-in-law Brouillette mowed for her with a scythe at least twice a summer, stood three tall, slender poles made of saplings of cedar. At the top of one hung the frayed, graying remnants of red and black ribbons. Wind and weather had reduced the cloth to almost nothing in the six years since it had been raised to mark Deaf Man's grave. By a short loop of tarnished silver wire there hung from the same place the ragged quill of an eagle feather, his mark as a war chief. Deaf Man had long before his death given over those duties to Palonswah, being too old and deaf to continue with them. She looked up at the shreds, which stirred slightly in the evening breeze. How she missed her old husband! Such a life they had shared. They had watched the once vast domain of his Miami people be pared away in treaty after treaty. They had raised their daughters to have hope and honor and kindness and good humor. They had begun their marriage in domed *wikwams* covered with bark and mats among dozens of similar *wikwams* under the shade trees, and ended with a rectangular two-room log house on a piece of land that looked like a white man's farm, with zigzag rail fences, their daughters' cabins nearby, with more than a hundred horses, large fields of corn and pasture, and a great herd of beef cattle.

It had all changed from the old ways when the Miami people had lived together in villages, when they had all worked together to plant the Three Sacred Sisters, when they had found and grown all their foods and medicines in Mother Earth with the blessing of Mother Corn. Now behind everything there was the spirit of "dollars" and trade. It had become this way because there were not enough lands or game animals left. Maconakwa and Deaf Man, like the rest of the people, had trapped animals and sold their pelts until there were few animals left. They had gathered and sold ginseng and goldenseal and sassafras. She had made and sold buttons and then brooms, and then chairs, the kind Tuck Horse made.

Now the Miami people all had mirrors and pistols and utensils and metal hoes and shovels. They had metal axes, which made it too easy to cut down trees; even the lives of trees were wasted now to get more white man goods or money.

Now the People had tin lanterns and saws and scissors, and wore clothes made of calico cloth that had to be bought. And they drank whiskey that needed to be bought. The People had grown selfish with these goods, and did not share and give away as they had in the old times. Somehow it was easier to give away things one had made than things one had bought.

Now the money came not so much from furs and handmade goods as from a thing called "annuities." It was money the *wapsi* government gave the chiefs for land. The man Ewing was always in the place called Washington arranging for more land to be sold. Maconakwa had only a vague idea of how all that was done. She knew that the former Long Knife general named Tipton was a friend of Ewing, and Tipton was the Indian agent at Logansport. The annuity money came from Washington through Tipton, and much of it got into Ewing's pockets. She knew that Ewing arranged for clearing and plowing of lands along the Mississinewa Sipu and that the work was paid for by annuity money meant for the Miamis. She knew that when Miamis got in debt for trader goods, Tipton and Ewing got their lands. Another man who was called the governor of Indiana was also a friend of Tipton, and that governor wanted the Indians out of the way so white men could have all the land. Palonswah had explained much of it to her, but some things he would not say because he too was selling his people's lands. He had said it was not simple for Ewing, who wanted to make money both from trading and from land, and so he wanted the Miamis to stay and go at the same time. And Chief Peshewa Richardville knew how hard it was for the white men to make their schemes work, so he squeezed as much money as he could from them for the lands he sold.

To think of all this made Maconakwa shut her eyes and shake her head, and she was always afraid that some trick would be done to her by those clever people and she would lose her home, as so many others had. She wanted to trust Palonswah and Richardville, because she knew they did love their people. Many who had lost their lands had gone to live on Palonswah's land and Richardville's land, and the chiefs spent much of their wealth supporting them. It was mainly on those chiefs' lands that enough Miamis could stay together to do the old sacred ceremonies. The Bread Dance and Green Corn and thanksgiving ceremonies were held in lesser ways than they had used to be, shorter, and with some of the words wrong and movements left out as the old people died and the younger ones forgot, but at least those chiefs still provided safe places where councils and ceremonies could be done. The People were being changed, little by little doing as the white men did.

Deaf Man had remained as much an Indian as he could, leaving the management of his property, the trading, the sale of beef, to Maconakwa and Brouillette, while he provided for his family as a Miami man should: by raising horses and hunting, almost to the day of his Crossing Over. She could remember times when he had ridden out on his favorite hunting horse, forgetting to take off her bell because he could not hear it, then returning all grouchy because he could find no game, complaining that the whites had scared it all away. Brouillette still liked telling that funny story, in a fond way. Brouillette and Deaf Man had been content with each other; Brouillette had bestowed upon him the help and affection that his own two sons had not lived to give Deaf Man.

Those other two poles standing on the burial place marked the sons' graves. They had been dead so long that not a shred of the ribbons remained on their markers. If the poles had been other than red cedar, they would have rotted and fallen by now.

Maconakwa stood among the graves and tried to calm her spirit.

She had not wanted to believe that the gray-haired visitor was her brother; that was too troubling. But his knowledge of the finger accident so long ago had virtually convinced her, although he might have known it by hearsay somehow.

And another suspicion was beginning to enter her mind: that what he wanted so fervently might not be her land, but her return to her family in the white people's world. All the captives had been ordered returned long ago. That general so long ago, Wayne, had demanded it.

She tried to imagine how things were planned and conceived in the white men's great councils far away. She knew they were incredibly cunning, and that their great councillors must be men of crafty genius, because the things she had seen done by them to the Miami people could not have been devised by ordinary minds.

I was born with a white person's brain, she thought. If I were one of those councillors, what might I think up for an old Miami widow who was supposed to go back there but instead stayed with the Indians and has nice land they would like to have?

She thought: I might send Colonel Ewing the fur trader to gain her confidence and find out her name is Slocum. Then sell that name to the white Slocums back there. Then send a Slocum to take that widow back East. Then take her land from her because she left it!

E heh! That is the kind of thing the whites would do!

She held her walking stick with her left hand and rubbed that hand with her right, and gazed over her fields, and remembered the evening she had told Ewing.

She had been sick that night and afraid she was going to die, and it seemed to her then that she should not take with her to the grave that lifelong secret—that it might be terribly selfish to leave the Slocum people forever in doubt about the fate of their relative. It had been a bitter cold night, and the man called Colonel Ewing stopped before dark and ate dinner with her family. Being in too much discomfort to sleep, she sat up by the fire long after her family went to bed. And then, although a bed had been made up for him, that Ewing sat up late with her, talking about little things. Sitting so long alone with the white man, she had been taken with a powerful notion that unless she revealed her history, she would find no rest in the Spirit World, to which one must not go burdened with lies. Out of her agitation, she told Ewing that she had something important on her mind and could not die peacefully until she told it. But then she was seized with the old fear that the whites would try to take her away from her country if they knew. So she had rocked to and fro in her chair for a long time before getting the courage to state it. Ewing seemed to have suspected that that was what she was going to tell him, and he had assured her he would protect her from any attempt to separate her from her home or children. And then as she poured out to him all she could remember, she felt as if a huge, crushing weight were floating off of her. After they bade each other good night, she had lain down in her bedding with her pain so diminished that she slipped off into such a long, deep, pure slumber that her illness began to mend by the next day. Then for two years she had wondered and worried what might have come of her confession. She had seen Ewing once since then, and he told her about sending her story back East to be put in printed language of the white people, which left her feeling confused and betrayed for a while—though she had not asked him not to do such a thing—until, nothing happening, she had quit worrying, even thinking, about it. The truth had made her well and had not hurt anything in her life.

Now this Isaac man had come, and her fears had returned.

I did not lie to this Isaac today, she thought. But in a way perhaps I did. I did not tell him the thing he had come so far to hear. So now I am toting the secret again, and it is heavy.

In a distant cornfield she could see her family at work harvesting. They had a tent there. Even though within walking distance of the house, they followed the tradition of staying in the corn until the harvest was done. Brouillette had his oxen team and wagon out there. Maconakwa's daughters and grandchildren were helping. Those harvest camps were happy. Maconakwa could remember how the spirit of corn, Mondahmin, as the Miamis called her, Kahesana Xaskwim to the Lenapehs, could be heard and felt in the corn. Maconakwa regretted being old, with painful hands that kept her from helping with the harvest. If she had been out with her family harvesting, she might not have had to talk to this Isaac person. Miller would have explained to him that the harvest spirit could not be troubled by such business.

But that Isaac would be coming back when his old brother and sister arrived in a few days. The harvest would be done by then, the ears of special corn hung up in bunches by their braided shucks, hung from ceilings where rodents could not get them; much more would be shelled and stored for the winter. And then when all those Slocums came, if Slocums they really were, Cut Finger and Yellow Leaf and Autumn Brouillette would be around her and she would be more at ease with the visitors.

You should not fear them anyway, she told herself. Are they not Quakers?

If they truly are Slocums, she thought, I will not deny who I am. I do not want to bear that secret around again.

But I really wish I had not told Ewing anything. He is one of those who do anything they do for just one reason, and that reason is money. He sends me troubling things, and he will profit by it.

She reached out with her left hand and with her stumped forefinger touched the marker of Deaf Man's grave. "Old husband," she said aloud, "I promise I will not let anyone take me away from our place. When I Cross Over, I will lie beside you as before. I have not forgotten our vow that we will not lose each other even in Crossing Over."

She pinched tobacco powder out of a pouch and sifted it over the graves, then limped off the mound and across the fields of the river bottomland where the leaves of the trees in the copses were reddening and yellowing. The lazy dogs greeted her with wagging tails, without getting up from their sunny places, and she went in the cabin, filled and lighted her clay pipe, went back out and sat in a patch of sunlight by the cabin wall on a hickory splint chair she had made when her hands were still good. She sat among the sunning dogs and listened to the breeze in the treetops and the flowing water of the river and watched her smoke swirl away and the leaf shade tremble on the ground. She thought of her long-ago travels to come to this place, and the longer time she had lived here in war and peace, and she thought that no matter how cunning the white people were, they were no more likely to move her from this home place than to make the Mississinewa go someplace else.

* * *

Joseph Slocum jounced and swayed on the buggy seat, his shoulder now and then bumping Isaac's. Whenever he heard Mary groan in the backseat, he would crane around and give her a sympathetic smile. She was going on seventy, the oldest surviving one of their generation, and had endured an eternity of bouncing and jarring over the ruts and the log corduroy roads of Ohio and Indiana to meet her brothers here.

Joseph felt so good being in the presence of his brother and sister again, and so excited about the end of their lifelong search, that this Wabash Valley seemed like the most enchanted place he had seen in his life. It wasn't rugged and steep like the Susquehanna country, but the placid, misty river and deep soil and the magnificent hardwood trees in their fall splendor seemed like a garden of paradise.

Their young guide, Miller, reined in his horse until the buggy was alongside him and said, "Gentlemen, Mrs. Towne, if you don't mind fording the Mississinewa, we'd do well to stop at Godfroy's trading post before we go on up to your sister's. It'll ease her mind considerable to know he's looked you over. She puts much store by his judgment, y'see."

"Well, lead on then, if it's not too far out of the way," Joseph said, and he flicked the reins as Miller spurred ahead to join his fellow horseman, a young friend named Fulwiler who had come along because of his fascination with the story of this lost sister. Joseph said, "When I think of all the wilderness we all scoured looking for Frannie—and now we find her in a place that's almost as civilized as Wilkes-Barre." He shook his head and chuckled. There were plantations all along the river road.

Isaac pointed to a cluster of cabins, huts, and fields ahead. "They say this was the town where Tecumseh walked in on the Miami Council, just before the war, and tried to whip them up to fight General Harrison. Of course, Harrison burned down the town a time or two during the war, but there's always been somebody living here. Watch for Harrison to run for president again, by the way. He showed pretty strong out here last time."

Joseph laughed. "What's this, a Quaker talking on worldly politics?"

Isaac nodded with a shame-faced smile, then pointed ahead. "There's the mouth of the Mississinewa. Godfroy's store is on the far side."

They rattled and clopped down through the collection of huts, through wood smoke and the sour smells of hide-curing. A few Indians, most dressed in calico, were working or idling outside their dwellings, or off in their cornfields harvesting. There was a forlorn, sullen look about them. Joseph felt reproached for his whiteness. Though some of the Indian men raised a half salute to Miller, they seemed never to look directly at these three somberly dressed elders in the rattling buggy. Still, Joseph felt that he was being studied hard. They went up the Mississinewa a little way and crossed at a riffled place, climbed to an elevated clearing, and entered a fenced compound of log buildings, one very large. Here Joseph stopped the buggy where the young men had dismounted, and the three got down stiffly from the buggy and followed Miller into the store, wending among barrels, counters, stacks of hides and blankets, shelves of tools, stacked bags of meal, saddles, hanging harness, pots and china, coils of rope, and Indian men and women. The big room smelled of pitch and oakum, hides, tobacco, sassafras, smoked meat, tallow. Suddenly the aisle before them was filled with the form of a giant, brown-faced man.

He was majestic and solid, dressed in a long blue calico ruffled shirt with a broad finger-woven sash around his middle, breechclout, leggings, and moccasins. Joseph guessed the man must weigh at the least three hundred pounds. His face, though broad, russet, and jowly, gave no impression of fat-man softness. His eyes were big, dark, intense, and canny.

"Chief Godfroy," said Miller, who seemed a mere slip beside him, "here are Mr. Joseph Slocum of Pennsylvania, Mr. Isaac Slocum of Sandusky, and Mrs. Mary Towne of Centerville in Ohio. They believe that Maconakwa, Deaf Man's widow, is their sister, as Colonel Ewing has told you, I believe, and they have come a long way to meet her."

"E heh," he replied in a resonant bass voice, appraising them so penetratingly that his gaze was almost palpable, then extending a huge brown hand and a half smile—not one of those mocking half smiles that men in Quaker garb were accustomed to receive from ungentle men, merely a reserved half smile, as if the rest of it would be forthcoming when it was earned. "I expected you. Come back to the quieter room, where we may sit and have a few words of understanding, and a refreshment if you like." He turned to lead them back and up toward a sort of office room with hewn puncheon floors and a huge stand-up merchant desk. The room was clean and pleasantly lit by a northern window overlooking not the

little Mississinewa, but the broader Wabash. As he led them in, Joseph found himself admiring the sheer presence of this man— not because he admired physical power, except in terms of the work a strong man could do, but because here was a combination of might, elegance, and self-containment such as he had seldom seen in anyone. Godfroy, he knew, was war chief of the Miami Nation, but in the absence of war he was making himself a great merchant and, Miller had declared, was one of the richest men in the state. Godfroy's cupped hands seemed to row his bulk through the air as he crossed the room. He offered chairs. His thick ebony hair, glossy and full of silver strands, was combed smoothly back around his huge, shapely skull and braided into a thick, neat queue that hung nearly to his waist, and he seemed very clean. His posture was erect and his step light and silent despite his bulk. Joseph Slocum, himself a judge at law, felt as he entered Godfroy's chamber as if he were a humble cipher presenting himself to be appraised for worthiness.

It was apparent that Chief Godfroy already was aware of their mission and some of its particulars, and was prepared to speak as well as listen. He greeted them warmly, lit and offered a pipe all around, which they obligingly put to their lips. Then he congratulated them upon what apparently was the joyous conclusion to a sadness that had lasted for generations. He explained his deep personal interest in and affection for Maconakwa: that she was the widow of a good chief and fine man who had approved him as his successor as war chief, but more important, that she was a woman of courage and honesty, high principles, vast generosity, and devotion to the Creator. All this was heartwarming, but when Joseph glanced at his brother and sister, he saw that little edginess in their eyes that made him sure they were wondering, as he was, what *was* her concept of the Creator by now? It did not seem a proper question to ask Godfroy; better to hear it from her, if their visit with her should permit the discussion of such things. So many Indians had become Christianized in the peace since the last war with England; perhaps she had. It was something Colonel Ewing had not stated in his letters, though they hinted that she was totally an Indian by habit. Now Godfroy had begun talking in earnest, leaning forward in his groaning chair:

"Brothers, if it proves that my old friend is your relative, it will not be easy for her. She has held this in her lone heart so long that it will frighten her to have it known. She will be afraid of anything it might bring. I ask this, as her friend:

"Approach her as if you were going to look at a little four-legged. Go quiet. Do not startle her. Do not get all around her to make her feel trapped. I mean with your bodies or your words. Keep thinking this: whenever whites have come to this valley where she lives, they have burned down her house or taken more land. She is like an animal that has learned that two-leggeds are predators with guns. When it sees a two-legged, it runs.

"You appear to be gentle. I trust that you will not corner her or rush upon her. Do not be surprised if she is timid like a rabbit, or cold and coiled like a snake. Much has happened to her. Her younger daughter is three times married because of whiskey troubles, and Maconakwa is suspicious of your race. Give her ease until she grows used to you."

"Don't thee be cast down or surprised," Isaac said as the wagon swayed and bumped along the riverside path toward Deaf Man's village, "if she doesn't so much as break a smile. She didn't for me, and if thee asked me whether she has so much as a tooth in her head, I couldn't answer because her lips were set tight the whole time I was there."

"Mr. Slocum," Miller called back, "yonder comes her *sober* son-in-law!" Miller was pointing across the fields toward a slender figure coming at an easy canter on a fine-looking bay saddle horse.

"This is, ah, Brouillette?" Joseph called.

"Yes, Brouillette, sir. T'kwakeaw. Means 'Autumn.' "

"Ah, this is good!" Isaac exclaimed. "I was given to understand she wanted to have Brouillette and her daughters at hand when we came. She might not be so timid with them at hand."

"Grand fellow," Miller said loudly over his shoulder. "Couldn't ask for a better Indian."

The man was perhaps in his early forties in age, graceful in the saddle, wearing leggings, a sashed frock coat, and a turban of red cloth whose long tied ends billowed and fluttered like banners over his shoulders as he rode. Joseph thought he had never seen so beautifully wild-looking a horseman ever, and his admiration grew as the man drew closer.

And, best of all, he was smiling. That was a good sign; after Isaac's description of Frances' dour demeanor, Joseph had been worried that their whole reunion might be considered an invasion of her world. This man's dazzling smile at least indicated welcome, though how sincere remained to be seen.

The rider gave the Slocums a hand salute and then wheeled his mount to fall in beside Miller and Fulwiler, and as his horse pranced along the path, he talked cheerfully with them in the Indian tongue. When the wagon forded the Mississinewa again, Brouillette rode behind, keeping an eye on the stability of the buggy, ready to help if anything happened. Then they moved on southeastward on that bank for a short while, until Isaac said, "There it is, our sister's farm."

Joseph loved the look of the place at once. It sat in a bend of the green river, overarched with gigantic cottonwoods and spectacular sycamores whose white limbs spread upward and outward through their yellowing foliage. On the bottomland close to the river stood a few log cabins and sheds and cribs, and on the second level of the bottomland was the main house, two log rooms connected by a breezeway under the same roof, the whole village pleasant and free of undergrowth and dappled with sunlight and shade. Beyond, he saw the open, bright yellow-brown and green of pastures and cornfields, through which snaked picturesque zigzag fences of stacked split rails. Remarkable numbers of horses and cattle grazed in the distance. "By heaven!" Joseph exclaimed. "I was dubious where Mr. Ewing's letter called her a 'wealthy Indian,' but I see now!"

Brouillette took away the saddle horses while Miller helped the elderly Quakers out of the buggy. Then he returned, shook hands with them with small bows, and led them into the house. Joseph was suddenly so wrought up inside that his heart quailed.

There in the clean and fragrant room sat the woman he had been seeking all his adult life; he was sure of it.

She had risen from her chair for the introductions. She was about as tall as Mary. Her posture was not stooped. She was in every regard an Indian woman—except her coloring. The reddish auburn hair, thick with gray, was parted in the middle and slicked back behind her ears to hang in a braid, and from her lobes hung several intricately made sets of earrings. Her wrinkled, weathered face was stoic. Much of its darkness was from massed freckling—a contrast to Mary's protected paleness. Joseph, himself ready to burst out with tears of joy, was almost intimidated by the severity and control in this woman's face. She was every bit as forbidding as Isaac had warned she would be. Joseph was vaguely aware of others standing in the dim background behind her chair and of Brouillette moving about, but at this moment the center of the world was in this space of an arm's length between them, and that space seemed so dense with the power of the moment that if he could have thrown off his reserve and tried to go forward and embrace her, he would not have been able to move through the compressed atmosphere. She looked at him for just a moment, then nodded recognition of Isaac—still without a smile—and then her eyes met with Mary's.

Maconakwa was only half hearing Miller as he made the introductions in first one language and then the other. What had seized her attention was the face of the old woman who stood before her in a dark travel cloak.

This was supposed to be her sister. Even though she could not remember her sister, and even though she had never seen her own mother as an old woman, this face stirred something in her memory. There was a familiar prominence of the jaw muscles, something about the wide-set eyes. Was she remembering her mother's face by looking at this old woman?

Then she knew where she had seen those characteristics: in her own mirror.

The woman's eyes were filling with tears. Maconakwa had to turn away from that sight. She made her way back to her chair, saying to Miller, "Tell them welcome. Daughters, come around and greet these visitors." She realized that she had not even offered them her hand. Well, never mind that now, she thought. They were already busy being introduced to Cut Finger and Yellow Leaf. Both daughters were dressed in their finest, with ruffles and ribbons, earrings, calico blouses almost entirely covered with rows of little silver brooches, embroidered skirts to the ankles, beribboned leggings and quill-worked moccasins beneath. Her daughters were so beautiful, these white people would be impressed, and probably would forget how awkward she had been in greeting them.

She sat down in her chair with all the talk swirling around her. She had tried to prepare her spirit for this meeting. She had prayed all the time since the one called Isaac had been here. Sometimes she had prayed for a certain knowledge that this was her birth family, but mostly she prayed that it would be proven a mistake and they would go away and not trouble her life. It was a good life, and she did not want it changed or complicated by more white people.

Now the introductions were done and her daughters and her son-in-law had eased back around behind her chair and there were no bodies between her and the three old white people, and she had to sit here and watch the agitation they were suffering. These people seemed to have no strength. The brothers would not sit down in the chairs that had been set out, but kept pacing about, wringing their hands, their chins trembling, looking up at the ceiling and sighing, while the old woman named Mary sat with a handkerchief, trying in vain to keep tears mopped off her pale cheeks and red nose, sobbing and snuffling. Maconakwa's heart squeezed at that sight until it hurt, but she just clenched her jaws and would not let tears come to her own eyes. This was terrible. Now even Miller's young friend Fulwiler was going red in the face and starting to leak tears, and he suddenly went gasping out the door into the yard, wiping his sleeve across his eyes. And he was certainly not one of the relatives. Maconakwa turned and glanced quickly at her three loved ones, Cut Finger, Yellow Leaf, and Brouillette. They were beginning to look dazed, but when they saw the set of her face, they braced themselves not to weep.

Every now and then one of the brothers would turn a beseeching face toward her and open his mouth as if to ask something, but then would squeeze his eyes shut and tilt his head back and give a sob and walk around some more. It was becoming too awkward and pathetic to bear.

One should not let something like this happen in one's home, she thought. This shames me! I will have to talk with them!

I suppose I need to know, as much as they need to know. "Miller," she said, "make them sit. I am going to talk about Slocum to them. What is wrong with them?"

"As I understand them, they are hurt because you are cold to them, Grandmother."

"They are strangers, Miller."

"They do not believe that. Do you?"

"I do not know, Miller. Have the men sit and I will tell my life."

Miller said some words and the men turned and sat, one on each side of the white woman. Their souls were in their eyes and they were eager. Seeing the three faces side by side, Maconakwa now was looking not at the different degrees of grayness in their hair or their different postures or their expressions, but at the essential faces, and yes, they now were so obviously old people who had once been children who must have looked all alike, their lives having changed the outsides in various ways. She could not remember the child faces but saw that these were brothers and sister to each other. And perhaps to me, she thought. That notion set her mind to whirling and she was speechless for a while, and at last the man who had not been here before began speaking to her. Miller translated the words.

"Joseph Slocum says, they three have come from several places. They had not seen each other for many years, but each always knew where the others were. You, they have not seen for nearly sixty years. But they always believed that you were alive somewhere. He says that your mother crossed to the Spirit World thirty years ago knowing you were alive, and she made her sons promise never to stop seeking you. The other brothers who searched for you even as far as Canada, they are all dead now. Their names were Giles . . . William . . . Ebenezer . . . Benjamin. Your oldest sister Judith died in Ohio more than twenty years ago . . ." Miller kept pausing as the man called Joseph gave him the names one by one. They sounded familiar, in a vague and haunted way, but she could not envision any faces when she heard the names. The gray-haired man spoke some more, looking intently at her face, and Miller continued. "Your youngest brother, named Jonathan, is still alive, but he lives away even farther east, in New York, and was not well enough to come so far."

The man called Joseph spoke some more, his voice warming and growing more cheerful, and his was a good voice, she thought, and though she could understand few of his words, she thought he might be some kind of an orator or chief among the white people where he came from; now that he was not gasping and rolling his eyes to the ceiling, he was an impressive man.

"He says your father was killed by Lenapeh warriors one moon after you were carried away, and your grandfather with him. And so now, he says, you four in this room, and the one left in New York, are the elders of the Slocum family from your time. All have children who are adults now, and most of them are married and have given them many grandchildren. He says all the Slocums are prosperous; that had they not been, they could not have searched for you so far and so often, or come here now. He says they prayed together when they met in Peru town and thanked God for Colonel Ewing, who was so kind and concerned, and they thanked God for letting them live long enough to come to you at last."

She sat for a long time thinking of all that she had just heard, so long that the white people began to look distressed again. She remembered that white people have a strange sense of hurry and are afraid of silence; she had noticed that when visitors came. So she perceived that her silence was upsetting them. And so she stopped thinking back over the things the man named Joseph had said and forced herself to think how to answer. She said to Miller:

"Tell this man he has spoken well and now I know about Slocums. And tell him these things. My father's name was Slocum, but he did not look much like these people; I can remember him a little. He was Quaker. He wore a wide black hat. The number of my brothers I believe was seven, and two sisters."

She held up her left hand for them to see. "The end of this finger was hammered off by a brother. But not to hurt me. He was making something and I wanted to help him by holding it. I was never angry at him for it." The old people nodded and talked excitedly among themselves. She went on.

"Three Indians came one day when it was cold. They were Lenapeh, whom you call Delaware. They pulled me from under a stairway. There was a boy they took also. He was not a brother of mine. I do not know what became of him. . . ."

Joseph raised a hand and spoke, and Miller translated. "Wareham Kingsley was that boy. He was returned later and told of being kept in a village where you were, but later separated when General Sullivan's army came through. He lived in Rhode Island later and has passed away."

"Yes," she said. "I remember it was when that army came. That was the first of the Town Destroyers. The Lenapeh fled to the Great Falling Water. Niagara. Maybe you have heard of it. It is a sacred place. I was adopted there by Lenapeh elders to be the resurrection of their daughter who was killed by soldiers . . ." She told them of her first marriage, ruined by whiskey, and said, "I do not even yet permit drinking liquor in this family."

"Amen," Joseph said, and his brother and sister repeated it. It was a word that Maconakwa slightly remembered; it meant something like *a ho*!

She then told them of the long and terrible years of being burned out and pushed back, naming each burned town she could remember, and watched the expressions of horror and dismay as they listened. Often they dabbed at tears, shook their heads, moaned.

"Forty summers ago I became married to a Miami war chief. A gun shot in his face made him deaf. He was a kind man and a strong man. He gave me these two beautiful daughters who live close by me and keep me happy. He gave me two sons, but they were babies when they Crossed Over.

"This one, Yellow Leaf, has given me three grandchildren. Her husbands were ruined by the spirit water. It was not her fault what happened to those marriages. It was the white man's drink. Though they have not burned our towns for some years, they still destroy us with that. Perhaps you saw their liquor houses along the road. Twice, soldiers burned my husband's town here, but we rebuilt it better. Here I have had some years of peace. My husband and sons are buried here. I will let no white men take this place. It is a very good place. I have put down my roots in this place, like a tree. I do not want any more treaties that would take it out from under me. I would die at last.

"That has been my life. I have peace now. Brouillette, who stands behind me, husband of my older daughter, he is very good to me. He runs all the outdoors for me. Only he among the Miamis turns the earth with a plow and oxen. He is not too proud to provide all my firewood. He is a good husband to my daughter and does not drink liquor. Only they have no children. I am a widow for six winters. That has been my life. Now you are here. You believe you are my birth family. When white men come, they are after something. What are you after?"

She leaned against the chair back and felt the tightness in her shoulders from saying so much and trying to say it right. With her arms straight and her hands on her knees, she took a deep breath and sighed and waited for Miller to finish translating and watched the faces of the old white people. She felt that her heart should reach out to where they sat, but it was not happening. She did not trust white people, and the question she had asked them was still holding in her heart: What are you after?

It was the first thing the man named Joseph said in his reply: "We are only after *thee*. Thee's always been in our hearts and our prayers even though thy person was lost to us all our lives. Look at us. We are thy flesh and blood, thy brothers and sister! Is that not enough to bring us here? We would have been with thee forty, fifty years ago, had we known how to find thee! What thee's just told us about the capture is just as it happened. We *know* thee's one of us. Our own sister. Born a Slocum. A parent and a grandparent, like us, with, God forbid, not many more years. And we've found thee, by the miracle of a good man's kindness. Mary, Isaac, would thee have a better way of saying this? Sure I'm the only lawyer here, but must I be the only talker?"

Isaac leaned forward in his chair and said, "Sister, we were born Friends, just like thee; we've never hurt the Indians, or anybody. We were not the white men in those armies!"

And while Miller was translating that, using the word Quakers instead of Friends, the white woman called Mary stood up from her chair and extended a hand, almost touching Maconakwa's wrist, and then she said:

"Dear sister! All we're after is thee, as Joseph said. To see the face we've but remembered all this time. To hear thee speak our names again! Can thee just speak our names, dear?"

She remembered two of their names from somewhere far back. "Jo-seph. Mayl ... May ... Mary." She paused and thought. "Isaac."

"And thy own name, sister," said Joseph. "Does thee remember it?"

"Slocum only. Not the other."

"Would thee remember it if thee heard it said, sister?"

With such a melancholy sinking in her breast that it made her sigh, Maconakwa answered, "It is a long time."

Mary said, "Dear, was it Frances?"

"Oh!" Maconakwa shut her eyes. There seemed to be a jump in her heart, an echo in her ears. She bit her lower lip, and when she looked up at old Mary, the woman's form was dimming a little; she felt tears. She blinked and blinked. Something lifted up inside her. *Palan* ...

In far memory she heard the name as it was said by beloved Neepah, so many, many summers ago. *Palanshess*. Like *Palonswah*.

E heh! Palanshess, eh. She tried to pronounce it as Mary had, and her heartbeat quickened, and she could feel that her whole face had eased into a wide smile; she could feel it in her cheeks and lips, the delight of smiling: "Fuh-ran-ses!" she exclaimed, nodding her head.

And Joseph, sitting just in front of her, clasped his hands

together, his own face suddenly gone radiant, and he cried, "Look at that lovely smile! It's like a sunrise!"

Maconakwa stood outside the cabin door waving as the three old people left in their buggy.

The rest of the visit had been cordial. She had proudly made tea in her beautiful teakettle and served it loaded with maple sugar. She gave them corn bread with wild plum conserve, served on china plates she had acquired and learned to use in the last few years. She watched Mary's eyes for signs of approval in the way she did these niceties, and Mary complimented everything. The old Quakers had seemed very tired by their emotions and needed to go back to their inn in Peru town; this day, added to the fatigue of their long journey to Indiana, had worn out the woman even more than the brothers, who were strong for their age. While their carriage could still be heard, Maconakwa picked up some sewing she had been doing before their arrival, a ruffled blue calico blouse that would be a gift for old Minnow, who still lived upriver at Metosinah's Town. She would have to be careful what she told Minnow about all this when she saw her.

Yellow Leaf went to tell her children about the white people's visit. Cut Finger and Brouillette hung close by Maconakwa, and Cut Finger asked whether she was convinced the old ones were kin.

"I believe them to be," she said. "*E heh.* I am satisfied of that."

"Do you like them?" Cut Finger asked.

"Those are good white people. I always did believe the Quaker white people are good. I said so. If all whites were Quaker whites, perhaps we would be living in peace with them all over Turtle Island. I believe the land is big enough for all people, if they are all kind and fair to each other. I believe they never would have sold our People spirit water."

"Will you go to visit them at Peru town tomorrow?"

Maconakwa glanced up from the sewing to her daughter's lovely russet face with its vermilion dot on each cheekbone.

"Perhaps. I will go down to the trading post maybe, to ask Palonswah Godfroy for his thoughts. He knows white people."

"If you go, may I go with you?"

"To the trading post or to Peru town?"

"To both."

"Eh. Ask your husband to saddle horses for us. And for himself if he wants to come."

"We go now?"

"To see Godfroy now. To the town tomorrow, I don't know yet."

Maconakwa could still ride as well as anyone, but she had to mount from standing on a bench because of her knees and hip sockets. There was not much evening left after the white people's visit, but Maconakwa rode at a walk instead of a canter, not wanting to overtake the Slocum carriage on her way to Godfroy's. She did not want them to think she was following them, nor did she want to have to explain why she was going to see Godfroy.

Palonswah led her into his office room while Brouillette and Cut Finger looked at things and talked to people in the store. He acted surprised to see her, but a little amused smile made her suspect that he wasn't so surprised. "I am troubled," she said, then told her of her visitors and of their invitation and wondered whether she should go tomorrow to see them at Peru. "Do you see any trickery in it?" she asked.

He smiled and slowly shook his head. "I met those people. They are certain they are your very kin. Their hearts were full of joy and shyness as they went toward your house. Do you believe you are their sister?"

She sat for a moment with head bowed and eyes clenched shut, too swollen in her heart to speak at once. "*E heh.* I do believe. They have moved my heart. So old, and such a long way. It is this, Palonswah: For all the time I can remember, I have seen white people are after something and cannot be trusted. I . . . how much of my heart can I give to such people? What will they do with my affections if I give them?"

He leaned forward in his chair and it creaked under his bulk. He looked straight into her eyes, nodding, and answered: "They will return them just as much. I believe I could see that in them. I know we have not seen much of it, but some white people will give without tricking. What do you have that they would want to take?"

Yes, she thought, yes! What *could* they really want to take from me? They are rich and old and live far away. By coming so far to me, they were giving to me, not trying to take anything.

"Palonswah, tomorrow I will go and visit with them at their inn."

"Good."

"Nesawsah, brother, thank you for your advice."

He chuckled and said, "I gave none."

That made her smile, then laugh softly, and suddenly all that had been dammed up by her caution overflowed and she was convulsing, her face wet with tears. She felt as if her heart were being bathed. When she was calm again, she said, "I am glad the white people did not see me like that, all crying in the face."

"Were they like that?"

"Yes. The old woman—my sister—was."

He compressed his lips and tilted his head.

"I suppose I should take them a gift," she said.

"You should. That would be a good gift for you to give them," he said, "a face crying with tears, like that."

"Hah! Only if I cannot prevent it!"

"Then if a weeping face is not to be your gift, you will be buying something in my store for them?" He rubbed his hands.

"No," she said with a mocking smile, and got up from the chair.

"Ah, no? A gift that you cannot buy here? Then I suppose you mean to give them a jug of whiskey?"

She swatted at him, but, big as he was, he dodged, and they were laughing when she left.

When the church bell began ringing so close by, the horses almost bolted; with less capable riders, they would have. Maconakwa and her daughters and Brouillette held their mounts under control and rode on up the street, watched by the many well-dressed white people who were in the vicinity of the church. Maconakwa, when the weather was right, could vaguely hear these bells all the way out at her farm but had never realized how powerful their sound was. It hurt her ears, and it was obviously hurting the horses' sensitive hearing even more. They kept starting and prancing at each clap. She held the reins hard and corrected the mare and thought, Even my husband could have heard those noises!

So it was the white people's religious day. She thought of that, how strange it was. As she understood it, they were religious every seventh day, instead of all the time.

The people of the town of Peru were accustomed to seeing Indians. But Maconakwa and her family, in keeping with the special nature of this visit, wore their brightest clothing and silk sashes, and were riding on good saddles, and their bridles were decorated with tufts of dyed horsehair and feathers and jingles. On Maconakwa's breast hung a hammered silver cross as big as a hand. Women on the way to church gaped at the sight of these Indian women riding astride instead of sidesaddle, and their husbands noticed too. Maconakwa knew pretty well how the burgeoning whites and the diminishing Indians perceived each other, all the good ways and all the bad ways. She knew how the whites had got the Miamis addicted to spirit water and then scorned them for their addiction, and how the white traders would hold out a promise called "credit" and keep stretching it until they had an Indian's belongings and soul in their hands. She knew how the white men's wives considered the Indian women inferior even though they themselves were rather helpless in most matters and could not even vote or speak in their husbands' councils. Most of the town white women were disdainful of the "squaws," as they called them, but at the same time feared them and envied them. Maconakwa had heard and seen much of all that, even though she stayed at her farm most of the time and let Brouillette do the town trading and cattle selling. And the white town women's attitude toward Maconakwa herself was even more complex because most of them knew she was of white blood. She knew that many of the town women referred to her as the "Indian queen" because of her wealth and her power to manage her own affairs, with the dashing Brouillette working for her and dedicated to her well-being.

But most of the white town women did on certain occasions and for certain purposes treat the Indians kindly, and there were a few who were always honest and kind toward them.

And the attitudes of the town men toward the Indian women was in its way even more complicated, and sometimes it made her angry while other times it made her laugh.

Therefore, as Maconakwa and her daughters and her son-in-law rode up the street toward the hotel in all their silver and bright apparel, they did not meet the eyes that were staring at them, but looked straight ahead and neither smiled nor frowned—except Brouillette, who, as a sober, smart, and well-to-do half-French man, would salute any man and look him in the eyes, usually with a bright smile as well. No one could make Brouillette look down, just as no one could make Palonswah Godfroy look down.

Still, riding through this town of the white people on a religious day with the bells clanging was, she thought, much like going through a gauntlet. And what if her brothers and sister had gone into one of the religious buildings and would not be at the inn? It might be unpleasant to have to wait, surrounded by whites.

Or it might be amusing.

She glanced aside just in time to see a plump, richly dressed man and woman staring at her with scornful eyes and tight mouths, and she thought:

I have brothers and a sister who are as white and proper and rich as you, but they do not hold their mouths tight and funny like yours. Then she thought:

I myself am as white and rich as you.

She looked straight at them and tightened her mouth like theirs, and then she had to laugh. It seemed to make them angry and they jerked their heads away and strutted off toward the church. Maconakwa heard Cut Finger giggle to herself.

There was the inn, a new, white wooden building with the shadows of the autumn leaves blue on its walls, and, with a lifting of her spirits, she saw her three gray-headed kin coming down off the hotel porch to greet her, and she was surprised at how glad she was to see them. She had dreamed of them last night—once she had finally gotten to sleep—and the dream was warm and bright.

The brother called Joseph, and the sister Mary, were coming off the porch close together, her hand hooked in his elbow, and Maconakwa remembered something they had said yesterday at her house while talking of the day when she was carried away. It was that this woman Mary, who had been just a ten-year-old girl then, had rescued this man Joseph, who was only two then, by dragging him toward the fort.

And the little boy had run so hard his breeches had fallen down.

And now see them, she thought: he helps her walk.

Pakot wehsah, she thought. That is good.

Miller was already there, standing nearby. Strangely, there were almost as many people milling around by the inn watching their approach as there had been around the church.

They dismounted and their horses were taken to a water trough and rail close by. A large bundle in white cloth lay tied behind Brouillette's saddle.

Joseph, Mary, and Isaac came looking rested and happy, and each in turn took Maconakwa's hand, holding it warmly with the right and covering it with the left, and in each such hand-greeting she could feel a genuine good vibration of spirit. Then they gestured for her and her family to enter the inn. She turned, caught

Brouillette's eye, and pointed with her chin to his horse. He had forgotten the gift. He raised his eyebrows, nodded quickly and trotted off to his horse, untied the bundle, heaved it onto his shoulder, and came back. Cut Finger took it from him and went into the room. There she put it on the table, and Maconakwa summoned Miller with a tilt of her head. "Bring my old sister to that table, will you?"

"Gladly, Grandmother." He went through the crowded room and brought Mary to face Cut Finger across the table. Cut Finger was not accustomed to looking into the faces of white people, but she looked at Mary, her pretty, pale old face aglow with nervous pleasure. When Miller had hushed the babble of voices and people had gathered around, Cut Finger reached to her mother's sleeve and pulled her closer, and then began:

"*Kiji Moneto, mehgwesh!*" Thanks to the Creator. "The Master of Life brings my family together with brothers and sister of my mother. Now my family brings to these travelers this gift. This gift speaks to them of our trust and friendship."

"*A ho,*" murmured Maconakwa and Brouillette.

When Miller had translated that, the old Quakers appeared deeply touched.

Cut Finger said, in a quavering, sweet voice: "If the woman will now take it to see what it is, and wants it, that will speak to us of their trust and friendship in return."

Moist-eyed, nodding and mouthing "Thank you," Mary Towne bent over the table, taking an edge of the cloth and starting to unwrap it. She had to turn the heavy object over and over to unwrap the long white cloth. As she did so, her expression grew strained. The inner folds of the cloth appeared blood-pink, like bandages being removed from a wound. She hesitated, glanced at Joseph, saw him nod, and lifted back the last edge of cloth.

It was a fresh hind quarter of venison, neatly trimmed.

Cut Finger said now, "This flesh of the deer is the best food Creator has made for us to eat. The meat of cows fills our belly but the cow does not have good spirit like the deer. The deer is strong and free and generous. She hurts no one. She knows she was put here to feed the People, and when we eat her, those good spirits of her become ours. They feed our bodies and our souls and keep them healthy. Will you accept our gift?"

Mary Towne blinked and nodded as she heard this translated. "Yes. We accept it with happiness and humility. And . . . and we take your trust and your friendship to our hearts. And . . . we offer you ours. Like the deer, we hurt no one. Thank you, my dear niece. And thank you, Sister Frances."

"*E heh,*" said Maconakwa. "May this flesh keep my kin healthy for a long time, so they can come to see us again."

Now all was as good as Joseph had so long dreamed a reunion would be. Frances was no longer cold or severe. She listened, seeming deeply moved, to the story of her birth mother Ruth Slocum and her refusal to lose hope. Joseph told of their mother dying with her face turned toward the place where she had last seen Frances carried away, and Maconakwa sat with a long, far-away expression thinking of that, recalling her distant memory of the place.

Then she was told descriptive details of current Slocum family life in the Susquehanna Valley—of the great meetinghouses and courthouse, the academy, the churches, all bigger and more magnificent than the buildings here in Peru; she heard of the wharfs on the riverfront, the great, floating boats called arks that carried coal and farm products down the river to even bigger cities of the East, and of the steamboats, huge ships that ran on mere steam, steam such as that coming from the hotel's tea urn—yes, she said, some of her Miami people had seen such ships, on the Ohio or far down the Wabash—and she heard with awe and dismay of how the white people in that valley, including some of her brothers, dug a black stone from under the ground everywhere, a stone that would burn with white heat, called "hard coal," and sold it for great sums of money everywhere on that side of the eastern mountains; she looked almost frightened as Joseph described the honeycomb of black tunnels that was growing under the town and the farms as that coal was dug out, and the black, stinking hills of what he called "culm," which was the waste after the coal was smashed and screened; and when he talked of the black dust everywhere and the smoke, and the clanging of mechanics' foundries, she did her best to envision such horrors, which to her seemed almost like the Afterworld she had sometimes heard of when Christian religious shamans had stopped at her house on their way to the Wabash towns. She listened and watched Miller try to aid his translated descriptions by making shapes in the air with his hands. It seemed that the words he had to use most often were *maco,* black, which was a part of her own bear name, and *kotawe,* which was fire, and *kepekotwe*, which was iron. He talked of how some of their brothers had made iron and flour, and she stopped him with a blazing look of anger when he said that some of them had made whiskey and sold it.

"Joseph does that?" she asked.

"No. I never have made whiskey."

"Isaac?" she asked.

"No."

"Where are those brothers now?"

"They are dead," he said, and started to tell her where and when they had died, but she cut that short simply by saying:

"Eh! Good!" His mouth dropped open when he realized what she had just said.

"Well, Mr. Miller," he said, "I'm certainly glad I never made whiskey! I'd be put back farther than where we started yesterday!"

"Might be, sir. She's very strong on the subject."

Brouillette, standing behind Maconakwa's chair, began speaking in Miami, with a terrific intensity in his eyes, Joseph thinking he had never seen a man of a more electrifying appearance, and Miller translated:

"Brouillette says he is a sober man. That the people of Peru know this. That her sons are dead and he stands in their place to her, and will maintain her well as long as she lives. That if he had been a drinker, he would have been worthless to her, and she would not have lived to this age."

It was like a creed, Joseph thought. The devotion this sister had from her family was one of the best things Joseph had ever seen. He tried to remember the Miami words and, standing up, he reached out and took Brouillette's hand, and said, "*Pakot wehsah! Megwesh*, Captain Brouillette! Good! Thankee!" Brouillette looked near bursting with pride and pleasure after that compliment.

The room was packed with townspeople, curious spectators who had heard through town gossip about this meeting of the elderly Pennsylvanians with the old Miami Queen. Men were smoking their cheroots and clay pipes and crowding all the windows and the door, and the room was a clamor of voices. Joseph had turned to hear something young Fulwiler was trying to tell him, and when he turned around, he was facing an empty chair where Frances had been sitting. Gone to the jakes, no doubt, after all this tea, he thought. He had so many things to ask her and tell

her, and was eager for her to come back in. He had made arrange-
ment for a scrivener from the town to write down her history of
captivity as she told it—in more detail, he hoped—so the wondrous tale and its happy ending could be shared through the press
in both the Susquehanna and Wabash valleys. The Wilkes-Barre
journals had already reported Joseph's hopeful journey to the
West following Colonel Ewing's miraculous letter; the towns
along the Wabash had no idea yet that the history of the "white
Miami Queen" in their midst was so fascinating or that it had
turned out so joyously. And Joseph intended that it would all end
even more wonderfully when, if they could, the Slocums could
persuade their sister to return with them to the comforts and gen-
tility of Pennsylvania civilization. He did not intend for this day's
gathering to end until that offer had been broached.

But where was she? "Mr. Miller," he said, "does anyone know
where my sister went?" He had the sudden horrible fear that she
had found the society in this room unpleasant and departed for her
woodland haunts. Although he could see Brouillette and Cut
Finger still in the room nearby, being talked to by Isaac through
Fulwiler, she still might have ridden off with her other daughter.

Miller went through the crowd toward the door, and Joseph followed him, beginning to fret. They stepped out onto the bright
porch and looked toward the hitch rail. All four horses were still
there.

"Where in the world do—"

"There," said Miller.

At the far end of the porch lay a bundled blanket with a pair of
moccasins sticking out from the near end. It was the blanket
Frances had been wearing. Alarmed, Joseph hurried with Miller
toward that end of the long porch, and Miller knelt beside her. She
was lying on her back, eyes shut, ankles crossed. When Miller
spoke to her in a querying tone, she turned her face toward him,
opened her eyes, and said something. She swung her feet down off
the edge of the board porch and sat up, yawning. Miller stood up
and came back, shaking his head and smiling.

"She said she just needed a nap in the fresh air. Too many
people, too much talk, too much smoke."

Joseph bit his lower lip, chuckling, as much amused as relieved.
"We might do well to thin the crowd a little. I appreciate the
townspeople's interest, but they've had years to visit with her and
didn't. It would be pleasant to have just the family—and thee and

the journalist, of course." Just then he saw a movement over by the wooden privy: a whitewashed door had opened and Yellow Leaf, the younger daughter, fairly leaped out, holding her nose with one hand and with the other fanning the air with an edge of her blanket. So. She had not deserted the reunion either.

After the curious bystanders had been politely shooed out to the porch and Frances was seated in a comfortable chair with a cup of sweet tea at hand, Joseph introduced a gangly fellow with ink-dark fingertips who was a compositor and scrivener from a nearby newspaper, and asked her if she would mind telling the story of her life with the Indians, from childhood through womanhood, with more details about her travels and the wars.

That did not seem to please her. She looked askance at the pencils and sheets of paper the printer had taken from his writing box and laid out on the table. "That man intends to capture my words?" When Miller assured her it was only to help her brothers and sister remember her story better, she seemed to relent. But Mary could not let it go at a half-truth, and had Miller explain that the story was to be published, and what that meant, and Frances had to think about that awhile, but finally shrugged and began at the exact place: "When I was a little girl and my father was a Quaker with a wide black hat, three Lenapeh warriors came one day . . ."

She described the little she could remember about that day, including the story she had heard only yesterday about Mary rescuing Joseph with his breeches falling, and forward through the decades from there. Because of the pauses for translating, the writer had no trouble keeping up.

"This is wonderful," Mary remarked once. "We ought to write a copy to be mailed to family, so they can hear it all the sooner."

At one point Joseph asked her whether she had known that her brothers, and even her mother, had traveled on the frontier searching for her. She thought awhile and said, "I think I remember my Lenapeh parents were afraid someone would come and find me, that someone would sell my name . . . but I thought little about my first family after a while. Always I was treated well and kindly by all the Indians. Always they taught me and fed me and protected me. Always the armies were coming after us, and I grew afraid of whites. For long times I would not even think that I had been a white before. But sometimes something would remind me . . ." She sat quiet awhile, remembering Wells, the Wild Potato with his red hair and freckles like hers. "I do not remember one thing or another of the wars, they were so common and so bloody and so much alike each time. I did not like to see the scalps our warriors brought home, I never did like that, but I liked it that we won, when we did. That was not often, and even then, armies came again the next season. There were so many winters without food because of the soldiers. . . . I remember a war that came just when we lived at Kekionga, Fort Wayne now. The army of Harmar came. The women and children were all made to run north, and we got away and then the warriors beat him good. They were Lenapehs, Miamis, Potawatomi, Shawnee. As I told you, I was always well-treated by the Indian people. I was married young to a Lenapeh I had to put out, then older to a Miami, but even long before I was ever married, I was red in my heart and I did not think so much about my white family."

She said it matter-of-factly, without any sort of apology for having forgotten them.

Now Mary Towne was sitting close before her, saying, "No matter. Now you do see us and remember us. We were not in those armies. Joseph and many of our offspring live where our father and mother used to live, the place you remember, the banks of the Susquehanna so beautiful." Maconakwa thought of the blackness and smoke Joseph had been describing, and wondered whether Mary was lying about the beautiful valley. Or perhaps it had been changed after she moved to Ohio. Mary was saying now, "They have a way of doing things there. You may sell your farmland or house, but you can keep the mineral rights and—"

"Ma'am," said Miller, "is there some other way of saying that? There's no Indian words I know for 'mineral rights,' and I don't even know what they are myself."

Fulwiler leaned closer and said, "It means if there's coal under land you've sold, you can keep rights to the coal and get paid for it when they dig it."

Miller expressed that to her in the best way he knew how.

Mary said, "The Slocums have made a great deal of wealth selling land, and coal too."

Maconakwa shook her head. "Nothing has been worse for people than selling land."

"What we are saying, sister, is that if you went back home to the Susquehanna with Joseph, you could live so richly and well. We could give you property, and a big, good house, and everything you desire. Oh, do come back to your family!"

Maconakwa shut her eyes and nodded. So that was what they were after. I was right. She seethed for a while but decided not to be unkind. These people meant this with good hearts. It was only Ewing who had done this in hopes of getting her off her land. These Slocums just didn't know the color of her heart. She was tired and all this talking and meeting white people was making her head hurt, but she would have to make them understand her heart now or they would keep trying to take her away. She held out her hand and looked at the three siblings one by one.

"I have always lived with the Indians; they have used me very kindly. I am used to them. The Great Spirit has allowed me to live with them. I wish to live and die with them."

She saw their faces growing long and sad as those words were translated. But she could see them already starting to think of protestations and arguments, and knew that what she had said was not yet enough.

"In my house you saw my mirror. Your looking glass may be longer than mine, but if I went with you and you gave me a great, long, fine looking glass, I would still see what in it? This face. But that fine looking glass would not give me a finer face. It would give me a sadder face, because I would be far from my home. Sister, brothers, I do not wish to live any better, or anywhere else.

"I believe the Great Spirit has permitted me to live so long because I have always lived with the Indians. I should have died sooner if I had left them." She had to press her lips tight together to keep them from trembling while the interpreter talked. She blinked rapidly with her thoughts. The things she was going to say came to her mind in images. She saw a grassy mound with three cedar poles on it bending slightly in the wind and ribbons fluttering at the top.

"My husband and my sons are buried here. The day my husband died, he charged me not to leave the Indians. . . ." She stopped, looking down, remembering how she and Deaf Man used to talk about Crossing Over hand in hand so they would not lose each other in the great journey. How could he take her hand if she went away to a distant valley? She tried to moisten her dry tongue to say more.

"I have a house and large lands. Two daughters, a good son-in-law, three grandchildren, and everything to make me comfortable. Why would I want to go to something else? Would a fish choose to go someplace besides water, where he would die?"

It was getting too hard to talk now. She had to squeeze her mouth and her eyes shut so these white people would not see her cry. She did not want them to travel away with a memory of her crying. She rocked back and forth with her hands clutching each other, trying to get herself able to say more. Just then Brouillette's voice spoke behind her.

"I am married to this woman's daughter," he said. "About thirteen winters. I was born far down the Wabash at Fort Harrison, near Terre Haute, but I live here now, with thanks for this marriage. The whites in these towns have known me since they settled here. They know me to maintain my family respectably. I stand in the place of this woman's sons. I mean to maintain her well as long as she lives, for the truth of which you may depend on the word of Captain Brouillette."

Eh, Autumn, she thought, you are so good, but you are not making it easier for me not to weep. She straightened her back and took a deep breath. "What my son-in-law says is true," she told them. "He has always treated me kindly. My relatives should have no uneasiness about me here. The Indians are my people. I do not even have to work. I sit in the house with these my two daughters, and they do the work inside, and he does the work outside. I do not need any richer care. There is none." She had to stop again. She did not want to sadden these good old white people. But they were saddening her. Miller told them all she had said.

"Sister," said Joseph in a gentle voice, "won't you at least come and make a visit to your first home? And when you have seen it and visited with us, then return here to your people?"

Already she was shaking her head, even before Miller finished with the question.

"I cannot, I cannot. I am an old tree. I was a sapling when they brought me away. You know you can plant a sapling in another place but not an old tree; you cannot even move an old tree a little way and bring it back. It is all gone past, the time when I could go about. I am afraid I would die and never come back. I am happy here. I shall die here and lie in that burial place, and they will raise the pole at my grave with the white flag on it, and the Great Spirit will know where to find me. I would not be happy going away with my white relatives. I am glad enough to see them, but I cannot go, I cannot go. I have done."

When that was translated for them, the Slocums looked as if they were praying, with their heads wearily down and eyes shut and their hands folded in their laps. There followed a painful silence, and Brouillette apparently was too happy with her refusal to let gloom prevail. In a happy and animated voice he said, "When white men take an Indian woman as their 'squaw,' they make her work like a slave. It was never so with this woman. She has always been honored here, at Deaf Man's village, named after her husband. So she has lived to this age. I have done with my words."

Now followed Cut Finger's voice, almost like singing, it was so lyrical and rich in tone. "We have been happy to see you. To see my mother again, later, you will be welcome at my father's village and our home there. But not to take her to the East." She glanced at the venison quarter they had brought as their gift of friendship. She added, "A deer cannot live out of the forest."

Now even Yellow Leaf, who had been painfully shy around the white people, said, "My mother should not go even on a visit. A fish taken out of water dies quickly."

After that the silence was so deep that even the people on the porch sensed it and quit murmuring. A few people cleared their throats. Maconakwa sat looking at her hands and then shut her eyes and thought of the village, the poles over the graves, the big shade trees, the river, the spring at the foot of the hill whose delicious cold water had always quenched her family's thirst. Just this one day away from that place had already made her feel sick and feeble. Of course she could not leave long enough to go to their black valley of coal and smoke and iron.

With a sigh, Joseph got up from his chair and looked around. "It is late, time for supper. Mr. Miller, please ask them to stay here and eat with us."

Miller talked with them, and replied: "Sir, as they feel now, and smelling the way the inn's man cooks, they ask not to have to, and ask that you not be offended if they go home. They would like to ride home before it grows too dark, this being a night when there'll be no moon."

And so the four Indians, including the one who had been born his sister Frances, held the hands of the old Quakers for a few moments, and with sad smiles, and barely glancing at their eyes, and not backing away when Mary and Isaac and he pressed their cheeks to theirs, went out to their horses. There was not a bench near the hitch rail. Brouillette stood by her horse and laced his fingers to make a step for his mother-in-law and hoisted her to her saddle, while the two daughters seemed to spring like rabbits onto their saddles. Then he turned toward the inn, gave them all a nod of his turbaned head, and swung onto his mount. The few people who were left on the porch were smoking and looking curiously, sympathetically perhaps, back and forth between the departing Indians and the gray-haired white people.

Maconakwa and her family rode half a block away, slowly, through low-slanting evening sunbeams, and then, like one of those flights of birds that seem to act all of a single mind, they were suddenly at full gallop down the street and vanishing around the church, toward the river, leaving only dust full of sunbeams under the yellow trees.

CHAPTER TWENTY-SIX

October 1846
Deaf Man's Village

Day after day Maconakwa heard the pitiful sounds up and down the valley and along the river road and she thought: To be deaf like my old husband, eh, that would be a blessing now! But I hear as well as ever! She stood in the rain by the road, day by day.

She could not keep from hearing the soldier guns. Not many guns at a time, like war. One shot at a time echoing up or down the valley of the Mississinewa. Just a few most days, some days none.

An Indian's dog would be howling or barking far away. Then there would be a gunshot and no more sound from that dog. But always somewhere in the distance there were dogs howling.

Some of the soldier bullets were not shot at dogs, but at Indian people. She knew about many of those: Some Miami man would refuse to leave his cabin to march down the road, and there would be a gunshot. An Indian boy being driven down the muddy road toward the canal boats by the bayonet soldiers would dart out from his family and dive into the river, and there would be a gunshot. A woman crying at the grave of her grandmother would hang on to the grave marker when soldiers tried to drag her away, and she would draw her sheath knife to cut the soldiers or perhaps to kill herself, and there would be a gunshot.

All these pitiful sounds were in the valley because the white people had finally gotten their way and the last few thousand Miamis were being rounded up like livestock to be put on canal boats and sent away west beyond the Missi Sipu, taking only what they could carry on their backs and leaving their dogs behind.

It was the worst of all times for the Miami People. To make it even harder to bear, cold rain kept falling and the paths and roads

517

were sticky with mud that sucked their moccasins off as the soldiers prodded them along with bayonets.

To make this worst of all times worse for Maconakwa, she was not going with her People.

Her brother Joseph had made a paper with the white council in the East called Congress, and Congress had sent a paper that allowed Maconakwa and her Miami relatives to stay here because she was white.

She could stay here with Deaf Man's grave as she had promised him she would do. But the Miami People she had chosen to stay here with instead of going back to the Quaker family in the East were being sent away from her, out of their homeland, and she knew they must hate her for this now. They had reason to.

All the Miamis had used to like and respect her. They had thought it fine that a woman with white skin had a red heart. She had been praised for generosity and admired for her understanding of plant medicine, and for helping deliver babies. Older people remembered Deaf Man, respected her as his widow, and remembered how brave and helpful she had been during the war.

Now the People she loved, and who had loved her, hated her because she was allowed to keep her part of their homeland, while they had to tie up their dogs to keep them from following them, and go down and be put on the canal boats. And her square mile of that homeland was now surrounded by white settlers, who called her a squaw and her family half-breeds. She was already having trouble with them because they felt that their thing called "law" would not care if they stole horses and cows from a squaw. So they sneaked around and took her horses and cows. Now Cut Finger's husband Brouillette, and Yellow Leaf's fourth husband, Bondy, patrolled the edges of her square mile carrying guns, and she lived in dread of the day when they would actually meet one of the white thieves. Brouillette and Bondy had Miami blood in their veins, and if they ever killed a white man, even for stealing her livestock, the whites would call it an Indian uprising and use it as an excuse to hang her sons-in-law and probably take her land away from her in spite of her paper from Congress.

And so now, standing in cold drizzle near the road to say farewell to her old friends as the soldiers herded them past, Maconakwa, who was seventy-three years old according to the count made by her Quaker brother Joseph, thought it might have been better if Joseph had never found her. Maybe better, maybe worse.

Joseph had meant well. He had come out a second time, bringing his two daughters. He had hired a painter to make pictures of Maconakwa and her daughters. She had tried to give him land here, so he would stay and use his "law" to protect her from her white neighbors. But like her, he was too old to move, and went back East. Then in good heart he had done that Congress paper.

In the cold her nose was red and running, and she raised her arm and wiped the tip of her nose with the edge of her blanket.

Joseph is good, she thought. With that Congress paper, he was just trying to help me keep my land.

Another family was coming down the road and two soldiers followed them wearing capes, soldiers with bayonets sticking up. Maconakwa recognized the lean young Miami man of the family. He was one she had helped deliver from his mother's womb twenty summers ago.

Now see how he looks at me, she thought. As if he would kill me.

"Ningeah." She felt a hand on her arm. It was Yellow Leaf, saying, "Mother, come up to the house or you will get sick in the rain." She shook her daughter's hand off and would not turn around to speak to her. After a while she heard her feet squishing away in the mud toward the house.

Maconakwa had told her sons-in-law that if they saw any running-away Miami people crossing onto her land to hide, they must pretend they did not see them. She knew that people slipped away. When Black Hoof's Shawnees had been driven out of their reservation in Ohio to go west, many of them had simply turned off into the woods. When the Potawatomi were herded out of their country north of the Wabash Sipu a few years ago, some had slipped off the side of the trail when soldiers were not looking and were now living hidden wherever the whites hadn't filled in the space. She knew these things. She knew that the slipping-away people were hiding also on the lands of Palonswah's family at the mouth of the Mississinewa, and on Meshingomeshia's reserve up the river, and wherever wealthy or half-breed Miamis, through cooperation with the white government land people, had been allowed to keep sections of country. Of course, there would be troubles caused by these hideaways, some kinds of troubles easy to foresee and probably many kinds of trouble no one could even imagine yet. But she prayed that the ones who tried to escape from the bayonet soldiers would escape without getting hurt.

I do not want this valley all emptied of its True People, she thought, peering up the muddy road for someone she wanted to see but dreaded to see. This would be too sad a place with all of them gone, and nothing left but the howling of their tied-up dogs and the abandoned spirits of their dead.

It was not only that the Miami People wanted to stay near the graves of their ancestors, in this rich land that had always been theirs; it was not just that the land they were being sent to was far away; but that it was not a good land. Last year five Miami men had been sent by the government to see the place beyond the Missi Sipu where the People were to be sent, and one of the five had been her son-in-law Brouillette. The place was called Kansas Territory. Autumn Brouillette had come back telling of the terrible heat there and the thin, dry soil, and the dried-up creeks. Those descriptions had spread through the Miami Nation as fast as the wind, so all these who were being sent there believed they were going to a scorched place where they would have to die from want.

Far up the road she saw another group of people in the drizzly grayness, coming down the road toward her. She thought she recognized one of the horses, but it was too far to tell yet. But she felt that this would be the one she was waiting for and dreading to see. She waited, wiping her nose again. Below, the gray surface of the river was made misty and spattery by the unceasing drizzle.

Because of brother Joseph's Congress paper, the man called Ewing had not been able to get Maconakwa's square mile. But he had made so much money on the other Miamis' lost lands that this little piece probably didn't matter much. It was almost funny in a way that his letter to her Quaker family had, instead of removing her to the East, resulted in a Congress paper that kept her here so he couldn't profit from her land, this which had been Deaf Man's Town.

But Ewing was making money even from this last misery of the Miami people. Maconakwa knew this from Brouillette too: the white government had paid many thousands of dollars to somebody to do this removal of the Miamis, in something called a "contract," and Ewing with his brothers was among the white people who had that contract.

And Ewing was also setting up to do more Indian trade business in Kansas Territory, so he would keep making money off the Miamis even when they got there. And so would others: Brouillette had seen on his trip to that far country that the route went through long gauntlets of whiskey sellers.

Brouillette, in answer to her constant prayers, was still a sober man. And he kept studying the schemes of the white men so he could protect this family against them. He had even been learning their tongue so he could hear things they didn't know he could understand. Now he was able to advise her on the sorts of matters for which she used to go and ask Palonswah. It was important that Brouillette was learning such things, because Palonswah had Crossed Over just a few years ago.

Yes, Brouillette she still counted among the best gifts the Creator had put into her long life. He was still a good husband to Cut Finger, though they still had made no children. She had given up hope that they would. Even if they might have someday, it was unclear whether their children could stay here, because the Congress paper had written on it the names of all the people who could stay, and it said nothing about people who might be born yet.

Eh! Maconakwa now saw that the people coming down the road were the ones. She shut her eyes for a moment and prayed for the strength she would need.

She recognized two blaze-faced horses descended from a mare that she and Deaf Man had given long ago to Minnow. Minnow was now too old to be one of those walking in the mud. She would be the little, humped figure riding with a blanket over her head, on one of the horses. Maconakwa watched her coming with the soldiers following and thought of the time thirty winters ago when Minnow and her daughter had escaped in the snow. Minnow was now at last too old to escape white soldiers anymore.

Maconakwa reached inside her blanket and closed her hand around a small object. Her heart was pattering fast with cold and dread.

This person Minnow had saved her life in the old days, and helped save the life of the wounded warrior who had become Deaf Man. Minnow had been her one friend since the beginning.

She sees me, Maconakwa thought. How terrible her eyes are!

But she should remember that I have saved her life too.

Now Minnow's horse was almost beside Maconakwa, its breath making fog puffs in the cold. It saw Maconakwa and nickered.

The horse knows me and does not hate me, she thought.

The horse stopped. Minnow was looking down, her face dark and wrinkled under the cowl of the blanket's edge. She was wearing under the blanket the blue calico dress Maconakwa had made for her years ago when Minnow had been unable to afford trading-store cloth.

For days while waiting, Maconakwa had thought of how she would say things to Minnow if she saw her, but now she could not remember any of that. Instead she drew her hand forth and showed Minnow that she was wearing the medicine bag Minnow had made for her from a soldier's scrotum.

Minnow showed no expression. She stuck one hand out from her blanket. The hand was a solid fist. A soldier was speaking angrily behind her, probably telling her to move on. Minnow ignored him. She held the clenched hand close to Maconakwa's face and opened it, palm up, the hand with which Minnow had combed her hair one cold morning long ago, one morning when soldiers attacked. Now the hand was full of dark, damp earth, so wet it was almost a fistful of mud, and rain was drizzling into it.

"This is from the grave of my husband. I have to take it far away with me," Minnow rasped. "You get to stay with yours!"

Then, looking straight ahead, she kicked the horse in the flanks and went on, not looking back, down the river, down to where the three canal boats were waiting to load all these hundreds of wet and weeping Indians. How would they crowd so many people on three boats?

What would become of all those tied-up dogs left behind? She could hear them barking and howling far up the valley.

Minnow, she thought, if you could hear my soul as I watch you go, it would sound to you like all those dogs!

I have to go in now. As my daughter said, I will get sick in this rain, and die. But if I did, what would it matter?

March 1847

That winter the abandoned dogs that had been left tied up starved to death, or grieved to death, or were killed by wild animals, and for a while there were always buzzards in the sky over the valley. The dogs that were loose or got loose joined into packs and overran the valley, getting wilder and meaner than coyotes and wolves had ever been in the old days. Those feral dogs seemed to be full of bad spirits. Some had come near Maconakwa's house in the first snow and watched her with what looked like witch eyes. Then Cut Finger got very sick. Brouillette brought her up to Maconakwa's house for healing.

It was some kind of long, weakening sickness, with a bloody flux from her bowels. The medicine man had been sent west with the People. Maconakwa finally decided on a tea of sumac root bark, which slowed the flux, and then began feeding her corn soups and succotash with no meat to try to bring her strength back. The pain diminished but she did not get stronger. The continued weakness made Maconakwa worry about a witch spell. She burned herbs in a mussel shell around the bed every day, and prayed with all her concentration against bad spirits. Yellow Leaf came up every day and helped with the nursing and the prayers. Maconakwa seldom slept, but paid little attention to the passage of days and nights. Sometimes she would look at the food stored in the house and be surprised that so much had been used up. She would fall asleep in her chair by the hearth and would be awakened by a faraway gunshot, probably white settlers shooting another wild dog, and the fire would be down to embers, so she would put wood on and then go tend to Cut Finger.

Then she would wonder if the gunshot might have been not a white person shooting a dog but Brouillette or Bondy shooting a white person they had caught stealing, and she would fret about that until she saw them.

Through the winter the whole outdoors seemed to have something terrible and invisible sitting over it. Sometimes she would stand at the door in the early morning and look out at the snow and the gray river and the trackless road, and the absence of the People would seem like a great, silent, unseen force in the valley, and she would have to shut the door to keep it from sucking her spirit out. Nobody ever came from Palonswah's family or from Meshin-gomeshia's reserve up the river. So she thought they too considered her white.

One day Brouillette was loading axes, saws, and kettles into his wagon, and he asked her if Cut Finger was well enough for him to be gone a few days.

"Gone where, Autumn?"

"Up into the sugar trees. The sap is rising."

She said, "Will it be worth the trouble? You don't have enough people to work a sugar camp."

"Perhaps enough," he said. He was wearing a fur *gustoweh* instead of his turban, and his chin was stubbled. She saw in his eyes that there was something he wanted to say or did not want to say. She stared at him until he knew she knew there was something, so he sighed and said, "There are some people up there."

"What people?"

He smiled slightly and said, "Such as those you told me to pretend not to see if I saw them."

"Those who slipped away from the soldiers and did not go to the boats, perhaps."

"*E heh.* I saw smoke in the woods, and snares. The footprints in the snow were not white men's boots. So I went in to them and told them I knew they were there. They have had a hard winter."

She said, "I wonder if you ever took food from this house to them."

"Now that you ask, so I have, a little now and then."

"Aha. I wondered where it was going so fast."

He did not look in the least ashamed. He said, "They told me to thank you. I can, now that you know."

She swallowed. "They said to thank me?"

"*E heh.*"

After a moment she said, "If we had a cow less, or a few chickens, I would just guess white men stole them."

He nodded, trying to hide a smile. "They will thank you for that too."

A few days later Brouillette rode in from the sugar camp through melting snow, his wagon muddy, and he was grinning. First he went to sit beside Cut Finger, his palm on her forehead, and they talked softly. Then he got up and came smiling to Maconakwa.

"She says you are taking good care of her, and she says she feels well enough that Yellow Leaf could stay with her tonight and you would be free to come out for the sugar dance."

"You joking man. How can I go to a sugar dance?"

He leaned down near her, an eyebrow cocked. "The hiding-in-the-woods people helped us make much sugar, and it is customary to give thanks for the sugar. They asked me if you would come out to the camp and dance with them."

Her first feeling was annoyance, because she presumed that he was teasing her, and this was too serious. But she saw in his face that he was not joking, and her heartbeat quickened. "Miami people would celebrate with me, the white woman who was permitted to stay?"

"We have been feeding them and hiding them and have not told the whites they are here. By now they know your heart is as red as it always was when you made them medicine and helped their babies come."

She clenched her left fist in her right hand, squeezed her eyes shut, and was quiet for a long time, until Brouillette said:

"I could not speak for you that you would come. I told them, Maconakwa might protest that she is too old to dance."

She looked up at him and saw that now he was teasing. She frowned at him, cleared her throat, and said, "Have they a drum?"

"They made one. A deep drum."

"*E heh! E heh!* Go shave your face. Then make me a seat in the horse wagon!"

Eh o weh
Eh o weh o weh!
Eh o weh
Eh o weh o weh!
Eh o weh o weh!
O weh o weh o weh!

All night the drum had been like a heartbeat, and the voices sometimes loud, sometimes soft, sometimes joyous, sometimes sad. If the whites living within the horizons heard this, they were probably scared. Eh, let them be scared, she thought. It has been too long since we scared them! Since Tecumseh was alive. And this is my land and I can dance in the woods in the middle of it.

The hiding-away people had started with an honor song for her, and it had swelled her heart so big that she could feel nothing else—not the fatigue in her old legs, not the chill of her muddy, slush-soaked moccasins, not the icy night air on her head and face. She was a Miami, and could dance all night. She shuffled in two-step around the bonfire countless times, sang, nibbled maple-sugar snow and chunks of pure sugar and drank tea sweetened with it; she ate meat and corn bread now and then to keep up her strength for dancing. She smoked her clay pipe while resting between dances and watched the others. It was not as large a circle of dancers as in the old days, nor as colorful; these were ragged, hiding-in-the-woods people. But they seemed as happy as she was to be dancing, and if they had been timid and quiet here in her woods the past winter, they were not now. They had been assured that it was her land and she had a promise written by the highest white chiefs that she could never be chased out of it. That had been promised to them too, all the Miami people, often enough, and the promise always broken, but they were willing to believe her. So there should be no fear if their fireglow was seen, or the drum heard. This was the first Miami thanksgiving dance since the bayonet soldiers came, and it was too good to stop.

It was in the middle of the round horizon, in the middle of her land, in the middle of the woods, in the middle of the circle of dancers, and it was the fire. Everything else was around the fire, which was the center. It melted the snow and made the dance circle muddy. Whether Maconakwa was dancing or resting, there was the fire, the spirit of fire, simple and honest.

Fire made her remember. For almost seventy years she had lived with Lenapeh and Miami peoples, and almost every night of those years she had looked into their cookfires and campfires. She had listened to their stories and learned their languages and beliefs by those fires. By a fire pit Neepah had given her a medicine bag, and by another fire Minnow had given her another. Around the fires she had danced with the People, and she had coupled with her husbands and borne and nursed her babies by those fires, and had brewed the medicines to heal their wounds and illnesses by the fires, had melted lead to mold their musketballs, had baked the funeral bread by the fires, had treated the frozen hands and feet of the People in winter war. She had fired pottery by corncob fires in the ground, and made charcoal and heated paint pebbles to make war paint, and had carried wood to make bonfires for the war dances as well as the thanksgivings. She had dropped meat in fires as sacrifices to the Master of Life and crumbled tobacco into fires to make the smoke that would carry her prayers to him. Over fires she had parched corn and boiled maple sap for the trail foods for hunters and confections for children. Everything useful and necessary and comforting came from fire heat, and all the stories and plannings, counciling, mourning, and laughing of those long years had had fire in the middle. Fire made her remember Rainbow Crow, who brought it from the sun when the earth was cold, and it made her remember Tuck Horse, who had always said that it was alive, a living spirit without which life would be only winter.

But she remembered too, as she watched the embers shimmer

and shift and the flames and sparks shower up, the fires of the Long Knife Town Destroyers that had consumed her homes one after another, fire from cannons and guns, fire in the whiskers of a whiskey seller, one of the few times she had ever hurt anyone. Fire could be a destroyer.

And she remembered how the People, after each burning, after each war, would come back and rebuild their *wikwams* and replant the next year's crops, using fire in a shell to make smoke for the Three Sisters prayer. . . .

Always there was fire at the center of everything, fire, the gift of Rainbow Crow, and as Tuck Horse had told it, there was fire in the heart where life burns in a person.

Maconakwa danced on and on around the fire and the heartbeat drum, until the sun was almost up and the wisps of clouds above the eastern horizon glowed a vivid vermilion, the color of the dots the women painted on their cheekbones to identify themselves to Creator so he could find his own True People when they died. Whenever Brouillette asked her whether she had danced enough, she smiled and kept dancing.

She was older than anyone here, two or three times as old as most, and their tongues were almost hanging out, but no one tried to make her stop dancing. With her they danced on and on, around the drum, around the fire, around the heart of their story.

AUTHOR'S NOTE

Two days after that dance at the sugar camp, Maconakwa died of pneumonia.

On March 11, 1847, she was buried on the knoll beside Deaf Man and their sons, with a white flag on a pole over her grave, her favorite brass teakettle and cream pitcher in the coffin at her feet. Her daughter, Cut Finger, died two days later and was buried beside her. There the family lay beside the Mississinewa for 120 years, their legend growing and their descendants assimilating into Indiana society, until the graves were moved to higher ground when the river was dammed to create a reservoir.

Maconakwa's square mile of land had been put in Yellow Leaf's name—Ozahshingkwa's Reserve—and she managed to keep it the rest of her life. She died in 1877, leaving Peter Bondy with nine children.

By then he was Reverend Bondy. Both he and Autumn Brouillette had been converted to Christianity by Isaac Slocum's youngest son George, so Maconakwa's beloved sons-in-law ended up as Baptist preachers. Their lives characterized the extreme social changes wrought upon the Miamis, both east and west of the Mississippi, by the encroachment of white settlement. The resourcefulness and adaptability of the Miami people, from Little Turtle's time to the present day, make an epic story both heartbreaking and inspiring—and not concluded even yet.

Though the defeated Little Turtle has been reviled for signing land-cession treaties throughout the first decade of the 1800s, it is hard to see how he could have done otherwise. He had promised not to fight the white men anymore, and he was a man of his word. President Jefferson's Indian policy was to make all tribes within U.S. territory dependent upon the national government, through any means including indebtedness. Jefferson wanted the tribes to take up white men's agriculture and give up their traditional hunting culture. He recommended that traders extend credit till the Indians were in debt, noting that "when these debts get beyond what the individuals can pay, they become willing to lop them off by a cession of lands." Jefferson's method of dealing with any recalcitrant tribes was bluntly stated: ". . . seizing the whole country of that tribe and driving them across the Mississippi, as the only condition of peace, would be an example to others . . ."

And the man who governed the frontier Indiana Territory at that crucial time, William Henry Harrison, had no qualms about carrying out such policies. If a chief did not want to sign away his people's land, Harrison might try to make him more agreeable with liquor. If that didn't work, he could resort to getting some other Indian's mark on the treaty, whether that other Indian had any authority to sign or not.

It is interesting to speculate whether Little Turtle would have remained pro-American during the War of 1812 when Harrison ordered his scorched-earth campaign against all Wabash Valley tribal towns whether hostile, neutral, or even friendly. But the seventy-year-old chief had died that summer.

Little Turtle's successors as chiefs of his people were mostly Miami-French mixed-bloods, wealthy and well-educated men, who no longer had recourse to war; for many years they yielded Miami lands bit by bit under the pervasive pressure of government policy and white settlement. Well versed in law, politics, and trade, such chiefs as Richardville, Godfroy, Le Gros, and LaFontaine drove hard bargains; they manipulated the various ambitions of land speculators, traders, and bureaucrats against each other. But liquor, credit, and Manifest Destiny prevailed, and soon all the Miamis were living in widely separated pockets of land surrounded by white settlers.

Like most other tribes, the Miami did not embrace Jefferson's assimilation theory very well, and since the government didn't want enclaves of native culture lingering behind the frontier, the next plan to evolve was that of exiling Indians from their homelands to the far side of the Mississippi. That required a sweeping betrayal of existing treaties and promises, and over it hung the threat of renewed force.

The greed of traders, Indian agents, and politicians took various forms, and the plan to exile the Miamis created a dilemma. While living like parasites on the tribe and sucking up its annuity

moneys, the whites also coveted the rich Wabash lands that would
fall into their hands when the natives were expelled.

George Ewing, the trader whose correspondence had connected
Maconakwa with her Slocum family, was a clever enough entre-
preneur to make money off the Miamis at both ends of their trail
of tears. He and his brother had been influencing and profiting
from virtually every transaction made by and about the Miamis in
Indiana, running tribal members into debt. After raking in a huge
proportion of the money paid the tribe by the final removal treaty,
the Ewings began transferring much of their business to posts in
Kansas, the exiles' destination. If getting Maconakwa's land had
been part of George Ewing's motive for trying to help the Slocum
family find her, he was disappointed when Congress gave her dis-
pensation to keep it.

The names Frances Slocum and Maconakwa remain legendary in
Indiana and in the Susquehanna Valley of Pennsylvania. There is
a Frances Slocum State Recreational Area in Indiana and a
Frances Slocum State Park in Pennsylvania. Several histories of
her life were published in the late nineteenth and early twentieth
centuries. There was at least one narrative poem. A pageant about
her was performed for a few years by the Miamis themselves. But
all those stories ended with her poignant refusal to return to her
white family's civilization, and left off the awful irony of her last
years: spared from exile by her white blood and thus separated
from the people her red heart had chosen.

The course of Frances Slocum's life among the tribes, from her
capture until her reunion with the Slocums, is based upon her own
sketchy account told from memory to her brothers Joseph and
Isaac and her sister Mary. The map in this book is derived from
that account. She may have traveled with her adoptive Lenapeh
parents to places in Canada and among the Great Lakes that she
neglected to tell the Slocums; a child in those circumstances
probably would not have been cognizant of national and territorial
borders.

The gradual route from her childhood home at Wilkes-Barre to
Niagara can be presumed from historical accounts of the war
roads and refugee trails used in those turbulent years. It is logical
that their flight from Wyalusing would have been in the path of
General Sullivan's well-documented 1779 invasion, that is, up the
West Branch of the Susquehanna, through Tioga, north to the

Finger Lakes country, then westward through the "Longhouse Road" of Iroquois nations to the rugged Genesee River gorge and on to Niagara, a place she was to remember clearly for the rest of her life. She remembered that she had been taken to Detroit. Her brothers knew those routes and followed them in their tireless searches over the ensuing years. Her mother, Ruth Slocum, actually did go to the prisoner exchange at Tioga.

Maconakwa in her old age remembered enough to tell her brothers about her Lenapeh father Tuck Horse, the chair maker, about her Lenapeh name Wehletawash, her brief and unsuccessful marriage to a Lenapeh warrior who treated her badly, and her family's rescue and treatment of the wounded Miami warrior Shapahcahnah, who became her second husband and eventually was known as Deaf Man. She could not, or would not, recount details of specific battles that had affected her tribes, saying only that they were many and bloody; that she didn't like to see scalps but knew white men took them too; and that she had been helpless to do anything about the conflicts. Of course, a quarter of a century had passed since the end of the fighting until her first conversation with her white relatives. Because Maconakwa told so little, I have had to take the liberty of presuming just how certain battles and raids would have beset her home communities. As traumatic as these events are in my portrayal, they probably were far worse.

In twenty years of writing about the Revolution and the Indian Wars, I have had the exhausting task of researching and re-creating scores of battles and campaigns. Such labors were minimal for this book because most of the military actions take place "offstage"—that is, outside the protagonist's point of view. Here I wanted to emphasize the ways those actions would have disrupted the lives of the innocents, and I think this is a worthwhile theme because wars are generally more devastating to women, children, and elders than to the fighting men, who usually at least get a notion of glory and some bragging rights out of what they're doing.

A body of forgotten literature exists documenting the role of Quakers as friends of the dispossessed tribes, and it is terribly poignant, worth the reader's research.

The struggles of the Miami people—both those who were exiled beyond the Mississippi and those who stayed in their homeland—continue to this day. With the Removal, the struggle diverged into two separate travails, each peculiar to its own set of geographical, political, and cultural factors. What both tribes had in common was their patient and stubborn efforts to hang on to whatever small rights and entitlements the U.S. government's treaty documents had promised them. These were constantly revised and diminished by the government. Both tribes were hurt by the General Allotment Act of 1887, which broke up the reservations they had been given into private holdings, with the surplus put up for sale to whites. Upon this action, tribal governments were supposed to dissolve as entities, meaning that the U.S. government would then be free of its promised obligations. A federal court ruling soon afterward was used to deny the Indiana Miamis recognition as a tribe, and they have been working ever since to regain that recognition.

As for the deported Miamis, as soon as they tried to establish themselves on the reservations made for them in Kansas, they were hit by a surge of white settlement and land speculation on that side of the Mississippi, spurred by the route of railroads through their newly assigned lands. That white invasion was augmented by an association of white settlers whose founding goal was to thwart government protection of the exiled Miamis. And still ahead lay further uprootings, and assignment to hardscrabble reserves in Oklahoma.

That either Miami tribe still exists is a wonder, and it is due to their stubborn belief in themselves as a people. That belief has kept them in the courts, the state legislatures, the Capitol, and the newspapers for most of a century, fighting intelligent and dignified battles for rights and recognition, for the well-being of their people. A detailed and inspiring history of those complex struggles—*The Miami Indians,* A Persistent People 1654–1994, by Stewart Rafert—was published this year by the Indiana Historical Society. It is recommended to readers interested in the fate of Frances Slocum's descendants and the Miami people she loved.

At the time of this writing, Frances Dunnagan is acting chief of the Indiana Miami Tribe, and Phyllis Miley is Tribal Secretary. Both are direct descendants of Frances Slocum. Lora Siders, a chiefress and historian of the Indiana tribe, and Chief Floyd Leonard of the Oklahoma Miamis, have been kind and helpful to me over the years, busy as they are in the present-day conduct of their tribal affairs. Believing that their predecessors must have been as levelheaded, resourceful, wise, and firm as they are, I think I understand how the Miami people have survived and adapted in the two centuries since the Treaty of Greeneville, in the century and a half since the Removal, and in the century of struggle for recognition. It is no wonder to me that Maconakwa came to love the Miami people so much that she refused to leave them.

> —James Alexander Thom
> Bloomington, Indiana
> November 1996